THE MacGREGOR TRILOGY

Book One
MacGREGOR'S GATHERING

At the beginning of the eighteenth century, one of the most exciting and romantic periods in British history, the famous Rob Roy MacGregor and his gallant nephew Gregor, a fierce young Highlander, loyal to the cause, led the MacGregor clan in battle against the Duke of Cumberland and the English army.

Outlawed and landless, they clung to Glengyle, one small remaining corner of their ancient territories, and held fast in their loyalty to the Stuart King over the water. But in the midst of the political struggle young Gregor still managed to pay court to Mary Hamilton, a lovely girl from the Lowlands who at first rejected his rough Highland ways . . .

THE MacGREGOR TRILOGY

Book Two
THE CLANSMAN

In 1715, declared an outlaw by the Secretary of State, the Duke of Montrose and the Duke of Cumberland, Rob Roy MacGregor, steadfast supporter of the Stuart cause, left home and clansmen to avoid bringing disaster upon them.

In his absence, Montrose's factor came to his home, attacking his proud wife, Mary MacGregor, frightening his children and setting fire to Inversnaid House. For which Rob Roy vowed a terrible revenge . . .

THE MacGREGOR TRILOGY

Book Three
GOLD FOR PRINCE CHARLIE

In 1745 the Highlanders limped away from the bitter field of Culloden. Soon the Duke of Cumberland was offering a huge sum for the capture of Prince Charles Edward Stuart, dead or alive. Duncan MacGregor, great-nephew of Rob Roy, volunteered to join the small band of men escorting the Prince to safety.

Just one day after the Prince's escape, a large amount of French gold was landed at the very spot from which he had sailed. Thus it was that Duncan became involved in a desperate attempt to save Prince Charlie's gold, helped by beautiful, headstrong Caroline Cameron.

The MacGregor Trilogy

MacGREGOR'S GATHERING
THE CLANSMAN
GOLD FOR PRINCE CHARLIE

Nigel Tranter

CORONET BOOKS
Hodder and Stoughton

First published as three separate volumes

MacGregor's Gathering © 1957 by Nigel Tranter.
First published in Great Britain in 1957 by Hodder and Stoughton Ltd
First published as a Coronet paperback in 1974

The Clansman © 1959 by Nigel Tranter.
First published in Great Britain in 1959 by Hodder and Stoughton Ltd
First published as a Coronet paperback in 1974

Gold for Prince Charlie © 1962 by Nigel Tranter.
First published in Great Britain in 1962 by Hodder and Stoughton Ltd
First published as a Coronet paperback in 1974

This edition 1996
A Coronet paperback

A CIP catalogue record for this title
is available from the British Library

ISBN 0 340 40572 4

Printed and bound in Great Britain by
Cox & Wyman Ltd, Reading, Berkshire

Hodder and Stoughton
A division of Hodder Headline PLC
338 Euston Road
London NW1 3BH

MacGregor's Gathering

Book One

MACGREGOR'S GATHERING

The moon's on the lake, and the mist's on the brae,
And the clan has a name that is nameless by day.
    Then gather, gather, gather, Gregalach!
    Gather, gather, gather.

Our signal for fight, which from monarchs we drew,
Must be heard but by night in our vengeful halloo,
    Then halloo, halloo, halloo, Gregalach!
    Halloo, halloo, halloo.

Glen Orchy's proud mountains, Kilchurn and her towers,
Glen Strae and Glen Lyon no longer are ours.
    We're landless, landless, landless, Gregalach!
    Landless, landless, landless.

But doomed and deserted by vassal and lord,
MacGregor has still both his heart and his sword.
    Then courage, courage, courage, Gregalach!
    Courage, courage, courage.

If they rob us of name and pursue us with beagles,
Give their roofs to the flames and their flesh to the eagles.
    Then vengeance, vengeance, vengeance, Gregalach!
    Vengeance, vengeance, vengeance.

While there's leaves in the forest and foam on the river,
MacGregor despite them shall flourish for ever.
    Come then, Gregalach! Come then, Gregalach!
    Come then, come then, come then.

Through the depths of Loch Katrine the steed shall career'
O'er the peak of Ben Lomond the galley shall steer,
And the rocks of Craigroyston like icicles melt,
Ere our wrongs be forgot or our vengeance unfelt.
    Then halloo, halloo, halloo, Gregalach!
    Halloo, halloo, halloo.

WALTER SCOTT.

AUTHOR'S FOREWORD

THIS is fiction – though the background and most of the characters are factual. The legends adhering to Rob Roy MacGregor's name are legion, some of them fairly well authenticated, others less so. Vastly less has been written about his nephew, Gregor Ghlun Dubh (Black Knee) Mac-Gregor of Glengyle. The character of Rob Roy was obviously a highly complex one, that of his nephew considerably less so. I have sought to cull, from the mass of lore and legend and history, such incidents as seem to me to present a recognisable and fairly consistent picture of these two men, set against the stormy background of Scotland in the first decade of the eighteenth century, not hesitating to invent wholly imaginary incidents and individuals where such seem necessary for my story and for the fuller delineation of the characters that I conceive these two to have borne.

Much herein, therefore, is no more than a product of my fancy – but I have sought to keep the background of the times as accurate as I know how, and not to traduce any historical character unduly. John Campbell, first Earl of Breadalbane, is the villain of the piece, and while this tale may do his memory less than justice in some respects, in others it holds a more charitable silence. All authorities seem to be unanimous that he was a man whom no one in Scotland trusted and everyone feared, and his dexterity at changing sides was unrivalled in an age when such gymnastics were commonplace. He had his reward.

Rob Roy led his clan again in the next Jacobite rising of 1715 – and suffered some diminution of esteem in the process. Gregor, his fame unsullied, fought both in that affair and in the later attempt of the Forty-five.

The politics of the day ought not to be wholly without their lesson for us today. Politics, indeed, seem to change but little with the centuries.

NIGEL TRANTER.

ABERLADY, 1956.

CHAPTER ONE

YOUNG Gregor Ghlun Dubh MacGregor of Glengyle uplifted his golden head and hearty voice and shouted great
laughter to an understanding heaven – the pure unsullied
and spontaneous laughter of a happy soul. Not the laughter
inspired by amusement or humour or mockery or still less
worthy emotions, but the joyous variety born of sheer goodwill towards all, and a lively appreciation of the excellence of
life. Gregor Ghlun Dubh was a great appreciator of life, and
consequently a notably happy young man.

And certainly the scene was an inspiring one. Indeed, seldom could the little market-place of Drymen have seen anything more lively and altogether heartening. Cattle milled
everywhere in glorious and loud-voiced confusion – not only
the small black kyloes of the glens but the more substantial
products of fat Lowland pastures – steers, bullocks, milch-
cows and calves, in an endless variety of size, colour, shape
and temperament. There were hundreds of beasts there, uncountable – though undoubtedly Gregor's puissant uncle
would be having a count kept somewhere – and their
bellowing protest ascended up as a hymn of praise to a
benign Providence, and the steaming throat-catching scent
of them was as incense in a MacGregor's nostrils. Laugh?
The tall young man in his best tartans slapped his bare knee
– the same that bore the hairy black birth-mark, so strange
on a young blond giant, that gave him his by-name of Ghlun
Dubh, or Black Knee – slapped and out-bellowed the
cattle.

It was Lammas quarter-day, the year of Our Lord seventeen hundred and six, and the Captain of the Highland
Watch was at the receipt of his dues and customs – the Mac-

Gregors' Watch, Rob Roy's Watch – Gregor of Glengyle assisting for the first time since coming of age.

A less vigorous and lusty young man than Glengyle might have been weary of it all by this time – for this business had been going on all day, and now the August sun was beginning to sink behind Duncryne and all the serried blue hills beyond Loch Lomond. These cattle had come from far and near, in droves great and small – for Rob Roy MacGregor cut a wide swathe. From the Graham lands of Aberfoyle and Killearn to the Buchanan territories of Touch and Kippen, from the uplands of Fintry and Kilsyth to the green plains of Stirling and Airth, from Menteith to Callander and Allan Water to the Vale of Leven, the droves great and small had come to this convenient tryst of Drymen – convenient for the MacGregors, that is – representing the tribute of some seven hundred and fifty square miles of fair Scotland to Robert MacGregor Campbell, alias Robert Ruadh MacGregor of Inversnaid, alias Rob Roy, Captain of the Glengyle Highland Watch, or, as his own Clan Alpine put it, Himself. Proud earls had contributed – even a marquis, said to be in line for a dukedom – lairds of large acres and small, fine Lowland gentlemen and canny Highland drovers, the Church and the State, all were represented there. Which was as it should be. Rob Roy was worth paying tribute to – and he made a point of leaving none in doubt of it.

It was the Church speaking now, just at the young man's back, in the sober, indeed somewhat lugubrious person of the Reverend Ludovic Erskine, Minister of Drymen. 'Man, Glengyle – that's a terrible lot of beasts,' he said, without proper enthusiasm – undoubtedly because there was a cow of his own included somewhere in the total. 'I canna think what your uncle can be needing with them all.' He shook a grizzled foreboding head. 'There is danger in it, mind. The grievous danger of greed, of the worship of Mammon, Glengyle.'

Gregor Ghlun Dubh, like his uncle, was a great respecter of the Church, as of all worthy and proper things. Also he was newly enough of age to appreciate that introductory 'Man, Glengyle' of the minister's. Therefore he did not turn and rend the maker of such infamous suggestions as undoubtedly he deserved. Moreover, the man had recently lost his wife, and Gregor was of a soft heart.

'There are many MacGregor mouths to feed,' he mentioned, still smiling. 'You would not be having them starve in the midst of plenty?'

'Starve, is it!' Mr Erskine cried, his harsh voice vibrant with power and emotion. It had to be to counter the bawling of the beasts. 'The starving will be nearer home, I doubt! And there will be no plenty in Drymen after this day.'

Gregor knew what was coming, of course. The minister was not the first to seek to approach Rob Roy through his nephew, as the less alarming individual. All men knew of Rob's affection for his dead brother's son, the young chieftain of Glengyle, whom he had cherished and brought up from the age of ten. Tutor of Glengyle had been one of his uncle's proud titles, only recently relinquished – and, if the truth was known, sometimes relinquished only in name at that.

'I am thinking the good folk of Drymen will not be letting their shepherd starve,' he observed.

'Little you ken them, Glengyle – backsliders, reprobates, withholders of God's portion! And now my cow is riven from me – my best cow, the only brute-beast that is worth its keep, indeed! It is hard, hard. If you would but speak a word into your uncle's lug, Glengyle. He is namely as a man respectful to the Kirk, kindly towards the poor and the widow. Och, and the widower is the worse off, indeed . . .'

Young Gregor groaned in spirit. That the creature should spoil this bonny day and its good work with such shameful whining! He shook his yellow head impatiently. 'Himself is throng with business, *Mhinistear*. Later, may be . . .'

Glengyle paused, grateful for a diversion. A new drove was coming at the trot up the little hill from the south-west into Drymen's slantwise market-place, mixed beasts as Rob liked them, stirks, cows and followers, but all prime conditioned stock. He pointed.

'Oho – see you!' he cried. 'My Lord of Aberuchill is late. But better late than sorry, as they say!'

'Aberuchill . . . ?' the minister echoed. 'Man – does the Lord Justice-Clerk of Scotland himself pay your Hielant blackmail?'

'Blackmail, sirrah!' Gregor's voice rose menacingly, all laughter gone. 'As Royal's my Race – I'd have you remember to whom you speak, *Mhinistear*!' His uncle could hardly have improved on that himself. 'Choose you your words to a Highland gentleman, see you, with more care . . . !'

As well for the Reverend Erskine and any hopes in the matter of his cow, perhaps, that just then a sudden high-pitched squealing overbore even the speaker's vehemence. At the trotting heels of the new herd a six-month calf was outdoing all rivals in ear-piercing protest, as a burly drover twisted its tail savagely as a means of propulsion. The press of beasts in the market-place was already so great that the newcomers were holding back, and the fellow was using this method to urge them on past the narrows of the street which sundry MacGregor gillies were endeavouring to keep open for incoming traffic from the east.

Gregor wasted neither breath, time nor opportunity. Leaving the minister without a word, he strode down through the little crowd of gaping townsfolk and round the near edge of the milling throng, thrusting aside men and cattle with equal disregard. This was more in his line. That calf could be injured by such treatment, for tails could break – and a broken tail took the value off a beast. Moreover, its bawling was an offence to the ear, and unsuitable. Again, the offending drover was obviously nothing but a Lowlander. And, as has been seen, Glengyle was of a notably soft heart.

The last few yards to Lord Aberuchill's drover were covered at a pace which allowed little opportunity for Gregor's rawhide brogans to touch the cobbles. One of the hulking fellow's two colleagues cried a warning. But it was too late. Before the man could turn, Gregor's arm reached out and did the turning for him, swinging him round with such force as almost to overbalance him. As he staggered, still clutching the calf's tail, Glengyle's other hand grabbed the substantial stick that the other held, and wrenched it from his grasp.

'Fool! Knave! Scum!' he cried indignantly. 'Would you damage MacGregor's cattle? Hands off, lout!' And without allowing even a moment for the transgressor to question the authority of that, he swung the heavy stick and brought it down with a resounding thwack upon the creature's forearm.

The drover yelled, in tune with the calf, and both arm and tail dropped limply. A spluttered volley of oaths, incomplete and incoherent but nevertheless hoarsely heartfelt, followed on.

But the Lord Justice-Clerk's drover did more than swear. He lashed out with a great ham-like left fist for Gregor's head – which branded him for a rash and impetuous fellow indeed. Perhaps he was so much of a Lowlander that he did not recognise the significance of two eagle's feathers in a Highland bonnet. Though probably his folly was the result of mere spontaneous reaction.

It was as well, undoubtedly, for all concerned, that the blow did not strike home – for the consequences would scarcely have borne consideration. As it was, Gregor avoided it with a full inch to spare – despite the shock that such a thing could be possible. And quicker than thought, of course, he drove home the much-needed lesson.

Coming up from his hasty sideways duck, he clutched the other's shoulder to slew him round into a more convenient position, and drove down the staff in his other hand with all his force on the man's bullet head. The stick broke, too.

The drover grunted, swayed drunkenly, tottered on his toes, and then slumped full length on the dung-spattered cobbles, mouth open and eyes shut.

Gregor Ghlun Dubh tossed the two sections of the stick on to the body of the unconscious miscreant, wiping fastidious hands thereafter on the seat of his philamore or great kilt, as though to avoid contamination.

'Remove it,' he jerked, in the Gaelic, to the nearest of the gillies. And to the two remaining gaping drovers, in English, 'Begone'. And without further ado he stalked off to return to the minister.

Not unnaturally he felt considerably better. He was prepared even to be patient with the Church-Supplicant. But as he approached his former stance before the ale-house door, a third man came hurrying from the other direction, another gillie, naked save for short kilt and brogans. They met in front of Mr Erskine.

'Himself would be having a word with you, Glengyle,' the newcomer said, panting a little. 'Down in the church.'

'Yes. I will come,' Gregor assured, and almost started off there and then. But he recollected. Those days were past and done with. He was Glengyle now, chieftain of his house. 'Tell Himself that I will be there very shortly, MacAlastair,' he amended graciously. And repeated the message in English for the benefit of the minister, without the 'very'. 'Off with you.'

The dark-avised and sombre-browed messenger gave him a meaning look. He was Rob Roy's own foot-gillie, and something of a privileged character. He nodded, unspeaking, and padded away silently whence he had come.

'About this cow of yours, *Mhinistear*,' Gregor mentioned handsomely. 'What colour did you say it was ? Is it a kyloe ?'

The other eyed him a little askance. 'That man . . . ?' he began, and swallowed. 'Is he . . . ? Was it needful to be so . . . so hasty, Glengyle ?'

'Hasty . . . ?' The younger man wrinkled his brow. 'Myself hasty – to MacAlastair ?'

'Not him. The other man. Down there. The herd . . . '

'I do not follow you, sir.' That was said with deliberation and a remarkable clarity of diction.

'Oh. I . . . ah . . . ummm.' The minister glanced sidelong at the young chieftain's elevated profile – and decided to revert to the subject of cattle. 'My cow, yes. Och, she is just an ordinary sort of a dun-coloured creature. But a grand milker, man – a grand milker.'

'Indeed. I am going to speak a word with, er, Inversnaid. I think it best that you accompany me, sir,' Gregor said, somewhat stiffly formal.

'Me . . . ? Och – no, no. Not at all. No need, Glengyle. Yourself will do fine. Just a word in his lug, like I said. . . .'

'Come,' the other commanded, and turning on his heel, strode off.

Reluctantly, with no urgency upon him, Mr Erskine followed on, the space between them growing at every step. They made quite a notable contrast, the tall, gallant and swaggering young Highlander, in his vivid red-and-green tartans, stepping Drymen's cobbles as though very much upon his native heath, and the lanky stooping divine, clad in patched and sober grey, shuffling doubtfully after, out of the market-place and down the curving brae towards his own parish kirk.

* * *

The Kirk of Drymen could hardly have been more conveniently placed. It sat squarely above the climbing narrow road which led into the little town from the west, and nothing could pass its door unseen. Moreover, directly across the trough that the road had worn for itself was another ale-house, Drymen being namely for its numerous places of refreshment. Again, around the back, a lane encircled the town, by the water-meadows, linking up with the road that came in from the east and all the wide lands of Forth. So all that was necessary was to have a couple of stout fellows stationed at the east end of the town, directing the flow of traffic from that side down the lane to where it must join the west-coming droves, and all had thus to come surging up the hill below the kirk door, where it could be scrutinised, counted and received in business-like fashion.

Rob Roy MacGregor sat decently in the church doorway behind a table, quills, ink and paper before him – for he was almost as good a hand with pen as with claymore and dirk.

These latter, of course, also lay upon the table. He was something of a stickler for the niceties of procedure. Mac-Alastair stood at his back, another man sat counting silver at the board, and three or four plaided gentlemen of the name lounged around. As Gregor came up the steps from the roadway, his uncle was in process of interviewing a stout red-faced little Lowland laird in cocked hat and good broadcloth, who appeared to be essaying the difficult task of keeping civil, paying over hard cash, and suggesting a rebate, all at the same time. Some clients of the Watch elected to pay their dues in silver.

'Er . . . just that, Buchlyvie,' Rob said pleasantly. 'My nephew, Glengyle. Mr Graham of Buchlyvie, Greg.' And he got to his feet as he spoke.

Rob Roy seated and standing gave two very different impressions. Seated, he looked a huge man, for he had enormous breadth of shoulder, a barrel-like chest, and arms so long that he could tie the garters of his tartan hose without stooping. Standing, he proved to be less tall than might have been anticipated – though nowise small – with stocky and just slightly bowed legs that gave an extraordinary impression of strength. That impression of strength, indeed, was the most notable quality about the man – and it was not confined to his peculiar physique. A man in his late thirties, he radiated personal power and a latent energy. His fiery red hair, fierce down-curving moustaches, and the rufus fur that clothed wrists and knees as thickly as on one of his own Highland stirks, did not lessen the effect. He was not a good-looking man, as his nephew Gregor Ghlun Dubh was good-looking, but no one who glanced once at Rob Roy MacGregor failed to look again. The brilliance of his pale blue eyes saw to that, if nothing else did. He was clad now, like Glengyle, in the full panoply of Highland dress, great kilt and plaid, tartan doublet, otter-skin sporran, silver buttons, jewelled brooches, buckles and sword-belt. Only, his bonnet, which lay on the table, flaunted but the one eagle's feather to Gregor's two.

'Nephew,' he said now, quizzically, in the English,

16

'Buchlyvie here poses us a nice problem. He contends that since there has been no villainous thievery of his cattle, nor raids on his district, this past year, we ought to be reducing his rate of payment. From five percentum of rateable value, he suggests, to four. How think you?' He sounded genuinely interested in the proposal.

'*Dia* – I think Mr Graham is ungrateful!' Gregor declared strongly, as required. 'Because our Watch is successful, and preserves him in peace and plenty, he would deny us our poor sustenance. I cannot congratulate him on his reasoning!'

'And there you have it, Buchlyvie!' his uncle laughed genially. 'My nephew has the clearer brain to us oldsters. *Maxima debetur puero reverentia.*' Rob was a great one for Latin tags – for education and all its benefits indeed, and so had brought up young Gregor. 'I cannot think that there is any more to discuss, eh? Unless indeed you would have us withdraw the Watch from you altogether?' He was glancing down at the end of the table where one of his henchmen had the silver coins all neatly counted and stacked, and who nodded his head briefly that the tally was correct. 'Now is the time, whatever, if you would wish it, Mr Graham?'

'No, no! Mercy on us – never think it, Rob . . . Inversnaid!' the laird assured hurriedly. 'The thought never crossed my mind.'

'That is well. We are of one mind, then?' The MacGregor signed the handsome receipt under his hand, with a flourish, and passed it over – a document worthy of Edinburgh's Parliament House. 'Eh, hey – it is good to deal with reasonable men. I bid you a very good e'en, Buchlyvie.'

'I do also,' Glengyle agreed.

All the MacGregor gentlemen did likewise, as the little man bumbled out. Politeness was a great matter with Rob, and none laughed out loud.

'Well now, Greg,' his uncle said, in their own tongue, resuming his seat. 'It was not to listen to such as Buchlyvie that I brought you here. Would you be after liking a small bit of a task, and this something of a special occasion for yourself?' Taking his nephew's acceptance for granted, the Captain of the Watch went on. 'It has been a good day, and all has gone well. The tally has been kept, and only three droves have not come in. Ballikinrain, Kerse and Gallangad. But Ballikinrain and Kerse are on the way. They have been spied from up the tower, there. There is nothing from the direction of Gallangad.'

'Ah!'

'And only last quarter-day, see you, Graham of Gallangad was after grumbling about his payments – just the way Buchlyvie was at just now. I am thinking that it is maybe a little small lesson that he needs.'

'That could be,' the younger man acceded gravely. 'And you would have me teach him it?'

'The notion occurred to me that you might welcome the exercise, Greg. It serves no good purpose when cock-lairdies grow too cocky, whatever. The disease could be catching! You know the place?'

'Surely. No great distance off. Behind Duncryne, yonder. Five miles, or six?'

'Eight, make it, and the ford to cross. It will be sundown within the hour. If his beasts were to be here in time, they should have been in sight ere this. Man, Gregor – go you and fetch them in for me. All of them, you will understand? All. It will keep you from wearying.'

'Yes, then. They are as good as here, just.'

'No – not here, lad. Bring them to Inversnaid – to Glen Arklet. We shall be gone long before you win them back here. But . . . see you, Gregor – is that the minister that is dodging and skulking down the steps there, like a rock-rabbit?'

'Och, yes – I had forgotten him. The man is desolate because of his bit cow that has been taken. Bewailing like all the daughters of Babylon!' Gregor glanced sidelong to see how the other MacGregors had taken this erudite allusion. 'God's shadow – it is a great plague for one small cow!'

'Ministers' cows always low the loudest,' Rob Roy observed. 'But you are speaking for him, Greg?'

'Och, well . . . '

'Call him up, then.'

The Reverend Erskine came up to his own kirk with little of the Church-Militant about him. 'Mr MacGregor,' he began, with an incipient bow, 'you'll forgie me, I hope? I winna waste your time forbye ae meenit.' Perturbation, it is to be presumed, was driving him into his broadest Fife doric. 'I was just speiring at Glengyle here . . . '

'See you, *Mhinistear*,' Rob Roy interrupted, but easily. 'Let us be discussing your matter, be it what it may, on a right footing, whatever. Myself, you may name me a number of things – but not Mister! Inversnaid would be proper, or Captain maybe. But Rob I will answer to – or even Mac-Gregor. But, as Royal's my Race – no man shall Mister me within my hearing or the reach of my arm, *Mister* Erskine!' It was mildly said, but there was a certain sibilance of enunciation, which had a notable effect.

The growl of approval that arose came from all in hearing save Mr Erskine.

That unhappy man all but choked. 'I . . . I . . . och, nae offence, Inversnaid! Nae offence meant, I assure you. A slip o' the tongue, nae mair. Just oor Scots usage. . . . '

'Are you for informing me, sir, what is Scots usage?'

'Na, na – guidsakes! You'll have to forgie me, Captain. I'm a right donnert man become since my wife died on me. And noo the coo . . . '

Somewhat donnert he certainly sounded. Gregor, beside him, perceived that the lean veined hand actually trembled as it gestured feebly – the same hand that undoubtedly would beat the Good Book in thunderous authority in the pulpit back there of a Sabbath. And soft-hearted as ever, he intervened.

'It is but a little small matter, Uncle, to be wasting our time over. One small bit of a cow! Think you we could spare . . . ?'

'The cow is nothing, Nephew – but the principle is everything, whatever,' Rob Roy declared, sternly now. 'Mr Erskine, like others, has had my protection, and gained thereby. He cries penury now – but so does every subscriber, from my Lord Marquis downwards. Restore him his cow, see you, and I should have a tail of others demanding the like. The thing is not to be considered. But . . . ' He paused, toying with his silver-mounted dirk, his glance switching between the faces of his nephew and the alarmed presbyter. ' . . . my respect for God's Kirk and religion is known. Mac-Alastair – take you Mr Erskine and let him be choosing any two beasts from the *spreagh* that he will. *Two* – you hear me? As free gift and thank offering, from Robert MacGregor of Inversnaid.'

Into the divine's subsequent incoherent babble of grati-tude and blessing, and Gregor's great laughter, Rob Roy held up his hand. 'Wheesht you, *Mhinistear*!' he comman-ded. 'What is that outcry? A truce to your belling, Greg – what is the to-do upbye?'

They all listened. Sure enough there came down to them a considerable din other than the day's norm of bovine pro-test. There was much shouting, the clatter of shod hooves and the unmistakable cracking of a whip.

'See you to it,' Rob directed, with a brief jerk of his red head in the direction of one of his lounging gentry.

'I will go,' young Glengyle announced, born an optimist, and turned him about.

*   *   *

It was a large travelling-coach that was the cause of the pother – a heavy, brightly painted affair drawn by four matching greys and equipped with whip-cracking jehu and shouting postillions. It was jammed in the throat of the market-place where the road from the east came in, along with perhaps fifty miscellaneous cattle-beasts, and making nothing of the business. Sundry gillies were hallooing round about, and cocked hats were poking through the coach windows. An interesting situation.

Gregor strode thitherwards laughing, pushing his way amongst the beasts. The coach doors were emblazoned with a florid coat-of-arms, ermine cinquefoils on a red field. How the equipage had got even thus far was a mystery. Determined folk, evidently.

A heavy-featured handsome man, handsomely clad and bewigged, beckoned imperiously to Gregor from one of the windows as he approached. 'Is this a fair, or what ? A tryst ?' he called out. 'Young man – these damned animals are not yours, by chance ?'

'They are not mine, no. But a tryst it is, after a manner of speaking.'

'Thank the Lord that you speak the Queen's English, at any rate!' the gentleman exclaimed. 'Will you kindly request these jabbering heathen to clear me a passage. 'Fore God, it should be obvious enough even to such as these! I believe that they are wilfully misunderstanding me!'

'What was it that you were after calling them, sir ?' Gregor Ghlun Dubh enquired interestedly.

'I said jabbering . . . ' The other's masterful voice tailed away as his arm was grasped from behind and another and older man's face appeared near his own, to mutter in his ear. Gregor heard only the words ' . . . MacGregor tartan . . . ' of whatever was said. But the effect of the whispering was on the whole beneficial. 'Well, dammit . . . we can't have this! Shrive me, it's a scandal, just the same. This is Drymen, is it not ? In the same Sheriffdom of Stirling as is Bardowie! Not some Hieland clachan! Blocking the Queen's highway . . . !'

'To which Queen do you refer, sir ?' Gregor asked then, more interestedly than ever. To counter the press of bullocks around him, he was now holding on to the handle of the coach door.

There was a musical tinkle of laughter from within. '*Touché*, John!' a woman's voice said, as with enjoyment.

The heavy gentleman swallowed, all but gobbled, and drew back from the window a little, turning his head. Gregor took the opportunity to jump up on the step and peer within.

He found the coach to contain two women as well as the two men, both young and both merry-eyed. But the younger, and the larger-eyed if anything, was sitting at this side of the vehicle, only a yard from Gregor's face. And he recognised her there and then, with a decision and certainty that his uncle must have commended, as quite the most lovely and desirable creature upon which his chiefly grey eyes had yet fallen. In token whereof, despite the difficulty and the balancing feat involved, he swept off his feathered bonnet in an impressive sweep – a thing that could have been done for no man save only the unfortunate Archibald MacGregor of Kilmanan, High Chief of Clan Alpine.

'Your servant, ladies!' he announced happily. And though he included them both, courteously, he rather concentrated upon her who was nearest. The Gregorach had always been notably impressionable as regards the sex – as centuries of blood and tears bore witness.

'Enchanted, sir,' one of the ladies said – the other one. 'You are an improvement, I swear, on the other faces that have been examining us! Is he not, Mary?' She was a plumpish comely creature, patched and prinked and power-fully well dressed for travelling – save over a bulging bosom.

Despite the bosom, Gregor's eyes still were magnetised by the other female attraction whom she called Mary, a less voluble young woman, and much less fussily dressed, but still more spectacular in her own way. Tall and slender, though dark-eyed and dark-haired and of a sculptured and arch-browed patrician loveliness, there was nothing of the chill and aloofness that frequently complements such beauty. Indeed, conversely, she had a lively warm eagerness of ex-pression, a gaiety of spirit, that was as notable as her good looks. From her comparatively plain attire, and the fashion in which the curling masses of her seemingly unruly hair were ineffectually enclosed in a mere kerchief, instead of the elaborate headgear of the other woman, she might have been a superior servant, or perhaps a paid gentlewoman-com-panion – only, no one with half an eye could have taken that one for any sort of servant; certainly not Gregor Ghlun Dubh MacGregor of Glengyle.

'But still more dangerous, I would say!' this other

charmer declared – without by any means cringing back in her corner.

'Oh, most assuredly. The others, after all, were only bullocks!' The rounded lady veiled her eyes momentarily, and with effect. 'And a Jacobite into the bargain, if I mistake not. A *professing* Jacobite . . . unlike some!'

Both the men opposite cleared their throats. 'That's enough, Meg,' the younger heavily handsome man jerked. To Gregor he said: 'I'll wager the ladies will esteem your service the higher, sir, when you set about removing them from the God-offending stink of these cattle!' And he treated himself to a couple of liberal pinches of snuff, as deodorant.

Gregor managed to withdraw his gaze from the young woman – but sufficient of the effect remained to markedly tone down the automatic resentment aroused in any Mac-Gregor by a derogatory remark anent their staple and stock-in-trade. 'The Mother of God took no offence at the smell of cattle – in Bethlehem!' he mentioned levelly. And silenced all in that coach very thoroughly.

Which was the state in which Rob Roy found them. His great shoulders suddenly filled the other window, and he gazed in, from amongst the cattle, frowning just a little. Then his glance lightened.

'Arnprior!' he cried. 'Well, well – here is an unexpected pleasure. And Miss Meg, it will be? Beautiful as was her mother, too!' Rob's eyes did not miss the other young woman either, on their way round to the fourth traveller. 'A coachload of worth and beauty, whatever!' And he smiled that guileless smile of his that so little matched his reputation.

'Rob! Yourself, is it!' That was the older man speaking, and he thrust his hand out of the open window to shake the red-furred fist of the MacGregor. 'Well met, indeed. Man – you're looking fine and prosperous. Better than the last time we forgathered, eh! You mind, in that damnable business in Edinburgh – when they pulled Atholl down with the forgeries, and near got some others o' us, forbye! Three years past, it would be . . . ?'

'Three years, yes. Seventeen and three. Three bad years for the Cause, too. But . . . ' The Highlander shrugged those shoulders. 'Och, for myself, I have managed, man – I've managed! And you, Arnprior – you've been furth the country, they tell me?'

'Aye, aye, Rob – I thought it wise-like, after you-know-what. France, where I saw you-know-who. Then to the Americas – to try to save something from the Darien business, see you. Then London itself – the lions' den. But och, the lions are purring now, with plenty to digest in their bellies, and auld Scotland dead just, dead – save maybe for yourself, Rob. . . . '

'Sleeping,' the other amended mildly.

'Well . . . maybe. But here's no place to discuss politics. Man, I saw the MacGregor tartans, and wondered what was all the stour. And this young man . . . '

'This young man, Arnprior, is my nephew Glengyle.' That was significantly said.

'Ha – the Colonel's grandson!' Rob Roy and Robert Buchanan of Arnprior had served as comrades-in-arms under the former's father, Lieutenant-Colonel Donald MacGregor of Glengyle, in the bad stirring days after Killiecrankie. 'I am proud to shake your hand, Glengyle.'

'Buchanan of Arnprior, Greg. And Mistress Meg Buchanan. . . . '

'Alas, no,' the plump young lady declared, pulling a face. 'No longer, I'm afraid!'

'Och, mercy on us, and my manners all gone gyte!' Arnprior cried. 'Here is my son-in-law, John Hamilton of Bardowie. And Miss Mary Hamilton, his sister. Rob Roy MacGregor.'

The impact of this introduction on the Hamiltons was noteworthy. John Hamilton half rose from his seat, recovered himself, made as if to thrust out his hand, thought better of it, and bowed his full-bottomed wig instead – a strangely uncertain performance for such a substantial citizen. His sister was more forthright.

'Rob Roy MacGregor – the noted ... er ... !' Her forthrightness faltered there, and she bit a red lip lest any more should emerge.

'Exactly, Miss!' Rob laughed, and slapped the side of the coach so that the entire affair shook alarmingly. 'None other.' He turned to her brother. 'Bardowie is a known name to all men,' he said civilly. 'Myself, I thought that I recognised the red and white of the Hamilton scutcheon. Arnprior travels in better company than sometimes he has done, sir!'

'In more cautious company, anyhow,' Mrs Hamilton amended, smiling. 'You will have poor John quite dumbfounert with all your seditious talk! Though not Mary, I think ... !'

Her father changed the subject. 'But what do you here, Rob – in Drymen? And whose are all these cattle? Is it some new fair, established since I've been gone?'

'The beasts are mine – or, say, the Gregorach's. Though, if you are after looking closer, friend, you'll maybe can make out your own mark on two-three of them, whatever! Your factor at Arnprior, I thank God, has an excellent memory!'

'Save us all – you mean ... ? Don't say ... ? Not all these, man ... ?'

'Business is expanding, yes.' Rob shrugged. 'A man must keep pace with the times, as they say. It is Lammas quarter-day, see you, and the dues fall to be collected. And you-know-who gets his share, too.'

'Eh ... ? Ah! Ummm.'

'Also, your Arnprior herds, sir, have not lost a beast in these three years,' Gregor mentioned, coming back into the conversation after a feast of pulchritude. 'Ask you your factor when you get there.'

'Aye. I see. Just so.' The laird did not sound just entirely converted even so, perhaps.

25

'Come – we will have to be getting you out of this,' Rob Roy declared, in suitably businesslike tone. 'A plague on't Greg – we'll need more gillies. Where's MacAlastair . . . ?'

*   *   *

That coach was extricated from the bottleneck of Drymen only by means of a major operation wherein cattle were coaxed, cajoled, whacked and manhandled by a vociferous host of wiry and half-naked Gregorach – and during which stirring proceedings the young chieftain of Glengyle contrived, amidst much buffeting, to remain at the desired window of the coach, and from there to point out much that was amusing and edifying. And that some part of his audience at least was fully appreciative of his show and his showmanship seemed to be established by the consistency of the laughter, melodious but little constrained, that rose to join his own throughout.

It was with a distinct sense of disappointment and anti-climax, indeed, that Gregor at last saw the way clear for the coach to take its onwards road eastwards round the lower rim of the great Flanders Moss, to Kippen and Arnprior. He did suggest to his uncle thereafter, as a matter of some urgency, that a mounted escort to conduct the equipage for the remaining dozen miles or so might be a wise precaution – but the older man did not seem just wholly convinced of its necessity. If his nephew insisted, needless to say, they could always send along one of the MacGregor gentlemen . . . ? But meanwhile wasn't it time and more that Gregor went off about the serious business of Gallangad? Unless, of course, Glengyle preferred squiring Lowland females around the country to the man's work of teaching Gallangad his lesson?

After that, naturally, there was no more that could be said with dignity. Gregor bade an abruptly stiff and formal farewell to the travellers, and curtly ordered MacAlastair to find him half a dozen sturdy gillies – insisting with a stern loftiness that when he said half a dozen he meant only half a dozen; wasn't he only going to doff the bonnet of a mere bonnet-laird for him? Thereafter he stalked off to collect his garron.

His uncle smiled after him, stroking his small red beard.

CHAPTER TWO

GREGOR got over his disappointment with commendable speed, of course, for as has been stressed he was of a cheerful disposition and no repiner. Also, it falls to be admitted, he was on a ploy that any young MacGregor, any Highlandman almost, would relish. Moreover, the sunset into which he rode was particularly fine – and, as has been made equally clear, he was a young man with an eye for beauty.

He rode south-westwards through the August evening, then, on his sturdy short-legged Highland garron, his own long shanks trailing in the already turning bracken. Six deep-breathing but tireless gillies ran at his heels. They would do the eight miles in well under the hour, thus – for this was a tame country of gentle green slopes and whinny knowes, of patches of tilth and winding purling burns, and these men would run forty steep mountain miles in a day – and then ten more after supper; also they had been townbound all that day, and now rejoiced in the fine freedom of flexing muscles. And at *their* heels loped two lean and shaggy deerhounds, trained to cattle working. So ran the Gregorach.

Gregor maintained the bold steep sugarloaf of Duncryne on his right front, where it thrust like a jagged black fang out of the green braes, dividing the level rays of the dying sun, keeping between its base and the shallow valley of the Catter Water. They rode through a blaze of gold and crimson, with inky shadow brimming from every hollow and dip, and magnifying every least projection. Away in front, across the loch, the massive hunched shoulders of the Mac-farlane hills above Glen Fruin were etched jetty black against the glare. To the right, their own Ben Lomond and all its stalwart satellites thrust noble brows into the burning heaven to win crowns of glory. And to the left, southwards, the gentler rolling Lowland hills of Kilpatrick lifted round bare breasts out of long purple-brown shelving moors. It was a fair scene – and the fairer for the good work that was toward.

Gallangad sat amongst the green skirts of those long brown moors, across the Catter Water, an open breezy place amidst wide cattle-dotted pastures, visible for miles off. No sort of cover did its approaches boast, save for a few crooked wind-tortured trees – not that Gregor, of course, contemplated for a moment approaching the place under any other cover than his own chiefly bonnet. The house itself, set amongst the huddle of its farmery, was a modest two-storeyed crow-step gabled place grown out of a squat square tower, whitewashed but solid and without pretensions.

The MacGregors forded the Catter at a point actually slightly west of their objective, for Gregor desired to assure himself that they could get cattle across the stream here, on the best line for his eventual formidable droving back to Inversnaid so many rough miles to the north-west. Then up over all the green braes to the house they went, their leader whistling blithely as he rode.

There were cattle scattered about those braes, however, and it seemed a pity to be passing them by. So Glengyle gave the word, and the gillies and dogs spread out, working together in a nice harmony – the consequence being that young Gregor approached Gallangad House with a tail of a round dozen fine heifers. Nobody was going to accuse him of being underhand or ungentlemanly about the business.

Graham of Gallangad thus had fair notification of what was to do, and the size of his problem. He was out in front of his steading as Gregor rode up, a big raw-boned glowering man, clad in hodden-grey homespuns and blue bonnet, a stout blackthorn cudgel in his hand. At his back was only an old cattleman – yet there had been two others only a minute or so before, Gregor had noted. From the windows of the house female faces peered anxiously.

'Hech, sirs – what's the meaning o' this, ava?' Graham grated – though he must have had a fairly shrewd idea. 'I'll thank ye, whaesiver ye are, to leave my beasts alane, b'Goad!'

Gregor tut-tutted, mainly to himself, at the harsh coarse Lowland manner and voice, so unlike his own soft and sibilant Highland tongue. But he greeted the man civilly nevertheless. 'A good e'en to you, Gallangad,' he said. 'Dry it is, and the brackens going back early.' The fellow, however rude and uncouth, was laird of his own heired thousand acres, and the rights of property and line fell to be respected. 'I am Glengyle.'

'I care'na whae ye are, Hielantman – but thae queys are mine, and I'll hae ye return them whaur ye got them!'

Gregor was interested. This was not the reaction that might have been expected. After all, the fellow knew that he had flouted Rob Roy and the Highland Watch. He would hardly have expected his defection to be overlooked. And yet he was apparently prepared to be defiant. Which could only mean, surely, that he believed himself to be able to defend himself and his cattle? With what? He had sent two men away, presumably to bring up support. But from where? Gallangad himself would not have more than four or five cattlemen and herds on his thousand or so acres of rough grazing. Had he then been brash enough to raise some sort of a confederacy against the Gregorach? The thing was next to unthinkable – but what else would serve? His neighbours, small farmers, cottagers, the miller at Mavie, merest peasants all, would scarce dare lift their hands against Rob Roy – however little they had to lose. Who else could Gallangad have got, then? Not any minions of the law or the government, certainly, when even the Lord Justice-Clerk himself had to pay for protection. They were much too near to the Highland Line for Edinburgh's writ to run.

Intrigued, Gregor considered the man in relation to all this. A modicum of circumspection might be indicated. Though naturally the fellow must be taught how to speak to such as himself. 'I think you forget, sir,' he observed, pleasantly enough. 'Perhaps your memory is failing on you – a thing that could be happening to any man? But these beasts – and of course two-three others forbye – now belong to Robert Ruadh MacGregor of Inversnaid . . . and to myself. As witness our bond and agreement. The agreement said, moreover, that you should deliver eight prime beasts to Drymen at Lammas-day – that is today – before sundown.' Noting the other's swift glance to the left and behind him, Gregor bethought him to gesture to his own henchmen, indicating further cattle which grazed on the slopes above the house. Four gillies and the dogs slipped off unobtrusively forthwith, leaving two with the heifers they already had. 'Alas that your memory has played you false, Gallangad – and caused the Watch no little inconvenience, whatever. But, as between gentlemen, matters may always be settled decently, and we shall say no more about it . . . save to recoup our extra trouble with a poor extra beast or two.'

'Y'will, will ye – dirty Hielant stots!' the other cried. 'I'll see you damned first! You with your saft mincing words and your gentrice – ye're nae mair'n a wheen red-leggit robbers and thieving sorners! I've paid enough o' your mail, and mair.'

Sitting his pony, Gregor sighed – for he greatly disliked unseemly bickering. 'Not quite enough, Gallangad – not quite. A year of Rob Roy's peace you have had – and that's a thing better men than you esteem worth paying for.' He could not help noting that the man was for ever glancing over to his left, westwards. There was a dip over there, some three hundred yards off, tree-filled – a dene of some sort. 'And I must urge you, sir, to mend your manners – or I shall be forced to have my gillies teach you better with, say, your blackthorn there!'

Gallangad took a wary pace or two backwards, so that he might slip into the narrows of the steading if necessary. 'It'll need mair'n you and your like, my fine fellow!' he said. 'I've gien you the last beast you'll hae frae Gallangad.'

'You prefer that I select them myself . . . ?'

There was an interruption to drown Gregor's soft Highland voice. Up beyond there, where the deerhounds were circling to bring in a mixed scattering of milch-cows and followers to the gillies, a grey-and-white half-collie had appeared out of nowhere and launched itself, barking and snarling, on one of the busy hounds. As dog-fights went it was a brief and inglorious affair, a short sharp tussle wherein the lean and long-legged deerhound seemed to coil itself round the shorter body of its attacker, silently, almost as a snake might, fangs flashing. The other dog's snarling ceased abruptly in a strangled yelp, and then there was no sound from the heaving rolling squirming pair for a few seconds. Then, seemingly leisurely, the deerhound appeared to disentangle and shake itself, before leaping in great springing bounds on its interrupted task with the cattle, leaving an only faintly twitching ragged bundle on the grass.

'Aye,' Gregor sighed. 'Sorry about that I am, man – for I am fond of dogs. I am hoping that you will have no more of them loose, to be getting hurt, at all? There could be a lesson in it, too, for a wise man. How think you . . . ?'

But Gallangad's attention was on him no more, nor even on his unfortunate dog. He was looking away to his left again, and this time with no furtive squinting. The speaker followed his glance. A group of men, indeed a company of men, had emerged from the tree-lined dene and were advancing towards them with an easy resolution – as well they might, for there must have been between two dozen and thirty of them. Moreover, they were tartan-clad men, ragged, dirty, unkempt, but indubitably tartan-clad – a red-blue sett, as far as the grime let it be seen, as distinct from the MacGregor's red-and-green. They seemed to be very liberally armed, too, with staves and billhooks and sickles and knives. Two Lowland cattlemen escorted them from well to the rear.

'Well, now,' Gregor Ghlun Dubh said to himself softly,

in his own tongue. 'The unwashed Sons of Parlan the Wild!'
And he laughed – not his usual hearty bellowing, but a
soundless brief chuckling. And he loosened his claymore in
the silver-mounted sheath that hung from his gleaming
shoulder-belt – quite unnecessarily. MacGregor swords
seldom needed loosening.

*　　*　　*

Gregor knew who they must be, of course, the only people
they *could* be, there and then – Macfarlanes from across the
loch, of the broken clan of Glen Fruin, dispossessed these
many years by the Colquhouns, landless and little better
than tinklers. The Gregorach knew what it was to be landless – not his own sept of Glengyle, of course, God be
praised – even nameless, and they were theoretically outlawed with a price on every MacGregor head even now; but
they had never degenerated to ditch-dodging bog-wallopers
who would sell their swords for Lowland silver against their
own kind.

Swords was wrong, Gregor amended. There did not seem
to be a single sword or claymore amongst the advancing
throng – only dirks; as was only suitable, of course, for none
could possibly be gentlemen.

Gallangad must have dug deeper into his pouch than any
eight stirks to buy this crew.

Gregor spoke to Graham, quite gently. 'I think it would
have been less costly to keep faith with MacGregor, Sassunach,' he said.

He did more than that, of course. He raised his voice, and
cried powerfully, 'Ardchoille! Ardchoille!' the dreaded
rallying cry of his clan – partly to bring back to his side the
four gillies with the hounds, and partly to help strike caution
into the minds of the oncoming Macfarlanes.

Up on the braes behind the house his henchmen, already
on the return with another dozen cows and calves, responded by yelping high yittering versions of the same
slogan, and came racing downhill, driving the affrighted
cattle in a lumbering gallop before them.

The Macfarlanes came on steadily, secure in their numbers, a little dark lively monkey of a man seemingly their leader.

Gregor sat his garron motionless, even if his eyes were busy. He noted swiftly, automatically, such features of the layout of the buildings and the lie of the land as might be useful if this foolish affair came to blows. Seven to thirty, such considerations might have their value.

Gallangad was biding his time, just waiting and glowering, like one of his own bullocks. As the Macfarlanes came up in a solid phalanx, silent but menacing, however ragged, he turned towards them heavily.

But Gregor forestalled him, speaking easily in the Gaelic. 'You are on the wrong side of the loch, are you not, Sons of Parlan ?' he wondered. 'What do you amongst the Sassunach ?'

'We eat,' the small dark fellow answered him swiftly, briefly.

The MacGregor nodded. 'All must do that,' he agreed. 'But dog does not eat dog – much less eagle eat eagle! I hope that you feed well on Gallangad's beef ?'

The other looked just a little uncertain at this line of talk. He glanced along at some of his fellows, and then over at Graham. That individual raised a hand to jab at Gregor.

'Yon's your man!' he cried hoarsely. 'Dirty thieving MacGregor scum! Gie him his paiks, lads – and teach him to come lifting honest men's gear. . . . '

Gregor ignored the creature, addressing himself, in the older tongue, still to the little Macfarlane. 'I am Glengyle,' he mentioned. 'It may be that you have come to help us lift our dues from this close-fisted borach ? In which case, my thanks . . . and there are beasts enough for us all!'

'You are generous, Glengyle – with other men's goods,' the dark man said, in his quick squeaky voice. 'But we mind of other times when the Gregorach were less generous. In our own glens!' There was a rumbled growl behind and around him, and an incipient but distinct edging forward.

The Macfarlanes and the MacGregors had ever been un-
friends – and Highland memories are long.

'Hae at them, damn their red hides!' Gallangad roared.
'I didna pey ye tae blether, ye gangerels. . . . '

There was a commotion behind Gregor, as the cows from
upbye came plunging down to join the heifers, and, more
quietly, the four gillies at their heels slipped into their
places at their chieftain's flanks, bare chests heaving with
their running, but hands on their dirks. The deerhounds
loped round and round the augmented herd, red tongues
hanging, with the strange effortless tittuping motion of their
kind.

The young man on the pony emitted a sigh of relief –
though not visibly, of course. His talking had gained what
had been required – time to gather his little force tightly
about him. Now, he need be less painfully diplomatic.

'Are you with MacGregor, or against MacGregor, Sons
of Parlan?' he shouted, then, and whipped out his claymore
with a thin high-pitched skreak of steel. 'Choose you!'

He did not give them long for the choosing, either – not so
had the renowned Tutor of Glengyle brought him up.
While still the Macfarlanes shuffled and muttered, he dug
bare knees into his garron's broad sides, and the beast
plunged forward. Close and tight as an arrowhead, at his
flanks and rear his six gillies moved with him, herding-staves
in one hand, dirks in the other. 'Ardcho-o-o-oile!' they
yelled in unison, a fine heartening shout.

That first notable charge was as great a success as was
usual – and the Gregorach were namely for their first
charges, which in fact not infrequently won the day for
them; not with the odds at thirty to seven, of course. But
their tight arrowhead formation would bore through any
throng not unreasonably deep, and when the point of it was
mounted and the opposition was not, and moreover was the
only man with a sword in his hand, the thing was child's
play. Gregor plunged straight at the little dark fellow, flashing his great blade in a beautiful and symmetrical down-
bent figure-of-eight pattern – left and right, left and

right, the back stroke just clearing his nearest gillies' noses by inches, the forward reaching well out and round in an arc wide enough to ensure that no man could use anything shorter than a billhook against them, with effect. And billhooks are unhandy things to wield in a crowd. Only once did the claymore falter in its sweet rhythm, and that was when, passing Gallangad himself, Gregor turned it sideways-on to give the laird a good whacking buffet with the flat of it, and send him spinning to the ground satisfactorily. It would have been more satisfactory still, of course, to have given him the edge of it, but Glengyle realised well enough that running through even a low-country cock-laird such as this, in the way of business, might arouse all sorts of troublesome repercussions and enquiries, whereas nobody in all the land was going to worry about a few bare-shanked chiefless Macfarlanes more or less.

They drove through the tinkler rabble then, like a knife through cheese, men going down like ninepins on either side, falling back against their fellows, getting in each other's way, billhooks being sheared off by that terrible slicing blade, their butt-ends even doing their own damage in the rear. The gillies actually had little to do, save in the way of dotting an i or crossing a t, only the two rearmost managing to really redden their dirks. They were through the mass in almost less time than it takes to tell, with no more hurt than a long scratch on Gregor's bare thigh caused by a splintering billhook shaft, and a glancing wound on one gillie's cheek made by a thrown sickle, bloody but insignificant.

This sort of manoeuvre was simple, satisfactory, and could be repeated till either the enemy was largely dispersed and scattered or till the chargers became exhausted. But it had one weakness, and that was when each rush was immediately through, and when the arrowhead bared its more or less unprotected rear – that, and the subsequent period of reforming when the components thereof turned around and steadied, regaining their wind. Gregor knew of these possibilities, needless to say, and had chosen to drive through towards a certain alleyway in the line of the steading, a narrow dung-strewn gap between a byre and a stable. Herein they could turn and pause and pant a little, their flanks and rear protected by the walling.

Gregor was laughing again, though a shade gustily with the vigour of his swording. 'How ... choose you ... now ... Parlanach ?' he called out.

No one actually answered his enquiry this time, either. The Macfarlanes were too busy picking themselves up, sorting themselves out, examining their hurts, tripping over their fallen, and generally cursing. Their evident confusion indicated that they were not used to fighting in a body; broken men seldom were, of course. Moreover, Gregor had made certain in the first rush that their monkey-like leader would do no more leading. Also indicated, at least to his uncle's nephew, was the precept that in war confusion in the enemy was a thing to be encouraged. Therefore he jerked a brief word forthwith to his faithful tail, and once more the Ardchoille slogan rang out as the arrowhead bored forward again.

This time they were not quite so successful – not through any failure or lack of vigour on the part of the Gregorach but solely because the Macfarlanes were still involuntarily scattered and uncertain, and therefore less conveniently compacted. As a result, the charge swept through them almost without opposition, and only those unfortunate enough to actually get in the way tended to fall – a disappointing business. Perceiving that most of the throng had drawn away over to the left of them, Gregor gestured and pulled his little cohort round in that direction, in as tight a circling movement as they could make it, causing considerably more of the admirable dispersal and confusion. They returned to their gap beside the byre breathless but intact.

They waited a little longer, now, for the recovery of wind. But the Macfarlanes were undoubtedly rallying, to some extent getting over their first bedevilment. Somebody seemed to be taking the lead. The last memory of the sun had gone, and though the August night was not dark, individuals were becoming difficult to identify at any distance. Gregor gave them a minute or so to decide whether or no they had had enough.

It quickly became clear that that stage had not yet been reached. Despite all the spectacular tumbling and chaos, they had suffered very few real casualties and still outnumbered the invaders by more than three to one. Further lessons were going to be necessary.

Gregor was about to give the order for still another sweep, when a sound behind them drew their glances. A man was darting about at the other end of this alley in which they were wedged. It was deep in shadow there, but by his jerky stiff motions it seemed to be the old cattleman who had stood at Gallangad's side when first they arrived. It was unlikely that such could be of any danger to them, however, and when the character promptly disappeared into one of the sheds, Gregor forthwith dismissed him from his mind. There were more potent folk to deal with.

Strangely enough, he was wrong there, as it happened. Just as Gregor filled his lungs to bellow their slogan once more, a different and still more deep-throated bellow sounded at their backs, jerking all heads round. A great white shape had emerged from a doorway at the head of the alley, and had turned down its narrow length, prodded on apparently at the back by the old man with a pitchfork. It was a bull, most obviously, a massive white and dauntingly horned bull – even allowing for the magnifying effect of the twilight, quite the most bulky and brawny specimen of its kind that even these experts in cattle had ever set eyes upon. And it had its great head hanging low, swaying from side to side, while it scrape-scraped at the ground with an angry forefoot.

Even as they stared, the brute's bellowing rose a degree or two, in tone as in volume, so that it became more like a savage trumpeting. It seemed to try to lash out to the rear at its tormentor there, but could not turn in the confined

37

space of the alley. So, instead, it started off down the passageway at a lumbering gallop, roaring its fury, while the ground and the buildings shook to its challenge.

Gregor Ghlun Dubh delayed no longer. Swallowing whatever it was that had risen into his throat, he gestured forward with his blade – and at that barely beat his gillies to it. The Ardchoille that rose from those lips as they plunged out into the open once more was a poor and wavering effort that Rob Roy would never have recognised. Like the charge that accompanied it. Even a MacGregor charge is seldom up to standard when the chargers' glances are apt to be as much rearwards as front.

CHAPTER THREE

GALLANGAD's white bull changed the whole aspect of that battlefield, changed it radically and entirely and in a ridiculously short space of time. It was a great evil-tempered brainless brute undoubtedly, and what was more, did not know one clan from another. Perhaps the fact that both tartans had a deal of red about them confused even as it enraged the creature, dusk or not, for it hated and attacked them all with equal blind ferocity. From the moment that it came charging out of that alleyway at the heels of the somewhat malformed arrowhead, the interest and enthusiasm went out of the entire battle, as such. It was every man for himself.

At first, the animal merely thundered in the wake of the MacGregors – and the Macfarlanes, with a spontaneous appreciation of the situation, drew aside respectfully to give the whole procession space and passage. The thing thus might have remained attached to the charging Gregorach as a sort of rearguard had it not developed such an unsuitable turn of speed for so clumsy a brute. As it was, with the spray and draught of its puffing snorts beginning to reach the backs of their bare legs, the running gillies became increasingly preoccupied with other issues than keeping due tight formation and uniform pace. In fact, Gregor began to find them actually passing him on his horse – which was no way to conduct a charge, at all. It was not as if he was going slowly himself – for good garrons were valuable beasts, and not to be lightly hazarded. Gradually, then – at least, in so far as anything so headlong and breakneck could be termed gradual – the MacGregors fanned out, and since those on the flanks quickly perceived that the bull seemed to be considering the pony and its rider as its ultimate objective, they kept on fanning. Soon Glengyle discovered himself, his mount and the bull to be assuming the roles of major actors while everybody else looked on enthralled. Presumably the creature had an objection to horseflesh, or else the extra quantity of red tartan represented by his philamore and plaid acted as magnet.

Needless to say, Gregor found all this both unseemly and quite unfair. He was not quite sure, in a race, whether his short-legged stocky garron would have the heels of the short-legged stocky bull, or vice versa. Certainly the latter seemed to be uncommonly nimble for its weight. Or again, whether he might not be better on his own feet, he who was neither stocky nor short-shanked? But dignity and prestige entered into that, of course. He was Glengyle, after all, and could not be seen actually running away from anything under heaven. Moreover, he was in process of teaching Gallangad and this Macfarlane riff-raff a lesson, and was not to be distracted. Therefore, he ascertained where the somewhat farflung enemy was thickest, and thitherwards slewed his pony at maximum speed. He managed a rudimentary Ardchoille too, claymore waving.

It was to be hoped that once amongst the Macfarlanes the annoying animal behind would become suitably involved.

Gregor was not disappointed in this, at least. The Macfarlanes on this occasion saw no reason to impede the Mac-

Gregor's progress, and gave way on either side with an alacrity worthy of better men. Two of them, indeed, in a haste unbecoming in Highlanders, collided with such force as to lose their balances and fall. The more agile was up and off again before you could say Loch Sloy. But the other was less effective at getting to his feet in time. Over this miserable specimen Gregor lifted his garron in a jump, disdaining even to poke him with his sword in the by-going. The bull, however, allowed itself to be distracted by the squirming and convulsing red apparition in its path. Which was no less than the foolish fellow deserved, probably.

Gregor knew almost a momentary pique at the lack of attention that his single-minded charge seemed to be receiving from the Parlanach. They all appeared to be much more interested in how their grounded fellow dealt with a rapidly developing situation. And to give the creature his due, he rather redeemed himself, managing now to leap to his feet as though spring-loaded, and so effectively to take to his heels that only the ragged folds of his stained kilt caught on one of the hurtling bull's thrusting horns – where it remained. Fortunately or otherwise, the wretch was not too firmly attached to this his only garment, and leapt off, naked but vociferous. The bull, disappointed and temporarily blinded by this tattered tartan draped over its face, slewed round and charged hither and yonder in short rushes, tossing its head, stamping its feet, and bellowing. Gregor was able to pull up, a short distance off, evidently forgotten for the moment by all and sundry.

There could be no point in seeking to chronicle any coherent and consecutive account of what happened thereafter. A state of general, stirring but quite chaotic activity ensued. The bull quickly got rid of most of its kilt – though it retained one fragment which fluttered like captured colours from its horn – and thereupon hurled itself at anyone and everyone that came within its range of vision. And it had a wide-ranging if choleric eye. Entirely catholic and quite unpredictable, it flung itself around, attacking Macfarlanes, MacGregors and its own Lowland keepers with a fine impartiality and with an unflagging vigour that indicated a virility patently quite unsatisfied by the demands of Gallangad's paltry herd.

Occasionally, of course, some brave fellow would take a whack at the brute, as it were in passing, with billhook or cudgel. But such were few and far between – and apt to be unplanned. It was extraordinary how swiftly everybody lost their identity too – the deepening dusk assisting, of course. Gregor alone, because he was mounted, remained kenspeckle. For the rest, it was quite impossible to establish who was which, all being merely identical and individual targets for an angry quadruped.

Very soon it was apparent to Gregor that there was no hope of restoring the field to anything like order, or even of resuming the battle. Everybody had lost interest. Already there seemed to be markedly fewer folk about – which, since there was no routh of bodies lying about the scene either, must mean that the combatants were just quietly betaking themselves off as occasion offered. A reasonable and sensible attitude, he decided, for the Macfarlanes. But for the Gregorach, of course, it was different. They had their errand to fulfil, and the cattle to consider. . . .

He considered these, then, scattered around eastwards, but none far away, ghostly shapes in the gloom, apparently watching the entire affray with interest. It occurred to him that if he could just get this lot rounded up and on their way, leaving the remaining Macfarlanes to the bull, it would probably be the best outcome of the situation. The trouble was – where were those miserable gillies of his?

Raising his voice, Gregor emitted a sort of modified Ardchoille – nothing that would sound too like a challenge to either bull or Macfarlanes, not so much a warrior's rallying-cry indeed as the call of say a hen eagle for her errant chicks.

There was no audible response. But presently he found a couple of somewhat hang-dog-seeming individuals at his side. He gestured imperiously in the direction of the cattle, and, uttering brief high yelps for the hounds, the pair darted thankfully off. Other shamefaced miscreants appeared, one by one, out of the mirk and confusion, and were sent about the same business. The only thing – Gregor was not quite certain that the odd Macfarlane might not have got included amongst them.

In a gratifyingly short space of time the unified herd of some two dozen beasts was on the move – not directly towards Gregor admittedly, with beyond him the bull's circus, but aslant and northwards – which after all was the way in which they had to go eventually. Which was all right. But one of the young heifers, white also and by her behaviour almost certainly a daughter of the wretched bull itself, chose to be awkward. Breaking away from the others, she came lolloping across, as though to join her sire, mooing warm invitation.

Gregor managed to nip that in the bud, turning the creature back a little. But unfortunately the damage had been done. Perhaps the bull had been getting tired, not physically most assuredly, but of chasing shadows; perhaps it was pining for its own kind; perhaps it just recognised that flutelike lowing, and deep responded to not-so-deep? At any rate the big brute abruptly gave up the harrying of elusive Macfarlanes, produced a really major but quite touching bellow, very different from all its angry trumpetings hitherto, and came pounding over to join the gentle heifer. And therefore, unhappily, the heifer's herders.

Gregor Ghlun Dubh found himself faced with a nice problem. That bull was not to be shooed away – but unfortunately neither was the heifer. She was cavorting joyfully to his right, ululating urgent goodwill. Gregor's abuse and gesticulations and sword-slapping were of less than no effect. The foolish animal would not go away, but only bawled the louder. And the bull, bearing down on his other side at full ground-shaking speed, made answer.

Gregor came to a decision at commendable speed, too. What was one heifer, more or less? Gallangad could be left with one beast to him – or, rather, two. The rest of the herd was streaming away downhill northwards at a fine pace, gillies well up – disappearing into the gloom, in fact. Without further debate, the chieftain dug his knees into his garron and set off in pursuit.

And with a high-pitched silvery belling of sheer *joie de vivre* the heifer followed on, kicking up her heels.

Farther back the deep roar of infatuated maturity intimated that the bull had duly noted the change of course and was now heading northwards also.

Gregor cursed vehemently and comprehensively. He cantered after the herd, and the white heifer cantered after him, and the bull cantered after the heifer. In such fashion the Gregorach retired from Gallangad.

*   *   *

The long half-mile down to the Catter Water was covered in what must have been record time, with the rear gaining noticeably on the van. What would happen at the riverside was a matter for real speculation.

Gregor had joined up with the gillies ere that. No hearty greetings were exchanged. There was a definite tendency for the drovers to spread out, left and right, leaving ample space for the white heifer to rejoin her sisters. Glengyle did nothing to discourage this. Unfortunately, the frolicsome creature seemed to have taken a fancy, like the bull before her, either to the young chieftain or to his horse, and now insisted on clinging to his heels with annoying fidelity. The bull, ignoring the rest of the herd, lumbered in her wake.

By the time that Gregor and his immediate tail reached the waterside, the remainder of the cavalcade, now unaccountably slackening speed, had dropped fully a hundred yards behind. The young man rather blessed that dark and chuckling water. He put the pony straight at it, and splashed across its thirty feet or so in fine style – making as much pother as possible, in fact. Now they would see. . . .

But when he got to the far bank and looked back, the heifer was already half-way across, and loving it, even kicking up her hindquarters skittishly as the water splashed her underparts. Her faithful sire plunged in after her, unhesitant.

Gregor groaned.

Up the rather steeper gorse-grown slopes beyond he urged his garron, hoping somewhat desperately that the climb would deter and weary either progeny or progenitor. It did nothing of the sort, only too clearly. The heifer was apparently in the same elevated state in which young females of other sorts, for instance, frail and delicate as they may seem, can dance away the entire night and appear with the dawn fresh and lively as kittens beside their tottering and haggard-eyed escorts. And the bull most obviously was nothing less than a manufactory of energy and vigour, the devil damn it! It was the rider, and possibly to some extent the mount, that began to weary. And there were still fully twenty-five rough and difficult miles to Inversnaid.

It was not until he and his personal procession was high on its long hummocky ascent to the base of Duncryne, round the east side of which lay their route – and the stodgy and uninspired remainder of his retinue had long been lost to sight and sound, far below – that it began to dawn on Gregor MacGregor that this might not all be quite so humiliating and unsuitable as it seemed. Suppose, instead of seeking to shake off this vast and terrible bull, he considered delivering it intact at Inversnaid, as a personal and monumental booty, an epic of single-handed valour and devotion? Might not that be something truly heroic, so much more worthy of his stature and name than merely to bring home the few cows and stirks that his uncle had ordered – or rather, requested? Indeed, might it not be just the sort of thing that the sennachies and song-makers in time to come would sing about and hand down to on-coming generations – how Gregor Ghlun Dubh brought the Great White Bull of Gallangad to Glengyle? That would sound very fine, magnificent.

The notion did not require any period of gestation and growth in Gregor's mind – it flowered forthwith and immediately, fully grown, and was as promptly accepted, MacGregor like. And, of course, thereupon the whole situation was changed, transformed. The bull became at once a subject for coaxing and managing, not for terror, a source of possible triumph instead of a menace. From being afraid that the brute might overtake or outrun his garron, the man incontinently began to fear that it would soon grow tired, lose interest, give up the chase. The heifer, from being an infuriating little nuisance, was translated at once into a major blessing, the essential bait for the trap, to be cajoled and cherished instead of shooed away. The human mind is a truly exceptional mechanism.

As they climbed, Gregor was now looking back over his shoulder even more frequently and anxiously than heretofore – in case the creatures behind him should be slackening pace and falling off. But the heifer did not fail him, right up to the low ridge between Duncryne Hill and the lonely place of Cambusmoon – and though the bull's heavy puffings were now more indicative of laboured breathing than majestic wrath, its interests still seemed to be wholly engaged.

It was downhill thereafter, happily, all the way to the Endrick's levels around the tail of the loch. Keeping the few lights of the village of Gartocharn well to his left, Gregor plunged on north-eastwards, having to even restrain his garron a little – it apparently not yet having discovered that they were now leading and not running away. But at least the beast was notably sure-footed, like all its kind, so that its rider needed only to give it the general direction and leave it to pick its own route over the shadowy broken shelving ground – which was a great convenience for a man whose head was turned rearwards for most of the time. It would be a tragic thing, he now was perceiving, if the bull was to fall and break a leg in any of the numerous holes, burns and steps with which this benighted territory was littered. Or the heifer either, of course. . . .

Once across the Dumbarton turnpike, new problems arose to worry the leader of the little procession – literally arose, and went lumbering off affrighted into the night. Cattle. These broad lush flats and water-meadows flanking the mouth of the Endrick were dotted with sleeping beasts,

45

My Lord Marquis of Montrose's beasts – and who could tell whether one of these might not at any moment take the bull's fancy, in place of the heifer, and divert it off into the gloom?

But that bull was of a worthily tenacious mind, undoubtedly, and not to be turned aside from whatever it was doing. And for the time being it was following and pining after its own little white heifer. Other bovine charmers might plunge off with inviting woofs, or low siren songs from all around, but her sire, that most adequate animal, that was even now butting and bull-heading its way into legend, folklore, even into history itself, just kept boring on, head down, breathing gustily, short thick stamping legs shaking the soft ground.

And that was Gregor Ghlun Dubh's next worry. The nearer that they came to the sluggish mouth of the coiling Endrick Water, the marshier became the terrain. Would his bull perhaps sink into the mire, get bogged, and have to be abandoned like a stranded leviathan from the loch? Fortunately the season had been a dry one, and the place was not nearly so wet as he had known it; he had been perfectly content to lead a herd of ordinary beasts across these flats and over a ford he knew of. But this bull must weigh three times as much as any normal beast. . . .

In the event, however, it was the heifer that got into trouble, not her sire. At the very edge of the river, as Gregor did some quick prospecting for the ford, she came up, still skittish and fancy-dancing, and seeking to cut off a corner that the garron's turning up the river's bank had made, plunged straight into a quaking pot of black mire covered by a skin of moss, and sank almost to her belly. Promptly a piteous heart-rending plaint rang out, markedly different from her previous utterance, to which the faithful bull made loud and confident answer. But the big brute had more sense than to lumber in beside her, just the same, and came to a halt a few yards off, testing the ground with tramping forefeet, great head stretched forward towards the other, snuffling and bellowing by turns.

This was where Gregor of Glengyle's calibre rather fell to be tested. It was one thing to lead the way, keeping a discreet distance between himself and his self-attached tail, and altogether another to turn back and actually approach that bull. He did not do so off-hand or without consideration, either. But he did it. Let that stand. What was more, he went on his own two feet – since the garron would on no account co-operate. Dismounting, and without exactly striding, he moved back to the heifer.

Actually, the bull paid him not the slightest heed. The brute's entire attention was concentrated on the bleating animal in the pot of the bog. After a few wary moments, so was Gregor's. Man and bull stood on opposite sides of the little quagmire, considering the situation.

The heifer was not struggling nor floundering about, just standing still and wailing her dismay. Gregor scratched his head. Just what to do was less than crystal-clear. He could not reach out sufficiently far to touch the creature without falling into the hole himself – not that touching would have been a lot of use anyway. He had no rope with him, to loop round her and seek to tug her out. He tried speaking coaxingly to her, urging her to make the effort to get out herself. But that produced only enhanced complaints – each answered by a sort of groaning blast from the sympathetic bull, the draught of which reached across to the man distinctly.

Then he had an idea. Unlooping his sheathed claymore, which hung on its silver-mounted shoulder-belt, he held the weapon out by its tip, and after the third throw managed to toss the loop of the belt over the heifer's head. Twisting the thing, and moving a little to the side so that it did not slip off, he tugged. It was not the sort of thing that he would have liked anyone to have seen him doing with MacGregor of Glengyle's broadsword.

He tugged to no purpose for a few moments – and it was galling to consider the power and vigour represented by the great brainless brute standing there at the other side of the hole, useless, and that yet could have hauled this cry-baby

47

out in two shakes could it only have been harnessed. Then suddenly his efforts had effect. The pressure on the heifer's neck evidently decided her to do something for herself, for after a series of convulsions she got first one foreleg out on to firm ground, and then the other, and finally, with a great slaister and splattering of mud – much of it over Glengyle's finery – she heaved herself right out, to stand, bemused, bemired and trembling, on the brink. And silent for the moment.

The bull moved round the hole, now, with a sort of sober circumspection noteworthy in so rampant a brute – and Gregor, detaching his sword, moved back to his garron with similar circumspection. But there, looking round, he discovered that the heifer had not moved at all, but was standing still, apparently all the wanton whimsey-whamsey drained out of her into the bog. The bull was nuzzling her rear tentatively.

Gregor compressed his lips, sighed and shrugged in one, and taking the reluctant garron by its shaggy forelock, led it back to the cattle. He had to tug hard here, too. He elected to come up on the other side of the heifer from her sire, the which was making a deep rumbling noise in its throat, that sounded daunting in the extreme but was probably a species of purring; and went only close enough to reach out his sword and its belt once more, loop it over the heifer's head, and vault on to the pony's back. That wise animal was nothing loth to continue its northward journey promptly; the heifer came along meekly, deflatedly, at the pressure; and, chin resting contentedly on her rump, great puffs from its nostrils blowing along her back, the bull came too, waddling grotesquely.

Thus, in sober file, they walked down and into the Endrick Water, and across, with no more fuss than might the Senators of the College of Justice proceed to a hanging, and up on to the firmer ground at the far side. And thus they continued across the darkling flats, to the drove road beyond that led to Balmaha. And every now and again the bull sighed mightily, the heifer coiled a long tongue round the chased sheath of the noble brand that led her, and the garron blew doubtfully through flaring nostrils.

Presently Gregor began to sing, gently to himself, to them all. He made up the words and the tune as he went along, since there was nobody in all the night to hear him – save a bull, a heifer and a pony. And it had the makings of a good, a noble song in it, too.

*   *   *

There is no need to tell of the long long walk that they all had thereafter – for that was in fact all it was. Crossing the Endrick had amounted to crossing the Highland Line, and the drove road that they followed took them northwards between towering dark mountains on their right hand and the great isle-strewn expanse of Loch Lomond on their left. Once through the narrow Pass of Balmaha the unrelenting rampart of the hills drew even closer, until it was pressing them for much of the time almost on to the loch shore itself. But despite the constriction of their going, the climbing and the plunging and the twisting of the track, the innumerable streams draining the land mass that they had to cross, and the endless wooded bays and headlands that fell to be circumnavigated, the heifer and the bull followed steadily on behind the pacing garron, the one with a mild acceptance, the other with a growing but determined stolidity. And at the one side the tiny wavelets whispered and sighed, and at the other the muted singing of a hundred burns accompanied them, to fill in the periods when Gregor's nocturne died on him. Otherwise, only the occasional lost cry of some bird of the night interrupted the even clop and scuffle of hooves.

They did not make any great speed now, of course; probably if they averaged two twisting coiling miles in an hour they were doing as much as could be expected. Gregor calculated that they had all of eighteen difficult miles to cover after reaching the drove road – which was of course no road at all, but only a rough track for most of the way and sometimes not even that – a long walk for a stiff-legged heavy-built bull indeed.

Before long, the rest of the herd had caught up with them – or almost. When the gillies perceived the white shapes in the gloom in front, they slackened pace judiciously behind, so that a suitable interval should be preserved between the chiefly and the merely subordinate sections of the expedition. And that they maintained throughout, whatsoever the difficulties.

It was at least a couple of hours past midnight before they reached the clachan of Rowardennan, half-road to Inversnaid, and a MacGregor outpost. Gregor would much have liked to knock up the ale-house, whatever the hour, for well-deserved refreshment, but regretfully decided against it; who knew, if once the rhythm of this tranquil progress was disturbed, when and how the bull could be got to resume it? His people behind him, under no such pressure, were some time in reaching their due station in the rear thereafter.

Beyond Rowardennan the mountains pressed still closer and the track deteriorated accordingly, so that now they were merely clinging to a steep hillside grown with oak and birch and hazel, now high above the wan glimmering floor of the loch, now down at its dark wrack-littered beach. They were, in fact, here circling the massive base of soaring Ben Lomond itself. It was hereabouts that the white bull began at last to show signs of weariness, to stumble on its knee occasionally, and to grumble abysmally in its throat. But it kept doggedly on after the tireless heifer, nevertheless.

The pale dawn found them at the lonely place of Cailness, crouching under the great sleeping hills, the house of a sort of cousin of Glengyle's own. And here the bull decided that it had really had enough for one night. But with Inversnaid a mere three miles farther, Gregor was determined to complete his epic. The wills of tired bull and tired man clashed – and the man's won. MacGregor of Cailness was roused out of his bed, a rope and a pitchfork required of him, and the hounds and gillies whistled up. The bull and the heifer were tied loosely together, and another rope looped round the former's horns. Gregor redonned his sword and belt, and took the end of the rope, while dogs and gillies whooped and yelped discreetly in the rear. Only a couple of prods with the pitchfork were required. The party resumed its weary progress up the side of surely the longest loch in all Scotland, the bull led on like a lamb. Cailness, in parting, mentioned that he had never seen such a gentle animal.

Strangely enough, Gregor found himself to be somewhat nettled by this remark. The unsuitability of it remained with him for all the rest of the way over the rock-strewn wooded mountainside that the track was now slowly but surely climbing. His sleep-starved mind was perhaps less nimble than heretofore, but by the time that they had at last turned away from the loch altogether, and were making a laboured slantwise ascent of the precipitous pass of the Arklet Burn, he recognised what he must do to put the matter right. Admittedly, the just-awakened folk that peered at them from the doorways of the grouped croft houses of Clashbuie, first of the Inversnaid townships, gaped in awe at their white monster – but that was not enough. He and his men were now dragging and even pushing the drooping wayworn brute up that gruelling climb, hoisting it almost by main force, a labour of Hercules indeed. So, at the crest, with the level new-risen sun pouring golden light in their faces down the high east-lying trough of Glen Arklet, Gregor, panting, ordered thistles and whins to be collected from the hillside around. A bundle of these was then tied under the tail of the gasping heaving colossus, Glengyle remounting his garron the while. At first the creature merely stood, head sunk, exhausted. But when the gillies, bold now, slapped and poked it with their sticks, it rumbled, swung its head – and swished its tail. The startling hurt widened its dulled eyes. It emitted a cracked bellow. It took a pace or two forward, swished its tail again, and roared its pain and ire. Like milk on the boil, its fury rose within it and poured over. Lashing its spike-loaded tail now, and shaking all the enclosing hillsides with its trumpeted indignation, quite outsoaring and drowning the widespread lowing of beasts that came out of the valley ahead of them, it tore the turf with its forefeet, ripped it with its horns, and then lurched forward at the only live objects visible in front – Gregor and his garron. Neither required the gillies' shouted warning. They proceeded.

And so they tore out through the scattered birches, over the rushy levels where the Arklet and the Snaid Burns met, and round into the lovely green glen of Inversnaid itself, the bull temporarily recovered its strength in its choler, Gregor keeping ahead of it with a nice judgment, the heifer dragged along willy-nilly sprawling and stumbling, and the rest of the herd streaming behind amidst yelling men and baying hounds.

It was a notable entry, worthy of any chieftain of all the long line of Glengyle, or Clan Alpine itself. From all the profusion of the hump-backed cot-houses of the glen floor the folk emerged, to point and shout and laugh and cheer. 'Ardchoille!' Gregor ululated, above the din, and again 'Ardchoille!' and all the watchers in that valley took it up, the men chanting, the women skirling, the children screaming. Straight for the grassy terrace formed above a wide bend in the burn, where Rob Roy's two-storeyed house stood, Gregor rode, and the bull charged. Rob, stripped to the waist, in short kilt, scratching his red-furred chest, was outside his door, head back, laughing his strange silent laughter. At his side a man stood, open-mouthed, clad in once elegant breeches and once white frilled shirt. And from behind their legs children peeked.

Across the shallows the peculiar cavalcade swept, almost to the watchers' feet. There Gregor leapt lightly from his horse, casting away the rope that linked him to bull and heifer at the same time. For a grievous moment he knew doubt, the spectators knew doubt, possibly even the bull knew doubt, as to which it would follow – the careering pony, or the red-tartaned man? But the moment passed, and so did the bull – on at the affrighted garron's heels, pounding the earth and driving itself into further paroxysms of fury by the lashing and liberal self-application of whin-prickles to its tenderest parts, the heifer dragged alongside.

Gregor let them go without so much as a backward glance. No harm in the brute giving the glen a taste of its calibre, he decided – no harm at all. Travel-stained, mud-spattered, heavy-eyed, but chin even a degree higher than his wont perhaps, he swung his plaid back over his shoulder, and strode up to his uncle, hand on the guard of his claymore.

'I have fetched you a few beasts from Gallangad,' he mentioned. 'Just like you said, whatever.'

'As Royal's my Race – you have so, Greg!' Rob Roy cried. 'Yon bull, now – did you fetch it, or did it fetch you, I'm wondering?'

'Sir!' Young Glengyle frowned. 'I'd have you to know ...' Then he stopped, eyed his uncle from under one raised eyebrow, and then opened his mouth and laughed loud and long, Gregor Ghlun Dubh's own laughter. 'Shadow of God – I couldn't be telling you that my own self!' he declared. 'And that's a fact.'

Uncle smote nephew on the back, then, and despite the younger man's notable size he all but went sprawling. 'Bless you, boy,' he chuckled. 'You're a MacGregor, whatever!' And then, sobering quickly, he turned to the other man in the Lowland garb, a gentleman, and mystified obviously. 'But we are not all MacGregors. Colonel – my nephew, Glengyle, Chieftain of our branch of Clan Alpine. Greg – Colonel Hooke ... from St Germains!'

'Oh! Ah!' said Gregor, and swallowed his laughter. 'Your servant, sir.'

Perhaps that swallowing of his laughter was symbolic, there and then. For the man before him sought to bring not laughter to the glens but blood and tears.

It might be said indeed that, between them, the White Bull of Gallangad and Colonel Hooke closed the door on

Gregor's carefree youth. The bull galloped away with that chapter, and the Colonel pointed through into the next. Man's estate opened before Glengyle. There are more ways of coming of age than one.

CHAPTER FOUR

GREGOR MACGREGOR had earned his sleep out, surely – but he was denied it nevertheless. Rob Roy would drive men hard, on occasion – though seldom as hard as he would drive himself – and when events were astir, he had scant patience with slumber. By noon he had his nephew shaken out of the log-like sleep into which he had sunk immediately after the merest gesture at breakfasting, and hailed owlishly down to the groaning littered board set outside the front door of Inversnaid House, whereat Rob and his guest were just finishing their dining. He was not much of a man for being indoors, either, when he could be out. Gregor's Aunt Helen-Mary, a quiet but striking-featured woman with a very direct eye – indeed, it was said, the only living eye which could quell that of her husband – gathered the amplitude of broken meats, cold salmon, venison, oatcakes and curds laced with whisky, round her nephew's place, patted his shoulder, and withdrew indoors with her seven-year-old son Coll. Which meant men's talk.

'See you, Greg,' Rob Roy said, feeding his deerhounds scraps from the table now that his wife was safely out of the way. 'Colonel Hooke here has work for us to do. The word has been long of coming, but now it is here at last, God be praised. He was here awaiting me last night, when I was after reaching home from Drymen. He has come from Fife, and requires of us swift action, in the name of the King.'

54

'Fife . . . ? King . . . ?' Gregor mumbled, blinking the sleep out of his eyes. The noonday sun set up a great dazzle from the plashing Snaid Burn below their terrace. 'You mean the Chevalier . . . ?'

'Tut, lad – wake you! The King – our only king, Jamie Stewart the Eighth, by the grace of God. The Colonel has come from his Court of St Germains, in France, with the word that we have been awaiting. . . . '

'From Fife, did you not say. . . . ?'

'Och, from Fife, yes,' Rob explained patiently. 'He was after sailing from France to Anster, in Fife. He has been talking to the lairds in the Kingdom and in Angus, and now comes to raise the clans, Greg. The King will make a bid for his own, at last.'

'We are rising, then – now?' Gregor's voice rose a little, as his mind rose to shake itself free of the cobwebs of slumber.

'Not quite, young man – not yet.' That was Colonel Nathaniel Hooke speaking, a lean, sober, unsmiling man of middle years, liker the Kirk in looks than the battlefield, yet an old soldier of Dundee's and an Irishman into the bargain. 'Pray it will come to that. But as yet it is plans and promises that we are drawing, not swords.'

'But you said swift action, Uncle, did you not . . . ?'

'To be sure – but there is other action, whatever, than just drawing swords, *a dhuine*,' Rob said. 'We are to be getting the chiefs assembled to a great meeting, a gathering, so that the clans may be raised. Myself, I am to go round them, it seems . . . '

'You are the best man for the task, MacGregor,' Hooke assured. 'No man can cover the ground as you can – especially these wild mountains. You will do in a week what would take me a month and more.' That was no more than the truth, at any rate. 'Moreover, your name and your fame are known to all. You will be able to act as ambassador, my deputy, not merely my messenger. I have His Majesty's commission for you in my bag. And again, you are Breadalbane's kinsman, which, since he is to be host to the gathering, is of advantage. For, h'mm, not all men unfortunately love my Lord Breadalbane!'

Rob frowned. His mother, the Lady Glengyle, had indeed been Margaret Campbell of Glenlyon, first cousin to John Campbell, first Earl of Breadalbane – but it was not every day and in all company that Rob liked to be reminded of the fact. The connection could be useful at times, of course – indeed, had he not had to take the name of Campbell in lieu of his own, in 1693, when the Clan Gregor was outlawed and proscribed again so that no man might legally bear the name of MacGregor? In the eyes of the law – but only the law, to be sure – he was still Robert Campbell. But the Campbell connection had its disadvantages, as Rob was the first to admit – and Breadalbane was kittle-cattle even for a Campbell. Had he not been the main instigator of the MacDonalds' massacre at Glen Coe, of ill memory? Powerful as he might be, ho man was less trusted in all Scotland.

'I mislike this forgathering with Breadalbane,' Rob declared gravely. 'Myself, I misdoubt his attachment to the King's cause. It is something sudden, is it not? He stood neutral in 'Ninety, and came out for Dutch William after Cromdale fight. Kinsman or no, I'd liefer see the gathering held some other where, Colonel.'

'You must allow His Majesty's advisers to be the best judges of that, MacGregor,' Hooke asserted, a little stiffly. 'And you will recollect that whatever Dutch William's attitude may have been, Anne's present Government has not looked over-kindly on Breadalbane. In politics, men in high places must sometimes be, h'mm, allowed to change their minds!' He sipped at his horn beaker of whisky fastidiously. 'Moreover, if Clan Campbell can be persuaded to declare for King James, then Scotland at least is as good as won.'

'Man – you are right there, whatever!' Rob Roy cried, but jeeringly. 'Breadalbane may do what he will, but Argyll himself will never declare himself till Scotland *has* been won! As my Race is Royal – that is the way it will be! Man, I know the Campbells, see you – I know them fine.'

It was his guest's turn to frown. 'Maybe you do, Mac-Gregor – but I think perhaps that you do not fully realise the present state of Scotland, which will force the Campbells' hands for them, force Argyll's as it has already forced Breadalbane's. This Act of Union that they are forcing on the Scots Parliament, this surrender of Scotland's independence – it will be signed before the year is out, and the whole country will rise in revolt. . . . '

'It will *not* be signed, in God's name! Scotland will never sign her own death warrant, whatever!' That was Gregor Ghlun Dubh, awake at last.

His uncle eyed him thoughtfully.

Hooke's long upper lip seemed to grow the longer.'There speaks innocence! Scotland's death warrant will be signed, never doubt it, Glengyle. Enough pens have been bought to ensure it! Already the golden guineas are flowing north. A flood, it is. The Scots Parliament will meet for the last time in October . . . '

'The dastards! The traitors!' the young man cried. 'There are not crawling renegades enough, even in Edinburgh, to carry the day.'

'Think you so?' The other actually smiled, if thinly. 'Many bearing the noblest names in Scotland have already come out for the Union. All thirty-two Scots Commissioners have already agreed it, in London . . . at a price! But *we* need not distress ourselves, my young friend. Leal men should rather rejoice, and grasp the opportunity with both hands – while these others are grasping the English gold! Scotland will be aflame with resentment by the spring. And then King James will come – and when he lands, the entire country will flock to him. It is all, h'mm, most opportune.' That, from Nathaniel Hooke, might be esteemed as enthusiasm. 'Argyll, like Breadalbane, is no fool, whatever else he may be. He is one of the leaders of the Union party, yes – and who knows what his share of the guineas may be – but he knows the temper of the people very well, and what will happen if King James were to land at the right moment. It would not be beyond him to keep his gold, and yet to be ready to join the winning side in time to undo the deed that the gold had wrought!'

'God's death – do men sink so low?' Gregor gasped.

Rob Roy cleared his throat strongly. 'That may or may not be so, Colonel. Time will tell. I agree with you that if the Union is signed there will be trouble from one end of Scotland to the other. Even the Lowlanders may find themselves a modicum of spirit! And that will be the time for Jamie Stewart to land, indeed. But still I mislike this gathering to Breadalbane. I fear the other clans will mislike it also. . . . '

'Tush, man – you misjudge not only your kinsman but the situation,' the Jacobite emissary declared, almost impatiently. 'Do you not see – it is a sign of success? That the tide is with us. Breadalbane will not adhere to a losing cause. All will see that, and take heart. Indeed, the Earl has been most helpful. I had much converse with him at Blair-in-Atholl. This hunting match at Kinloch Rannoch is his own suggestion. All may attend it as his guests, without fear of suspicion.'

'Aye,' Rob said heavily. 'Aye. I'ph'mm. Maybe. And what says Atholl?'

'Atholl is, er, somewhat indisposed. A sick man. But he is with us in spirit. . . . '

'Aye,' the MacGregor said again, significantly. 'That is Atholl. Och, well – *non omnia possumus omnes*, eh? We all have our limitations, whatever. I will do what I can to bring the chiefs in to your hunting match, Colonel. But it will take time – for I will have half the Highlands to be covering.'

'I will come with you,' Glengyle declared, then.

'No, Greg – I think not,' his uncle said. 'There is other work for you. The King's army will be needing gold as well as men – and it will not get its gold out of the heather. Save for my cattle, that is – much of our fine haul here can be turned into good Scots pounds at the Crieff and Falkirk Trysts. The Colonel will go talking with the lairds in Gowrie and Strathearn and the Carse of Stirling. But the real money in this land is otherwhere – what is left of it after the Darien business! It lies with the merchants in Glasgow. Their poor shilpit souls are with their ledgers, whatever – but not all of them will look kindly on this Union. To tap them, we need the help of such as Buchanan of Arnprior and Hamilton of Bardowie, men with their fingers in the pie of the Indies trade. Ha – I see your eye light up, boy! I wonder why? You took a fancy to Arnprior, or maybe his goodson Bardowie, yesternight, did you? Aye, so.'

His nephew examined the stripped haunch of roebuck that he held in his hand, before passing it on to the hounds. 'I preferred his ladies,' he said, judiciously frank. 'They seemed . . . more fervent for the cause.'

'Is that so? Oh, aye. Anyway, I jaloused that you might not be averse to taking a message to Arnprior? And maybe to Stirling of Garden too, who has his links with Glasgow. And to two-three others that I can think on. Fine, then. And again, see you, something more. The Colonel thinks – and I am agreeing with him – that the chiefs and captains of clans that I will be after assembling at this Kinloch Rannoch ploy might be heartened and stablished and in some degree convinced if, as well as seeing Colonel Hooke and each other there, they were to see a sizeable body of armed and determined men!' Rob smiled gently. 'Gillies for the hunting match, of course – entirely necessary, whatever! Now, it so happens that in the deplorable and downholden state of our Highlands today there is only our own Gregorach that could be making such a muster at short notice, belike! A coincidence. It is against the law, of course – but, *dia*, are we not outlawed and proscribed anyhow! So gather you, Greg . . . ' His uncle recollected, and stroked his beard. 'So if Glengyle will be so kindly as to gather his sept, and such other of the Gregorach as he can raise betwixt here and Balquhidder, to the number of, say, three hundred, and bring them to Kinloch Rannoch three weeks from now – och, that will be fine, just fine, see you.'

'And His Majesty will be duly grateful, Glengyle,' Nathaniel Hooke added gravely.

Gregor was on his feet, eyes shining. '*Dia* – I shall be leading the first men under arms for the King in all Scotland, then?' he cried.

'You could put it that way,' Hooke agreed.

'*Ro mhath* – I will do it! Do it all. This will be better than droving cattle, whatever. I will go now. At once. . . . '

'Wait you. Wait for the message, at least!' Rob Roy laughed. 'And think you it would not be kindly to go say farewell to the Lady Christian your mother, over at Glengyle?'

'M'mmmm.'

'And the bull? You will wish to take your bull to Glengyle?'

'I . . . ah . . . I will go see my mother,' Gregor said handsomely. 'Give me your message, and let me be gone. And, Uncle . . . you may keep the bull!'

* * *

The green valley of Inversnaid, fair and grassy and spreading open to the south and the sun, was in fact little more than a high sheltered corrie and no real glen at all, some two miles in length before it tailed off into the lofty crags and rocky buttresses of Maol an Fhithich, the Bluff of the Ravens. A thousand-foot ridge separated it on the west from long Loch Lomond, and to the east a higher barrier of three tall hills divided it first from Corryarklet and then from Glen Gyle. To reach his home from Inversnaid, then, Gregor Ghlun Dubh could either go the long way round the hill masses, by Loch Arklet and Loch Katrine, or over them by a high bealach between Stob an Fainne, the Peak of the Ring, and Beinn a Choin, the Mountain of Weeping. Needless to say, as a matter of principle he chose the latter. Seldom indeed were conditions such as to force the former upon him, practically two thousand feet high though the saddle lay.

It was not all a matter of youthful masculine esteem, or a point of honour. Aesthetics entered into it too, for assuredly the vista from the lofty pass was something to move even the dullest perception. And Gregor's was not that – especially when, as now, a fierce pride in it all possessed him, and an aching, yearning yet eternally unsatisfied sense of identity with all that prospect. On every hand the mountains stretched away into purple infinity – save to the south, which was blocked out anyway by the majestic bulk of Ben Lomond. No fewer than eight lochs lay below him, in blue tranquillity, sparkling in the sun, or glooming deep in shade. Far down the stretching arm of salt Loch Long the Firth of Clyde reached out to the western sea, past all the peaks of Arran. Through the great gap of Glen Falloch and Strath Fillan to the north, the vast Moor of Rannoch sprawled, the playground of the winds, flanked by the serried mountains of Black Mount and Glen Coe and Mamore, with, far beyond, the shadowy giants of the remote north-west, pale and austere and streaked even now with the white of eternal snows. In every other direction the jagged succession of countless summits and spurs and ranges, green with deer-hair, purple with heather, brown with peat and raw earth, and black-and-white with naked quartz-shot rock, shouldered and jostled and enclosed this verdant sanctuary of Clan Gregor, and, over all, the cloud shadows sailed and flitted. It was a panorama that could speak with many voices to the beholder. To Gregor that day it represented Scotland, the ideal, the lovely and forlorn, the betrayed but inviolate Alba, mother and mistress both, the land to draw sword for, if necessary, to die for.

Thus uplifted, he slanted down into his own Glen Gyle.

Here was a very different valley from that of Inversnaid, a true glen, deep and narrow, between soaring rugged peaks, through which raced a sizeable river in rushes and falls and linked gleaming pools. It was a place of scattered open birch-woods and hazel-fringed water-meadows, of great outcropping rocks as big as houses, and long sweeping grassy aprons scored by burnlets innumerable. Five miles it stretched, all seen clearly from up here, from the head of fair Loch Katrine at its foot, to where the thrusting shoulder of a mountain divided it neatly into two upper corries that rose fully five hundred feet above its floor, where the twin headwaters were born. And the whole was dotted with croft-houses with their patches of tilth and their peat-stacks, and cattle grazed high on all the hills. Down near the loch shore Gregor's own House of Glengyle stood amidst its sheltering trees, surrounded by its orchard, its herb garden, its steading and offices, its smiddy and its tannery and its duck-pond, like a hen amongst her brood. Heritage enough for any man – and an excellent place for coming back to.

Gregor had soft-heartedly walked his garron up to the bealach, for it could have been tired from its night's cantrips, but he rode it down all the long sweeping slopes to his home in the glen, letting it pick its own way, what time he sent cattle plunging left and right with his cheerful shouting, called and waved to such of his people as were to be seen about their crofts, and fetched his hounds racing up to meet him from the House by his long ululant halloos that the hillsides tossed to and fro in blithesome echo.

Glengyle House was a much superior place to Rob Roy's fairly recently built establishment at Inversnaid, three storeys high, narrow, whitewashed, with a steep crow-step gabled roof, stone-slated not reed-thatched, however much moss-grown. Moreover, it had a stair-tower attached, wherein was the handsome moulded doorway surmounted by a weather-worn heraldic stone panel showing, even though dimly, the crossed tree and sword of his race – bearing suitably the crown on the top of the sword – and the motto S'RIOGHAL MO DHREAM, My Race is Royal. Slapping his mount away to find its own place, Gregor strode in under this ancient stone, all his leaping barking hounds around him, to shout for his mother and acquaint her of the good tidings.

The Lady Christian was a gentle soul who had tackled the business of being wife and mother to MacGregors rather more acceptingly than had, say, Rob Roy's Helen-Mary – who of course was of the Gregorach herself. Six years a widow, she was still under forty, with no grey in the golden hair that was one of the few non-Gregorach characteristics which she had managed to transmit to her elder son. She listened now to his excited and joyous tale, did not seek to chasten his enthusiasm, swallowed her own mother's fears, and sighed a small sigh. For herself, King Jamie could have bided very happily in France.

There was much to tell, much to envisage, many instructions to give, not a few immediate demands to make. Christian MacGregor received all with the quiet compliance that was expected of her. Indeed, her son would have been quite put out had she done otherwise. Nevertheless, even as he made it all known to her, Gregor was looking at his mother as he had never quite looked at her before – as an individual rather than as a sort of comfortable institution to be taken for granted, as a woman indeed – and as at least temporary mistress of his domain of Glengyle. For the first time some detached portion of his mind was contemplating it as a possibility that one day she might be displaced in that mistress-ship. It was a strange and exciting conception – if mildly perturbing too.

As it happened, in all the flood of his talk, the enchanting Mary Hamilton of Bardowie quite escaped mention. There were so many other issues to be dealt with, of course. . . .

To the Lady Christian's highly mother-like if tentative suggestion that King James's cause might not suffer irretrievably if her son did not rush off on it that very afternoon, but spent one night in his own bed, Gregor of course gave short shrift. When Scotland's future was at stake, it behoved men to be up and doing. He was, after all, Gregor Black Knee of Glengyle, and no slug-abed. Had not his Uncle Rob demanded – or at least urged – prompt action? Well, then. With a fresh garron he could cover the twenty-five miles to Arnprior, by the Pass of Aberfoyle and across the Moss, in four hours. He could be there well before dark. A whole day saved. . . .

Christian MacGregor understood, of course.

CHAPTER FIVE

GREGOR GHLUN DUBH rode at a steady mile-eating trot, up hill and down, by track and no track, by lochside and bog, by birken brae and bracken dene, by ford and narrow pass, till at the Clachan of Aberfoyle they won out of the mountains and into the green and spreading plain of the great Carse of Stirling. At his pony's heels loped two running gillies, their bare chests heaving rhythmically, like well-regulated bellows. They ran thus from preference, for they could have ridden ponies also had they wished – indeed, the elder, Ian Beg, who had been foster-brother and body servant to Gregor's young lamented father Ian More of Glengyle, and now liked on occasion to serve his son in the same capacity, actually possessed a couple of garrons of his own. These clansmen were no bidden slaves, but name-proud cousins of their chieftain – however far removed – who served of choice and esteemed it honour.

This matter of the size of his tail had been Gregor's major problem before coming away. Going through and into populous country as he was, it behoved Glengyle to sustain his dignity and status with a suitably large following of armed supporters – especially when, at least theoretically, he was the representative of an outlawed and proscribed clan entering settled country, whose members were forbidden by law to carry anything more lethal than a broken-pointed eating-knife, or to assemble in numbers exceeding four. On the other hand, this business that he was engaged upon was in the first instance highly secret, confidential and not to be shouted about. The time for shouting would undoubtedly come later. That did not mean, of course, that MacGregor of Glengyle was going to skulk about like any tinkler or Colquhoun or something of that sort. He had decided that just a pair of gillies probably would be best –

distinguishing him as a Highland gentleman deserving of due respect without actually drawing unnecessary attention to himself. So that quality should compensate for quantity, he had them armed suitably, with claymores, large and small dirks, and metal-studded leather targes. Here was no cattle droving.

A pair of Gregor's own deerhounds completed the little procession.

With the hills behind them, they took to the lonely empty wilderness of Flanders Moss, that vast waterlogged plain of sedge and reeds, of willow and alder and general quaking bog, that practically filled all the western half of the wide carse, and through which the River Forth linked and coiled and doubled fantastically, an uncertain and daunting quagmire of some fifty square miles, wherein whole armies might enter and never reappear – the Gregorach's first line of defence, indeed. The routes across its mighty and treacherous expanse – for routes there were – remained jealously guarded secrets, some of them known only to a select few, all of them, with the fords of Forth which complémented them, known only to one man – Rob Roy himself. There were islands of firm ground in that huge morass where whole herds of cattle could be hidden and maintained; lochans without number whose waters could be loosed and decanted to flood great new areas; causeways of stone set unseen a foot deep under peat-stained water, the pattern of which was the key to territories as large as a lairdship.

Across this trembling haunted place, where the reeds nodded and whispered and sighed endlessly, where the roe-deer slipped away silently like russet shadows into deeper shade, and the wildfowl squattered and quacked and flew, Gregor picked his roundabout intricate way with entire confidence, his general direction east by south. His followers trod exactly in his garron's footsteps.

Deliberately Gregor took a line that would keep them in this floundering Moss till directly north of Arnprior, a line that entailed more than the usual amount of zig-zagging and gave them fully eight miles of bog-trotting before, at last, with the sun already behind Ben Lomond, they came out on to firm ground once more, in the vicinity of Merkland.

After that it was straightforward riding through populous farmlands where humble cotter folk stared, but discreetly, silently, at the tartan-clad travellers, who spared them not so much as a glance, and into the wooded lands of Arnprior across the Glasgow-Stirling turnpike. Robert Buchanan, as befitted a substantial Lowland landowner with a hand in the America trade and a mind beyond mere cattle and rents, dabbled in this new-fangled pleasantry of enclosed parks and policies, and even planted ornamental trees – presumably for the benefit of hoped-for Hamilton grandchildren.

Arnprior House was a much more pretentious place than was Glengyle, needless to say – indeed, though only twenty-five miles apart, they might have belonged to different hemispheres, representing two utterly distinct and opposing ways of life. The one was the purely functional home of a patriarch amongst his people, on land for which he was only trustee and chief guardian; whilst the other was the private demesne of a magnate, the wherewithal for the costly support of which was earned elsewhere.

Gregor and his supporters rode up to the front door of this handsome establishment, enlarged beyond all recognition of the modest square tower-house that had contented earlier Buchanans. Here was a place where golden guineas surely would accrue to King Jamie's cause. He could see his approach being watched from more than one window – which was hardly to be wondered at since his two henchmen, aided by the promptly baying hounds, had been hallooing and bawling summons since ever they came in sight of the house, lest a chieftain of the Gregorach should be insulted by being kept waiting, even momentarily, on any man's doorstep.

Gregor was spared that, at any rate. Arnprior went in for the latest type of windows also, that opened by the entire frame being raised. One of these was raised now, on the first floor, and two female heads were thrust out – in grievous danger of being beheaded were the contraption to descend upon their fair necks.

'Welcome! Welcome, Mr MacGregor!' the feminine voices rang out. 'Gregalach! Gregalach!'

Delighted, Gregor swept off his best bonnet – with two new feathers in it, too. But that hardly seemed adequate, somehow, despite that unfortunate Mister that had crept in. So he whipped out his claymore instead, and tossed it spinning up into the air, under the young women's noses, its silver basket-hilt and gleaming blade flashing and scintillating in the golden rays of the setting sun, to catch it again dexterously as it came down – even though he cut his hand a little in the process.

'Ardchoille!' he answered them cheerfully – and for good measure the two gillies repeated the slogan loyally. 'Ardchoille!'

Another window went up, on the floor above. 'What a' God's name's to do?' That was Mr Hamilton of Bardowie, playing-cards in hand.

'It is young Mr MacGregor come visiting,' his saucy piece of a wife called up to him. 'At least, I think that is what he is doing. Though I must say, it's not very civil to throw swords at us like that!'

'Perhaps it's more cattle that he wants?' the younger girl suggested. 'Has your father one or two left, for him, do you think?'

'Dear me – I hope so. Or it will be us he'll be off with, instead! Mercy on us – what a fate! Can you conceive of it, Mary?'

'Well . . . ' Mary Hamilton was non-committal. 'The Gregorach don't really do that sort of thing any more, do they, Mr MacGregor?'

'We do not have to, whatever,' the young man said, a little stiffly, for he believed that he might be being made game of somehow. He returned his claymore to its scabbard – and tried to keep the blood on his thumb from

67

showing. 'And you may call me Gregor, see you.'

'Oh.'

Mistress Meg's laughter spilled over. 'And you can make a kirk or a mill out of that, Mary Hamilton!' she cried.

Robert Buchanan, who knew something about the niceties and civilities required by Highland gentlemen, appeared in person in his doorway, buttoning up his long-skirted waistcoat. 'Glengyle – this is a pleasure and an honour,' he declared, holding out his hand. 'Come away in. Your fellows will take your beast to the stables, and get a bite of supper in the kitchen. Come you – and pay no heed to those lassies' havers from upbye. They're a skirling pair.'

'I like them both, sir – very well,' Gregor said, dismounting and stepping indoors, hounds at heel. 'The younger one – Mary. She is not wed, or bespoke, or otherwise embroiled, I hope?'

'Guidsakes, man – you're blunt!' Arnprior gulped, blinked, and faltered a pace, all at once. 'Lordie – you Hielantmen don't *aye* mince your words!'

Gregor eyed him enquiringly.

'Aye. I'ph'mmm. Well . . . no. Mary's a free woman, as yet. At least, so far as I know. . . . '

'That is good,' his guest commended, lifting off his shoulder-belt and claymore attached, and handing the lot to his host, as was suitable – though noting keenly enough what the man did with it.

'Did you come here . . . ? Was it to . . . ? H'rr'mm.' Arnprior hung the sword from a convenient pair of stag's antlers on the vestibule wall, and gestured a little doubtfully towards the wide square stairway. 'Oh, aye,' he said. 'This way, Glengyle.'

Gregor was fairly straightforward in most matters. 'King Jamie is for making a landing, and there is to be a rising in Scotland,' he mentioned. 'Men we will be finding in plenty, but money, it seems, will be required also.' He enunciated that word money with more than a hint of the Highlander's theoretical contempt therefor. 'You and your like have your hands on the money, Arnprior. That is why I am here. My uncle has sent you this letter.' And he held out a missive drawn from his doublet.

'Eh . . . ? Good God, man! Save us a' . . . no' so loud!' Buchanan stared, and actually seemed to start backwards there on the stairs, as though to withdraw himself from all such rash and dangerous association. 'Guard your words, Glengyle, for the Lord's sake!'

Surprised, Gregor looked at him. 'Must you whisper in your own house, Arnprior?'

'Damnation – that kind of talk needs whispering any-where!' Only as it seemed reluctantly did the laird accept the letter that the younger man still held out to him. 'What sort of folly is this you've got hold on, boy?'

Gregor frowned – as much at the boy as at the deeper implications. 'If my words do be needing guarding and whispering, sir, I'd suggest that yours could do with better choosing, whatever!' he declared strongly. 'The folly you speak of is the decision of His Majesty's Council, in St Germains, announced to us, to my uncle and myself, by Colonel Nathaniel Hooke.'

'Hooke, you say! Does that storm-cock crow? Is he here, then – in Scotland?'

'I ate with him, this midday, at Inversnaid.'

'So-o-o-o!' Buchanan was obviously impressed. 'Not six months agone I had word with him in France. . . .'

'Then you will know of how they conceive that this Act of Union will set Scotland aflame. . . .'

'Tut, man – hush you! Sssshh!' They were nearly at the first-floor landing now, and there the two young women stood awaiting them, a striking eye-filling pair, both good-looking and both attractive, but so very differently – though neither, it must be admitted, made quite such a colourful picture as the young man climbing up to them.

'Ah – so Scotland's to be set aflame, is she?' Buchanan's daughter cried down to them. She obviously had sharp ears to add to her many other evident attributes. 'Splendid – and high time, too! She's plaguey dull the way she is, I vow!'

69

'*I* don't think so,' her companion asserted, smiling. 'Especially when there are MacGregors about!'

'But aflame, my dear – the whole country! Think of it. It's Jacobite talk – I'm sure of it! A revolt – a rising? That's it – look at poor Father's face!'

'Guidsakes, Meg – hold your tongue!' Arnprior exclaimed. 'What way is that to talk! You clatter like a bell in the wind! Never heed her, Glengyle.'

'It *is* a rising, isn't it?' his daughter questioned, ignoring him.

'It is, yes,' Gregor agreed, since he saw no point in denying it.

'Oh, good! I'm glad,' Mary Hamilton declared, eyes shining.

'When?' Mistress Meg demanded. 'When will it be? I've said all along we'll have to rise. That's what's needed. The country's ripe for it, too. Even the English are . . . '

'Silence!' her father commanded hoarsely. 'Not another word. Have you forgotten, addle-pate, that I've got Killearn upstairs? And Garden. And that man Buchlyvie.'

'Stirling of Garden is a good Jacobite, is he not?'

'Maybe. But Killearn is Montrose's factor, and a Government man. And I'm no' so sure of Buchlyvie, either. . . . Come ben here, to my study, Glengyle. We'll no' can go upstairs. I'll have to read this letter. . . . '

'Leave Mr . . . *Master* Gregor with us, while you go read your letter, Father,' his irrepressible daughter urged. 'You will get the more out of it, belike. I am sure that he came all this way just as much to see *us* as to carry letters to you! Say that I am right, young man?'

'Yes,' Gregor said, readily enough – but he looked at Mary rather than the speaker.

That young woman sketched a curtsy, but said nothing with her lips.

Buchanan grunted, and scratched under the edge of his wig. Obviously he was as putty in Mistress Meg's hands. Probably, too, he felt that he could do with time to collect his thoughts and con Rob Roy's letter alone, in view of the momentous tidings. He nodded, then. 'Very well – as you will. I will see you presently, Glengyle. But, for the good Lord's sake – for everybody's sake – be careful what you say to those prattlers!' And he stumped off.

'Come, Master Gregor – and tell us all about it,' Meg cried, leading the way into a large bright west-facing room, handsomely furnished and hung with tapestries and pictures, woven carpeting on the floor-boards. One of the windows still was raised.

The young man bowed elaborately to Mary Hamilton, and she preceded him into the apartment. At his brogues' heels the two large hounds followed him – to be eyed somewhat askance by the women.

'You will have a glass of wine? You will be tired with your journey? And one or two of my cakes? I make superb cakes. . . . '

'He does not look tired, Meg!'

'You think not? Do you not note the delicate brush of shadow under the eyes, my dear? An improvement possibly, I agree – a refinement. . . . '

'I am not tired,' Gregor asserted – though he smothered a yawn as he said it. 'But I will accept your wine, Mistress, gladly. You may give the cakes to the hounds, here – they have run far.' And he took the proffered chair, and stretched the long limbs that thrust out from his red tartans luxuriously. The dogs sank down one at either side of him.

'Oh!' said Meg – and with nothing more to follow.

It was the other girl's turn to laugh, joyously. Seldom was it that her sister-in-law was thus effectively quietened.

*   *   *

Gregor had no intention of obeying Arnprior's unmannerly warning about being careful of his speech before these two girls. For one thing, he was not in the habit of weighing words like a huckster at other men's behest. But also he conceived it that these two were probably better Jacobites than their menfolk. Clearly this Meg had a deal of influence on her father, too, if not her husband – and he might well

71

serve the King best by enlisting the ladies to bring pressure on the others. Moreover, it had not been Gregor's experience – limited as such was, admittedly – that women were less able than their betters at keeping secrets, in things that mattered. His mother, and his aunt, for instance, were safer to confide in, he had discovered, than even Rob Roy himself.

So his fair hostesses by no means had to winkle and squeeze everything out of him – as undoubtedly they had been prepared to do. He told them all of what was to do, what was planned, and what he knew of how plans were to be translated into action. He hid nothing – save his uncle's grave fears of Breadalbane's part, which might conceivably alarm the uninitiated – only adding, as casual rider, that now he had put men's lives in their slender hands . . . including his own, of course. Which was not without its effect, either.

He got round to the money fairly promptly, explaining what was required and where it could best come from. He found his hearers quick in the uptake there, too. Perhaps they took up more even than he told them, more than he knew indeed, as is the way of women – but if so, no slackening of their interest or sympathy transpired. In fact, before Robert Buchanan reappeared, the two young women were not so much sympathisers and partisans as partners in the business – and not wholly sleeping or inactive partners either, it appeared.

So much so that when Arnprior, spectacles on nose and wig awry, but expression magisterial, suggested that Glengyle should accompany him to his study where he could inform him of what was what, Meg pricked that balloon forthwith, announced that they knew all about everything, and wanted to be informed how much her father proposed to contribute, in the first instance? Not enough, she would vow!

Buchanan's carefully authoritative demeanour wilted noticeably under this flank attack, and for a few moments he was reduced to puffings and growls and incoherencies. He turned his reproaches on Gregor, of course, but was not permitted to get away with that, either. Nor the assertion that young females knew naught about affairs of state, were qualified to say nothing, and at least ought to respect their parents' wisdom and judgment. He eventually was reduced to confessing, indeed, that money was tight and the times difficult, security extremely doubtful, hare-brained schemes were to be deplored, and the dangers of implication grievous. In fact, that in the circumstances His Majesty would probably be well advised against the whole project – unless, of course, he came over with a large French army and coffers well filled with golden *louis*.

The outcry which greeted this level-headed and business-like assessment of the situation was such as to send the laird rushing over to close the window, to hush and shush imploringly, and to invoke Heaven's merciful deafness on Graham of Killearn upstairs.

Gregor had apt and dignified answers to give, needless to say, points to make, and morals to draw. But he got little opportunity to enunciate any of them. His companions did that for him, the one vigorously, shrewdly, mercilessly, the other pleadingly, reproachfully – but both eloquently. The young man could only sit back and listen, listen and marvel and enjoy – but also in some measure sympathise and know some small disquiet at this demonstration of masculine defeat and discomfiture, wholesale and unscrupulous.

Also, needless to say, Arnprior was forced to change his tune. First to the tune of fifty guineas. Then to a hundred. And finally to two hundred and fifty. Also to agree to use his influence, to some unspecified extent, with others of his kidney. Of course, as is frequently the way with hardheaded men of the world, he may have intended all along to come round to some such concession in the end, after being suitably cautious and sceptical. Who could tell ? After all, he was in theory a supporter of the Stewart dynasty, and his daughter presumably had got her Jacobite sympathies from him. But for all that, the process represented a noteworthy piece of ruthless female aggression, a feminine triumph, that should have been an object-lesson to Gregor Ghlun Dubh – and a warning.

The immediate objective gained, tactics gave way to strategy, in a dutifully daughter-like atmosphere. What others were to be brought in? How were they to be approached? And when?

Gregor mentioned some that his Uncle Rob had named for him to call upon – Stirling of Garden, who was apparently upstairs playing cards; Kerse of Kerse; Sir Hugh Patterson of Bannockburn; Leckie of Croy Leckie; Graham of Arnfearn; Bailie Drummond in Dunblane; and so on. He would just have to make a tour of them – and any others that Arnprior might think of.

That man was horrified at the suggestion. For young Glengyle to go traipsing the country calling on all these respectable lairds in turn would be as good as to shout aloud from the top of the Abbey Craig at Stirling what was to do. Didn't he know how kenspeckle he was – a chieftain of the MacGregors, nephew to Rob Roy himself, as notorious a Jacobite as there was in all Scotland? Did he imagine that he wouldn't set folks talking? Strange questions to put to Gregor Ghlun Dubh.

The younger man protested that that might well be so, but that he would be thought to be on the business of the Watch. But Buchanan would have none of it. Since when had Rob run his Watch like that – sending round an ambassador? And there was no harrying and rieving going on, to account for anything of the sort. And was it not directly after the Lammas mail-gathering? No – it would not do.

The ladies took over here, again. The thing could and should be done discreetly, judiciously. Only a little common sense was required, they declared. Instead of dashing around the country with his gillies and his hounds and his claymores, Gregor should lodge here quietly at Arnprior, taking sundry inoffensive trips with them in the coach to make polite calls upon the ladies of some of the gentlemen mentioned. Others of the gentlemen could be asked to visit here. Thus no Jacobite clamour would be raised, and all would be well. It was simple and obvious.

Arnprior, soul of hospitality as he was, embraced this programme with little enthusiasm. But Gregor saw distinct possibilities therein. The coach might limit his calls in some measure, of course, since not all of his quarry would be conveniently situated on turnpikes where wheels could reach them. But on the other hand, he had never experienced coach-travel; it might be a pleasant change – especially in select company. And the others could very well come to see him, indeed; on second thoughts it seemed highly suitable that they should, whatever.

Glengyle therefore signified his assent. Though it seemed doubtful whether anything of the sort was necessary, or really competent.

Time was not limitless, however, he felt bound to point out – distasteful as it was for a Highlandman to be preoccupied with mere hours and days. He had much to do, elsewhere than in this tame low country, before he made his rendezvous with Rob Roy and the rest at Kinloch Rannoch in three weeks' time. He could only spare, say, five days to this business.

Buchanan agreed that his guest's duties elsewhere ought by no means to be neglected.

The young women accepted this understandingly, too. But much could be achieved in five days, they indicated significantly.

There turned out to be a fairly unified opinion against Gregor starting his campaign there and then, on Stirling of Garden upstairs – or, for that matter, on John Hamilton of Bardowie either. They had been drinking at their play, naturally, and were likely to be in no state to deal with matters of high politics and patriotism. Another day would be more propitious. Garden was a near neighbour, anyway. In fact it would be best, probably, if Gregor did not meet the card-players at all that night, and get himself involved in all sorts of unedifying discussion and claret-inspired argument. Let these have their supper, with their host, aloft in the card-room, and the latest guest could dine down here with the ladies. For the safety of the cause.

The cause was in good hands, very evidently.

CHAPTER SIX

So commenced a week – for a week it became, of course – such as Gregor MacGregor had never before experienced, contemplated or even could have visualised. An education might be the best description of it. He made a fairly apt pupil, it had to be admitted.

There was much to be tasted, tried and savoured – beyond coach-travel. Though that had its rewarding moments, to be sure. He discovered quite a lot about women, for instance, that had not been crystal-clear to him; quite a lot about gentle dalliance that could be more dangerous than any of man's noisy challenges; pretty ways that masked unbending resolution, melting looks that represented anything but fluidity. Perhaps by inference, as it were on the rebound, he even learned a little about himself.

Achievements were not unimportant either – if not achieved altogether without his self-appointed coadjutors' help. Reluctant promises were wrung out of not a few pessimistic patriots – the fact that their cattle might always be used as a form of security for fulfilment of contract never being actually mentioned by the MacGregor. But strangely enough his successes with these fairly consistently purplefaced and heavy-paunched realists whose venturesomeness in the commercial sphere seemed to be so surprisingly more vigorous than in other realms, impressed Gregor on the whole as little more than a by-product of his week's activities. Other matters tended to bulk still larger, unexpected as this may have been.

How far these other matters managed to develop, in six days, like extra sturdy plants in fertile soil – with some little deft husbandry here and there perhaps – will be apparent from what transpired on that final day of Gregor's stay as a guest at Arnprior.

All the gentlemen named by Rob Roy – and even one or two others – had been seen and prevailed upon one way or another, with the exception of Sir Hugh Patterson of Bannockburn. This was one of the most important of all, being a man of far-flung interests and reputed zeal for the Stewart cause. But he had resisted any attempt to get him to come to Arnprior, and Bannockburn of course lay considerably farther south and distant from the Highland Line than did any of the other properties. It was on the wrong side of Stirling, country where the MacGregor writ did not run, and the Government's frequently did.

This day, then, Gregor being adamant, an expedition was made by coach to Bannockburn, a journey, by devious ways, of some twenty miles. They avoided the constrictions and possible dangers of Stirling, skirting well to the south of the town, past the Buchanan lairdship of Touch and the village of Cambusbarron, the great castle-crowned rock rearing up away to their left. They reached Bannockburn House in due course, achieved an encouraging measure of success with the wary Sir Hugh – who proved, like many of his kind, to be more susceptible to feminine charm than to Gregor's histrionics and challenges. It was on the way home that things began to go wrong. Just after they had come down off the moor and passed through the little village of St Ninians, south of Stirling, the coach, negotiating a bad stretch of the road, lurched heavily into a larger hole than usual, broke three or four spokes of its off front wheel, and came to a jarring drunken halt.

This was not Bardowie's handsome equipage, with postillions and quartette of matching greys, but an older lighter two-horse carriage of Arnprior's, less conspicuous, with an aged coachman to match. This veteran now dismounted amidst dire lamentations, to wring his hands and call upon his Maker, proclaim his innocence of all fault – and do nothing more constructive. The two young women twittered and exclaimed and were less effective than usual. Gregor Ghlun Dubh ordered the coachman to unhitch the horses, and strode off masterfully back to the village for a wheelwright or a blacksmith. So much for coaches.

Unfortunately, St Ninians, a poor inadequate bit of a place, did not boast a wheelwright, and the hulking smith whom Gregor ran to earth and dragged protesting back with him continued to protest, on the spot, that he could do nothing with spokes and wood. The Highland gentleman would have to go to Stirling.

It was a bare three miles to the town. The girls were for the coachman going, but Gregor would not hear of it, asserting that he would be as useless there as he was here. Let him be getting the wheel off. The evening was approaching, hirelings would be leaving their work and would be loth to come to their aid perhaps – he had had to convince even this miserable blacksmith in no uncertain terms. He would go himself, taking both horses so that the wheelwright could ride back on one.

The dangers of a proscribed MacGregor entering the garrisoned town and citadel of Stirling, though eloquently pointed out to him, had quite the wrong effect on Gregor of Glengyle, of course. Mary's rather faltering suggestion that she should accompany him as screen and diversion – for she was certainly not dressed for bareback horse-riding – was dismissed with scant gratitude. Let them sit peaceably in the coach and leave man's work to a man, he advised – possibly even thankful to be able to assert himself after his week of leading-strings. Where would he find a wheelwright conveniently in Stirling, he demanded of the smith?

So Glengyle trotted the two horses down the Edinburgh turnpike into the tall town that dominated from its thrusting crag the flat carselands of Forth – or such part of them as were a little too far east and south to be dominated by the still more masterful ramparts of the Highland Line that reared majestically filling all the prospect to the north. Past the huddled hovels of the Craigs he rode, and up the steep cobbled streets towards the citadel's churches and palaces and ultimate frowning castle. And tall Gregorach though he was, he knew a certain sense of smallness and loneness in the process.

He did not ride unnoticed, naturally. It was not every day that betartaned Highland notables clattered over the Stirling cobbles on what were obviously heavy coach-horses – especially with chin in the air and eagle's feathers cocking higher still. The narrow streets held their full quota of hodden-clad and beshawled strollers and idlers this fine August evening, with the day's toil over, folk leaned comfortably out of windows and gossiped in alleys. Children skirled and pointed, and even acted as escort – though that could be in the nature of a compliment, of course. There was no sort of hostility evident, even from the odd redcoats amongst the throng.

Near the foot of Broad Street a short wynd turned down, giving access to an open yard wherein a couple of carts and an old coach mouldered, wheels entire and broken lay about, and wood was stacked and littered. At the rear was a house, around the door of which fowls picked and scratched. And on a bench nearby two men sat, tankards in hand. They stared at their visitor.

One was a small wizened man, decently dressed in coat and breeches only a little patched, and a greasy cocked hat. The other was large and muscular, in uprolled shirt-sleeves and leather breeches. Both middle-aged men. Gregor addressed himself to the latter, fairly enough, bidding him a good evening and enquiring if he was Calder the wright, and announcing his need, civilly if firmly.

The man hummed and hawed, oooh-ayed and just-so-ed, and repeated the salient points to his companion whom he referred to at every other word as Bailie – and who thereupon joined in the humming. A lack of appreciation and urgency was apparent.

Patiently Gregor explained the situation, pointed out the spare horse for transport, and mentioned that payment would be prompt and adequate. But the wheelwright remained unimpressed. The day's work was done. He would see to it in the morning. And there was an inn at St Ninians. . . .

Gregor was not used to this sort of treatment – and made the fact reasonably clear.

The other mentioned, apparently more to his companion than to the enquirer, that there were other wrights in town.

The visitor expressed no interest in this information.

The wright, from ooohing and ayeing and head-shaking, became more specific. 'Since when,' he wondered, to the Bailie, 'has Hielant gentry taken to riding in coaches? I havena heard tell there's ae road fit for a cairt much less a coach north o' the Hieland Line!'

The smaller man tee-heed appreciatively. 'Ye're richt there, Deacon,' he agreed.

'An' div ye no' think yon tartans could be MacGregor, just – red an' green? Eh, Bailie?'

'Man, they could that. As you say.'

'Oooh, aye. I'ph'mmm. MacGregor.'

Gregor drew a long quivering breath. 'MacGregor it is, by God – and I am Glengyle!' he cried. He was about to say considerably more when a long tuck of drum rolled distinctly on the evening air from the castle walls above, presumably sounding for some military duty. The noise reminded the younger man rather forcibly of the possible advantage of a modicum of hateful discretion, ladies' comfort being involved. 'Come, you,' he merely said then, authoritatively.

The other did not stir. 'Is that a fact?' the wright mentioned, and sipped his ale. 'It's a bold lad this, Bailie, is it no'? An' in the deil's ain hurry!' To Gregor he said, with some dignity: 'I am Sam'l Calder, Deacon o' the Wrights' Guild. An' here's Bailie Livingstone o' this toon.'

'I am still in a hurry, whatever,' Gregor answered. But his mind was turning the situation over quickly, nevertheless. 'For myself, the coach matters nothing. But there are ladies in it. Their coach it is – not mine. I seek to aid them, just. They must be at Arnprior before darkness.'

'Arnprior . . . ? Man – did ye say Arnprior ?'

'I did. It is Buchanan of Arnprior's coach.'

'Och, mercy on us – d'ye hear that, Bailie? Arnprior's coach.'

'Tsst-tsst,' the wizened man deplored. 'Houts, man – that's a wee thing different.'

'Oooh, aye. Just that. As you say, Bailie . . . '

It was not a little galling for Gregor to perceive the very different impression made on these smug Lowland townsmen by the Laird of Arnprior's name as against his own. Obviously Buchanan meant a deal more in Stirling town than did MacGregor – a situation that certainly seemed to call for some rectification. But at a later date, assuredly – not just now. Swallowing the words which would really have done justice to the occasion, and keeping his fists tight clenched beneath the folds of his plaid, the Highlander nodded.

'One of the ladies is Arnprior's daughter – wife to Hamilton of Bardowie. It is an ill thing to be keeping them waiting, at all.'

'Bardowie . . . ? Dearie me – Bardowie too! Man, man.' Deacon Calder was on his feet now. 'Andra!' he shouted. 'Here, Andra. Whaur the deil is the limmer . . . ?'

An answering call preceded another man who emerged from a tumbledown lean-to erection across the yard, hitching up tattered breeches behind a leather apron, a stolid bull-like workman, in no sort of hurry. To this individual, Calder gave instructions to get his tools and go with the Highland gentleman to repair the Laird of Arnprior's coach-wheel. He indicated that the man was a qualified wright and would be well able to do the work expeditiously and to Mr Buchanan's satisfaction – giving the impression at the same time that he himself, as a Trades Deacon of Stirling's Guildry, had still more important matters to attend to.

Gregor maintained a lofty silence while the man Andrew was gathering his gear – even when it transpired that the

Deacon was now assuming that he, Glengyle, had been merely a passing traveller who had come upon the coach in difficulties. That assumption, insulting though it was in its implications, might at least spare talk and gossip. He let it pass.

His leave-taking of Deacon and Bailie thereafter was as frigid as he knew how to make it.

With his silent, indeed morose companion, Gregor rode back down Stirling's hilly streets and out on to the Edinburgh road once more – keeping a suitable distance ahead of the fellow, needless to say. They collected some shouts and witticisms *en route*, and a few barking dogs, but nothing more serious.

At the coach the girls seemed to be gratifyingly pleased and relieved to see him back. Setting the wright to work forthwith, he saw no need to enlighten them on what had transpired in Stirling. There were things that even intelligent women could not be expected to appreciate.

*　　*　　*

The sun had set and the grey dusk was beginning to make things of mystery out of the scattered thorn trees and whins of the grassy hill above St Ninians – the same hill whereon Robert Bruce had drawn up his scratch army before Bannockburn fight of glorious memory – when, the new spokes fashioned and the hub repaired, the wheel was ready to fit on to the axle again. Gregor was assisting at this task when the drumming of hooves from down the road drew all eyes in the direction of the village. A sizeable group of horsemen were approaching – and at a spanking pace.

'Oh, Gregor! It's not . . . I hope it's not . . . ' Mary Hamilton began breathlessly, and did not finish.

'I fear it is,' Meg faltered. 'Are those not redcoats? I fear they are. . . . '

Gregor straightened up, peering. 'Red they are,' he agreed. 'But fear you nothing, *a graidh*. Fear is not for the likes of you and me, at all.' Fine words, but the man's hand dropped to the region of his hip, and he cursed beneath his breath that no claymore hung there.

With a great jingling and clatter the newcomers drew up around the stationary coach, a party of a dozen heavily armed dragoons led by a young Ensign on a handsome black charger.

Gregor got in the first word, as soon as he could make his voice heard above the din, addressing the officer. 'A good evening to you, Captain,' he said civilly. 'I take it kindly that you have come to escort these ladies to Arnprior.'

'Eh ... ?' The other, a young man of about Gregor's own age, looked a little nonplussed. He bowed stiffly from the saddle to the young women who stood beside the coach. 'My respects,' he jerked. 'If escort is required, I can provide it. But I am here to apprehend one who calls himself MacGregor.' He turned back to the Highlandman. 'You, I take it, sirrah?'

'I do not call myself MacGregor – I *am* MacGregor!' he was told strongly. 'I am Gregor Ghlun Dubh MacGregor of Glengyle, Chief of the Clan Dougal Ciar of Clan Alpine!' A drum to roll with that would have sounded well.

'M'mmm. Indeed!' The Ensign cleared his throat. 'I ... ah ... well, you are our man, then. You will accompany me back to the Tolbooth of Stirling.' He spoke with the accent of the north country English. And added, as an afterthought: 'In the name of the Queen!'

'That would be inconvenient for my arrangements,' Gregor informed him, conversationally. 'And you refer to Anne Stewart in London, I take it? What has she to do with Gregor MacGregor of Glengyle, at all?'

The officer drew himself up, on his fidgeting mettlesome horse. 'Have a care how you speak, sirrah, of the Queen's Majesty! And how you flaunt the name of MacGregor!'

'Can you name a prouder, sir?'

''Fore God – are you crazy, man?' the other cried. 'Know you not that the name of MacGregor is proscribed?

That it is contrary to law to use it? That the whole rascally clan of you is outlawed, by royal statute? And that no man of that race may bear arms other than a blunted eating-knife?'

Gregor laughed. 'Och, och – a sad tale, that! Did not another king downbye one time order that the waves of the sea hold back?'

'Eh . . . ?' The Ensign, frowning, did not catch the allusion, unfortunately. 'There is a reward offered for the apprehension of any man who uses the name of Mac-Gregor. That reward has been claimed this day by a burgess of Stirling. You must come with me. . . . '

'Of how much, pray, is this reward?'

'Forty pounds Scots, I believe. But the . . . '

'Faugh! Forty pounds, the price of a stirk, whatever – for Glengyle! Is that not monstrous!' Gregor cried. '*Dia* – but the wheelwrighting must have fallen on ill days in Stirling for its Deacon to have to be selling his fellow-men at such paltry price! I fear that I cannot let myself go for such a figure, Captain!'

'Enough of your talk, fellow – it will serve you nothing. Sergeant Tod . . . '

'Officer!' That was Mary Hamilton, urgently. 'You cannot do this, sir! This gentleman has done no wrong. He went to Stirling on our behalf, to get us aid. For this kind action you would injure him . . . ?'

'For no kind action, ma'am – but for flouting the law!' the Ensign gave back. 'You heard him – glorying in the name of MacGregor. And look – he carries a dagger, there! He is armed. . . . '

'A dirk is part of every Highlander's dress,' Meg exclaimed. 'You must know that. . . . '

'Tut – let us not be squabbling over the small matter of a dirk,' Gregor intervened. 'You shall have it if you want it, Captain. But let the ladies be on their way to Arnprior. Here is no business of theirs.'

'The ladies have my permission to continue their journey.'

'No!' Mary Hamilton cried. 'If you take him to Stirling, sir, then we go too!'

'Exactly,' her sister-in-law agreed strongly. 'We all go.'

'But *I* am not going to Stirling, see you,' Gregor said, very softly. Louder he declared, 'The gentleman is after wanting my dirk. Here it is!' And whipping out his *sgian dubh*, he leapt like a coiled spring released.

The single great bound brought him to the side of the officer's tittuping charger. A brief jab with the point of the knife sent the already nervy brute rearing and dancing. Its rider's hand, darting down towards the heavy cavalry pistol holstered there, grabbed at the saddlery instead, to hang on. Gregor Ghlun Dubh grabbed at the saddlery too, and, bracing himself on his toes, sprang for the second time. He had been vaulting on to garrons' backs all his days – and though admittedly this charger was taller than any garron, its haunches were well down as it reared, its forelegs pawing the air. Out of the flying leap Gregor landed, tartans sailing, square on the beast's black back, behind the saddle. As he came down, all in the same movement his left arm crooked tightly round the neck of the man in front, who still was struggling to retain his seat. Bare knees gripping fiercely at the prancing horse's silky flanks, Gregor flicked the dagger viciously before the other's eyes. 'Still, you!' he hissed. 'Or . . . !'

The entire sudden outburst of violent action had occupied no more than four or five seconds. The watching ranks of dragoons were wholly taken by surprise. The Highlander was up behind their officer before they could do anything to stop him. And once there, they were not very effective – they could not be. Disciplined men, they tended to wait for orders – and no orders were given them. They tugged out sabres and pistols, but with the Ensign's black cavorting round and round, they would have been just as likely to hit their officer as his assailant had they attempted to use them. The sergeant shouted for them to close in – but a dozen mounted men closing in simultaneously on a given spot must inevitably get considerably in each other's way. More especially if the spot keeps caracoling around and lashing out.

A high degree of confusion developed around that coach. Also considerable shouting mixed with some feminine screams.

Gregor alone was not confused – for only one course was open to him. He took it forthwith. The ring of jostling red-coats was not complete, because of the coach's bulk. And since they had come up from the east, from the direction of St Ninians, the coach lay to the west of them. The angle of his left arm still all but throttling the unfortunate officer, Gregor grabbed at the reins which the other still gripped, at the same time giving a sharp flick with his dirk at the charger's arching neck. Also he kicked hard with brogue-shod heels at its heaving flanks. Under this provocation that black leapt forward instead of merely upward, had its head slewed round to brush past the coach, almost knocking over the young women, wheelwright and coach-man in the by-going, jumped the trace-pole in its stride, and sent the two waiting coach-horses stampeding. Then, lengthening its pace from a scrabbling canter into a raking gallop, it went, head out, nostrils flaring, pounding along the road to the west, its double burden swaying precariously on its back.

Shouts, curses, screams and incipient hysterical laughter rose from those left behind as they stared after. But even as the sergeant's swearing pulled the mass of the dragoons out of their tangle, to spur their mounts in pursuit, high above all the uproar a ululant cry came floating back to them on the evening air.

'Ardchoille! Ardchoille!' it skirled. 'Gregalach!'

The Tutor of Glengyle had tutored well.

*   *   *

Gregor did more than skirl as he pounded along that dusty road. He laughed loud and long – which must have been disconcerting for the semi-choked victim in front, whose impression that he had been sent out against a madman may well have been reinforced. The fugitive – though that description hardly applies somehow – was not worried about the pursuit. This horse was doubly laden admittedly – but it was, quite naturally, far the finest and fleetest beast of the bunch. Moreover, he could jettison the Ensign quickly enough – and though that would be to discard his cover and lay himself open to be shot after by the dragoons, he did not anticipate much danger from pistols fired from horseback at extreme range. Indeed, he was out of range, he imagined, as it was. The redcoats would be tenacious undoubtedly, but with the dusk he could probably lose them when he cared. And only a few miles ahead lay the great wastes of Flanders Moss. . . .

No shooting developed – for pistols took a deal of repriming and charging, as well as aiming. Gregor reckoned that he was just about holding his lead. He could have thrown the officer overboard there and then – but as has been said he was a soft-hearted man, and he bore this unhappy Sassunach hireling no ill-will. Thrown to the ground at the gallop, he might well be injured – and after all, he was only a harmless dweebly sort of Englishman doing what he was paid to do, who might not be expected to understand what it meant to insult a MacGregor. If it had been a Scot, now . . . !

So Gregor waited for perhaps a mile, until they had thundered round a bend in the road – and then waited further still, for Cambusbarron village was just ahead, and it would be a pity indeed to deprive such villagers as might be out and about at this hour of the rewarding spectacle of how Government officers should be dealt with. The man's thoughtfulness had more than the one facet, it will be seen.

They clattered through the hamlet, then, Gregor giving the inhabitants a slogan or two for good measure, the dragoons pounding along strung out perhaps two hundred yards behind. A heartsome sight, undoubtedly. And round the next bend he pulled up the black a little, at the same time speaking into the ear so close to his lips – and that was nicely clear and accessible owing to the owner's cocked hat and bob-wig having landed on the road some distance back.

'I am for setting you down, Captain,' he said politely. 'And I would not like you to be hurting yourself. I will draw over to the grass, and drop to a trot, and you will jump, see you. If you are wise, that is.'

The officer may not have been suitably grateful, affable, nor even civil. But he was prepared to be wise, apparently, to this extent. As his charger was slowed down to a head-tossing sidling canter, the vice-like arm was removed from round his neck – and the dirk flickered in a last significant gesture before his eyes – he kicked heavy-booted feet free of his stirrups, swung right leg over before him and, aided by a little push from behind, slid down, to land on all fours on the grassy bank, and roll over.

'A good night to you, Captain,' Gregor shouted. 'Tell yon Deacon Calder that he'll need to work harder for his forty pounds Scots if he would . . . ' The rest was lost in the beat of hooves as the black was kicked into a gallop again.

A glance over his shoulder showed Glengyle the Ensign picking himself up a shade dazedly – and the first of the troopers just rounding the bend in the road. Seventy or eighty yards had been lost, perhaps – but the runaway could spare them. This excitable piece of horseflesh could now show its paces.

Gregor settled down to mere hard riding.

Quarter of an hour later, in the vicinity of Gargunnock, with some woodland behind him, he turned the black down a narrow lane that led through willows to the river. The sound of the pursuit was not so much a thunder or a drumming now as a mere vibration on the still air. He splashed through a ford across the Forth. Ahead, to north and west, lay all the empty spectral wastes of the great Moss. Dismounting, since this beast was no nimble-footed garron, he led his mount into it.

He heard the dragoons pounding past, across the smooth-flowing river, on the straight road to Kippen, and sighed for the folly of men.

*   *   *

It was fairly late, nearly midnight indeed, when Gregor came again to Arnprior House. He had left his fine new horse hobbled down at the water-meadows of Forth, as he came out of the Moss, and had approached the house cautiously and unobtrusively, on foot.

The household did not yet appear to have retired for the night, for lights shone from sundry windows. But there was no sign of dragoons' horses about the place. A visit to the stableyard disclosed the coach returned and in its place, and a discreet call at the back door of the mansion found it open and his own gillies waiting for him in the kitchen, with the hounds. They revealed that the coach and the ladies had come back hours before, escorted by six soldiers who had gone again with little delay. All was well – but the Laird was in a great to-do about something, apparently.

Gregor retraced his steps so as to come in at the front door, now locked and bolted for the night. His bangings thereon brought him fairly prompt entry, and thereafter he strode up to the first-floor room that he had seen to be lit up. The family was there assembled, Robert Buchanan pacing the floor.

Quite an emotional scene followed – the emotions varying considerably. Relief, joy even, praise, anxiety, displeasure and sheer outrage were all represented, and notably mixed. The young women were loud in their acclaim, Meg going so far as to rush forward and throw her arms around the prodigal guest – to the tut-tutting of the menfolk, Gregor included. Mary, though not so demonstrative, seemed only little less affected, laughing and clapping her hands and biting tremulous lips by turns. Arnprior was less appreciative, however, a man in the throes of misgivings – in fact, in a fever of anxiety. And John Hamilton of Bardowie made no bones about it – he was angry, massively angry. This, as far as he was concerned, was the end.

It seemed that there was more than the one way to view the day's lively proceedings.

A little bedevilled by this distinctly mixed reception, Gregor made a false start or two, and then, as usual, suddenly seeing the funny side of it all, burst into hearty laughter. Which commended itself to fifty per cent of the company at least. Arnprior, he assured, had nothing to worry over; nobody was going to accuse him of anything. Bardowie he considered it best to ignore entirely.

'Nothing to worry over!' Buchanan cried. 'Man – you have openly defied the Government, assaulted one of the Queen's officers, and stolen his property – all whilst a guest under my roof! And you say that I have nothing . . . '

'Sir!' Gregor interrupted. 'Do you accuse a MacGregor of *stealing*?'

'Eh . . . ? Och, well – no, no. Of course not. But *taking*, call it.'

'I could do no less, and keep my liberty, sir. And that does not implicate you, Arnprior. I let all believe that I was only a passing traveller offering aid to these ladies in their need.'

'Yes, he did!' Meg declared. 'He was splendid. . . . '

'You nevertheless involved my wife and my sister in an unsavoury and highly dangerous scrimmage, by your folly and hot-headedness,' Bardowie said heavily.

'John – how dare you!' his sister demanded. 'You are entirely at fault. It was no blame of Gregor's.'

'Of course it wasn't! We told you.' That was his wife joining in. 'The blame was anybody's but his. . . . '

'The blame was wholly his,' Bardowie insisted. 'For publicly admitting that he was a MacGregor. If he had held his tongue about that, all would have been well.'

'Shadow of God, sir!' Gregor roared. 'Were you a MacGregor – which all Heaven forbid – would you deny your own name and fame?'

'I . . . I cannot conceive of the situation arising, young man.'

'Nor can I, John – and that's a fact!' his sister agreed, hot where he was cold.

'The former Laird of Bardowie is to be congratulated on his daughter, at least,' Gregor said ponderously.

Meg all but choked. 'Oh, splendid! Splendid, Gregor!'

'Sir – this is beyond all bearing . . . !'

'Guidsakes – peace! Peace – all of you!' Arnprior exclaimed, snatching off his wig. 'Flyting at each other will get us nowhere. You, Meg – speak your goodman fairer, or hold your tongue! The damage is done, whosever the blame. Our names will now be linked, in the Government's mind, with outlaws and rebels and Jacobite MacGregors.'

'*Dia* – some would consider that same an honour, whatever!' Gregor said, stiffly still. 'But since *you* do not do so, it is evident, I shall withdraw myself from under your roof, sir! Now! Forthwith! As Royal's my Race – this minute!'

'Gregor . . . !' Mary wailed.

'No!' Meg cried.

'Yes. Where my name is not honoured is no place for Glengyle!'

'Toots, man – don't be so touchy!' his host said, slapping on his wig again. 'There is not all that hurry. . . . '

'For yourself, Arnprior, perhaps no. But for myself, yes. Nothing else is possible, at all.' Since Gregor had had every intention of being away from the house before daylight anyway, he could be the more positive in this assertion of his due dignity.

'Well – you know best, no doubt. But I am sorry, lad. . . . '

'So am I, sir. I have to thank you for your hospitality, up till this time.' That was rigidly formal. 'And these ladies for much kindness.'

'You will explain to your uncle, Glengyle, how I am placed . . . ?'

'My uncle will know fine what is what,' the young man assured cryptically. 'Now, with your permission, Arnprior, I will relieve you of my presence. . . . '

'Where? Where are you going, Gregor!' Mary demanded.

'Och, here and there, lassie – just here and there. On

King James's affairs.' That sounded just a little too much, even in his own ears. Rather hurriedly he added a rider. 'But up beyond our Highland Line, see you, where a man can breathe clean air, and free.'

'And . . . and you will not be back?'

'Think you I have not spent overlong here, as it is?' he asked her, and held her eyes with his.

She shook her head, and bit her lip, wordless.

'The first sensible words you have spoken this night!' her brother observed flatly.

'Oh – you are hateful!' Mary cried at him. Meg moved over to put her arm round the other girl's shoulders.

'Aye,' Gregor said, with the deliberate and sibilant enunciation that he reserved for his most impressive pronouncements. 'You are the big man, Bardowie – safe behind this lassie's skirts! But, see you – you, who would not wear the name of MacGregor – come back I may, one day. And if I do, it could be to change the name of one of your family to that same MacGregor, whatever!' He bowed. 'A good night to you all!'

And while still his hearers drew gasping breaths, Gregor Ghlun Dubh swung on his brogue's heel, reached the door, slammed it, and went striding hugely down the stairs, shouting loudly for his gillies and his sword and his hounds.

If his entry had engendered emotion and babblement, his exit did no less. Above the clamour of talk the whole house shook and the candles danced and flickered as the front door crashed behind the Gregorach.

CHAPTER SEVEN

THE three men made no great journey that night – for the
Flanders Moss was no place for even a MacGregor to
traverse in the dark – but settled down some half-a-mile
into the morass, dined off some portion of the considerable
spoils of the Arnprior kitchen which the gillies had had the
foresight to bring along, and slept in their plaids amongst
the whispering reeds, the untroubled sleep of men more
easy in their minds than they had been for a week.

Sunrise saw them picking their devious way northwards
through the place's early-morning mists, Gregor, all wrath
and hard feelings dead in him, rivalling the larks at their
carolling. He rode his garron, and Ian Beg led King
Jamie's new property, a matter which required a certain
amount of care and patience, for the charger did not seem
to like either bogs or deerhounds.

They fetched a course which, skirting the islanded
higher ground of Choille Mhor, took them past the west
end of the great lake of Menteith, wading on a spongy
carpet of underwater roots amidst man-high bulrushes,
and up beyond on to firmer ground. Here Gregor mounted
the black charger, for the prestige of Clan Alpine, and
Ian Beg climbed on to his garron. By a fortunate coincidence Duncan Og, the remaining gillie, disappearing for a
little, presently made up on them, himself mounted upon
a useful garron of piebald aspect. It was only Graham
country hereabouts, and Gregor forbore to seek paltry
details.

They climbed the long long scarps of the long Menteith
hills into the heather, and rejoiced with the myriad humming bees and the whirring chattering grouse at the sweet
and honest scent of it in the smile of the sun. Over the
watershed, they slanted down to the birch-clad shores of

Loch Drunkie and across the hummocky moors beyond to the wide strath, where they forded the peat-stained shallows of the Black Water between Lochs Achray and Vennacher. Here, at the ale-house of the township of Brig o' Turk, they made their first halt, a dozen rough miles covered. There was quite a population at this spot, paying lip-service to MacGregor, but of mixed clans – MacLarens, MacNabs, Stewarts and the like, professional drovers in the main, whose services were much in demand for transferring the cattle of a thousand Highland glens to the Lowland markets. They were tough and broken men, handy with a dirk undoubtedly, and would have their uses in due course – but it was not such scrapings as these that Gregor sought today. He accepted the respects of all whom they clapped eyes on, and proceeded on up Glen Finglas.

At Achnaguard, the seat of the MacGregor thereof, it was a different story. Here was a gentleman of his own sept of Dougal Ciar, and a following of genuine clansmen. It was part of Glengyle's calling to know exactly how many men each laird could raise. He greeted Glenfinglas with a nice mixture of authority and respect – for he was an elderly man – and requested fifteen armed men with all reasonable expedition. When the other wondered if it was in Rob Roy's name and behalf he was told, a little coldly, that it was not. It was Glengyle speaking. The men were promised by the morrow, and Glenfinglas's own son would make the sixteenth, for good measure. Meanwhile his house was at Glengyle's disposal, and all within it.

So next morning Gregor turned off up Glen Vane, beneath the tall frowning ben of the same name, with seventeen men at his heels and one, a boy two years younger than himself, at his side. This was more in Glengyle's line than asking dour and grudging Lowlanders for guineas.

At midday they came down, over the Pass of the Faggots and through the narrows of Glen Buckie, to the lovely shut-in vale of green Balquhidder. Here was another place of divided loyalties and interests. If rights were right, it should have been MacLaren territory, but the Duke of

Atholl and his Stewarts and Murrays had gained the title to it in law, the MacGregors dominated it outside the law, and the poor MacLarens had to do the patient best they could. Here had been Rob Roy's first independent holding, where his father had set him up as farmer of Monachyle Tuarach at the age of twenty-one. From here many of his most stirring exploits had been essayed, and his name still spoke loudest of all in Balquhidder.

Gregor did not delay in the Kirkton, at the eastern extremity of the long valley amongst the mixed folk – beyond paying his kindly respects to the Minister. The upper western end was solidly MacGregor, and thither he repaired, with his trotting tail of warriors, by the pleasant cattle-dotted shores of Lochs Voil and Doine. At Invercarnaig House, across from his uncle's old farmstead, he deposited himself and his entourage with the laird thereof. One hundred and fifty men, he calculated, the Braes of Balquhidder ought to supply him. Would Glencarnaig kindly see to it? In the name, this time, of Rob Roy.

Murray, alias MacGregor, of Glencarnaig was a substantial figure, alike in person, property and influence in the clan. He was not of Gregor's Dougal Ciar sept at all, but a two-feather man in his own right, head of another branch altogether. Indeed, he might well be claiming *three* feathers one of these days – though that of course Glengyle for one would have to contest strongly.

It falls to be explained here, perhaps, that at the time the Siol Alpine – that is, the entire race of the descendants of royal Kenneth MacAlpine, founder of the Scots monarchy in the ninth century, including its senior clan of MacGregor – was to all intents chiefless. The last High Chief of Clan Alpine in the direct line, Gregor MacGregor of the house of Glenstrae, a somewhat fushionless character, had been gathered to his fathers thirteen years before, and his dying had been the best of him. His first cousin, Archibald MacGregor of Kilmanan, who succeeded, was an irresponsible and a brawling sot. That might have been borne, but having committed a pointless and undignified murder in a fit of drunken frenzy, and not having the wit to cover it with any cloak of decency, he had lit out for Ireland and had not been heard of for some years – leaving Rob Roy, who had sought to sustain him for the clan's sake, his principal debtor. Kilmanan's two sons had predeceased him, and though dead he himself might not be, he was as good as dead to Clan Alpine. And the Gregorach were the kind of people who needed a chief, and a strong chief at that.

There were no fewer than four tentative contenders for the office, chieftains of the most ancient and senior septs. MacGregor of Roro, in Glen Lyon, probably had the best claim, on parchment. This Glencarnaig would have disputed, claiming that Roro's ultimate progenitor, though elder brother to his own, had been illegitimate. Drummond, alias MacGregor, of Balhaldie, was another claimant, with moreover a fortune and Lochiel's daughter as wife to back it. And, of course, Glengyle himself was in the running. But, in point of fact, Rob Roy ruled the clan by sheer force of personality.

Therefore, it was in Rob's name that men were to be raised in Balquhidder. Gregor had his moments of vision.

Balquhidder was a hospitable convivial fertile place – if you bore the right name therein. It outdid itself in both respects towards Rob Roy's nephew, as was only seemly and proper. Indeed, the gentry thereof so outdid each other in their hospitality as in their man-raising efforts, as a matter of credit as well as esteem, that the one effort tended to interfere sorely with the other. Gregor found himself in no state to proceed, or even to efficiently count or inspect the assembled manpower, for the best part of a week. Sunday intervened, too, and the claims of divine worship by no means were to be overlooked. It was the Tuesday, then, and six days after his arrival, before Glengyle was able to disengage himself and lead his now truly spectacular tail up out of the western amphitheatre of Balquhidder and southwards over the high Pass of Weeping below the jagged peak of Stob a Choin, down to Loch Katrineside, and so on to his own Glen Gyle. As far as he could make it, in the present state of his faculties, the total amounted to between two hundred and two and two hundred and twenty men, of whom seventeen were mounted gentlemen of name and property and eleven were pipers. Or thereabouts. They made a gallant sight and sound along the shores of Katrine, at any rate, and no little impression on Glen Gyle itself.

The Lady Christian had been as good as her son's instructions. Fifty-odd of his own men had been assembled and twiddling their thumbs for the best part of a week. Forty more were waiting at Inversnaid and Glen Arklet, and at least as many again in the clachans between there and Aberfoyle. Gregor sent messengers to fetch them all in to Glen Gyle, and meanwhile set about the task of scraping together the necessary wherewithal to fittingly entertain and feed this host. He decided, without a lot of debate, that the sooner they could all be gone from Glen Gyle the better, however stimulating their presence. Moreover, of course, he had only a bare week left till his rendezvous with Rob Roy at Kinloch Rannoch.

His mother, who being of a housekeeperly disposition was good at figures, assured him that she had exactly three hundred and forty-four extra mouths to feed, before they moved off for the north the following day. A plague of locusts, she called them – which was not like Christian MacGregor. Her son could only assume that some woman's ailment had her in its fretful grip.

For some reason they did not seem to be able to travel so fast and so far as was Gregor's wont – which might mean that he would have to curtail his intended itinerary a little through the MacGregor lands to the north, now so largely Campbell-ridden. They went over to the head of Loch Lomond, up long Glen Falloch to Crianlarich, collecting adherents and refreshments on the way. Then on up populous Glen Dochart, a far cry, and into the mighty strath of Tay – Breadalbane. This was all Campbell country now, but it had been MacGregor once, before the proscriptions and the harryings and the persecutions of the clan that was

97

to be blotted out, nameless. But there were still more sons of Gregor than of Diarmid in the humble cot-houses and crofts, even though they might call themselves Campbell before the law – and without a doubt this notable demonstration of armed might, clad in the old red tartan, did them all a power of good. Many a leaderless man dropped mattock or peat-spade or herd's crook and ran to join the pipe-led gallant throng, little bothering to ask on what business bent.

Happily the feeding and supplying of this multitude became now perforce a matter for the Campbell lairds *en route*, a source of considerable satisfaction to all ranks. The fact that the assembly was apparently proceeding to some hunting match at Rannoch on the invitation of their own chief, the Earl of Breadalbane, for some extraordinary reason, rather tied Campbell hands. And, of course, four hundred men are not to be argued with too strongly in their own right.

All this took time, and Gregor was forced, after leaving Killin, to cut short his triumphal progress along the shores of Loch Tay and turn his cavalcade up over the lofty shoulder of Ben Lawers and so down into lovely sequestered Glen Lyon. Here he had Roro to call upon, the only MacGregor of note who had managed to hold place and lands in the very heart of the territory engulfed by the Campbells, and the man with most right probably to the chiefship – not, of course, that Gregor was going to admit or imply anything of the sort. Roro, as was scarcely to be wondered at in the circumstances, was not in the habit of making displays of strength or independence, having indeed gained something of a damaging reputation, for a MacGregor, of chronic caution and discretion. But Gregor had hopes that since Breadalbane was the host in this affair, Roro's circumspection might be relaxed somewhat. And he could, if so he desired, raise at least seventy men.

Roro did not do anything on that scale, it has to be admitted, despite all his visitor's oratory. But he did send eventually twenty men and his third son – which represented quite an achievement on Glengyle's part, though it took him two whole days to work it. Another day might have achieved still more – but Gregor's time was up. Tomorrow he was due at the foot of Loch Rannoch, to meet his uncle, and pride forbade that he present himself there one minute later than noonday.

The sun was still a good hour from its zenith when, at last, Gregor at the head of his impressive company topped the final long heather ridge that marked the northernmost bounds of Breadalbane, and looked far and wide out over the long sparkling loch, the rolling hills and valleys of Struan of the Robertsons, the endless ranges of Atholl, and the vast and daunting desolation of Rannoch Moor, to the majestic peaks of Glen Coe and Lochaber. But few with him had eyes for even such a prospect. Below them, a great dark mantle of trees reached almost from their feet right down the hillsides to the water, clothing all the southern shore of the loch – the Black Wood of Rannoch, and relic of the primeval pine forest that had once clothed all Caledonia. And plain to see, from up here, in a large clearing down near the eastern end of the loch, were numerous white and coloured tents and pavilions pitched, around them a stir of men and horses and the blue plumes of wood smoke.

Gregor pointed. 'Yonder is my Lord of Breadalbane!' he cried. 'Forward the pipers. Unfurl the banners. Ian Beg – bring me my standard of Glengyle. Let us show the proud Campbell that the Gregorach has come to Rannoch! That we have a name to us, yet! Come, you!'

*   *   *

John Campbell, eleventh of Glenorchy, first Earl of Breadalbane, Viscount of Tay and Paintland, Lord Glenorchy, Benderaloch, Ormelie and Weick, and second man only to Argyll himself in the great Clan Diarmid, stood outside his gold-and-black pavilion and stared uphill. At his side lounged Rob Roy MacGregor, and at his back were ranged a dozen chieftains and leading men, few of them Campbells, Colonel Nathaniel Hooke included.

Breadalbane was frowning, whereas Rob was smiling. They made a strangely matching pair standing there, strong men both. The Earl was elderly, but gave little impression of his years. Of a pale complexion he had heavy-lidded piercing eyes, a long thin nose and a still thinner mouth that turned down notably at the corners. A small man in body, he seemed the smaller for the enormous wigs that he affected and the inordinate richness of his clothing – Lowland-style clothing. Beside Rob Roy's virile hirsute bulk he appeared the merest puppet of a man.

But there was nothing of the puppet about John Campbell. He had a peculiar reputation in Scotland, and furth of it, little of it inspired by love, but none of it scornful. The Master of Sinclair, who had cause to know, had said that he had the finest headpiece in the land, but that he knew neither honour nor religion save when they were mixed with interest. His greed was notorious, and his double-faced cunning a by-word. Yet it was declared that he could charm any bird off its bough, any man out of his allegiance, or any woman out of her virtue. He had held the highest offices in the land, was one of the richest men in Scotland, and had married an English heiress – yet he was not looked upon as a representative of Lowland interests, as was Argyll, and he was known to oppose the Union with England and had not once attended Parliament in Edinburgh while it was being discussed. At the moment he was out of favour with Queen Anne's Ministers, who no doubt found him an awkward customer, used as they were to long-spooned supping with the Devil.

He was speaking now, somewhat testily. 'Coming from that airt, Cousin, they can be only my people – or yours. I did not invite either.'

'But I did,' Rob declared easily. 'Just two-three Mac-Gregor lads as gillies for the beating, see you. You cannot have too many beaters at a hunting match!'

'That will depend upon the quarry!' the Earl said shortly.

'And how many pipers need they to beat with, Cousin?' Breadalbane affected a semi-royal mode of address – and of course Rob was indeed his cousin, twice removed.

The MacGregor had been rather wondering that himself – though he showed no sign of concern. 'It can be wearisome work, the beating – and nothing keeps the lads in better heart for it than a tune on the pipes, Iain Glas,' he said. He was probably the only man in all Scotland who would call Breadalbane his Gaelic by-name to his face.

The Earl shot him a glance that was not all cousinly affection. 'I wonder ... ?,' he began – and then stopped. Over a minor fold of the wooded hillside fluttering banners appeared – many banners streaming in the breeze.

The Black Wood of Rannoch was no close-grown forest, but a far-flung hummocky area of scattered pines, great-girthed noble-boughed individual trees, growing loosely out of a rich carpet of heather and blaeberries, cranberries and brackens, and even broom. There was much open space, though few lengthy vistas. In consequence, Gregor's company became apparent rather than just appeared, did not all materialise at once, or in the same place, as it came plunging long-strided down hill amongst the knowes and the hollows. Probably the effect was more striking thus than even was intended. Horsemen emerged over a wide front, picking their way amongst the tall heather clumps, and disappeared again. Pipers, singly and in groups, surmounted knolls and crests, blowing lustily, only to plunge out of sight and be succeeded elsewhere by others. Colourful banners came and went. And everywhere red-tartaned armed men emerged and broke out, so that the entire wood seemed to be full of them, ever more following over the farther ridges.

'Great God – it is an army!' Breadalbane gasped. 'What is the meaning of this?' He looked around and behind him. His own Campbell minions numbered a score or so, no more.

Sundry other proud faces in the waiting group bore just a trace of uneasiness as they watched.

Rob Roy drew a great red-furred hand over mouth and beard. 'Have no fear, my lord,' he said. 'These would seem to be my people . . . and will do as I say!'

The other's swift look at him did not give the impression of being wholly reassured by that.

Out into the wide clearing that the Earl had selected for the gathering the Gregorach streamed, and drew together and formed themselves into some sort of order, the pipers leading now, then Gregor Ghlun Dubh on his fine black charger with some two dozen mounted gentlemen at his back, and behind them most of five hundred grinning foot gillies. Almost they danced as they came down to the tents, to the lively tune of The Laird of MacGregor's Rant.

Gregor waved to his uncle, bowed towards Breadalbane and his guests, but took off his bonnet for no man. Also, he waved right and left for his host to halt, and at the pipers to cease their blowing. The latter with indifferent success. All men perforce had to wait till the solid phalanx of musicians saw fit to conform – which was not until the due end of the rant.

It was Rob Roy, however, whose powerful vibrant voice dominated all when the music ended – as indeed it was apt to do. 'Greetings, Nephew!' he cried. 'You have brought us some bonny beaters, I see! We should not lack sport. Greetings, Gregorach! You warm the cockles of my heart, whatever. Come, Greg, and pay your respects to *Mac Cailein Mhic Donnachaidh.*'

The Earl swallowed. He swallowed the Highland title of Son of Colin, Son of Duncan – which was not the one by which he preferred to be addressed. He swallowed Rob Roy's speaking first. He swallowed the possible threat of this invasion, and all it might mean. He swallowed other things, too – for the moment. 'H'mmm. You will be Christian's boy,' he said, his voice sounding notably thin after Rob's. 'You have grown aplenty since last I saw you, boy. You must have been eating a sufficiency . . . of beef, Gregor Tarbh Ban!'

Gregor blinked at that. Tarbh Ban meant White Bull. Which meant again either that his uncle had been talking – or that Breadalbane was alarmingly well informed of what went on amongst the MacGregors.

A great shout of mirthful appreciation went up as the Gregorach saw the point of the Earl's greeting. There was a Wry-mouth for you, a Campbell indeed!

Gregor laughed too. Dismounting, he stalked forward. 'My respects, *Mac Cailein Mhic Donnachaidh*,' he said. And meant it.

CHAPTER EIGHT

THE great gathering was by no means yet complete. Most of the nearer-at-hand chiefs were in, including Struan Robertson from across the loch, Cameron, Younger of Lochiel, MacDougall of Lorne, Menzies of Shian, the Stewarts of Ardshiel and Ardvorlich, Farquharson of Inverey, Gordon of Glenbucket representing Huntly, and Grant of Invermoriston. Each had come, at Breadalbane's invitation by the mouth of Rob Roy, with only one or two of their gentlemen and a handful of attendants, inconspicuousness being the watchword. Highland lairds of broad acres frequently held hunting matches, social occasions where they all could get away from their womenfolk, relax, forget their dignities, feuds and problems for a little, and concentrate on junketing, hard drinking and fine talking just as much as on hunting deer. Large numbers of retainers at such were neither necessary nor desirable. The fact that Rob Roy had thought it worthwhile to assemble a major portion of his clan on this occasion, therefore, intrigued all. Almost as much as why Breadalbane was holding it at all.

And why he should be staging it here, at Rannoch, on the very northern limit of his vast territories, where he had no castle or house. That the Earl was a slippery customer and not to be trusted went without saying. But Rob, on the other hand, was known to be honest after his lights. And he had given every chief his personal word that no hurt would come to them in attending this affair. It might be that all these Gregorach were some sort of surety for that promise. The implications of which would be interesting, indeed.

The MacGregors, of course, quite swamped the camp, and upset all Breadalbane's victualling arrangements. Nevertheless, he would not have them going off foraging for themselves, as they cheerfully offered to do, preferring apparently to meet the extra cost himself than to be at the charges of outraged tenantry.

That afternoon three more chiefs came in, weary after much garron-riding across the roughest country in these islands – Cluny Macpherson, Chisholm of Chisholm and MacDonald of Keppoch. The other MacDonalds, the Mac-Kenzies, the Macleans, and the representatives from the far north-west could not arrive till the next day at the earliest. Not all men were prepared to travel at the speed that Rob Roy and his man MacAlastair had done.

In the evening Breadalbane dined and wined his principal guests and their gentlemen in his own great pavilion with its black-and-gold Campbell hangings – a colourful occasion to which, however, only Rob and Gregor and one other MacGregor were invited. The rest of the Gregorach gentry consequently held their own celebration outside – which by the sound of it was a still more colourful and certainly more lively occasion, and at which Gregor at least would much have preferred to attend. Breadalbane made an assiduous host, and though he did not unbend greatly, his witticisms and shrewd asides were well received – for the Highlander dearly loves a good talker, even when his tongue is barbed. He drank less than most of his guests, and seemed to grow the more sober as the others did the reverse.

Rob Roy, on whom liquor seemed to have no effect, kept the company amused in a different fashion, and Gregor, much aware that for once he was not only one of the youngest but the least important present, was content to sip and watch and listen. It was not often that it was a young man's – or any man's – privilege to sit down with no fewer than ten three-feather chiefs and thrice that number of chieftains of his own rank. In this tent was represented the cream of Highland Scotland, the cream of Scotland itself. Gregor was young enough to be just a little bit overawed – though as he listened to the shouts and songs of his colleagues outside he knew a certain division of allegiance. Especially when he heard a new ballad evidently in process of being composed and tried out, with many interpolations, dealing with the white bull of Gallangad.

In the great pavilion a slightly less carefree atmosphere prevailed, despite the Earl's witticisms, Rob's stories and raillery, and the effect of the wines and the whisky. The mutual suspicions and rivalries of generations were not to be wholly banished. Politics were studiously avoided – save that the loyal toast was drunk to The King, and not The Queen.

Later that night, Rob and Gregor, with MacAlastair as a pale shadow in attendance, sought privacy and cleared heads in walking the dark aisles of the wood. It was their first opportunity for confidential talk.

Rob took his nephew's arm. 'Now, young man,' he said, 'what is the meaning of it all? Why the multitude? I said three hundred – and you have brought double that. *And* a score of *duine-uasail*. And a regiment of pipers. Your grandfather did not lead as many at Killiecrankie, Greg. Why, now?'

Gregor drew himself up. 'The clan's honour demanded it, whatever,' he asserted.

'The clan's honour could have got along with less, I think,' his uncle observed. 'My object was to prevent Breadalbane from attempting any trickery, and to reassure the chiefs, who trust him but little. But this host looks like a challenge to them all, a threat, maybe. Something of an embarrassment to my own self. Did I not teach you – *est modus in rebus* – that there can be too much even of a good thing ?'

Gregor thought of blustering, but recognised that it would be of no use. Not with Rob Roy, not with the man who had taught him all that he knew. He scratched his head instead. '*Dia* – it started at Balquhidder,' he revealed. 'Each of them – Glencarnaig, Marchfield, Monachyle, Craigruie and the rest – all vied with each other as to how many men they could raise. I could not deny one and accept another, without offence. They were so very . . . hospitable. The story of the bull had somehow become known. Too much was made of it, I think. I . . . och, at the end of it, Uncle, I was after finding I had more men than I needed, just. But there could be no sending them back, at all. And after that, every glen we entered added more to the tally, see you. . . . '

'Aye, Greg – there is more to being a chieftain than cocking feathers in your bonnet and strutting on your heels!' the older man said – but not harshly. Then his tone lightened, and he clapped his somewhat crestfallen nephew cheerfully enough on the back to send him stumbling forward over the pine-needles. 'But never care, lad – it may all work out for the best. We will see if we can turn the business to good purpose. And how went your errand to Arnprior ?'

Gregor was on firmer ground here, and did the theme full justice. The financial account he could give made a striking enough total – though Rob seemed to be less impressed with magnates' promises than he might have been. The matter of the coach breakdown and the dragoons, of course, he turned into an epic – with all due modesty, naturally – his uncle laughing his silent laughter and only commenting that he had wondered whence came the notable black horse. Not a great deal was said about young females, despite Rob's civil enquiries. Gregor did indicate, however, that in his opinion Arnprior and Bardowie both were extraordinary poor creatures to have such exemplary womenfolk. Rob nodded sober understanding.

Then it was the younger man's turn to do the questioning. How had his uncle's mission gone? Were the chiefs rallying as they ought? None had mentioned the forthcoming campaign at the meal; were they half-hearted? What was Breadalbane's game? And how had he come to know about the white bull?

All that took a deal of answering. As to the last, Rob had not mentioned that saga of Gallangad – which ought to give them pause for thought. On the whole he was satisfied with his private talks with the chiefs and their reactions to the proposed rising. But they were not unnaturally chary of committing themselves openly to an active part in a revolt until sure of the dependability of everyone present. Moreover, few if any trusted Breadalbane himself, and only Rob's own guarantee had brought most of them here into Campbell territory. . . .

'Yes, then,' Gregor interrupted. 'And why is it here, at Rannoch, that he has chosen to have this gathering? He has a dozen castles and houses. He has better hunting than this. There is nobody here . . .'

'And there you have it, Greg,' Rob intervened. 'There is nobody here! I have thought about this, my own self, not a little. Iain Glas is a shrewd and clever man – never forget it, or underestimate him. I know none shrewder. He always will have good reasons for what he does – good for his own interest. Here are some few reasons for why he might choose Rannoch. If things go wrong and no rising takes place, the fewer folk that have seen this gathering, and his connection with it, the better! Perhaps he does not trust his own Campbells! For the same reason, he might not wish it said that he had entertained rebels in any house of his. Again, Rannoch is not all in Breadalbane, at all – at least the half of it lies in Struan Robertson's country. That might make useful explaining one day in, say, London town!'

'*Diabhol!* You believe his mind works that way? The dastard!'

'I believe that he is a man who takes every precaution – that is all. He has been so doing all his days – and seems not to have lost by it! And there is another reason that might have weighed with him. Few of the chiefs might wish to place themselves deep in Campbell country without a large fighting tail at their backs. But Rannoch, practically on Robertson land, is another matter. See you?'

Gregor nodded. 'I see, yes. I see, too, that not only do you not trust Breadalbane, but you believe him traitor. And yet you have brought all these chiefs here and put them into his hands. Why?'

Rob stopped, to lean against one of the sturdy stocky red-trunked pines that somehow had such a strange affinity with his own build and stature. 'You see things over-simply, Greg – all black and white,' he said. 'But you will perhaps grow out of that. I told you – we are dealing with a clever man in Iain Glas. It is easy to name a man traitor, and be done with him. But no clever man will turn traitor until it pays him to do so. Breadalbane is not a traitor – yet!'

'But . . . but he *may* betray us,' Gregor cried. 'I say this is madness – playing with fire, whatever!'

'All war is playing with fire – like marriage, lad! And rebellion more so. He may betray us – yes. But so may many others. What does the Good Book say – that a man can be weighed for a price? Breadalbane's will be no petty price, I warrant. He will not fail us so long as we are winning, I think – only if we are losing. Then will be our time to watch him.'

'You thought otherwise back at Inversnaid, with Colonel Hooke. You said that you misliked this forgathering with Breadalbane, doubting his attachment to the King's cause . . . ?'

'Aye – so I did. And still I would liefer have had other host than him for this gathering. I had to use some powerful persuading to bring some of these chiefs to Rannoch. But that is not the issue, now. I have considered the matter well. Also I have had speech with the man. Hooke was

right, Breadalbane sought this meeting. There was no need
for him to do so. He is with us, then . . . for the nonce.
Which means that he thinks that we shall win, whatever!
And his name, see you, is a great accession of strength – for
all men know that he does not love lost causes. He will turn
many waverers. When it is widely known that he is with us
– as you and I shall see that it *is* known, Greg – then King
Jamie will be a deal more likely to see those golden guineas
that your Lowland lairdies have so bravely promised!
Breadalbane could mean Jamie's throne for him – and
himself the power behind it, maybe! You are over-previous
with your traitors, lad.'

Gregor stared through that half-light at his potent uncle,
and wondered, his mind plunging, whether he saw feet of
clay in his idol for the first time. He was shocked – shocked
at many things, but worst of all at this revelation of the
older man's philosophy. 'You . . . *you* do not believe it?
That every man has his price?' he demanded, his voice
urgent.

Rob shrugged. 'Experience has not wholly convinced me
otherwise,' he said.

'But that is monstrous! It is against all that you have ever
taught me. . . . '

'In precept, aye. In practice . . . !' Those great shoulders
lifted again. 'It depends on the price, see you. With one, it
may be two pounds Scots – or thirty pieces of silver. With
another, all but the Kingdom of Heaven!'

'No!' Gregor grated. 'Not *all* men.'

His uncle smiled, then, that winning heart-warming
smile of his, and his hand came out to clasp the young
man's plaided shoulder. 'No – not all men,' he agreed. 'I
will make an exception of *you*, Greg – 'fore Heaven I will!'

'And you, Uncle?' That was hardly, levelly, said, and the
regard that went with it as level.

'I am as God made me,' Rob Roy MacGregor answered,
no less evenly. He withdrew his hand, and straightened
up. 'Come, you.' And he turned away, back towards the
camp.

Gregor Ghlun Dubh stalked half a step behind him for most of the way, with hardly a word to either of them.

*   *   *

Though hunting was, of course, a minor consideration for this assembly, a gesture in that direction was made the next day. The business was arranged in two distinct phases – one for the young and vigorous, the other for the more mature and dignified. The first was practised on horseback, with deerhounds; the second from behind butts and hides, with flintlock muskets. Deer were required for both, running free for the huntsmen, and driven for the marksmen. Deer being deer, to arrange that both practices could be engaged in simultaneously required considerable organisation and very extensive territory.

For, of course, the fleet and wary red deer of the Highland hills cannot really be driven at all. At the first hint of orthodox driving they would be off, singly and in herds, streaming and drifting over the skyline and far away, free as the cloud shadows, to be seen no more of men. They had to be manoeuvred, not driven, worked upon without them being aware of the fact, impelled not constrained – and never alarmed. To achieve that, against the keenest noses and ears of God's creation, leaving eyes and instinct out of it altogether, demanded a high degree of knowledge, cunning, patience and fitness.

The scheme went thus. Sizeable quantities of deer having been located – and that was the simplest part of it – expert beaters were sent out, over a wide area, to try to work the beasts in towards a given locality, preferably a sort of bottleneck, from which they could only escape by dashing through the neck or by breaking back whence they had come. The marksmen lined the bottleneck, and the horsemen and hounds waited hidden to chase the breakers-back, In theory, at any rate. The difficulties, which were many, made the sport.

The success or failure of the day rested not really with the sportsmen at all, but with the beaters. The moving of the deer, the wildest of the wild, had to be done by merely slightly unsettling them, never alarming them, so that they drifted and fed gradually in the right direction – which had to be down-wind, of course, or the brutes would scent the waiting hunters and bolt. This meant that the beaters had at all times to be off-wind to right or left – which in the eddying air currents of the hills was in itself no easy task. They must not disclose themselves to the deer, nor let them get more than the merest hint of their wind; yet they had to cause the creatures just enough disquiet to make them move away in the required direction. This, over vast acreages of mountainside, and with different herds of deer, called for exceptional hillcraft. Compared with it, the mere shooting or riding down of the game with hounds, however exciting and difficult it might be, could be dismissed as child's play.

The MacGregors of course were there ostensibly as beaters, but it went without saying that no large proportion of them were expert enough for this task. They were sent, in the main, by devious ways that would not arouse the quarry, to block various passes and gaps and valleys, for the horsemen's benefit. Both Gregor and his uncle, though expected to be of the hunters, being old hands at the game, insisted on joining the beaters, placing themselves under the orders of local men who knew the ground and something of the wind currents. Not all their chiefly colleagues approved.

They had a fine exhilarating day of it, nevertheless, on the great heather slopes above the Black Wood, a day of physical action such as both men loved, pitting their wits and skill against a wily and worthy adversary on his own territory – or hers, rather, for the old hinds represented three-quarters of the difficulty – working in fine and instinctive harmony and co-operation with their fellow hillmen, irrespective of name or rank. And all under the spell of great skies and endless vistas and the clean scented airs of the high tops. A clean good day altogether, the object of which, in the ultimate banging of flintlocks and the halloo-

III

ing of headlong hunters and the baying of racing hounds, seemed comparatively unimportant, if not actually a pity. The taste of politics and suspicion and cupidity, and worse, was for the time being washed away and forgotten. Uncle and nephew worked as a team again, with MacAlastair and Ian Beg in fullest sympathy. Coming off the hill that evening, weary, peat-stained and begrimed, their laughter and singing nevertheless rang out for all men to hear. The fact that the life's-blood of only a mere sixty-odd stags had dyed the heather, not one of them an outstanding head, and that my Lord of Breadalbane was annoyed, was of supreme unimportance.

It transpired that the proud Sons of Donald, from the west, had arrived at the camp in the interim – ClanRanald, Glengarry and Sleat. With them Matheson of Lochalsh, and MacKinnon of MacKinnon from Skye. And not with them, by any means, but a decent distance apart, the MacKenzies, under the young Earl of Seaforth and Sir Alexander of Gairloch.

The tally was now complete – for the Frasers and the Rosses, with sundry lesser clans, had made excuse, and Rob Roy had not had time to reach the Isles or the far Mackay country.

That night there was more feasting in honour of the MacDonalds and the MacKenzies – though, with the Glen Coe incident far from forgotten, the former were only frigidly polite towards their host. On the morrow, the real business of the gathering would begin.

*　　*　　*

The assembly was held in Breadalbane's pavilion again – however uncomfortable many of those present must have found it to be discussing politics under the black-and-gold Campbell colours. To avoid the ever-thorny problems of precedence, there were no formal placing arrangements, individuals and groups seating themselves where they pleased – though amidst a deal of shouldering, edging, stiff bowing and steely stares. No man discarded his bonnet. Apart from

'Colonel Hooke, only Breadalbane himself was hatless, in his great heavy wig – and as the heat in the tent grew oppressive he eventually laid that aside, and promptly, strangely, became infinitely more potent and dangerous-seeming, with his thin scrawny neck and bare bald vulturine head revealed.

The Earl made a brief carefully-worded introductory speech, declaring that they were all leal and good-intentioned Scots gathered for no other purpose than to further if possible the well-being and best interests of their native land. A Union with England was being negotiated, a Union that was no union but an incorporation, a swallowing up. If that was to the benefit of Scotland, well and good. But if it was not, if it spelt the end of their independence, then it behoved them to resist it. Good or bad, there was no doubt that the mass of the Scots people were against it. Which, in the circumstances, was a highly significant factor in view of the dynastic situation. Seldom indeed was the mass of the people aroused. Not for many generations had the people of all parts of their ancient kingdom been so concerned, or the Government and Parliament so out of step with the desire of the populace. Occasion and duty knocked at their doors. It behoved the Highlands to listen. He himself was an old done man – but his hearing remained to him yet, God be praised!

He then introduced to them Colonel Nathaniel Hooke, and sat down, having spoken no treason and committed himself to nothing, yet having created an extraordinary impression of crisis and opportunity. Rob Roy caught Gregor's eye – but did not hold it.

Nathaniel Hooke made a very different impact, the plain soldier, downright, unequivocal, unemotional. He read them a message from the nineteen-year-old James Stewart, subscribed at the Court of St Germains, by the grace of God, King of Scotland, England and Ireland, in which he assured his leal and trusty cousins, friends and subjects in Scotland of his love and affection for them, his gratitude for their continued loyalty to his House and throne, and his determination to come to them at the earliest opportunity. Also he commended to them Nathaniel Hooke, his trusted courier and emissary, who would explain to them what he and his Council proposed. God undoubtedly would be with them, and would defend the right.

Rob Roy, perceiving nobody else about to do so, raised a cheer here. 'God Save the King!' he shouted.

It was hearteningly taken up – even though men tended to watch their neighbour's lips as they supported it.

Hooke went on to reiterate the opportunity afforded by the widespread dissatisfaction in Scotland over the proposed Union. He told them that undoubtedly the Treaty would be signed sooner or later, a sufficiency of the Parliament in Edinburgh having been either bribed, threatened or compromised. There would be revolts and disorders up and down the country. Then His Majesty would land. Then the standard would be unfurled. Then they must strike.

'When?' ClanRanald demanded – thus asserting the MacDonald right to speak first and indicating their readiness for the fray. He was an impatient man at any time.

'Our information is that Godolphin, and Anne's Government, expect the Acts of both Parliaments to be passed by April next. That is in seven or eight months' time, sir. The glens will be free of snow and floods by then, and His Majesty intends to land about the first of May. Public indignation should be at its pitch by then, and the campaigning season just starting.'

'The time would seem to be well chosen, whatever,' Glengarry said swiftly, before his fellow MacDonald could rush in with his inevitable hasty talk about delay, faintheartedness and the ClanRanald motto of Gainsay who Dare.

There was a general growl of approval. Seasonal conditions meant a great deal where the clans were concerned, not only because snow and flooding made large-scale movement practically impossible for five months of the year in the mountains, but because of the needs of sowing and harvesting the winter feed for the hill cattle, on which the entire Highland economy was based, and the droving south of the surplus stock for the autumn trysts. Clan armies always had one eye over their shoulders during campaigns for these serious matters – and who would blame them? May undoubtedly was the best time for adventures of this sort, with four clear months ahead.

'Is it all Scotland that is to rise – or only the clans . . . as usual?' the young Earl of Seaforth asked.

'It is the whole country, my lord,' Hooke assured. 'I have been travelling round the country of Fife and Gowrie and Angus and Aberdeen. I have been in correspondence with many of the leading men to the south. And everywhere the cause is well received, and goes from strength to strength . . . '

'In Lowland promises!' Chisholm of Chisholm interpolated cynically.

'Promises – yes, sir. But what would you have? We do not wish to see men assembled just now. . . . '

'When you *do* wish to see men, I'll warrant it will be Highlandmen you will see, Colonel!'

'In the forefront, naturally,' Breadalbane intervened smoothly.

'His Majesty relies on the clans to give the lead, of course,' Hooke hastened to agree, casting a wary eye around the gathering. 'But there will be large numbers of men from the Lowlands. Many great lords are committed. Errol, the High Constable; the Earl Marischal; Panmure, Kinnoull; Rollo; Strathallan; Linlithgow; Winton; Carnwath; Southesk; Ogilvie; Stormont; Nairn. The shire of Fife is almost wholly ours, as is . . . '

There was such a muttering from the assembled chiefs that Hooke paused, unsure of how to proceed, unsure whether these proud Highlanders were resenting too much Lowland intervention or too little. Rob Roy came to his aid.

'That is fine, just,' he said, his vibrant voice, though seeming but little raised, sounding clearly through the hubbub. 'There will be tasks for all. Our own selves to do the fighting, and the Lowlanders to garrison the towns and hold the bridges and the like. And to keep us fed, see you . . . !'

The growling changed to a laugh, at that, and the ever-present Highland-Lowland problem lowered its ugly head for the moment.

'His Grace of Hamilton is much interested . . . ' Hooke was going on, hopefully, when again he was interrupted.

'How much is His Grace being paid for his kindly interest ?' Cluny Macpherson demanded. 'King Jamie must have gold, then ?'

There was another laugh, from some. Breadalbane raised his hand. 'Gentlemen,' he said, 'I take it that it is practicalities that Colonel Hooke has come to discuss with us – not personalities. I counsel that we should hold to that.'

'*Mac Cailein Mhic Donnachaidh* is right,' Rob Roy supported. 'We have not assembled from the half of Scotland to be teasing at tassels.' Though for Breadalbane to hint that gold and the price of support were less than practicalities did not fail to strike him as quaint. That others thought on similar lines was evident by the asides.

Coll of the Cows, MacDonald of Keppoch, an old and seasoned campaigner under Dundee, brought the issues back to earth. 'The clans will rise, undoubtedly,' he asserted. 'The Lowlands will assist. The populace will be sympathetic, belike. But what about King Jamie ? What is he bringing with him ? And what about France ?'

'Aye, aye.'

'Just that.'

'Tell us that, man.'

There was no doubting the generality of the concern.

Nathaniel Hooke cleared his throat. 'His Majesty will land, somewhere on the east coast, with a sufficient force to at least protect his person,' he announced. 'Gold he will bring with him. But . . . not in unlimited quantities, I'm afraid. The King of France is sympathetic – but preoccupied with his own wars. He will help – but the extent of his help is as yet uncertain.'

'Aye,' Keppoch said heavily. 'And there you have it!'

'No, no. Do not mistake me, gentlemen. His Most Christian Majesty's support is sure. Only it is as yet unspecified. . . . '

'Then it will have to be specified, sir, in no uncertain terms!' The old chief brought down open palm on bare knee. 'Our Highland broadswords may overrun Scotland – but they cannot hold it. We need muskets, ball, powder. But above all we need artillery, to reduce the great fortresses. The castles of Edinburgh and Stirling and Dumbarton and Inverness will be held against us – and we cannot bring them down with claymores and dirks. Artillery we must have. And engineers. If the King of France does not supply them, then we are beat before we start.'

The deep rumble of agreement was eloquent.

'My lords, gentlemen – that is understood,' Hooke cried. 'King James is well aware of the need. Only details are yet undecided. There is time yet, for that. Louis will be sending many soldiers with His Majesty. He will not send them without the services that they require. Let your minds rest easy on that score.'

'And money?' Glendaruel, the only other Campbell of note present, wondered. 'A rising cannot be maintained without money. Fighting men must be paid and fed. Horses, weapons, ammunition bought. Compensation paid . . . '

'His Majesty will bring what he can. Undoubtedly King Louis will help there also. But the Court at St. Germains is far from wealthy. It would, I daresay, wring the hearts of some here to see how His Majesty must live. His clothing threadbare, footwear down-at-heel, food of the plainest.' Hooke did not actually look at Breadalbane, but his glance just flickered in that direction. 'Some French gold will come, assuredly. But His Majesty is relying, in the main, on the generosity of his loyal subjects here. . . . '

Rob Roy stood up. 'Gentlemen,' he said, 'I for one do not seek to see my country saved by foreign gold! While I have a plack in my sporran and a beast on the hill I'll not be after shouting for *louis-d'ors!*' He changed his tone, a little. 'As some of you will have heard, likely, my Lammas herds are new in. Half of all that I shall sell of them, at Crieff and Falkirk trysts, in October, shall go to the King's purse!'

That raised a cheer and flattering acclaim. But also some sidelong glancing and thoughtful beard-tugging. Not all men were so well supplied with cattle of other folk's rearing as were the Gregorach.

Rob noted the glancing, and went on quickly. 'My nephew, Glengyle, here, is just after calling on Lowland lairds in the Carse of Stirling, see you – men of the size of Arnprior and Garden and Keir, who dabble in the America trade. And Patterson of Bannockburn. Up, Greg, and tell them what these will give.' No hint there of the doubts that he had thrown on the said promises the day before.

It was a new experience for Gregor Black Knee to feel self-conscious and embarrassed before his fellow-men. But this was a distinctly special assembly. He looked round him, as he rose, clearing his throat.

'Up, the Gregorach!' somebody said.

'Up, the White Bull!' another amended. There was a laugh.

Gregor felt better immediately. Gallangad's bull was serving him well. 'I gained from these lairds promise of around 25,000 pounds Scots.' That was only some £2,000 sterling, but it sounded well. 'That was from but some eight men.'

'Promises again . . . ?' the cynical Chisholm commented.

'They are all within the area of my Watch,' Rob Roy put in mildly. 'They might possibly be held to their words!'

Gregor took a quick breath. 'You can be adding another thousand to that, gentlemen, from my own self,' he said, greatly daring. 'Scots.' And, as there was a distinct murmur from his assembled seniors and betters, he added a wholly rash, 'And if anyone wishes to buy a notable bull, the price can be added to my contribution, whatever!'

'Damnation! Were you not after giving that bull to me?' his uncle demanded. 'I tell you . . . '

The rest was lost in a great shout of mirth. Financially, at least, the day was saved. No more was heard of *louis-d'ors*.

Men were now the question. And of course men meant commitment. A chief who once had his name linked with so many men could nowise go back on it, dare not, for pride's sake, contribute one clansmen less. Rivalry, caution, ambition, suspicion and sheer vainglory played a major tug-of-war now.

Again the MacGregors were in a position, of course, to lead the way. They had 600 armed men outside there and then. What proportion of that number could be mustered for a lengthy campaign as distinct from a day or two's cantrip like this remained to be seen. But this was by no means the scraping of the Gregorach barrel. And there were always the broken men and drovers and suchlike from Balquhidder and Brig o' Turk and thereaway who could be enrolled at a price. Rob Roy said 750, at any rate – and set the standard high. Higher than he was likely to fulfil, perhaps.

ClanRanald promptly weighed in with a haughty 1,000. And thereafter young Seaforth, glaring, mentioned 2,500 MacKenzies, with a casualness that his looks belied. That brought the other MacDonalds to their feet. 700, Glengarry cried. 500, old Coll of Keppoch added. There was a brief pause as the more circumspect Sir Donald of Sleat calculated just how many would be needed still to decently beat the MacKenzies. He made it 400, and announced that figure cannily – though, successor of the Lords of the Isles himself, he could have more than doubled it. But they had outbid Seaforth and his MacKenzies by 100. That should ensure them the right of the line.

Sir John Maclean of Duart, another veteran, named 600 for himself; added that his kinsman Maclaine of Lochbuie was good for 300; and reckoned that another 100 could be got out of Ardgour. 1,000 in all.

But after this exciting interlude there was a notable pause. It was all very well for these great outland clans from the Isles and the remote north-west to commit themselves thus in their ancient rivalry. They could never be brought to heel in their distant fastnesses. If things went wrong, major punitive expeditions were never likely to reach Skye or Mull, or even Kintail and Applecross and Torridon of the MacKenzies. The MacGregors, likewise, had little to lose. They were outlawed and proscribed already, living on their wits. For more accessible and responsible folk, it was all rather different. . . .

There was much humming and hawing, much discussion and consultation and prevarication, much head-shaking and beard-tugging. Rob Roy worked hard, as did the MacDonalds and MacKenzies and Macleans, who were already committed. Hooke, of course, dared not intervene; and Gregor was much too junior to do more than pose as a good example. It was decided to adjourn for dinner and see what victuals and liquor could do to loosen stiff tongues and wills.

They were still eating when Lochiel's son almost came to blows with Glengarry, and thereupon threw 400 Camerons into the scales. Cluny Macpherson could not thole that, and committed himself to 450 of his folk. Alexander of Struan, the poet, had no option but to go one better, and came in with 500 Robertsons. Thereafter the contagion spread, and before the afternoon was out 17,000 men were vouched for, and half as many again hoped for, once the go-one-better-than-my-neighbour process really got going.

And, of course, with the men committed, the chiefs also were committed. The rising was assured. There only remained to draw up the usual Bond of Association, decide the assembly points, who were to command the brigades, and so on.

All that could be done on the morrow, after another hunt. Meanwhile certain clerkly ones amongst them, Rob Roy included, should draw up the terms of the Bond of Association, concoct a Loyal Address to King Jamie, and also a Memorial to His Most Christian Majesty Louis XIV of France, pointing out how ripe was the time, how fair were the prospects and how urgent the need of engineers, ammunition and artillery. Breadalbane offered to assist in this task.

Gregor wondered how many others, beside himself – and his uncle, of course, for it was not the sort of thing that Rob Roy would miss – had noticed that the said noble earl was the only man present who had not committed himself to providing some tally of men for the venture. Even Campbell of Glendaruel had offered 100.

*   *   *

The deer-hunt the next day amounted to no great shakes as these affairs went, a drizzling rain damping the ardour of the sportsmen and a fitful wind making the driving more difficult even than usual.

Gregor hunted this time with his hounds, and achieved one or two exciting kills. But he was used to better sport amongst his own hills around Loch Lomond and Loch Katrine; this Rannoch had altogether too much wood for this sort of hunting, the deer tending to bolt downwards for this forest cover instead of upwards for the open tops, as was usual and suitable. However, it all served as excuse for the gathering, which was what was required; moreover, the Laird of MacKinnon grassed a huge woodland stag of no fewer than fourteen points, past its best and creaking at the joints admittedly, but still with a spread that few had seen bettered, a trophy to take back with him for the Skyemen to make a ballad out of when compared with their poor small island deer. Not a few felt that it was a pity, however, that thi should have fallen to such a dull fellow as MacKinnon.

In the evening there was another session in Breadalbane's pavilion, to approve the form of the Memorial to King Louis, the Loyal Address to King James and to sign the Bond of Association. Louis, whose aid was so unspecified, but who nevertheless would so greatly gain in his other interests were London to be actively preoccupied with a rising in Scotland, was specifically requested, with all respect, to provide 15,000 muskets and equivalent ammunition, 4,000 barrels of powder and 12 brass field-pieces. Also

8,000 soldiers, to include an adequate number of engineers. No harm in pitching it high, as Rob explained, indicating the peculiarities of the Latin temperament. James was assured of all love and loyalty, and of the impatience with which all awaited his personal appearance amongst them – but was urged in the next paragraph that the value of his royal presence would be vastly enhanced if he brought with him the supplies and troops demanded of King Louis.

The Bond of Association was in the usual terms. It bound its signatories to reassemble at points to be decided later, together with armed forces to the numbers agreed, within twenty-one days of receipt of an authorised summons, to support with their blood, strength and treasure the legitimate title and claim of their *Ard Righ* or High King, James Stewart, against the present most calamitous and illegal usurpation.

There was some inevitable discussion and some heat engendered on the subject of who was first to sign this decl: ra tion. Not only were the MacDonalds vociferous that he honour lay with their house, rather than with, say, Sca-forth, whose earldom was a mere modern nonsense not to be mentioned in the same breath as the ancient Lordship of the Isles; but there was internecine strife as to which of themselves should pen the premier superscription – Sleat claiming that he represented the senior branch of the clan, ClanRanald asserting that he was supplying the most men, and Glengarry pointing out heatedly that he was not only the eldest but the only veteran of the wars amongst them. In this pass Rob Roy it was who declared that the obvious name to be first on the Bond was that of Breadalbane, their host, who had summoned this gathering and so great y assisted them to their decisions. No man's name would lock better at the head of this historic list.

There was a moment's silence in that pavilion as the significance and worth of this suggestion sank in – for it had been pregnantly delivered. Then there was a great and general outburst of acclaim, even the Sons of Donald perceiving that here was a trap out of which the wily Campbell would find it hard to wriggle. Breadalbane's signature, first on this Bond, would do what he had so skilfully avoided doing hitherto – implicate and commit him in no uncertain terms to this venture. All men cried their approval.

All except Breadalbane, that is. With thin-lipped modesty he urgently declined the honour. He was an old man, and past days of active campaigning, good only for the conference table. He would not dream of superseding the resounding names present, scores more notable than his own. Et cetera. But Rob would have none of it – and the entire assembly supported him gleefully now. The quill was thrust into the Campbell's hand.

The Earl looked at the ranked faces around him, and then smiled bleakly. He stooped down, and signed – not Breadalbane, nor even John Campbell, but *Mac Cailein Mhic Donnachaidh*, Son of Colin, son of Duncan. And then, bowing, handed the pen to Sir Donald of Sleat.

Those near enough to see stared at that signature in silence. Rob Roy drew a long breath. Himself, he was not so clever after all, apparently. It took a long spoon to sup with the Devil, indeed.

CHAPTER NINE

THE Gregorach rode and ran southwards in different fashion from their coming. Late in the night, after that signing of the Bond, a weary courier had arrived in the camp from Glen Gyle, for Gregor Ghlun Dubh. He came from the Lady Christian, to tell her son that soldiers had descended upon Glengyle House, from Stirling, seeking him. She urged that he keep away until she could be quit of them.

The message had quite other effect upon Gregor to that

intended. He had questioned the courier and discovered that the troops were dragoons to the number of some fifty, or half a squadron, under two officers, and he had thereupon gone to wake Rob Roy and inform him that he was off home forthwith to cleanse Loch Katrine-side of such gentry. Rob had listened, nodded in the dark, grunted, and then advised against unseemly haste. Was he going to let a few red-coats spoil their sleep? Let Gregor wait, in Christian fashion, till morning, and he would accompany him. They would see to this matter in a manner befitting gentlemen.

So, taking ceremonious farewell of all the assembled chiefs, and of their host, and insisting on leaving the major part of the MacGregors, under Roro's son, to assist at the final day's hunting and to provide escort for any of the guests who might wish it – little needed as these services might be – Rob and Gregor, with their own immediate followers from Glen Gyle and Inversnaid, had set off southwards up the Dall Water, going as only the Gregorach knew how. They numbered some 120 picked men.

As the crow flies they had perhaps a bare forty miles to cover – but over no fewer than five distinct ranges of mountains. And almost as the crows flew went the MacGregors, scorning drove roads, paths and tracks, at a long-legged steady mile-eating trot, over great heather shoulders and ridges, across rolling moors, down winding glens and through quaking bogs. Over into Glen Lyon at Innerwick and out again by the savage Lairig Breisleich, the Pass of Confusion. Down into Glen Lochay, to climb once more over the massive hump-backed hills beyond into wide Glen Dochart, fording the river at Innishewan. Then up under the towering heights of Ben More and Am Binnein, down the Monachyle Glen and so into green Balquhidder. There remained only the Pass of Weeping's harsh ascent, and Loch Katrine was glittering golden below them, with the sunset flooding down Glen Gyle. Eleven hours the journey had taken them, practically non-stop, and none would name them laggard.

They slanted along the high ground, some 500 feet above the loch, leaving such horses as were with them behind a shoulder of hill, and halting at a discreet distance above the whitewashed house in the mouth of the glen, in the cover of a scooped hollow. Looking over the lip of this they could discern the rows of horses tethered with military precision in the green haugh below the house, and the blue feathers of wood-smoke drifting up from the area of the steading and outbuildings at the back. Otherwise the impression was one of undisturbed peace and normalcy, amongst the lengthening shadows of evening.

Rob Roy looked from the scene to his nephew. 'Well, Greg?' he said. 'What now?'

The younger man was grateful for that question, and for what it implied. His uncle was going to leave it to himself, as Laird of Glengyle. This was his own affair, and men were to know it.

'I am thinking that my guests downbye have probably overstayed their welcome,' he observed thoughtfully. 'All those horses will have consumed a deal of forage needed for our winter feed. It is perhaps time that the redcoats returned to Stirling?'

'It could be that you are right,' his uncle agreed.

'It seems that I will need to be having speech with the officers.' Gregor fingered his chin. 'To do so suitably and without fuss, I think it would be best if sóme portion of us were to be slipping down by the Yellow Burn, there, and maybe working along between the steading and the house. That would be the most of us. And another portion could be for going down the Black Burn, here, and along the front between the house and the horses, see you. And then maybe the horses could just be getting a fright, the way horses will whatever, and off with them?'

Gravely Rob nodded. 'I could see all that happening,' he admitted. 'Always supposing that the sentries that these soldiers do be setting were after looking the other way.'

'Yes, then. But supposing that small little belt of trees

and bushes to the west of the house was to be going on fire, some way, and the smoke blowing over in the wind? The sentries could be distracted, just.'

'Why not?' the other conceded.

'A gentleman might then be having a quiet bit of a talk with two officers in his own house, in these circumstances, might he not?'

'Man, Gregor – I shouldn't wonder, at all!' Rob chuckled. '*Dia* – you have been well trained, I swear!'

Gregor slid down from the lip of the hollow to inform and instruct his men, men most of them, like himself, already in sight of their homes, and wondering. Being Gregorach, they were in a brittle mood. But he soon had them grinning. He ended on a note of warning.

'It is not yet war, *a graidh*, see you. That will come later,' he explained. 'Here is only an exercise in the civilities. There is to be no killing. If use your claymores you must, let it be the flat of them. These redcoats must be taught that Gregorach territory is no place for such as them – but let us be teaching them it with all courtesy. Coll Carach – you will take the Yellow Burn, with, say seventy men. Ian Beg – you, the Black Burn, with thirty. Myself, I will come with you. A score will remain here, in reserve, to come down with much noise if it seems that they are needed. Dougal, ...' he turned with a smile to his cousin of Comar, '... you have the loud voice, as Heaven's my witness! You will bring them?' Then he glanced at his uncle. 'You ...?'

'I will be keeping Coll Carach company. And maybe lighting that fire,' Rob declared. 'An old man I am getting, just. But, see you – old or young, I have noticed here and there that dragoons, saving the officers, do be keeping their swords and their pistols attached to their saddles, and not to their persons. A strange custom – but a great convenience, on occasion.'

'Aye. You all hear that, my friends? The saddlery you will look for. Coll – you will not move in towards the steading from your burn-channel till you are hearing the curlew call three times. The same for the smoke. Is all understood?'

There was a murmur of assurance.

Gregor laughed, happily, but quietly. 'Home-coming is sweet, they say! Let us be tasting it!'

The entire lengths of the long green hillsides that flanked Glen Gyle were scored by innumerable narrow burn-channels, most of which were filled with birch and rowan scrub in their steep crevices where the winds and the cattle could not get at them. The big house lay embosomed in its trees between the outflows of two such streams, both coming down within a hundred yards of the buildings, that on the west, the Allt Buie, the Yellow Burn, actually skirting the back of the steading, into which an artificial channel was diverted to water stock and to provide for the duck-pond. Nothing was easier than for men wise in hill-craft to slip soundless and unseen down these clefts of burn-channels to within a few yards of the house, the hounds that accompanied them everywhere padding silently at their heels.

In the event, the entire business was absurdly simple, what with the excellent cover available, the deep purple shadows of the creeping dusk, and the fact that obviously the soldiers were at their evening meal. The savoury smell of roasting beef came drifting down on the westerly air to Gregor as he and his party reached the foot of their stair-way-like descent into the scattered dark pines to the east of the house – an appetising scent for ravenously hungry men who had not eaten since breakfast. That it was undoubtedly Gregor's own beef only added piquancy.

From here, peering through the trees, they had an excellent view of the area in front of the house – though of little behind it. The ground sloped down to the loch shore in two shallow grassy terraces and then a reedy water-meadow. On the second terrace the cavalry horses were tethered in two long lines. And nearby, but a little closer to the house, two corresponding rows of neatly arranged small heaps upon the ground could only represent the saddlery – though the dusk made it impossible to distinguish details. As far as could be seen, only two sentries were posted here, who strolled about casually, apparently from a base at the far end of the horse-lines. Lights were already lit in the house – which Gregor took to indicate that the officers were even now within, for his mother was less prodigal with her dips. Now and again a figure appeared in the moulded front doorway in the stair-tower – probably another sentry.

Gregor touched Ian Beg's arm, and pointed. Between the water-meadow, in which two or three milch-cows grazed, and the actual loch shore was a long dyke or raised grassy bank, built to preserve the haughland from flooding in the winter storms. 'Along behind that, with you,' he whispered. 'Line it. When you are in position, hoot like an owl. Then crawl over the bank and through the rushes of the meadow, see you, amongst the cattle. It is low-lying, and they'll not be seeing you. You will get almost up to the horses, I think. Then dirk work amongst the beasts' halters. The moment that you are seen, howl all of you like the doubly damned – get those horses bolting, whatever. Then disarm the sentries – gently, see you – and round the back to aid the others. You have it?'

'Och fine, just – yes,' Ian Beg assured. 'There is nothing to it, at all.'

'Not a thing. Go, then. And fortune go with you.'

Gregor kept back two gillies, one of them his own Duncan Og, while the others dissolved into the dusk, hounds at heel. They waited. From down at the lochside mallards quacked sleepily. Now and again a tethered horse blew through its nostrils. From far up the glen a stirk's bellow sounded faintly. Somewhere a man was singing monotonously – none of their own Celtic melodies, and therefore a dragoon.

Suddenly a pair of duck flew up from the shore, with the flap of wings beating on the water before changing into the whistle of flight. The single owl's hoot from behind the bank came almost immediately, sooner than Gregor had anticipated. Thereafter, stare as he would, he could see no sign of men, no hint of movement about the dyke or in the meadow. Was Ian delaying, holding back? Had he perhaps

seen some obstacle, not visible from here? More
sentries . . . ?

Then one of the cows amongst the rushes moved jerkily,
out of the rhythm of her quiet grazing. He could see her
moving along, now, on a line towards the house, head low
but not feeding, curiosity in her gait. Some gillie would be
cursing her.

That was all that Gregor required. Pursing his lips, he
whistled clear and true the long liquid yittering call of the
curlew, three times, trilling lonely and lovely on the evening
air. Then, gesturing to his companions, he slipped forward
through the trees.

Circle round as they would, there was an open space beyond the last of the pines some forty yards to the gable-end
of the house. They must cross it. Their rawhide brogans
making no sound, the three men paced out these yards,
unhurrying – even though every instinct said to hurry, to
run; in the gloom were they seen, they would be but three
walking figures, no cause for alarm, but running they
would have been three intruders. Still no commotion arose,
front or back of the house.

Gregor reached some fruit trees under the gable-end,
presumably without being observed. Against the wall of the
house they waited.

Not for long, this time. They heard the crackle of fire in
dry undergrowth, and in a moment or two even glimpsed
the faint reflection of flame amongst the tree-tops. A man
called out, enquiringly, not actually alarmed – an English
voice. Another answered him, from farther away. Somebody shouted rather than called – perhaps a sergeant. The
first acrid smoke clouds began to drift over, so much more
pungent than the aromatic tang of the small cooking-fires.

Suddenly a horse whinnied, loud and high – and the
waiting men jumped at the sound. And immediately thereafter chaos was let loose in that quiet valley under the
brooding hills. Eldrich howls and yells and halloos rent the
air. Hounds bayed. Shod hooves clattered and pounded.
Challenges and orders and demands resounded, alarmed

enough now in all conscience. A pistol banged. And then another. Steel streaked and rang.

Intrigued and concerned as he was to judge the progress of events by the noise, Gregor did not wait to listen. He slid round the gable-end and along the front of the house, behind him his two shadows. Over to the left the grassy slope was commotion materialised now, with nothing to be distinguished in the massive confusion. Gregor edged round the semicircle of the stair-tower. Only a split second after he came in sight of the door, a man appeared therein, staring out. Gregor drew back swift as thought. The man stepped out, shouting something questioning. Gregor let him get two paces beyond the line of the tower – and leapt. The general hullabaloo deadened any sound of his coming. The haft of his dirk crashed down upon the bare bullet head of the unfortunate soldier. His breath came out of him in a shuddering groan, and he sank to the ground limply.

Gregor jerked his head towards the house, and strode for the open doorway, his two gillies close at his heels, claymores in their right hands, dirks in their left.

Scared faces peered at them along the ground-floor passage, from the kitchen door. They were his own people, and Gregor waved a reassuring hand to them. He was turning to race up the twisting turnpike stair to the first floor where were the principal rooms of the house, when he halted. Hurried footsteps were coming clattering down those same stairs. He stepped back, signing to his henchmen to flank the foot of the stairway. He had not drawn his own sword, and now he put away his dirk, and folded his arms. He was in his own house, was he not?

The long spurred and gleaming thigh-boots of a cavalry officer appeared, preceding a heavy figure, down those winding stairs at an awkward run. The rest of him showed the frogged and gold-braided red coat unbelted and flying open, the long waistcoat underneath also undone, one of Lady Christian's own lace-edged napkins still tucked in at the throat to protect the cravat, and then a square-chinned cleanshaven face, brows dark but jaws still chewing. At sight of the three motionless tartan-clad figures below, two with naked claymores barring the way and glimmering in the light of the guttering dips, and the other leaning casually against the farther wall, this hurrying dragoon sought to come to an abrupt stop, did not quite manage it, slipped spurred heel on a worn step, all but fell headlong, and only recovered himself by grabbing at the rope which hung down the newel. At his back a second, younger man, coming down just as fast, collided with him, nearly pitching him farther down still. They came to a halt only a few steps above those gleaming swords. The second officer was the Ensign of the St Ninians road.

'Good evening, gentlemen,' Gregor called out to them, civilly. 'I hope that I have noways interrupted your supper ? I regret that I was not here to greet you in person. But now, perhaps, I can be making up for it ? Welcome to Glen Gyle!'

*   *   *

The military men were perhaps not wholly to be blamed if it took them a few moments to recover their due poise and aplomb. A series of stuttered ejaculations and appeals to the Deity came from the older man, while the Ensign first drew back as though to return upstairs, then gulped and pointed, to announce that that was the man, MacGregor himself, the miscreant Glengyle. From without the uproar maintained, if it did not actually increase. Gregor was glad to hear only three or four reports of firearms.

'Perhaps I may be honoured with your names, gentlemen ?' he suggested, politely.

The older man pulled himself together with an obvious effort. 'I am Captain Somers, 4th Light Dragoons,' he said. 'This is Ensign Davies. And you, sir, if you are James Graham, calling yourself MacGregor, of this place – then I am here to arrest you in the Queen's name. On the authority of Her Majesty's Commander-in-Chief, General the Earl of Leven.'

'Och, man – tut-tut,' Gregor deplored. 'Not so fast,

surely. Here is no sort of talk between gentlemen. If you will be returning upstairs, now, we can maybe be discussing matters like . . . '

'Damnation – a truce to your chatter, sirrah!' Captain Somers broke in. 'I am not here to bandy words.' He made as if to step farther down the stairs, perceived only too clearly how the two broadswords seemed to leap quivering to life – and thought better of it. 'What in God's name is going on out there?' he demanded, instead.

Gregor cocked an attentive ear. 'That, I take it, is some of my people trying to catch your horses for you, sir – they would seem to have broken loose, somehow. Och, but they will soon have them, safe and sound.'

'Eh . . . ? Loose?' Somers turned to look at the Ensign. An appreciation of the situation seemed to be in progress, as became good soldiers. 'Deuce take it – this is armed revolt!'

Young Davies, for a brief moment, looked almost smug. If he did not actually enunciate the words 'What did I tell you?' he managed to convey his sentiments clearly enough. 'Undoubtedly, sir,' he said.

'You!' Somers swung back to Gregor. 'Do you realise what you are doing, fellow?' he demanded. 'You could hang for this – taking up arms against the Queen's Majesty!'

'Me?' Gregor looked suitably shocked. 'I do no such thing, Captain, at all. I take up arms against no one – not even Anne Stewart, of London.' He held out his empty hands to prove it. 'These gillies of mine are apt to carry their claymores that way. A mere formality it is. Like your sentries, outbye!'

'You . . . you insolent bareshanked jackanapes!'

'Sir – under my roof, I'd suggest more moderate language, whatever,' Gregor said coldly. 'I would not wish to have my friends here teaching any guest of mine a lesson in manners.'

'Are you threatening me, sir?'

'Not so. Merely informing you, just. Indeed, I am offering you further hospitality – requesting that you go upstairs, gentlemen, and proceed with your interrupted meal. At

132

which I shall be glad to join you, for I am hungry. And I have much travelling ahead of me this night yet – as indeed have your own selves, sirs. So I advise that we eat well.'

'You . . . devil take you, sir! What do you mean? Travel . . . ?'

'To Stirling, Captain.'

'Dammit . . . to Stirling you'll be taken, certainly. But not tonight, Graham. . . . '

'The name is MacGregor. And tonight it is. You have been away overlong as it is. I insist, whatever. In fact, I will escort you there, my own self.'

'Lord save us – are you mad, fellow?'

'I said that I feared he might be, you'll recollect, sir,' Davies mentioned a little unsteadily.

'I am concerned for your comfort, rather,' Gregor announced, head ashake. 'Our provision and means of hospitality here at Glen Gyle is limited, I fear, for such a large number of guests – however boundless our goodwill. I find that we have unhappily reached the limits of our provender. Now. It is unfortunate – but I know that you will be understanding. You must return to Stirling – tonight. When we have managed to catch your runaway horses, of course.'

'Now, by all the Powers of Heaven!' Somers swore. 'I . . . '

That was as far as he got, then. A press of men was surging in at the front door of the house, to fill the stone-flagged vestibule. All wore Highland dress, save one – a dishevelled and distinctly frightened-looking sergeant of dragoons. Rob Roy was in the forefront.

'*Dia!*' his great voice rang out. 'Pretty work! As Royal's my Race – it was a diversion, no less! How is it with yourself, Greg?'

'Passing fair. I was just after informing these gentlemen . . . Ah, forgive me. Captain Somers. And Ensign Davidson, is it? This is Rob Roy MacGregor of Inversnaid, Captain of the Glengyle Highland Watch. I was for informing them that they would be in Stirling before daylight, see you. We would see to it, our own selves, and no trouble at all. Once we have their runaway horses caught for them. Och, we can do no less.'

'Surely, surely. A good evening, gentlemen. It is a pity about the horses.'

'Sergeant Cooper . . . !' Somers got out, in a strangled voice. 'What in God's name has happened? Where are your men?'

But the sergeant only shook a woebegone head, dumbly.

'Och, your men are fine, Captain,' Rob answered for him. 'Our lads are after sharing their supper with them – a pleasing sight.'

Mystified and confounded, Somers looked behind him at his subordinate. He got no aid there, the younger man wagging his head helplessly. Whether it was the sight of their unhappy sergeant a prisoner, the potent name of Rob Roy MacGregor the redoubtable freebooter, or merely the self-evident fact that all this crew of Highlanders could not possibly have come streaming in at the front door of the house unless the troopers had been quite overwhelmed in some extraordinary fashion – whatever the cause, the fight and the spirit seemed to have drained out of the two dragoons. Gallant officers as they no doubt were, they drooped rather. This sort of situation was not provided for in any military precept or instruction.

Gregor nodded, then. 'I am suggesting that we follow the others' example, then, Uncle. Upstairs with us, and let us be eating. I think that we disturbed these gentlemen at their meat, also. We must delay them no longer. Up with us.'

He moved forward to the stair foot, Rob following. The two gillies gestured with their drawn claymores. And, heavy-booted, heavy-footed, the two officers turned and climbed sourly up whence they had come.

*   *   *

In the dining-room above there was a touching reunion with the Lady Christian – who had undoubtedly been listening at the stairhead to all that had transpired. Rob made much of her, Gregor a little less, as was but natural. She did not seem to be wholly reassured by either – but females were like that, seldom accepting even the bounty of Providence without niggling doubts. But at least she fed them, and did not argue – two essentials where women were concerned, whatever their role.

The officers seemed to have lost their appetites and refused Gregor's further hospitality, sitting like spectres at the feast while the MacGregors cleared the table. Gregor did not think much of their manners, and indicated as much, without of course being rude enough to say so.

Assured by his uncle that all was satisfactorily in hand outside, and everybody getting sufficient to eat – the soldiers having killed beef in plenty – Gregor enjoyed his meal. Then, replete, leaving Rob to entertain his guests, he hurried downstairs and outside, to cope with the further needs of the situation.

He found the troopers all penned up in the steading, and being very little trouble at all. They had been caught by surprise, cooking their meal, separated from their arms and equipment, confused by smoke and the dusk, and out of touch not only with their officers but with the sergeant and two corporals, who also liked to show their superiority by eating apart – in this instance in the kitchen, from which they had emerged too late to give any real lead. Theirs had been the pistol-shots, other than those of the sentries. Fortunately nobody was dead, or nearly so. One or two had sore heads, contusions and scratches – the worst hurt probably a young MacGregor who had stumbled over a cooking-pot of stewing beef collops and scalded his bare legs.

Already most of the stampeded horses had been caught again, or had come back on their own, none having run far, being disciplined brutes. A strong guard was sitting over the saddles and arms, having food brought by the others. The Gregorach, being used to the activities of the Watch and the droving, were good at looking after themselves in most circumstances. MacGregor of Comar had come down from the hill, with their own horseflesh, aggrieved that neither his services nor his noted voice had been required.

Gregor urged one and all to eat heartily – but to be quick about it, as he had work for them yet. He gave his instructions. All the army horses were to be saddled up. Nothing was to be taken from any of the soldiers, save actual powder and shot. Every grain and ball of that was to be taken. But no weapons. Cavalry swords were to be collected, bundled up, and carried in panniers on garrons' backs. The pistols, chargeless, could be left in their saddle-holsters. Then the troopers were to be mounted, willy-nilly, a MacGregor sitting at each man's back, dirk drawn. That would account for some fifty of them. A score more should get themselves garrons and be ready to ride. The remainder could go home. That had better be the Inversnaid people, probably. Was it all understood?

Gregor returned to his own dining-room. 'All will be ready for you gentlemen in two-three minutes,' he informed. 'But first we must all have a drink for the road, and us maybe needing it.' He filled generous glasses with amber whisky, for all present, officers and Gregorach gentlemen. 'Here is a toast for us all, my friends,' he cried. 'On your feet and let us drink to our beloved and rightful Sovereign! The Sovereign!'

There was a shout of mingled laughter and acclaim as glasses were raised and drained. Gregor had done well – enabled them all to drink to King Jamie's health, and obviously so, in the presence of these officers of Queen Anne, yet had neither shown bad manners to the guests under his roof nor left them with any excuse for not drinking the loyal toast with them. All eyes upon them, the two unhappy dragoons exchanged glances, frowning and hesitant, saw no way out of it, and lifted glasses to sip doubtfully. The joyous shouting redoubled, Gregor's own uninhibited laughter outringing all. He clapped Captain Somers on the back, next to choking the man.

'Your sentiments are sound, sir!' he cried. 'Come you, now. Gather your hat and your gear. And your sword, whatever. Yes, indeed – your sword! Stirling, it is.'

Rob Roy took leave of them at the door downstairs, claiming that a respectable man of his years was better in his bed over at Inversnaid than traipsing the countryside in the middle of the night. Moreover, they had no need of him, most evidently. He bade Captain Somers convey his respects to the Governor of Stirling Castle, and pointed out that this was the first body of troops ever to honour the MacGregor country with a visit, in his lifetime. He forbore to add that if 600 MacGregors had not been engaged elsewhere at the time, they might not have been even thus honoured.

The Captain and the Ensign, sitting their own horses and with their swords at their sides – but flanked fairly closely by Gregorach mounted on shaggy garrons, nimble if short-legged, their right hands a shade ominously hidden in the folds of their red plaids – rode away from Glengyle House, amidst the valedictory cheers of those left behind. At their backs trotted their half-squadron, more or less in parade-order, but each charger bearing a double burden – in every case the pillion-rider being noticeably the more cheerful of the two. Behind them again another swarm of garron-borne Highlanders crowded anyhow, with three pannier-ponies.

South-eastwards, round the head of the darkling loch, they rode, for Stronachlacher and the drove road for Aberfoyle.

*   *   *

It was approximately thirty miles to Stirling by the drove road that wound between the ramparts of the Highland Line and the northern rim of the long desolation of Flanders Moss – but a little longer by the route that Gregor led the dragoons, and by which, once their own clachan of Aberfoyle was past, they avoided all villages and haunts of men. The edge of the Moss itself received them more than once – where Gregor was urgent that all should follow exactly in the tracks of the horse in front if miry death would be avoided, himself leading. That he led on Mr Davies's former fine black charger was not actually commented upon by anybody.

Indeed there was little comment or chatter of any sort throughout, the Gregorach finding the military but surly companions.

They had left Glen Gyle after ten o'clock. Hurrying was out of the question in the circumstances, and it was almost four in the morning before Gregor drew rein near Drip Bridge under the tree-clad Hill of Drip that rose like a stranded leviathan amongst the flats of the Carse. Ahead, just over a mile away, against the already paling sky to the east, the loom of the great Castle-rock of Stirling just could be descried. He let Somers come level with him, and pointed.

'Yonder is your Castle, Captain. You will excuse us from coming farther ? My people have travelled far since yesterday's dawn, and it is a far cry for dismounted men back to Glen Gyle.' He yawned, himself, as he said it.

Somers stared straight ahead of him. He did not speak, nor even glance in Gregor's direction.

The latter, who had a modicum of pride himself, knew a certain sympathy for the other man. 'Och, man – it is none so ill an ending to this ploy, at all,' he pointed out. 'You were a brave man to be entering the MacGregor country at all. More, with but fifty men to you. And you have brought them all out again, too. The first man, belike, to ever have done such a thing!'

'You can spare me your condolences, at least, MacGregor,' the sorely tried soldier said tersely. 'And do not think that you have heard the last of this night's work! By God – you have not!'

'Do not be taking it so hard,' the soft-hearted Gregor urged. 'It could have been a deal worse, whatever. You have lost not a thing, at all. All your men are here. Your weapons are in the panniers, there. Also the ball and powder for your pistols. You have lost nothing.'

'Except my reputation, sir ! And my self-respect. What do you think I will tell my Colonel of this night's affair ?' That was a *cri de coeur* indeed, however harsh the tone in which it was uttered. 'I was ordered to bring you in to justice. . . . '

'*Dia* – what is an order, when it cannot be carried out? What will you tell your Colonel? That you braved many perils to reach your destination. That Glengyle was not at home when you got there. That he was away in the north, it was said. That you waited as long for him as you felt was safe and proper. That you left the word for him to come forthwith to Stirling Castle when he got home – and then returned your own self to report, wasting no more time. That would be the tale I would be telling, whatever.'

'May be, sir. I could well believe it. S'wounds – a likely story!'

'I think that there will be none to gainsay it! Your men will be glad to have it so.' Gregor turned. 'How think you, Ensign?'

Davies cleared his throat strongly, but did not commit himself to more positive answer.

Gregor shrugged. 'I have done the best that I can for you, gentlemen,' he said. 'I suggest that you keep this side of the Highland Line, in future – for peace's sake!' He pulled his horse round, and in his own Gaelic tongue called to his people to unload the pannier-ponies, dumping their loads on the ground. Then he ordered all the pillion-riders to dismount. They were for home.

'Good-night, gentlemen,' he said, in English again, to the officers, to all the company. 'In fair fight you might have been the end of us, whatever!' He laughed as he said it, happily, heartily, for that hour of the morning. 'Sleep you on that. Good-night!'

Not a word of response did he receive from any of them as the Gregorach turned away and slipped back into the mists and shadows of the great Moss.

CHAPTER TEN

EVEN for such as Gregor Ghlun Dubh – or Gregor Tarbh Ban, Gregor of the White Bull, as he was beginning to be known – even for such as he, life could not continue at the rate that he had been living it since that Lammas day four weeks before. Scaling the heights of experience and bestriding the pinnacles of destiny may be all very well – but there are the valleys and flats of existence to be covered also, slopes down as well as up, and even sober levels, even for a chieftain of MacGregor. Moreover, these are not only inevitable but highly necessary for the avoidance of both physical and emotional exhaustion. Gregor's need for the level plains and the quiet pastures was undoubtedly greater than he either knew or would have acknowledged.

All of which is not say that he was in any way grateful or appreciative of the quiet – or the relatively quiet – weeks that followed. Dull, he found them – thoroughly dull. Also humdrum, tedious and stale. Which was doubtless ungrateful of him, as well as foolish and illogical.

It was unusual, too, for those golden September days, the pride of the Highland year, had been always the season that he loved best in Glen Gyle – the season when the oats were harvested, the hill cattle were rounded up and brought down preparatory to the autumn trysts, when the heather was in fullest bloom, the honey was flowing, and the stags were at their best, and all the land of the mountains smiled and was glad. All that still applied, of course – but in comparison with what had gone before it seemed to have lost something of its savour for Gregor MacGregor. His thoughts tended to be elsewhere. And by no means all of them were deep in high politics, affairs of state, or battles to be fought when King Jamie landed, either. More often indeed, traitorously, they sped away southwards into the soft lush Lowland country, drawn by the magnet of a pair of dark eyes.

Not that Gregor failed to throw himself, physically at least, with a fair semblance of his usual enthusiasm, into the daily round, as was expected of him. Unlike the Lowland gentry, who would, of course, find field-work shockingly demeaning, he laboured amongst his people with a sickle at the thin oats till his long back ached with the bending and his hands were full of thistle-pricks and thorns. He rode on exhilarating round-up gallops over the boundless hills to herd the three-parts wild cattle into the glens. He stalked stags in the high corries and roebuck in the birchwoods, and lured salmon in the rivers and shallows of the lochs. He even turned his hand to compiling verse and writing it down – though this he did more privately than was his wont. The fact that in none of all this did he achieve any great degree of satisfaction was ominous.

The Lady Christian watched him at it, and sighed.

There were no repercussions from Stirling Castle. Not that he had anticipated any, strange as this might seem to anyone not versed in the situation. Though only thirty miles away, Stirling might have been in a different land. Stirling and its fortress was only an outpost of the world of government and soldiers, promulgations and parchments. Beyond the Highland Line the Governments had to depend upon the chiefs for carrying out their precepts. And if the chiefs were otherwise inclined, the precepts got no farther than Stirling, or possibly Perth. The MacGregor's south-west corner of the Highlands was particularly immune from outside interference, protected almost as much by sheer geography as by the highly practical independence of its people. The clan had been proscribed and outlawed for just over a hundred years – yet only the Campbells and other inimical Highlanders under their wing had dared to put the royal Letters of Fire and Sword into effect, even then leaving the central stronghold area of Balquhidder, the Trossachs, Glen Gyle and Loch Lomondside strictly alone. Rob Roy had been put to the horn time and again, rewards offered piously for his capture, and solemn proclamations made forfeiting his goods and chattels. Yet he was not only still at liberty and increasing in gear and substance, but officially appointed Captain of a Highland Watch – since only he could keep any sort of order along the Highland Line, and Rob's order was better than anarchy – and the Lord Justice-Clerk himself continued to pay for his protection. Captain Somers, or whoever sent him, had been bolder than he knew – and luckier. Only an army could have wiped out his humiliation – and Queen Anne had more to do with her armies in 1706.

After all the excitement of the projected rising, too, only one interlude seemed to provide any echo of it all, meantime, any relief to the feeling of anti-climax. That was a meeting of the Clan Council of the Gregorach, to elect a Captain of Clan Alpine. The meeting was held at Glen Gyle, as the most central and suitable spot – and of course Rob Roy was duly elected, there being no other real contender. A clan was normally led by its hereditary chief in war or battle, but where such chief was incapacitated by age or youth or failing in character, then it was necessary that it should have a duly appointed and accepted warrior to take over his military functions. In fact, of course, this had been Rob's unofficial position for years. But with war envisaged, and the Gregorach committed, a more explicit command was required. Had Rob not been there, who could tell what might have been the outcome, for many would have considered themselves bound, in self-respect, to seek the office. And Roro was too old and cautious, Glengyle too young, Glencarnaig unwarlike, Balhaldie untrustworthy, and so on. As it was, all were content, since Rob's fame was an asset, his prowess acknowledged and generalship proved – and moreover, as a mere second son, he had no claim to the actual chiefship, and therefore was no rival to these tentative contenders.

The Laird of Inversnaid, Captain of the Watch and former Tutor of Glengyle, then, became Captain of Clan Alpine and undisputed war-leader of the Gregorach, with all due authority to raise such numbers of the clan as the circumstances should demand. He also could now wear three eagle's feathers in his bonnet, as representing the absent chief.

The said Rob stage-managed the business beautifully, achieved all that he required, and sent everybody home happy. Gregor was particularly pleased, since his lieu-tenancy now could be assured. Also, he had never been really comfortable about being senior to his puissant uncle, wearing two feathers to Rob's one. It was better this way – and after all, he still remained head of Clan Dougal Ciar and in line for the ultimate chiefship.

But all that, of course, rousing as it was, represented only one day's excitement and junketing that sunny September, a very brief interlude in Gregor's deplorable humdrummery. Frustration returned.

He put up with it till the end of the month, when the harvest was cut, if not in, in all his glens, and the cattle were lowing protest in a score of valleys under the watchful eyes of the herd-boys. Then, one afternoon, he dressed more carefully than of late, informed his mother a shade curtly that he had business to attend to, stalked out, took his garron and not his black charger, and without a single gillie at heel, or even a deerhound, rode off eastwards along the loch shore.

Not a few eyes lifted from sundry tasks to watch him go, and gleamed with quiet smiles – even if the Lady Christian's were not amongst them. Even gillies will talk.

*　　　*　　　*

Already the evenings were shortening, and it was dark before Gregor won out of the Moss and rode up through the quiet farmlands. Even here, twenty-five miles away, he noted the difference in the harvest. The oats, so much heavier than his own, were all in stack and the stubbles bare.

Arnprior House was less brighly lit up than when last he had approached it. Lights shone from only two windows to the front. He indulged in no hallooing or slogan-shouting this time, quite content to wait at the front door like any unchiefly mortal, after he had banged thereon.

The manservant who opened, lamp in hand, gaped at sight of him, but admitted him hastily and hurried off with his news.

It was Mistress Meg who came flitting down the stairs amidst a rustling of petticoats, a few moments later, to greet him. 'Gregor!' she cried, 'It *is* you? How good to see you! Is all well? What have you been doing . . . !'

Gregor doffed his bonnet, and bowed. 'Och, yes – fine. Nothing at all, that is. Och, I mean – everything is good and fine. And you, Mistress Meg?'

'I'm all right. But the better for seeing *you*, my braw Hielandman! But Father is ill. That is why I am here. He has the gout again – his old trouble. And the spleen, to make it worse! So I stayed behind to look after him, when the others went.' She sighed prettily. 'And, dear me – it is a dull business.' That made two of them.

'Eh? The others went . . . ? You mean . . . ?' He swallowed, and recollected himself. 'Sorry I am, whatever, to hear about your father,' he declared hurriedly.

She gave a little laugh. 'Quite, sir. Exactly. I understand! Still – I'm pleased to see you!'

'I am glad of that,' he said, and sincerely. 'It is good to see your own self, too.'

They eyed each other then, she quizzically, he trying not to show the disappointment that he felt.

'You came a long way . . . to see Mary?' she asked.

He nodded, wordlessly.

'I am sorry, Gregor. They . . . she and my husband, returned to Bardowie just a week ago. He had affairs to attend to. Naturally I should have gone too, but for Father. I could not leave him like he is. Mary will look after John meantime. She will be sorry to have missed you.'

'Yes,' he said.

She considered him keenly. 'You are fond of Mary,' she put to him, not as a question but as a statement.

He accepted it at that. 'Fond is a poor word, I think.'

'Poor Gregor. Poor Mary. Lucky Mary! Or . . . is she? Heigh-ho!' That young woman's sighing was apt to be never very far away from laughter. 'Come upstairs, and take a little refreshment with a lonely woman, Gregor – even if it is the wrong one. We can at least *talk* of Mary!'

'Ummm,' he said, and followed her.

But they did not talk as much of Mary as he would have wished. Meg was not the one to do any such thing. Gregor did gather, however, that she was well, displeased with her brother, sorry to be gone from Arnprior, and that, if she had not actually left a message for himself, should he make an appearance, she did not lack goodwill towards him – though he had to pick out all this from the spate of his hostess's more personal chatter.

'Now – tell me all that *you* have been doing, Gregor,' she demanded, at the end of it.

'Nothing. Just nothing at all,' he assured. 'It is a long way to Bardowie Castle, is it not?'

She shook her head over him. 'Much too far for you, anyway,' she declared. 'Too far from your Highland Line. It must be thirty miles from here, forty miles south of your barbarous fastnesses, Gregor. It cannot lie more than five miles north of Glasgow. No place for the likes of you, my man.'

'Forty miles by your roads, it may be – but not as I travel,' he asserted.

'Perhaps. But all through country hostile to you and your kind. And, recollect – my husband does not feel so loving towards you as I do, Gregor MacGregor! I would not like to test him too sorely with your safety!'

'You . . . you do not sound the most respectful of wives, Mistress!'

'I had not the choosing of my husband, sir!' That was short, almost sharp.

'Ummm,' Gregor said again. 'Oh.'

There was a moment or two's silence. Then she spoke again. 'You have not told me what you have been doing since you rode away from us that night, so dramatically –

banging all the doors behind you! You need not inform *me* that you have been doing nothing. . . . '

'I have been cutting oats and herding beasts for the trysts. Dull work, see you. . . . '

'You were going to raise your clansmen, I understood – lots of them. For some mysterious meeting. Would they not obey you? The Gregorach would not rise . . . ?'

She wormed most of it out of him, of course, before, half an hour later, thumps from above indicated that Robert Buchanan's patience had run out, and gave Gregor his excuse for leaving.

He begged off visiting the invalid, promised that he would come again, and enjoined strictest secrecy over all that he had told her.

She assured him that his information would be safer in her hands than in his own – which was probably true enough – and said that she would be writing to her sister-in-law. Had he any particular message that he would like her to transmit?

'Tell her that I was after meaning what I said, that night – the last time that she saw me,' he declared strongly. 'Tell her . . . och, tell her to be watching out, after the Crieff Tryst is by with, Bardowie or none! Good-night to you, Mistress Meg – and my thanks.' And he clapped on his bonnet and strode off, downstairs and out. That door banged again, loud as ever.

CHAPTER ELEVEN

CRIEFF Michaelmas Tryst was the greatest cattle-fair in all Scotland. To it came the exportable products of most of the Highlands, an area covering two-thirds of the land. Other fairs, at Crieff and elsewhere, had their points, but this occasion was unique. Herds travelled from as far away as Ross and Sutherland and even the Hebridean isles, some taking as long as six weeks to the journey, and buyers came from all over the Lowlands and the North of England, from as far south as Darlington and York. Thirty thousand head of cattle, and more, would change hands at this three-day event, mainly the shaggy kyloes of the glens.

Climate and geography dictated this vast annual transference. The Highland pastures and hill grazings would feed young stock handsomely enough from April till October, but thereafter the forage died away to nothingness. The sparse poor oats and bog-hay that could be grown in the narrow glen-floors were never enough to keep alive over the winter any large proportion of the stock that could be raised in the summer shielings, and only the hardy mature beasts would survive the snows and storms and floods on the open hill. So it was necessary every autumn to dispose of these great numbers of young animals, keeping only the minimum of breeding stock to face the winter.

And there was a great demand for the stirks, as beef stock, for they were the hardiest cattle in all Europe, and moreover, brought up the hard way, they fattened most spectacularly and profitably when transferred to lush Lowland pastures.

On cattle the entire economy of the clans was based, one way or another. And Crieff Tryst represented the major harvesting thereof. By common consent and for mutual advantage a truce was called for the occasion, not only in the internecine clan feuds but in the unending bickering with the Lowland authorities.

The MacGregors' droves made an even larger contribution to the total this Michaelmas than was usual. They had had a highly successful season – which, for the Gregorach, might have a slightly different shade of meaning than when applied to other and less enterprising cattle-rearers – those connected with the Highland Watch in particular having more animals to dispose of than ever before. Rob Roy himself was anxious to make a good showing – and not solely because he had promised half of the resultant sales to King James's coffers; with war envisaged and highly unsettled conditions liable to prevail, and moreover himself and most of his clansmen away from home, it behoved a cattle-owner on the verge of the Lowland country to turn as much of his stock safely into golden guineas as was possible. Then, if his lands were to suffer the misfortune of being overrun, by whichever side, in his absence, he would have the more to show for it. Others of his kind, needless to say, thought along similar lines. The Inversnaid and Glengyle herds, linked up, made the impressive total of nearly 2,000 head.

Crieff was a stirring place those days. Droves, great and small, converged on it from all quarters. The wide haughlands of the Earn were a-move with cattle almost as far as the eye could see. The noise was deafening. Highlanders were everywhere, their encampments covering the green hillsides. The houses were full of Lowland buyers, factors, farmers, merchants and packmen – and every second building was an ale-house.

Tinkers and cadgers were there in their hundreds. Drovers, temporarily in the ascendant and largely drunk, swaggered at will. Lords rubbed broad-clothed shoulders with half-naked gillies. Douce townsmen looked askance at swarthy gesticulating Islesmen. Proud chieftains hobnobbed with Northumbrian dealers. Crafty gypsies outbargained urban cheapjack hucksters. Money and liquor flowed in a spate, strumpets paraded the streets – and not a redcoat was to be seen in all Strathearn.

Rob Roy and his nephew had more to see to than merely the selling of beasts. It was an ideal occasion for many ploys, including the sounding of political opinion, the converting of doubters, the threatening of backsliders, and the spreading of useful rumours. Before the first evening, for instance, everybody in Crieff knew that the Earl of Breadalbane was committed to King James's cause, and the Campbells with him. Also that sundry high-placed traitors were accepting bribes from England to vote for the Union. And that Scotland would assuredly rise and rend all such, whenever the Treaty was signed. And so on. Even that Rob Roy was going to give every plack he made at the Tryst to the Jacobite funds – and that others were following his example. If the resulting climate of opinion was that war was obviously near and that beef, like other things, might well soon be in short supply – and consequently cattle prices tended to rise sharply – that was only just and suitable.

In consequence, too, by the close of the first day's business there were a lot of very happy MacGregors about, and rather looking for something to do about it.

Rob was nothing if not an enthusiast, once he took up a cause. Nor was he a spoil-sport. There was always some other little thing that might be done to further King Jamie's affairs, and at the same time keep his spirited lads amused and in good heart. He approached one of the numerous smugglers who thronged the town at such a time and expended some small portion of his day's profits on a cask of finest duty-free brandy – since naturally he could not in honesty subsidise Queen Anne's Revenue – and rounded up a dozen miscellaneous pipers, of whom there was no dearth. Thus equipped, all the MacGregors that he could find marched through the streets and alleys of the old town, dark but far from deserted, to the Cross, picking up adherents on the way. At the ancient Cross the cask was set up, broached ceremoniously, and the health and success of King Jamie the Eighth drunk by all present, with musical honours. Then parties were sent out into the highways and the hedges, into every street and lane and all the roads radiating from Crieff, to hale to the Cross all found stirring, of whatever kind or degree – at the point of the dirk, if need be – to taste of Rob Roy's fine hospitality and pledge a similar toast, with a damnation to the Union included. They caught some curious fish. Some were initially diffident – but none ultimately refused. Loyalty was complete.

The business took the Gregorach most of the night, and a second cask of brandy.

Gregor slept late the next morning, and reached the saleyards without breakfast but with a sore head. His uncle was distressingly active, vocal, and seemingly on top of his form. Prices, it appeared, were even better than yesterday. God bless King James!

It was almost midday when MacAlastair, Rob's personal gillie, sought Gregor out to inform him that a lady was seeking for him, beside the Tolbooth.

'A lady!' Gregor cried hoarsely. Ladies, with any pretensions to the title, were apt to be scarce in Crieff at Tryst time.

A lady, the sombre MacAlastair agreed disapprovingly, and took himself off.

Gregor did not actually run through the town to the Tolbooth square, but neither did he daunder. He saw the coach drawn up beside the great ponderous iron stocks that were supposed to be the terror of the Highlandmen – the same coach that had spelt trouble for him two months before.

He recocked his bonnet, tossed plaid across shoulder, and pushed his way thitherwards as though Provost of the place at least.

*　　*　　*

Mistress Meg Hamilton was alone in the coach – which said something for her courage. She sat forward eagerly as he appeared in the doorway.

'Oh, I am so glad to see you, Gregor,' she declared, a little tremulously for that young woman. 'All these horrible drunken men . . . ! But I was sure that you would be here, somewhere. You said that you would.'

He got into the coach beside her. 'You are alone?' he demanded.

'Yes. Father is in no state to make the journey to Crieff Tryst. Besides, I doubt if he would have approved.'

'You have not beasts to sell here . . . ?'

'Of course not. It is you that I came to see, Gregor. I told

Father that I was going to see Jean Stirling, of Kippendavie. So I did. I stayed at Kippendavie last night.'

Gregor was puzzled, and a little uncomfortable. This young woman had gone to a lot of trouble to reach him here. Which was flattering, of course – but could be embarrassing. After all, she was somebody else's wife, even if she did not think a lot of her husband. 'Crieff, at the Tryst, is no place for the likes of yourself, Mistress Meg,' he told her doubtfully.

'Lordie – I do not need you to inform me of that!' she returned. 'But it was important. At least, *I* thought so. Whether you will do so or not, is a different matter. But I felt that you had to know. I had a letter from Mary, two days ago. Aye – I see that alters matters for you. She writes from Finnary . . . '

'Finnary! That is nowhere near to Bardowie,' the young man interrupted. 'It is in Graham country. Near to Drymen. Finnary marches with Gallangad, does it not?'

'Maybe it does. I do not know. But there she is at present. My husband has taken her to lodge with Hugo Graham of Finnary. It seems that he thinks that it is high time that she was wed – and he considers Finnary a suitable husband!'

'My God!' Gregor cried – and it was no blasphemy but a cry from the heart as he said it. 'Wed? Never!'

'That remains to be seen. But so John would have it, apparently. And besides being her elder brother, he is her only male relative, and legal guardian.'

'But . . . in the Name of Heaven – this cannot be, surely? Has she any fondness for the man?'

'She barely knows him, I think. I have met him only once, myself. He is a friend of my husband, engaged with him in some of his Americas ventures. A man of wealth and with a good estate. Moreover, a safe Whig. A match, I take it, after John's own heart!'

'But not Mary's?'

'She does not write as though it was! But does that matter so greatly? In my own case it made little difference!'

He stared at her. 'Her brother can marry her to whom he will?'

'It comes to that. One way or another. What can she do? She is only twenty – as I was. In the eyes of the law she is his property.'

'No!' Gregor denied vehemently.

'But yes,' she insisted. 'I *know*. That is the position. And you are in some measure responsible.'

'Me? My own self? What do you mean?'

'You it is that have frightened John . . . with the things that you said, that time. When you last saw him. It is because of you, I am sure, that he is hurrying Mary into this. There was no word of it previously. It is largely your doing, Gregor.'

'You believe that?'

'Yes. There is also this, I think – that he does not want any part in this rising of yours. No link with the Jacobites. Having a wife a Jacobite worries him. He would have his sister wed to a substantial Whig, for safety's sake.'

'Aye. And a Graham, sib to the Marquis of Montrose, that is the Government's own man! That will be the way of it. But, *Dia* – I think that your husband is going to be finding himself on the wrong side, at the end of it!'

'I hope so. Then, no doubt, it will have to be his wife that is the saving of him!'

Gregor looked away. 'Another Graham!' he said slowly.

'That makes it worse, does it?'

'It means that I shall be enjoying doing the business the more, whatever.'

'What . . . what are you going to do, Gregor?'

'What has to be done, just.'

'You are going to Finnary?'

'To be sure. You did not think that I would do other, did you?'

'No,' she admitted. 'That is what I expected you would do. After that – what?'

'Time enough for that,' he said briefly.

'Well . . . ' She considered him closely. 'You could

always tell her that her room is waiting for her at Arnprior.'

'Yes.'

'I do not know what else to say. What to suggest.' Meg shook her head. 'It is all so difficult. To know what is best. I only felt that I had to come to tell you – that you had to know.'

'Thank you.'

Obviously the man's mind was not on what she was saying. Though he was looking at her, Meg perceived that he was not seeing her. 'I am fond of Mary too, you see,' she said, then.

'Yes.' Already he had his hands on the door.

'You are going – now?'

'Now,' he agreed. 'I should have gone to her before this. I blame myself, whatever.'

Doubt grew in her. 'I hope that you will be . . . I hope that I have been wise . . . ?' she faltered.

He got out. 'You are for home now – Arnprior? I will find you an escort of my people, to put you down to Kippendavie at the least. There are some ill characters about at this time.'

'Thank you. You will not travel with me? Arnprior is on the way to Drymen.'

'Not by the ways I shall be taking. The roads take the long way round. I go straight. Good-bye, Mistress Meg. You are a fine woman, indeed. You should have been after marrying a MacGregor!'

'I wonder,' she said, as she watched him go.

Returned to the sale-yards, Gregor sought out his uncle. 'I find that I have business otherwhere,' he announced cryptically. 'I shall not be needing any of my people – only Ian Beg. I shall not be back, see you, before the Tryst ends. You will look after my guineas for me?'

Rob Roy eyed him shrewdly. 'Surely. Your business is urgent, Greg?'

'Yes.'

'You will be needing no assistance?'

'I think not. It is my own business, just.'

'I see. Was it Arnprior's daughter in the coach?'

His nephew frowned. 'Yes.'

'Just that.' Rob smiled. 'You will be seeking no advice from an old fellow the likes of myself, and be damned to me?' he suggested.

'M'mm. I had not, h'mm, thought of it.'

'Nor did I, lad, in like circumstances! Off with you – and do not forget that your name is MacGregor!'

'I could do no less,' his erstwhile pupil agreed.

*   *   *

Garron-mounted, Gregor and Ian Beg rode fast and far, up Strathearn, over into Glen Artney beneath the soaring peaks of Ben Vorlich and Stob a Chroin, through the Pass of Leny and along the rolling flanks of Ben Ledi to Brig o' Turk. They were on a longer journey even than that from Kinloch Rannoch to Glen Gyle. But they had no footmen to think of, and their mounts were fresh. Fifty miles, Gregor calculated the distance between Crieff and his destination, a long day's trot for even the freshest and sturdiest of garrons.

Dusk found them nearing the borders of their own Flanders Moss. Another two hours. . . .

Finnary, though adjoining Gallangad to the north, was a very different kind of property. It had its hill-farms and its moorland grazings, yes – but they were rented out to tenants. The mansionhouse itself, recently rebuilt, lay snug and sheltered in a wooded dene of the winding Cadder Water, convenient to the Glasgow turnpike, a fine place of gardens and ponds and statuary, with no single cattle-beast in sight to mar the aesthetic purity of the scene. Graham of Finnary, with revenues well invested in Glasgow, required to pay no mail to Rob Roy and his Watch. That was his tenants' affair, not his.

Gregor and his companion arrived on the scene just before nine of the evening. The big house was lit up from end to end, all downstairs windows ablaze, riding-horses stood at the front door, carriages thronged the stableyard adjoining, and the sound of music drifted out across the ornamental waters in the little valley to the Highlanders' point of vantage amongst the trees. Appreciatively they sat their tired horses, and watched. Graham had more guests than the Hamiltons, apparently.

It was an interesting situation, and a lively scene. The stir and movement indoors could be sensed, if not actually viewed. And even out of doors there seemed to be considerable activity, as coachmen and postillions shared the gaiety with the maids in the stableyard to the left.

For a time Gregor considered it all. Obviously they were going to have an extended wait. This party could go on for hours yet, no doubt. His plans were of the vaguest. He had hoped that something would give him a hint as to which was Mary's room – if necessary, a dirk at a servant's throat – and thereafter, once the house was settled for the night, he would seek to reach her there, less than simple as that might be.

But now, watching, another notion came to him – a notion that would not take so long to put to the test, and that might in the end prove simpler. It was risky, of course – but it might work, he decided. With boldness, and a modicum of good fortune that boldness merited, it might work. He mentioned the matter to Ian Beg. The funny side of it struck him forcibly as he enlarged on it – as it was ever apt to do with that man – and he began to laugh. He could hardly get it out, indeed, for mirth, and soon he had the gillie laughing too. Dignity, on this occasion, looked like being a casualty.

They settled down for a prolonged wait, content that the weary garrons should have time to rest and graze.

At length a coach-and-four drew out of the yard and up at the front porch of the mansion, the coachman climbing down and proceeding into the house. The first of the guests was about to leave. It was nearing midnight, probably.

Gregor nodded to the gillie, doffed his plaid, and laid his sword beside it. Leaving the horses to feed peaceably where they were, the two Highlanders slipped down through the trees and the bushes, waded quietly across the artificial stream below, and up amongst the clipped shrubbery and statuary beyond towards the house.

Another coach was driving round to the front door as they came up. It was to be hoped that this was the beginning of a general but gradual exodus, as was the way with most parties. The first coach was moving off, a group at the porch steps waving the guests away amidst shouted farewells. The group consisted of three men and a woman – but though one of the men was almost certainly Hamilton of Bardowie, the woman was not his sister. That would have been too much to hope for, probably.

The MacGregors, unseen in the gloom beyond the circle of yellow light, edged farther to the left, towards the stableyard entrance. Two more coaches were coming out, to line up behind the others. There seemed to be a further two still remaining in the yard, in the light of the lanterns and the flaring torches. These, like the last of the three already out, were two-horse carriages – no doubt with shorter distances to go. If they would but stay there for a little longer. . . .

Gregor moved close up to that third and last coach of the little queue. There was no need for exaggerated crawling and skulking. The shadow was deep on their side, and the statuary and shrubs were kind to men who desired not to be noticed. Anyhow, the coachman was looking consistently in the other direction, towards the porch. There was no postillion on this two-horse vehicle, of course.

With a breathed word to Ian Beg, Gregor sprang into action. He leapt lightly up on to the space between the box and the coach proper, and before the coachman had an inkling that there was anybody behind him, an arm was round the unfortunate man's neck with a choking grip – the same grip that he had used on Ensign Davies one time. The jehu was dragged over, backwards and sideways off his seat, to the ground, Ian Beg assisting at his silent downfall. In the shadows beyond the coach, the astonished man found himself hustled round behind a bush, and the point of a dirk tickling his constricted throat.

'Not one sound out of you!' Gregor panted. 'Do as I tell you, and you will suffer no hurt. I want the clothes off you, whatever.'

Already Ian Beg was tugging off the long many-caped coat, muttering Gaelic threats the while. The fellow did not struggle, either out of wisdom or sheer surprise. Gregor transferred the coat to his own broader back swiftly – and found it tight across the shoulders and chest. But the multiple capes would hide that. Its long skirts had come down to its owner's ankles – but the man was no giant, and on Gregor the coat came only to a little below the knee, leaving tartan hose exposed beneath. The coachman was wearing breeches – but the Highlandman was damned if he was going to discard his kilt and soil his limbs with any Lowlander's trousers. But there were also knee-length felt gaiters, and these might serve.

Getting the gaiters off, and buttoned up again on Gregor's more muscular calves, was not so speedy a process as the latter would have liked. The second coach drove away from the front door while he was so engaged, and the next two equipages moved up. That the third did not do so might look strange. Though its driver might have got down from his box for any of a number of reasons. Probably no suspicions would be aroused. ...

The gaiters on, they tied up their victim. Then, before gagging him with his own neckcloth, Gregor demanded of him the name of his master.

'Edmonstone of Alderpark,' the man gasped. 'Sirs, ye wouldna ... ?'

'Quiet, you!' he was ordered, curtly – and was silent.

Leaving him, with the gillie skulking in the background, Gregor stepped out. He picked up the coachman's cocked hat that had fallen in the struggle, and clapped it on his own head. It fitted better than the other items. Reaching the horses, he took their bridles and led the coach forward to immediately behind the previous vehicle, the driver of which, he noted, was still seated on his box. Then, leaving the horses, he strolled over to the lighted porch, as casually as he could while at the same time seeking to take sufficiently short steps so that his bare knees and tartan did not reveal themselves above the gaiters.

Another party came chattering out even as he approached, a coachman preceding them. Once again John Hamilton and the woman were with the departing guests, along with another fashionably-dressed man who was no doubt the host, Hugo Graham. None of them so much as glanced at Gregor, naturally enough.

The Highlander took a deep breath, and moving respectfully round the rear of this group, he mounted the few steps and in at the great doorway, sidelong as it were.

There was a small outer vestibule and a large inner hall, blazing with light from a great central chandelier and numerous candelabra. About a dozen people stood laughing and talking therein, besides two or three waiting servants.

Gregor saw her at once. She was standing a little way apart, talking with an elderly gallant, who waved hands, snuff-box and cambric in a positive flurry of self-satisfaction. He had never seen her looking lovelier, in a low-cut gown of ivory brocade with a filmy shawl of deep crimson. But he had seen her looking a deal happier. She had a listlessness about her that was wholly foreign to the young woman whom Gregor knew, a remoteness to all that went on around her that made her companion's complacent gesticulations seem the more out of place. Gregor willed her to look towards him, with all the willpower that was in him.

But it was a bewigged and elaborately-liveried majordomo who looked at him – and from much nearer at hand, within the vestibule. 'Weel, Cockie – an' wha're ye for?' this potentate demanded – and Gregor had just time to be struck by the markedly ordinary braid Scots voice to issue from so much exotic magnificence before realisation of the danger of his position swept over him. To announce that he was Edmonstone of Alderpark's coachman might well result in this creature here shouting out that laird's name, drawing his attention – to the immediate unmasking and downfall of his fraudulent servant. His mind racing, Gregor extemporised desperately, taking an enormous risk.

'Mr Hamilton – Bardowie – would have his sister come to the door. Miss Mary. He is out there.'

'Ooh, aye. Miss Mary. She's ower there.'

'Yes. I see her. I will tell her . . . '

'Ye'll dae nae sich thing, Hielantman,' the other asserted – and Gregor jumped at that. His voice, of course – it would never sound like any Lowland servant's accent. 'Ye'll keep your place, my mannie. *I'll* tell her.' And turning, he stalked off with all the dignity of his office.

Gregor swallowed. He had only seconds now. Would she – *could* she possibly . . . ?

The major-domo reached her, bowed and spoke, gesturing towards the doorway. Mary nodded, barely glancing in Gregor's direction, and after a moment and a word to her companion, started to walk unhurriedly towards him, her elderly cavalier still in attendance.

Gregor bit his lip, his attention almost as much on what went on behind him as before. If Hamilton and the others turned and came back inside now, before Mary reached him, there would be added complications. Fortunately, from the sounds of it, their group of guests were still lingering.

Mary Hamilton raised her eyes to look at him when five or six yards off and found his gaze directly upon her. The impact was immediate and unmistakable. Her hand went up to her throat, her lips parted, a flush flooded over face and shoulders. Gregor was frowning, shaking his head. Her step faltered.

As clearly as though he spoke to her, Gregor urged her to come on, to show no sign. He saw her gulp, dart a glance right and left, and resume her progress. Only a bare couple of seconds had elapsed. The man at her side, hand on her arm, talked away, perceiving nothing amiss. Behind them came the major-domo, strutting.

They were nearly up to him, Gregor moved a little over

to the side, the side that would ensure that the girl's escort would not come between him and her. The fellow at the back was a nuisance.

As Mary came level with him, within the arched entrance of the vestibule, Gregor turned away, to face the front door as did the others, so that for a brief moment he was moving beside her, a bare foot away. 'Your brother asks for you, ma'am,' he said, aloud. And, below his breath. 'He does not! But go to him. Say anything. Then get you away. Get you to the stableyard. Somehow. The stableyard.'

She gave no sign of having heard him. But Gregor was sure that she had heard. He let her pass on ahead of him.

He found the major-domo looking at him strangely, whether in suspicion or in mere disapproval he knew not. He walked out behind Mary and her escort, slipped away to the right, down the steps, and out into the blessed night air, stalking back to his coach. He must have seemed a very stalwart and long-striding coachman, at that. Fortunately, there was no one in front to perceive his knees.

The door of the carriage at the steps slammed shut as he reached his horses' heads, and the equipage rolled away amidst wavings. The next carriage moved forward to the porch, just as the host's group turned back inside. Mary Hamilton turned back with them.

Gregor led his horses forward the required few yards, to keep station, and leaving them there edged away into the darkness at the far side.

He found Ian Beg awaiting him anxiously in the shrubbery. 'I am for the stableyard,' he announced tersely. 'Watch you the front, here. If there is trouble about the coach, come and tell me. If you hear an owl hoot thrice – back to the garrons with you.'

Reconnoitring the stableyard swiftly from its entrance, he found the two remaining coachmen still hobnobbing with the maids around the back door. Keeping to the shadows, he moved in and round. His disguise was unlikely to avail him anything here. He halted within the doorway of a lean-to building that smelt sweetly of fresh hay.

Would she come? Had she heard him – understood? And if she did come, how was he to deal with her, here under the eyes of all these servants? Would they make an outcry? If, at the same time, the loss of Edmonstone's coachman at the front was discovered, what would he do?

There was one thing that he could try. He slipped over to the nearest carriage. The lamps were already lit. He lifted out the nearside one from its socket, to examine it behind the bulk of the vehicle. The oil-container's lid opened readily enough. Keeping his body between the light and the group across the yard, he moved back to his hay-shed doorway.

He was barely there when the skirling and chatter of the servants' voices suddenly stilled. He peered over. Another figure had appeared within the doorway at the back of the house – a female figure from which the giggling maids fell back a little in surprise and embarrassment. Gregor took a deep breath – and acted.

Turning within, he splashed out some of the oil from the lamp on to the hay with which part of the shed was filled. Then, stooping, he took a handful of dry stuff, held it to the burning wick, and as it blazed, flung it on to the oil-soaked heap.

The flames shot up, almost too well for the incendiary's safety. Brows and hair singed a little, Gregor backed hurriedly out. He raised his voice. 'Fire!' he shouted, 'Fire!' And hurried along into the shadows again as he did so.

Chaos ensued in that stableyard. Leaping flames lit up the scene, and thick smoke rolled out of the hay-shed. Women screamed. Men shouted and came running. Horses reared and whinnied and bolted. One coach went rocking right out of the yard. The other was merely dragged hither and thither.

In the commotion, Gregor slipped round the perimeter of the yard, and so to the back door. Mary now stood a few feet out on the cobbles, staring wide-eyed. Pushing past a pair of gabbling maids, Gregor reached her and grasped her elbow.

'Come!' he cried. 'Quickly. This way.' And with an arm round her middle he led her, ran her, part-carried her, across the yard, over to the entrance, and out.

She came wordless but unresisting.

Just outside they all but ran into the concerned and excited Ian Beg, who was hopping about from one foot to the other at the edge of the bushes.

'To the garrons,' Gregor jerked briefly. Had he had any available breath he would have sighed with relief as they plunged out of the area of light and down through the shrubbery towards the quiet water and the climbing woods beyond.

CHAPTER TWELVE

MARY HAMILTON was not clad for clambering up through dew-drenched benighted woodlands, but Gregor's arm was strong about her waist and she kilted up her long brocade skirts and did her best, uncomplaining, unspeaking. To cross the ornamental water the man picked her up bodily in his arms, and more than once he did the same on the hillside beyond. He was breathing deeply, then, when at last he set her down beside the placidly grazing garrons. Clutching her flimsy crimson shawl to her, she was doing likewise.

Converse was spasmodic, incoherent, difficult. 'Oh, Gregor!' she gasped. 'What . . . ? Where . . . ? Gregor!' She shook her head, helplessly.

'Everything is . . . fine now, *a graidh*,' he assured. 'Fear nothing . . . at all.'

'No. No – but . . .'

He was casting off the coachman's coat, and ripping away the leggings. 'You are all right? You are not hurt?'

'No, no. I am . . . well. But – I do not understand . . . ?'

'You were not happy . . . in that house?' he demanded.

'No,' she agreed.

'Well, then. You are . . . out of it, whatever. You are to be the happy one! Always.' He picked up his sword, and slung its belt over his shoulder. Then taking the voluminous red tartan plaid that it had lain on, he wrapped it round her person. 'That is . . . better colours . . . for you to shelter under! You will be fine now, my dear.'

'Thank you. Yes. But what am I to do . . . ?'

'Nothing at all, at all,' he assured. 'Just nothing. Wait you.' He leapt lightly on to his garron's broad back, and pulled its head round, beside her. Ian Beg came forward to assist, but his aid was not required. Leaning over, Gregor crooked an arm under the girl's shoulders, and picked her up in a single sweeping motion. to deposit her before him on the horse, seated sideways. 'T..at is you,' he declared, and heeled the beast into a trot.

She gulped. 'Where . . . are we going, Gregor?'

'Where would you like to be going, *a graidh*?'

'Oh, I don't know. I don't know. We must talk. . . . '

'Surely, surely. We can be talking as we go. Fine.'

'Yes – but where?'

'Arnprior is one place that we could be going to. Mistress Meg was after saying it. But maybe we will be thinking of a better. . . . '

'Meg?' Mary cried. 'She sent you?'

'Sent is maybe not the word, just. But she was after telling me where to find you.'

The girl said nothing for a little while, as they rode up out of the trees, and on to the bracken and whins of Finnary Muir. Gregor glanced behind him. The house was already out of sight, but the reflected glow of it could be distinguished amongst the tree-tops – a glow that flickered now. There was no sound of any pursuit, nor did the man expect any.

'Gregor.' Mary turned round and faced him, gripping his wrist. 'Do you realise what you are doing? What *we* are doing?'

'Fine I do, yes.'

'Riding away, like this. You are not taking me back . . . to the house?'

'No.'

She bit her lip. 'Not even if I ask you to?'

'Och, it would be hard for me to be refusing you anything that you were asking in all the world, Mary,' he assured her warmly. To add: 'So do not be asking me, whatever!'

'Oh!' she said.

'There is nothing for you in that house.'

'But . . . ' She shook her head over him. 'I am a, a prisoner, then?'

He laughed, at that, joyfully. 'A prisoner! That is it – a prisoner, just. You are my prisoner, Mary Hamilton – for always! Och, mutual it is, too.'

She had nothing to say to that, at all.

He told her then how Meg had come seeking him at Crieff, to inform him of the situation, and how her brother would marry her off to this Hugo Graham. That obviously could not be allowed to happen. So he had come hot-foot. He had said that he would come for her one day, had he not? Well, then – here he was.

The girl listened in silence, and at the end of it burst out in no paean of gratitude and acclaim. He peered down at her, wondering. So far as he could see in the gloom, she seemed to be biting her lip again.

'You did not want to marry that Graham?' he demanded, then, a little roughly.

She shook her head.

'Well, then – there is something to be thanking me for. He will not marry you now.'

'No,' she agreed, a trifle heavily perhaps. 'He will not marry me now!'

Gregor decided that she was tired, unstrung, not at her

best. Let her rest, remain quiet, be at peace. Perhaps she would sleep, there within his arms. The best thing it would be. 'Hush you,' he urged. 'Quiet, now. Everything will be fine, just fine. You will see.'

She did not deny it, in so many words – in any words at all. He had never known that one so silent. Which was strange. But women were unpredictable, ever.

*   *   *

Untroubled by thoughts of pursuit or consequences, the men trotted their garrons northwards through the night. They went by the base of Duncryne Hill again, but to the east of it this time, and down into the wide Endrick valley, through the country of shadowy hummocks and knolls, and past small sleeping homesteads. And all the time that other ride was in Gregor's mind, when he had had so different a problem and responsibility, when he was homing with a bull and not a woman. And some comparison and association rankled and rankled in his mind.

Just when he actually took the decision, it would be hard to say. Perhaps it had been at the back of his head somewhere, all the time. Perhaps there was just a hint of pique in it – a lesson for her, whatever. Perhaps there was good logical reasoning behind it – MacGregor reasoning. Perhaps, indeed, the man being a MacGregor, it was inevitable. But when, the Endrick crossed, and Drymen skirted, and they were climbing the long long braes above the little town, with all the emptiness of Flanders Moss unseen but not unsensed on their right front – then Gregor kept his garron's head due into the north, instead of turning it when he might have done, due into the east. And held to that course, as the hillside lifted and lifted, out of rough grazing, through gorse and bracken, to the ultimate heather. The great hills loomed black ahead of them.

Mary had been silent for a long time, but the man knew by the tenseness and uprightness of her carriage that she by no means slept or dozed. At length she spoke.

165

'We are climbing hills,' she said. 'We are in the heather. This is not the road to Arnprior?'

'No,' he agreed. 'It is not.'

'Where are you taking me, Gregor?' There was a tremor there.

'Home, just,' he told her, simply.

'Home? You mean – *your* home? Glen Gyle?'

'Glen Gyle, yes.'

'But . . . no! No!' She turned round to face him again. 'You cannot do this, Gregor. You *must* not! Don't you see – I cannot go to your house. Not this way. Oh, don't you understand . . . ?'

'The best place it is, for you,' he asserted. 'You will be safe there. My mother will look after you. I will, my own self. It is where you ought to be, Mary.'

'You said Arnprior,' she accused. 'I thought that you were taking me there.'

'I was thinking,' he justified himself. 'Arnprior would be the first place that your brother would be looking for you. He would have you away again tomorrow. You have got to be safe from him. He would be finding you anywhere in the low country, and take you away. To be safe from him you have to cross our Highland Line, where he cannot follow you. You will be safe at Glen Gyle, whatever. No Lowlander can reach you there.' His voice rose a degree or two. 'Stirling Castle itself cannot reach you there!'

'But . . . but don't you see what this means?' she cried. 'Riding away with you, like this, is bad enough. My, my reputation will not go unscathed. But to go away into the mountains with you, to your own home! It means that I am committed to you – that, that our names are linked for always. That either I become a woman of no repute, or, or . . . '

'Or my wife,' he ended for her. 'The Lady Glengyle. We shall be married, my dear, just as soon as we can hale the minister from Balquhidder!'

'We shall, shall we!' she exclaimed spiritedly. 'Who

says that we shall? It takes two to make a marriage, Gregor MacGregor!'

Astonished, he stared at her. '*Dia* – what is this? Do you not *want* to be married, now?'

'No. I do not. Not like this. Not like a, a kitchen-wench in trouble! Not taken for granted. Not without, without . . . ' She was thumping at his chest with her small fists now, for emphasis, almost unseating herself. 'Turn round, and take me back,' she cried. 'Take me to Arnprior.'

Gregor frowned. Such illogical and unsuitable behaviour was quite beyond him. 'If I took you to Arnprior, I would just be at pains to be rescuing you again, in a day or two,' he pointed out, with a noble effort at reasonableness.

'Nobody asked you to rescue me,' she returned. 'At least, *I* did not.'

'Would you rather that I had left you for Graham of Finnary, then?'

She did not answer that. 'Take me to Arnprior,' she repeated.

'I will not do that' he told her levelly. 'It would avail nothing. We will go to Glen Gyle. And we shall be married. I told you, that time when last I saw you, that one day I would come for you. To marry you. To change your name for you, to MacGregor, I said. You knew my mind. . . . '

'And what about *my* mind, sir?'

'You came away with me, tonight, knowing my mind,' he reminded her, more stiffly.

'But . . . I could do no other!' she claimed, her voice rising unsteadily. 'To do anything else would have been to betray you, to fail you utterly. . . . '

'So you were after coming away with me only to save me from your brother, woman – is that it? Me – Gleagyle!' His voice could rise, too.

'Oh, do not be foolish!' Mary cried. 'You know the way it was, perfectly well. For the last time – will you turn, please, Gregor, and take me to Arnprior?'

'No, then. I will not.'

'Oh . . . !' She drew herself up, her knuckles gleaming white in the gloom as she gripped the plaid tightly to her. 'Then you will regret it, sir. You will regret dragging me off to your, your barbarous mountains like the spoils of war across your saddle-bow!'

He laughed then, but shortly, harshly. 'There has been many another bride come to Glen Gyle that way,' he told her. 'And lived to be glad of it, whatever!' He kicked up his garron into a fast and jolting trot, despite the uneven terrain, that put all unprofitable converse and argument outwith possibility. 'Enough of this,' he ended abruptly.

And ended it was.

It was a far cry yet to Glen Gyle, twenty miles as the crow flies, but half as much again by hill and heather and ford and lochside. They followed the contours of the eastern flanks of the Ben Lomond range, down eventually to ford the Duchray Water near the lonely place of Blair-vaich, and so round the boggy head of Loch Ard to the drove road that threaded the Pass of Aberfoyle. In all those rough miles Gregor and the girl hardly exchanged as many words – though he asked her with stiff solicitude twice whether she was tired and would wish to lie down and take a rest? Also whether she was warm enough in his plaid? To which she made answer with merely a shake or a nod of the head. Sometimes Gregor endeavoured to sing a little, but aggressively rather than spontaneously, his heart not in it. And now and then he chatted, in the Gaelic, with Ian Beg, determinedly casual. But most of the time they rode in silence through the silent night, with only the clop of unshod hooves, the swish of the heather, the cry of a night-bird, and/the age-old chuckling of a thousand streams, as accompaniment for their several thoughts.

The grey and desolate dawn began to pale the night behind them, accompanied by a chill smirr of rain, while still they trotted by the birch-clad shores of Loch Chon. Gregor drew the plaid more closely about his charge. There was no sunrise that wan morning, only the mist heavy upon crouching hills. The blue smoke of morning fires was rising above the clachan of Stronachlacher as they reached Loch Katrine. Gregor acknowledged a few greetings from the folk, his own Gregorach, but declined refreshment, with only a few miles to go now.

The great trough of Glen Gyle was shrouded in cloud and mist as they came to it that cold grey morning – and the man was a little grieved that it should be so on such an occasion. But he was too weary to care greatly. And Mary was in no state of mind for the due appreciation of scenery, anyway.

The deerhounds sensed him from afar, as ever, and came bounding and baying in joyous welcome. Thus forewarned, the Lady Christian was on the front doorstep of Glengyle House waiting, still-faced, calm, when they rode up.

'Mother,' Gregor called out, before questions could be asked, 'I have brought you home the woman that I am going to marry. Mary, she is – Mary Hamilton of Bardowie. We have travelled far, and she is tired and cold and wet. You will be kind to her, I know.'

The Lady Christian drew a deep long breath, and her hand went up to touch the still-golden hair at her brow. 'Yes,' she said. 'Of course. Of course.' Then she smiled, slowly, gently. 'Mary,' she repeated. 'Mary is a lovely name. Come, my dear.' And she stepped forward, arms out, towards the garron and its double burden.

And the girl, after a moment's lip-biting hesitation, slipped to the ground and ran, tripping over her bedraggled brocade, the two or three steps to the older woman. Into her open arms she sped, and there burst into choking sobbing tears on the other's shoulder.

The Lady of Glengyle stroked and smoothed the dark and unruly rain-wet hair, and held her close. 'There, there! *De' tha 'cur ort? Tha mo bheannachd agad,*' she crooned. '*Mhairi, Mhairi, mo chreach.* There, there.'

Considerably embarrassed, as ever by woman's tears, Gregor cleared his throat. 'H'rr'mmm. She is distraught a little, I think. Tired, like I said, see you,' he declared, rather loudly. 'Myself, I must see to the garron.' And digging in his heels, he urged his mount quickly and thankfully round the side of the house and into the steading behind.

Ian Beg looked sombrely after him.

And the Lady Christian MacGregor turned her new charge around, and led her, arm about her, over the threshold of Glengyle House.

CHAPTER THIRTEEN

GREGOR MACGREGOR's unspecified but inborn suspicion that women were strange, unpredictable, unreasonable and ungrateful beings, indeed God's most illogical creation, was more than substantiated in the days that followed – in the weeks that followed. A little piqued and tired and put out himself, he had been prepared for some small exhibition of the effects of similar influences on Mary Hamilton's part, for a brief period after her arrival at Glen Gyle – if only as an allowable and perhaps required display of feminine spirit. The last thing, after all, that he wanted as wife was any meek-and-mild milk-and-water miss. He was, too, prepared to make allowances, recognising that it had all been somewhat sudden and abrupt – though that, surely, was no fault of his. But that she should develop and maintain and continue to cherish an attitude of distant, remote indeed, reserve, of chilly aloofness, polite and calm and patient as it was utterly inflexible, almost steely, was quite ridiculous and insufferable. And that his mother, his gentle mild and reliable mother, should not only seem to acquiesce in this irritating performance but actually tacitly support it by her own demeanour, was almost as deplorable.

The whole thing was so unrealistic too, so lacking in practicality. After all, the deed was done, the milk was spilt. No display of sorrowful reproof or pained injury would alter the fact that she was here in his house of Glengyle, under his roof, and likely to remain so. She could not leave on her own, and nobody from her world could reach her here. Common sense, at the very least of it, dictated that she should make the best of what, after all, many young women would esteem a very excellent situation. Or so it seemed to Gregor MacGregor.

But not to Mary Hamilton, evidently. After the first silent day or two, when she kept her room and saw no one but the Lady Christian, she did not sulk or make scenes, admittedly. To that extent she accepted the inevitable. Nor did she actually idle or seem to pine. She found things to do, made little excursions with her hostess, and did not hide herself from the people round about. But to Gregor she was armoured in cool dignity and formal civility. All talk of marriage she either ignored or turned aside. She refused to discuss or to argue. His pleas, his reasonings, his inducements, even his threats to fetch the minister from Balquhidder and have them wed whether she willed or no – all she evaded or dismissed or rejected. There was no compromise, no weakening, no hint of response.

And all the time, strangely enough, she seemed to grow in beauty and desirability, the aura of patient sorrow and gallantly-borne tragedy actually seeming to enhance her dark-eyed chiselled-featured patrician loveliness. Everyone exclaimed at her cool graciousness and good looks – and in consequence tended to take her part. A more maddening situation for a spirited and well-doing young man would have been hard to envisage.

Gregor's well-doing was notable, too. He did not pester her, or force his attentions upon her, as some might have done in the circumstances. Indeed, presently he came to keep himself out of her sight as much as possible – and knew himself grievously the loser in so doing. He seldom actually lost his temper with her. And he wrote a letter to John Hamilton, as he need not have done, informing him of her whereabouts and that she was safe and well, and assuring him that she would be well looked after. Strangely enough, Mary did not choose to avail herself of his offered facility for sending a letter or even a message to her brother on her own, merely shaking her head and suggesting that Gregor include her sisterly regards. So he himself had to add the request that Bardowie send back certain of her effects by the hands of the present bearers. He also wrote a brief note to Mistress Meg at Arnprior; and here Mary did elect to include a letter of her own – and quite a long one. What she said therein the man would have been interested to glimpse. Ian Beg with three or four armed supporters was charged with the delivery of both missives.

The messengers brought back, eventually, an answering letter to Mary from her sister-in-law, and nothing at all from John Hamilton – no letter, no things for his sister, no message. Unless the threats and bluster and tirade to which he had subjected Ian Beg could be termed a message, and the fact that he vowed that he would move heaven and earth to lift his poor misguided and unhappy sister out of the hands of barbarous ruffians, and bring down due and terrible retribution on her abductor's head. Et cetera.

And that, of course, was not worth calling a message, much less a threat. All the heaven and earth that Bardowie could move, or considerably more highly placed folk than he was, could not winkle out his sister from Glen Gyle of the MacGregors, nor produce the retribution that he desired. The Queen's Ministers might be invoked – and no doubt were – Parliament House, the Lord Justice-General, and the Court of Session, even the Commander-in-Chief. None were in any position, or in any mood, to dispatch an army over the Highland Line, provoke the clans and stir up trouble in a Scotland already seething with discontent. And nothing less would serve – no edict or manifesto or official trumpeting would affect the MacGregors one iota –

so long as they stayed on their own side of the Line.

Gregor himself, perhaps, would almost have welcomed attempts at reprisal, or some such excitement, in the circumstances – something to make time go a little faster, some action to allow him to assert himself. Action, he felt instinctively, was his forte.

He was almost grateful, then, when after a couple of weeks of this infuriating stalemate Rob Roy came to him, apologising for interrupting his courtship – Heaven forgive him – and seeking his nephew's assistance. It was King Jamie again. Though Grant of Invermoriston had been at the Kinloch Rannoch hunting match, and had agreed to rise, his High Chief, the Laird of Grant himself, was staunch for the Government and was holding the main clan back, a serious loss to the cause, for they were strategically placed on Speyside and were having a bad effect on their smaller neighbours. But MacAlpin Grant of Rothiemurchus, one of the most potent septs of the clan, was a strange wayward man, with moreover a fondness for the theory that the Grants and the MacGregors were of one original stock. Indeed, he elected to be known as Mac-Alpin rather than Grant, much to his chief's annoyance. Colonel Hooke thought that if one of the Gregorach, highly enough placed, were to go to work on him, they might bring him in on the King's side. And if MacAlpin came in, others might follow, with Invermoriston already committed, and the Laird of Grant might find himself left high and dry as it were. And this was important, for the clan had a regiment under arms for the Government. Rob Roy himself, unfortunately, could not make the journey, for he was engaged to attend a conference of commanders at the Earl of Panmure's house in Angus. Would Greg go to Badenoch and try to win over MacAlpin for King James?

Gregor, of course, could nowise refuse. He explained to Mary, elaborately, that whatever his own inclinations, His Majesty's cause must be maintained. He would have to leave her for a little – a couple of weeks, perhaps, no more.

His mother would look after her. And she would probably never miss him anyway. As an afterthought, he mentioned that it was not really likely that he would be in any great danger. He left fairly explicit instructions with Ian Beg, who was to keep an eye on things – especially on Miss Hamilton – and with a tail of half a dozen gillies he set out next morning on his long ride northwards to the Spey.

And, though he had certain misgivings as he left Glen Gyle, he was not over into Balquhidder in the golden October sunshine before he was singing again – as he had not sung since Crieff. Which was a strange thing, too.

*   *   *

It was almost four weeks before Gregor saw Glen Gyle again, four weeks of strenuous riding, most of it spent chasing MacAlpin down the long banks of swift-flowing Spey through Badenoch's endless pine forests. The laird of Rothiemurchus derived most of his very impressive revenues from felling and floating his timber down the Spey to the sawmasters and charcoal-burners of the Moray coast. And most of the way thereto Gregor had had to pursue him, before he could catch up with him and his lumbermen and rafters, and discuss high politics. He had found the man a handful indeed, queer, fiery and more concerned with upsetting his chief than with setting King Jamie on his rightful throne. But he had got some sort of assurances out of him eventually, and did not feel that his journey was wasted.

The first snows of winter had been crowning all the world of the mountains as he rode south again, yet all the blaze of the Highland autumn lingered in the valleys. Gregor sang practically the whole long road home, and laughed at every least opportunity. His men were happy to have him himself again. He counted the last fifty miles, one by one – and did not think to name himself a fool for so doing.

He came back by the Trossachs and Loch Katrine-side rather than by the more usual route through the Pass of Weeping from Balquhidder, solely to avoid the delay that the hospitable and merry lairds of that green valley were bound to impose upon him. He reached his own place just as the last glow of light was fading out of the autumn mist-wreaths that draped most of the corries and high valleys – though the topmost peaks, snow-clad and austere, still reflected a pale sun that the rest of the world had lost.

His mother greeted him no differently from any other occasion, quiet accepting woman. But her glance slid beyond him and around. 'You have been long, long, Gregor,' she said. 'But have you not brought Mary?'

'Mary?' he wondered. 'How could I be doing that? Mary is here. Why – where is she?'

'She is up the hill. She went, as she has gone each of these last afternoons, up the hill to the Pass, to look down into Balquhidder.'

'Why? Why should she do such a thing as that?'

'Who knows, Gregor? Who knows why young people do what they do? Perhaps she was watching for somebody – somebody who would come that way, and who should have come long ere this . . . !'

'Dia! You mean – my own self? Watching for me?' His voice thickened. 'She would not do that . . . ?'

Christian MacGregor shrugged slightly. 'Perhaps not. You it is should know, Gregor. Perhaps it is just the view that she likes. But these last three afternoons she has ridden up there to the Pass, on a garron – alone.'

Gregor left her then, without a word, to hurry round to the back of the house and gaze uphill. There was no sign of anything but a scattering of cattle on the shadowy slopes directly above. But higher, patches of mist rolled greyly. He came back, elation and anxiety struggling within him.

'She should be down by this,' he told his mother. 'There is mist up there.'

'Yes. She has been down earlier than this, the other days. The mist may have delayed her. But she has a good garron. It will bring her home. . . .'

'I told Ian Beg to be looking after her,' Gregor declared, frowning. 'Where is he?'

'Ian Beg has done more than enough,' his mother said. 'He went after her the first two times. Then she asked him not to, the girl. She said that she did not like being spied upon. You cannot be blaming her. Besides, Ian Beg has his wife to think of. She is having another baby just now. . . .' She shook her head. 'But Mary will be fine, I am sure. She will be down in a little.'

'I will go up and meet her, just the same,' her son declared.

'Are you not tired? And hungry, Gregor? Some food, and then she will be down. . . .'

'No. I will eat after,' he decided, and turned to leave her again.

He took a fresh garron, and set it slantwise at the steep braeside straight away, his two deerhounds at heel. The hill directly behind Glengyle House was called the Stob an Duibhe, and with two others formed the western side of the high Pass of Weeping. By climbing straight up and over the fairly easy saddle between it and its neighbour to the south-east, the summit of the Pass could be reached much more expeditiously than by the usual roundabout route. Half an hour on a garron would do it.

The higher out of a mountain valley one lifts, the more light there is of an evening. It was still not dark when Gregor reached the saddle between the hills. But feelers and wraiths of clammy mist were now eddying about him, and dense cloud cowls had come down to shroud the summits above. When he looked over into the gut of the Pass, it was as into a seething cauldron of billowing vapour.

The man paused, uncertain, the hounds questing the air. He had seen no sign of the girl. If he went down there he might very easily miss her. She might be coming up, and pass within a hundred yards of him, and neither be the wiser. But surely that was a chance that he had to take? She could hardly be lost – but she might well be frightened. She might still be down in the floor of the long Pass, uncertain at which point to start to climb out. If he did not miss her on the way up, he would be sure to find her in the Pass itself, narrow as it was.

He went down into the swirling silent gloom.

Slanting down, he stopped his garron every few yards, to listen. No sound but a strange recurrent sigh of air broke the eerie hush – but Gregor knew how effectively mist can blanket sound. Presently he called a long 'Halloo-oo!' And again, 'Halloo-oo!' Not even an echo responded, as his cry was swallowed up.

It was much darker down in the pit of the Pass. The man, at the foot, peered down at the peaty path that threaded it, seeking to discern hoof-marks. But he could see nothing in the gloom. At a particularly muddy spot, keeping his hounds to heel, he dismounted again and felt gently about the mud surface with his finger-tips. No single track of any kind could he trace thereon, horse or deer or bird. The peat-broth and gravel was smooth. And cast about as he would, right and left, he found nothing.

The conclusion that he had to come to was inescapable. She had not come down into the Pass at all – whatever she had done on the other days. Nothing had threaded that narrow way since last night's rain. What, then? Where else could she have gone?

Only the one answer presented itself. On the other side of this central hill of the Stob, a much higher ridge than the saddle that he had crossed connected it with the next summit to the north-west, Meall Mor. This link was no saddle at all, but a high stony escarpment, a narrow place of rocks and crags and pinnacles. But from it there was an excellent view down into upper Balquhidder, a better and wider vista than from the Pass here. The only other spot, in fact, on this range where there was such a view. If she had indeed come up to watch for him . . . ?

Gregor wasted no time, but set his mount to the steep hillside again, climbing whence he had just come down. That ridge, vantage point as it might be, was no place to be caught in the mist. There were drops all round it, jagged lips, out-cropping brows. The thought made the man drive his sturdy sure-footed beast hard.

A six-hundred-foot climb, the last part of it on foot, and he was up on to the saddle again. It was dark now, even though up here the mist seemed to be a little less thick than down below. He had to contour round the southern face of the Stob. It was not difficult, though steep, even in the darkness, for a man who knew every foot of the way. He called as he went – and even the sound of his own voice was lonely, lonely.

He had still to climb to reach the final ridge. He was actually in cloud, now. As the rocks grew rougher he dismounted, leading his horse. He shouted when he could spare the breath, and he sent the hounds ranging ahead.

He searched that jagged ridge, foot by foot, clambering over the rockfalls, circling the outcrops, slithering on the rubble and scree, picking a way not only for himself but for the garron that followed on so patiently. Searched, but found nothing. He had seldom felt so helpless. He did not even know that she had come here. . . .

The sudden baying of the hounds ahead of him, followed by the high whinny of a horse, sent Gregor's heart up into his mouth. He went racing forwards, shouting his presence. But no voice answered him. In a panic he came stumbling. A white garron, one of his own, stood there beside a huge rock, ghostly in the gloom, a folded plaid across its broad back. The hounds sat panting nearby. And that was all.

Really frightened now, Gregor went scrambling around in concentric circles, peering, quartering the uneven ground, calling – and cursing the darkness. There was no sign nor sound of her.

He grabbed the plaid from the horse's back, called the dogs, presented it for them to sniff, and then sent them off, ordering them to seek, seek. Noses down, twisting this way and that, they disappeared into the night. The man noted that they both were trending away northwards, towards Balquhidder, not southwards towards home.

Over there lay, first, broken rock and short precipitous

drops, worse than on this side. Then a vast gently shelving tableland of peat-hag and heather knoll and quaking bog, extending for miles at the high head of Balquhidder, the very womb of waters, where most of the streams of that green valley were born. A sanctuary for old rogue stags, the playground of the winds, and an ill place to cross at any time – in the dark and mist it could represent its own hell indeed. If she was down there . . . !

At the black edge of the abyss of it, Gregor filled his lungs to the utmost, cupped hands to mouth, and cried with all the power than was in him. 'Halloo-oo! Halloo-oo!' again and again. Five or six times he cried, desperately, half-crazedly, changing the direction of his facing a little each time. And then he stopped abruptly. Was it imagination . . . ? An echo? A ringing in his ears? One of the hounds answering him? A night bird? Or was it . . . ?

No! By God's Glory – it was none of these! It was an answering human cry, thin and tremulous and infinitely forlorn, coming from afar, somewhere half-left, out of that grim desolation. Almost beside himself, Gregor yelled again, differently now, joyfully, reassuringly, incoherently – and all in his own Gaelic. Then, urgently noting the line of that faint reply, and where on this ridge he was leaving the garrons, he started to scramble down the steeps before him, slipping and sliding, over the mist-wet rocks and ledges, the rocks at the foot of which he had so recently feared that she might be lying.

*   *   *

It took him the best part of half an hour to reach her, for it was by devious quaking desperate ways that he had to go, with scarcely a dozen consecutive yards in a straight line. He leapt and floundered and sank knee-deep. He ran light-footed, and plunged heavily. He balanced on tussocks and old heather-clumps, and tripped over bog-pine roots, jagged as fangs, and splashed through pools. And all the time Mary Hamilton drew him on, calling, calling, directing him, wisely not moving apparently. The fear that she would so move, attempt to come to him as he drew near, grew in the man. She might plunge deep in one of these black bottomless hags.

'Mary! Mary!' he cried. 'Stay still. Do not . . . be moving . . . till I come.'

'Gregor! Gregor!' From the sudden changed ring in her voice, it was evident that for the first time the girl realised the identity of the man who was making for her. Her quick high-pitched cry ended in a choking sob. She sounded as though she would be no more than perhaps a couple of hundred yards away.

That last stretch was the worst. She seemed to be stranded on what was almost an island of long heather grown up round a cluster of ancient pine-roots, and surrounded by particularly evil stretches of black treachery. How she had got there remained to be discovered – but Gregor was not able to join her without very considerable tacking, retreating and a weltering that was next to wallowing. Time and again he was almost engulfed. Then, at last, soaked, black with peat-mud and slime, gasping, he was able to reach a jutting crooked arm of root, and haul himself up. She was crouching across from him, only two or three yards away, a slight black figure only a little darker than the surrounding menacing world of blackness. The two hounds were moving shadows nearby. He leapt across to her.

'Mary! Mary, my dear, my beloved!' he cried.

She came into his wide-stretched arms, to grip and cling to him convulsively. 'Oh, Gregor!' she said – and could say no more.

*   *   *

For how long they remained thus, clasped to each other tightly, panting, stammering incoherences, is not to be known. In such a situation time counts for little. At length, it was Gregor's foot slipping on the precarious stance of root that caused him to move, to step aside, to loosen his hold of the girl. And immediately she sank down into the crouching position that she had been in before.

'What is it?' he wondered. 'You are hurt? or Unwell?'

'It is my foot. My ankle,' she said. 'I twisted it. Between some roots. There is nothing serious, I think. But it is swollen. . . . '

Promptly the man was down on his knee beside he feeling her ankle with gentle skilful hands.

'Oh, it is nothing – now that you are here,' she assured. 'Oh, Gregor – I was afraid. I was terrified. In this awful place. And the mist . . . '

'I know it, *a graidh*,' he agreed. 'It is bad. But you will be fine, now. Your leg will be sore, sore. It is swollen, yes. But nothing is broke. It will be all right. You will be fine, just fine, now.'

She almost choked. 'Oh, Gregor – I've heard you at that before!' she got out, with something between laughter and tears. 'Always I am to be just fine!'

'And so you are,' he agreed, seriously. 'Always. But . . . you are trembling! Shivering. Lassie, lassie – you are cold? Wet?'

She nodded, biting her lip. 'A little.' Great tremors were racking her, intermittently.

'Och, my dear – this will not do,' the man cried. 'See – my plaid is damp a bittie, but it will serve, maybe.' He stood up, unfastened the plaid that was belted about him for ease in climbing, and wrapped it round her. His arms lingered about her, and she leaned against him gratefully.

'See, you,' he said, as another tremor shook her, even to the rattling of her teeth. 'Warm we must get you.' And selecting a firm spot, he sat down, and took her bodily on to his lap, to tuck in the ends of the plaid around her, and hold her close to him. Then he ordered the two hounds in to him, and pressed them to lie down against them. A notable warmth came out of them, as well as a powerful smell of wet dog. The shivering girl protested at none of it.

He found her hands, and rubbed them with his own, to encourage the circulation. Then he told her to put them under his arm-pit.

Presently her shuddering and jerking died away. But

now he found that she was sniffling, regularly. Gulping too. He peered at her, so close to him.

'You are weeping?' he exclaimed. '*Och, ochan, mo chreagh. Ciod so?* You must not weep. It will all be just . . .' He stopped, gulping also. 'I mean – you must not be sad, at all.'

'I am not sad,' she mumbled, and sniffed again.

'Is it sore, then? Your ankle? A shame, it is . . .'

'No, no. It is not that. I am not weeping. Not really. It is just . . . well, you are so good. So kind. And strong. So, so thoughtful. I . . . I am sorry, Gregor.' That was a whisper.

'Eh? Eh-hey – what is this? Sorry? You?'

'Yes. I have been so foolish. . . .'

'Och, wheesht, lassie. Anyone can be getting lost in a mist, whatever. Easy it is. Myself, I do not know what direction I am facing now.' Which was not strictly true, but it might well have been.

'I didn't mean that. Though there, too, you are kind. Not to reproach me. I don't know where I went wrong. I do not know where I am, indeed, in this horrible marsh – though I think that I must be at the wrong side of the hill. I had left the pony, and climbed some way up that pointed hill – yes, the Stob – for a better view down into . . . well, for a better view. When the mist caught me, I thought that I knew my way down well enough, back to the pony. But – well, evidently I went wrong. I got into steep places. And the mist got thicker. I kept going down, as well as I could. I thought that I was getting down towards Glen Gyle. I knew I had missed the pony, but so long as I kept going downhill . . . But I must have been wrong. I got into this dreadful place of bogs. I knew that I was wrong, then. There is nothing like this on the Glen Gyle side. I . . . I was not very clever, I fear.' She shook her dark damp head. No word of the terror that she had undergone as she floundered and struggled, lost, across that endless quagmire. Her sniff had stopped. 'How did you find me, Gregor?'

'Och, it was easy,' he lied. 'I just could not help myself, you see. I came straight for you, just. I could not help but find you, Mary. I would have found you if you had been at the other end of the world, whatever!'

She drew a deep breath, but said nothing now.

He warmed to his theme. 'You were drawing me, drawing me, see you – all the time. I could not miss you. Like the star that guides the shipmen, you were drawing me. All the way from Badenoch. My star, just. That is you, Mary my dear.'

There was the beginnings of another sniff, there.

'Och, now. There, there. Hush you, my dear one, my beloved, my fawn of the woods.' He was stroking her hair. 'Do not cry, at all, my pigeon, my dear heart. Never . . . '

And then she suddenly came to life within his arms, twisting round, her hands gripping his arm. 'Gregor! Gregor – do you realise what you are saying?' she cried. 'Listen to yourself, Gregor! You are . . . you are . . . ' Her voice broke.

'I am telling you that you must not weep, just,' he said. 'You will not be looking half so beautiful if you weep, my lovely Mary. . . . '

'No, no!' she burst out. She thumped at his chest with her fists, as she had done once before – but with so very different emotions. 'No – not that! Oh, Gregor – how foolish you are! Don't you see? You are calling me beloved! Saying that you love me. . . . '

'And why not?' he demanded. 'Haven't I been loving you from the day that I set my eyes on you, whatever? In the coach, that time. Can I not say it, when it is God's own truth? A man cannot help it when he loves. . . . '

'Oh!' she cried, almost sobbed. 'Oh – you fool! You dear, beloved, adorable fool!' And abruptly her arms were up and around his neck, and her lips were pressed to his, quiveringly, passionately.

Gregor was surprised, naturally. But he got over it with commendable speed, and put off the questioning till a more convenient occasion. Something of an opportunist always, he took what Heaven was so liberally giving, and was thankful.

* * *

Time and place was of even less consequence thereafter. The night stretched ahead of them – for of course it would have been folly to have attempted to move the girl, handicapped as he was with her sprained ankle, over that evil morass in the darkness – and its long chill hours might have been honeyed minutes, their cramped and unpleasant stance a cushioned arbour, for all the difference that it made to them. The seventh heaven may be reached by strange routes, and curiously located.

But, in the fulness of experience, rather than of time, the man did learn, more or less incidentally and bit by bit, something of the reason for Mary's notable change of front – if reason it could be called, with a woman involved. She had, it seemed, merely wanted to be wooed. In essence, it was as simple as that. She had not been content with being just chosen, firstly, and then carried off. She had looked for gentle dalliance, apparently, tender words, the declaration of love, and her suitor's passion – and she had received none of it, only an implied admiration and a somewhat high-handed being taken for granted. Pride, it transpired in effect, had been what was wrong with her – a virtue suitable enough in Highland gentlemen but unlooked for in a woman. She herself, it seemed, had loved him all along – but it had not been for her to say so. That he had not seen fit to actually do so either was his failing. A failing for which she was prepared to forgive him, now. A little nonplussed by it all, Gregor, however, did not attempt to argue or defend himself. A practical man, he found the matter to be of only hypothetical interest now, anyway.

All of which only goes to underline something or another.

Marriage of course was a different matter – something practical, involving dates, plans and details, as well as unquestioned delights. She was not still against the idea of marriage . . . ?

Of course she was not! She would marry him just as soon as it could be decently arranged. She had all along intended to marry him – one day. It was only . . .

He would build a new wing to Glengyle House for them,

he declared, at this stage. The place was on the small side. And there were things that he had seen in his travels which he would wish his wife to have. And there were the children to think of. They were going to be very busy.

And what about the rising and the King's cause, Mary wondered, a little doubtfully?

'Damn the rising and the King's cause!' Gregor declared, quite violently. Anyway, that was not till April or May. Who could tell what might have happened by then?

Gregor MacGregor did not know what a good prophet he was.

So passed the night. They talked, they clung to each other, the plaid now rearranged to envelop them both. They embraced. They slept, in snatches, sometimes one, sometimes the other, sometimes both together. And they found no fault with any of it, even with the stiffness and cramping pains that they suffered, and the grievous emptiness of their stomachs – and the effect of strong fumes of dog thereon. They were young, they had found each other and themselves, and they were alone.

The grey dawn stealing over that black and dreary place, mist-free now, found them fast asleep, the girl curled within the man's arms, his face buried in her hair. It did not awake them. It was the shouting that did that, distant hailing, later, as a watery sun began to gleam palely above the peaks to the east. Ian Beg and the gillies were out searching for them, and had discovered the garrons on the ridge. Almost, Gregor was sorry to have to raise his voice and answer.

Even in daylight, and with hillmen to help, getting the young woman out of that tumbled sea of peat-hags was no child's play. But skill and great patience, allied to a masculine conception of gentleness and a deal of shouting, achieved it in time. A peat-stained and dishevelled crew they reached the horses, and set off downhill. And Gregor's great laughter filled all Glen Gyle ahead of them.

CHAPTER FOURTEEN

THEY were married within the month, in the ancient squat little Kirk of Balquhidder in the mouth of the valley, amidst a flurry of December snow – a chilly business, for the doors of the church had to be left open since most of the congregation inevitably had to remain outside. This had the merciful effect of reducing the length of the sermon. Most of the hierarchy of the Clan Gregor was present, as well as folks of lesser name, come at considerable difficulty through the winter glens. Apart from the bride herself, no single Lowlander was there. They both would have liked to have had Meg Hamilton up for the auspicious occasion – but Meg was now back with her husband at Bardowie, her father much recovered, and it seemed hardly feasible in the circumstances to invite her under Gregorach safe-conduct as it were, alone. And, of course, the journey in winter would have been trying for a lady, to say the least of it. Rob Roy, most suitably, gave the bride away – as a friend of the family, he said. Gregor's young sister Catherine attended her. It was a good wedding, as these things go – though undoubtedly not such as Mary's virginal dreams might have visualised a year before.

There was almost as much warlike talk thereat as there was nuptial congratulation.

But the young people were little aware of anything of the sort – or of anything at all except each other. A proper and felicitous state of affairs, which persisted thereafter likewise. The clouds of war might gather and lower over all Scotland, but for Mary and Gregor they did not obscure the sun which shone in another sky altogether. Alarms might be sounded, Government grow desperate in its bribery, riots occur in Edinburgh and Glasgow, the cry of No Union link up with the cry of King James, rumours run through the glens as they did through the streets and alleys – but at Glen Gyle other matters held sway.

They were very busy, as Gregor had said that they would be. Adjusting themselves to their new state was an absorbing task, and what energies were left over were occupied with building the new wing to the house, on Gregor's part, and in learning to become mistress of Glengyle on Mary's. In this latter business the Lady Christian was tact and sympathy itself, removing herself and her two younger children to the house of Portanellen a mile down the lochside, but making herself available every day to help and advise if desired. Mary, who had not known a mother of her own since early childhood, soon loved her more deeply than she would have thought possible.

So the winter passed. Rob Roy was seldom at home, covering the countryside, ostensibly on the affairs of his Watch, but frequently surprisingly far afield. The Watch was indeed busy, for unsettled times bring out unsettled men, and Rob was responsible for order over a wide area, many men paying him sweetly to keep the peace. Sometimes, of course, Gregor as his lieutenant had to be involved. But his uncle fondly spared him as much as possible, knowing full well that there would be demands enough later.

But as the months rolled on, a change came over Rob Roy MacGregor. A cheerful and hearty man ever, he became addicted to unaccustomed silences. Sometimes he even managed to look grim. Which was strange, for news from all over the country was almost consistently good; good for the Jacobites, that is. The clan chiefs were everywhere committing themselves; the low country lords were coming in; the populace and the burghs were seething. Petitions against the Treaty were streaming in from all quarters of the country – and being refused by the Lord Chancellor Seafield. The local militia and fencibles, and the heritors, were forbidden to meet, as required under the Act of Security, in case they turned against the authorities. Copies of the projected Treaty of Union were being burnt at market-crosses, kirk doors and other public places up and down the land.

Effigies of the Queen's Ministers hung on gallows, trees and town gates. In Edinburgh, where Parliament was signing its own death warrant, the said Ministers skulked by dark ways or rode deep in armed guards about their occasions. The country was ripe for revolt.

But it was the news that came secretly out of the castles and mansion-houses along the east coasts of Fife and Angus, in touch by sea with France, that furrowed Rob's brows – and more than Rob's. In France King Jamie's cause did not go quite so prosperously. Louis was being difficult, vacillating, playing hot and cold, promising much one day, cancelling his promises the next. James himself, a young man of only nineteen, melancholy and taciturn, brought up in an unreal atmosphere of make-believe and intrigue, was proving weak, incapable of facing up to the arrogant French king, and surrounded by ill-chosen advisers. The rivalries in his court were notorious. There were violent disputes over who was to command the expedition, the fleet, the army of liberation. The clash of personalities resounded as far as Scotland.

Spring came but reluctantly to the hill country that year, and with it April, the melting snows, and the start of the campaigning season. With it also came the fatal day, April 25th, 1707, when the Chancellor made his celebrated remark, 'Now there's an end of ane auld sang.' The completed Treaty of Union, signed, sealed and established, was presented to the Scots Parliament, which thereupon dissolved for the last time. Popular resentment reached fever pitch, mobs rose and wrecked and looted, buildings were set afire, trade came almost to a standstill.

And no King Jamie arrived, no expedition sailed, no orders were issued.

Up and down the Highlands and Islands the clans were either mustering or ready to muster. The Gregorach, being comparatively close at hand and readily available, did not need to assemble yet. Rob did not give the word. Indeed, nobody gave any word. No beacons were lit. No fiery crosses went out.

May came and went. Scotland simmered, and waited. Word came that the Duke of Berwick, James's half-brother and a Marshal of France, had been appointed to command the expedition. Then came the news that Louis had forbidden his release, as a French citizen. The Marquis de Matignon was selected in his place – and Admiral the Count de Forbin, in charge of shipping the expedition over, refused to co-operate with him. The clans waited – though some indulged in a little local raiding and innocent spoilery, just to pass the time and keep their hands in.

June passed into July, and if Scotland still waited she was off the boil now. The clansmen were returning to their summer shielings. The towns settled down sullenly. Lawlessness still was rife – but the Government began to breathe more freely.

Colonel Hooke arrived again from France, almost exactly a year after his first appearance, a disappointed man. He told of dissension, irresolution and divided counsels at St Germains, of King Louis's obduracy and haughty pride, and the rivalries of the French military leaders. They were still talking of an expedition that year, but he himself and all knowledgeable of Scottish conditions advised against it, knowing the clansmen's objection to autumn harvest-time campaigning and the closed state of the Highlands in winter. The expedition would undoubtedly sail in the spring, then – a year late, and having missed the first fever of anti-Union resentment. But who could tell how much more Scottish anger and indignation might be stirred up in the meantime by the working out of government from London, highhanded activities and contemptuous treatment? Had not Mr Speaker himself said, 'We have catcht Scotland and will keep her fast'? and the Lord Treasurer of England declared indignantly, 'Have we not bought the Scots, and a right to tax them?' Waiting another six or eight months might be no great misfortune in the end.

Rob Roy was more than doubtful. Reviving damped-down fires was ever an uncertain business, he contended. Promises and commitments made for one year might not always stand carrying over to another. There were some that he knew who would be hard to turn out a second time.

Many other Jacobite leaders undoubtedly felt as did Rob. But there was nothing that they could do to alter the case. A rising against disciplined troops and great defended fortresses, without the necessary artillery, ammunition and engineering equipment, would be useless and worse than useless. They could only wait for France.

Gregor was not amongst those who fumed and fretted and frowned. He was quite content to remain at Glen Gyle minding his own business. The exterior of the new wing to his house was completed, and very fine – but the interior, to be worthy of Mary and to come up to his own conceptions, was demanding all his ingenuity and a lot of his time. Moreover, it seemed as though Mary already might be pregnant; it would be a terrible thing if he was to go and get himself killed before he had either got the house finished or seen his own son that would be chieftain of the sept of Dougal Ciar after him.

That is what a woman, given time, can do to a hero.

*   *   *

But it must not be assumed that all spirit had died quite out of Gregor Ghlun Dubh, even if the range and scope of it had suffered a curtailment. As example, there was the little matter of the tax-collector, in November. Tax-collectors, like a general scale of taxation itself, were new phenomena in Scotland, and one of the earliest and most exotic fruits of the Union. But England had this attribute of modern progressive government, and Scotland must now have it too. English tax-gatherers, assessors and preventive-men were recruited by the hundred and sent north over the Border in a flood. They were less well received than either they or their masters would have wished.

Word of the presence and activities of these interlopers reached the MacGregor country from time to time, but was hardly to be taken seriously or considered in relation to such as themselves. It was with something betwixt consternation and profound offence, then, that one grey November day the news was brought to Glengyle House that one of the noxious breed had actually penetrated as far as the clachan of Aberfoyle, this side of Flanders Moss, and was going about poking his nose into other folk's affairs and generally behaving in an ungentlemanly way. That something had to be done about it went without saying. There were sundry vigorous Gregorach suggestions, that only awaited chiefly sanction.

It fell to Gregor to take the appropriate decisions – for Rob Roy was away in the Lowlands, *incognito*, on a delicate mission; no less than in mortgaging the estates, his own of Craigroyston and Inversnaid, and Gregor's Glengyle, for ready cash. That he had not felt it necessary or wise to do this previously was perhaps a significant reflection on his changed attitude towards the entire projected rising. Now, he considered, the possibility of failure and consequent forfeiture of participants' estates at least fell to be envisaged – and if one's estates might be forfeited anyway, it was no bad thing to have the cash value of them safely in one's sporran beforehand. An elementary precaution for a far-looking man like Rob Roy. So his nephew had to deal with the tax-man.

Perhaps as a result of his new status as a man of family and husbandly responsibility, Gregor went about the business in a slightly less bull-headed fashion than had been his wont. Instead of going himself, forthwith, and throwing the creature off MacGregor territory neck and crop, he sent scouts to spy out the exact position. These in due course came back to report, what had not emerged before – namely that the fellow had a couple of redcoats with him as escort, that he was working his way westwards towards the real hill country, going from house to house, enquiring after numbers of occupants, how many beasts were owned, and other property, what tribute was paid to the laird or land-owner, and so on. All of which sounded thoroughly ominous. If people were to be penalised for owning a few cattle, then it was past time that all right-thinking citizens rose up and put a stop to it.

Thus well-informed and well-intentioned, Gregor set out eastwards. He took only Ian Beg with him, much to his people's chagrin. Since the Union, the military forces had been much strengthened in Stirling and Dumbarton Castles, as elsewhere, entire English regiments being sent up. Colonel Hooke had sent urgent orders that no head-on clashes should be provoked on any account, meantime. These troops were all badly needed elsewhere to support Marlborough's new campaigns. If they seemed not to be needed here in Scotland, they would almost certainly be withdrawn – which was what was urgently required for the King's landing in March or April. This call, this *command*, for moderation and discretion fell in quite conveniently with Gregor's new-found mood of married responsibility. A nice moderation would be his watchword, then.

Accordingly, his plans were simple and unambitious to a degree. He ascertained that the tax-man had just begun to work along amongst the crofts at the bottom end of Loch Ard. He and Ian Beg consequently started to visit the houses at the head of the three-mile loch. They instructed the occupants in how they were to treat the tax-gatherer, how they were to be civil, not threatening, but very very distressed for him personally. How they were to assure him that he was a very brave man indeed. That there was another tax-gatherer had been working amongst them, out from Glasgow and Dumbarton, who was not nearly so brave – who, in fact, was after having a very bad time of it, to the danger of his life, who hadn't been seen for some time, indeed. The MacGregors of the hills were hard, hard on tax-gatherers. Thus and thus the story went, that they were to tell, with slight variations and embellishments, all around Loch Ard head and over the water-meadows of the isthmus to Loch Chon. Gregor returned thereafter decently to wife and fireside.

The next day he was back again, this time with an extra garron loaded with bundles of clothes and gear. He had been raiding his grandfather Colonel Donald's trophy chest. They found that the tax-man was still at Loch Ard, but near the head of the loch now. Leaving the mile or so of the isthmus between them, Gregor and Ian Beg selected one of the few empty houses at the foot of Loch Chon, a fairly isolated place. They borrowed a few armfuls of bog-hay from the nearest neighbour. Unloading the garron, they took its burden indoors.

Thereafter they spent an amusing hour or two, with hay and rope and paper and the gear that they had brought. Plus the red keel that they used for marking the cattle.

When they had finished, they shut and barricaded the door. They also told the neighbours what to say if they were questioned. And retired to Glen Gyle. Discretion and moderation could not have been better exemplified.

The next afternoon the tax-gatherer, with his two soldiers, arrived on the shores of Loch Chon, busy methodical man, now undoubtedly highly conscious of the risks that he was apparently running and the evil reputation of these mountainy MacGregors. They duly found the barricaded cottage, could gain no entrance, prowled around it, and perceived signs of recent activity. Suspecting smuggled brandy, or an illicit still, or worse, they broke down the door. And there they were confronted with three bodies dangling from the roof-timbers, two in the red coats and cocked hats of the military, that in the centre in good civilian broadcloth. And around this central figure's elongated neck hung a roughly inscribed legend which said THUS PERISH ALL TAX-GATHERERS.

As the trio staggered back from the doorway, a great outcry arose from the cover of a nearby birch-wood, shouts of 'Gregalach! Gregalach!' and 'Ardchoille!' and the like. Also a considerable baying of hounds.

The tax-man ran for his horse. But he was less active than his two guards. He had to follow them, indeed, pounding in their dust, down the drove road by Loch Ard eastwards. According to the good folk of Aberfoyle, they clattered through the clachan, much strung out, without pause and as though the Devil himself were at their heels. Which may well have been an exaggeration. But eastwards they did go, with some expedition, at any rate. And the MacGregors saw no more of fiscal authority that winter.

Rob Roy's laughter sounded just a little rueful when he returned from his journey and heard about it all. It was the sort of story which would have sounded still better coming from himself.

However, Rob also had success to report. He had managed to mortgage both estates for an excellent figure. Half of it, of all people, he had got from no less a personage than James Graham, now Duke of Montrose, himself. Montrose was land-hungry always, of course – but that a man so close to the Government, and a close-fisted man at that, should have been prepared to do the business, and to do it thus generously, was interesting. It showed that he, for his part, was no more confident than was Rob about the future, and thought it wise to maintain a link with the Jacobites.

Perhaps Hooke was right?

CHAPTER FIFTEEN

AND indeed, as the winter of 1707 passed into the spring of 1708, Nathaniel Hooke's prophecies were very adequately fulfilled. The Union grew steadily in unpopularity – not only with the mass of the people, who had always been against it, but amongst the influential circles that had supported it, the aristocratic and commercial interests that had hoped to do well out of it. Westminster's abrupt imposition of the Salt and Malt Taxes were serious blows to the Scottish economy – as they were intended to be. The trade in salted herrings to the Low Countries, Germany and the Baltic was one of the basic Scots exports. The Salt Tax hit it hard, dealt the fishing and shipping communities a sore buffet, and set the East Coast merchants growling. The Malt

Tax hit the manufacture of both whisky and ale, the drinks of the common people of both Highlands and Lowlands. The outcry ought to have been heard as far south as London. The entire farming policy of a mainly agricultural country was upset – and with it, of course, the landowners' revenues. Two more damaging taxes could not have been conceived. A duty was levied on linen, another of Scotland's staples, that ran down the looms and started riots up and down the land. And to add insult to injury, simultaneously the duty was removed from Irish linen. Then the bribes for many who had steered the Union through remained only promises, whether in cash, positions or honours. Even the Equivalent was still unpaid – that mass bait of nearly £400,000 sterling that was to compensate Scotland for having to shoulder a share of the English national debt, and which had been the carrot dangled before the noses of the growing commercial classes hard hit by the collapse of the Darien Scheme. Scottish trade with France, England's enemy, went by the board. Trade from the colonies, even when consigned to Scots ports, now had to be carried only in English ships. It was apparent that Scottish trade and interests, where they rivalled or conflicted with those of the larger partner to the Union, were to be firmly put down.

Repeal the Union became the cry from all over the land. But now there was no Scottish authority to act on the cry. Gradually the people began to look to their ancient monarchy to save them. Not Anne Stewart, lethargic and sickly in London, needless to say, but James, her nephew in France. Rob Roy's brows began to lighten again.

None of all this directly affected the MacGregors, of course. Save to push up the price of cattle, at which they made no complaint. The new wing of Glengyle House was completed and ready for occupation by Christmas – and a fine house-warming it got. And the Heir of Glengyle was born a month later, and christened Ian, amidst the rejoicings of the entire clan. Life was good for Gregor and Mary, and war could well stay away from their hospitable door indefinitely.

But that indefatigable courier and herald of fate, Colonel Nathaniel Hooke, was not to be balked. He arrived at Inversnaid and Glen Gyle again, new come from France, in late February. And this time he brought definite tidings and instructions. All – or almost all – was settled. King James would sail at the end of March or beginning of April. The fleet was already assembling at Dunkirk, some thirty frigates and transports, with five great men-o'-war as escort. Five thousand regular troops were being detached and mustered, equipped with all necessary artillery, ammunition and supplies. Even money was forthcoming. At last Louis, with the effects of Marlborough's successes at Ramillies beginning to pinch, perceived the value of a diversion in Scotland. All now would be well.

There was work for Gregor, at last. Work which could nowise be put off or shirked. The clans had to be informed and assembled. And there was no great surplus of time for the business. In four or five weeks James would be sailing.

So Gregor Ghlun Dubh, sighing, kissed his wife and baby farewell, accoutred himself with targe, claymore, pistols and dirk, and rode away northwards, not on his fine black charger, along with Rob Roy and the other MacGregor notables.

He had managed a longer honeymoon than most – but it was over now.

*   *   *

As usual, the MacGregors were acting as couriers – for none could cover the difficult upheaved country so swiftly as they. And it was the very worst time of the year for such travelling, with the snows beginning to melt on all the mountains, every stream a raging torrent, every valley flooded, and every flat a quagmire. Fords were lost beneath swirling yellow spates, fallen trees and landslides jammed the passes, soft and sodden snowfields cloaked the heights. In driving chill rainstorms, never warm or dry by day and seldom by night, the Gregorach rode, fanning out north and west. And none who saw them envied them their task.

Rob went to the west, but Gregor proceeded right up the centre of the country, through Breadalbane, Atholl, Badenoch, the Great Glen and beyond, calling on the Robertsons, the Macphersons, the Cattanachs, his old friend MacAlpin Grant of Rothiemurchus, the Macintoshes, Glengarry's MacDonnells, the Invermoriston Grants and up as far as the Chisholm in Strathglass. Turning south again, he skirted the country of the Frasers, who were refusing to come out, and the main mass of Clan Grant, but warned the Gordons, with the help of the fiery Glenbucket, and reached the Farquharsons at the head of Dee. Then south through the long empty gut of Glen Tilt, and into Atholl again. He was home four weeks to a day after leaving, weary, exhausted almost, and a deal thinner than when he had set out. He was not the first home, but not the last. One by one the Gregorach messengers returned – though Rob Roy himself, with the farthest to go and sea passages to make amongst the islands, still was absent.

All had the same tale to tell. The clans would rise, assuredly – were now rising. But few, if any, could be mustered before the beginning of May, whatever the Lowland forces might be able to do. Sheer geography and climatic conditions prohibited. Word to that effect was dispatched forthwith to Colonel Hooke at his headquarters in Fife.

The messenger returned from Fife on the same day that Rob Roy got back from the north-west. He brought a peculiar reply from Hooke, for the Captain of Clan Alpine. It was to the effect that it did not matter now that the clans would be delayed in their assembling. The expedition had indeed set sail, but it had turned about and gone back to Dunkirk. King James had contracted the measles. The attempt was postponed.

That silenced even the eloquent Gregorach.

*   *   *

Rob Roy, tired as he was, made one of his famed lightning journeys thereafter, across Stirlingshire and Kinross to Fife this time. There he delivered heated representations to

Colonel Hooke – practically an ultimatum, in fact. The Colonel assured him that all would yet be well; that this was only a very temporary set-back. The expedition would sail again later. A month's delay would do no great harm – and it did give time for the clans to gather. Rob repeated his warning, reinforcing it with some plain speaking and unpalatable reminders. The other promised to transmit the gist of it all to France forthwith.

Rob returned to his own place, and the MacGregors began to gather, in earnest.

There was a great deal to be done in the assembling and equipping and organising of some hundreds of armed men – as well as in arranging for the everyday life of the rest of the clan to continue during the absence of the bulk of its man-power. A chieftain was the father of his people, to some extent, as well as their ruler and magistrate. Gregor was kept very busy.

Mary watched all the preparations with a heavy heart. But she took Christian MacGregor as her model, and sought to be as good a warrior's wife as the other was a mother.

CHAPTER SIXTEEN

MORE than five hundred men were standing to arms in the valleys of the Snaid, the Gyle and in all the side glens of Balquhidder. The smell of roasting beef hung over all, with the smoke of the cooking fires, perpetually, and the sound of the pipes never ceased from morn till midnight. Races, trials of strength, feats of endurance, and the less reputable diversions of fighting-men with nothing to do, went on with unremitting vigour. It was an awesome thought to consider that similar conditions would apply in a goodly percentage of the glens of all the Highlands.

It was May 16th, and the climax of long preparations was at hand. His Majesty, recovered, had set sail. The expedition was encountering gales and contrary winds, and was being shadowed by the English Fleet under Admiral Byng. But it was definitely on its way, at long last. Thirty-six sail all told. All this information had just come by swiftest relays of dispatch-riders from London to Queen Anne's Commander-in-Chief in Scotland, the Earl of Leven – from whose entourage a judiciously placed Jacobite promptly passed it on to Colonel Hooke across the Forth.

Such was the situation that blowy May day of sun and shadow and scudding clouds when Hooke himself arrived at Inversnaid, in haste and some agitation for that sombre man. He was seeking Rob Roy, found him not, and was directed on to Glen Gyle, where Rob and Gregor were hard at work on organisation and supply. He found them, amidst the cheerful clamour of an armed camp, superintending the serious business of doling out the by no means plentiful powder and ball.

'There you are, MacGregor! I am thankful to have run you to earth,' he cried. 'You are plaguey inaccessible folk.'

'We are where God put us,' Rob answered mildly. And then in a different tone of voice, almost menacing, 'You are not come to tell us, Colonel, once more, that . . . ?'

'No, no,' the other assured hurriedly. 'All is well with the expedition. Though these thrice-damned winds from the north-west will hold it up. Always the Stewarts have bad weather! No – it is not that that brings me. I need your help again, MacGregor – the cause needs your help. Word has just reached me, through my Lord of Breadalbane, of a piece of folly which must be undone, and quickly. Two French officers on a special mission to MacDonald of Sleat and the Laird of MacLeod have been landed by some rascally sailing-master in Lorne, of all places.'

'Lorne!' Rob exclaimed. 'Amongst the Campbells? In the heart of Argyll's country?'

'Exactly. Whether by accident, wretched navigation, or evil design, I know not. But according to Breadalbane's information, they have been put ashore below the Oban somewhere, a hundred miles south of their destination in Skye. And they must be rescued, at all costs.'

'*All* costs, Colonel?' Rob repeated. 'Are they so important, these two Frenchmen?'

'They are,' the other nodded decidedly. 'Not so much the men themselves, perhaps, as what they have with them. I knew of their mission – and it is an important one, and must be completed.' Hooke lowered his voice a little. 'You will know how MacDonald of Sleat has gone back on his word, given at Kinloch Rannoch, and is not now rising? Some petty jealousy is behind it, I understand, with ClanRanald. But the effect is serious. He is the most powerful figure in Skye, and he is affecting others. The MacKinnon is hesitating. The Macleans to the south are unhappy at leaving all those MacDonalds at large behind them, with their territories unprotected. Others too. You know how it is.'

Rob knew all this only too well, being not long returned from the north-west, where he had done his best to improve this very situation. He nodded. 'What could the Frenchmen do that I could not?' he wondered.

'That is the point,' Hooke declared grimly. 'They carry, h'm, inducements, these two. Honours, from both James and Louis, for Sleat and for the Laird of MacLeod, who has always been a waverer. The price of being difficult! But much worse – money. Many hundreds of gold *louis*. Money that can ill be spared. Money that we need here. When I was in France I advised strongly against this sending of money. But others have known better. If that gold falls into Campbell hands . . . !'

He did not require to stress his point. Gregor and his uncle exchanged glances.

'Moreover,' Hooke went on, 'and perhaps as serious – these two are colonels straight from Matignon's staff. They know his plans – *our* plans. If they were to talk – were *made* to talk . . . !'

'Yes,' Rob nodded. 'This was an ill landing indeed. South of the Oban, you say?'

'Yes. At a place called Minard, on Loch Feochan, Bread-albane's message said.'

'So Breadalbane is still with us!' Gregor commented. 'I had scarcely expected as much!'

The Colonel glanced at him sharply. 'One can perhaps be over-suspicious, Glengyle,' he reproved. 'And his lordship is your kinsman.'

Gregor pulled a face, but held his tongue.

Hooke turned to Rob Roy. 'Will you go to Lorne at once, then, MacGregor, rescue these Frenchmen and put them on the right road to Skye?'

'Me?' Surprised, Rob stared. 'Man, myself I have a clan to lead, in war. I will be sending somebody to find them, never fear. But not my own self.'

'Yes,' the other insisted, in his dour sober fashion. 'You it is that should go. And I suggest that you take young Glengyle here with you. You are one of the few men who could pass through Argyll's country unmolested. Your mother was a Campbell. So was Glengyle's. You know the Campbell lairds – and I have heard you say that you have had dealings occasionally with the Duke himself. And there requires to be two of you. You may well have to separate. One may have to use guile on the Campbells while the other deals with the Frenchmen.' He smiled then, his wintry smile. 'There are not many fitted to trade guile with Campbells!'

'But the clan ... ?' Gregor protested. 'We are captain and lieutenant of our forces.'

'The clan will not suffer,' Hooke assured. 'I know your value to our cause. You will be back before any of your people are required. There will be no action for the Highland forces for two weeks yet, at the least. Here is how it is planned. The expedition will sail up the Forth to Edinburgh. Or Leith. His Majesty will land there, about a week from now. It was to have been sooner, but these contrary winds are causing delay. I have it from a reliable source close to General Lord Leven that he does not believe that he can hold Edinburgh if the King lands. He will abandon it, if there is a landing, leaving only the Castle defended, and retire on Stirling. We want him to do that. Once the Capital is ours, and His Majesty in Holyroodhouse, we have achieved the equivalent of a notable victory. So Leven must not fear to retire on Stirling. There must be no demonstration of strength in these parts, threatening Stirling, *before* he gets there. You understand ? Even Perth must not seem to be threatened too soon by our forces. Once the Government troops are safely concentrated at Stirling, then the clans may show themselves. Not till then. Is that clear, now ? So your MacGregors will not be into action for two weeks yet, at the soonest – ample time for you to get back from Lorne.'

After that there was no more to be said. All that Hooke had asserted about the unique suitability of Rob Roy and his nephew for any difficult mission into Campbell country was entirely true. And so long as there was no danger of them failing their clansmen, or missing any of the first heady excitement of the rising, they were both quite happy to be off on a lively-sounding jaunt of this sort, foot-loose, pitting their wits against the Campbells and leaving all this humdrum business of equipping and organising to others. They could hand it all over very nicely to Cousin John of Corryarklet, Cousin Dougal of Comar, Cousin Alastair of Corryheichen and the rest. Which would undoubtedly be very good for the said cousins.

So be it, then.

*   *   *

With only Rob's MacAlastair in attendance, Gregor and his uncle rode off early the next morning, westwards over into Glen Falloch, and still westwards, through the high pass of the Lairig Arnan to narrow Glen Fyne. Already they were in Campbell country here, and avoiding the populated lower reaches of the valley where it ran down to the head of the loch – the Duke of Argyll's own loch, with Inveraray Castle itself a bare dozen miles away – they got out of the glen as quickly as possible by climbing up to a lofty saddle over a shoulder of mighty Ben Buie, and so down by winding deer-paths through wet peat-hag country into the head of Glen Shira. Twenty rough miles covered, they rested their mounts for a little, hidden amongst the birches above the lonely farm-place of Benbuie in the valley, with the cuckoos calling from all the hillsides around. By a coincidence, that house down there was one in which Rob Roy himself was to find sanctuary, with his family, many years hence. Then on, over another range, to upper Glen Aray, and into the welter of low brown hills and bleak lochans and bogs beyond that flanked the great inland barrier of Loch Awe.

All this way the travellers had been deliberately keeping to high ground and unfrequented places, and had seen no more than an occasional upland shieling and a herd or two pasturing the hill cattle. But now they were forced to come down into low-lying and populous country. Loch Awe, stretching across their path for twenty-five miles, had either to be crossed or circumnavigated – and along its shores quite a proportion of Clan Campbell dwelt. There was no avoiding them. Rob chose to head for the little clachan of Boat of Ballimeanach, one of the many places where there was a ferry to cross the loch, but which was next to unique in having no laird's house in its vicinity. Argyll and Lorne were thicker with lairds, great and small, than anywhere else in the Highlands, the Campbells tending that way.

The travellers routed out the ferryman from his house with no sort of modesty or reserve. 'Ho! The boat!' Rob Roy shouted. 'Ho, there – the boat, I say. In the name of *MacCailean Mor* – on the Duke's business! Rascal – the boat, quickly! I pay well.' That was the way to talk to Campbells.

The ferryman came out promptly enough to that – even if he seemed somewhat surprised to note the red MacGregor tartans. He had to use his larger boat, apparently, since there were garrons to transport – which meant that he must go for a couple of men to help pull the sweeps. Rob sent Mac-Alastair with him, on this errand, just for safety's sake.

They were put across the mile of the loch in the wide old

flat-bottomed scow, with no undue delay, by a frankly inquisitive crew. Rob, far from attempting to hide his identity, boasted of it, talked largely of his closeness to Red John of the Battles, Duke of Argyll, and of the importance of his present mission – sufficiently so to embarrass Gregor, who felt that even to Campbells this was unseemly. But his uncle always knew what he was doing – and would nowise heed any frowns and tut-tutting anyway. He most handsomely paid off the ferrymen at the farther side, below the hanging woods of Inverinan. Then, heading as though for Inverinan House till the trees hid them, they turned abruptly southwards and then west to ride at all speed into the vast wilderness of little hills that lay between Loch Awe and the sea.

They slept the night in the heather, by a sad and lonely lochan, where the oyster-catchers piped and the curlews called and called inconsolably.

The next day, with the salt tang to the hill air that heralded the ocean, they spent their time working by devious ways over towards the green Minard peninsula that jutted into the Firth of Lorne between Loch Feochan and the Sound of Kerrera, seeking to avoid the valleys and all haunts of men. By late afternoon they were looking out over the wide blue waters of the Firth to the far mountains of Mull. And nearer at hand, below them, the winding rocky-shored inlet of Loch Feochan probed the valley. At its square head, amongst the flats and meadows of the River Nell, lay the Kirkton of Kilmore. Away at the mouth of the sea-loch, off the Point of Minard, according to Breadalbane's message, the French ship had set ashore its unfortunate passengers. No ship showed there now, at any rate, nor anywhere on the seascape.

There was an inn down there at Kilmore – but also, unfortunately, nearby was the castle of Campbell of Lochnell, a prominent chieftain of Clan Diarmid, and still nearer the lesser house of Campbell of Glenfeochan. They could wait till darkness, and then slip across the haughlands around the head of the loch, amongst the croft-houses, and so on to the Minard peninsula. On the other hand, if information was to be gained, that inn at Kilmore would be an apt place to gain it, sitting at the base of the peninsula as it did. Rob decided that information was necessary.

Halting in a hollow of the heather, Rob effected a transformation. Doffing his weapons, tartans, doublet and fine bonnet, he drew out from a bundle of gear that his garron carried the patched and dingy clothing of a travelling packman – hodden breeches, torn hose, grimy shirt, and stained and ragged plaid of indeterminate check. A pack too, which he stuffed with heather. All this he donned with practised ease, and told his two companions to wait for him there. Gregor thought that he might have sent MacAlastair about this business, but Rob would have none of it. So, thus garbed, the Captain of Clan Alpine went off downhill long-strided, pack over his shoulder. But it might have been observed that, long before he reached the inn in the Kirk-ton, he was limping heavily and with a stoop to his enormous shoulders like a dog scraping a pot. Going thus, his long arms reached almost to his ankles, and perforce he had to keep them tucked away in the dirty folds of the tattered plaid.

It was hours later, dusk indeed, and Gregor was not only impatient but getting anxious – unnatural as it might seem to be anxious about Rob Roy MacGregor – before his uncle came back uphill, actually singing, through the drizzling chill rain that had set in on the everlasting north-westerly wind. He was in excellent form. Apparently the Campbell innkeeper dispensed refreshment worthy of better folk. Which was a matter of only academic interest to one who had sat shivering in wet heather for the intervening hours.

But Rob was full of information, as well as good cheer. There was no need to go over to the peninsula and away down to Minard, he revealed. The Frenchmen had been captured, and were even now on their way, under guard, to the Duke's castle at Inveraray. *Finis coronat opus!*

The innkeeper had not required overmuch prompting, apparently – in fact, he had been agog with news. The ship had been sighted off the point six days before, evidently a foreigner, and it had lain offshore in the mouth of the loch till nightfall – but had been gone by the morning. It was obvious that somebody had been landed. Campbell of Lochnell, who was a captain of one of the Independent Militia Companies, had instituted a search – and sure enough, five Frenchmen had been discovered, two days later, hiding in a deserted croft-house some miles to the north. Or at least two French officers, two servants and some sort of Irishman. Jacobite agents, for certain. They had been taken and locked up in Lochnell Castle. And only this same morning Lochnell had set out with them for Inveraray, passing that very inn *en route*.

Gregor sighed. 'We might have known it!' he said. 'What else should we have expected? And the money?'

'There was no mention of money,' Rob told him. 'And I could not be asking.'

With Rob dressed in his own clothes again, they set off southwards through the half-dark of a wet May night.

*   *   *

Wrapped in their plaids, they followed the road that ran south, from the head of one dark sea-loch, over high ground to the head of the next, and so on, by Kilninver and Kilmelfort and Craignish. It was a populous settled country, interspersed with ribs of low rocky hills, but they rode openly through the night, unchallenged save by the occasional dog from croft or farmstead. Rob sang cheerfully but grievously out of tune – till Gregor was forced out of sheer aesthetic integrity to put him right with his own more melodious voice, and once started quite forgot to stop.

They were making for Ardmoine, on Loch Craignish. Campbell of Ardmoine was father-in-law to Lochnell, and since the place lay almost exactly half-way to Inveraray, a moderate day's journey, and just before the track thither cut away from the drove road and through the rough hills, it could be taken as more than probable that the party would be halting there for the night. It was likely enough to take a chance on, at any rate.

The trio came to the place in the darkest part of a May night – an hour or so before the dawn. But even so, the rain having stopped, there was light enough to distinguish the tall stone house with its high chimney-stacks and pepper-box turrets, set on its own little grassy promontory jutting into the wan mystery of Loch Craignish. No lamplight showed about the house or its vicinity.

MacAlastair, on foot, was dispatched to spy out the land – and to be reasonably quick about it, for time was not un-limited, with dawn in an hour. He slipped away soundless – and his eventual returning was like a shadow materialising beside them. Briefly, factually, utterly unemotional as ever, he declared what he had discovered. Fifteen horses were tethered in the stableyard at the back of the house. Men were asleep in the stables themselves – how many he did not know. The doors of the big house seemed to be locked or barred. There was no guard or sentry set, that he had seen.

'Why should there be, whatever?' Rob demanded. 'They are safe in the heart of their own Campbell country – and MacCailean Mor rules with a sure hand. What need they of sentries? But Lochnell and his captives are here, for sure. Fifteen horses? Five for the prisoners. Lochnell himself and nine of an escort. Lochnell and the two French officers and this Irishman at least will be in the house. The others in the stables. It is our task to get them out. How think you it is to be done, Greg?'

'The stabling – is it roofed with thatch?' Gregor asked MacAlastair.

'Aha – your mind runs yet on firing stables, boy!' Rob exclaimed.

'Why not? It has proved profitable hitherto, has it not? A fire in the stable will open Ardmoine's door, I think.'

'Very well so,' his uncle agreed – who had thought along similar lines himself. 'And when it opens, we slip within. The stable roof will be of thatch, surely – even Campbells will not slate their stables, I think. But it will be damp. It may need assistance in its burning.' He sighed, and turning, rooted about amongst his gear, to produce a bottle that the others had not seen hitherto. 'A pity to be wasting good whisky – but this will help, maybe. With some hay.' Rob scratched his red-bearded chin. 'If you were Lochnell – which God forbid – what would you do with all that money, overnight, in another man's house ?'

Gregor, for whom money had less importance than sundry other commodities, shrugged. 'Lock it up somewhere, I suppose ?'

His uncle raised an eyebrow. 'So ? I am thinking that would be . . . disrespectful! Myself, I would take it to bed with me – closer than any wife! And the man is a Campbell, mind you! Now – have we all got flint and tinder . . . ?'

Their several duties were swiftly rehearsed. The garrons would be left here. They would all take a hand at the fire-raising, but MacAlastair would be left to make the most of it, and if necessary shout the alarm when all was well alight. He would then see that the tethered horses were loosed and stampeded if possible – making sure that he kept a grip on three or four of them, to bring up here. In the dark and confusion it was to be hoped that he would pass as one of Ardmoine's men to Lochnell's people, and vice versa. Meanwhile, Rob and his nephew would move in close under the walls of the big house near the back entrance, and endeavour to slip inside once the door was opened. What happened thereafter would be dictated by circumstances.

MacAlastair leading, the trio moved quietly down across the cattle-dotted rough pasture, and through the belt of shelter trees that backed house, farmery and gardens. A few branches of dead pine picked up on the way would much assist their fire. They came without hindrance to the rear of the range of stabling and byres, which formed half a square at the landward and northern side of the tall old house. The roofing was thatch, sure enough – old reeds from the water-meadows. The walls were of stone, save for one corner, presumably an addition, where they were composed of birch planking. From the somewhat musty smell that issued from between the cracks, last season's bog-hay had been stored therein. Rob changed that smell for the better, by pouring whisky against the timbers and on to tufts of hay that projected. The reed thatching, save for the topmost layer, seemed to be as dry as their tinder.

The three men went to work with flint and steel, Gregor taking the middle of the range, using pine clusters to aid him, and MacAlastair working at the farther corner.

All that was needful was done in a few seconds. With the materials so highly inflammable there was no need for coaxing or tending – and the strong wind at last proved advantageous. As the dry reeds began to crackle noticeably, Gregor and Rob left it all, and hurried round to the front.

A small cobbled yard lay between the stabling and the rear wall of the house. The two MacGregors ran across this, aware of the stirring of tethered horses, to fetch up crouching on either side of the only back door. They were well enough there for the moment, in the dark – but whenever that thatch really blazed up, they were bound to stand revealed in the glare. Rob darted out again, over to the nearest of the horses, slashed its tether with his dirk, and led the beast back to beside his nephew, its hooves sounding painfully loud in that hollow place.

'We can crouch behind this,' he panted. 'Not attract much attention here. There will be confusion, I think. . . . '

He was right about that, at any rate. The flames were licking up from four or five points now, highest at Rob's plank building. Suddenly, with a distinct *whoosh*, this hay store turned itself into a blazing beacon, however, lighting up the entire scene in a vivid orange glare. Dense clouds of smoke were now seen to be pouring out from the thatch everywhere. Simultaneously, shouts, howls, curses and coughing rang out. Horses whinnied and began to sidle and stamp their hooves. Men came stumbling out into the yard, yelling. Sparks, blown on the wind, came flying over. Gregor had to hold in their covering horse, tightly.

Now the yard was a pandemonium of excited men and frightened horses, of wildly leaping shadows, billowing smoke, and soaring flaming fragments. And noise. For how much of it all MacAlastair was responsible was not clear.

Nothing was clear. Rob Roy, eyes streaming, ran to the closed door of the house, banging thereon with his open hands.

'Fire! Fire!' he shouted, his voice choking, affected by the smoke. 'Fire!' And went on banging.

They had not long to wait. Pounding footsteps preceding the sounds of bolts being drawn gave Rob warning, in time for him to leap back from the doorway to Gregor's side. Then the door was thrown open and two men came running out, one barefooted and struggling into a coat, the other booted but pulling up his breeches as he ran. They paused only for a moment at the sight that met their eyes. Then the booted man went plunging out into the mêlée, while the other turned back within, shouting.

The entire roof of the steading was now alight from end to end, a roaring inferno fanned by the breeze. The heat was intense, even over where the hiding men crouched. They had much ado to keep their horse held. The other beasts seemed largely to have got away from the yard by this time, either having been loosed or having dragged their tethers. In the rolling smoke and cavorting shadows it was difficult to distinguish details – especially with flooding eyes.

Three more men came running out from the house, variously garbed, and then a fourth. A woman also appeared in the doorway, wrapped in a plaid, and screeching. Rob touched Gregor's arm, and nodded.

Leaving the rearing horse to its own devices, the two of them hurried to the door. They brushed past the staring squawking woman without a word – and she did not so much as spare a glance for them. There was a long passage ahead of them, with doors opening off it, lit only by the fitful glare from behind them. Hands on dirks, they dashed along this. At the far end it opened out into a larger hallway. As they turned into this, Rob, in front, collided with another man hurrying in the opposite direction.

'Devil scald you – out of my way, fool!' this individual cried. 'What hell's work is this ?' His was the angry voice of authority. He seemed to be an elderly man, and portly. Probably the master of the house himself.

Rob took a chance. 'Lochnell?' he shouted. 'Where is Lochnell?'

'Damnation – if he's not out already, he will be up in his room!' The other gestured vaguely behind him, and up. Dimly the foot of a stairway could be perceived at his back.

'The prisoners,' Rob cried then. 'We must look to them. Where are they . . . ?'

But the laird, if such he was, was hastening on along the passage, and did not answer.

Rob hesitated for only a moment. 'Come,' he jerked, to Gregor, and led the way to the stair foot.

Side by side, three or four steps at a time, the MacGregors raced up the worn stone treads of the winding turnpike stair, slipping and stumbling a little in the darkness. But at the first-floor landing there was light, partly from a window in a passage that must face the rear of the house, whence a ruddy glow radiated, and partly from a lamp held up by an elderly woman in a nightdress who stood within an open doorway, twittering and exclaiming, one hand on her thin bosom, grey hair about her shoulders. There were two other doors on this landing, one of which also stood open.

Rob sought to moderate the manner of their approach. 'Ma'am,' he cried. 'It is the stables, just. It will be all right. Where is Lochnell?'

The lady only mouthed and gulped, the lamp swaying in her hand.

Almost certainly this would be the Lady Ardmoine. The chances were that her husband had come out of the same bedroom whose doorway she now filled. These, on this first floor, would be the principal bedrooms of the house. That other that stood open, then, might well be that of her son-in-law, Lochnell. 'Is that Lochnell's room?' he demanded, pointing.

She nodded.

Lochnell was downstairs, then – out at the fire, no doubt.

211

'The prisoners, Ma'am,' he questioned her, now. 'We must see to the Frenchmen. Where are they?'

'Mercy on us – what's to befall us?' the lady got out. 'Dear God – is the house afire? Am I to be left to be burned . . . ?'

'No, no. You are fine, Ma'am – just fine,' the soft-hearted Gregor assured. 'There is no danger, whatever. But the Frenchmen. We must see that they are safe. Where are they, at all?'

'The Frenchies? They are in the dairy – locked in the dairy,' she gasped. 'But what's to become of us all . . . ?'

'Wheesht you!' Rob cried. 'Down to the dairy, Greg! I'll be with you in a little.' And he ran into the room indicated as Lochnell's.

Leaving the lady to wail and appeal to her Maker, Gregor sprang down the stairs again.

The dairy – that would be to the rear of the house, for sure? Probably along that very passage by which they had first entered. One of those doors? Which one? As they had come along, there had seemed to be not a few. . . .

Pounding down the passage again, fairly well lit now by the lurid glare, Gregor halted at the first door. It opened to his touch. All was dark within. There was a smell of fish. And something else? Hams. A larder, only? No hint of life or movement within. He backed out.

A man was coming hurrying along the stone-flagged passage from the open back door. Gregor paused, hand ready on dirk. But the fellow brushed past, intent on his own errand, bawling something about pails and buckets.

Gregor was moving on relievedly, when swiftly his mind reacted. 'See, you,' he called after the man. 'The dairy! There will be pails in the dairy, man. That's the place – the dairy.'

The other halted, and turned back. 'Hech, hech – that is so, yes. The dairy, yes. But, *dia* – the Frenchies are in there. . . . '

'Never care!' Gregor cried. 'First things first, whatever! *I'll* look after the Frenchies for you.' He drew his claymore with a flourish. 'They'll not be getting past this! Quick, man.'

The other, an undersized runt of a man, undoubtedly a house gillie, was evidently used to receiving authoritative orders, and reacted unquestioningly to the tone of voice. Pushing past down the passage again, he stopped at the second door on the other side, and standing on tiptoe sought to reach a shelf above the lintel. Promptly Gregor was after him, and feeling along the ledge, grabbed a large key that lay there. He handed it to the little man. 'Quickly, now,' he commanded.

But the other paused doubtfully, the key in the lock. Not because of Gregor, it seemed, but on account of the noise that was coming out from behind that door. Fists were obviously beating against the panels, and shouts in French and English could be made out.

'Och, heed them not,' Gregor exclaimed impatiently. 'We'll soon quieten them. They are not armed, at all. They will not argue with my steel! Pails we must have.' And pushing the other aside, he turned the key, and kicked open the door.

There seemed to be but three men within – whose shouts died on them as they drew back before the blood-red gleam of firelight on a naked sword.

'*Bon chance, messieurs!*' Gregor cried. '*C'est bon. Vive le roi Jacques! Vive le Grand Monarque!*' That was the best that he could do at short notice. In English, which was probably as unintelligible to the gillie, he went on. 'Do exactly what I am telling you. I am your friend. You understand. Friend. *Ami.* This man wants pails. *Seau. Buquet.* Pails to put out the fire that we have started. Let him get them quickly. Then we shall be quit of him, whatever. *Comprenez?*'

'Indade yes. Shure, sir,' a rich Irish brogue assured him. 'Mary-Mother and all the Saints be praised! An honest Christian. . . . '

'Quiet!' Gregor rapped. And turning to the wondering gillie, he spoke in the Gaelic. 'Quick – the pails, man. I have

213

warned these wretches. They will not challenge my sword. Get you the pails.'

In the ruddy uncertain glow that illuminated the chamber from a small high-set window barred with ironwork, it was to be seen that the place was equipped with stone shelves furnished with many bowls and pails and churns, like the dairy of any other large house. The little man scurried forward, grabbed two of the pails and edged out warily.

'Haste, you,' Gregor urged him. 'I will bring more. These Frenchies are safe enough with me. . . . '

'The door . . . ?' the gillie panted.

'I will lock it behind me,' he was assured.

The little man ran off down the passage, his pails clanking. Swiftly Gregor swung on the captives. 'Take you pails too,' he directed. 'Coggies, bowls – anything. Anything to carry, see you. To seem to fight the fire. *Vite! Vite!* Then follow me.'

With considerable chatter and exclamation the two Frenchmen and the Irishman did as they were told, taking up receptacles, emptying the contents out of some where necessary. They seemed to Gregor to take an unconscionable time about it – and to make a deal more noise than was called for. He had sheathed his sword and got himself a large earthenware jug. Impatiently he fretted at the door.

'*Diabhol!*' he cursed, suddenly. Somebody was coming down the passage again. Had he been seen, standing in this doorway? Was it best to slam the door shut on them, himself included? The key was still in the lock. No time to take it out now. He would be a prisoner himself that way. . . .

Then, with relief, he recognised something familiar in the shape of the approaching man. It was Rob, stooping a little, carrying something fairly bulky and heavy under his plaid apparently.

'I have them here,' he called out. 'All ready. Carrying pails to put out the fire. Two French and an Irishman.'

'Good. Good.' Rob grunted. '*Dia* – this gold is heavy! Under Lochnell's bed, as I said! Man, I'm going to find dirk work difficult!'

'Damn the gold!' Gregor declared, forcefully. And in English, 'Come, you.'

Gregor leading, and Rob bringing up the rear, they hastened down the passage to the back door, clutching their various burdens. The worst of the fire was already over, with the blazing thatch fallen in at one or two points, but the clouds of smoke seemed but the denser. There was a murky hellish quality about the scene outside. But it was considerably more confused and obscure than when they had left it.

Peering, Gregor could make out only two or three vague figures amongst the eddying smoke clouds. It was difficult to be sure, but it seemed that there was more activity at the other end of the steading, the west end. A small wing jutted out there. Possibly they were trying to save that. There were no horses to be seen, now.

Strange as it might seem, it looked as though they were going to be able just to walk out of Ardmoine. Apart from the grievous fumid fog of smoke and the chaos occasioned thereby in the darkness, nobody seemed to be interested, in them or anything other than the fire. None of these people were regular soldiers, of course, just local militia, untrained and little disciplined. They had lived secure too long to compete adequately with MacGregors.

Scarcely crediting their good fortune, the five men slipped away, along the side of the house, round the corner of the steading to the east, and into the trees behind, seeking to swallow their coughing and choking, half-blinded by their streaming eyes. In the wood they deposited their pails and containers, amidst a considerable outburst of voluble French and accented English. But Rob Roy cut it short with crisp orders for silence and the saving of breath. It would be a long while yet before they could start to congratulate each other. There was much that could yet go wrong.

The validity of this warning was borne out all too soon. When they reached MacAlastair and the garrons, it was to find that he had been unable to retain a hold on more than two of the Campbell horses in the stampede – and of these one had lamed itself in the panic. In his sour cryptic way the gillie was apologetic – only to Rob, of course. The fire had gone too fast for him, and most of the beasts had broken their fetters and bolted before he had got round to them. Only these . . .

The problem before them now required no emphasising. There were five horses, one of them lame, for six men. And they would have to ride far and fast, for the entire country would be raised against them before they were many hours older. Argyll and Lorne would be buzzing like two nests of angry wasps, and it would take fast movement and sound hillcraft to avoid being stung.

Rob wasted no time in making up his mind. Quick decisions were a speciality of his, anyhow. First things had to come first. That was almost a MacGregor motto. Getting the two French colonels safely on their way to Skye was his prime task and major responsibility. The Irishman, who it seemed was only a sort of guide and interpreter – and a poor guide at that, judging by results – must take his chance. MacAlastair could take him, and the lame horse, and seek to get back to MacGregor country as best he could. The rest of them would head north with all speed on the four beasts.

Gregor was sorry enough for the Irishman to plead for him, in Gaelic. But his uncle was adamant. That was the way that causes were lost. To hold together would mean that they must go at the pace of the slowest. They would never get the Frenchmen out of Lorne that way. It was going to be no joke, as it was. Besides, MacAlastair and the Irishman would no doubt do very well on their own, anyway. They would probably be best to abandon the horse, and disguise themselves as a pair of wandering masterless men. He would leave them his packman's gear. Taking their time, keeping to the high ground, and living off the country, they would get back to Loch Lomond-side safely enough, in due course. MacAlastair had had harder tasks than that to perform in his day!

The gillie nodded terse confirmation of that.

So it was accepted, as all Rob Roy's decisions were apt to

be accepted, and the little company separated there and then, the French officers distinctly bewildered and vocal, but the Irishman less concerned than might have been expected when informed that his destination lay less than fifty miles away, as the crow flew, whereas the others had four times that amount of ground to cover.

Without ceremony or more than the briefest leave-taking, Rob Roy led his remaining three companions away at a brisk pace northwards. He had hung the two heavy leather bags of gold *louis* behind him on his own garron.

CHAPTER SEVENTEEN

THEY did not continue along the north-going road down which they had come, but quickly cut off north-eastwards up Glen Doin, following the Barbreck Burn. Ten miles or so up there lay Loch Avich, embosomed amongst its wilderness of low identical hills – and it was into that brown labyrinth that Rob would have them before the sun was fully risen.

His plan was to head north by east, travelling only by night and hiding by day, seeking to leave Campbell country, via Glen Etive, for the fastnesses of Glen Coe. It was necessary to do more than merely win out of Lorne and the Campbell territory; he had to find somebody who was actually anti-Campbell, and prepared to work actively against that powerful clan – and most of the Campbells' neighbours undoubtedly would not be prepared to do that. But the MacDonalds of Glen Coe were different from others. The iron had entered their souls. MacIan, their young chief, would do anything in his power to hurt the people who had slain his father and massacred his clansmen fifteen years previously. Moreover, with his vessels on Loch

Leven, with access to the sea, he could ship out the two Frenchmen direct to Skye. And, of course, he was a Jacobite.

Glen Coe it should be, then. But that savage valley lay a long way from Glen Doin and Craignish – a hundred miles by the roundabout routes that fugitives must take to avoid the populous Campbell glens and the great water barriers of Lochs Awe and Etive, a hundred weary miles of benighted heather and peat-hag, of rock and scree and flood. A weary wary journey, indeed.

It would be a weariness, too, to seek to set down the record of their patient circuitous seemingly endless travels, by the hills of Kilchrenan, the Sior Loch, Glen Nant and the Pass of Brander, by the high ridges of mighty Cruachan and its sisters, by the upper reaches of Glen Kinglass and the wild peaks of the Starav range and into Glen Etive. And so, at last, over the grim but happy Pass of the Lairig Gartain, out of the Campbell lands and into Glen Coe of the Mac-Donalds. Let it suffice to say that it took them five nights of most difficult heart-breaking marching and counter-march-ing, made possible only by the MacGregors' masterly hill-craft and Rob Roy's uncanny sense of direction, to reach MacIan's new-built house down beside the weed-grown shores of long Loch Leven – five nights of marching and five days of hiding, wherein they grew to know each other tolerably well, wherein the MacGregors grew to like and appreciate the laughing and debonair Colonel de Cloquet, and to utterly loathe and abominate the stiff and complain-ing Colonel Robinet – and wherein Gregor came to admire his uncle's abilities more than ever he had done. Five days and nights in which all Lorne and Argyll were looking for them, all the powers of the Duke of Argyll and his brother the Earl of Islay, Lord Justice-General, were mobilised against them, and in which never once was their presence revealed to their enemies.

So much for *MacCailean Mor*, Red John of the Battles, lately gazetted Major-General of Her Majesty's Forces.

On the 23rd of May, then, Rob Roy MacGregor handed over his two charges to MacIan MacDonald of Glencoe, who accepted them warmly and promised to have them delivered safely by sea within the week to his fellow-clansman in Skye, Sir Donald of Sleat.

The parting, and the close of the entire satisfactory mission, was marred by one brief incident. Rob would not hear of stopping overnight with MacIan, but insisted on riding away south again forthwith, by the Moor of Rannoch and Glen Orchy, claiming overlong absence from his clan as it was. In the end, in so much of a hurry to be off was he, that the Frenchmen had to come dashing out of MacIan's house after him.

'*Monsieur* – the gold!' Colonel Robinet cried. '*Mon dieu* – you forget the gold!'

Rob Roy stroked his beard, but shook his head. 'No, *mon Colonel* – I do not forget. But the gold will be safer with me than with you, I think, in this unchancy Scotland of ours. *I* shall look after your *louis-d'ors*.'

'*Mais, non! Ma foi* – *ce n'est pas possible. Il est* . . . the gold, it is *essentiel, de la dernière importance!* To . . . to our mission. It is the most necessary that you give the gold to me.'

'I deem it otherwise, *monsieur*. And I think that I know the situation best, see you. The gold will be safe with me.'

'*Non, non.* The gold, it is for me to give! It is not your gold. *Nom de Dieu* . . . !'

'It is not *your* gold, Colonel. It is King James's gold – Scotland's gold. And here, in this part of Scotland, *I* decide what is best for King James's cause, whatever!'

'But surely, Monsieur MacGregor,' the other colonel, de Cloquet, intervened. 'Our mission to Monsieur de MacDonald and Monsieur de MacLeod is *sans valeur*, valueless, without the gold . . . ?'

'Not so, my friend. If Sleat will not bring in his clan for honour's sake, he will not bring it in for gold, that is certain. And MacLeod will not fight anyhow. There is better work for the gold than that. I take it.'

'*Voleur! Brigand! Traître!*' Colonel Robinet shouted,

almost screamed. 'Miscreant – you shall suffer! *Parbleu* – you shall suffer . . . !'

'Sir!' Rob drew himself up on his travel-worn garron, thrusting forward his red-bearded chin. 'Those are no words to use to a Highland gentleman! Men have died for less! I leave you, sir – and I do not congratulate you on your manners or your wit. Good-day. And to you, de Cloquet – a pleasant journey, and good fortune.' And pulling round his mount's head, he kicked the beast into motion.

'*Dia* – I do not like this!' Gregor began unhappily. 'Might it not be best to . . . ?'

'Your opinion was not asked, boy!' Rob Roy snapped back at him. 'Come, you.' His garron broke into a canter.

Gregor looked at de Cloquet, sighed, shrugged wide shoulders, and rode after his uncle.

*   *   *

'That was not well done.' Gregor had taken a long time to come up with the older man, under the soaring smoking precipices that frowned down on dark Glen Coe – and he had been doing no little thinking in the interim. 'It ill became you,' he said.

His uncle turned to look at him. 'Still croaking, Greg?'

'I say that you should not have done it. That you have spoiled a good enterprise at the end of it.'

'Spoiled? I say crowned, rather, boy! The gold is the best of it, whatever!'

'I think otherwise.'

'Tcha! There speaks experience! Mature judgment! Glengyle – the man of the world!' Rob Roy laughed, loudly for him. 'Spare me more of your discernments, lad!'

Doggedly Gregor went on – though of all things he hated being thus laughed at. 'Nevertheless, you had no ease in the doing of it, your own self,' he averred. 'It was unseemly to leave MacIan so.' He looked sidelong at his companion. 'I believe that you intended this, from the first? To take the gold? That you were more interested in the gold than in the Frenchmen? Or the Irishman!'

'You are very free with your beliefs today, Greg,' Rob said. 'I did what Hooke laid it on me to do, did I not? And was not Hooke himself after saying that the money should never have been sent to Sleat? That it was needed here? MacDonald of Sleat would have put it in his chest, and that would have been the end of it, whatever.'

'And is it so certain, then, that MacGregor of Inversnaid will not be doing the same? Or with some of it?'

'*Diabhol!* This is too much!' his uncle cried. 'A truce to your puppy's yappings, sir! Remember to whom you speak, my God!'

'I had not forgotten,' the younger man said flatly. 'More's the pity. Nor have I forgotten that night at Rannoch, when we spoke of treason and of Breadalbane!' And he drew on his garron so that it dropped well behind Rob Roy's beast.

And thus the MacGregors rode southwards.

*   *   *

It was a silent journey that they made of it, across the boundless desolation of Rannoch Moor and down green Glen Orchy that had once been MacGregor but was now Campbell – but Breadalbane Campbell. They went discreetly still, avoiding men – for *MacCailean Mor's* arm was long – and certainly they went harder and faster than they need have done. And the barrier between them rode as fast as they did.

It was two days later, at evening of the 25th of May, when they reached home, and geography brought them to Glen Gyle first. And if it had been a silent ride, it was no less a silent reception that awaited them there. The great throng of warriors had gone from the glen – though the marks of their sojourn were everywhere evident. The women it was that greeted them, strainedly, Mary and the Lady Christian, with an unhappy Ian Beg in the background. No, the clan had not been moved to another area, they said. They had gone home – all of them. Home, just. The rising was over. King James had been – and gone. The clans were to disperse quietly to their homes. Orders from Colonel Hooke. Messengers were out, up and down the land, with the word to disperse. The King was on his way back to France. All was over.

Dumbfounded, Gregor looked from the women to his uncle. Rob's gaze was far away, but his clenched hairy fists were trembling.

'The fool!' he said softly. 'The poor weak ignoble faint-hearted fool!' It was not clear of whom he spoke – and his nephew did not question him. Then the older man's eyes narrowed, and his voice changed, notably. 'As well that we did not let go of that gold, boy,' he said. And smiled twistedly.

The Irishman had reached Inversnaid three days previously, with MacAlastair, and had been sent on to Fife.

CHAPTER EIGHTEEN

IT took two or three days, and the arrival of Colonel Nathaniel Hooke himself at Inversnaid, for the entire sorry story to emerge. Hooke came, as usual, seeking Rob's aid. An authoritative explanation of the fiasco must be got out to the clan chiefs if their loyalty was to be preserved. James Stewart still had need of the MacGregors' services, it seemed.

It was all the fault of the French Admiral the Count de Forbin, apparently. All the way north, in the face of those contrary winds, he had been nervous, with Byng's English squadron at his heels, lying off but never losing touch. He had feared a trap, outsailing, an attack whilst disembarking troops and materials. He was at odds with both King James and with Matignon the French military commander.

On the night of 23rd May the fleet reached the mouth of the Firth of Forth. The plan was for them to sail up the twenty miles or so to Leith, which they had reason to believe would not be defended against them, and there disembark. But de Forbin feared that once in the Forth estuary, Byng would bottle him up, that he would not get out again. He hove to off the Isle of May, in a fever of indecision, and only one frigate, which had missed the Admiral's signals in the darkness, sailed on westwards according to plan. This vessel duly arrived at Leith, found no opposition, landed a party – and could have made the port its own. Indeed, had King James been on that frigate, history would have been changed. He could have proceeded almost unchallenged up to Edinburgh and walked into his ancestors' palace of Holyroodhouse – for the Earl of Leven, afraid of the populace, afraid of the loyalty of his own troops, was packed up and ready to bolt with his Staff – or such of them as he could trust. But there was no King, no commander, no person of importance on that single ship, nobody with authority to exploit the situation. It had waited till daylight revealed that it was entirely alone in the Firth, when it had hastily re-embarked its shore party and put to sea again.

Meanwhile the French fleet had lain heaving off the May Island, while the battle of wills continued. And craven irresolution won. Admiral de Forbin decided that safety was all. He was a servant of France, not of Scotland. He refused to sail into the Forth, or to permit a landing on the nearby Fife coast at the mouth of it. He refused even to allow the King to put off in a small boat – though James, it was said, even went down on his royal knees begging, with tears in his eyes, to be allowed to land, alone if necessary, on his ancient kingdom. He was too valuable, he was assured, for any folly of that sort to be allowed – too valuable a pawn for the French, it was to be assumed. Signals to the other ships were flashed out, and the entire fleet stood out to sea, on the first stage of its expeditious return to France, with the favourable wind behind it. But before the flagship got under way, two young Scots officers of Matignon's Staff, the Captains Seton and Ogilvie, with their servants, had managed, with the connivance of sympathetic French sailors, to lower a small boat and get away. They rowed to the Fife coast, at Anstruther, only five miles away. That was how the news reached Colonel Hooke.

That was all. That was the end of all their hopes and plans and strivings. James Stewart would be back in Dunkirk by now, with the north-westerly wind behind his sails. Westminster could breathe freely again.

The MacGregors were silenced. All Scotland indeed was silenced. What was there to say?

Only this did Rob Roy eventually find to announce. Nathaniel Hooke could find somebody else to take that melancholy and shameful story round the clans. Himself, he had more profitable things to be doing. And on this occasion, when he heard about it, Gregor did not disagree with his uncle.

A disheartened man, Hooke went on his way empty-handed. Gregor did not hear, either, that he went burdened with French *louis-d'ors*.

CHAPTER NINETEEN

IN the weeks that followed, Scotland waited – waited for news, guidance, reassurance, leadership, anything that she could lay hold upon. Like a rudderless ship, she yawed and veered and plunged, at the mercy of every drift and puff and current. No leadership was vouchsafed her. And all the time the Government grew bolder, more active, more resolute. And vengeful. It had had a fright. It had been made to look weak, unprepared, unsure of itself, foolish. Somebody had to pay. A display of strength was called for, now that the danger was over. Examples must be made, lest the like happen again.

There were arrests up and down the land – though not over the Highland Line. Edinburgh's numerous jails and cells were soon crammed to overflowing. Proclamations were issued demanding information anent traitorous acts, and offering rewards. Dire threats were made.

But it was largely sound and fury. Few really important people were held. Lord Drummond, admittedly, caught at the head of 200 men, was hustled away south to be immured in the Tower of London – which much offended Scotland, being contrary to the terms of the Union, and he had to be released. Dragoons called upon the Duke of Atholl, but found him confined to bed, with a resident doctor to say that he had been unable to leave his room for months. Other apprehensions hung fire. Evidence was not forthcoming. Despite the enticements and threats, the necessary evidence remained stubbornly amissing. Scotland was in surly mood, and folk would not talk. There had to be releases. Stirling of Garden, Arnprior's old friend, who had been rash enough to ride towards Edinburgh with some of his servants to meet his sovereign and had been held ever since, was freed – for the same lack of evidence. After all, it was no offence for a gentleman to ride armed about the country in unsettled times – self-preservation demanded no less. The Court of Session required more than suspicion and animus to convict of high treason, even in post-Union Scotland.

So the uneasy summer went in. Rumours abounded, even reaching to Glen Gyle. The Government found scapegoats on its own side. Various gentlemen came up from London, and sundry Scottish nominees' heads toppled.

Such was the situation as it drew near to Lammas-tide again, and the dues for Rob Roy's Watch fell once more to be collected. And in Glengyle House thoughts inevitably turned towards Drymen and Arnprior – and Mary Mac-Gregor sighed just a little, happy, busy, and secure as she might feel.

Her sighs, curiously enough, few as they might be, were answered rather remarkably. Late one golden afternoon as Gregor was scything the hay with long slow rhythmic strokes in the meadows below the house, and Mary was rolling and bouncing young Iannie in the sweet-smelling coils that she was supposed to be building, their laughter was interrupted by the arrival of a deep-breathing gillie who came out of the hills to the south and brought strange news. They had found a woman, wandering in the heather, with a lamed horse, many miles away, near the head of the Duchray Water. She had not the Gaelic, but she had made it clear that she was meaning to be heading for Glen Gyle, far from the route though she was. They had brought her, on another garron – see, there they came, over the hill. Her name? Och, yes – her name, she said, was Hamilton.

Gregor went running, then, just as he was, the hounds bounding by his side, and Mary calling messages after him. A mile or so away, over the low shoulder of hill that lay between them and Stronachlacher, a small party was approaching, three or four on foot and one figure mounted.

Stripped to the waist and covered with the seeds and dust of the hayfield, Gregor came up at his effortless lope. But he had little need to concern himself with his appearance. For Meg Hamilton was less than presentable also, her fine riding-habit stained and soaked and bedraggled, her hair unbound, her whole person mud-spattered and dishevelled. Evidently she had had at least one fall. And she looked very weary. Yet even so, her dark eyes gleamed with some hint of their old sparkle as the man came running up to her.

'Gregor! Gregor!' she cried. 'My splendid braw Hielandman! Oh, but you are a sight for sair een, Gregor! And ... and my een are just a small bit sair, I will admit!'

'Och, never say it, Meg.' He gripped both her hands – and saw that one of them was badly scratched and mud-encrusted. 'They never looked bonnier. Fine kind brave eyes – I am glad to see them, I tell you. It has been a long time.'

'Be quiet, be quiet – or you will have them weeping tears!' she told him, a little unsteadily. 'I have contained my tears till now, on this hapless journey of mine. I must not loose them here.' She managed to change and control her voice. 'How is Mary?'

'Well, God be praised.'

'And happy?'

'I think so, yes.'

'She had better be – or I will know the reason why!' That was strongly, if unevenly, said. 'And the young man?'

'Och, a giant. A terror. A Hercules, just! And you, Meg? And . . . and your husband?'

'We have our health,' she assured briefly.

'Ummm.' They were moving on, he pacing at her garron's side. 'Yes,' he agreed, 'it is a great thing the health. You have come from Arnprior?'

'From Bardowie, really. Though I came *by* Arnprior.'

'A long road, lassie.' He shook his head. 'You should not have come alone. The wonder it is that you got this far. . . .'

'I was best alone. None of my father's servants would have been of help to me to reach Glen Gyle. I think. I dared not trust them, anyway. Not on this errand.'

'You have come on an errand, then? An especial errand?'

'Yes. I could not get a message to you – even if I could have risked sending one. I had to come myself. I have come because I think that you are in danger, Gregor. You and others. Many others. I had to come.'

'Danger? Me?' He did not manage wholly to keep incredulity out of his voice.

'Yes. You. And Rob Roy. And scores of others. Have you forgotten my Lord of Breadalbane?'

Gregor glanced at her sharply. 'No,' he denied. And that was only half true. 'What of him?'

'Do you trust him?'

Gregor ran the tip of his tongue over his lips, but did not answer her in words.

'Has he the means of betraying you, Gregor?'

'Betraying . . . ?' Swallowing, the man parried that with a question of his own. 'What do you know, woman – about Breadalbane?' he demanded, a little hoarsely.

'I know very little. Nothing certain. Nothing definite. Only scraps and pieces that I have managed to pick up from my husband's unguarded speech with two callers at Bardowie. One of them was an officer from Dumbarton Castle.

From them, eavesdropping and putting two and two together, I have gathered something. Not a lot – but enough to make me very afraid for you, Gregor. You and Mary. I gathered that Lord Breadalbane must have in his possession some paper, some document, that implicates you in . . . in what happened. Or what did not happen! Evidence to convict you of high treason – you, and your uncle, and many clan chiefs, apparently. Is there such a document, Gregor ?'

Stiff-lipped, the man nodded.

'Then you *are* in danger! For the Government have been informed of it. Breadalbane is suspect – known to have been implicated in the rising that was to be. Now, he is willing to buy his immunity – and office with the Government too, it is suggested. He has been in correspondence with the Queen's Ministers. He offered them this paper, as price of his preferment!'

'My God! It cannot be! No man could be so false. So great a dastard. To betray us all – to betray the whole Highlands! I'll not believe it. Even of that fox. . . . '

'How then does my husband come to know of it ?' the young woman demanded. '*He* believes it, if you do not! God forgive him, he glories in it. He hates you, Gregor – perhaps with cause. And now he sees you ruined, dead probably, and his sister free of you! He is close to many in official positions – and he is not easily misled. You will know that hitherto most of those arrested over this affair have had to be set free, for lack of evidence against them. But here is evidence, it seems – written evidence that the Courts could hang men on – hang *you* on! Oh, this horrible thing is true, I am sure. That is why I had to come. I said that I had had a message from my father, needing me. That I must go to him at Arnprior. John was going to London, anyway. He let me go – not knowing that I knew, of course, that I had overheard. . . . '

Gregor was not really listening, now. He was looking out over Glen Gyle – and seeing it as he had never quite seen it before. All the fair settled peace and seeming security of it, embosomed in its guardian mountains. But how secure was it, if this black treachery was true? It had always been inviolate, yes. His uncle was an outlaw already, yes. The Government's arm had never been long enough to reach them here. But would that still stand? After all, there was no denying that what had allowed this last remnant of the landless Clan Gregorach to remain secure was not only its inaccessible mountains and its vigorous right arms but the fact of the Glengyle sept's relations with the mighty Clan Campbell – however they miscalled them. His own mother had been a Campbell, as had Rob's, his grandmother. And the MacGregors had cleverly played off the one branch of the Campbells against the other, the Argylls against those of Breadalbane, while keeping in with both. It suited both, probably, to have the usefully disreputable MacGregors as a small buffer state between them, and many a handy turn had Rob Roy done for both houses that they would not like to have done for themselves. But now – if both were turned against them, Argyll over the matter of the Frenchmen, and Breadalbane to save his own ancient hide? Could Glen Gyle remain inviolate? If Breadalbane and Argyll let the military pass readily through their territories that flanked Gregor's own to north and west, could anything save the Gregorach if the Government was determined? If Breadalbane had done this other deed of shame, would he boggle at that? The clans might fight amongst themselves, but they kept out the invader from their glens. If Breadalbane was deliberately betraying the clans, could Glen Gyle survive, and the Gregorach become other than finally and completely landless – and leaderless – at last?

So the man was seeing his heritage, now, through suddenly different eyes. And seeing his wife and son there below them, coming hastening to meet them across the meadows, Mary flushed and excitedly happy, the toddling Iannie tumbling and squealing, naked as a trout. And Gregor felt a lump rise in his brown throat.

Meg also saw, and her voice tailed away. Then, her tone changed, she was waving to the other girl, and speaking.

'We will talk of this again . . . later. Shall we, Gregor ?' she suggested.

And he nodded, gratefully.

*　　*　　*

After the two young women had fallen on each other's necks and wept a little, Meg held Mary at arm's length and looked at her through glistening eyes.

'Oh, my dear – you are looking fine, fine,' she got out. 'And bonny. Bonnier than I have ever seen you. And me such a fright!' Foolishly her hand went up to her hair, her neck. 'And the little man – he is a darling, a precious, a joy.' She snatched the chortling baby up in her arms, and hugged him to her, almost hungrily.

The fond mother laughed and blinked and gulped in turn. 'He is a scoundrel!' she asserted. 'A handful, indeed. Worse, much worse, than his father. Gregor I can manage. But this one . . . ! What shall I do with another of them . . . ?'

'Another!' That was Gregor. 'What are you saying? Another . . . ?'

'Just that, Glengyle, sir.' Mary sketched a curtsy. 'With your permission, of course. But I think that there is another of the wild Gregorach on the way! A determined pushing lot. . . . '

'*Ciod so?* And you did not tell me! *Mè!* You said no word. . . . '

'I was saving it up . . . saving it for the next time that you were hard and cruel to me, you great ogre! Then I would have tamed you. But, this . . . this is a great occasion. Dear Meg. . . . '

'*Dia* – an occasion, indeed! Here is news! Another son for Glengyle! Donald, he shall be named. After my grandfather. Meg – how think you of Donald ? I tell you . . . ' Suddenly Gregor's eyes clouded, and his voice fell. 'Och yes, then,' he ended flatly.

But Mary did not notice. Moreover, Meg Hamilton spoke quickly. 'I am so glad, Mary – so very happy. You are the lucky one. But it will not be Donald, at all. It will be a girl.

You could even call her Margaret, if you were at a loss. . . . '

'It is a promise. Eh, Greg?' Mary laughed. 'But come – the house for us. You must be very tired, my dear – almost as tired as I was the first time I came here! Come away. I am so glad to see you, Meg, so very glad. . . . '

Chattering happily, Mary led them housewards, Gregor carrying his son. 'Is it not a lovely place – this Glen Gyle?' she demanded. 'I declare, it is worth putting up with Gregor and his brood and all his wild men, just to live here! So green, so safe, hidden away amongst its hills.'

Her husband cleared his throat, opened his mouth to speak, thought better of it, and shut it again.

'Safe, yes,' their visitor agreed levelly. 'It must always remain that, for you, Mary my heart.'

The other girl looked at her friend, her brows raised. 'Ah – you mean John? Our poor silly obstinate John? No – he cannot reach us here. I used to fear that he might. But not now. Gregor soon convinced me. And now that all the wars and troubles are past and done with, I am so glad, so happy. It was an anxious time when Gregor was going to be fighting. Always ranging the country, in danger. Perhaps it is wrong to say so, but I thanked God when the rising collapsed. It is not so easy to be a good Jacobite when you have husband and children and home at stake! But now – all is well. And your coming, Meg, crowns it all. I have only the one desire now – that you should be as happy as I am!'

'Thank you, Mary,' the other girl said. And left it at that.

Gregor set down young Ian on the threshold of Glengyle House. 'You will look after Meg, lassie?' he said to his wife. 'And you will forgive me, Meg? I have to go over to Inversnaid for a small while.'

'Now? Must you go now, Greg?'

'Yes. I have to see my uncle – about something that I had forgotten. A matter of, of trading. He would not want to be left uninformed, I think.'

'Tell your uncle, if he is looking for trade,' Meg Hamilton said, 'that he should have a word with Campbell of Invercroy.'

'Invercroy?'

'Yes. Campbell of Invercroy. I have heard that he is a warm man . . . for trade, just now.'

'M'mmm. Invercroy.' Gregor eyed her thoughtfully, and turned away. 'Thank you,' he said. 'I will not forget.'

*   *   *

Rob Roy smashed his great fist hard down three or four times on the massive table that always stood just outside the door of his house of Inversnaid.

'Fool!' he cried. 'Fool that I am! Fool thrice over. That I should not have thought of it. That Bond of Association – it ties a rope round half the chiefly necks of the Highlands! That it should have been left with Breadalbane, of all people! Who was madman enough to leave it with him? We had to be leaving early, you'll mind – to deal with your dragoons. But somebody should have had the wit to take it away – not to let Breadalbane keep it in his hands. Hooke. Struan. Cluny. ClanRanald. Any of them. The height of folly, it was! Yet I blame myself. I thought no more about it. I ought to have thought of it, whatever.'

'*I* ought to have done, assuredly,' Gregor asserted. 'For I esteemed the man a traitor, from the first. You will recollect, you said to me once, that the time to be watching Breadalbane would be when things went amiss with our cause. That it would be a failing enterprise that he would betray, not a succeeding one. Wise words. Yet I forgot them. We both forgot them.'

'Aye,' Rob sighed heavily. 'Well – now we must make up for our forgetfulness, lad. Or pay for it!'

'Yes.'

Their eyes met.

'The question is – has Breadalbane still got the Bond? Or has it left his hands?'

'I do not know. I cannot think that Mistress Hamilton can know that, either. But there is this – she hinted to me that Campbell of Invercroy may know something about it. You know him?'

'Invercroy? Yes. *Dia* – yes! He is a captain of one of the Independent Companies. Like our friend Lochnell! A good Whig. I sold cattle for his father, one time – a close-fisted old fox. The father, that was.'

'Is he of Breadalbane, then – or Argyll? Invercroy is in Benderloch, is it not?'

'Near enough. On the edge of Duror of Appin it is. He has a foot in both Campbell camps, has Invercroy. He is of Breadalbane's line, but his land is over-near to Argyll's, and he is apt to act like one of the Duke's men. As I say, he is a Whig, and a captain in the Government's pay.'

'How think you, then? Do we journey to Duror? Or to Loch Tay?'

Rob stroked his beard. 'Breadalbane is wily. And well guarded. At his castle on Loch Tay-side we could not do much with him – even with all Clan Gregor at our backs. Which would be less than wise, at this juncture, anyhow! Only cunning could serve with Iain Glas – and we have few cards to play, to that master. No, I think that we must see this Invercroy first. It is common sense, no less, to strike first at the weakest link of the chain. But we must seek to ascertain if what this young woman says is so, Greg. Whether Invercroy is indeed involved. You must question her more fully.'

'Yes. But, see you, if we could discover whether the man had visited Breadalbane recently, it would help us, would it not? Breadalbane would not travel to Duror, or anywhere else. He is claiming to be a sorely sick man, is he not? Like Atholl! And if Invercroy rode to see him at Loch Tay, he must do it by Glen Dochart – or else run the gauntlet of the MacDonalds in Glen Coe.'

'You are right,' the older man agreed. 'At the mouth of Glen Dochart it will be known if Invercroy has visited Breadalbane. That we can find out.'

'And if he has, it would be something that took him, a Whig, all that road to visit his chief who is under suspicion as a Jacobite?'

233

'I would not deny that, either, Greg. Hector Ban would
know.'

'Yes.'

'Very well. Go you back to Glen Gyle, and find out all
that you can from Robert Buchanan's daughter. We shall
ride in the morning.'

'Good. I mislike the feel of hemp at my neck, whatever!'

'Wheesht, lad. They would have to be catching us, first!
And they would need to be wide awake for that. It is other
necks than ours that I am more concerned for. Men whom *I*
invited to that gathering at Rannoch – and promised safe
conduct to. My own honour is in this business.'

Gregor bit his lip at that word honour. But he did not
comment. 'Myself, I am thinking of some that cannot take
to the heather,' he said sombrely. 'Some nearer home, who
risk more than a hanging!'

His uncle eyed him closely. 'Aye,' he said.

CHAPTER TWENTY

JUST before noon next day Rob and Gregor, MacAlastair
and Ian Beg, rode down to Hector Ban MacGregor's, or
Campbell's, ale-house of Farletter in the narrow western
throat of Glen Dochart. No traveller that followed the
lengthy transverse valley that linked the west Highlands
with the east could pass old Hector's door unnoticed. And
few did indeed pass it, either, without making at least a brief
call within, for ale-houses were far from thick on the
ground, and this one's hospitality noted.

They had no difficulty in gaining from Hector Ban the information that they needed. Yes, Campbell of Invercroy had
passed that way – twice, of recent days. He had travelled
eastwards about two weeks before, and had returned three

days later. No, he had said nothing of his errand, or where he had been. He had had half a dozen soldiers with him. No, not redcoats – militia. On each occasion they had stopped only for a short while.

That was enough for the MacGregors. It looked as though they were on the right track. They turned westwards, up Strath Fillan, heading for Glen Orchy.

Keeping out of Argyll's territory, the four of them spent the night in the heather on the edge of Rannoch Moor, crossed it obliquely next day, and avoiding the head of Glen Coe came down into Etive, through which they had brought the Frenchmen. That second night they stayed with Mac-Donald of Dalness, and from him made sundry enquiries about Invercroy, who ranked as next door to a neighbour. Only a single range of mountains separated them from their destination now – even if it was a range that demanded no little climbing, between mighty Bidean nam Bian and many-peaked Ben Finlay.

They looked down on the House of Invercroy in its bare overshadowed glen the next afternoon – and already the tall frowning hills to south and west, Ben Finlay and Ben Vair, had blocked out the sunlight. A sad and soured place to live, that could be. They went straight down to it, openly. Here was no occasion for skulking and creeping – the approach to the establishment of a friendly laird, a Breadalbane Camp-bell, to whose chief they were related, and moreover with whom they were bound in terms of alliance. Right to the front door they rode, announcing Rob Roy MacGregor and Glengyle, to see Invercroy – and announcing it with considerable flourish.

The laird, who proved to be a youngish man, dark, saturnine, almost swarthy, in keeping with his home, did not altogether succeed in disguising his surprise and perturbation. But he was civil, almost over-civil, next to effusive. His hatchet-faced spouse was markedly less so. She set about preparing her visitors a meal, without enthusiasm. Neither mentioned French prisoners, my Lord Breadalbane, or the Jacobite cause.

Rob waited, talking pleasantly of this and that – though Gregor's honest tongue would not so wag – until the repast, such as it was, was set before them. Then he rose to his feet.

'Sir – before partaking of this handsome entertainment and tasting of your salt,' he said formally, 'it is only proper for us to ensure that we are in fullest accord with you. It would be an ill thing for us to be discovering afterwards that we were not in sympathy, just. That would not be seemly, you will agree? It could tie our hands, see you!'

Invercroy licked his lips, at that somewhat ominous pronouncement, his eyes flickering swiftly from uncle to nephew. 'No, no,' he declared urgently. 'There is little fear of that, gentlemen, I am sure. Sit in, sit in. We shall agree fine, I vow.'

'I am glad to be hearing that,' Rob assured, more genially. 'Nothing else is to be expected, of course – and you a good clansman of Breadalbane's.'

The other looked none the happier for this mention of his chief's name. He glanced at his wife, and then, rather longingly, at the door.

Rob did not resume his seat just yet, but began to perambulate, his patrol covering that doorway. 'For it is on Breadalbane's behalf that we are here,' he informed. 'You will have his well-being at heart, I know. And so have we, whatever – so have we.' He nodded his red head strongly, to emphasise the point. '*Mac Chailean Mhic Donnachaidh* is a sort of kinsman of ours, as you will know. His health, well-being . . . and honour, concern us deeply.'

The Campbell swallowed. 'Quite,' he got out, but without the crispness that was called for.

'Yes. And unhappily, sir, these are all in danger. It is most unfortunate. There is a paper, that has his name upon it. A paper that, in the wrong hands, might cost Breadalbane a deal, even perhaps his noble head. We are seeking that paper. For its greater safety, just. And his.'

Invercroy's knuckles gleamed whitely. 'I . . . I do not understand you, sir. What has this to do with me? I am not so deep in his lordship's confidence. . . .'

'Tut – you are too modest, Invercroy. We have it otherwise. You went to see him the other day, did you not? On the subject of this very paper. This Bond. You see, we do not underestimate your importance, sir. Where is it?' That last came out like a whip-crack.

'Eh . . . ? I . . . I have not got it.'

'So! You . . . have . . . not . . . got . . . it!' Rob stared down at him, great shoulders hunched, long arms hanging horribly loose, a potent figure. 'Where is it, then?'

'I . . . sir, I will not be questioned thus! About confidential matters. In my own house!' Campbell had risen to his feet – or almost thereto. 'You have no right, sir, no authority . . . '

'Sit down!' Rob snapped – and such was the explosive authority of that command that their host did resume his seat promptly, almost subconsciously. 'I have every right. My name – and that of Glengyle here – is also on that paper. Yours is not. We are parties to it, principals to an agreement. It is *our* Bond, as much as Breadalbane's.' His tone of voice underwent one of its lightning changes. 'Have no fear. We are concerned only for Breadalbane's safety and honour. Your chief's interests are ours. Where is the paper, sir?'

'I cannot tell you. It is nought to do with me, I say . . . '

Gregor interposed, taking a chance. 'Our information, Invercroy, was to come to you for it.'

'No,' the other denied strongly. 'No. I no longer have it.'

'Ah!' The MacGregors exchanged glances. So the man had actually had the Bond in his possession. Meg Hamilton had learned even better than she knew.

'And now?' Rob Roy demanded. 'Where is it now?'

'That I am not in a position to tell you,' Invercroy answered. Though he did not altogether look it, he was a brave man even if not a bold one.

'No?' Rob smiled his wintriest smile. 'I foresee that you may swiftly be in a position to tell nothing else – if you do not remember, sir!'

'Are you threatening me?'

'Not so. Prophesying, shall we say. You may have heard of

237

Rob Roy's powers . . . of prophecy ? When the mood comes
upon me, I am seldom wrong!'

An unlovely sound, a squawk, part choking sob, part
moan, part sniff, came from the woman of the house, at the
other side of the room.

Gregor eyed the plain-faced lady compassionately. His
uncle did more. He bowed.

'Ma'am, I congratulate you. On your excellent woman's
perception. Lady Invercroy, sir, is of a sound judgment.
And she has your best interests at heart, I am sure. That is
clear. You would be wise to take heed to her. What did you
do with our property ? The paper ?'

The man shook his head. 'I did only what Lord Breadalbane told me to do with it.'

Gregor said quickly, 'You took it . . . to Inveraray ? To the
Duke ?'

'No.'

'Where to, then ? If you brought it here, from Loch Tay ?'
The other looked unhappy, but was dumb.

'Why else would you bring it this way ? For safe keeping ?
It is still here, then ?'

'No. No.'

'God – will you speak, man ? Or shall we make you ?'
Rob cried.

It was the woman who spoke. 'It is not here,' she panted.
'He took it to Fort William. To Colonel Sandford.'

'*Diabhol*! So that's it!' Rob exploded. 'You gave it to the
military, damn you! You rat! You wretched grovelling cur!
Dealing in better men's lives! How much did they pay you
for that ?'

'Nothing.'

'Liar! That Bond was worth a fortune!' Suddenly the
speaker had a naked dirk in his hand – though swords and
pistols had been left at the front door as was customary and
suitable. Now Rob lunged forward and the steel was darting
under Campbell's long nose. 'How much, dog, I say ?'

'Nothing – I swear it! I did only what I was told. I acted
only on behalf of Breadalbane.'

'Liar!' Rob repeated savagely.

'It is true! It is true!' Lady Invercroy cried. 'Not a penny did he receive. It was his duty, his duty . . . ' She jumped up.

'The door!' Rob jerked, to Gregor – who, anticipating her move, had already leapt to deny the lady egress.

'My duty – my duty it *was*!' the unhappy Campbell asseverated. 'Duty to the Queen's Majesty. To the Government. I . . . I am no Jacobite. . . . '

'That you are not!' Rob Roy agreed. 'Your duty – to betray your fellow Highlandmen to the English! Faugh! You stink in a decent man's nostrils! You would be cleaner with the foul breath let out of you, cur!'

'No! I tell you. I did only what Breadalbane enjoined. His work it is, not mine. I was messenger only. Because I am in touch with the Fort. Because I know Sandford, the Commandant. I am Captain of a Company. . . . '

So that was it. It seemed likely enough. But it did not suit Rob Roy to accept that, yet. 'You make a traitor of your chief, then?' he challenged. 'Not you – but Breadalbane! *Dia* – let us be thanking the good Lord that we were not born Campbells!'

'What is your Commandant doing with the paper?' Gregor demanded. 'When did you take it? How long has he had it?'

'Nearly a week ago, I took it. I do not know where it is now.'

'A week!' Rob exclaimed. 'Then he could have sent it south by now?'

'I do not know. I do not know, at all.'

The MacGregors exchanged glances. What could they do? They could wreak their wrath on this wretched man – but that would avail them nothing of value. If the Bond of Association was in Fort William it was quite beyond their grasp, however bold.

'Damnation!' Rob swore. 'I ought to slit your treacherous throat, fellow!' And certainly the dirk flickered closely enough to draw a choked scream from their hostess.

'Quiet, woman!' Rob ordered, less gently than was his

wont with the other sex. 'Would you have your servants up, to witness your man's shame? Or his end? I tell you . . .'

Gregor interrupted. 'Invercroy could maybe be writing a letter?'

'Eh . . . ?'

'A letter, just. To this Commandant at the Fort. A letter of introduction, as you might say.'

'Ah!'

'Yes. Commending ourselves as good Campbell bravoes. Useful men for his ill work. To get us into the Fort. Once inside, we might be able to do something, whatever . . .'

'Ummmm,' Rob said.

'Yes. I do not suppose that a letter from Invercroy could get the Bond back into our hands – but if we were inside that Fort it would be a poor business if we could not be finding out where it was.'

'Surely. Surely. But, see you – I fear that *I* would be the stumbling-block,' Rob demurred. 'The pity of it, but I am over well known. And kenspeckle. Every redcoat has a description of my person, with rewards offered for my capture. Rob Roy MacGregor would not likely be mistaken for anybody else, whatever!' The man did not sound as though he wholly deplored the fact, either. 'A great foolishness – but there it is.'

'Then it must be myself, just. With Ian Beg. Or Mac-Alastair.'

'It might not be so easy, Greg, laying hands on the Bond, even once within the Fort,' his uncle pointed out. 'The Colonel-man will be holding it secure.'

'At the least we could be finding out where it was. Whether it was still at the Fort, or had already been sent south. If it is still there, then we could bring up our people, have every route out from the Fort watched, covered.' Another thought occurred to Gregor. '*Dia* – Invercroy could write that we are noted Campbell guides! To conduct the redcoats by safe and especial ways.' The young man's eyes gleamed as his imagination excelled itself. 'He could say that he had heard that the Jacobites have got wind of the Bond being at the Fort. That the party taking it south will be attacked. So he sends these trusted guides, to escort the soldiers by little-known routes through the mountains!'

'No!' Invercroy cried.

'Hush, you!' Rob Roy ordered. 'What it is necessary for you to write, that you will write!' He turned back to his nephew. 'This will require some thought, lad.'

'Invercroy could loan us some Campbell tartans.'

'But . . .'

'Silence!'

'But I tell you – it is no use!' the urgent Campbell insisted. 'The Bond is already gone. It is not there – at the Fort. It is gone south.'

'God's death! Where is it then, now?' Rob thundered. 'What are you saying? Think you that we are infants, to swallow your miserable lies? As Royal's my Race – you will find that it pays not to lie to MacGregor!'

'But it is the truth – I swear it!'

'You said that you did not know whether the paper was still in Fort William.'

'No. No – I said only that I did not know where it was, now. As I do not. But it left the Fort three days agone.'

'How do you know that?'

'Because I came back with it. With the officer that carried it south. From Fort William. As far as Duror. I took it to the Fort. I stayed there two days. Then I travelled back with the escort, by the Boat of Ballachulish, and left them at Duror, to come home. That is truth. I swear it. . . .'

'Three days back?' Gregor exclaimed. 'Then by now, where will it be? Which way went they?'

'Aye,' his uncle reinforced. 'Which route were they taking? By Duror, you say? That means that they were keeping to Campbell country – avoiding the MacDonalds. No large party, heh? Not looking for trouble? They would be going by the coast, by Loch Creran and Connel. And then, man?'

'I . . . I cannot be certain. But I think that they intended to travel by Taynuilt and Brander to Dalmally, and on by Tyndrum and Strath Fillan.'

'Aye – as I say, keeping to Campbell territory all the way. Though it is the longer road. That means that they are not sure of themselves, those redcoats. How many, man – how many?'

'A half-troop, just. Under an Ensign. All that Sandford could spare of his garrison . . . '

'So! A half-troop. Thirty men. Redcoats or militia?'

'Redcoats. Regulars. Dragoons.'

'Then they will be mounted on chargers, not garrons?'

'Yes.'

'That means that they must hold to the roads. They cannot risk the heather. Regulars on heavy chargers. They will travel the slower. Let me see, now . . . '

But Gregor already had been calculating. 'It is twenty miles from Fort William, by the ferry at Ballachulish, to Duror. Ferrying thirty men across the loch would take time, in the small boats. You would not reach Duror till perhaps mid-afternoon, Invercroy?'

'No. It was later. Evening. We did not start early.'

'The soldiers would not get much farther, then, that night?'

'No. They were stopping for the night at Duror.'

'So! They are not rushing it, then. That was three days agone. Twenty miles for the first short day. Thirty for a long one. And ferries at Creagan and Connel. Two nights back, then, they would rest at Connel. The Pass of Brander makes bad going for the surest-footed garron. I cannot think that they would risk it on chargers. They would take the longer route by Glen Nant and ferry Loch Awe at Sonachan. That would be another day's journey. So, tonight, they cannot be farther than Tyndrum. Tomorrow they will be threading Strath Fillan.'

'Ha!' Rob said, and his eyes met those of his nephew. 'Yes. Strath Fillan. I think that you have the rights of it, Greg. Thirty men . . . ' He tapped his teeth, a habit that he had when thinking deeply.

'We have some hard riding ahead of us, then, this night, I think,' Gregor summed up.

'Yes. *Diabhol* – we have so! But first, lad, we shall eat. We shall need the food. Here it is, spread before us. We shall not partake of your bread as guests, cur!' he declared, to Invercroy. 'We buy it!' And reaching into his sporran Rob Roy drew out a golden *louis* which he tossed down scornfully on to the table. 'That for the food – and overpaid you are! Set to, Greg.'

Tight-lipped, smouldering-eyed, the Campbell watched while the MacGregors wolfed down the spread repast, his wife plucking at her dress and biting her lips the while. But neither stirred from their places, or spoke any word.

In a surprisingly short time the food was all gone. Rob Roy stood up. 'Campbell,' he said, wiping beard and moustaches, 'you are a fortunate man to be still alive. Perhaps I am foolish not to be making a widow of this woman, here and now. But we have more important matters to attend to, just. You will value your treacherous hide, no doubt? Well, watch it well! If a word of this visit of ours leaks out, we shall be back, see you! With time and to spare for what has to be done! You will hold that false tongue of yours between your teeth, Invercroy – or it will wag no more. You have Rob Roy MacGregor's word for that! Ma'am, I regret this upset of your house – but I regret your mismarriage more! Good-day to you.'

The MacGregors flung out of the room and downstairs, shouting for their gillies.

*   *   *

Gregor had not exaggerated when he declared that they had hard riding ahead of them that night. Tyndrum lay no more than twenty-five miles away, as the eagle might fly, but to reach it by the most direct route possible to the ablest of hillmen they must cover more than twice that mileage. And across two savage ranges of mountains, the Forest of Dalness and the Forest of the Black Mount. Fortunately they still had almost four hours of daylight, so that they won back into Glen Etive, across it, up Glen Ceitlein, over the harsh pass at its head, and down to the swampy levels of Loch Dochard, before the night closed upon the hills. Thereafter, by following the south shore of Loch Tulla, they reached the River Orchy, difficult boggy riding in the darkness. At Bridge of Orchy they were on the drove road that ran southwards below the soaring cone of Ben Doran. That was well after midnight. But then they had only dogged riding ahead of them, down to the head of Strath Fillan.

There was good reason for all this effort and haste. It was almost certain that the military party which they were seeking to catch up with would be lying that night at Tyndrum, at the head of Strath Fillan – at least it was not likely to have moved beyond there, and halting-places in that great and empty watershed of the Central Highlands were few and far between. After Strath Fillan its route would be through comparatively open and populous country. If anything was to be done about halting that column, without a large force of men to achieve it, the thing must be attempted in Strath Fillan's bleak narrows. And Strath Fillan, of course, was made for ambushes. Generations of warring clans had recognised the fact. King Robert the Bruce himself had been ambushed there, by MacDougall of Lorne, escaping with his life but not his cloak – and the spot was known as Dalrigh, the Dale of the King, to this day. What had so nearly brought low Scotland's greatest general might well prove a hazard for the Ensign from Fort William.

It was unfortunate that the MacGregors had no time to go to collect any of their clansfolk. Long before they could reach even the outskirts of their own territory the soldiers would be safely in the heart of populous Breadalbane. Anything that they might do, they must attempt on their own. Four men against thirty. Rob had known greater odds than that – but it certainly provided the travellers with ample food for thought during their long ride through the night.

They came down into the narrow strath about two miles below Tyndrum, at three o'clock in the morning, in a thin and depressing drizzle of rain that restricted even the limited visibility of the late August night. Almost automatically they had made for Dalrigh itself, scene of the most famous ambush of all. But once there, despite the mist and the gloom, it was apparent to them all that the best place for ambushing a king and an army was not necessarily the best for four men to hold up a half-troop. Dalrigh was actually the widest and flattest part of all the upper valley, a boggy haugh through which the river wound, now dotted with the shadowy humps that were sleeping or cud-chewing cattle. Four men, however bold, could do little here. But farther up, nearer Tyndrum itself, the river's channel ran through a broken rocky ravine, and at one point the drove road was pressed close to the river, now high above it on a steep bank, now low at the water's edge. Inevitably it was narrowed to a single track. That was more like the place.

Dismounting beside the murmuring river, the four weary travel-worn men held a brief council-of-war – and pooled the results of their cogitations. Certain considerations were obvious and needed not to be discussed – the necessity for cunning, surprise, exact timing, the best use of the terrain. But more specialised notions had been simmering in all four heads, and now they emerged. Cattle, said Rob Roy – whose mind tended to run on such. Fire – or at least, smoke – said Gregor, inevitably. Shouting, suggested MacAlastair the silent. Water, added Ian Beg. And in considering all four possibilities, eyes began to gleam, laughter to ripple, and weariness fell from MacGregor shoulders like discarded plaids.

They had two hours till sunrise, and probably another hour or so thereafter, before they might look for the column of dragoons. They were going to require every minute of it, they decided.

They went to work.

*   *   *

In the event, they had time on their hands and to spare.

Dawn came, with wet cloud heavy upon the hills, and if thé sun rose thereafter, it made little impact up there on the high watershed of Scotland. The mist rolled and eddied endlessly around them, visibility was reduced to a few yards – and nobody came along the track from the west, from Tyndrum. Only the complaint of disturbed cattle broke the hush of early morning.

Rob and Gregor lay on a little shelf of the steep braeside, amongst the already turning bracken, with just behind them their garrons standing hidden in birch scrub. They had chosen this exact spot with infinite care, after much prospecting. On either side of them, only thirty or forty yards apart, small tributary burns cascaded down to the river, cutting quite sizeable clefts for themselves in the steep banks. A mere twenty yards below the watchers the road wound and dipped and climbed, here reduced to no more than a yard-wide track. It crossed the first burn by a carefully undermined small bridge of birch-logs. It did not cross the second at all – considerable digging with sticks and dirks and hands having gone to ensure the fact, leaving a gap that no horse would jump. Some hastily thrown brushwood camouflaged this, however, save from close inspection.

MacAlastair and Ian Beg were elsewhere, out of sight, but in no less carefully prepared positions.

Despite the tensed-up excitement of their waiting, and his occasional shivers of cold, Gregor's eyelids drooped. His uncle seemed not to miss his sleep.

Their vigil prolonged itself into hours, that seemed the longer for the countless number of Gregor's dozings-off and wakings-up. He began to fret. Had their calculations been amiss? Were the soldiers away ahead, or away behind? Were they perhaps on the wrong route, after all? Had the enemy gone directly south, by Inveraray– unusual though that would be? Or was it just that they were slow in starting of a morning?

The mist was clearing only very slowly – not that there were any complaints about that; it would assist their purposes. If there was to be any fulfilment of them, anyway. . . .

Rob Roy counselled patience. It was much more probable that they were too soon rather than too late. In which case they would just have to wait, and go on waiting. In due course their quarry would appear.

They did, too – just as Gregor was proposing a reconnaissance to Tyndrum itself to see whether they were indeed there. The thin calling of a curlew twice repeated, from a little way upstream, alerted the watchers. That was to be MacAlastair's signal, only to be given when the soldiers were in sight. And in sight, in this mist, meant very close at hand.

And now all tension and fretfulness left the two men. They reverted to calm and efficient men of action. They threw aside their plaids, loosened claymores and dirks, checked the priming of their pistols. Everything now depended upon timing – and cool heads.

The mist was hanging in white wreaths in the trough of the river, so that Rob and Gregor heard the clop of hooves and the jingle of harness and accoutrements for quite some time before the first figure loomed out of the fleecy obscurity. Both gave a nod of satisfaction. It was neither an advance-guard nor a scout, as they had feared, but a young officer – the Ensign himself. He was wrapped in a long black travelling-cloak, but the gold braid on cocked hat and on the heavy scarlet uniform cuff that extended towards the reins was unmistakable. A few paces behind him a sergeant emerged from the mist. And then a trooper. And another. They were in single file, inevitably.

The officer rode at a walking pace, hunched in the saddle, eyes sensibly on the narrow slippery track ahead of him. The MacGregors had carefully drawn heather bunches over the mud of that road to ensure that none of their own or their garrons' tracks remained. He was approaching the bridge over the first burn now. There was no reason for him to be suspicious of this; all the way down that steep-sided valley he had been negotiating identical little birch-log bridges. He crossed it, and came pacing on.

The watchers held their breaths, now, awaiting the outcome of all their plans and calculations. Everything depended upon feet, inches even, of distance, and seconds of time.

They could see eight soldiers now – ten. The officer was almost directly below them, not twenty yards from where they lay, and almost at the edge of the second burn-channel. He was drawing up his horse, perceiving now that the bridge was gone. The sergeant and three others were behind him, across the first burn, and another trooper was about to negotiate the bridge.

Rob Roy raised his pistol, took careful aim, and, as the Ensign turned in his saddle to call out something to those behind, he shot the horse through the head.

The vicious bang of that shot seemed to let loose pandemonium in that quiet valley. Though, as far as the MacGregors were concerned, it was sternly controlled and planned pandemonium. To attempt to describe the sequence of events coherently and in due order would be to essay the impossible – for a great deal happened simultaneously, and the entire action took place in the briefest space of time.

The officer's horse pitched forward, forelegs splaying under it, and its rider was thrown headlong into the burn-channel. Even as the dragoons' shouts rang out, their horses were pulled up, and hands went groping for weapons, their cries were outdone if not drowned by higher, shriller, fiercer yells of 'Ardchoille! Ardchoille!' and 'Gregalach!' – ominous slogans in any redcoat's ear. For four men, the MacGregors made an almost incredible din. Gregor's lungs were never the least of him. Much of the noise came from considerably farther up the glen – two hundred yards at least. And not only shouting. A great boulder came bounding and crashing down the braeside, back there, bringing a small landslide of scree and rubble with it – and though the troopers directly below saw it coming and were able to urge their mounts out of the way in time to avoid it, the effect of threat and disorganisation was strong. And there was a further ominous confused sound from where it had come, the sound of much movement, of snortings and clatterings.

The sergeant, abruptly in command of the lengthy strung-out column, four-fifths of which he could not see, because of the mist and the bend in the ravine, was hardly to be blamed if he hesitated, swithering between going to the aid of his fallen superior, turning back to rally the main body of his force, or attempting to deal with his immediate assailant. That he decided on the last is hardly surprising, seeing that Gregor was now bearing down on him at a breakneck pace, claymore drawn, roaring challenge, his garron sitting down on its hind-quarters, its hooves scoring deep red weals in the steep bank. He got his heavy cavalry pistol out of its holster, appeared to realise that he had no time to deal with its priming, wisely threw it from him, and dragged out his sword instead.

Then Gregor was upon him, preceded by a hail of gravel and stones. Straight at the sergeant's horse the Highlander drove his stocky garron, and though the former was much the heavier beast it could do no other than stagger back from the cannoning impact. And staggering back meant that its hooves left the slender muddy pathway. Down the abrupt slope beyond it slithered, iron-shod hooves striving for a grip and finding none. Over the brute toppled, and its rider with it, after only a single clash of sword and claymore, and down man and beast went in a sprawl of flailing limbs. Gregor's garron, carried on by its own impetus, went a little way over the edge too – but surefooted and bred to the hill as it was, it recovered itself quickly, and got all four feet back on the track again.

Laughing aloud, Gregor turned to the next dragoon.

This man had his sword out also. And he stood his ground gallantly. But he was only an ordinary trooper, good enough for the cut and thrust of a cavalry charge, but no swordsman in the way in which a MacGregor chieftain must be a swordsman. He did his best, but in half a dozen strokes his sword arm was slit from wrist to elbow, and with the seventh, a mighty back-handed swipe, his opponent knocked him right out of his saddle with the flat of his claymore.

'Gregalach! Gregalach!' the victor shouted.

There were still two troopers left this side of the burn – the man who had been crossing the bridge when the attack began had prudently drawn back. But these two, observing what had happened to their betters, and hearing the commotion behind them and the ominous noise from above, had their heads turned as much backwards as forwards. In fact, not to put too fine a point on it, they decided that they would be of more use back at the other side of the little bridge amongst the mass of their fellows. So, as Gregor yelled the slogan of his clan at them, they turned their horses' tails on him and applied their spurs.

But now a new factor complicated the situation. The noises from up above were still confused. But one of them now resolved itself into the roar of water. Down the narrow deep channel of the first burn came a wall of foaming peat-brown water, a torrent, a flood, surging and leaping, throwing out a shower of sticks and stones and debris before it. Glancing up, Gregor saw it, and shouted his mirth. Ian Beg's dam had worked, then – and the demolishing thereof! The two troopers also looked up – and desperately redoubled their efforts. The first one got across before the torrent reached the level of the track. But the second man's charger did its own calculating, and decided that it could not make it in time. It drew up sharply, haunches down, all but unseating its rider. And the pent-up frothing tide roared down, swept the undermined bridge away as though it had been made of straw, and effectively isolated the segment of track between the burns.

The remaining redcoat, glancing round at the oncoming Gregor, threw his sword away downhill in an eloquent gesture, swung his right high-booted leg over his sidling mount's neck, and leapt, landing on all fours on the slippery ground, to go sliding and glissading downwards after his sword, to the safety of the riverside below. A man as wise as his horse, undoubtedly.

Gregor and his two troopers were not the only observers of the flood. A leaderless group of dragoons had been bunched a little way back from the far side of the bridge, uncertain whether to come on or turn back. Now there was little question about it. One or two fired pistol-shots at Gregor – but they were fifty or sixty yards from him, and he took no hurt. And anyway, the soldiers' attention was further distracted. The snorting and scuffling and clattering sounds were now waxing mightily, egged on by a continuous volley of blood-curdling yells. MacAlastair, for a taciturn man, was excelling himself. Moreover, smoke was beginning to billow over and down on them, borne on the westerly air-stream, in acrid rolling clouds, growing ever denser, to thicken the mist. And out of it loomed movement, massive substantial movement, bearing menacingly downhill. New and urgent shouting from all the strung-out line of unseen soldiery rent the already tortured air.

As a substitute for a charge of mounted warriors, perhaps, a stampede of angry frightened Highland cattle may lack something. But as an alarming spectacle and a deranging influence – especially when shrouded in smoke and mist, and possibly being used as a screen for the said charging warriors – it has its own terrors. Driven on by yells and hurled fronds of burning heather from the barrier of dry stuff that had been collected up there and duly lit by MacAlastair, the brutes came thundering down the slope, heads low, tails high, great horns clashing – and it would have been brave men indeed, and braver horses, that would have stood firm in their way. The dragoons scattered left and right. But mainly left, back westwards whence they had come, for it was down to the vicinity of the swept-away bridge that the cattle were being driven. The uncertain group of men who had fired a shot or two at Gregor came to a conclusion, now, as to their immediate future, and turning their mounts round, went pushing and jostling back up the valley, no one of them being the hindmost.

All this while Rob Roy had by no means been idle –

though, indeed, little time had actually passed. When his nephew had run to throw himself upon his garron and thus to enter the fray, Rob had jumped up and plunged long-strided downwards on foot, empty-handed, even thrusting the smoking pistol back into his belt. Straight for the lip of the second burn-channel he ran, to where the fallen Ensign floundered amongst the brushwood that they had thrown in to hide the removed bridge. Down the little bank of the stream he slid, to bend over the unfortunate officer.

'Och, och,' he cried, concernedly, 'here's a misfortune, whatever! Here's no place for a gentleman! Are you hurt, at all? Your horse threw you, just. Here, man – out with you.' And reaching down a great hand, he almost bodily plucked out the young man from the branches and leafage, to set him on his feet beside him.

Unsteady feet, for the Ensign was still dazed with his fall, his brow cut, his shoulder limp, cocked hat and wig gone. 'What . . . ? Deuce take it, where . . . ? God's death, man . . . !' he muttered, and reached a shaking hand to his brow.

Rob was glancing swiftly around him, even as he supported with a hand the reeling officer. But he let no note of urgency or anxiety sound in his voice. 'A scratch – nothing more, sir,' he declared. 'You will be all right. Fine, just. A judgment, you might be calling it – eh? A judgment – for harbouring stolen property!'

'Eh . . . ?' The other peered at him uncertainly. 'What . . . what are you saying? My horse . . . was shot. You . . . ?'

'Tush, man – you'll soon get another horse!' Rob Roy reassured. Then he rapped out, 'Your dispatches? Where do you carry them?' Without waiting for an answer, he ran his hands over the other man's person, beneath his muddied cloak. And though the officer struggled against the indignity, in his dazed and shaken state he was as putty in the older man's huge hands. But there was obviously nothing like a dispatch-case attached to him. Swiftly Rob turned his attention elsewhere. The horse and its gear? Letting go of the officer, who all but fell in consequence, he strode over to the dead horse. First of all he abstracted the heavy cavalry pistol from its saddle-holster and tossed it down to the river. Then he turned to the rolled valise, strapped behind the saddle. His dirk whipped out, Rob ripped this open expertly. On top of the blankets and spare clothing was a worn black leather case, embossed with the Royal Arms. The point of the dirk had scored a line right through that official symbol.

Snatching the case out, Rob prised it open, breaking the sealing-wax which bound it, ignoring the cries of the Ensign. Inside were four or five papers. There was no mistaking, however, the one that he wanted. It was a large parchment, handsomely inscribed, and with many signatures appended. Even folded up it made more bulk than the others, mere letters, put together. Taking it out, Rob put the other missives back.

The officer had started forward, exclaiming broken-voiced. Rob Roy bowed to him, flourishing the Bond of Association.

'Hush, you,' he adjured. 'I am not hurting your dispatches. Och, no. Just this one bit paper I am taking. It belongs to . . . to friends of mine, see you. It is stolen property, and you should never have been given it, you an honourable officer. I am relieving you of a stain on your honour, just! And other men's. My apologies for upsetting your column-of-march, Ensign. And a very good journey to you, from here on.' And Rob thrust the dispatch-case back into the ravaged valise.

Then he was running up the bank a few feet, to stare around him. The cattle were in process of hurling themselves down the hill amidst clouds of brown smoke. Of troopers there appeared to be no sign. His nephew was sitting his garron about twenty yards off, laughing uproariously, twirling his claymore. Rob raised hand to mouth, and called out a long halloo, vibrant and sustained, that sounded high above the general clamour. He waved the parchment in the air, triumphantly.

And as he strode on hugely up for his garron, two other calls answered him faintly out of the din.

Spaced out along the valley, the four Gregorach set their horses to the steep braeside, leaving the chaos to sort itself out.

* * *

Three hard-riding hours later, the four men drew up their weary garrons on the rocky summit ridge of Maol an Fitheach, the Bluff of the Raven, high above Loch Lomond's head. They had not been pursued, so far as they could ascertain in the mist, but they had taken the roughest route, over the lofty shoulder of Ben Dubh-chraige and down the harsh Fionn Glen into Glen Falloch, to climb again up hither. But now the mist had gone, gathered its trailing skirts about it and lifted silently, suddenly away, and the sun shone down on a glory of glistening colour and a far-flung vista that could utterly bemuse the eye. The Mac-Gregors were not bemused, however, heavy as were their eyelids. They gazed down into the fair green sanctuary of Glen Gyle, from its farthermost head. Far down there, beside the dreaming blue waters of Loch Katrine, Gregor could just make out the white speck that was his home. He pointed to it, but his lips would frame no words.

His uncle nodded. Delving into his doublet, he brought out the crushed and crumpled Bond of Association, and opening it up, spread it before him over his garron's shaggy mane. 'There it is, then,' he said. 'There is the paper that should have set James Stewart on the throne of his fathers. There is the paper that can put a noose round scores of the finest throats in Scotland – our own included! There is the evidence Queen Anne's hangmen need to choke the life's-breath from the cream of the Highlands! See the signatures, there – Lochiel, Drummond, Struan Robertson, Cluny Mapherson, ClanRanald, Sleat, Glengarry, Keppoch, Seaforth, Duart, MacKinnon, Chisholm . . . ' Rob read off the resounding list of names slowly, sonorously. 'Aye, and first of all, *Mac Cailean Mhic Donnachaidh* – not Breadalbane, or John Campbell! Who would that outlandish name apply to, I wonder? There is a paper that is worth more golden guineas than you or I could spend in a lifetime!' Almost he sighed. 'A paper worth a dukedom, and what was left of his honour, to Breadalbane. . . . '

'A paper that could have parted Glen Gyle from those that love it!' Gregor put in, unsteadily. 'That could have turned yon pleasant place into a wilderness, and driven those within it homeless into the heather. Those who trust all in me. Aye, and others similarly.'

'Aye, Greg. Even so.' His uncle nodded again. 'A potent paper, indeed.' And putting both enormous hands to it, he rent that parchment from top to bottom, And then again, and again, until the thing was no more than a heap of fluttering fragments. He tossed these into the keen air of the high tops, and they were carried away on the wind like a snow shower. 'The Bond is redeemed,' he cried. He laid a hand on his nephew's arm. 'Your Mary can sleep sound o' nights now, Greg lad.'

Gregor nodded. 'Yes,' he said thickly. 'Yes. And myself at her side. I am not a warring man, at all, see you. I am a man of peace, just . . . for all your training! An ill thing . . . for a MacGregor!'

Rob Roy looked away and away. And slowly he began to laugh, his great silent frame-shaking laughter. 'Aye,' he said. 'Just so! Gregor Ghlun Dubh MacGregor of Glengyle – Dove of Peace! So be it. Away you down to her then, man – to the Lowland Mary that has tamed you! But, see you – be at Inversnaid the day after tomorrow's noon. There is the Watch's Lammas mail to be collected – and already we are late in setting about it. Folk must not be getting wrong notions, whatever! The proper and profitful concerns of peace must go on, let kings come and go as they will! The Gregorach have work to do.'

'Very well so,' Gregor acknowledged. 'I will be there.'

And with a waved hand he was digging heels into his garron's flanks, and away downhill with him towards Glengyle House, Ian Beg at his streaming tails – and having to ride hard to keep up, weary beasts or none. And soon his great home-coming shouting was ringing round the glen-sides, back up to where Rob sat his mount, still-faced, and down forward to the populous heart of the green valley, echoing and re-echoing from a hundred hills. And presently the baying of hounds could be heard through and beyond it.

Rob Roy turned to MacAlastair, and their eyes met, and held.

The Clansman

Book Two

PRELUDE

JAMES GRAHAM, first Duke, fourth Marquis and eighth Earl of Montrose, looked down from his window on to the busy London street, and laughed. As a laugh, it scarcely matched the nobility of his Grace's style, background and power. In fact, it might have been described as a girlish giggle in anyone less august.

'I think that we have him, Johnnie,' he said. 'Yes, this time, damme, I think we have – God rot his soul!' And he sniggered again, and lovingly caressed one of the tight black curls of the enormous full-bottomed wig that he affected. His voice was gentle, delicately modulated.

'Aye, your lordship . . . your Grace. I'm glad o' that.' John Graham of Killearn was not yet quite used to his master being a duke. 'No' before time, either.' That was a very different voice, broad, strong, using the unvarnished speech of the Scottish Lowlands. 'We've had him before, mind – but no' to hold. He takes a deal o' holding, does Rob.'

'Think you I don't know that, man! But this time, I'll hold him. I am going to isolate him, knock his damned hairy legs from under him – bare his dirty red backside for all Scotland to gawp at!' The coarseness and indelicacy sounded strange in that fastidious high-pitched voice. The Duke reached into a pocket of his long yellow satin waistcoat for his gold snuff-box, and flicked back the lace from his wrist gracefully. 'Preparatory to the application of a good honest length of rope to his unwashed MacGregor thrapple, 'fore God!'

'A bonny day that'll be, aye,' Killearn agreed, but still doubtfully. 'It's maybe a wee thing easier thought on here in London than up on the Hieland Line – as your Grace weel kens. The man's clan are ay thick aboot him as the lice in his ain red fur! And he uses the very land to fight for him, damn him!' Montrose's factor spoke feelingly.

'His clan, and his land! That's the beauty of it, Johnnie. I'm going to make the fellow's very strength work against him.' The Duke turned back from the window to face his companion, laughing again. His voice, now, was seen not to belie him – whatever might be said of his laughter. James Graham, like most of his illustrious family, had extraordinary good looks – even though it might be said that they would better have graced his father's daughter than his son – from his high noble forehead, wide strong arching brows, deep glowing eyes, finely chiselled nose, and small pouting shapely mouth, to the delicately pointed chin. If the effect, enhanced deliberately by the cascading black ringlets of the vast wig and the touches of rouge at the cheeks, was rather more feminine than was everybody's taste, no one who knew him would have therefore read any hint of weakness into the features of Her Majesty's new Lord Keeper of the Privy Seal.

Graham of Killearn, factor of his Grace's great estates in Scotland, where the Lowlands joined the Highlands, certainly had no such illusions. A hard strong man himself, he knew a harder when he saw one.

'It is all most convenient and opportune,' the Duke went on, dabbing at his red lips with a lace-edged handkerchief now; he was always doing something with those slender pointed fingers of his. 'Now that I have the Privy Seal, the Lord Advocate is in my pocket – as, for that matter, is the whole Law of Scotland. Useful, Johnnie – useful. Argyll, who might befriend our Rob, out of unwarranted spite of me, is away in Spain at his ridiculous soldiering. And both Atholl and Breadalbane, poor fools, are in disgrace for being unwise about the Union, of glorious memory!' Montrose himself, of course, had worked hard for the Union of the Parliaments of Scotland and England five years before – hence his dukedom and new-won high office. 'Rob has no one to turn to.'

'Save his own damned MacGregors!' Killearn growled.

'Ha – but they are not his own MacGregors any longer, you fool! His nephew, young Gregor of Glengyle, now no longer needs his uncle to run his people for him. Glengyle is very much the chief, I'm told, with two fine sons of his own. 'Tis said, indeed, that he finds Rob an embarrassment at times – as well he may! Do not think that I have forgotten the barbarous MacGregors, my dear Johnnie.' The Duke was quite capable of naming a man a fool and his dearest Johnnie in the same breath. 'Here is the way of it. It has been a bad year for the cattle trade and the droving, as you know. Prices have never been lower. At the recent trysts at Crieff and Falkirk, Rob Roy has chosen to keep his beasts rather than sell at the prices. That means he has a great many cattle to winter – an expensive business, as we have found to our own cost, eh? He cannot do it in his own Highlands. And it is too late to sell now, with the trysts past. I am told that he is devilish short of silver.'

'Who is not, in Scotland today, my God?' Killearn returned. 'The Union looks like costing us dear. . . .'

'Tush, man – leave that. Do you mind the money I loaned to Rob that time, for the cattle-dealing? Back in '08?'

'I mind the one thousand pounds Scots your Grace invested with Rob Roy, for the supply of beef to King Jamie's army – before we kenned just which way the cat was going to jump,' Killearn admitted cautiously. 'Is that the money you mean?'

'That is something like the sum, yes – less interest accrued. Considerable interest. But I think you both mistake the terms, Johnnie, and put it badly. Badly, yes.' The Duke

9

spoke softly, gently. 'It was a pure loan, to a man in need. And would I, think you, who was Queen Anne's Lord President of the Council in Scotland, have any truck with Her Blessed Majesty's enemies? Would I, oaf? Would I?' Long and hard James Graham looked at John Graham, out of those dark luminous eyes.

The factor cleared his throat, and his own glance fell. 'As your Grace says,' he muttered.

'Exactly, Johnnie, I intend, you see, to demand the repayment of that loan, together with full interest, forthwith. Considerable interest, in view of the unsettled and risky times, as is only just. And, alas – poor Robbie cannot pay! Heigho!'

'Aye. But we tried that before, you'll mind. And Rob claimed you were his partner, and must share losses like you shared profits. He'll claim the same again. . . .'

'Aha – but then I was not Lord Keeper of the Privy Seal, Johnnie, and the Lord Advocate did not have to do what I told him! Rob cannot pay – not till the spring sales. I'll have the Court grant me an immediate citation against him, and have him declared a fraudulent bankrupt. . . .'

'But he still has his lands, y'Grace. He still has Inversnaid and Craigroyston. He can sell you these, and keep out o' bankruptcy. They're worth far more than the debt. . . .'

'But he won't my good clod – he won't. He looks on these as MacGregor lands. Clan land – and he is too fond of his filthy bareshanked clansmen to sell. That's what I meant when I said I'd make his strength fight against him. He'll do many things will Rob Roy MacGregor – but he'll never sell MacGregor land. I want Craigroyston, yes – and I'll have it, too, by God! But not that way. I want it for nothing, you see. And once he's declared bankrupt. . . .'

'But, guidsakes, y'Grace – he'll never attend your Court. Rob'll never put himsel' into your hands. He'll stay snug in his ain Hielands. . . .'

'Of course he will, Johnnie. Whereupon I shall have him

declared outlaw! And, see you, an outlaw's property is forfeit to the Crown. The Crown, Johnnie – and, for the time being, *I* am the Crown, in Scotland! Craigroyston will round off my Buchanan lands nicely, as I think you will agree?'

Killearn blinked small eyes. He was not in the habit of admitting admiration for God nor man, but he could scarce withhold it now. 'Aye,' he said heavily, licking his lips. 'Aye – that's clever. But he'll fight, mind. We'll no' get possession easy.'

'I think we will. Again, he will think of his clan, see you. Any of the lieges who support an outlaw against the Crown become outlaws also, forthwith. Will he turn his beloved Gregor of Glengyle, with his wife and bairns, into outlaws too? And all the rest of his MacGregor rabble? Or will *they* allow it? I think not. Rob has fought us off before, in his damned mountains – yes. But that was in the bad old days before the blessed Union! And it was just our local clodhoppers and levies that he fought – not the Crown. This time, mark you, it will be Her Majesty's forces. The Army. For, of course, the Crown must protect its own property. I shall see that an adequate force is sent to Craigroyston to take and hold it, in the name of Queen Anne. In fact, it strikes me that it might well be excellent Government policy for a new fort to be built thereabouts, with a permanent garrison – to clip the wings of the deplorable Gregorach for the future. Such a garrison ought to keep Buchanan Castle and the Montrose estates reasonably snug and comfortable, think you not, Johnnie?'

Killearn was now lost in admiration. 'My God,' he said 'you think o' a' things, y'Grace. I cannot see how Rob can win oot o' that tangle.'

The Duke's laugh was positively silvery now. 'Frankly, Johnnie, I cannot see it, myself! So, my good animal, if you can bear to tear yourself away from your sordid lecheries amid the stews of London ...' The rosebud ducal lips curled in distaste. '. . . and repair forthwith to Scotland, I will have work for you in plenty. Within, I hope, the month. Merry work – work that I think you will enjoy. You have never greatly loved the MacGregors either, have you, Johnnie?'

'No,' the other acceded briefly. He was a curt man, was Killearn. 'Have I your Grace's permission to retire?'

'You have, Johnnie. See that you are posting north by tomorrow. Oh – and for the proper furtherance of Her Majesty's law and order in the good shire of Stirling, I think it would be as well if you were appointed to be a sheriff-substitute of that county! Then you could lead the forfeiting expedition to Craigroyston in person, with all due authority. I will write the Lord Advocate to that effect at once. Authority to take all necessary measures, Johnnie – all necessary measures. You take me?'

John Graham's heavy features creased to a grin. 'Aye, your Grace – I do. Fine, I do.'

CHAPTER ONE

PROVOST DRUMMOND of Crieff looked apprehensively from one visitor to the other, and cleared his throat. 'Did . . . did ye bring many men along wi' you, sirs?' he wondered. 'More than just them, oot there?' And he nodded his greying head towards the knot of red-coated dragoons who stood outside the Tolbooth window.

'There are a dozen stout fellows, there,' Captain Plowden said impatiently. 'Ample, surely, to apprehend one man! Our information is that the fellow rode into Crieff yesterday, alone, and put up at the house of one Lucky MacRae. He is said to have business with a dealer and corn-chandler of the name of Patrick Stewart.'

'Aye – I daresay.' The Provost's grizzled eyebrows rose a little at the accuracy of the Stirling military's information. They must have passing good spies in Crieff town. He wondered how much more they knew? That Rob had business with himself also, as tanner and hide merchant? 'But maybe a bigger troop, see you, would ha' been wise. A kittlish customer, he is. And no' just alone, mind. MacAlastair's wi' him – MacAlastair's ay wi' Rob. . . . '

'Tut, Provost – this is a law-abiding town, isn't it?' the Sheriff Officer interrupted. 'You're no' suggesting that a round dozen o' Her Majesty's sodjers are no' enough to arrest two men in the middle o' the burgh o' Crieff – wi' all your good honest townsfolk at hand to support the Queen's officers?'

The little tanner, who was Crieff's chief magistrate, moistened his lips. 'No, no – never think it, sirs. It's just that ye never ken what Rob'll be up to. And he has a deal o' friends – amongst the baser sort, see you. Rob's ay a great one for the common folk. They like him, some way. I've seen him giving away whole sides o' beef, at the Cross oot there, for the poor. . . .'

'Not good enough friends to make themselves the Queen's enemies, for any nameless MacGregor, I'll warrant!' the Captain snorted. 'You don't foster rebellion in this town of yours, Provost – do you?'

'Guidsakes – no! Och, mercy on us – nothing o' the sort! We're a' right loyal subjects o' Her Majesty. . . .'

'I'm glad of that.'

'You've no MacGregors in the town, to worry you, Provost?' the Sheriff Officer said. 'You're far from the Mac-Gregor country here – twenty good miles and more. There are no MacGregors nearer than Strathyre and Balquhidder. Our word is that Glengyle is away in the south, visiting Arnprior. And Rob Roy's own folk are all out scouring the country for winter fodder for his beasts.'

Again the Provost marvelled at the authorities' informa-MacGregors like hawks. They had waited until he was well outside his own country, and alone, to strike. Biding their time, knowing that come out he must, desperate for winter feed for his swollen herds of cattle. Did they know, too, that Rob was here seeking to barter hundreds of hides to himself, for his tannery, in exchange for great loads of Lowland hay from Patrick Stewart?

'Is that a fact, sirs?' he stalled. 'Och, no doubt you've the rights o' it. There are no MacGregors in town, no. But . . .'

'Devil take it – enough of this!' Captain Plowden cried impatiently. 'We have wasted time enough as it is. I want to be back in Stirling, with our prisoner, before dark. Where is this Lucky MacRae's house, man? Lead us there – in the Queen's name!'

Drummond swallowed. He was not a valiant man. He

had done what he could, put off as much time as possible, kept these officers talking, in order to give opportunity for Rob to slip away, out of town. Whenever they had arrived at the Tolbooth, from Stirling, and sent for him, he had contrived to get a messenger out of the back door, with the word for the MacGregor. He could do no more.

'As ye will, sirs. Lucky's howff is up in the Kirk Wynd. I'll hae the Town Officer to fetch ye there. . . .'

'As well if you came yourself, Provost. As chief magistrate . . .'

The Sheriff Officer paused, listening. Above the stir of the blustery November wind, another sound penetrated, faint but clear, within the massive walls of Crieff's ancient Tolbooth. It was pipe music, thin and high. Not such a strange sound to hear in the streets of the capital of Strathearn, on the very edge of the Highland Line, at some times, no doubt. But strange on a November day in the year 1713, with the Union Government supreme, the Jacobites in eclipse, and the clans in disgrace for having lately preferred James Stewart across the water to Queen Anne in London, and weapons proscribed by law to all but the Queen's forces. Not that bagpipes actually ranked as offensive weapons, of course – but when they played martial music they could be equally dangerous in Scotland, a barbarous challenge to sound order and authority. And the present strains sounded martial enough, in all conscience.

Soldier and Sheriff looked at each other. 'What is that?' the former demanded sternly.

'I . . . I dinna just ken,' the Provost muttered. Which was less than honest. For whether or not these two knew it, he and everyone else in Crieff – except for the dragoons outside, probably – recognised the stirring strains of *My Race is Royal*, the MacGregor march, when they heard it.

'Who would blow the devil-damned pipes in front of Her Majesty's dragoons?' Captain Plowden went on, angrily.

15

'God kens, Captain!' the little man quivered. And again, though undoubtedly true enough, his statement lacked fullest candour.

The soldiers outside had moved forward, to gaze up the climbing High Street of hilly Crieff, pointing and gesticulating. Their commander barked an oath, and turning, stamped out of the room and down the steps to the cobbled street, spurs jingling. After him hurried the soberly-clad Sheriff Officer, clutching his parchments. And, less eagerly, the Provost followed on.

They were not alone in their interest, needless to say. All up and down the street, heads were thrusting out from windows and doors and close-mouths. Many of the good folk of Crieff had already been keeping a discreet eye on the scarlet-coated dragoons, undoubtedly – but this latest development was of the stuff to temper discretion. Miraculously people appeared on every hand, staring.

What they stared at was not, in itself, spectacular. A mere three men – and two of them far from impressive. But people's breath caught in their throats nevertheless – and more than one goodwife hurriedly turned to whisk children and self safely in behind a shut door.

Coming down the very centre of the High Street walked these three men. The first two went side by side, and a comic pair they made; one small, deformed and twisted, with a hunch to his back; the other long and lean and lame; both filthy and unshaven, both clad in tattered rags of tartan so stained as to be unrecognisable, and both puffing away strongly at the bagpipes, hirpling and hobbling. Comic indeed – but no one in all that street so much as smiled. Save one. Obvious to all, they were gangrels, Highland tinks, strolling pipers, routed at a moment's notice out of some back-street den or other, and scarcely sober by the looks of them. But at least they both could play *My Race is Royal*, and approximately in time.

Behind them, a good dozen paces behind, strode another man, alone. And there was nothing comic about this one, save perhaps in his astonishing length of arm, so that his hands hung down to his bare knees – though, again, few would have found that cause for laughter. He was an extraordinary figure of a man, in more than his arms, not seeming so tall as he was in fact, owing to his enormous breadth of shoulder and very slightly bowed legs. But the impact of him had nothing of deformity about it, nothing freakish nor apelike – only strength, a notable and singular impression of personal strength. Those near enough to meet the shock of brilliant pale-blue eyes knew another and still more potent strength, as of a smouldering explosive energy only just held in leash – eyes that many could only look at askance. But they were smiling now, those eyes – for the man was laughing as he walked. His hair a fiery red, the curling hair of his head, of his fierce down-turning moustaches and pointed short beard, the thick furring of wrists and hands and knees, that contrasted so vehemently with those startlingly blue eyes, seemed all part of the latent power of him. A man in his early forties, he was dressed in the full panoply of a Highland gentleman, in great kilt and swathed plaid of red-green MacGregor tartan, a long-skirted doublet of brown-and-white calf-skin, great jewelled clasp at shoulder, silver buttons, otter-skin sporran, woven and diced half-hose, buckled brogues, and sword-belt with basket-hilted claymore. On his head was a bonnet of blue, with a diced band, sporting a sprig of Scots pine, badge of his clan, and a single eagle's feather. Rob Roy MacGregor was always clothes-conscious. He strode down the crown of Crieff's causeway now, alone, apart – but never lonely-seeming – and while it would be unfair to say that he swaggered, his whole bearing and carriage proclaimed a proud and genial satisfaction with the day, the place, the good Lord's providence, and the splendid heartening strains of the MacGregor's march.

Down the street, at his back, but keeping a respectful distance, thronged a growing crowd.

Captain Plowden spluttered his wrath and sense of outrage, incoherent at first from sheer dumbfoundment. He pointed. ' 'Swounds – the damned insolence of the fellow!' he got out, with difficulty. 'It's him – MacGregor! Look at him! *Look* at him . . . !'

The Sheriff Officer was looking, sure enough – and not too happily. But not nearly so unhappily as was Provost Drummond, who was twisting his hands together in major distress, and blinking fast. It was hard, hard on a peaceable man who wished no harm to anybody. Rob had certainly made strange and wicked use of the precious few minutes' grace that he had so generously bought him. 'He . . . he's an awfu' man . . . a right borach!' he stammered. 'Did I no' tell ye – ye never ken what he'll be up to? Och, sirs – this is difficult, difficult, see you . . .'

'Difficult?' the soldier repeated harshly. 'It's a scandal, sir! To add to all his other offences, he's deliberately making a public riot. But at least, we do not need to go find him – he's coming to us! Which will save time.' Plowden raised his voice. 'Sergeant – draw your men across this street. I want that man stopped, held, and taken.'

'Aye, sir.' The sergeant of dragoons ordered his troopers to mount, and after a certain amount of backing and sidling of horses, led his dozen men out into the centre of the street, amidst a clatter of hooves on cobbles. Hands on sheathed sabres, they turned and halted, to form a barrier of scarlet and black across it. The crowd pressed back and out of their way. All eyes turned away towards the single figure that still came striding downhill.

Rob Roy gave no sign that he had noticed the soldiers' manoeuvre. His glance lingered right and left, rather than forward, as he nodded and smiled and raised a hand to townsfolk at door and window.

The pipers, undoubtedly, were less unconcerned. Though

they continued to puff and blow, they were getting very near to the dragoons now, and their heads tended to turn a little, so that *their* glances could flicker backwards towards their temporary employer. Their unease was patent.

The Town Cross of Crieff rose just a few yards uphill of the Tolbooth and Town House, and therefore stood in front of the line of stationary dragoons. As they neared it, Rob Roy barked a word or two in the Gaelic, and with most evident relief his two instrumentalists swung left and right, to turn and face inwards, stationary as the troopers now, but tapping each a foot to the beat of his music.

The red-headed man strolled on, still at one with the world apparently, right up and on to the three steps of the Cross itself. These he climbed, and swung round, presenting a broad back to the soldiers who sat their restive mounts a mere dozen yards further on. The chatter of the crowd had died away altogether.

There was a shouted command from the sergeant. One of the pipers, the hunchback, stopped his blowing, and his instrument hiccuped and wavered sadly. Rob Roy's hand jerked out at once in a peremptory and eloquent gesture that most clearly indicated that a work of the virtue and nobility of *My Race is Royal* was not to be interrupted and cut short in mid-verse under any circumstances. The sergeant bellowed again – but the human voice, however military, is at a distinct disadvantage when in competition with two pairs of bagpipes at close range, and willy-nilly all present must listen to the final triumphant and sustained bars of the MacGregors' march.

Rob Roy, of course, had the advantage of knowing at just what point the recital would end, and it was his great voice therefore that was able neatly to fill the throbbing void the moment that the instrumentalists had bubbled and wailed to an ultimate close, the sergeant being seconds late. His rival did not so much as glance at him, anyway. He was looking towards the Tolbooth doorway.

'Aha, Provost!' he cried gaily. 'I call it civil of you to accord me a civic welcome to your good town. I do so. I pledge you, and Crieff, my thanks.'

The little tanner could not even look at the speaker, in his embarrassment. He mumbled something inaudible.

Captain Plowden did not mumble, by any means. Lifting his voice to its most commanding, he shouted. 'You! MacGregor! Enough of this foolery. Come here.'

Evidently his shouting was not loud enough, for Rob Roy went on talking to the little man. 'If you had told me now, Provost, I'd have brought some of my lads along with me, and made a better showing of it, whatever. Just a private visit it is, you see . . .'

'Silence, mountebank!' the Captain rapped out. 'I spoke to you. I said, come here!' But he started forward himself. Less urgently, his two companions followed.

'Would it be to myself you were after speaking, Captain?' The Highlandman wondered, civilly, still standing on the Cross steps. 'I am thinking you must be having my name wrong, some way. Och, it's easy mistaken, and you an Englishman by your voice. MacGregor it is, see you – MacGregor of Inversnaid and Craigroyston, just.'

'And that is a lie, to start with!' Plowden returned strongly. 'There is no man in this kingdom lawfully bearing that name, today. And the lands that you name are no longer yours, but your creditors'. But enough of this. Give me that sword, fellow – that you are carrying in defiance of the law. I arrest you, in the name of the Queen's Majesty!'

'Och, tut sir – what's this?' the MacGregor protested, but mildly. 'It grieves me sorely to have to controvert a gallant officer of the Queen – but *you* cannot arrest me, Captain. You have not the authority. I am no notary, God knows – but I have enough of the legalities to know that. I am a free citizen of this realm of Scotland – and I know my rights.'

'Fool! Quibbling over words will not serve you now. I

carry you back to Stirling Castle, free citizen or none! But if you must have my authority, sirrah, the Sheriff Officer here will let you have the form of words. Read it to him, sir.'

The Sheriff Officer had stopped quite a few paces further back. He glanced behind him, and over at the substantial line of soldiery, for comfort, unrolled his parchment, and cleared his throat.

' "*To all whom it may concern,*" ' he read out, in something of a hurry. ' "*Proclaimed at Edinburgh, by the Lord Justice General, at the instance of Her Majesty's Lord Advocate for Scotland that:*

' "*Robert Campbell, commonly known by the name of Rob Roy, or Robert MacGregor, or Robert MacGregor Campbell, or otherwise, being lately entrusted by several noblemen and gentlemen with considerable sums for buying cows for them in the Highlands, he did most fraudulently withdraw and flee, without performing anything on his part, and therefore is become unquestionably a notour and fraudulent bankrupt. The said Robert Campbell moreover, being treacherously gone off with the moneys, to the value of £1,000 sterling, which he carries along with him, all magistrates and officers of Her Majesty's forces are entreated to sieze upon the said Robert Campbell and the moneys which he carries. God Save the Queen!*" ' That resounding pronouncement admittedly might have been read with more of a flourish.

There was a silence over the High Street of Crieff, as the Sheriff Officer finished, nevertheless, in which the lowing of cattle from up on the Town Moor could be heard distinctly. Citizens eyed each other askance, and many a head was shaken.

Plowden spoke. 'Are you satisfied, sirrah?'

'Me, Captain?' Rob Roy's voice sounded entirely unconcerned, if a little surprised. 'What is it to me? Who is this Robert Campbell? A terrible man he must be, indeed, to have defrauded all these noblemen. One thousand pounds sterling, was it? A fortune, no less. A strong man he must be, too, to carry it all with him, in gold pieces, whatever! Och, I've heard some queer-like tales of those Campbells in my day, yes – but this beats all. And to buy cows . . . ?'

'Silence!' the Captain cried. 'Such clowning will gain you nothing. I arrest you, now, in the Queen's name.' He turned to his men. 'Sergeant – take him.'

Rob Roy's hand came up, with a swift and strangely authoritative gesture. 'No,' he said. 'That you may not do. It is contrary to the law of this land.'

'What? God in Heaven, man – are you beyond your wits?'

'You stand, Captain, in the town and burgh of Crieff, in the presence of its chief magistrate. No arrest may be made therein, see you, save by the Provost or by his authority – this country not being in a state of war. I call Provost Drummond and the citizens of Crieff to witness! And the Sheriff Officer likewise.'

The soldier took a further pace forward, wrathfully. Then he paused, and shrugged. 'Very well. It matters not who says the words – so long as I take you to Stirling. Provost – arrest me this man. You have heard the proclamation.'

Drummond swallowed, and shifted his feet. 'Aye,' he said thickly. 'Ooh, aye. Dearie me.' He looked from the soldier over to MacGregor, and then to the ranks of his own watching townsfolk. 'I hae no choice. The proclamation speaks plain. . . .'

'Surely, surely, Provost,' Rob acceded readily. But this time his glance was not bent on the speaker but turned uphill, away up the street that he had recently come down. It would be untrue to say that he peered, but there might have been a hint of urgency in his gaze. 'Do what you must do, friend. But read you the form of words again, Provost, so that all is done right and in order.'

'Nonsense!' Captain Plowden exclaimed. 'What folly is

this? The proclamation has been read, and is clear to all. Have done, Provost.'

'No, sir,' the MacGregor insisted, firmly. 'The law is the law. If the Provost is for making an arrest, he must do so as the law prescribes. Read the proclamation, Provost.'

'Maybe he is right, then,' Drummond said uncertainly. 'Och, no harm in reading it again, to be safe, see you.'

'Lord preserve me from such lawyer's hair-splitting. . . !'

So the proclamation was read once more, even less eloquently than before.

'Thank you, Provost,' Rob acknowledged gravely, at the end. 'But it is as I feared – the thing is faulty, whatever. You cannot arrest a man on false authority.'

'My soul to God!' Plowden choked.

'What . . . what . . . ?' the tanner croaked.

'Your paper is made out against one Robert Campbell. That is not my name, as well you know, Provost.'

'Och, we a' ken that, Rob. But . . .'

'But, nothing. We must be accurate, in matters of law.'

'Damnation – this is beyond belief! None knows better than you, man, that the name of MacGregor has been banished and proscribed by law since, since . . .' The Captain swallowed. 'Well, for years. And that every one of your wretched cut-throat clan has had to take another name. You, who prate of the law, are known as Campbell before the law. Can you deny it?'

'Ha! As Royal's my Race – and there you have it, my friends! I do not deny it. Before the law I may be *known* as Robert Campbell though my name is MacGregor, as were my forebears back to Gregor son of Alpin, King of Scots. But that is not what your paper says, see you. It says Robert Campbell, commonly known as Robert MacGregor. And there is none such in this realm – for no Campbell would ever take the name of MacGregor, for fear of his skin, whatever! The thing is faulty, as I say, and will not serve.'

That was declared like a fanfare of trumpets – but, at the

same time, the speaker's eyes flickered away momentarily to his right again, up that steeply climbing street.

Plowden actually gobbled in his efforts adequately to express his feelings. Nor was he alone in his incoherent comments. Of all the watchers, only the dozen dragoons sat silent and apparently unmoved. The crowd stirred and buzzed like a bees' bike.

'Silence!' the Captain roared, at length. 'Quiet! You!' He swung on the unhappy Provost. 'Say that you arrest this fool, and be done.'

'You cannot do that, Provost — you would break the law,' Rob Roy's great voice carried clearly, vibrantly. 'The law of which you are a magistrate. You must admit the paper is wrongly worded.'

'Aye — och, maybe. But I canna help that, Rob. What can I do . . . ?'

'You can give the proclamation back to the Sheriff Officer, and tell him to go have it amended. Then he, or the Captain, can come with it to me, any day, at my own house of Inversnaid, and present it again. Lawfully.' Rob Roy smiled. 'They would be warmly received, I promise you!'

'For God's sake! I've heard enough,' the sorely tried Plowden cried. 'Not another word. Forget the proclamation. I am taking this man into custody as a proscribed MacGregor bearing arms contrary to Act of Parliament. On my own authority . . .' He had to keep raising his voice, to be heard.

But it was a losing battle. A louder noise than his authoritative shouting was beginning to fill the air. And to turn all heads — Rob Roy's, the crowd's, even humiliatingly his own dragoons'. Furiously the Captain jabbed an imperious finger first at his sergeant and then over to the MacGregor on the steps of the Cross — a gesture surprisingly clear and eloquent, words or none.

But good soldier as that sergeant might be, he did not obey. In fact, he just was not looking. Not at his officer, anyway. As who was to blame him? He was staring up the street, like everybody else. And what he saw might well have given pause to the boldest of warriors. For coming charging and careering down the hill to them was a great mass of cattle, filling every inch of the street as in the trough of a narrow valley. Tight-packed, heads down and tails up, bellowing their alarm, horns clashing, hooves thundering, they came in crazy stampede under a cloud of steam, the half-wild, shaggy, long-horned cattle of the hills. Behind them, the flicker and smoke of brandished bog-pine torches was just discernible through the dust and reek.

As though by witchcraft the street cleared before them – since nothing would withstand or survive the impetus of that cataract of beef. There might have been anything up to a couple of hundred of the brutes, rounded up from the near end of the Town Moor, not a few of them Rob Roy's own beasts, brought in the night before to sacrifice to the tan-yard as hides to buy fodder for thousands more. Like rabbits into their burrows the townsfolk disappeared into doors and closes, none being hindmost.

The MacGregor was laughing now, in his relief, a changed man. It was not the first time that he had had re-course to this trick – though the first time in a town's streets. He roared his mirth as his two decrepit pipers went running and stumbling for shelter to the nearest close-mouth, and then turned, still standing on the Cross, to stare directly at the row of dragoons. He was all there was now, between them and the oncoming stampede.

No soldier's eye met his own. They had other things to look at. Already some of the horses were rearing and back-ing, whites of eyes showing in fear. Troopers' glances swivelled between the menace in front, the sergeant and their commander. The Provost and the Sheriff Officer were already scuttling to the Tolbooth doorway. Captain Plow-den, more courageous, lingered a few seconds longer. Then he began to back, then to turn and stalk with such dignity as he could muster, in the same direction, and finally to break into a run.

At that the sergeant hesitated no longer. Pulling his mount's head round, he waved his hand in a round-about motion which clearly meant scatter – and more than one of his troopers were already anticipating the order. Unfortunately, mounted men could not just disappear into houses and entries – and in the narrow confines of the street scattering was a manoeuvre more readily ordered than carried out. The dragoons interpreted the command in the only way possible; they turned and fled in a ragged straggle of scarlet and black, down the High Street, their chargers' hooves striking sparks from the cobblestones. Rob Roy MacGregor's great laughter followed them, though unheard.

The Town Cross of Crieff was the usual stone column, standing in the middle of the street, raised on three or four steps so that pronouncements and public statements could be proclaimed from its platform. Even so, its top step was not more than three feet or so above the cobbles – but fortunately for Rob the shaft of the Cross rose out of a sort of plinth of its own. Eschewing any flight or scuttling, the MacGregor climbed up on to this, one arm round the column, and so gained a further eighteen inches. There, like a mariner clinging to the mast of a wreck, he stood.

He was only just in time. In a surging red and brown tide the cattle swept round him, a sea of heaving shaggy bodies, snorting nostrils, tossing horns and rolling eyes. The man all but choked with the stench and stour of them. On and on the brutes pounded and plunged. The street shook to their weight. Wide horns came perilously near to the man's legs. The drooling slavers of foaming mouths splashed his colourful finery. But the splayed steps saved him, and the herd thundered past.

Behind them, the group of nondescript youths and boys, discarding smoking torches, had halted and were in process of melting away discreetly. Only one man came on, a dark-haired, dark-avised unsmiling gillie, dressed in short kilt and plaid of stained MacGregor tartan and little else, sitting a shaggy Highland garron and leading another. Close in the wake of the streaming cattle this man rode, to pull up beside the Cross.

'*Dia*, man MacAlastair – the time you have been!' Rob Roy cried, in the Gaelic, but cheerfully. 'I was thinking you would never come. Were you after milking the cows first, or what? I near talked my tongue out of my head!' Leaping down from his stance, he vaulted on to the back of the second pony, in a flurry of limbs and tartan.

'The torches, it was,' the gillie mentioned, shrugging. 'Finding the torches.' A man of few words, he sat his mount calmly, unmoved and unmoving.

His master turned to face the Tolbooth. He bowed from the waist, and sketched a graceful salute with his hand – for his bonnet was to be raised to no man save his chief and perhaps James Stewart in France. And slapping his short-legged garron's rump, brogues almost trailing on the cobbles, he set off at a trot uphill, his attendant at his heels. He did not forget to bow right and left either, as he went – as he had done on the way down, of course.

Only a pair of flattened and ragged bagpipes remained to show for it all in the town centre of Crieff.

CHAPTER TWO

THE barking of the deerhounds caught Rob's ear, and he set down his two-year-old second son Ranald, and stepped over to the window.

'It is Greg,' he reported. 'And in a hurry, as ever.'

Up the side of the headlong Snaid Burn rode a splendid figure, a young giant of a man on a big black horse – no stocky Highland garron, but a handsome Barbary charger. Even so, the horseman's long tartan-clad legs trailed low, for he rode without stirrups, in the Highland fashion. His plaid streamed out behind him in the wind, and two tall eagle's feathers thrust proudly above his bonnet. At his back loped two running gillies, deep-breathing but light of foot still, plaids wrapped around their middles, though it was November, leaving their muscular torsos bare. And behind them three graceful deerhounds bounded, baying in answer to the yelped welcome of Rob's own dogs.

'Alone? From down the glen? From Arklet, not Glen Gyle?' Mary MacGregor asked.

'Aye. And bravely dressed. For visiting, surely.' Rob gently pushed the little boy away. 'To your mother, my cock ptarmigan. Run, you.' And turning, he strode to the door, and out.

Inversnaid House stood on a grassy terrace above a bend in the stream, within the open mouth of the lovely green and secluded glen of the Snaid Burn, near to where it joined the wider and greater Glen Arklet. The waters of long Loch Lomond lay only a mile away to the west, but unseen and many hundreds of feet lower. It was a comparatively modest house of two storeys, reed-straw thatched, that Rob had enlarged from a mere farmhouse to bring his bride to when they were married. It was no fortified strength or castle, for your Highland laird was apt to rely for security on walls more potent than stone and lime – the inaccessible mountain fastnesses, and the loyalty of the clan's folk in whose midst he dwelt. Outside his ever-open door, now, Rob Roy stood, in his oldest tartans and worn leather doublet. His voice rose in shouted welcome to his nephew, pupil, friend and chieftain, to wake new echoes alongside those of the hounds, from all the tall and mighty hills that hemmed them in.

Gregor MacGregor of Glengyle came clattering up from the waterside in fine style, to leap down lithely, for all his size, and toss his charger's reins to a gillie.

'Ha, Rob!' he cried. 'As well that I find you at home. I have come hot-foot from the Clachan of Aberfoyle. . . .'

'Aye, Greg – and when did you ever come cold-foot from anywhere?'

'*You* to talk!' Gregor Black-Knee of Glengyle, chieftain of the Clan Dougal Ciar branch of the Gregorach, snorted. He was an open-faced yellow-headed young man – an unusual combination in his race – and notably good-looking in a vigorous and gallant fashion. Clad today all in tartan, but with long and almost skin-tight trews instead of the kilt, cut on the cross and hugging an excellent leg lovingly down to the ankle, he made almost as eye-catching a figure as his uncle – almost, but not quite. Of a cheerful, uncomplicated and laughter-loving habit, he was, at twenty-four, almost seventeen years younger than Rob – but a mere babe nevertheless, if compared with the complex character of his famous relative and guide. And, for once, there was no laughter showing about his eyes and mouth.

'It is crazy-mad! Beyond all belief,' he said, the words tumbling from his lips. 'But you are put to the horn, Rob – outlawed! They have proclaimed you outlaw!'

'What! *Outlaw*, did you say?' That was a woman's voice. Mary MacGregor stood in the doorway behind her husband, the little boy in her arms. 'It . . . it cannot be!'

'True it is. I saw the paper, myself. Some misbegotten Lowland scum had dared to nail it up outside the inn, during the night. Our people tore it down, of course – but the dominie has it. He showed it to me. I was on my way to visit Buchanan of Arnprior – but I came back here, right away. I saw the paper. It said that you had put yourself outside the law, failed to submit yourself to justice, and a deal more. Aye, and that you, by open fraud and violence, had embezzled much money. And kept a guard or company of armed men, in defiance of the Crown. *Dia* – the insolence of it! You, Rob – Captain of Clan Alpine, Captain of the Highland Watch, descendant of kings . . .'

'. . . and stumbling-block in the path of James Graham!' his uncle finished for him. 'So-o-o! It has come to this, has it? I did not think that he would dare so far.' His voice was even, deliberate, with none of the violent outburst that Gregor had expected. Rob Roy raised those piercing pale blue eyes to the lofty summit of Beinn a Choin, the Mountain of Weeping, that soared to the north between his own fair valley and that of Glen Gyle, and stroked his pointed red beard.

'If Montrose has dared so far, he has dared too much, 'fore God!' Gregor cried, the more strongly for the other's unlikely restraint. 'Does he think, because the woman Anne in London has named him duke, that the Gregorach will bow the knee to a Graham, and do his bidding?'

'Hush, you,' his uncle mentioned, and jerked his head to the side. A boy had appeared from around the gable-end of the house, a lad of ten or eleven, bright-eyed and eager, who was darting his glance between his elders and the handsome fidgeting charger, obviously torn between interest in what was being said and admiration for the horse. It was Coll,

Rob's eldest son. 'I'm thinking we might continue this discussion indoors.'

'The Gregorach bow the knee only to God, don't they? Though they'll touch their bonnets to King Jamie across the sea,' the boy's voice came, high-pitched and earnest. And then, equally fervent, 'Can I have a ride on Barb, Cousin Greg? Please! I will be very careful.'

'A short one then, Coll – for I must be off again, to Arnprior. Down to the Arklet and back – no more.'

'I wish that I could vault right up on to Barb's back – the way you did when you stole it from the dragoon officer, Cousin Greg. I wish . . .'

'Stole?' Gregor repeated sternly. 'Watch your words, young Coll. Glengyle does not steal. He takes!'

'That is an old story, boy – and better forgotten perhaps.' his father observed, smiling. 'Your cousin is now a respectable married man. Like your father. And does not harry the Queen's officers! *Maxima debetur puero reverentia!*' Rob always had a weakness for Latin tags. He led the way indoors.

Mary MacGregor was waiting for them. She had passed the toddler on to one of her house-women. 'What does it mean, Rob? Outlawry? How much will it harm you?' she asked, directly. 'And us?'

'It will not harm *you*, my love,' her husband said, quietly. 'That I shall ensure. Never fear.'

'What harm could be in it, for anyone – here in our own country?' Gregor declared. 'Montrose's writ stops short at Drymen and Balmaha and Aberfoyle. So long as Rob stops within our own country, the word means nothing. There is no *harm* in it – only insult and offence that cries to high heaven! And, by God's shadow, insult that Montrose shall rue! The man who slights Rob, slights all our race, all Clan Alpine – and shall pay for it. The Gregorach will teach such folk a lesson. . . .'

'Wheesht, Greg! A truce to your great swelling words,'

Mary MacGregor interposed, but not unkindly. 'A clear head is what is needed now, I think.'

Gregor looked abashed. As ever, this woman who was his aunt could silence and confound him – as to some extent she could her puissant husband also. Not by her words so much as by her sheer calm and unruffled beauty, some steadfast inner quality of mind and spirit of which her extraordinary loveliness of face and figure was but the outer symbol and sign. Gregor had a comely wife of his own at Glengyle House, another Mary, and fair indeed; but familiarity with her good looks left him none the less in awe of this prouder, classic, almost tragic beauty of his dark-haired aunt, however close a relative. For Rob, of course, had married his own cousin, daughter of MacGregor of Comar, from under Beinn Lomond.

Her husband nodded. Undoubtedly his nephew's news had made him more than usually thoughtful. 'Mary is right, Greg,' he said, now. 'This calls for more than slogan-shouting. Outlawry means more than just cocking my bonnet at Montrose. He has the power of the State behind him now, see you. And these are changed days in Scotland, since the Union. The power of the central government has waxed greatly. We are not so far from Stirling or Dumbarton or even Edinburgh as we were a few years back, lad.'

'But, *Dia* – you do not mean that you will submit to this thing? That you will not fight. . . !'

'Rob will fight, of course,' the woman said, level-voiced. 'Could he do otherwise, and remain himself? But there are more ways of fighting a mad bull than by butting it with your head!' She gave the glimmer of a smile. 'As *you* ought to know, Gregor Tarbh Ban.'

But no answering smiles were aroused by this reference to her nephew's famed exploit with the White Bull of Gallangad that had marked his entry into man's estate.

'Aye,' Rob said, a little heavily for him. 'Just that.'

Gregor looked from his uncle to his aunt doubtfully.

'Myself, I think that you are taking this a deal too seriously,' he maintained stubbornly.

'How legal is it, Rob?' Mary asked. 'How far will the law support this outlawry?'

'Does that matter, my dear – so long as the Advocate and the Justice-General support it? And Montrose has them both in his pouch, it seems. But I daresay that it could be made to stand in law, whatever. They will have it that, since I am not paying Montrose what he demands, I am bankrupt. And since I have not attended their court in Edinburgh, to be thrown into a debtor's cell, I am outside the law. Outlawed. Och, it fits nicely enough, I grant you.'

'It stinks to heaven!' the younger man cried. 'It is a dastard's trick! In the first place, Montrose has no claim on the money. He *invested* it with you, as he had been doing for years. He shared the profits – he must needs share the losses likewise. That is but business. And the man has more than doubled the sum, for interest, the thieving huckster! In the second place, how can you be bankrupt – you, with five thousand cattle to your name, and all the lands of Inversnaid and Craigroyston?'

The other shrugged his great shoulders. 'James Graham knows well the state of the market, the bad prices, and the cost of winter feed. He knows my difficulties – and he knows too that I would not pay his damned blackmail even if I could!' Rob Roy's voice vibrated there with a hint of its accustomed vigour.

'Aye, then. What will you do, then, Rob? My sword – every claymore in Clan Dougal Ciar – is at your service!'

'My thanks, fire-eater.' His uncle smiled a little. 'Can it be that you are tiring of wedded bliss, maybe? What of your bonny Mary? And of the two little small fellows? How will they take to your swording, Greg?'

Gregor frowned. 'Mary has them still with their Aunt Meg at Amprior. I was on my way to bring them home, just. They will be fine at Glen Gyle. With the honour of the

Gregorach at stake, I . . .' The young man's eyes caught those of his aunt, and he coughed, and let the important matter of the MacGregors' honour lie for the moment. 'What are we to do then, Rob?' he asked again.

'You – get you to Arnprior and bring your Mary home, lad. For me, I have a letter or two to write, I think.'

'*Letters!*' Gregor all but choked on the word. 'Is it pen-and-ink you would be at, in this pass! *Dia* – I'd have thought that Rob Roy MacGregor would have answered louder than with a pen's scratchings!'

'There are times when a whisper can reach as far as a shout, Greg.'

'Is it to Argyll you will write?' Mary MacGregor asked.

'No – the pity of it. He is still in Spain, I hear. It must be to Atholl. Set one duke against another. And maybe Breadalbane. . . .'

'That knave! That traitor! That broken reed!' Gregor cried. 'A mercy – if that is the way of it, then I'll leave you to your scratchings, and be back on my road to Arnprior!'

'Do that, Greg,' Rob Roy agreed, gently. 'My respects to Robert Buchanan. And when you have Mary and the lads safely home to Glen Gyle, we'll be over to see them. In a day or two.'

'Greet her warmly for us, Gregor,' his aunt added. 'But, think you that she might not be better staying at Arnprior, for a while? Safe in that great Whiggamore house of Buchanan's?'

'No. Not so,' the other said definitely, slapping his bonnet on his yellow head – though automatically adjusting it so that the eagle's feathers stood up tall and proud. 'In troubled times, the place for Glengyle's wife and bairns is in Glen Gyle. God keep you, both!' And swinging about, he went marching outside.

They watched him go long-strided down to the burnside, a gallant figure, his huge voice raised in bellowed commands for Coll, his horse, and his gillies.

'Heigh-ho,' Rob Roy declared ruefully, shaking his head. 'The lad's sore disappointed with me, I doubt. He judges me as failing him and his notion of the Gregorach. Aye – and that notion *I* instilled into him, whatever!'

'Does that count – so long as you do not fail your own self, Rob?' the woman asked quietly.

'Aye. As ever, you have the rights of it, Mary my dark love. Fetch me the quill and the paper, will you?' But the man sighed as he said it.

*　　*　　*

'*. . . his Grace of Montrose thought fit to procure an order from the Queen's Advocate to secure me, and had a party of men to put this order in execution against me. This is a most ridiculous way for any nobleman to treat any man after this manner. God knows but there is a vast differ between Dukes! Blessed be God for that it's not the Atholl men that is after me! If your Grace would speak to the Advocate to countermand his order, since it's contrary to Law, it would ease me very much of my troubles. . . .*'

Rob was reading over what he had penned, quill poised in a great hairy hand that seemed wholly unlikely to have formed the neat and indeed stylish writing before him – for however contrary to his reputation he was a man of education and culture – when he raised his head to the sound of a commotion outside. A man's voice, breathless and hoarse, was demanding to see Himself. Himself still meant Rob Roy to most of Clan Gregor, even though he was not their chief, nor even, like Glengyle, chieftain of a sept. He rose.

Mary showed a panting dishevelled gillie into the room. 'News, Rob,' she announced. 'For your own ear.' She would have retired, but her husband stayed her with a gesture.

'Ha, Murdo,' he greeted the ragged-garbed but lusty newcomer. 'What sets you running, this time? Has Cailness fallen into the loch again? Or is it your own wife chased you out of the house?'

35

'Boats, it is,' the other panted, briefly. 'Many boats.'

'Eh?' Not only Rob's voice but his whole posture and bearing changed, tensed. Abruptly he was a different man. 'Boats? On Loch Lomond? As far up as Cailness? Tell me, man.'

'No. Not so far – yet. But coming, see you. Ian Beg saw them. From Rowchoish. He came running up to Cailness. Cailness sent me to warn you. Myself, I saw them from the high ground as I came. A score of boats, at the least. Och, maybe more. They were creeping up the near side of the loch see you, and hard to count. . . .'

'*Diabhol* – a score, you say! That could make two hundred men!' Rob Roy's glance lifted, to meet that of his wife. 'Here is an expedition, whatever!'

'Yes, then. And Ian Beg said that he was after seeing red coats in the boats.'

'So-o-o!'

'They . . . they are coming here, Rob?' Mary asked.

'Where else – if they have got as far up the loch as that? And who else would they send hundreds of men for, up Loch Lomond, but Rob Roy MacGregor?' A keen ear might have detected just a hint of pride in that. 'From Dumbarton Castle they are, for sure.' He swung back on the messenger. 'Creeping up close to the loch-shore, you said, Murdo? This side? That means that they are not wanting to be seen, at all. A surprise it was to be. At this time of day, that can only mean a night arrival.' It was mid-afternoon, and the unseen November sun would be setting behind the great hills to the west in just over an hour. 'They want cover of darkness, then – so it is no peaceable visit!'

'Aye. So Cailness reckoned it. I was to say, Rob, that he was for gathering all the men that he could, whatever, and bringing them to you.'

'M'mmm. I see.' Rob Roy looked out of the window, stroking his pointed beard. 'How long have we got? Of a mercy, the wind is from the east. It will not speed the red-

36

coats' rowing. And if they are for hugging the shore, they will take the longer.'

'They were large and heavy boats, and going but slowly. . . .'

'Aye. If they were south of Cailness when you saw them, Murdo, I'd say that they would not reach Inverarklet for over an hour yet. Two hours before they come knocking at my door here, eh?'

The other nodded an unkempt head.

Rob drew himself up. 'To the kitchen with you, then, Murdo – and get you a bit and a dram. You will be needing it.'

'No need. Will I not be after running to warn others? Corrarklet? And Corrheichen? And Comar, and the rest? You will be needing all your gillies to rouse the clan.'

'No, no. Leave that to me, Murdo. Go you, now.'

When the man had gone, Rob looked at his wife. 'So James Graham has not let the grass grow under his ducal feet!' he said. 'I had not thought that he would act so fast. He must have had this planned for long enough, the man. I am sorry, my dear.'

'Rob – this is a great evil that has come to us,' Mary MacGregor said. 'I . . . I could wish it otherwise, indeed. At this time – with the children. . . . But what is to be, will be. At least, your conscience is clear.' Her lovely eyes gleamed to the suspicion of a smile. 'Clearer than sometimes, perhaps!'

The man grinned. 'Aye – and much good *that* will be doing me! Still, it is a change, is it not?' Then he was grave again, swiftly. 'This may well be an ill business for you, Mary. And the boys. As well perhaps that you should be off to Comar. To your father. You would be safe up there.'

'No, Rob. My place is here. I cannot whisk away two babes, into the hills, at an hour's cry. I will stay. You will not be fighting them round the house itself?'

'No,' he answered her, flatly.'

'But do not waste time on me, Rob. I will do finely. You will be needing to rouse the glens, to get the gillies running to Corraklet and Glen Gyle and Stronachlacher and . . .'

'No,' her husband said again, as flatly.

She stared at him, eyes widening, at the note in his voice. 'No . . . ?'

'No, Mary. No gillies. No rousing of the glens. Not this time.'

'But, Rob . . . ?'

'Flight, it must be this time, *a graidh* – not fight! For me. They will not catch me – but I will not fight them. They will come here and find me gone.'

Mary MacGregor shook her head. 'I do not understand you, Rob. *You*! To flee, without a fight? What has come over you, at all? Oh, I know that I said to Greg that it was clear thinking that was needed, not just big words and talk of war. But that was different. Now, the soldiers are at your very doorstep. Even if there are two hundred of them, you could raise men enough to keep them from here, to trap them in the pass up from the loch, to throw them back into the water . . .'

'Aye, I could do that, Mary – nothing simpler. And, belike, that is just what Montrose would have me do. But have you considered the cost? I am outlawed now, remember. And all who knowingly will be assisting and supporting an outlaw are liable to outlawry in their turn. Any measures can be taken against outlaws – *any* measures, Mary. If I flee, lass, there will be *one* outlaw only. But if I do rouse the clan, all MacGregors will be outlawed, whatever. How think you of that? All my people, at the mercy of Montrose and those others who do not love us. You – and the young ones. Greg, and his bonny wife and bairns. Your old father, at Comar. All – all outside the law. What do you think of that?'

'But . . . ?' She shook her head once more, dark eyes tragic indeed.

'No, lass,' he went on. 'The Gregorach have suffered enough. Already they are proscribed and denied their name, a by-word. I will not put them outside the law as well, my God! Not in the present state of Scotland. Not for *my* sake. Nothing would better suit James Graham, I think. And there is something else, see you. An outlaw's lands and property can be forfeit to the Crown. Inversnaid and Craig-royston are mine, yes – but MacGregors are living on them. They are the clan's lands, too. Make those clansmen outlaws also, and they can be swept off the lands and all property confiscate. But let them remain law-abiding subjects, tenants and tacksmen, and it will be a deal more difficult to dispossess them and take over the land. Do you not see it, Mary?'

'I do not know. I see Rob Roy MacGregor talking like any Lowland lawyer. Talking – not acting. You have ay been wont to act, Rob – not talk. I do not know, at all . . .'

'Where is the clear thinking now, then? Tell me lass – would you see Greg and his Mary and their boys in the heather, outlawed, hunted and homeless, because of what I have done, or have not done? Tell me!'

'So!' Almost shrilly for her, with her deep quiet voice of calm, his wife cried. 'It is your beloved Greg that you are thinking of! That is the way of it. Always Greg. You are not Tutor of Glengyle any longer, remember. . . .'

'I name him and his, because I esteem it little use naming you and yours, woman!'

For moments they looked at each other, the big powerful-seeming man and the beautiful woman, so contrasting yet somehow so complementary, strong characters both. Then Mary sighed.

'I do not know, Rob. You will do what you must,' she said. 'Always you have gone your own road – and will go it to the end, I do not doubt. If this is it, then you must take it – quickly. God grant that it is the right one!'

'Yes. The responsibility is mine, and I must carry it. I must have time, you see. Time for Atholl and Breadalbane to get my letters. Time for my friends to do something – for I have friends still, mind. More important – time for the winter snows to fill the passes and keep the red-coats out of MacGregor country. Give me a month, and Montrose will be baulked till the snows melt. After that – who knows? Argyll will be home from Spain, likely. And there will be a market for cattle again. . . .' He shrugged, as though putting all such considerations finally aside. 'Now – get me food, lass. For two. I will take only MacAlastair. Have him told. I will finish this letter, and be gone.'

Nodding, wordless, she left him.

Some twenty minutes later, the Captain of Clan Alpine, Captain of the Glengyle Highland Watch, famed warrior of the fierce Gregorach, and Laird of Inversnaid and Craig-royston, buckled his sword-belt over his broad shoulder, and turned from the two garrons and the impassive Mac-Alastair back to his waiting family. He gripped young Coll's shoulder and shook it gently, telling the boy to look after his mother and see that he was not too hard on everybody while he was master of Inversnaid. He picked up the two-year-old Ranald, tickled him, and chucked the baby James under the chin. Then he enfolded wife and child together in his long arms, and kissed the woman on hair and brow and lips.

'Do not fear for anything, *a graidh*,' he said. 'This is the best way. I will come to you, or send for you, as soon as I may. God remain with you.'

'Yes, Rob. But I would have preferred that you remained with me, also!'

Long and sombrely he looked into those great eyes, before shaking his head. Then he turned to the garrons. He mounted, but without his usual vigorous vault, raised a hand, and flung the ends of his oldest plaid across his shoulders. Mac-

Alastair mounted, without word or gesture, at his back. And waving away his deerhounds not to follow him, he pulled the pony's head round northwards. Quietly, with no single backward glance, the two men slipped away up the green Snaid valley and into the already shadowy hills.

From many a cot-house door, as well as his own threshold, eyes watched him go, doubtful, perplexed, uncomprehending.

CHAPTER THREE

It was later than might have been expected before the visitors announced themselves by a great and imperative banging on the front door of Inversnaid House. It had been dark for fully two hours. The callers had been very careful, taken every precaution. Mary MacGregor had been kept informed of their progress, of course, by fleet and silent-footed gillies, all the way from the landing at Inverarklet, up the steep pass that climbed through the woods for four hundred feet above the loch, to the entrance of the hanging valley of the Snaid. She had heard how there were scouts out before and to the flank, and how soldiers stepped softly with arms muffled and to whispered commands; how, where Snaid joined Arklet, there had been a halt and conference, while men, many men, had been sent off in parties into the night, right and left, obviously to surround the house and its vicinity. Knowing that the ring of armed men now wholly encompassed and enclosed her home, in the darkness, she had waited, with her children, the house-women and a couple of gillies. Rob's word that there was to be no fighting, no resistance, no gathering, had been obeyed. Rob was always obeyed.

The door was not locked, and without waiting for any sort of answer to the summons, it was thrown open, and men streamed in. First, a group of red-coated soldiers clearing a way for an Officer of Foot; then John Graham of Killearn followed by a rabble of civilians – bailiffs, constables, sheriff officers and Montrose hirelings.

It was as though a storm had hit that house in the green

glen, a violent uncontrolled cataclysm of insensate nature, rather than an entry of an official party or disciplined men. Without request or enquiry or even pause, men swept and stamped and surged through the building, shouting, swearing and knocking over furnishings. Mary MacGregor was flung roughly aside, and one of the gillies who sought to aid her was felled to the floor – but otherwise the occupants were for the moment ignored. Into every room and cupboard and cranny, upstairs and down, the tide of violent men poured, swords and bayonets drawn and sticks brandished, to swipe and prod and slash in a fury of destructive search. The house resounded and shook to the crash of broken glass and china-ware, the banging of doors and the splintering of woodwork. From outside came a corresponding din, as the outbuildings, stables and byres were similarly ransacked – and through the windows the ominous red glare of fire began to flicker, as thatched roofs were lit.

There was utter pandemonium for a while. But not for long, for Inversnaid was not a large house and its search no major task. The savage tide turned and ebbed, and men went streaming outside again in angry chorus. But not all of them. John Graham of Killearn, the officer in charge of the troops, and sundry others came stamping back to where the mistress of the house stood pressed back against the hallway wall, biting her lip, the baby James at her breast and clutching the sobbing Ranald to her thigh. Young Coll, nose bleeding from a swipe he had received when rushing to his mother's defence, stood close by, lower lip trembling, and striving hard to blink back unmanly tears. The gillies were gone, and of the women only the oldest remained, an apron thrown over her grey head and keening shrilly – though her cries did not wholly drown the screaming and the sobbing pleas of the other younger women from the kitchen quarters.

'Where is he?' Killearn demanded, halting in front of Mary MacGregor. He had to shout to make himself heard.

'Where's he hiding, the cowardly red-headed stot?'

Head up, white-faced, burning-eyed, she stared back at him, unspeaking.

'Answer me, woman – or by God it will be the worse for you!' Graham roared. 'We'll find him in the end, never fear – wherever he's skulking. *You* can't save him. Better look to yourself.'

From tight lips Mary spoke. 'Think you, if Rob was here, he would suffer you to insult his wife, ruffian!'

'Watch your words, woman! Where is he?' The man took a pace nearer.

'Think you, even if I knew, that I would tell *you*? Montrose's jackal?'

Killearn's open hand shot out to hit the woman hard across the alabaster white of her lovely face. 'Bitch!' he jerked.

The baby, struck by the heavy braided cuff of the man's coat, wailed. Young Ranald buried his face against his mother's side, screaming. And Coll launched himself bodily at Killearn, small fists clenched and beating – to be hurled aside by the factor's back-handed swipe. One of the Montrose servants grabbed him, flung him into the nearest room, and held the door shut on him.

The officer, a major of The Buffs, looked a little uncomfortable. 'There is no profit in this, Mr Graham,' he said. 'He is not here, clearly. He's been warned, and bolted.'

'He won't be far away,' Killearn grated. 'And this bitch will ken where he is, I'll wager.'

'If she does, it seems that she will not tell. . . .'

'She'll tell, all right, before I'm done wi' her!' the other snarled. 'Get your men outside, Major, searching these animals' cabins and hovels. Leave me to see whether or no' I can make this woman talk!'

The officer hesitated – but only for a moment. Probably he was glad to go, and to be spared responsibility in the business; and of course he and his men were there only in

44

support of the Sheriff-Substitute's civil activities, so that to that extent he was under Killearn's orders. With just a flickering glance at Mary MacGregor, the pallor of her face now marred and barred with a scarlet band, he turned and strode outside, calling the few remaining soldiers after him. From out there, the angry baying of a deerhound suddenly ended in an agonised choking yelp.

The feel of his hand against the woman's face seemed somehow to have affected John Graham, to have changed his attitude. He was actually smiling now, and gently rubbing that hand with the other, eyes narrowed but fixed on her features. Closely, comprehensively, he considered her – and the tip of his tongue emerged to moisten his lips in one or two places. 'Aye,' he said, on an exhalation of breath. Undoubtedly there was satisfaction in the sigh. He continued to rub his hand.

Mary met his gaze unflinchingly, her dark eyes blazing – though she could not wholly control the tumult of her bosom, against which she clutched the six-months-old James. Perhaps it was the baby's motion that spurred Killearn on.

'Take the brats – both o' them,' he barked.

There was some competition amongst his henchmen to obey – especially to grab the baby in arms. Two or three hands reached for it – and in the process of detaching it from the clutch of its mother, her gown was somehow torn down the front. She fought to retain the child, fiercely, silently, and the tearing went on. By the time that she was flung back against the wall, panting, her full breasts were uncovered heaving as though with their own life.

For a moment there was the silence of involuntary admiration. Then comment broke out, loud and appreciative.

'Dirty bitch!' Graham mumbled, peculiarly – but with no indication of revulsion.

Mary MacGregor was no shrinking maidenly girl, but a mature, beautiful and spirited woman – and a MacGregor

45

born as well as wed. Her arms came up, not to cover her body but to reach out still for her tiny son, in an instinctive gesture at once proud and pleading.

Killearn gestured, too. He jabbed a finger in the direction of the door behind which young Coll was already hidden. 'Put the bairn in there,' he rasped. 'This other one, too.' Again his finger stabbed, towards the open door of another room, the principal front chamber of the house. 'Tam! Wattie! In there wi' her. Take the woman in. God's sake – let's have a mite o' privacy, eh!' And he laughed.

Two of his own men, in the Montrose livery, grabbed Mary each by an arm, and knocking roughly aside the little yelling Ranald, half-pushed, half-carried her into the room. Graham came striding in after them, and slammed the door shut behind him.

It would have been dark in that large apartment had it not been for the red glare of the flaming roofs outside. In the baleful uncertain light the three men and the woman stood – and there was nothing kindly in the half-dark to offer cloak for her shame. For a little only the sound of panted breathing competed with the din outside. Nor was Mary MacGregor's breathing the loudest.

'Well – where is he?' Killearn asked, at length. He said it levelly. It was not a question at all, but only a necessary form of words.

She did not speak.

'A-a-aye!' Again that gusty sigh of satisfaction. 'All right, lads,' he said. 'I'll wager you can make the bitch give tongue! She's yours!'

For just a moment the two men stared at him, questioningly, in the flickering firelight.

Graham motioned with his hand, a gesture eloquent as it was obscene. And he barked a throaty laugh.

His henchmen required no further encouragement. They leapt on the woman, hands clawing. Rending and tearing at her garments, they forced her back and back to the wall.

Like wolves they worried at her, wrenching and pawing. She fought back, twisting, struggling, scratching, till a fierce buffet to the side of her head left her dazed and reeling against the wall. Merciless hands ripped the pathetic remnants of her clothing from her, till she stood naked amidst the fallen ruin of it.

The men drew back for a moment, gulping and gasping.

Even then she did not cringe nor huddle nor plead. Nor did she speak, at all. Swaying and dizzy as she was, she stood up straight, defiant, proud even, all her outraged loveliness erubescent in the leaping glow and shadows of the flames. The hand that lifted to her head was not to clutch her bruised temple nor to cover her blazing eyes, but to finally tug loose the fillet which still partially held up the coils of her dark hair. With a toss of the head that spoke louder than any words that she could have used, she shook down the long heavy tresses about her shoulders.

'Ha So there we have it, eh?' the factor said thickly. He had moved over to the side, the better to see and so as not to obstruct any of the firelight from the window. 'No' bad! Och, no' bad! I've seen worse, aye – dammit I have!' His voice rose. 'But the bitch's no' yelping yet, lads. Ye're ower gentle, I doubt. Is that the best ye can do, damn you? *You*, Tam!'

Again the men launched themselves upon their victim. This time it was not at clothing that they pawed. Savagely they wrestled with her, forcing her over towards a great wooden chest. Fiercely she fought back, using her nails, even her teeth. Her attackers were shouting now, though the woman said never a word. Suddenly the man called Wattie yelled with pain, as Mary MacGregor's teeth sank into his wrist. Wrenching his arm free, he swung his clenched fist to the side of her head, in his fury. She sagged limply to the vicious blow, and her struggles became feeble, semi-involuntary.

'Man, Wattie – you're no' up to your usual, the night!'

Killearn reproved, but jovially. 'Och, a bit spirit's ay as good as a sauce, man. Ye should ken that.'

Cursing and stumbling, the two of them as good as carried the swooning woman to the chest. And there, gripping her by the coils of her hair and her arms, they had their brutal way with her, one holding her down for the other. As well that she was only semiconscious. But before they were finished with her, she was struggling and twisting again, to the men's inevitable discomfiture – and to Killearn's evident glee.

Graham, a man with a distinct preference for the supervisory role in most affairs, was offering further practical and amusing advice, when the door burst open, and a sheriff officer's head thrust round.

'Maister Graham!' he cried. 'Maister Graham – you'll hae to come oot o' there. . . .'

'Devil roast ye, man – what's the meaning o' this? Did I no' say I was no' to be disturbed?' the factor roared. 'Get out – and shut that door!'

'But Maister, Graham – your pardon, sir. But, och – the hoose is afire! *This* hoose! The roof's catched alight, frae the others. D'ye no' smell the smoke? D'ye no' *see* it?'

'God's curse on it!' Killearn had been vaguely aware of the smell of burning for some time, of course – but had assumed that it was coming in from the blazing outhouses. And the illumination in that room was not such as to show up curling tendrils of smoke. Now, through the open doorway, it could be seen against the torchlight, billowing down the hallway. Anathematising all and sundry, and ordering his two panting henchmen to have done, to leave the filthy shrew, to put themselves to rights and get out of this, the new sheriff-substitute and county court judge of Stirlingshire stamped out of that ravaged room without another glance at its prostrate mistress.

Muttering, blaspheming, and already beginning to cough with the acrid fumes, his two minions disentangled themselves and went stumbling after him.

In only a comparatively few seconds there was not an intruder left in Inversnaid House. Only the crackle of flames, the wailing of women and the screaming of children resounded.

Mary MacGregor did not add to the din. After a moment she dragged herself upright to stare around her, wild-eyed. For a little she stood there, swaying, but otherwise unmoving. Then, as her mother's consciousness, despite all else, distinguished her Ranald's yelling amongst the rest, and the baby's feebler plaint, she tottered over to where the ruins of her clothing lay, and dazedly sought to cover herself to some extent with what had survived those rending hands. Back at the same chest that had supported her shame, she opened the lid and drew out a couple of large tartan plaids. In one she wrapped herself, and taking the other with her she staggered out of the room.

Young Coll and his two small brothers were locked into the apartment opposite. Their mother opened the door and ran to her children, picking up the baby James from the floor. She clutched them all to her, dry-eyed, wordless. Then, coughing from the now thickly rolling smoke, she put the baby into Coll's arms, with the other plaid wrapped round it, and took up his two-year-old brother herself, to lead the way out, through the kitchen and rear quarters.

The upper floor of the house was now a blazing inferno, fanned by a wintry east wind. Mary MacGregor led her brood, around the stair-foot and down the passage, as though sleep-walking, without expression or any comment. About the back door were grouped hysterical women in various stages of undress, a gillie lying with a broken head, and two dead deerhounds. At sight of their mistress the women's screams rose afresh, declaring their rape, their agony, and their ruination.

Mary MacGregor spoke to none of them, looked at none of them. Straight ahead of her she walked, past them all,

49

through the trampled kitchen-garden and orchard towards the birchwood behind, out of the red ruin and the grim radiance of its blaze, holding her children close, her head high. Darkness, blackness, anonymity, she sought fiercely. And her lovely eyes were wild, wild.

*　　*　　*

Up on the open hillside, about half a mile above the house, was a sort of cave contrived out of a great outcrop of rock that had split down the middle, with a narrow opening and lined with pulled heather – a favourite haunt from which young Coll MacGregor was wont to sally forth to do battle with the champions of all the lesser clans of Scotland. For this shelter his mother made, in the darkness, sure of foot as of direction. And in its draughty sanctuary, huddled close together under the two plaids for warmth, the wife and children of the famed and dreaded Captain of Clan Alpine passed that November night, while below them, on the low ground, the red glow of fires died away and the shouts of men faded. Not once did the woman close her eyes throughout.

At first light, on a grey chill morning of thin driving rain, Mary MacGregor sent Coll downhill, with specific instructions. He went, bent low, dodging, skulking, darting from cover to cover, as his father had taught him in stalking the deer, screening himself amongst the great numbers of somnolent cud-chewing cattle with which that green valley was filled. An hour or so later he was back, leading a couple of garrons. The sun still had not risen behind the mist-shrouded hills to the east.

On his mother's instructions he had avoided the smoking ruins of his home, just as he had avoided contact with any of their people. Except for Old Seana that had been his nurse, as she had been his father's before him. To her black-house of stone and turf he had made his inconspicuous way, collecting the two ponies from one of the in-fields. An old and bent crone, Seana had escaped molestation at the hands of the intruders – though most of her chickens were missing. From her the boy had brought a bag of oatmeal, some cold meat and one or two old pieces of women's wear for his mother. Also the news that the invaders had retired back to their boats at Loch Lomond, in the darkness, no doubt fearful of reprisals from the clan. No soldiers remained around Inversnaid meantime. He had spoken to none other, and, tight-lipped and great-eyed, he did not expiate on what he had seen.

Mary MacGregor asked no questions. Indeed she said but little, at all. Something seemed to have dried up within her. Anonymity she craved still, within herself almost, and certainly from her fellow men and women.

Presently, wrapped in a plaid against the chilly rain, the baby in her arms, and seated on one of the placid and sure-footed garrons, she led the way out from their shelter, Coll, with Ranald before him, riding at her back. She turned the beast's head northwards, keeping to the high ground. Well up on the side of the long ridge that separated the Snaid valley from that of Loch Lomond, she rode, heading into the wilderness of empty mountains between Glen Falloch and Glen Dochart. And not once did she glance down towards the scattered houses in the floor of the glen, nor backwards towards Glen Arklet, where help and comfort and sympathy were there for the asking, or over to Comar, her childhood's home under Beinn Lomond. Not even half-right towards Glen Gyle, where the Lady Christian, Gregor's mother, would have cherished her. Unspeaking, straight-backed, expressionless, she gazed directly ahead of her, from eyes that glowed with a strange smouldering fire.

The long-maned, long-tailed garrons paced deliberately, picking their way through stones and heather.

Rob Roy had a house at Corrycharmaig near the west end of Glen Dochart, on the fringe of the safe Campbell country of Breadalbane.

CHAPTER FOUR

IT was four days later before Rob Roy himself came riding down Glen Dochart to Corrycharmaig, MacAlastair at his back, with no hurry on him and all the time in the world to play with, a man philosophically seeking to enjoy the freedom of outlawry. Intent on involving no others, save MacAlastair, this shadow of his, in the displeasure of the authorities, he had lain up, the day following his departure from Inversnaid, snug on Eilean Dhu, a tiny island in the middle of Loch Katrine, waiting for nightfall before moving on again. Avoiding all contact with men – for he was too well known and eye-catching a figure to remain unrecognised anywhere in the Highlands – he had made his way north by east by the head of Balquhidder and Glen Ogle to the great strath of Tay, heading for the castle of Finlarig, seat of his own mother's cousin, *Mac Cailein Mhic Donnachaidh*, John, first Earl of Breadalbane, chief of the Glenorchy Campbells. He had decided to deliver his letter to Breadalbane in person. Not that he had any love for the man, nor even respect – save perhaps for his undoubted shrewdness and cunning – knowing that he would betray friend, ally and country whenever it suited his interests so to do; nevertheless, besides being undisputed lord of some hundreds of square miles of the Central Highlands, a powerful figure, and undeniably the cleverest rogue in all Scotland, he hated Montrose. In the circumstances, that was of vital importance. So Rob had gone to see Breadalbane, and for the very reasons that he sought to avoid and not involve other men in his outlawry he had come to Finlarig openly and with almost a flourish. As far as John Campbell was concerned he recognised no duty, no conscience; he would involve him if he could. How much good his visit to that wily and slippery customer might have done him, remained to be seen.

So now, Rob rode down Glen Dochart in the thin wintry sunlight, to his house of Corrycharmaig under the towering mass of snow-capped Beinn More. He was surprised to see, rising from one of its chimneys, a drift of woodsmoke, blue against the rich sepia of the old heather that soared beyond. He had not expected the house to be occupied – but perhaps some of his folk in the two or three cot-houses near by had installed therein some traveller of quality in need of shelter? Highland hospitality could demand more than that.

None of his people emerged to offer him warning of any hostile presence in the house, so Rob did not hesitate to ride right up to the door. His surprise grew still further as he saw a boy at play with a puppy up at the edge of the pine wood behind the house, a boy whom he suddenly realised was his own son Coll. Nor did his wonder abate anything when the lad, after staring at him fixedly, not only failed to answer his wave of greeting, but abruptly turned away and went slowly but deliberately into the darkness of the trees.

Fingering his beard perplexedly, Rob jumped down. Though the garrons' approach must have been audible, nobody was waiting in the doorway to greet him. He strode into the lobby – and all but tripped over young Ranald, who was crawling about the floor. At sight of him the child jumped up and ran screaming into the kitchen.

'Ho ho, small fellow, little frog-in-the-bog! What sort of welcome is this for your sire?' the father demanded, great voiced. But he prevailed nothing against the bawling.

Corrycharmaig was not a large house – for Rob had no use for large houses, being essentially a man of the open air, of movement, whom no hearthstone could bind. Three or four paces took him into the kitchen. And there he found his wife.

She stood facing him from the far end of the room, almost as though she had retreated there at the sound of him. But there was no expression of fear of an unknown intruder about her – nor of welcome or relief either, for that matter. No expression of any sort, indeed. Her proudly beautiful features were calm, still, almost impassive, as though wiped clean of expression. She did not smile to him. She did not speak. Her hands were folded in front of her. She did not move. Only those great eyes glowed. And the light in them was distinctly peculiar.

'Mary, my dear, my heart's love!' the man cried. 'Here is a great surprise.' Long-strided he came across the room to her, to enfold her in his arms, to swing and lift her right off her feet, to hold her aloft. 'What brings you here? What means this move? Did you . . . ? But, no – do not tell me! It is plain – och, you just cannot be doing without your husband, woman!' And setting her down, he kissed her.

The woman's lips did not stir under his. Her body did not stir within his arms. No word came from her.

Concerned, the man drew back from her. Holding her from him, his hands on her shoulders, he peered into those eyes – and somewhere near the base of his neck an incipient shiver was born at what he saw therein.

'What is it, Mary *a graidh*?' he demanded. 'What ails you, my heart?'

Slowly her dark head shook.

'Come, my dear,' Rob insisted, frowning. 'Is it ill you are? Or what, then?'

Almost as though it was a physical effort, her lips moved slowly. 'What . . . is that . . . to you?' she whispered.

Astounded, her husband stared. 'Dear God,' he besought. 'What has got into you, woman?'

'*That* you may well ask!' The first hint of emotion, that of bitterness, was there. 'What, indeed!'

Rob tossed his bonnet on to the table, and ran a hand through the curling thatch of his red hair. 'I do not understand,' he declared. 'For God's sake, Mary, tell me what this means! Tell me what sort of a woman you have become, to speak so!'

'Tell me, rather, what sort of a man *you* are, Robert MacGregor, to have turned your back on your wife and children, to have failed me as surely as you have failed your honour and your clan?' That was said levelly, without evident passion or anger, and was the more wounding therefore. 'You threw me to the dogs and rode away – you, the hero of men! You said that it was the best way, that I was not to fear anything. You preferred that God should remain with me, in the crutch of trouble – not yourself. And God did not do so. God turned His back on me, as did yourself. God and you, both, Robert MacGregor.'

He shook his head, wordless.

She went on evenly, as though reciting something that she had learned by heart. ' "The responsibility is mine," you said, and you must carry it. "I must have time," you said – and you bought the time with me! You said . . .'

'Stop it, Mary – stop it! What are you trying to tell me, at all . . . ?' That was little more than a whisper, but a fierce one.

'Little enough to you, perhaps, who have your mind on greater things. Only that your home is in ashes, your glen savaged, your children abused, and your wife shamed!'

'Wha-a-at!' The huge hands came out to grip her shoulders again – and though he scarcely knew it, they shook her bodily.

'But, you – *you* won clear. And the clan did not rise. So it may be that you are satisfied, whatever!'

'Be quiet, woman! Enough of that,' the man said roughly. 'Tell me what . . . ?'

'I have told you. They burned down your house and all within it. They abused your women. Your children they struck, and tore from my arms . . .'

'And you? They did not strike *you*, my God?'

'Me! Aye, Rob – they struck me! Would God that it had been with the sword, and that I had died at the first stroke!'

'Mary!'

She winced involuntarily with the pain of his grip. 'I would have done what little they left undone . . . with a dirk in my own heart . . . had it not been for the children. Jamie needed me. And Ranald. They need me yet. For a little time yet. Then, pray God, the grave will hide my shame at last! Though,' she paused, seeming to gaze through and past him to horror indescribable, 'my mother's bones will shrink aside in their grave when mine are laid beside them!'

'Merciful Lord!' her husband cried. 'What . . . I cannot . . . are you . . . ?' He gulped. 'By the Powers of Heaven – what have they done to you? What hellish thing is this?'

She shook her head, impassive again, but otherwise did not answer him.

'Mary, my love, my heart's desire – what have they done? What have *I* done to you? What? What, I say!' And at her blank stare, he abruptly all but flung her from him, and went off storming round the room, the extremity of his emotion exploding into compulsive physical action. Fists clenched and shaking, he stamped and strode and swore, cursing heaven and hell and men, tossing the heavy table out of his way as though it had been a toy, the room itself seeming to quiver to the vibration of his own fierce urgency. The woman herself shrank back instinctively, for Rob Roy MacGregor in the grip of passion was an unnerving sight. So much power and energy racking a human frame was something to be eyed askance. Men who did not love him had suggested that he was devil-possessed; others, rather that he had the spirit of the ancient heroes within him.

At length, with a tremendous and very evident effort, the man controlled himself. 'The soldiers did this – the damned red-coats?' he demanded, his voice trembling. 'I would not have believed it possible. Not at this day.'

'No? Have you forgotten Glen Coe and the MacIans? What they did there?'

'That was twenty years ago. In the aftermath of war. This is peace. The crime that I am outlawed for is that I have not surrendered to a charge of bankruptcy! A mere civil offence. And, for this . . .!' He swallowed, almost choked.

'It was not the soldiers,' she sad. 'It was . . . it was . . .' Almost it seemed as though she could not bring herself to speak the name. 'It was Graham. John Graham of Killearn.'

'*Killearn*? The factor?' The Blazing-eyed he strode up to her again. 'That . . . that oaf! That bullock of Montrose's! He it was that . . . that struck you?'

She nodded.

'Then . . .' Rob Roy drew a great shuddering breath. 'Then, as Royal's my Race – he shall pay for it! Pay in full. Pay for it with his wretched life! Before the throne of God Almighty I swear it – John Graham shall die!'

Coldly the woman nodded. 'Aye, he will die. Sooner or later he will die. But not as I died four nights agone. Would that he could!'

'I shall make him suffer first, Mary, I promise you . . .'

'Will you?'

'Yes, then. On my soul I swear it!'

'What will you give him to suffer? What that will recompense? A little pain, before the end? A little fear? What is that? Think you that will serve, Robert MacGregor?' The woman's eyes glowed again.

Rob's own brilliant eyes blinked a little at the intensity of feeling that he saw in them. He was a Celt himself, and well knew the black fire of hatred that humbled and slighted pride could engender in his race. But he had never before

57

seen it in Mary, a calm, serene woman, however strong-minded. But she was a MacGregor, of course. . . .

'Aye,' he said slowly. 'Rest assured, it will be sufficient.'

She said no more – but the man turned away at the blaze of something like contempt, mockery, in her glance.

After a moment, he said, 'Tell me how it was, Mary – the things that were done.'

'No,' she answered. 'The things that were done that night are not to be told. Not ever. Enough, and more than enough, that they happened. They cannot be undone. I cannot seek my grave yet awhile, as I would – but at the least the words can be buried!'

'But . . . och, Good Lord, woman . . . !' Helplessly Rob shook his head. 'Would you have me ignorant of the facts – myself, who must avenge what was done? Your own husband . . . ?'

'You will never avenge what was done. And what husband are you to me, who turned your back and left me? You chose ignorance when you rode away. Keep it. I have nothing for you, now – and want nothing from you. Save peace. Go, now.'

'But, Mary . . . !' Perplexed and uncertain as he had never been before, in all his life, Rob Roy spread his hands wide. 'What am I to do with you? How may I help you, my dear?'

'You cannot. Save perhaps in one thing. Find me another place to hide in. A secret place, deep in the mountains. Far from all men's eyes. Where I may hide myself and my children. That is all that I ask of you, Robert MacGregor.'

He sighed. 'As you will, *a graidh.* That I can do, yes. But is that all that I mean to you, now – after all our years together, lass?'

'Our years together ended four nights aback. You it was who ended them. Now go, please. That you can do for me, as well. . . .'

Rob picked up his bonnet. He looked at her, steadfastly

58

and sadly – and never had he seen her more beautiful. Deranged she might be, beside herself, a stranger almost – but she was still the most lovely woman on whom his eyes had ever rested. With a hand raised in salute, he turned and went.

*　　*　　*

He did not go right away and leave her, there and then, of course. Abruptly waving away MacAlastair and the ponies, he went striding savagely off up the hill behind the house, on and on, climbing ever higher up the steep side of Beinn More, as though he would leave below him in the valley all the heartache and ruin of his life there represented. To the very summit of the mountain he went, tireless, like a man possessed, there to sit in brooding stillness, unmindful of the chill that grew on him, eyeing without seeing all the far-flung vista of mountain and valley, and fighting his own battle with himself. It was almost dark before he came down, heavy-footed, to Corrycharmaig.

He found the situation as he had left it, as far as his wife was concerned. With young Ranald he managed to re-establish relations, but Coll remained distant and wary, despite all his father's efforts. It seemed that, in the boy's eyes, he was a shattered idol. From him, however, Rob learned, by questioning, what had happened at Inversnaid House four nights before up till the time when the children had been locked away in the inner room.

That night the master of the house slept, wrapped in his plaid, on the kitchen floor, excluded from Mary's room.

The day following he hung about the house and its vicinity, seeking to maintain a surface illusion of normality – with scant success. Mary fed him, replied after a fashion when he spoke to her, looked through him rather than at him, and made it obvious that she wished him away. He tried to break through this armour of reserve, tried honeyed words, pleading words, angry words, and no words at all.

But all was of no avail. And to a man of Rob's urgent and vigorous temperament and active habit, this state of affairs was more than trying. One day was as much of it as he could stand. Moreover, the fever for vengeance was burning within him like a searing flame.

At sunrise next morning then, he flung out of the house, shouting for MacAlastair and the garrons. They rode into a grey sombre morning, with mist low on the hills, everything dripping moisture, and Loch Iubhair below the house leaden as Rob's heart. Westwards they went, fording the Dochart to avoid the clachan of Crainlarich and the need to be civil to any man, and on up Strathfillan. At Tyndrum they swung right, to commence the long climb to the watershed of Scotland, high birthplace of rivers that ran east to the North Sea and west to the Atlantic, using the old zigzagging drove road that was Rob's favourite route for bringing down herds of cattle from all the north and west. The summit of the wild and lonely pass was thick in mist, but beyond the watershed, as often happens, the weather changed. Through a break in the clouds a few miles away the noble peak of Beinn Dorain frowned down on all that barren wilderness. Barren, that is, save for a single fertile island of green that crouched right below the savage mountain, a green startling and lovely as it was unexpected in all the waste of rock and heather, tucked into the mouth of a steep glen. And amidst the green haughland and watermeadows, a single small house stood, the only habitation of man as far as eye could see. It was the place of Auchinchisallan, or more commonly, just Auch. The men rode down towards it.

This was all Breadalbane country, and for a consideration its lord leased Auchinchisallan to Rob Roy, who found its extraordinarily rich pastures and fine shelter uncommonly useful for the assembling, sustenance and strengthening of his cattle droves, weak and hungry after long travelling, before they faced the final trial across the watershed. Moreover, the place was strategically situated – always an important consideration with the MacGregor – guarding the back door into Glen Lyon and covering the flank of Glen Orchy. He had found it a useful investment in the past.

All winter, with the droving season over, the little house was apt to stand empty. Now the two men set about putting it to rights and making it a reasonably comfortable place of refuge for Mary MacGregor and the children. Though a mere dozen miles, as the eagle might fly, from Corrycharmaig, Auch was more than twice that far as men must travel, and hidden deep enough in the wilderness for any would-be anchorite. A couple of days' work, and Rob was satisfied. Leaving MacAlastair to finish certain improvements, he rode back to Corrycharmaig, and the next day brought back a little procession consisting of his wife and children, a couple of elderly but trusty gillies with their unmarried sister, a number of garrons, four milk cows, and some poultry slung in wickerwork panniers. It was not a cheerful journey, even allowing for its slowness and the effect of driving rain.

Two mornings later, Rob made his farewells. Mary did not ask him where he was going, and he did not volunteer the information. She suffered him to kiss the alabaster-white of her brow – and in doing so he perceived silver hairs, amongst the raven-black, that he had not seen before. But she made no gesture towards him, did not unbend her stiffness, did not even come to the door to see him go.

Heavy-hearted, he turned his horse's head southwards towards the pass once more, MacAlastair silent as ever at his heels. When he looked back, only Coll and the gillies stood there. At least the boy raised a hand in valedictory salute.

CHAPTER FIVE

HIDDEN amongst boulders on the high ridge of Crèag an Fhithich, the Raven's Crag, with long Loch Lomond far below at his back, Rob Roy MacGregor looked down into his own fair and grassy glen of Inversnaid – and his mood was savage. He could see the blackened ruins of his house. He could see that many of the other habitations of the glen, the cot-houses and cabins of his people, were roofless and abandoned. Though it was drawing towards evening, he could see no blue columns of smoke from evening fires arising from any of them. Many of his cattle still grazed placidly on the valley sides, and especially around the little sheet of green water, Lochan Uaine, in mid-glen – but then, cattle were a drug on the market meantime. He could not see any of his large herd of horses, save for a scattered beast or two fairly high up amongst the cattle.

Not that he was looking for them with any urgency. The man's attention was concentrated on a spot within the very mouth of the glen, down where it opened into the wider and deeper Glen Arklet. Here, as distinct from elsewhere, was life, movement, activity – and colour. The colour, however, was rather noticeably scarlet. Though there *was* the blue of woodsmoke at the lowermost end of it. The movement was concentrated in three fairly closely linked areas – two in the valley floor, near the burnside down there, and the third a little way up the hillside near by, around a rocky projecting bluff in the very jaws of the valley. That bluff, Tom na Bairlinn, the Knoll of Warning, had long been used as a platform for a beacon-fire, since it commanded wide views up Glen Arklet to the east and out across Loch Lomond to the west. The activity seemed to be greatest at this point and at the higher of the two by the riverside – that only a short way below the ruins of Rob's own house – but the scarlet colour was confined to the group lower down, where the valley opened wider and it seemed that tents were pitched.

'What think you of it?' Rob jerked to MacAlastair, pointing. 'What are they at, down there, think you – damn them?'

That taciturn man shook his dark head. 'Busy, they are. At what, I cannot see. We could be going nearer.'

His master nodded. By keeping well over on the west side of their ridge, they could move down, unseen from Inversnaid, for another mile almost. Nor might they be spotted from Loch Lomond-side because of the steep overhanging woods of oak and ash that clothed the entire escarpment on that side. And there was no one to observe them from out on the surface of the loch.

The early November dusk was settling on the hills before the two men reached their final vantage-point, a little birchwooded hill that rose directly across from the rocky knoll aforementioned and a mere four or five hundred yards from it. The dusk helped to hide them, but it did not improve their vision – nor did the smirr of rain that was drifting between. Still, the situation was fairly obvious now, as from amongst the silver and shadow of the birches they peered.

'*Dia*! They are building,' Rob exclaimed. 'See – walls are going up. There. And there. And, look you – they are quarrying into the side of Tom na Bairlinn. They are winning the stone from there. See the men busy like ants at it, whatever!'

'Aye,' his companion agreed, briefly.

'Damnation! See you what it is – what it must be? Those walls are to be thick, strong, my goodness. It is a castle that they are making. A fort. As Royal's my Race –

63

they are for building a fort on *my* land! Mine, devil take them!'

There could be little doubt that such was the case. On a grassy terrace or shelf where the Snaid Burn made a loop before plunging over in a series of little cataracts in its descent into Glen Arklet, masons were active in erecting stout walls of the reddish stone that others were quarrying from the base of the rocky knoll behind. Those walls were of little height as yet – but clearly they were going to be both wide and substantial and of greater extent than any mere house. Rob saw where some of his horses had gone; many of them were being used to carry and haul the stone from the knoll to the terrace. The men involved were all dully-clad labourers; the colour came from further down, below the cataracts, where there was room for a small military camp, and where, amongst the tents and cooking-fires a company of scarlet-coated soldiers lounged – guards for the masons and quarrymen presumably, and too fine to be demeaned with manual labour.

The site selected for the building gave fine views in most directions and an excellent field of fire – almost as good as on the top of the nearby Knoll of Warning – with the added advantage that drinking-water could be gained without deep well-drilling through rock, which no doubt always was a preoccupation with fort-builders who had to visualise siege conditions. Nevertheless, Rob himself would have built that fort on the summit of Tom na Bairlinn. Not that he did not recognise the advantages of the chosen site; had it not been his intention, years before, to build his own new house exactly there, instead of merely enlarging the existing farm-house a little further up?

'So – we are to be permanently occupied, are we!' he said, in a tense whisper. 'As God's my witness, we shall see about that!'

As daylight faded, the busy men down there knocked off work, and went straggling away in groups and parties, some on the ponies, but most walking, by the steep track through the little pass that led down to Loch Lomond. Presumably the contractors for the work were not disposed to permit their unarmed hirelings to stay overnight up there in the open, surrounded by MacGregors, even under guard of the military. Only the red-coats in their camp remained. It would be chilly weather for camping, too.

When it was quite dusk, Rob and his attendant shadow slipped back out of the wood, leading their garrons and moving silently. Up the glen-side again they went, amongst the cud-chewing cattle, till it was safe to mount and ride once more. Then they turned downwards, crossed the Snaid Burn just below Lochan Uaine, and set their beasts to climb the steep hillside beyond that enclosed the glen on the east. This was a much higher ridge than that to the west, but the sure-footed ponies picked their way unerringly and tirelessly through grass, dying bracken and short heather till presently they were over the summit and slanting down into the pit of the valley beyond. This was Corrie Arklet, a parallel but shorter and less fertile glen than that of the Snaid, a couple of miles to the east. Down the track that followed its central burn the travellers rode, with the lights of Corraklet House gleaming ahead of them in the mouth of it.

But though the master of that house was Rob's own distant cousin, John MacGregor – and Mary's uncle into the bargain – they did not present themselves at its hospitable door. Skirting its many cot-houses – for Corraklet was the major centre of population for all the area – Rob took up his position amongst a group of boulders and thorn trees on the hillside above, and then sent MacAlastair on foot down to the lamp-lit house below, his instructions definite. The gillie melted into the blue of the night without a sound.

It was some time before the sound of heavier footsteps and still heavier breathing proclaimed the arrival of someone other than MacAlastair. Rob waited until he could just distinguish the blur of movement in the darkness before he raised his voice, from behind a great boulder.

'Wait you there, now,' he called, quietly. 'Greetings, John *mo charaid.*'

'Och, is that yourself, man Rob?' a panting voice replied. John MacGregor was getting to be an elderly man now, and heavy for hurried climbing. 'What sort of nonsense is this, at all . . . ?'

'Wait where you are, John, I say,' the younger man repeated, as the other continued to come up. 'And put you your plaid over your head, see you.'

'Och, for the Lord's sake, Rob – what ails you, man? Have you lost your wits . . . ?'

'No, Cousin – other things I have lost, but not my wits maybe. Hold him, MacAlastair. 'Tis for your own good, John – for the clan's sake. Tomorrow, I want you to be able to say, on your oath, that you have not seen me, that I have not been to your house. Otherwise, you may well find yourself outlawed likewise, for aiding and abetting myself. And you have seen what outlawry means, in this year of our Lord, seventeen and thirteen!'

'*Dia* – so that's it! Think you that I am afraid of them, Rob? That I am afraid to acknowledge you? Think you that I fear the dirty, skulking, burning women-fighters? Think you that I cannot take to the heather, yet, with fifty good claymores with me, and teach this Sassunach scum what it means to insult a MacGregor! I tell you . . .'

'Aye, John – aye,' Rob interrupted heavily. 'I could have done that same, too – with three hundred blades instead of fifty. And written the final death-sentence on our clan! Should I have done that, John? Should I, man?'

'Hech – what way is that to be speaking, Rob? The Gregorach are not so easily disposed of, my God! We have had them hounding us before, and thrown them back. In the old days . . .'

'Aye – but these are not the old days, *mo charaid.* These

are the new days, in Scotland. London rules now, in Scotland – and the nominees of London. Our true king twiddles his thumbs in France. Scotland is at peace – and the Government has many soldiers, and little for them to be doing. I could have thrown this parcel of ruffians back into Loch Lomond, yes – but only with the help of the clan. And with what result? The Government, with no one else stirring against them in all the land, could have sent their hundreds, their thousands of soldiers against this corner of the Highlands, to wipe our houses and our families off the face of the land – however snug we fine sworders might be in the heather! Was that the price that I should have paid? We know that many in high places, and one James Graham in especial, just wait their opportunity to destroy, once and for all, the very name and memory of MacGregor. *Dia* – of all the wide lands that once were ours, Glen Orchy, Glen Strae, Glen Lyon and Glen Lochay, Strathfillan, Glen Falloch, Glen Dochart, Glen Ogle . . .' The man's deep voice quivered as he named them, like the proudest notes of a lament. 'All these, and more, are gone. Only this little corner – Glen Gyle and Glen Arklet, Inversnaid and Craigroyston, are left to us. We have clung to these, though hated and proscribed, through all. They would have been the price of my swording, John. Would it have been worth it? Even at the cost I have had to pay? And nothing, I wager, would better have pleased the man who sent those soldiers – James Graham of Montrose.'

Save for a long exhalation of breath, the older man was silent.

It was a strange interview, up there on the bare hillside in the darkness, with the curlews calling and calling wearily around them and no other sound to the night but the sigh of the wind over heather – one cousin hidden behind great rocks, the other with his plaid-end tossed across his face, and MacAlastair standing by, silent, expressionless.

There came a pleading note into Rob Roy's voice, such

as few men could have heard before. 'You understand why I did it, John?'

'Aye. Aye – it could be that you are right. But . . . my God, it is an ill day for the Gregorach when Rob Roy MacGregor turns the other cheek for the Sasunnach to spit upon!'

Beyond a sharp intake of breath, the younger man answered nothing to that.

'Are we then to swallow their spittle? Do we stand by and bow our heads, man?' Corrarklet went on. 'We have done as you bade us. We have not risen. We have not touched a hair of a soldier's head. It has been hard to do, as Heaven's my witness – but we have done it. I do not know if I can be holding our people in much longer. . . .'

'You must, John. You must. What of Gregor – what of Glengyle? How does he take it?'

'Och, he is away yet. He is not back from Arnprior. Had you not heard? His wife is sick, and he waits with Buchanan of Arnprior. By the Powers – if Gregor Black-Knee had been home, no red-coat would be remaining in these glens!'

Again Rob was silent.

The older man wagged his head, so that the plaid dropped. 'And you, Rob?' he demanded. 'You, of all men! Do you accept it all, just? They name you outlaw, and burn your house, insult your wife – even strike her, it is said, my God – and turn her and your boys out of doors! Is that nothing to you . . . ?'

'Fool! Fool!' The sudden violence and fury of that eruption from behind the boulder made even the speaker take an involuntary backward step, so fierce and unexpected was it. 'Damn you – think you that I am a crawling reptile! A cold-blooded worm and no man! As Royal's my Race – I'll make them pay for what they have done! Montrose and Killearn shall rue the day that they did this thing. Before the throne of Almighty God, I swear it! They shall pay, pay, pay . . . !' There was anguish and pride and hate and a savage determination in that throbbing rising voice. But by an effort that must have been tremendous, the mounting wrath was checked, disciplined, and the voice steadied. 'But I myself shall pay my debts, see you. Not the clan,' Rob went on. 'What has been done has been done to *me*. What is done in return shall be done by me! They can do no more to me, now, save take my life. But I can do a deal for *them*, before that day! Fear not that they shall not pay, John *mo charaid*. Only, *I* shall set the price, and no other. Is that understood, Cousin?'

'Aye, Rob. Aye – if that is your wish.' Corrarklet's enunciation of the words was thick. Any man who had abruptly borne the full impact of Rob Roy MacGregor's unleashed anger was apt to be dry-mouthed for a little. 'What . . . what would you have us do, then?'

'Two things, John. Keep the clan quiet – and keep me informed. I want information all the time. I shall need it, whatever. Our folk must not raise their hands – but their eyes and their ears must be mine.'

'They will know that you are fighting back, Rob? That your pride – and theirs – is not lost on you?'

'They will know, by Heaven! But they must help me in the way that I say.'

'And Glengyle . . . ?'

'I will attend to Gregor. Now, John – I want information from yourself, here and now. Tell me how the soldiers are placed, just? What are their numbers? How goes it down at Loch Lomond-side?'

'Aye, then. This is the way of it, Rob . . .'

* * *

By the dark waters of Lochan Uaine Rob halted, and dismounted. MacAlastair was still his sole companion, but they had three ponies now, the third one fairly heavily laden. Away to the south, in the mouth of the glen, they could see the red glow of a single large fire; evidently the soldiers had let their numerous cooking-fires die out, but kept one blaze going, no doubt equally for its light and for the comfort of unfortunate sentries. Apart from that red gleam of light, the night was black. It was after midnight, starless, and with a drift of fine rain in the cold air.

They had halted at the lower end of the lochan. The water was high, after days of rain, lipping over the dam that Rob had built a few years before. Always there had been a natural pond there, a mere widening of the burn in a hollow, more reeds than water at the height of summer; Rob, as the cattle-droving business expanded, had found it expedient to dam up this lochan, as he had done with others elsewhere, to provide storage reservoirs for watering large numbers of beasts in dry weather.

While MacAlastair unloaded the pack-pony, Rob ferreted about at the lower side of the dam, peering and feeling and testing. Since it was he who had erected it, he knew the construction and points of weakness therein; but it was difficult to trace the exact conformation in the darkness, and to find or contrive the cavities and corners that he required. He had never looked upon himself as an expert in demolition.

They had appropriated the major part of the Gregorach's cherished store of gunpowder. MacAlastair was unpacking it slowly, handling the stuff gingerly, much less sure of himself than usual. It was a pity about the threatening rain, since they must keep the powder dry.

In order to create a cavity large enough to be effective, and placed so as to give maximum disruption, the two men had to labour long and uncomfortably, in a cramped position, digging with dirks and bare fingers, loosening, prising and extracting stones and rubble and soil. It seemed to be an extraordinary expenditure of effort when explosive was supposed to be doing the work – in fact, Rob more than once snorted that they might as well forget the gunpowder and pull the thing to pieces by hand. But at length they had a hole large enough and deep enough to accommodate their supply of powder. To keep it dry from trickling water, they lined the cavity with an old dear-hide rug from Corrarklet House, and thereafter filled in the explosive. This had all to be packed in again securely with replaced stones and turfs, to conserve the force of the blast – but a small gap had to be left, through which the igniting charge could be led. The total toil was considerable, and it was a couple of hours before Rob was satisfied.

He sent MacAlastair off, then, to try to drive away out of the floor of the glen any cattle that might be passing the night therein. Cattle represented life to the MacGregors. Meanwhile Rob had to lay his detonating contrivance. This was a problem, for he had no slow-burning fuse, nor anything which he could produce at short notice which would serve with any certainty. The only thing for it was to lay a line of gunpowder itself to a sufficient distance for his own safety, and in due course ignite this. And it would not do for such a train of powder to get wet, in the interim.

While giving MacAlastair the time he needed, Rob prospected as best he could an unimpeded and sheltered route for his fuse-line – with a view to his own hasty retreat once it was lit. Just how fast the flame would run, he had small idea. So he plotted his own line of flight with fair thoroughness also.

At length he decided that MacAlastair had had long enough – he was not to go too far down the glen anyway, for fear of alarming the soldiers' camp. Rob laid his trail of black powder – difficult to do evenly in the darkness – hastily reassured himself as to his line of flight, and got out his flint and tinder from his sporran. Striking sparks into the tinder, he blew on it, saw it flare up, and tossed the little blaze on to the gunpowder line.

He turned and ran.

He did not run far. There was a large rock-fall about thirty yards back and uphill, behind which he had intended to hide himself. But he had gone barely half as far before he felt the ground convulse beneath his feet. Without a moment's hesitation he flung himself flat, to join that heaving earth. It seemed to co-operate, as though it rose up to meet him. Indeed, the unanimity appeared to be almost too urgent, all but knocking the breath out of the man – though possibly that was the effect of blast. Curiously enough, Rob was aware of no great uproar, no huge explosion of sound. Probably that also was the effect of blast on his eardrums. Gasping for breath and clawing instinctively at the ground for some sort of security, the first sounds of which he was aware, after a period of seeming suspended sensation, were the thud and clump and patter of things, large and small, raining down around him and upon him – stones, sods, gravel, water. But this was quickly drowned under a much more potent volume of sound, an uproar now, authentic enough if delayed, and rising mightily – the swelling irresistible voice of pent waters released. From a drumming rumble it rose to a thunderous roar, and the ground beneath the sprawling man, that had been heaving, now began to quiver and tremble. Somehow he managed to drag himself to his feet, and went stumbling and staggering on, higher, out of reach of the clutching tearing flood that he had unchained.

Behind the rock-fall that he had selected as refuge, Rob turned and gazed back. Dark as it was, there was no difficulty in seeing the result of his handiwork, for the waters were black no longer, but foaming white, leaping and spouting in a wide and headlong cataract. On and on they poured, completely overwhelming and submerging the modest bed of the burn. It seemed astonishing that so comparatively small a lochan could have contained so great a volume of water.

Rob stood watching, bemused, fascinated by the violence of the power that he had unleashed, even a little abashed.

At length, with the noise beginning to abate and the level

of the torrent manifestly dropping, he climbed up to where the garrons still stood, restive. He soothed them with a word or two, mounted his own beast, and leading the two others, set off down the glen, keeping his distance well above the valley floor. He passed the sites of three of his people's cot-houses. They had had their thatches burned by the soldiers, and had been deserted – and now no trace of any of them remained, that Rob could see.

Presently a dark figure materialised from behind a whinbush. It was MacAlastair. Wordless he took his place behind his master.

Rob turned. 'Well, man – what of it?' he demanded, a little testily perhaps, for him. 'You saw? You had time enough – for the cattle? What think you of it?'

'It was an ill thing, that,' the other returned, flatly. 'You were after washing away every last stone of the house where I was born. And others too, whatever.'

'Aye, maybe. But maybe also I washed away more than that! Maybe I washed some little of the defilement from this glen, see you.' That was sombrely said. 'Come.'

As they neared the mouth of the valley, they dismounted and left the ponies, to proceed cautiously on foot. No red glow of camp-fire now beckoned them on. No sound other than the rush of the swollen stream and the sigh of the wind came to them.

From the shadow of Tom na Bairlinn they peered downwards, right and left.

MacAlastair spoke – and it was not often that he initiated any discussion. 'Think you that they are all drowned dead?' he wondered.

Rob shook his head. 'No. They would be hearing the noise of it, for sure. They would have the time to get out. Their sentries would wake the camp. And the glen widens there, below the falls. Och, some of them might be caught, yes – but the most of them would get out of it.'

'Your own house, too? It will be gone, like the rest? I

cannot see that far, in the dark . . .'

'Maybe – what was left of it.' Rob shrugged. But it was not upstream that he peered, to where the blackened walls of Inversnaid House had stood above a bend of the burn, but directly below, to that other shelf where the fort-building operations had been in progress. 'But what matter – so long as these other walls are down? Their castle. Their fort. Can you see them? See if they still stand? Or is the water still covering them?'

'I cannot see, no. But . . . can that be? Those walls they were building were thick. Strong. No house walls.'

'Aye. But the mortar is new. And better than that – that site is bad, see you, though it looks the best place in the glen, I grant you. It is undercut by the burn. A shelf of rock there is, yes – but underneath it is sand. That is why I did not build my house there. I started it, you will mind – but changed. After two days of rain, I saw the cracks appearing, whatever. So I moved away. Come – we will see.'

Cautiously they climbed down the steep and slippery slope, past the gaping hole of the new quarry and over towards that shelf above the stream. They had to pick their way amongst a litter of stones and boulders that had not been there previously, and their feet sank into gritty mud and sodden ground indicating that the flood had reached as high as this.

They did not require to go searching for what might be left of those new-built walls. The entire shelf, they found, had sagged and collapsed and side-slipped drunkenly into the deeper rock-bed of the stream. Whether or not the fresh mortar had held was now of no consequence, for most of that stone terrace was now merely a series of slantwise foam-forming obstructions in the snarling waters. And much of the bank behind, no longer supported, seemed to have come down in the form of a landslide, to complete the chaos. No fort would arise on *that* site, to tame wild MacGregors.

Grimly Rob Roy nodded. 'It is well,' he said. 'Very well. The first instalment of my debt paid, whatever. As Royal's my Race – Montrose will find that MacGregor is not quite bankrupt yet! I warrant he . . . Hist! Did you hear aught there, MacAlastair? Did I hear men shout? From down yonder?'

The gillie shook his head. To hear anything over and above the noise of rushing tortured waters, here in the gut of the glen, was asking too much.

Rob looked about him, seeking something – something close at hand, and not the source of distant voices. He found it, in the shape of a tall birch trunk, uprooted and brought down by the flood, and now securely wedged between two boulders at the upper end of the broken terrace. It was as near to the site of the projected fort as might be achieved. Reaching into his sporran, the man drew out a folded paper. He smoothed it out with a cut and muddied hand, and whipping out a small *sgian dubh*, or dirk, from his hose top, he skewered this firmly to the tree-trunk, adding a stone on top for further security. In the darkness he could not read again what he had earlier written thereon – but it would serve.

With a jerked word to his companion, Rob turned away and went climbing back whence they had come. Above the quarry he paused for a moment and faced back southwards, to raise his great fist, clenched above his head, and shake it, silently fiercely, with a world of menace, into the gloom, before slipping off up the glen towards the horses.

That gesture he left behind him – with a ruined site, a wrecked camp, sundry drowned and missing men, and a spreading desolation. Also a paper inscribed thus:

To All Whom it May Concern

No man builds stone upon stone in Inversnaid without my permission. What I have, I hold. I alone have done this. None other dweller in these glens has art or part of it. Any reprisal towards others I will avenge ten-fold. All men take note. In especial James Graham of Montrose, and John Graham of Killearn. These two have cost me dear. The first shall support me and mine hereafter, in return. The second shall die. This I swear, as my Race is Royal.

Robert MacGregor of Inversnaid and Craigroyston.

CHAPTER SIX

ROB ROY lay sprawled at ease on a couch of pulled heather, in the mouth of his cave. The aromatic smoke from his fire of resinous knots of bog-pine was drawn back over his head, deep into the cave, by the draught from a multi-mouthed chimney contrived with much care amongst the cracks and crevices of the roof. Neither smoke nor soot, nor the dispersed openings themselves, would reveal that refuge to the keenest eye. Not that the bog-pine, jagged stumps of the giant primeval conifers that once had covered all Highland Scotland to the summits of the highest hills, made a smoky fuel; impregnated with turpentine, it burned with a clear and intense orange flame that was fiercely hot.

And its heat was more than welcome, up there, high above the present tree-level, that late-November morning. Of sanctuaries innumerable that he might have selected, Rob had chosen this eyrie as his temporary headquarters, at the lofty head of the long smiling valley of Balquhidder. Tucked into a shallow corrie of broken rocky hillside, only a hundred feet or so beneath the summit of Cruach Tuirc, the Hill of the Boar, it held many advantages beside its wide prospect. It was not on his own land, not even on actual Gregorach territory – which was important; yet it was readily accessible – for the sure-footed and the stout-hearted – from all parts of the MacGregor country. Rob could turn downhill in three distinct directions; east into Balquhidder itself, a happy no-man's-land of broken clans and independent characters, where no authority ruled save a sense of humour, a fleet foot and an agile wrist; south into Gregor's

Glen Gyle, Loch Katrine-side, and beyond to Snaid and Arklet; and west into Glen Falloch and the head of Loch Lomond. Moreover, this Hill of the Boar rose out of a veritable moat of black and treacherous peat-hags, which only the initiated would cross save at their peril. Nothing less than an army – and an exceedingly well-informed and fast-moving army at that – could hope to corner Rob up here, much less to extract him.

One of Cousin John's gillies from Corrarklet, Finlay Broken-Nose by name, squatted before him at the fire, gnawing at a foreleg of cold roe venison. MacAlastair kept watch on the further, western, side of the hill.

Rob was pondering the information that Finlay had brought. Two days had passed since the shattering of Lochan Uaine and the projected fort. The soldiers, it seemed, had arrested Donald, Corrarklet's younger son, charging him with complicity in the outrage. Apparently he had been encountered by the alarmed red-coats as they fled before the devouring flood-waters. What Donald Mac-Gregor had been doing in the vicinity of the camp at that hour of the night, the gillie had not specified – but Rob had a fairly shrewd idea; Donald was something of a gallant, and though suitably married and with a fine son of his own, had not shown himself to be wholly insensitive to the charms of other ladies – in particular one, the generous and conveniently placed daughter of Malcolm the Mill, Seana by name, who lived at the mill-house in the pass between Inversnaid and Loch Lomond. The chances were that he had been on his belated way home from a nocturnal assignation when, all unwitting, he had blundered into the after-effects of Rob's explosion – and thereby presented himself as a most opportune scapegoat. At any rate, he had been accused of being an accessory, had been unable or unwilling to explain his presence on the scene of disaster, and was to be sent to Dumbarton Castle for trial. Moreover, it transpired that, later, his poor wife and child had also been taken into custody, as hostages to ensure non-interference by the MacGregors.

Rob Roy was concerned. He felt responsible. Though it might be that young Donald deserved a lesson, he surely had not earned the kind of justice that he would be apt to get at Dumbarton. Moreover, the older man had a soft spot in his heart for the unfortunate wife, Marsala, a gentle doe-eyed creature, who again was a far-out relative of his own. The MacGregors had never concerned themselves about the inter-marriage of cousins. In the circumstances, it was obvious to Rob that he would have to do something about it. Perhaps it was significant that the military had considered hostages to be necessary.

'You say that the red-coats are now all camped down at Loch Lomond-side, at their boats?' he asked. 'They hold their prisoners there?'

Finlay Broken-Nose nodded. 'That is the way of it, yes. But there are no boats in it,' he amended. 'The boats all are gone. Och, they were after sending all the masons and the building-men back to Glasgow in them – for there is no work for them at all, any more. All the boats were needed, and they have no boats left – some of our own people's boats they were after taking, indeed. They cannot be sending Donald Beg down to Dumbarton until the boats come back.'

'I see,' Rob sounded thoughtful.

The other leaned forward. 'Och, yes. This is what I was to tell you. It is a great chance, see you. Corrarklet says it.' Finlay gestured with his roe's leg to emphasise his point. 'If the clan was to be raised now, we could come down on those soldiers like the hammers of hell and drive them into the loch, whatever, and make an end of them! Before their boats are back. They could not be getting away from us. None would win back to Dumbarton, at all. Strike, it is – before the boats get back.'

'Aye,' Rob nodded slowly. 'Maybe, Finlay. Strike – but

not that way, I think. Those soldiers the clan might drive into the loch, yes. But there would plenty more come up in their boats from Dumbarton to avenge them – and all Glen Arklet and Glen Gyle would burn and die. No – there is a better way than that. The clan shall *not* rise – tell you John of Corrarklet that, from me! I will save his son for him, from Dumbarton Castle, never fear – but in my own way. When are they expecting the boats to be back?'

'Today. Before night. That is why I am here early. That is what the soldiers say. They are not happy, those ones, without their boats – God's curse on them!'

'Aye. I'ph'mm. They have twenty miles down the loch and ten more beyond, by the river, to Dumbarton. It makes a deal of rowing, for heavy boats, How many boats have they? Who have they at the rowing? Not red-coats?'

'Och, no. No work for soldiers, that. Some of the masons rowed, and they took some of our own folk. About ten of them. Near a score of boats, there were.'

'So! The masons will not be there to row back. They will be short of oarsmen – so they will have to be towing the empty boats. Time, that will take. Did many red-coats go with them?'

'The officer only – the major-man, Selby, who commands them all – and four others. Two of them hurt in the flood.'

'The major – this Selby – has gone, himself? For instructions, no doubt – about the fort, likely. The question is – will he be bringing back reinforcements?' Rob's query was put to himself. 'I think not. He has most of a company there – and only the two men to fight. The clan has not risen – he scarce can ask for more soldiers. Not yet, with not a shot fired! No . . . I think maybe that I see my way through this tangle, Finlay. Not just clearly yet, mind you – but it comes, it comes! Now – back with you to Corrarklet, man, and tell you my good and warlike cousin to be patient. Patient, just – no more is asked of him.'

The other, rising to his feet, grimaced. 'Patience, it is?

Be Patient, it seems, has become the motto of our clan, whatever! One time it was E'en Do and Spare Nocht!'

Rob's startlingly blue eyes narrowed as they met the other's wry glance. Not the most patient of men himself, words surged to the tip of his tongue. But he choked them back. He nodded curtly. 'Off with you,' he said.

He watched the gillie go, for a little, dark-browed. Then, rising, he extinguished the fire, and went in search of Mac-Alastair.

* * *

It was past noon when Rob and MacAlastair parted company, on the steep tree-clad hillside high above Loch Lomond, a good five miles south of their eyrie on Cruach Tuirc. Away below them, glimpsed through the hanging woods of oak and ash and hazel that were steadily losing their shrivelled leaves to a gusty wind, was the deep defile by which the brief River Arklet, reinforced by the Snaid Burn, made its abrupt descent of four hundred feet from its own loch to the great Loch Lomond. Down there, beside the little harbour near the final waterfall, were the few huddled houses of Inverarklet and the many scattered tents of the military. From so high above, all seemed remarkably peaceful and inoffensive.

'See you now – do not be killing anybody,' Rob instructed finally. 'That would only bring down reprisals on our people. Give the man this receipt for what you take – tell him, if you can keep him conscious, that it is for the use of Rob Roy MacGregor only. Then come you as fast as you may to the big bluff beyond Rowchoish. Four miles it is, from here, so you do not have over-long for it. I will be awaiting you there. Is it understood?'

His uncommunicative henchman nodded, and slanted off downhill through the scattered trees and the withering bracken.

Keeping to the high ground, Rob continued on his way

southwards, parallel with the loch. For this expedition the garrons had been left behind, as too conspicuous. He held to the uppermost limits of the trees, the best part of a thousand feet above the water, for he was almost as anxious to avoid the notice of his own people as that of the military – and Gregorach crofts and holdings dotted the area along the loch-shore for miles. This was his own domain of Craig-royston, comprising a dozen miles of steep forested hillside and rock and heather, flanking Lomond's eastern shore and extending right down to Montrose's northernmost property of Rowardennan. It might seem a somewhat rough and barren area to be the prime object of ducal covetousness, but looked at from another angle it certainly made a distinctly thrusting salient into the Grahams' more settled territory – and MacGregors could be restless neighbours.

Scrambling amongst the rocks, threading the tall crackling bracken, leaping burns innumerable, and seeking not to disturb noticeably the cattle that clung to even this precarious pasture, Rob nevertheless covered the difficult terrain at an impressive speed. He boasted, of course, that there was no man in all Scotland – save perhaps MacAlastair – who could keep up with him on the hill. It was no idle boast. Even tall Gregor of Glengyle, younger and with longer legs, was apt to be left behind.

Above Cailness, the home of another of his many far-out cousins, Rob began to dip down, discreetly. There were clearings and open meadows in the woods here, steeply slant-wise but fair, with much stock. To avoid them, the man, for much of the way down, crept actually in the rocky scrub-lined channel of the tumbling Cailness Burn – that was indeed more waterfall than anything else. He was wet – but he might well be wetter. Presently the grey-stone house of Simon of Cailness lay below him, with the usual scattering of cot-houses and cabins around it. Folk were moving about – but Rob had little fear of attracting their attention; it was the dogs, and to a lesser extent the children, that he had to watch for. Cailness himself, of course, like every soul there, would have been only too eager to hail and aid the fugitive. But he was determined that it should be otherwise; his fondness for these folk demanded more of him than sociable greetings and calls for assistance.

Making a wide detour, he approached the little bay below the houses, unobserved. Three boats lay on the shingle, at the water's edge. The smaller one would serve him finely. But extracting it unseen was going to be a little difficult. . . .

Moving away again, inland a little and to the south, Rob selected a small glade in the woods, with care. Through the trees he could still see the houses, a mere three hundred yards away. The wind was south-west as usual, gusty and sufficient. And there was ample dead bracken in the clearing. Quietly gathering some armfuls of the stuff, and adding some dry sticks for substance, he got out his tinder and flint and struck a light. In less time than it takes to tell, he had three well-doing fires blazing, spaced out and setting alight the standing bracken. As billowing clouds of acrid smoke rolled up, and, fanned by the breeze, bore down through the trees towards the homestead, Rob turned and slipped away in the other direction, satisfied. There was no hurry, for a little while.

He heard the shouts and cries of alarm before ever he reached the vicinity of the tiny bay. Give them a little while, and no man, woman, nor child would be left around the Cailness houses – for a forest fire was a most urgent challenge and had to be confined and beaten out immediately, or pasture and stock would suffer. Not that they would have much trouble in defeating this blaze; Rob had chosen this area carefully, anxious that it should not spread but only provide a diversion. In twenty minutes or so it should all be over – but meantime there would be much confusion and excitement.

His fire served him well. Not only did it distract the attention of all – including, very clearly from the noise, the dogs and children – but it sent down such a thick and choking curtain of brown smoke on the south-west wind as effectually to screen the shore from any eyes not already preoccupied with the threatening conflagration. Moreover, if Rob's own tears were anything to go by, no eyes were likely to be very efficient anyway, in the circumstances.

With only a gesture at hiding, then, he made his way round and down to the shingle of the little beach. The oars had been left in the boats, and all that was needed was for Rob to set his wide shoulder to the stern of the smallest craft, push it a yard or so down into the water, and jump in. No more than a minute of strong pulling, and he was out of the bay, and its little headland to the south intervened to hide him finally from Cailness.

Rob turned to stare southwards. As yet he could see no other boat on all the wide slate-grey spread of water. But Loch Lomond was long, over twenty miles long, with innumerable headlands and bays and inlets, to say nothing of its islands. The fact that the man could see no craft from where he was did not mean necessarily that he had unlimited time to spare. He recommended his rowing, pulling with long and powerful strokes that sent the little tubby vessel squattering forward at a great pace. He hugged the wooded shore closely.

There were other MacGregor cottages and cabins down that lochside – but not many, for the hillside was now merely the foot of mighty Beinn Lomond itself, and becoming increasingly steep, riven and barren. When Rob approached the vicinity of any such house, he pulled further out into the loch and covered his flaming head of red hair with his plaid; hunched and seated thus, he might just possibly escape identification, should he be seen – always a problem with that conspicuously made man.

Rounding the great headland of Rowchoish, he pulled on for a further mile and more, till he came to a small and narrow inlet, barely to be distinguished amongst the overhanging trees, and tumbled massive rocks. Into the mouth of this he rowed his borrowed boat.

It was a strange haven that he had chosen. A few yards in from its rocky constricted jaws, it turned sharply to the right around a steep soaring bluff, and then unexpectedly opened out into a wholly landlocked little lagoon, hemmed in by the hanging woods. It was all the work of a headlong turbulent stream that came in here, and, after carving through the solid rock at the lochside, had cut back and back through softer material behind to form this secret pool, into which the loch's waters had followed. Cascading down in a sizeable waterfall at the far end, the burn was still busy at its enlargement – and no doubt would be so until the end of time. It had proved a useful corner for Rob Roy Mac-Gregor ere this.

Tying his boat to a rowan sapling, he clambered out and went hastening up the hillside above, climbing at his fastest. He was heading for a tall and bare shoulder of the hill, where, unhampered by trees, he could gain a clear view for many miles down the loch.

He did not have to attain his vantage-point. Before he was half-way there he perceived the boats. Perhaps three miles away yet, these were not hugging the shore. In three distinct strings they came, a number of craft, perhaps half a dozen, to each string. From this distance it was impossible to count men – but the chances were that only the foremost boats would be manned, the remainder being roped together and towed behind.

Rob frowned. Even though progress was bound to be slow and the rowers would be tired, less than an hour would see those boats level with Cala nan Uamh, the Haven of the Cave, his hidden lagoon. They had the wind behind them.

It all depended on MacAlastair, now. If he was late, all was in vain. But how soon could he be expected? The gillie's task might well have proved more difficult than his own –

though it was MacAlastair's own choice.

Rob hurried back to his haven. He had work to do. From the top of the little bluff round which the entrance to the creek bent, he surveyed the possibilities. Quickly he saw the tree that he wanted – for there were many to select from, overhanging the narrow channel. His choice was a twisted red-barked Scots pine, growing at the edge of the rocky entrance passage near the bend, its sinuous roots gripping into the seams and fissures of the stone. A pine's roots are shallow.

Hastening round to this tree, he went to work. He had no axe available, and must just use his dirk, inadequate tool though it made. One after another he tackled the spreading roots of that pine, hacking, sawing, digging, severing. It was difficult, knuckle-barking labour, and frequently he used the enormous strength of those long arms and great shoulders to pull up roots by main force rather than cut them through. The rocky nature of the ground was a help, in that it kept the roots high and exposed – but it took the man all of half an hour before he was satisfied. Only two or three slender roots then held the tree, and it swayed ominously to the push. Propping some large stones against the trunk, to leeward, in case the gusty wind should bring it down before its time, Rob left it and returned to his bluff.

No sign of the boats yet. Time passed. He waited, but could not sit still. Soon he was pacing the limited area of his rock-platform like a caged thing. Where was MacAlastair?

It was the little armada that came into view first. Cursing, the waiting man eyed it. He could not have more than fifteen or twenty minutes left, now. What in Heaven's name was MacAlastair doing . . . ?'

In a few further precious minutes it occurred to Rob, ruefully, that he would be better employed in trying to think out some alternative course of action than in anathematising his faithful attendant. But nothing of the sort came to his impatient mind, rack his brains as he would. With only the two of them, the situtaion was difficult indeed. Not that his present project was likely to work out simply, to be fool-proof or assured of success. But at least it would give them a chance. . . .

Then, suddenly, MacAlastair was standing below him, at the edge of the lagoon, quietly waiting as though he had been there for hours. The fellow had an infuriating facility for giving that sort of impression. Rob went hurrying down to him.

'*Dia* – but you have taken your own time, man!' he cried, in greeting. 'The boats are out there, just. We have not a minute to spare. You got it – what was necessary?'

For answer the taciturn MacAlastair merely nodded, and unrolled the plaid that he carried bundled up under his arm. From its folds fell a scarlet brass-buttoned coat with buff facings, black breeches, three-cornered hat, bandoliers – in fact, the entire uniform and equipment of a private soldier in Her Majesty's East Kent Regiment of Foot, The Buffs.

'Good,' his master commended. 'Quick, then – get into the things, man. You chose somebody of your own size? You did not have to kill the fellow . . . ?'

'A sore head he will be having – that is all,' the other informed, shrugging. He was discarding his sword-belt, ragged kilt, and rawhide brogans, and with every appear-ance of distaste began to don the royal uniform. With urgent impatient hands Rob helped him on with the long heavy coat and clapped the three-cornered hat askew on the other's shaggy black locks.

'No musket?' he demanded, as he fitted the crossed ban-doliers in position over the other's chest.

'They do not carry the muskets to relieve themselves behind a bush,' the gillie mentioned heavily.

'Aye. Well, maybe not. Come, then – or it will be too late, whatever.'

They bundled into the boat, MacAlastair taking up pride of place in the bows, Rob handling the oars and pushing off.

He had doffed his own bonnet with the single eagle's feather, and put on his gillie's plain one, pulling it down hard over his head to hide as much of his ruddy locks as possible. He kept his plaid around his shoulders, too, to seek to hide his outline. At the entrance to their hidden harbour he turned to stare out over the loch.

The three strings of boats were now in full view, the foremost no more than five hundred yards or so away. It was as Rob had anticipated. Only the first vessel of each string was occupied, four men rowing in each of the three leading craft. These weary-looking oarsmen were clearly Highlandmen, bare to the waist. But in each of these same boats also sat one scarlet-coated soldier. Fifteen men in all.

'Aye,' Rob nodded. 'Just so. The fine fellow in that first boat there, with all the gold braid and the epaulettes, will be this Major Selby, no doubt. He has no reinforcements – or if he is to get them, he has not brought them with him, Heaven be praised! Now – listen you to me, MacAlastair.'

As Rob dug in his oars and pulled out towards that leading boat, he told his companion just what he was to do, very precisely. He was to screen Rob's person with his scarlet uniform, and he was to wave. But he was not to speak, or even to hail. Rob would do that himself – for he did not trust MacAlastair's English to be such as would deceive Major Selby, even at a distance. MacAlastair was to open his mouth and seem to be shouting – but the words would be Rob's. He would see that they did not come near enough to the other boat for the deception to become evident. And when he had to turn this craft round, to face the other way, the gillie was to transfer himself quickly to the stern, so as to continue to come between his master's noteworthy frame and the Major. There was more – but that was enough for the moment.

At Rob's word, MacAlastair, standing up in the bows, began to wave towards the other boats almost at once. Rob raised a halloo or two, to draw attention to the fact. He was approaching the advancing boats' course at a tangent – and crouching as low he might and still be able to row.

Promptly enough they received an answering wave from the foremost boat, and as Rob continued to halloo, the Major turned his craft a few points to starboard, towards them. So far, so good.

Carefully, his head turned back over his shoulder most of the time, Rob watched that decreasing stretch of water between them and the flotilla. To turn away too soon would look suspicious – but to get too close was to put too much of a strain on MacAlastair's disguise, however vivid his red coat, and to risk a recognition of his own person. It had to be nicely judged. Two hundred yards was as near as he dare allow – at this stage, at any rate.

When he reckoned that they were less than three hundred yards apart, Rob told his companion to put a hand to the side of his mouth, and seem to shout. Then behind him, he raised his own voice.

'Hi, sir! Major Selby, sir!' he cried, seeking to make his voice as like that of an uncultured southern Englishman as he knew how. 'Cap'n Taylor's compliments, sir. Will you come ashore, sir, he says? Follow us in? Cap'n's got that ruffian Rob Roy MacGregor cornered, sir. In the woods, here. You ahearing me, sir?' He was hailing into the wind, and was uncertain how his words would carry.

'Aye, aye. You've got Rob Roy, you say?' a thin high voice came clearly across the water to them. 'Where, man? Where is Captain Taylor?'

'Just in here, sir.' In a very different tone, Rob jerked to his gillie, 'Point, MacAlastair. Point towards the *cala.*' And raising his voice again, 'There's a creek, Major. Hidden. Follow us in, sir. Cap'n Taylor needs your help. In the woods. . . .'

'Very well,' the officer called back. He turned, and started to call and signal towards the other leading boats of his flotilla.

Rob decided that they were close enough. Throwing a command to MacAlastair to change positions, he swung the little boat round swiftly, rowing one oar and backing with the other, and commenced to pull for the shore again. Necessarily he was facing the little fleet now, but the gillie's person still screened him.

Soon they heard the Major shouting to them once more, asking for details of what was going on ashore. Rob affected not to hear him at first, for answering in the assumed English voice was a strain to him, and he did not want to risk more of it than was essential. But when the questions were repeated more loudly, he had to answer – hoping that Mac-Alastair's mouthings would still seem authentic at this closer range.

'Cap'n Taylor has him caught, sir,' he called, extemporising urgency. 'Has him in a cave. But Cap'n has few men with him. Dare not take him back to camp through the woods, sir. They might rescue him. Too many MacGregors about. We saw your boats. Cap'n Taylor reckoned safer to carry him back by boat. . . .'

'Aye, aye. Very good.' The Major obviously accepted all that.

Rob's boat drew ahead on the pull shoreward, being light and unencumbered. He was thankful to be spared more of difficult long-range explanations. He headed directly for the barely visible entrance to the little haven.

As they approached the rocky jaws of the place, Rob shouted his last instructions. 'In here, sir. Follow me in. There's a bend. Plenty of room round that.' The Major's boat, with its string of towed craft, was roughly two hundred and fifty yards behind him.

And now he was giving urgent directions to MacAlastair, in his own language. What happened thereafter must happen fast, and with all too many opportunities for mishap.

As the boat rounded the tight bend in the entrance channel, Rob tossed the oars to his companion, and leapt lightly ashore, leaving MacAlastair to row on up to the head of the little enclosed lagoon. He clambered swiftly up the steep side of the rocky bluff that towered over the bend. He did not allow himself to be seen on the top of it, keeping well back till opposite his propped-up tree. Then he threw himself flat, to peer over cautiously.

Major Selby's craft was just entering the outer channel, still with its towed tail astern. The leading boat of the next string was just behind, with a sergeant and four Highland oarsmen. The third group, necessarily, were some distance further off.

Rob had to calculate quickly. Obviously they could not all get round the bend and into the net of the lagoon in time. He would have to do the best that he could. He glanced behind him. MacAlastair, his boat now just below the waterfall at the head of the inlet, was jumping ashore.

Selby rounded that tight bend in the channel. He was delayed a little in getting his empty boats after him, so that the sergeant's craft drew level with the last of them. They were close under Rob's bluff now, so that he could edge much further forward without being seen. The third soldier, out on the loch with the last string, might spot him – but the fellow seemed to be concentrating on what his superiors were doing.

Rob waited, tense. Selby was well round the corner now, out of sight. The sergeant was about to negotiate the bend. MacAlastair was disappearing into the trees, climbing uphill, shouting vaguely and waving the Major on.

He heard a different kind of shouting from Selby then, with question and alarm in it. And promptly Rob acted. Leaping up he flung himself at that undermined tree, kicking away the supporting stones, and pushed with all his great strength. Slowly, majestically, the pine swayed and toppled, creaking, the remaining roots snapping like musket-shots. With a resounding crash it fell over and down. Right on top of the second boat behind that of the sergeant it pitched, shattering it with the impact and sinking the next behind it also by the spread of its branches. A vast spout of water rose up, drenching even Rob, and when it settled, there was the tree half-submerged and wholly blocking the narrow channel, two empty boats sunk and a third slowly filling. Major Selby's and the sergeant's craft, with seven or eight others, were securely bottled up within the lagoon.

The creator of the havoc delayed not a moment. As the babel of cries and curses uprose, he leapt across the top of the bluff to the far side, whipping the heavy cavalry pistol out of his belt as he went with one hand, and a wicked little dirk from his gartered hose-top with the other. Without waiting to charge or prime the former, he halted wide-legged above the little lagoon. From their boats thirty feet or so below, men stared up at him in alarm.

Rob's voice rang out, as he jabbed the pistol first towards the agitated Major Selby and then at the sergeant. 'Is it a ball in your chests, or your throats cut, at all?' he demanded ferociously. 'Say the word, make a move – and it will be your last, I tell you! I am Robert MacGregor of Inversnaid and Craigroyston – and I do not start what I cannot finish!'

There was a choking angry expostulation from the officer, and a stream of curses from the sergeant. Also some comment from the Highland oarsmen, mainly to the accompaniment of wide grins; most of them were MacGregors.

Rob cut it all short. 'Enough!' he cried. 'Silence! Mac-Alastair – come you and relieve these gentry of their weapons. You are my prisoner, Major. And you too, Sergeant. Or would you rather be dead men, whatever?'

There was no answer to that. MacAlastair, the scarlet coat discarded, materialised out of the trees, a pistol in his hand also. Major Selby wore a sword but apparently carried no firearms. The sergeant's musket lay on the floorboards of his boat.

Rob spoke tersely, in the Gaelic, to the oarsmen, while

his companion disarmed the two soldiers, telling them to come ashore but to take no part against the red-coats. There must be no suggestion that they were in league with himself, or the whole clan would suffer.

In only a minute or so it was all over, with Selby and the sergeant standing unhappily on the grass, disarmed, staring into the muzzle of MacAlastair's pistol, and the oarsmen in a whispering group a little way apart.

Leaving them for the moment, Rob turned back, on his bluff-top, to see what the remaining soldier was doing. He found that that perplexed individual had halted his rowers just off-shore, and was waiting events with every appearance of uncertainty. As well he might; he must have seen the tree crash down and could not have failed to hear the subsequent shouting – but what went on round the bend in the channel he would be at a loss to know. A mere private soldier, he obviously was in a quandary. He had picked up his musket, but held it without any confidence in its worth.

Rob ran back and began to climb down towards the sergeant's boat. 'Throw me up that musket there, MacAlastair,' he directed.

Taking the sergeant's weapon, he clambered back to a position of vantage on the bluff. The third boat, with its satellites in tow, still lay motionless, no more than seventy yards away. Rob rose to his full height, the matchlock aimed from his shoulder directly at the sitting soldier.

'Drop that musket, man – or die!' he shouted. 'Quickly, now – for I am an impatient man, by name Rob Roy MacGregor! Your major and sergeant have chosen to live, as my prisoners. Do you choose different?' He hoped that the fellow would not prove stubborn or stupid, for the weapon in his hands was not primed. To help the other's decision along, he spoke to the oarsmen. 'You at the oars – row you in here. Up to this sunken tree, see you. Quickly.' He repeated that in the Gaelic, adding that they were to do only and exactly what he told them.

The rowers did not require further invitation, and the bewildered infantryman, however heroic he may have desired to be, apparently perceived no advantage in opposing the very definite trend of events. He laid down his musket and sat his thwart glumly as he was rowed into the mouth of the inlet.

Rob ordered the rowers to jump ashore at the other side of the channel, where the rock walls were sufficiently broken to be climable – and the soldier to follow them, leaving his musket in the boat. In a few moments they were reunited with the rest of the expedition.

Now that the pressure of events was eased, Rob allowed himself to relax – though MacAlastair still stood by, pistol cocked and pointing unfalteringly – and addressed himself to Selby, civilly.

'My regrets to so rudely inconvenience you, Major, and interrupt your journey,' he apologised. 'But you see how it is? Just the two of us there are in it – MacAlastair and myself – so that we could not be so gentle as we would have wished. Och, pointing pistols and the like is no way to be dealing with problems between gentlemen.'

'A rope round your neck, MacGregor, will mark the end of *your* problems, never fear,' the officer said tensely.

'May be, Major – but not this afternoon, I'm thinking. Time enough for your ropes when I am *your* guest, and not you mine. I have better hospitality to offer you than that – a snug cave for shelter, good heather for your couch, a sufficiency of meats, and a dram to drink. Och, you will do fine, man – just fine. And the sergeant too, of course. Though likely enough you will not be with me that long, at all....'

'A truce to your chatter, man! You will suffer for this outrage against an officer of the Queen, I promise you. What you expect to gain by it, God knows!'

'That is easy. Your Captain Taylor has taken into his custody a friend of mine, one Donald MacGregor, an inoffensive lad. Moreover, he is holding his wife Marsala and his baby son as hostages. So now I have taken hostages too, Major. It is entirely simple. You and the sergeant, here, in exchange for Donald and his wife – och, and the Queen in London getting the best of the bargain whatever, as I think you will agree?'

'Ruffian! Do you think that I will agree to any such shameful transaction. . . . ?'

'I care not whether you agree or no, Major. It is Captain Taylor who will agree, I'll wager. The poor man can do no other.'

'He will lead a punitive expedition against you, forthwith. . . .'

'How will he be doing that? I shall sink every one of these boats in the loch – so that he cannot move from Inverarklet save through my heather. And think you that any Southron soldier could catch Rob Roy in his own heather? He cannot take Donald MacGregor to Dumbarton without boats – that I can promise you. I'm thinking that your captain will be happy to get his senior officer back at so small a price!'

The other stared at the MacGregor, biting his lip.

'Aye, then – here is the way of it,' Rob went on. He pointed at the private soldier. 'This bold fellow shall carry my message to Captain Taylor – and yours. These rowing men – who, you will note, have no part in this business – shall take him up through the woods to Inverarklet. It is five rough miles, so they will not be there till night. Mac-Alastair shall go with them, and wait at a suitable distance from your camp, for the Captain's answer. Tomorrow, I am hoping that you will be exchanged. Till then, sir, such poor hospitality as is left to me is at your disposal. Not the hospitality that I could have offered you under my own roof. But then . . .' Rob paused significantly. '. . . you burned that, did you not? My wife . . .'

Selby swallowed, and hastily looked away. 'That was

none of my doing,' he assured urgently. ' 'Pon my soul, that was Graham's work. Killearn's. The Sheriff. I had no hand in that. . . .'

'Aye,' the other said, softly. 'Just so. Graham's work!'

The Major began to speak quickly about what message should be sent to Inverarklet.

A little later, with the grey dusk already beginning to settle on the land, MacAlastair, with the private soldier, and all the Highland oarsmen in attendance, set off on the difficult walk northwards through the steep hanging woodlands. The gillie had his instructions. The two other soldiers, their hands tied behind their backs with rope from the boats, went with Rob in the opposite direction. There were many caves and crannies in the rocks in that country, and Rob Roy knew them all. The one that he was making for might not be so secure and lofty a refuge as was his sanctuary on Cruach Tuirc, and moreover might be a little damp – but it would serve admirably as a prison for gentry who thought house roofs were for burning.

CHAPTER SEVEN

MAJOR SELBY and the sergeant were exchanged for Donald
MacGregor and his wife and child the following day, in
an early flurry of the winter's snows. The transfer of hostages took place in a wooded glade about a mile from Inverarklet, with elaborate precautions on both sides against
trickery or bad faith. Rob Roy did not appear in person,
any more than did Captain Taylor – though undoubtedly
one was no further off than was the other. The MacGregor,
after parting from Selby with unreturned if marked courtesy, the sergeant's loaded musket retained in his hands,
watched from a rocky hidingplace as MacAlastair led forward their two prisoners to the rendezvous, pistol cocked
and prominent. After only a brief delay, the figures of
Donald and his wife Marsala, the child in her arms,
appeared, escorted only by the same private soldier who
had acted messenger before. How many more of the military might be hidden in the background could not be known.
There were no formalities, no sort of ceremony. The two
parties to the exchange merely stalked up to each other,
and passed, with scarcely a pause or a gesture, while the
escorts took over their new charges with no more civilities
than would pass between a pair of stiff-legged suspicious
dogs. MacAlastair came all the way back to Rob's cover,
walking sideways, eyes trained whence he came, pistol still
at the ready. He was a distrustful man by nature.

Rob did not delay their retiral by any prolonged welcome
for the rescued. A brief word to young Donald, and a warm
squeeze of the girl's shoulder, and he took the little boy

within his own arms and forthwith set off up-hill, long strided. The others followed on, with MacAlastair acting as watchful rearguard.

If there was any sort of pursuit or trailing, the fugitives saw nothing of it. Presently, Marsala breathless and distressed but holding them back only a little, they reached ground sufficiently high and broken to satisfy Rob that they were safe, for the meantime. They rested, to decide upon their further programme.

In fact, of course, there was little choice open to them. Donald MacGregor, now a marked man, and rescued thus, could not go back to his normal life and his father's house. Nothing was surer than that the military would seek to avenge their humiliation upon him, if they could lay hands on him again. He must either leave the district, then, or join Rob Roy in his defiance of the Government. Donald chose the latter course, without hesitation. And though Rob was by no means anxious to recruit any tail of supporters, he had to admit that there might well be occasions when he could use an extra pair of hands and perhaps an extra broadsword. Moreover, despite all his undeniable excellences, MacAlastair was not the most lively of companions, and Donald, a cheerful, ebullient and handsome young man, if somewhat headstrong and lacking in responsibility, was excellent company. As for his wife, the best arrangement was for her to go Auchinchisallan, where she could live with Mary. She was a gentle loving creature, and a closer relative to Mary than she was to Rob.

So it was decided. Rob was glad enough of the excuse to return to his wife with some token of vengeance taken. They would escort Marsala and the child to Auch forthwith, and give the turmoil here at Inversnaid an opportunity to settle down.

By devious hidden ways, around the head of Loch Arklet, they went, picking up their ponies *en route*, and leaving a message for the clan at the remote house of old MacGregor of Comar, Mary's father – at the same time borrowing two more garrons for Donald and Marsala. By evening they were at the head of Balquhidder and able to pass a cold night in Rob's cave under Cruach Tuirc. In the morning, with a thin covering of snow on the ground, they made their inconspicuous way northwards into Breadalbane. They came to Auch, in a blizzard, at dusk. It seemed a haven indeed.

But there is an inclemancy of climate that can chill even the warmest and snuggest haven. If Rob, not looking to be received exactly with open arms, at least had expected his wife to rejoice in some measure at the recital of his reprisals upon the forces of her hated enemies, he was disappointed. Mary, though she welcomed and accepted Marsala and the child with warm sympathy, greeted her husband with no more rapture than she did Donald or MacAlastair. His accounts of his exploits, even though they lost nothing in the telling – for Rob was no more inhibited as a story-teller than as a man of action – produced surprisingly little enthusiasm, or indeed reaction of any evident sort. Mary listened to what he had to say dutifully enough, but made only the one comment – to ask if Graham of Killearn had been involved. On learning that he had not, she betrayed no further interest. Rob was crestfallen as he was perplexed.

The weather was severe for the time of the year, with heavy and continuous snowfalls that tended to box the men up in the little house. And despite its warmth and comfort, Rob Roy at least, as the days and the nights passed, came to recognise that he would have been happier in his cave on Cruach Tuirc. It seemed to him that he just did not know this woman to whom he had been married for so many years. Had he never really known her? Or had she changed so entirely into a quite different person? Was that possible? She looked the same. Her beauty was no less, the near-perfection of her eyes and features and figure, tantalising him so that he ached for its solace in his body, and grieved and resented his loss in his mind. She was a passionate woman – or had been – a true MacGregor; but now she seemed to be not so much empty or frozen as encased in a hard shell, an armour of reserve. Was that it? Was the real Mary still there, hidden away and cowering? But Mary never hid or cowered; she was not that sort. And why cower from *him*, her husband and protector, her Rob?

If it was a shell that Mary had assumed, the man did all in his not inconsiderable power to pierce it. He coaxed and wheedled, he pleaded, he stormed and commanded, he wooed her again, using every art and stratagem and ex- pedient within an imaginative man's ken – in so far as she permitted and the crowded little house allowed – but to no avail. Mary remained encased, inviolate, unmoved.

His children, to some extent, he managed to win back to him – but that only seemed to underline his failure with his wife.

By the time that the weather cleared, a week later, Rob had had as much as he could stand – more especially in view of young Donald's all too evident enjoyment of *his* wife's favours. It was the heather for him again, he decided – and therefore for Donald and MacAlastair too.

Donald at least was accorded an affectionate, even tear- ful farewell.

CHAPTER EIGHT

ONCE again Rob Roy was ensconced amongst the rocks and thorn trees of the hillside above Corrarklet House, in the darkness of the December night, talking with the laird thereof. This time they sat, huddled in their plaids against the chill, and spoke face to face, for John MacGregor had refused to continue to talk with his unseen cousin from behind a boulder, asserting strongly that any lies that he might feel bound to tell to the accursed military were his own responsibility. Not that the soldiers were bothering the district much; they had come to Corrarklet, making enquiries and searching the place, after Donald's rescue, but had not since made themselves too objectionable. Rob, however, refused the older man's urgings to come down to the comforts of Corrarklet House, insisting that, in this area, it was best that he darkened no MacGregor doorway. Young Donald, however, had gone down to greet his mother.

John of Corrarklet's news of the local situation was not dramatic. After an initial and more or less token search of the vicinity for the fugitives, the red-coats had lain rather low, down at Loch Lomond-side. There had been no reprisals on the local MacGregors, nor on the oarsmen from the illfated flotilla. Almost certainly Selby was somewhat fearful about their security, and not anxious at the moment to provoke the clan into rising against them. This was hardly to be wondered at, in the circumstances. Rob had sunk their entire supply of boats – and left word for any loch-side MacGregors to scuttle or hide any odd boats of their own that still might have remained unrequisitioned; in consequence the soldiers' link with their base by water was cut, and any communications must be by the lengthy and highly precarious overland route through the mountains to Aberfoyle, by a series of passes that provided innumerable opportunities for ambush, and thence across the quaking wastes of the vast Flanders Moss where a dozen bold men could trap and drown hundreds. By this roundabout and dangerous route Dumbarton Castle was fifty difficult miles away, and Stirling Castle more than forty. There was no road down the precipitous east side of Loch Lomond, and anyhow, the Pass of Rowardennan could be made impassable by a couple of determined men. This was why the Gregorach had managed to remain uncontrolled, though proscribed and anathematised, for so long. Only by water were their fastnesses vulnerable. Again, the winter was no time for campaigning in the Highlands, and the low-country soldiers were at every sort of disadvantage.

So Major Selby was being cautious. He had issued sundry proclamations, to tuck of drum – one of them declaring Donald MacGregor to be considered an outlaw for having consorted and concerted with Rob Roy; another announcing that every boat whatsoever in the area was herewith requisitioned in the name of Her Majesty; and a third to the effect that anyone found abroad during the hours of darkness would be treated as an enemy of the Queen. But all this was largely face-saving, since he confined his men strictly to Inverarklet itself, down at the loch-shore. Tents made inadequate quarters in this weather, and the troops had moved into all available shelter – but this was scanty, houses being few, and overcrowding and discomfort was considerable. It might well be, Corrarklet thought, that the Major would soon recognise that the situation was unprofitable, and seek to advise his superiors to withdraw the expedition until more propitious conditions might prevail – if boats could be found to take his men south. Meantime, presumably on instructions that Selby had brought back from Dumbarton, a start had been made, in a tentative sort of way, at building the projected fort on a new site – on top of Tom na Bairlinn, the Knoll of Warning, where no floods could reach it. But this was mainly at the clearing and planning stage, for it was not the season for successful mason-work, and the soldiers were no builders.

All this gave the listener a modified satisfaction, since it indicated that for the time-being the tide was flowing his way. Montrose would gain considerably less satisfaction out of it all – which was good, so far as it went. But that was by no means far enough for Rob Roy. Somebody else was very much on his mind.

'And Killearn?' he demanded. 'John Graham – what of him? Has he been back – God's everlasting curse upon him!'

'No. No, I think not, Rob,' the other answered. 'I have seen and heard nothing more of the man. He keeps his distance, I trow. Unless . . . unless it could have been him at Glen Gyle? Och, but no – it would not have been him, whatever. Gregor would have said, for sure. . . .'

'What is this, man? What of Glengyle?'

'I was coming to that, Rob. Gregor sent me the word two days back that he had had a visitor at Glen Gyle in whom *you* would be very interested. He named no names, but said that when next I heard of you, to let you know. You were to go to him, there. It was important, he said. Gregor was not long back home, his own self, from Arnprior . . .'

'Important, he said? And secret, it seems? Two days back? Is this man, this visitor, still at Glen Gyle, then think you?'

'I do not know, Rob. I know no more than I have told you. But I think I would have heard, whatever, had it been John Graham of Killearn. . . .'

'Nevertheless, I shall go see. Right away,' Rob told him, grimly, rising up as he spoke. '*There* could be an appointment, John man, that could not wait! Tell Donald to be at the cave on Cruach Tuirc by morning. I shall be there, if you have further word for me.'

'As you will, Rob. But it is no weather for the caves. Bide you the night under my roof, man, in warmth. . . .'

'I have the wherewithal to keep me warm, Cousin,' Rob interrupted harshly. 'Hatred! Warm stuff – as good as any bed of blankets! Never fear that I shall suffer cold or discomfort while John Graham still breathes! Good-night to you.'

As he turned away downhill, and the shadow that was MacAlastair slipped past him, after his master, the older man thanked God that he was not John Graham of Killearn.

*   *   *

An hour or so later, but still on the right side of midnight, Rob Roy sat on another hillside, waiting, in a very similar situation. But this time the glen below him was wider and deeper and more populous, and many lights shone from the windows of the fairly large house within its sheltering screen of trees, while away to the east an emptiness seemed to yawn, that was the great nightbound expanse of Loch Katrine.

Presently he heard the faint swish of rawhide brogans in the deer-hair grass, and the deep breathing of climbing men, and he stood up. 'Well met, Greg,' he greeted. 'You were not abed?'

The towering figure of young Glengyle came striding up. '*Well* met, is it, Rob – and you skulking up here in the heather when my house and all within it is yours to command!' his nephew cried warmly. '*Ill* met, I call it! By God's shadow – what way is this to come to Glen Gyle? I near sent MacAlastair back to you with the word that if you wanted to see me, you could honour my house with your presence, whatever!'

'Hush you, Greg – if you do not want all Strath Gartney to know our business!' his uncle reproved – but not unkindly. 'What a terror you have become for the words, man! I'm hoping . . .'

'More than words I have for you!' the younger man interrupted, breathy as he was from his climbing. 'My sword and all I have is at your service, Rob. I will not be mewed up and confined any more, like some child. I am chieftain of Clan Dougal Ciar, and have suffered as much of the insults and presence of insolent soldiery as I intend to do. I have done as you ordered, hitherto, and acted the craven and the sluggard, raising no hand to protect my own honour or yours. But, as Royal's my Race, I've had sufficient of that! From now onwards . . .'

'Lord ha' mercy – the madcap! The drawcansir! Spare us, Greg, or you'll have me deafened! Was it thus I taught you, when I was Tutor of Glengyle?'

'You taught me that MacGregor bows the knee to no man, and doffs his bonnet only to his true and lawful king!'

'Aye. But not that MacGregor cuts his own throat when his true and lawful king happens to be interested in somebody else! Man Greg, the clan is more important than you or me, and honour an expensive commodity when it must be bought with other folk's lives.'

'Is that what you said when they burned your house, abused your wife, and drove your children into the night?' Gregor demanded sombrely.

'God's curse! You . . . you . . .' Rob's powerful voice deepened and vibrated like some great bass viol, so that even the young giant opposite took an involuntary pace backwards. 'What you your words, boy – or . . . or . . .' The older man controlled himself with obvious effort. 'This visitor,' he said abruptly changing the subject. 'This man you sent word of to Corrarklet. Is he still here? Is it Graham of Killearn?'

'Graham? No. Why should Graham come here? I'm thinking that cur will not dare show his snout in these parts again for a long time, my God! No – my visitor was another altogether. A friend of yours.'

'A friend? Why so secret, then?'

'Because of his errand, just. It was Colonel Hooke!'

'Lord – Hooke again! Does that cock still crow? Do not tell me, Greg, that it is the old story once more? Errand, you said? Not the old business over again?'

'It is, yes. The King is minded to try again, it seems. Nathaniel Hooke is spying out the land, once more. Making enquiries. He cannot travel the Highlands in this weather – but he made his way here, disguised as a packman. To see *us*. He was sore disappointed not to see you, Rob.'

'He is gone, then?'

'Aye. He went the night after he came. He could not wait for you. There is to be a meeting, see you, in a few days time – two days it is now, just – at the house of Harry Maule of Kelly, in Angus, brother to my lord of Panmure. Hooke had to be back for it. He left the word for you to join him there – in the name of His Majesty!'

'*Dia* – he did, did he! Across the breadth of Scotland! The man has not changed, I see! Here is folly, to be sure. . . .'

'Think you so? Such negotiations are needful, are they not, if the King is to be restored to his own again? Information he must have. . . .'

'Aye. But information from *Scotland* is the least of it, lad. Information from his own France is what will count. Here we will do our duty, yes. But, over there . . . ! I wager it's the King's own character that is the problem, and the delicate stomachs of his advisers in France that will decide the issue – not the loyalty of Scotland!'

Somewhat shocked, Gregor considered his uncle, peering at him in the darkness. 'But . . . but do not say that His Majesty should not try to regain his throne, surely?'

'Far from it. But after the last two fiascos I say that it is our own selves that will require information from Hooke –

not him from us! We have been made fools enough, already.'

'But it may be that Hooke *has* this information for us – the assurance you seek,' the younger man urged. 'That will be what the meeting is for, belike. He said that it was important that you should be there.'

'May be, Greg – may be so. Perhaps I judge over-fast. But the price – the price good men paid for folly, four years back – was costly. As you well know.'

Rob Roy drummed fingers on his bare knee. Five years before, Colonel Nathaniel Hooke, Irish emissary and spy of the exiled James Stewart in France, had arrived secretly in Scotland to plot and plan an armed uprising that would coincide with the signing of the unpopular Treaty of Union between England and Scotland. Rob, and to a lesser extent his nephew, had taken up the enterprise heart and soul, acting as Hooke's principal couriers and go-betweens to the clan chiefs of the Highland North and West. But when all was ready, the clans mustered, and the hour struck, King James took the measles at Dunkirk and turned back. The rising was postponed, the armies melted away, the clans returned to their glens, and London's hand clamped down heavier than ever. Then, a year later, Hooke returned. Scotland was now seething over the first effects of an incorporating Union, and a second attempt was made. This time James sailed, with a French fleet and troops in support. But with Queen Anne's ministers and generals packing their bags and preparing to change sides, and all Scotland ready to fall like a ripe plum, the French admiral had suddenly taken fright and turned back at the very mouth of the Firth of Forth, despite James's entreaties, carrying the young king with him. And the rising was off once more, leaving the relieved Government of Queen Anne to take reprisals consistent with the scare it had received.

Now Hooke was back again.

'It is a devilish nuisance,' Rob declared, out of his cogitation. 'I have more to be doing than traipsing across Scotland chasing a political rainbow. I have to . . .'

'But you *will* go?' Gregor put in, eagerly. To add, in a rush, 'I said that you would be there, whatever – and my own self with you!'

'You did, then!'

'Och yes, Rob – the honour of the Gregorach demanded. . . .' Glengyle coughed. 'In the King's name it was, see you. It is an appointment that is not to be rejected. . . .'

'I have another appointment that is not to be rejected, either,' the older man asserted grimly. 'With John Graham of Killearn!'

The other nodded. 'Aye – 'fore God, you have! We all have. But that is not yet. That one will not step north of our Highland Line for long enough, I think.'

'Then I will step south of it!'

'Och, but man, man – you cannot do that! Not far enough south. Not to Killearn and the Lennox. You would have no chance, at all.'

'I have stepped further south than that, in my day, and returned. Into England itself. . . .'

'Aye. But then you were not known as you are known today, Rob. *Dia* – everyone in the kingdom knows the name and fame, and what is more, the *looks*, of Rob Roy Mac-Gregor. With the shape of you, and the hair of you . . . and now you are outlawed with a price on your head . . . och, man – it is not to be thought of. That is, unless you are for taking a couple of score of good Gregorach broadswords south with you! Then we might achieve something. . . .'

'No. Alone I would go. This is my own business. The clan's name is proscribed already – I will not have it outlawed, on my account, likewise.'

'Then, even if you reached as far as Killearn, you would never win back home, Rob,' Gregor said earnestly. 'That is certain-sure. Surely you see it?'

'So long as I settle my account with John Graham, the

winning back here is of secondary importance,' his uncle told him, sombrely. 'You prate of honour, Greg – you will know that there are debts that must be paid whatever the price?'

'May be. But . . .' Gregor shifted his stance. '. . . you spoke of the clan's needs. The price that you would pay must be your own, you say – not the clan's. And yet your death would be the clan's price. Too great a price. We need you. You are the Captain of Clan Alpine. Lacking a High Chief, as we do, you are our war leader. And if Colonel Hooke speaks true, it looks like war again. No man north of the Highland Line is so potent and well-versed in war as is Rob Roy. The clan needs you. The King needs you. Would you be throwing all away for John Graham? Killearn will keep, Rob. He is better keeping. And if Scotland rises for King James – then you may travel where you will, and Killearn cannot escape you. Let him sweat in his fear till then – but come you to this meeting in Angus.'

'A-a-aye!' Rob sighed, raising and sinking great shoulders – but eyeing his erstwhile pupil with a strange mixture of exasperation, affection and admiration. 'Words and more words, Greg! Slay me – but you near drown me in the flood of them. Must I needs wrap myself in silk, for the clan's sake? And scurry across Scotland for the King's sake? And heed humbly to damnably lengthy sermons for *your* sake. . . . ?'

But the battle was won, and Gregor knew it. 'You come with me to Kelly Castle, then?'.

'What says your Mary to this?' his uncle countered, gruffly. 'She will not smile at Hooke's name again, I'll wager! She'll not be for you meddling in such matters, and leaving her. . . .'

'Mary is a good wife, and accepts what her husband decides is best . . . mostly,' the bold Gregor asserted. 'I . . . er . . she need not know where we are going, whatever. How soon can you start?'

'When I have filled my belly. I have not eaten since morning. We shall have to travel by night, and if the meeting is in two days just, the sooner we are on our way the better. But we can eat as we ride.'

Gregor MacGregor threw back his yellow head, and laughed into the December night. 'There speaks my laggard and reluctant uncle!' he cried. 'Come you down, and we shall see what Mary's larder can do for you.'

CHAPTER NINE

IN a couple of hours the two men were on their way. Mac-Alastair was left behind, at the cave on Cruach Tuirc, to keep an eye on the military – and also on the impetuous Donald MacGregor. Where the two travellers were going, Highlandmen would look conspicuous – which, for once, was the last thing that these proud sons of the royal race of MacAlpine wanted – so that they went clad in a strange and ragged assortment of ill-fitting Lowland apparel, with only their oldest plaids wrapped around them against the rigours of the winter's night. They rode their garrons, and each led another laden pony behind, to give the impression that they were travelling packmen – though unlikely packmen they must seem indeed, if anyone was to examine them closely in a good light, the gigantic blondly handsome Gregor and his enormously broad, long-armed and red-haired uncle, each with an inborn swagger of carriage and assurance of expression that no amount of play-acting would hide for long.

Rob did not cross the threshold of Glengyle House, despite his nephew's near-offence, and so did not witness Gregor's leave-taking of his bonny Lowland wife, nor hear what story he spun to her. Mary Hamilton in all probability was not deceived, anyway; she had been married to her Gregor for five years, and undoubtedly could read his not very subtle character like a book.

After crossing over the steep and rocky Bealach na Choin, the Pass of Weeping, difficult going even in daylight, but familiar to those two as the backs of their hands, they came down into the long and pleasant valley of Balquhidder and a beaten track for the ponies' hooves. From now on they maintained the tireless swaying trot that is the sturdy garron's unexciting but most profitable pace, eating up the long dark miles. For they had many, many miles to cover. All told, it would be fully one hundred miles to the Angus seaboard and Kelly Castle, near Arbroath, and roundabout routes and diversions might well be necessary.

Three times they were challenged, late as it was, down the length of Balquhidder – for this glen of broken clans, professional drovers more often named cattle-thieves, and confirmed individualists all, was as chancy a place for strangers as any in all the broad Highlands. But a brief word from Rob promptly cleared their passage. His name meant more in Balquhidder than that of any man alive or dead – some said than that of the Deity Himself; here, at Monachyle, Rob had had his first independent farmery and had started his unorthodox but lucrative career as a cattle-dealer.

Two hours after leaving Glen Gyle, they were at the mouth of Balquhidder and the head of Strathyre. By then it was nearly four o'clock, with sunrise still four hours ahead. Those four hours carried them along the south shore of Loch Earn, up Strathearn to Crieff – where Rob had embarrassed the little Provost – and over the hill to Glen Almond, out of the Highlands. They could have reached further by daylight, but preferred to lie up for the day, before reaching the more populous country of the Tay valley above Perth. In the chilly rain, they halted in dripping woodland on high ground above Logiealmond. The chances of being disturbed, up here, on a December day, were negligible. Hobbling their garrons, they found a cavity under the spreading roots of a wind-fall tree, wrapped themselves more tightly in their plaids, and lay down to sleep. They had covered some forty-five miles.

The early darkness saw them on the move again,

cramped and chilled but sustained from a leathern bottle of whisky, and chewing at forelegs of venison as they rode. They came down to the broad Tay in the vicinity of Redgorton. Crossing the great river, which was bridgeless and too deep to ford presented a problem, but there were ferries dotted along its course and nothing was simpler than for Rob quietly to slip down to the one below Redgorton, purloin the flat-bottomed scow without arousing the ferryman in his house, let it drift silently downstream to where Gregor waited with the horses, and so cross to the other side in comfort. Rob, being a man of sensibility, left a silver piece in the abandoned boat for the ferryman, Lowlander as he might be.

Thereafter they followed the Tay northwards through the flat cattle-dotted haughlands. They took its tributary, the Isla, when it led away to the east through the great vale of Strathmore, avoiding Coupar Angus and Meigle, nearly to Glamis, leaving it to strike seawards through the Sidlaw foothills to Inverarity and Carmylie. Long before dawn the fresh east wind had the tang of salt in it, and daybreak found them on Kelly Moor, near the little village of Arbirlot, with the grey North Sea fretting and sighing in front of them on a savage coastline. Many dogs had barked at them and some had even chased them – but never a man had they set eyes upon throughout. The canny Lowlander, it seemed, kept indoors after dark of a winter's night, and did not waste money on illuminations.

The travellers did not have to ask the whereabouts of Harry Maule's house, for the old grey tower of Kelly Castle thrust up above wind-twisted trees clear for all to see. The two Highlanders presented themselves at its heraldically decorated doorway in excellent time for breakfast – whereupon followed a somewhat undignified scene with the place's graceless servants before the visitors could vindicate their right to use the front entrance of the establishment. This at least had the effect of drawing the attention of all to the entry of two Highland gentlemen, as was only suitable.

Harry Maule, younger brother of James, fourth Earl of Panmure, was a quiet and capable man and no political firebrand – though possibly a more worthwhile adherent to the Jacobite cause than many who shouted a deal louder. His house had been chosen for this secret meeting, by his brother, as less conspicuous than the Earl's own castle of Brechin. It was his lordship, however who presided at the gathering.

Rob and Gregor, in the event, were welcomed with open arms – for they were the only true Highlanders present, and as such represented the most important source of actual manpower for any rising, however much of rank and title and wealth might be manifested otherwise. The remainder of the company, numbering perhaps a score, included the Earls of Southesk, Carnwath and Linlithgow, the Lords Kilsyth, Kenmure, Rollo, Duffus, Drummond, Strathallan and Ogilvy, Sir Patrick Murray of Auchtertyre, Sir Hugh Patterson of Bannockburn, Sir John Preston of Preston-hall, and other similarly resounding names. And, of course, Colonel Nathaniel Hooke, who was responsible for it all.

Hooke, an unlikely Irishman, grave, unsmiling and a Puritan, greeted Rob with as much enthusiasm as his nature would allow – and no doubt perceived a still more notable lack of the quality in the MacGregor, however cordial his address. He was a thin, dark, stiff man, fastidious of manner, soberly dressed amongst all the colourful Scots nobles and notables. Rob and he were apt to find, during that morning, their eyes fixed one upon another.

All forenoon further guests were arriving, mainly from the North-East, including the Earl Marischal and the Master of Sinclair. There were notably few from Edinburgh, Lothian and the South.

Gregor had brought his best tartans, wrapped in a bundle on the back of his pack-pony. In them he made an eye-catching figure, quite outshining the Lowland lords and achieving a notable success with the Maule ladies. In the matter of enthusiasm he more than atoned for his uncle.

* * *

'His Majesty is five years older – and, if I may make so bold as to say so, my lords, more than that wiser.' Hooke's voice was harsh, unmelodious, and with little trace of any Irish intonation. And though his steel-grey eyes swept the company as he spoke, they always seemed to come back to rest on those of Rob Roy MacGregor. 'He is determined, this time, to put his fortunes to the test, and under God's will, believes that what is his by right shall be his indeed.'

The statement was loyally acclaimed, Gregor being by no means backward in his plaudits. Rob Roy said nothing.

'His Majesty has been serving in King Louis' army, the better to fit himself for the stern tasks ahead. He acquitted himself nobly at Malplaquet, as I myself can witness. He now more fully understands the military requirements of a successful rising, gentlemen.'

There was some significant nodding, at that.

'Moreover, the time undoubtedly is growing ripe,' Hooke went on. 'As you all will agree, yearly, monthly, almost daily, the Union grows less popular in Scotland. This new Malt Tax is aimed deliberately at killing the Scots trade in malted liquors – just as the Salt Tax was to destroy your salted-herring exports, and the duty on linen to kill that industry. England covets your foreign trade, and will use her Parliamentary majority to see that she gets it. All trade with the Americas is to be carried only in English ships. . . .'

'Aye, we know all that, Colonel – only too well!' Panmure interrupted. 'But there is nothing new, there. 'Tis only a matter of degree.'

'Your Lordship will admit that degree, in timing, is vitally important, and that the trading interests in Scotland are ripe for revolt? The people always hated the Union, but the merchants were in favour. And now, with the lairds and landowners hit by the Malt Tax...'

'You were not after coming all the way from Lorraine to be telling us this, Colonel?' Rob mentioned, pleasantly enough.

'No, sir. But it is wise that we should have the background clear in our minds. There is more than that. One of His Majesty's agents in London is close to Queen Anne's court. He tells us that the Queen is sickening, of a disease which cannot but prove fatal!'

'A-a-a-ah!' Everywhere men sat up and forward at this intelligence.

'I need not inform you, gentlemen, of what this could mean. Anne's death would transform the political situation. Besides his gracious Majesty, there can be no other claimants to the throne than the aged Electress Sophia, and her bumbling son George of Hanover – a man who cannot even speak English! Moreover, Anne, it is known, cordially dislikes both of them, especially George, who refused her as a bride years ago. She has intimated that she will do all in her power to prevent him from ultimately succeeding her. In her dark days, it seems, she is turning more and more towards her gracious brother whom she has so grievously wronged, in remorse. And even a dying monarch can do much to influence the appointment of a successor.'

'How desperate is the woman's illness?' Lord Kilsyth asked forcefully. 'How soon can we expect the throne to be vacant?'

There were a few murmurs at this bluntness – but all awaited the answer eagerly.

'Only the all-knowing God can tell that,' the Puritan Hooke declared piously. 'But it is thought by her physicians that she cannot live more than perhaps a year.' He paused. 'In which case it behoves us, my lords, to have our plans laid and ready, the fire truly set and the tinder only awaiting the spark. That is why I am here.'

There was no doubting that Hooke had the company

with him, now. There was a clamour of excited talk.

The Irishman looked at Rob.

That man stroked his red beard. 'Is Queen Anne to put His Majesty on his throne – or are we?' he wondered, his voice stilling the chatter.

'Both, I hope,' the other answered. 'The Queen, His Majesty trusts, will name him as her successor. But there will be strong opposition from his enemies, from the Whigs and Hanoverians, and from, H'mm . . .' He coughed slightly. '. . . from those who cry Popery!' The religious problem was always a stumbling-block – especially so to the Puritan envoy of a Catholic Pretender. 'It will be necessary to have a large and well-equipped army ready to strike, here in Scotland – to take advantage of the situation as it develops.'

No one contested that – although it was noticeable that more glances than Hooke's flickered towards the Mac-Gregors.

Hurriedly the envoy went on. 'It may not be necessary to fight. But the presence of a powerful force, poised ready to strike in Scotland, would be of enormous encouragement and help to His Majesty's supporters in England. As you will know, the Tories are gaining favour and influence daily. Oxford and Bolingbroke have high hopes that Anne may turn to them to take over the government – and, with a demonstration of fervour from Scotland, they believe that they may be able to swing the whole Tory camp in His Majesty's support.'

The veteran Sir Hugh Patterson grunted. 'Aye, aye, man,' he declared in his broad Doric. 'Fine, that. But the Whigmaleeries still *are* the Government, wi' an army in Scotland to do their bidding. We canna openly raise a force here, and hold it standing awaiting Queen Anne's pleesure to dee! No' withoot a clash.'

'Yes, sir – that is true. As far as the Lowlands are concerned.' Hooke coughed again. 'But the Highlands are a different story, are they not? We all know that no southern army can really penetrate to any depth into the roadless Highlands. Behind the barrier of the mountains a Highland army could assemble and prepare without fear of interference. Word would leak out that it was there, no doubt – but it could not be brought to battle until it was ready to move out. The threat of such an army, my lords and gentlemen, in a few months time, might well be all that is needed to set King James upon his throne!'

A pregnant silence greeted this conclusion. All eyes were now frankly bent on Rob Roy – with varying expressions that ranged from anticipation and encouragement, through question and doubt, to suspicion and even alarm. The Highlands and the Lowlands ever made uneasy partners in Scotland. While most of the lords and lairds present undoubtedly would be well pleased if the Highland clans were to bear the brunt of the business and run the early risks, others would see the danger of the Highland influence growing too strong, and the rewards of success going in the wrong directions.

A born actor, Rob Roy took his time to speak. 'A Highland army is not a thing to be growing like leaves upon a tree,' he pointed out mildly. 'Indeed, there is no such thing, at all. Many little small armies there are, one to each clan – and och, they are not great at loving each other! It is a hard thing to bring them all to the assembly. And when you have them brought, to make them agree.'

' 'Pon my oath – that's the truth!' Keith, the Earl Marischal, said grimly.

Rob nodded. 'That being so, *ipso facto*, you cannot be having a Highland *standing* army. It just will not stand, whatever. The only way to be holding it together is to keep it moving and keep it fighting. Otherwise the clans will be at each other's throats, see you. I do not see any army raised and waiting for Queen Anne to die, behind the Highland Line.'

'I understand that,' Hooke said. 'I am not wholly ignorant of your Highland ways, you will recollect. I do not suggest that this army shall actually stand assembled. Only that each chief shall promise the King a certain number of men, and give his word that they will be at a certain place of assembly within so many days of a given signal. That is all.'

'You would trust to the chiefs' words so completely?' Viscount Fentoun, no lover of the Highlands, demanded.

'I would, my lord,' Hooke replied – and again looked at the MacGregor.

It was neatly done. Rob could not but uphold the honour of his fellow Gaels. He could not suggest that such a scheme would not work through any failure on the part of the chiefs. Nor could he claim that the clansmen might not follow their leaders. He was out-manoeuvred – and smiled slightly in somewhat rueful acknowledgment of the fact.

Gregor, however, did more than smile. He was not one to leave anything in doubt where Highland honour was concerned. 'Are you after suggesting, sir,' he cried, half-rising from his chair and staring at the viscount, 'that the word of a chief or any Highland gentleman is *not* to be trusted completely?'

'Lord – nothing of the sort, Glengyle, I assure you!' Panmure intervened hastily. 'Fentoun meant no such thing, I'll warrant. I take it that all he meant was could Colonel Hooke be satisfied with such word-of-mouth communications to assemble an army. That was your point, Fentoun, was it not?'

The peer from East Lothian mumbled something approximately affirmative.

'I think that you need have no fear,' Hooke went on smoothly. 'The chiefs all will be approached as soon as possible for their agreement and promises, and thereafter will be given as long warning as may be as to the date and place of assembly. I foresee no serious difficulties . . . if Mr MacGregor will consent to act as His Majesty's representative and ambassador to the clans, as he has done before?'

'And who would that man be, at all?' Rob asked gently, of the heraldic plaster ceiling apparently. 'This *Mister* MacGregor?'

'H'rr'mmm.' The Irishman blinked rapidly. 'Inversnaid, I mean, of course. I apologise, sir. A slip of the tongue. I have been away from the North for years. My regrets, Inversnaid.'

'Accepted, Colonel,' the MacGregor replied graciously. 'In this company, Rob will serve very well. But a gentleman of the MacGregors is Mister in no company, whatever, you will remember? *Dia* – he is not!'

The niceties of Highland and Gregorach dignity thus suitably established, Rob sat back. 'So it is myself that you will have to be doing all the toil and the striving?' he went on. 'Me it is that has to be seeing the chiefs and convincing the clans?'

'None could do it better. Or so well. The chiefs all trust you – even the Campbells! Which is a thing I doubt if any other man in Scotland could say!' And Hooke smiled his wintry smile.

'The Campbells may trust me – but that is not to say that I am trusting the Campbells!' Rob Roy observed dryly. 'But I'm thinking that more than trust is needed. The clans have rallied twice to King James's banner, already – and both times he has failed them. They will not be so eager now, I'm thinking.'

'All the more reason why it should be you who approaches them, Rob,' Harry Maule intervened quietly, fingering the long curls of his great wig. 'They will accept your assurances when you explain the situation in London. And that His Majesty has learned a great deal in these five years. And when you tell them that the prospects for the cause were never fairer.'

'For the cause, perhaps, friend – but what of the prospects for the *clans*? It would seem that they will bear the weight of any bloodshed that there may be. Not for the first time. I have to be thinking of them also, see you.'

Fentoun's chair scraped back. 'You put your chiefs before your king, MacGregor!' he cried.

Other voices rose in his support.

'I put the benefit of the people before that of any one man, my lord – even of James Stewart!'

'S'death! Is this His Majesty's envoy to the clans?' the viscount demanded hotly. 'God help King James if this is the voice of the Highlands!'

'No, no. Peace. Fentoun – in Heaven's name!' Panmure said. 'You mistake him. . . .'

'Would the gentleman prefer to play the envoy his own self?' Rob wondered. 'To go round the clans in person? I shall be happy . . .'

'Gentlemen – my lords,' Hooke broke in. 'This is folly. Let us not excite ourselves over nothing. Inversnaid . . . er, Rob . . . is perfectly right to concern himself for the people, *his* people. The interests of the country as a whole must be considered. His Majesty is equally concerned for the people, for his loyal clansmen – more so, if I may dare suggest it, as their divinely appointed ruler and protector. But fortunately, in this instance, the King's and the clans' interests coincide.' The Irishman tipped thin lips with his tongue. 'The usurping Government in London hates the clans. Witness our friend Rob's own personal predicament. The victim of animosity and greed, he is convicted in his absence on a trumped-up charge, declared bankrupt, and outlawed by the Government. He suffers more than any of us from the King's enemies. Therefore he has the right to be cautious, lest he suffers more.'

The MacGregor stirred in his chair. The man was wickedly subtle, seeing two or three moves ahead all the time. Never had Rob been manoeuvred so skilfully into a corner. To use his outlawry to commit him was clever; but to hint at over-caution, linked with the name and reputation of Rob Roy MacGregor, was masterly.

Gregor took the bait like an eager salmon. 'You are not suggesting, sir, that it is caution that concerns my uncle?' he demanded. 'God's death – you little know us if that is your opinion of the Gregorach!'

'Quiet, Greg lad,' Rob interposed. 'Colonel Hooke understands the MacGregors very well, I think – too well, perhaps!'

'I know that I have never yet called upon you in vain – whatever has been my experience elsewhere,' the Irishman said handsomely. 'I am sure that I will not this time either, my friend?'

'I fear that perhaps you will,' the other answered, shrugging. 'I have other things to do, see you.'

Gregor glanced at his uncle sharply.

'But . . . nothing so important that it can prevent you from doing this great service for your King, surely? And country likewise, of course,' Hooke added hurriedly.

'I think that it could, yes.'

'I need not mention, need I, that His Majesty will reward gratefully and suitably such services done to him?'

'As Royal's my Race – I do not serve my country for reward!'

'No. No – er, that is understood, of course . . .'

'But what is there that you must be doing, Rob, that is so important?' Lord Panmure asked. 'You are outlawed, more or less a fugitive in the heather, if all that we hear is true. How can you be so tied with affairs . . . ?'

'Sink me – I'd have wagered that you would welcome the chance, man, to get away from dodging the red-coats and living as a hunted man!' Lord Southesk declared. 'I vow *I* should!'

'Your lordship's preferences are your own. Put it that I have a debt to settle,' Rob mentioned. 'A notable debt.'

Hooke eyed the MacGregor shrewdly. 'I take it that you

mean with his Grace of Montrose?'

'With Montrose, yes. And with another.'

'That is understandable. And a debt of honour is not to be denied,' the other agreed sympathetically. 'But I put it to you that the best way to pay your debt to Montrose is to bring down the Government of which he is a member, to ensure his political downfall and the end of his position of privilege. Put King James on his throne, Rob, and Montrose is at your mercy! And others with him.'

'Aye, aye.'

'Truly spoken.'

There was sense in that, Rob could not deny. But a Mac-Gregor's vengeance was not of the sort that could be put quietly by till times were more propitious. 'That may be true,' he said stubbornly. 'But I do not intend to wait so long, at all.'

'But . . . mercy on us – the need for this service is urgent!' Hooke cried, for once nettled into irritation. 'The King's cause cannot wait!'

Into the silence, it was Gregor MacGregor's voice that spoke. 'If my uncle cannot find the time for this service, then *I* will go to the clans,' he said. 'I am not so notable a man as he, nor yet a famed warrior. Not yet. But I am chieftain of Clan Dougal Ciar of the Gregorach, and that is enough for any clan's chief under heaven, whatever! The King shall be served!'

There was a momentary pause as men looked from nephew to uncle and back again. Then the applause broke out and continued.

Rob stared straight ahead of him. Then his first quick frown was displaced by a smile. 'You are a brave fellow, Greg,' he said. 'A very paladin! But we will discuss this later, see you.'

Hooke judiciously decided that the moment was ripe to change the subject. 'Now, my lords,' he said. 'I think that we can turn to the consideration of how much each of you can promise to contribute in money, horses and materials. And men also, of course. You, my lord of Panmure, have already promised an excellent provision. As has Mr Harry. Now, perhaps my Lord Glamis . . . ?'

*   *   *

That evening, in the privacy of their own room, the two MacGregors faced each other, so dissimilar in appearance yet so basically alike.

'I tell you I am no longer your pupil! Your tutoring days are over!' the younger man declared warmly. 'Wanting a high chief of MacGregor, no man is my master. I choose my own road . . .'

'Aye, boy – but in matters of war I'd remind you that *I* am Captain of Clan Alpine still. And this is warfare.'

'Not yet, it is not. This is a matter between myself and my king! When the clan is to be led, you will lead it, and I will serve under you. But until that day, Glengyle is his own master!'

'*Dia* – you crow like any cockerel on a midden! How think you the chiefs – veteran fighters like Maclean of Duart, and Locheil, and old Coll of Keppoch – will heed the words of a stripling like yourself! How will *you* contest the evasions of that fox MacDonald of Sleat? Is the proud Clanranald likely to give his promises through young Gregor of Glengyle?'

His nephew swallowed, and his eager face sank a little at the mention of these famous and resounding names. 'I . . . I do not know,' he admitted, his voice suddenly subdued. 'I can but try them – do my best with them. Somebody must go to them, if you cannot. . . .'

'They will scorn you, boy – or cozen you. They will talk you round and about, and shout you down, and twist you round their fingers. They are devils for pride and doubletalking. I know them – I know the way of them, and the way round them. They have to be played off, one against another, played like salmon, handled like the slippery eels they are! Or the King will never see his army. . . .' Rob paused, tugging at his beard.

Looking at his uncle, Gregor opened his mouth to speak, and then shut it again – for once wisely holding his peace.

The older man took to pacing the floor of that little bedroom up within the steep roof of the castle. 'Difficult it is,' he muttered. 'If I thought . . . If James was to be failing the clans again, I would never have myself forgiven. Yet, if Anne dies, the word of a force in arms here in Scotland might turn the tide. . . .'

'Is it for policy's sake that you will not go to the chiefs, Rob – or because of John Graham of Killearn?' Gregor asked, then.

His uncle paused in his pacing. 'Both, lad,' he said. 'Both. Though it may be that Hooke has the right of it, this time. I swore that I would never again lead good Highlandmen out to risk their blood for a spineless fool, king or none! But, if Anne dies, and only a fat German is to succeed her . . .'

'It is not policy that holds you back, then, so much. It is Killearn, just?'

'Aye – I suppose that it is, lad.'

'But, Rob – Killearn will keep. I said that before, and it is truth. If the king wins, then Killearn's master falls, and Killearn with him. You can hunt him where you will – the Lowlands will be open to you. They will hide him no longer. You must see that?'

'Would you so wait, Greg, if it had been Glengyle House burned, and *your* Mary and bairns driven out into the night?'

'I do not know. I do not know, at all,' the other admitted soberly. 'Probably not, then. But you are a wiser man than I am, Rob. And, see you – there is this to it. How are you to get at Killearn, anyway? He keeps himself well hidden down there in the Lennox. If you make to go in there, you *may* kill Killearn – but you will never win back to Inversnaid. You, a man well known to all by sight, and with a great price on your head. And the clan is like to need its Captain. But if you wait – wait until February. The Quarter-day – Candlemas. Killearn always has to come north to collect Montrose's rents. *Then* you can reach him, in our own country. That is the time. A bare two months. As factor, he must come for the rents. Then you can pay him yours, my God!'

Slowly Rob Roy nodded. 'Aye,' he said, at last. 'The Candlemas Quarter-day. I believe that you are right, Greg – I do so! I had not thought of that. Yes, I will have him then. Even if he has a regiment of red-coats to guard him, I will have him! Aye.'

'Then . . . you have two months. You will go to the chiefs?'

His uncle smiled. 'I will go, fire-eater.'

'Fine! Fine! Then I will go with you. . . .'

'You will not. No, Greg. I go alone. With red-coats at Inversnaid, your place is with your Mary and the children at Glengyle. The clan needs you there, too. I go alone. But . . . I will be back . . . for Candlemas!'

Gregor sighed. 'Aye,' he said.

CHAPTER TEN

DESPITE all his legendary speed of travel, and the urgency that gnawed within him, Rob was only just able to fulfil his declared intention of being back in his own countryside by Candlemas Quarter-day. Traversing the remote and savage Highlands of the north and west at dead of winter, with snow-choked passes, every stream a foaming torrent, sea-lochs lashed with winds, and the islands often storm-bound for days on end, was a trying and unpredictable business, a succession of challenges, that made a mockery of haste. Nor were the calls that he had had to make such as could be rushed, or disposed of to any timetable. The chiefs, small kings in their own territories, and prouder than any en-throned monarchs, could not be forced into any definite undertakings to supply armed men for James Stewart in the course of, say, an evening's chat. The thing had to be approached suitably, discreetly, in accordance with dignity, and discussed with much diplomacy – frequently, the smaller the chief the greater the diplomacy required. Men had to be coaxed and wheedled, flattered and tempted, and played off one against another. If MacDonald of Barrasdale could be screwed up to promising fifty men, then the chances were that MacDonald of Arnisdale would feel bound to offer at least seventy-five – but again, MacDonald of Glenelg would not join in at all if he heard that the other two were involved, and *he* could produce at least a hundred. Then the great chiefs – Maclean of Duart, Clanranald, Glengarry, Sleat, Macleod, Seaforth and the rest – had to be angled for with probable advantages and honours and promises, as well as having their mutual jealousies and antagonisms played upon. Only the most expert, knowledgeable and trusted of emissaries, could hope to achieve any success in this task; even Rob Roy MacGregor could not rush matters as he would have liked.

So it was the last day of January, after leaving MacDougall of Lorne's castle of Dunollie, before Rob made his way, somewhat wearily for that man, up the fair Glen Orchy that had once been the MacGregors', and round below Beinn Dorain's cloud-hung peak, to Auch and his family. There, any hopes that he might have cherished as to the healing effects of his two months' absence on his wife's spiritual wounds were speedily dissipated. Mary treated him exactly as she had done previously. Her health appeared to be good, she ate adequately, cherished her children as a mother should, worked about the house and at spinning and weaving and dyeing, and in all other respects behaved as normally – save perhaps that her great eyes still held a strange light at times, and she showed less interest in her appearance than formerly; but where Rob was concerned – indeed, where any and all men were concerned – she was as blank as a wall lacking doors or windows. Her husband's stories of his mission to the chiefs, and what he intended for John Graham of Killearn when he came up to collect his master's rents in a day or two's time, equally failed to arouse any discernible reaction in her. The following morning, Rob flung out of the house under Beinn Dorain set-faced, thankful that his errand left him no time for delay.

That night he was at the cave on Cruach Tuirc, where he found only MacAlastair, living a hermit's life in apparent content. Donald, it seemed, had been gone for nearly a month, back to the haunts of men – and likewise women. It appeared that a couple of weeks after Rob's departure, a fleet of boats had come up Loch Lomond from the south, and had taken all the soldiers away. They had gone by night, as they had come, leaving no word, no explanations, no threats even – only much litter, equal quantities of scorn and hatred, and the foundations of the new fort up on Tom na Bairlinn. Presumably they would come back in due course. Meantime the MacGregors, without waiting for Rob Roy's instructions in the matter, had demolished such masonry as had been erected on the foundations, and carted the hewn stones over to the site of Rob's burnt-out house at the other side of the burn, for eventual rebuilding. Life in Inversnaid and the glens, therefore, had returned more or less to normal. MacAlastair forbore either to cheer or to prophesy.

Rob was well enough content with what all this might indicate – but at the moment he was more interested in the doings of Graham of Killearn than those of the military. The Duke of Montrose, from his base of Buchanan Castle in the low country at the foot of Loch Lomond, had inherited and acquired vast estates right up to the edge of the Highland Line – and in one or two instances, even over it. Much of this bordered on the MacGregor territories of Craigroyston and Aberfoyle, and was therefore, from the Lowlander's point of view, on the wrong side of the elementary safety line. It was the custom in Scotland to collect rents quarterly, at the term-days of Candlemas, Whitsun, Lammas and Martinmas – and since the tenants by no means would, or could, travel long distances to pay, it behoved the lairds to send their factors to recognised assembly points to receive their tribute in cash or kind. Thus, every three months, Graham of Killearn had to come north to visit various known venues on his master's behalf. The venues could not be changed without ample notification to all concerned – or no rents would be collected. Rob Roy could hardly go wrong.

At noon, for instance, next day, the second of February, John Graham was due to be at the ale-house of Duchray, only a few miles from Aberfoyle. Very well so.

The three men were in position early, amongst the heather and scattered pines above the clachan of Duchray. The small grey Graham castle stood on its knoll below them to the left, and to the right, beyond three or four cot-houses, lay the inn, scheduled scene of today's collection. It was a brilliant sparkling morning of hoar frost, and the snow-covered mountains gleamed and glittered in the dazzling sunlight, a trial to the eyes.

One or two tenants had arrived before Rob, and all morning they came in, singly and in little groups, driving a cow or a couple of sheep, or a pannier-pony laden with sacks of grain or crates of poultry – for by no means all paid their dues in cash. Hidden, the watchers high above, waited – and wished that they could help to keep the cold out with some of Colin the Inn's cheer, as did the over-punctual tenants.

Just before noon the still frosty air rang to a different sort of sound to the scuffle and clop of the hooves of cows and garrons – the ring of iron-shod hooves on the ice-bound track. Many hooves. Round a bend in the drove-road from the east trotted a purposeful cavalcade.

'*Dia* – he does not ride unprotected, does John Graham!' Donald MacGregor exclaimed. 'It is an army, whatever!'

'Half a troop, say,' Rob amended. 'And what did you expect? If I was John Graham, I would have brought more than that.' He paused for a moment. 'No, my God,' he added grimly ' – I would not have come, at all!'

The company consisted of about thirty red-coated dragoons, with three men in civilian clothing. They clattered past the inn, with scarcely a glance at the waiting countrymen, and on to the castle.

'He wants his dinner, from Duchray, before he attends to the tenantry scum!' Donald commented. 'Always Kill-earn loved his belly.'

The civilians and one of the soldiers – the officer, no doubt – dismounted and entered the castle doorway, while the dragoons disposed themselves as best they could. There was a sizeable crowd now, about the ale-house, and much livestock, some of it vociferous. All waited with what patience was in them.

Rob waited, too – waited for over an hour till the factor's party emerged from Duchray Castle and moved over to the inn, escorted by the soldiery; waited for longer than that, waited all afternoon in fact, despite the cold and Donald's increasing restiveness – while tenants came and went and the herd of beasts grew, and the soldiers scattered about and relaxed in their boredom. Donald was for action, unspecified but dramatic, all the time, but Rob would not be rushed. The longer that they could delay, the better, he pointed out; there would be the more beasts in the pens behind the inn, the dragoons were growing less and less watchful and drinking more and more of Colin's ale, and the more substantial tenants would be arriving late when, according to established custom, the factor would provide refreshments for these favoured folk at the end of the day. Moreover, dusk and the oncoming night, would aid them in anything that they attempted. The waiting game could be the winning game.

Lights indeed had been lit within the little inn before at length Rob decided that the time was ripe. Stiff and cramped with cold, the three men rose up out of the heather amongst the shadows of the dark pines, with the sun down behind Beinn Lomond and no certainty about anything in sight save the twinkling lights below.

'You have it clear, what you have to be at?' Rob charged his lieutenants. 'Work you down, unseen, to behind the house. Get a barrier down in the pens, there. Och, you will manage that, easy. Then out with the beasts – get them running downhill into the haughs of the Duchray Water. No torches this time, MacAlastair – you will have to be shouting, just. Noise is the thing, see you – once you are ready for them. Get the beasts running, and you amongst them – och, and the soldiers will be running after you. It is soft down in the haughs – boggy; they will not do much with their fine horses there. Splash you across the burn and up into the thick woods beyond. They will not find you in there, in the dark, those ones – but keep you on with the shouting, so that they follow you. You have it?'

'The cattle – the beasts, Rob?' Donald demanded. 'We'll never can manage the cattle through the thick wood. . . .'

'Let the beasts go where they will, man. Leave them. They will scatter – and take a deal of gathering again. In the dark, the soldiers will be hearing them crashing about and thinking it is yourselves. Och, it will be child's-play, just. All I am wanting is fifteen minutes to myself with John Graham – no more. Keep you the soldiers busy for that, and Killearn is mine. I will meet you, later, at the garrons back up here. You have your pistols primed, to be firing a shot or two. . . . ?'

Rob watched them slip away down hill like shadows. Very soon the dusk had swallowed them into its obscurity. He waited, once more.

His friends seemed to take an unconscionable time about their business. Not that this mattered greatly, for the darker the evening the better for their purposes – unless they delayed long enough for Killearn to finish his work at the inn and retire to the castle for the night, in which case all was lost. But that was unlikely, unless he was going to dispense with the usual refreshments. . . .

Then, abruptly, pandemonium broke out below. A shot, sharp in the crisp air, sparked it off, then a volley of yells, followed by much bellowing of alarmed cattle and the thunder of trampling stamping hooves. Cries and shouts rose from all around now, and two more shots rang out. In the din, Rob could distinguish the barked commands of authority. He nodded to himself, satisfied.

He gave them a minute or two, by which time the principal sources of noise were already obviously moving away down towards the water meadows, before looking to the priming of his own pistol and himself slipping away downhill.

Probably Rob followed approximately the same route as his colleagues. The pines and birches gave him cover right down to the level of the drove-road. He darted across it, and circled round towards the back of the inn. The hullabuloo was still proceeding, but it was now some distance off, down about the waterside.

Rob made for the inn's back door. There seemed to be nobody around the rear of the house – only one or two restive tethered garrons, a few agitated sheep, and the broken-down barricading of the cattle pens. So far, so good.

The back door was shut, but not bolted. However carefully he pushed it open, it creaked a little – but there was a chatter of voices upraised within that would cover the noise. He edged inside, closed the door behind him, and quietly slid home the bolt.

He was in a narrow passage, at either end of which were open doors through which light streamed. He was acquainted with the place, and knew that the apartment to the right was the large public room of the inn, that to the left being the proprietor's private kitchen. A ladder midway led up to rough sleeping-quarters in the loft.

Rob moved along the passage to the right, his rawhide brogans making no sound on the earthen floor. Keeping well back in the shadow, he approached the doorway.

There seemed to be about a dozen men within, all talking and gesticulating at the same time, some peering out through the open front door, some crowding around a window that faced down towards the waterside. All but three were dressed in the rough hodden grey and blue bonnet of the low country farmer. Colin the Inn was standing at the table with a steaming dish of collops. Of the two others, one was in Montrose livery, a thin stooping man who looked like a clerk – and an unhappy one. The last man, well dressed in broadcloth and wearing a cocked hat somewhat askew, stood well back from the outer door, turned away from Rob. In his hand was a drawn pistol – though he did not seem to be gripping it with any degree of confidence.

All this the MacGregor, with no eyes in his direction, took in during a swift survey of the room, by the wavering smoky light of the tallow dips. Bottles and tankards stood about everywhere; benches lay overturned as though upset when men rose hastily to their feet; the table, apart from its victuals, was heaped with ledgers and paper, with stacks of coins, and with bulging money-bags.

Rob's own pistol was now thrust forward, his thumb on the lock. He smiled, but not pleasantly, and took a pace into the room.

'Graham!' he said simply, not loudly but vibrantly enough for the word to penetrate the chatter.

The other man turned round – and as he did so, a dirk, hurled with savage force and accuracy, struck the wrist of his pistol hand. It was the haft that struck, not the point, but even so both weapons clattered to the floor, and the man uttered a yelp of pain.

Rob Roy uttered an exclamation too, part surprise and part curse. The pistol barrel that he had raised to point at the other's chest wavered for a moment.

'Gorthie!' he got out. '*Diabhol* – you! A plague on it – where is Killearn?'

'MacGregor!' the injured man gasped, his features contorted. 'I . . . you . . . God's curse on you, you devil!'

It was the wrong man – Mungo Graham of Gorthie, Montrose's chamberlain, not his factor.

*   *   *

Rob's upset and hesitation was short-lived – as was the wavering of that pistol. The weapon swept menacingly all around the room, for now every head was turned and every eye upon him.

'Your pardon, gentlemen all,' he called. 'I shall not be disturbing you for long, at all. Och, no. Colin – close me that door, man. Bolt it. Quickly. I thank you.' He turned back to Graham. 'This is strange work for you, Gorthie, is it not? I had expected to see Killearn . . . with whom I have my own small account to settle. Regrettable it is that he is not with us.'

The chamberlain answered nothing. No man spoke.

The MacGregor went on. 'My apologies if I have hurt your hand, Gorthie. I trust that it will not incommode you for the signing of receipts and the like? Colin – pick me up Gorthie's pistol; it will be safe with me.' He drew a long breath. 'Now, to business, gentlemen. I have not got long with you, more's the pity. All have paid their rents by this, I hope? Och, yes.' He scanned the many alarmed and anxious faces. 'Good. All have obtained their due and legal receipts from his Grace's chamberlain?' And, more sharply, as all gaped but none answered, 'Have you, gentlemen? For your own sakes it is important that you hold receipts.'

'Och, I'm no' needin' ony receipt,' one man declared.

'Nor me, neither. . . .'

'That is foolish. Is it not, Gorthie? Gorthie will give you one, now.'

Rob jerked his pistol at the thin stooping clerkly man. 'You, fellow – write these gentlemen their receipts. Gorthie will sign them. Quickly, man. His Grace would have all done in proper fashion, surely?'

'What . . . what do you intend, MacGregor?' Graham asked, biting his lip – whether with pain or agitation was a moot point. He was a very different man from the dour bull-like Killearn, older and more sensitive in manner, though of similar build.

'Nothing that is not·just and suitable,' Rob assured him

easily. 'Never fear, man Mungo – all will be done in order. *Exitus acta probat!*'

'You will suffer for it, I promise you. . . .'

'It may be that I have done my suffering already, my friend!' And to the clerk. 'Haste you with your scribbling, fellow.'

For a few moments there was no sound in that room save the scraping of the quill and some very deep breathing. From outside a lively shouting still prevailed, but it seemed to come from a long way off.

As the clerk laid down the pen, Rob took it up and handed it to Gorthie. 'Sign, you,' he directed. 'With your left hand, if need be.' And as the other hesitated, 'Go on, man – it is no more than your plain duty. These tenants have paid you – they are entitled to your receipt.'

With ill grace Graham took the quill with his left hand, and scratched some sort of signature.

'Good. Now, a piece of paper for my own self.' Rob transferred the pistol to his left hand, and took up the pen himself. 'Mark you all,' he mentioned pleasantly, 'that I can shoot equally exactly with either hand!' Leaning against the table, he dipped pen in ink and began to write, raising his eyes between each word. He enunciated the words as he wrote.

'Received from James Graham, Duke of Montrose, the sum of . . .' He paused. 'Does this excellent ledger tell how much coin has been received, fellow?' he asked of the clerk, 'As distinct from cattle and the like?'

'Eh? Aye – och, yes. But I've no' added it yet. . . .'

'Then do so now, man – and quickly. All must be done in order. Tell me at the end of this, and I will write the sum in. Just what you have collected in coin, see you. The beasts would be an inconvenience.' He started again, with the pen.

'. . . the sum of . . . being rents received in coin from all tenants due to pay at Duchray on this day Candlemas the year of grace seventeen hundred and fourteen, the said tenants all having received Gorthie's due receipts. I acknowledge that the said moneys have been duly accepted by me from Graham of Gorthie, as agent for his Grace, in part payment of the debt owing me by the said Duke James. As witness to which my signature is hereby appended.' And he signed the paper with a flourish, 'Robert MacGregor of Inversnaid and Craigroyston.'

'God damn you, MacGregor – you canna do this!' Gorthie burst out. 'It is plain and shameless robbery! Before all these witnesses, I charge you . . .'

'Wheesht, man – wheesht! Clerk – the sum total, if you please?'

'Och, sir – I canna just get it right. I'll tot it up again . . .'

'*Dia* – never trouble! I do not want it to the nearest groat. Give it to me in pounds Scots, man.'

'Pounds Scots . . . it'll be eight hunnerd an' saxty-five, aboot. I made it so the first time. . . .'

'That will serve well enough. Leave it now. Put you all the coin in the one bag – the large one. Quickly, now. In with it. Every groat of it, yes. Quiet, Gorthie, while I write in the figures. You would not have me make an error in an important receipt such as this, would you? Eight hundred and sixty-five, was it not? Pounds Scots. Good. That is it, then. Let the ink dry on that, and all is done in proper style. . . .'

'You are a villain, MacGregor – a barefaced thief and a murderous cateran!'

'Tut, man – not so. Not at all,' Rob denied, transferring the pistol and taking up the heavy bag of coin in his left hand. He seemed to weigh it, judicially, as he did so. 'Nothing has been done here but what is fair and seemly. Your master, Montrose, has unlawfully and maliciously deprived me of my ability to earn my living, whatever. Moreover he has had my house burned on me, my chattels destroyed, and much of my livestock purloined. It follows that he must keep me and my family, out of his bounty, until such time as I am permitted to do the same for myself again. . . .'

Rob stopped short. There was a rattle at the front door, and then a banging thereon. He grimaced. 'We seem to be disturbed, gentlemen. But och, I think our business is satisfactorily done. You have your receipts from Gorthie for your rents. You cannot suffer. Gorthie has his receipt from myself, for this payment on account. What could be fairer . . . ?'

The banging resumed, more urgently.

Rob shook his head. 'Impatient, they are. A pity. I'll bid you good-day, then, gentlemen . . . until the Whitsun term! God preserve all honest men!' And cocked pistol in one hand and money-bag in the other, he backed out of that room and into the passage. From the rear door he shouted, 'Colin, man open up and do not keep the gentlemen waiting!'

Then he was out into the night. Nobody seemed to be at the back of the house. Fleet as any deer he ran for the cover of the first trees.

As he had promised his friends, it had all been child's-play. But practically wasted effort, unfortunately. Killearn still went unpunished.

CHAPTER ELEVEN

ROB did not have long to fret over his disappointment. He had agreed to make a report on his mission to the chiefs to Nathaniel Hooke, and now there was nothing that more urgently demanded his attention. Taking Gregor along with him once more, with MacAlastair in attendance, and leaving Donald to keep in touch with the household at Auch, two days later he was on his way east to Kelly Castle again.

But Hooke was no longer based at Harry Maule's grey house by the grey sea. He had travelled north, it seemed, on receipt of an important message from London, making for Mar Castle on the upper Dee. Rob whistled when he heard this news – for John, Earl of Mar, was Secretary of State for Scotland in Anne's Government and no known Jacobite.

A day later the three MacGregors were on their way northwards likewise.

They went discreetly, as ever, avoiding Forfar and Kirriemuir and deliberately making for the snow-bound hills where, whatever the discomforts, they could travel openly and without skulking. They followed Glen Clova right up to its head amongst the great hump-backed Grampian mountains and then struck northwards over the high snow-choked passes that led down into Glen Muick and so to the wide strath of Dee near the Pass of Ballater. This was not the route that Hooke would have taken, undoubtedly, but it spared them many distractions other than the purely physical ones that anyway came to these three as second nature. Moreover, it gave Rob ample opportunity to ponder the problem of the Earl of Mar.

That Hooke apparently should be making a rendezvous

with London's Secretary of State for Scotland was on the face of it alarming. But the Colonel was no fool, and presumably his information satisfied him. Besides, it was significant perhaps that this journey was being made, not to Alloa House, Mar's Lowland home near Stirling, but to the remote and semi-ruinous Deeside castle from which the earl took his ancient title. This, surely, could only have been at Mar's own request. The man, known as Bobbing John on account of his facility for changing political parties, presumably must be considering changing dynastic sides – which could be a good augury indeed. His mother, of course had been Lady Mary Maule, a sister of Panmure, and his wife, recently dead, had been a sister of the Jacobite Earl of Kinnoull, while his own sister had married Sir Hugh Patterson of Bannockburn – so that, whatever his politics, he was closely connected with many of King James's most prominent supporters. Rob was doubtful, nevertheless, of the wisdom of having dealings with a man of his reputation who was in a position to do their cause infinite harm if he so wished; the uncomplicatedly honest and straightforward Gregor of Glengyle was not doubtful at all – he was dead-set against it.

Up the Dee, in darkness, they came inconspicuously to Mar Castle on its rock, to find it not only ruinous but deserted. Discreet investigations revealed that its lord was lodging at the house of Farquharson of Invercauld a few miles down the strath – a very doubtful Jacobite indeed. Not too happily the MacGregors repaired thereto.

They used MacAlastair to make enquiries. Colonel Hooke was found to be at Invercauld also. He came out to welcome Rob eagerly for so stiff a man, and took the MacGregors down to the inn by the riverside where they could talk freely. There he expressed himself as delighted with the report of Rob's mission in the North-west, and more than satisfied with the promises of men and support elicited from the chiefs. He further declared that this information had come at a most auspicious moment – for he could pass it on to Mar, to whose conversion it might well prove decisive.

At Rob's strongly phrased objection to any such betrayal of the chiefs' confidence, Hooke explained. Mar was a Jacobite at heart. Though a member of the Whiggish Government, he had been growing more and more convinced that the future lay with the Tories. With the prospect of Queen Anne's death, he was prepared not only to go over to the Opposition but to throw in his lot with the supporters of King James if he could be assured that they were in the temper and position to take fullest advantage of the dynastic vacuum. Mar himself had sought this meeting, and had gone to no little trouble to effect it. His declared concern, throughout the negotiations with the Colonel, had been doubts as to the numbers of troops that the Jacobites could put into the field quickly enough to keep the Government forces from dominating all strong-points in Scotland in the event of a sudden crisis. Rob's news and figures from the western seaboard would go a long way towards reassuring him.

The MacGregors' doubts about disclosing this information to the Government's chief minion in Scotland, incriminating the clans, were swept aside by Hooke, who pointed out that these chiefs of the North-west were known by all to be King James's men as it was, and the only question was how many broadswords they were likely to put on the field. The numbers that Rob had gained promises for, amounting in all to seven thousand, were highly satisfactory. There could be no harm in informing Mar – for even if he was minded to do the cause hurt, he could by no means reach these chiefs behind their endless ramparts of mountain.

But there was more to it than that. Mar was ready to be convinced, and the greater the weight of support that could be demonstrated for King James, the faster the earl would come over. And he was prepared, it seemed, to continue on in his present important position of Secretary of State, not to make any open break meantime with his Whig colleagues – and so could prove to be of the very greatest assistance to the Jacobite cause as an informer sitting at the very council table of the enemy. Moreover, a sympathetic Secretary of State could greatly ease Jacobite preparations in Scotland, and wink at much that might otherwise be banned. The stakes were high, as they must see.

Rob saw – though he did not fail to see, also, that an informer could work in two directions, and a double-dealer could play more sides false than one. Gregor, for his part, was entirely shocked, and said so.

But Hooke's mind obviously was made up. He was going to tell Mar, and all the MacGregors' doubts would not stop him. He left them at the inn, promising to see them again on the morrow. Being the Gregorach they were, once the Colonel was gone, they prudently left the hostelry and found less vulnerable quarters for themselves in a charcoal-burner's hut in the pine forest. It behoved those who entered the devil's kitchen, said Rob, to see that they left the door open behind them.

It was afternoon next day before Hooke contacted the MacGregors again. Then he came smirking his satisfaction. Mar was convinced. He would throw in his lot with the Jacobites – though not publicly of course – and act positively for them behind the scenes at Whitehall. A dukedom in due course, promised in the name of King James, had nicely clinched the matter.

Gregor made some remarks in the Gaelic which it was probably as well that Hooke did not understand.

It was decided that there was no point in the MacGregors seeing Mar. Hooke suggested that it might be an embarrassment for the Secretary of State to meet socially a wanted outlaw with a price on his head – though Rob gave it as his opinion that a minister who would swallow the salmon of betraying his own Government would not puke at a minnow such as that. However, as it happened, he had no desire himself to talk to the man – and Gregor would have refused to do so anyway.

Hooke, moreover, had other urgent plans for the Mac-Gregors. He himself was about to travel further north still, to fully implicate and enlist the Marquis of Huntly and all his Gordons. These were English-speaking; but the clans further inland, in Badenoch and the great Spey valley, were not – the Shaws, Macphersons, Cattanachs, Mackintoshes, Cummings and Grants. To these he desired Rob and Gregor to go, on the same errand as heretofore – especially to seek to use the influence of Rob's old friend MacAlpine Grant of Rothiemurchus to sway others of that large clan against the Whig tendencies of their chief, the Laird of Grant. Rob had performed an exactly similar service in 1707, with a certain amount of success. It would be a lengthy and diffi-cult employment, but Hooke, who appeared now to be in possession of considerable funds, no doubt raised from the low-country lords, promised that it would be a well-paid one. Gregor MacGregor tut-tutted at the introduction of such sordid considerations into the loyal service of His Majesty, but his uncle was differently minded and believed that the labourer was worthy of his hire – particularly when the said hire came out of the deep pockets of purse-proud Lowland magnates. Amongst other attributes, Rob Roy was not least a notable business-man. In agreeing to under-take this second embassy he drove a fairly shrewd bargain. Mary and the boys, back at Auch, would not starve yet awhile.

So the following day, as Mar rode south and Hooke north, the MacGregors headed westwards through the vast and daunting mountains of the Monadh Ruadh, by the passes of Glen Geldie and Glen Feshie, for Badenoch and the uplands of Spey. Rob was not altogether sorry, perhaps to have his mind and time so fully occupied with the King's business.

CHAPTER TWELVE

POLITICS and such high affairs did not so wholly fill his mind, however, that Rob forgot his promised engagement with Montrose's good tenants for the next rent day, the Whitsun term. His work on Speyside still unfinished – it had not only prolonged itself as the result of the evasiveness and obstinacy of men and the effects of melting snows on river-dominated terrain, but had extended itself into the heights of Moray and the Great Glen areas – he allowed himself a temporary respite and relaxation, and set off for the south at the beginning of May, in good time he trusted to do what had to be done. Gregor he had already sent home a good month previously – partly for his young wife's sake, partly to keep an eye on the Gregorach, and partly because his distinctly straightforward and all too honest nephew did not make the best of negotiators.

Rob and MacAlastair made their way out of Badenoch by the Pass of Drumochter, down long Loch Ericht-side and across the waterlogged wastes of Rannoch Moor to Orchy and Auch. This time Rob did not look for any notable welcome from his Mary – and so was not disappointed. But he had had ample time for thought and cogitation during his months in the north, and he arrived home with certain decisions firm upon him. Consequently, when he came to intimate something of his Whitsun Quarter-day programme, he added as an after-thought, but crisply, that he was going to take his wife with him on this occasion.

Mary's statuesque armour of reserve, almost impenetrable as it was, wilted just a little at this announcement. She actually blinked. 'What . . . I . . . such jesting is ill-judged,' she said.

'It is no jesting,' he assured.

'Then it is folly,' she gave back, as briefly.

'That is a matter of opinion,' he shrugged. 'But you come, nevertheless, *a graidh*.'

'Indeed I do not.'

'Yes, you do. You are my wife yet, see you – little as you may act the part these days. You will do as I say, woman.'

'Have you . . . have you taken leave of your wits?' she cried.

'It may be so – in which case there will be the two of us in that state! Still, I think not. But you will ride with me tomorrow, whatever.'

Helplessly the woman stared at him. 'But, why? Where would you take me? How can I be leaving here? The children – I cannot leave my children. It is unthinkable. . . .'

'The children will do finely with Marsala. It will not be for long, at all. A holiday it will be for them, just.' Rob changed his tone. 'Och, you rode with me on many of my ploys in the old days, Mary – and liked it well. We had good times together. You have been too long penned in a house. We used to work finely in harness. . . .'

'Those days are gone.' She shook her lovely head. 'Dead.'

'Perhaps not, *a graidh*. But sleeping, it may be.'

'Dead,' she repeated, flatly. 'You killed them.'

'I . . . ?' He raised wide shoulders. 'Have it as you will. But you ride with me tomorrow!'

'No! I will not! Are you crazy-mad? You cannot do this.'

'Some things I cannot do, woman, I grant you. But this I can! And will! As Royal's my Race – you ride tomorrow. Be you ready, early.' And turning about, the man stamped out of that house.

So, with the mists still low on Beinn Dorain next morning, a stiff-faced and stiffly-held woman was hoisted up in front of Rob Roy on his garron – for when he said that she was to ride with him, he meant just that, and did not allow her even a horse for herself. Her parting from the wondering children and startled Marsala had been strained, but there had been no scene – for Mary MacGregor was not a woman who indulged in scenes. They rode off, the impassive MacAlastair a discreet distance in the rear, with only Rob's hand waving farewell and his cheerful voice upraised.

There is little scope for distance-keeping and any effective display of sustained hostility and disapproval between two people on the back of a single trotting jolting pony. Rob found it expedient to hold his passenger fairly tightly within his arms throughout, a pressure which the passenger was in no position to resist. The jouncing motion of the horse flung body against body so consistently that any maintenance of attempts to avoid such would have been as absurd as it was fruitless. Markedly uneven ground and frequent steep climbing, both up and down, forced the woman to clutch the man's arm constantly for elementary balance's sake, and a sportive breeze continually blew her long dark hair in the rider's face with an undeniable sense of intimacy. Nevertheless, throughout a long day's riding, Mary MacGregor managed to preserve a detachment and cold aloofness that was little short of miraculous, giving the impression that she found her companion to be no more than some impersonal if deplorable force of nature that must be put up with. She did not actually refuse to answer all remarks addressed to her, but such responses as she made were so brief and non-commital as to serve only to emphasise her dissent and protest. Rob fairly soon gave up attempts at conversation.

It was not until they were plodding over the long braes that rise out of Glen Falloch and give access to the head of Balquhidder, after a full day's riding, that Mary, no doubt having struggled against it for hours, fell asleep. Thereafter she lay comfortably and naturally relaxed within the man's arms, her head nestled against his broad chest. Rob smiled then and frequently in the ensuing couple of hours that brought them down into Glen Gyle, holding her still closer. And more than once he surreptitiously brushed his lips over the heavy raven tresses so close to his chin, and grieved at the white strands so recently invading the black. Those were the happiest two hours that he had spent in half a year.

He did not take his wife to the cave on Cruach Tuirc, of course, but to the large and comfortable House of Glengyle – though still he held to his self-imposed ordinance of not entering under Gregor's, or any other clansman's, roof. Delivering Mary over to the welcoming arms of the younger Mary, and sternly refusing to be drawn into any explanations save that he would call for her again next morning, he drew Gregor aside and went walking with him through the May dusk, eating as they went.

The two men had much to tell each other, but Rob's questions prevailed, and were particular rather than general. Much anent Montrose's Quarter-day arrangements for this area he queried, and was answered just as he anticipated. Killearn was less likely than ever to venture north of the Highland Line, or anywhere near to it, after what had happened at Candlemas. But arrangements had been made for the grain collections to be held at different centres than was usual, and a day earlier than was normal – no doubt in an effort to circumvent any gestures by Rob Roy.

The Whitsun quarter was distinguished from the other three by the emphasis laid on the payment of rent by grain and meal, rather than either cash or cattle. This was understandable – at least from the landlords' point of view. The long winter was over, but the new season's pasture, up in these northern latitudes, was not yet available; consequently feed for the cattle, the basis of the Highland economy, was always in desperately short supply by May. Oats were all but worth their weight in gold. Shrewd landlords, therefore, made a point of insisting that at least some proportion of this quarter's rents should be paid in grain and fodder, albeit at a time when their tenants could least afford it – in the interest of their own hungry herds. Girnels, or collecting stores, were appointed in each area – and well guarded.

Rob learned more than all this from Gregor. He heard that the military were back – Major Selby and a full Company, at Inverarklet on Loch Lomond, plus a large number of masons and builders. They were working hard at the new fort on Tom na Bairlinn again. The soldiers were not otherwise proving themselves to be very objectionable to the clan, however, being there apparently, at this stage, purely to guard the builders and their work. The MacGregors, in accordance with Rob's unpopular instructions, were leaving them severely alone. For the rest, it had been a bad winter for the beasts, and Rob's great swollen herds were in bad shape, stock dying off every day for lack of fodder.

None of this was unexpected. Rob nodded grimly, and asked only for the brief loan of half a dozen Glengyle gillies, for service unspecified and anonymous.

* * *

Sometime during the next day, the majority of the Montrose tenants in the Aberfoyle, Gartmore and Menteith areas – all the more substantial ones, at any rate – were visited by a messenger bearing a short but authoritative letter, impressively stamped and sealed with the Montrose seal. This informed them that his Grace, having had warning of the rascal Robert MacGregor's baleful intentions, had decided to put the grain collection forward for still another day, and had changed the venue once again, in order to checkmate any knavish MacGregor tricks. The tenant was ordered to appear, therefore, with his oats conveniently bagged, on the thirteenth day of the month – that was, the day following – between the hours of noon and three o'clock, at the mill at Port of Menteith, on pain of his Grace's stern displeasure. God Save Queen Anne. If any of the said tenants noted that the messengers were not dressed in the usual Montrose livery but in assorted and ill-fitting Lowland garb and yet managed to sound extremely like Highlandmen – who were they, individually, to question the ways of their betters? And there was no arguing with that magnificent heraldic seal. Rob had retained possession of this trinket as a memento of a former business partnership, in which he frequently had had occasion to act on behalf of James Graham in the buying and selling of livestock. None of the tenants were likely to notice that the coronet depicted thereon was still that of an earl and not of a duke.

The following early morning, therefore, refusing any further assistance from Gregor – who of course had some of his own rent-collecting to attend to – Rob took Mary once more up before him on his garron, and again with only MacAlastair and Donald as lieutenants, rode off eastwards. Mary remained true to her former attitude – no relenting, no co-operation, but no scenes.

By a carefully thought-out route, avoiding the dwellings of men, even of MacGregors, travelling by the south side of Loch Katrine, the flanks of Beinn Venue, and the long ridge of high ground that stretches eastwards from there, they came down eventually to the wide green levels of the Forth Valley, to Port of Menteith on the north shore of its great lake, a good two hours before noon. Rob had selected this place with care. It was ideally situated for his purpose, the mill standing at the foot of a leafy lane beside a confluence of stream and loch, with only this one access road. Moreover, the miller was a Graham and a surly oaf, and so fair game.

They approached the mill quite openly, and while Rob installed Mary in such comfort as the main barn could offer, MacAlastair and Donald went in and locked up the miller and his wife and daughter in one of their own upper rooms, with fierce looks and blood-curdling threats. Thereafter they brought out a kitchen-table and chairs and set them up just inside the door of the barn. Then, after reconnoitring the neighbouring woodlands thoroughly, the two henchmen went to take up their positions to regulate the flow of traffic, Donald at the head of the lane, MacAlastair at the mill itself.

Rob sat Mary beside him at the table, facing the doorway, and with pens and ink and paper spread before him, filled in the time with the writing of receipts. He suggested, mildly, after a while that Mary might care to do likewise? She answered with a cold negative, whereupon he pointed out reasonably that what was being attempted was solely to the detriment of her hated enemies the Grahams and not for his own private benefit – so that she need feel no qualms about aiding him if that was her trouble. This specious argument received the response it deserved – but, after perhaps another twenty minutes of waiting, the woman suddenly reached out and took up a pen, and inking it, commenced to copy out one of Rob's blank receipt forms. The man at her side said nothing, but within him his heart lifted a little.

The two pens scratched thereafter busily, in unison.

The first tenant arrived well before noon, a substantial farmer, one Drummond in Ballabog, leading three pack-ponies laden with sacks of oats. MacAlastair directed him into the barn, where Rob greeted him pleasantly.

'Aha, Ballabog – you are more than punctual.' he cried. 'I trust that I see you well, whatever? An ill winter it has been. The Lady Inversnaid, maybe, you do not know?'

That the farmer was astonished goes without saying; flabbergasted might better describe his state. Mouthing like a stranded fish, he stared. No words came.

'A welcome on behalf of his Grace of Montrose,' Rob went on, genially. 'He cannot have the satisfaction of greeting all his tenants in person – so I am acting for him in the matter. But I have all the due receipts ready and in order, see you. Let me see, now – how much is your payment, at all?'

'Eh . . . ah . . . I . . . och, mercy on us,' the other stammered. 'Goad save us a'.'

'Tut, man – that will not be necessary, on this occasion! How much?'

'Och, T't'twal'bolls o' oats, an' forty pun Scots, jist. But . . .'

'But too much, I agree, Ballabog. Too much, after a bad winter. Don't you agree, my dear?' That to his wife.

Mary looked away biting her lip. But she nodded.

'Aye, then. Too much. What would you say, Ballabog, was a fair quarter's rent, in the circumstances?'

'Eh . . . ? Och, Goad kens, sir – I dinna!' the farmer faltered.

'Come, man – you must have some idea. If you have not, who has? It has been a hard time for the beasts, and prices are bad. What do you say – *eight* bags and *twenty* pounds?'

'Guidsakes!'

'That would satisfy you, eh? Very well, so. Eight bags and twenty pounds Scots, it is. His Grace perhaps lacks understanding in these matters – dukes often do. So I will make out your receipt for the full amount – the twelve bags and the forty pounds, you see – which will satisfy both his Grace and you – but I will take from you only the eight bags and twenty pounds, which will satisfy me whatever! Och, I am a reasonable man, as anyone will tell you!' Rob scratched busily with his pen.

'But, man – you canna dae that!' the perplexed farmer exclaimed. 'It's . . . it's no' lawfu'.'

'What is unlawful about it my friend? I am accepting payment on behalf of his Grace. Not for the first time. You will have heard that we were in partnership together – a partnership that has never been legally dissolved, see you? I am giving you a receipt, in his name, for the full amount of the rent. If I choose to take only part of it, the responsibility is mine. Is it not?'

'Well. . . .'

'Good, then. There is the one thing, just. I will be needing your garrons to be carrying the grain, see you. I see that you have three fine beasts out there. I will take two of them and leave you the one to be carrying back your four bags of oats – that will be a bit help for your own cattle-feed, I've no doubt? You will have my personal receipt for them, and the word of Rob Roy MacGregor that you will receive them back in good order within two days. You understand?'

'Och, aye – I mean, no! I'm hearing you – but . . .'

'*Dia* – you are no doubting my word are you, Ballabog!'

'No, no! Lordie – no! Save us a' – never think it! It's jist . . .'

'You *want* to be spared half your silver, and your four bags of oats, I take it?'

'Ooh, aye – surely. Surely. . . .'

'Very well, then. Here are your two receipts. Your garrons will be delivered back to Ballabog in due course. Mac-Alastair there, will show you to your ale and bannocks – refreshment that you may accept as a token of his Grace's goodwill! And a very good day to you, Ballabog. The Lady Inversnaid sends her greetings to your gudewife, likewise – do you not, my dear? Exactly. MacAlastair – show Ballabog his refreshment. Ah – you have another tenant waiting then? I fear that I do not just mind the name, for the moment . . . ? Och yes, then – Erskine, Gartfarren. Of course. Come away in, Gartfarren. You are welcome. My wife, the Lady Inversnaid . . .'

That was the pattern of the business. There were varying details with each tenant, but the basic strategy was the same. More effort and eloquence had to be expended on some than on others. Some were more difficult, others actually co-operated. None, when it came to the crux, refused to pay. Which was scarcely to be wondered at. Rob Roy was not a man to argue with, especially for small farmers – and he could be expected to have hordes of his fierce clansmen in hiding just around the corner, to enforce his wishes; by dealing with the tenants one by one, and then seeing that MacAlastair and Donald got them fairly quickly out of the way, he faced each with an individual choice and prevented any mutual encouragement to resist, any united front. Also, of course, none of them could be quite sure just how much of it all was trickery and how much fair dealing. Few of the payers had any love for their absentee ducal landlord, and most of their sympathies would lie with Rob rather than with Montrose – so long as it did not cost them dear. And Rob had baited his trap cunningly, remitting them a substantial part of their payments yet giving them a receipt for it all; he knew the minds of peasant-farmers. No doubt there was, too, that the presence of Mary Mac-Gregor sitting there, helped greatly to engender a suitably respectable atmosphere from the start, and to prevent acrimonious dispute; in a matter of this sort, first impressions were important.

Before mid-afternoon, then, an impressive concourse of garrons and pannier-ponies, with their burdens of grain and fodder, were tethered in rows behind the mill – necessitating the hiring of sundry small boys who had materialised as small boys will, to watch and ward them – and a sizeable heap of silver merks had accumulated in the barn. Rob was beginning to get just a little bit concerned, as time went on – for of course it could be taken as granted that the mulcted tenants would talk once they were away from the mill area, and the possibility of such excited talk rushing round the district and reaching ears hostile to the MacGregors could not be ruled out. Reactions might follow – though it was improbable that any large force could be summoned against them locally at short notice, or that the military escort for the factor's party would arrive in the district until the morrow.

At length, even with three or four tenants still to come, Rob called a halt. There was no point in risking all for the sake of a small fraction – for there remained much to be done yet. A band of sturdy Gregorach gillies would have solved his problems – but that was not to be. He pinned a writing on the barn-door instructing the late coming tenants to deliver their rents to such of the poor and needy as they might select, and left signed and sealed receipts for the full amount thereof skewered near by on a dirk; whether or not they actually followed these instructions was not the vital issue – which was to deny the rents to Montrose if possible. Then, piling all the coin into a bag, and recalling Mac-Alastair and Donald, he made ready to move.

There proved to be no fewer than sixty-three ponies assembled behind the barn, bearing on an average three hundredweights of oats apiece – a total of nearly ten tons of grain. They would make a long pack-train for three riders to control, most obviously. Rob turned to his wife.

'Mary, *a graidh*,' he said. 'You will notice that we are something lacking in hands. One extra rider, even, could be a help whatever. Will you do it?'

'Yes,' she said simply, quietly.

The man's blue eyes lit up, but he forbore to comment, containing himself with finding a suitable beast for her to ride, and sharing out its load elsewhere. He sent Mac-Alastair to release the miller's family.

Pairing up the horses, and linking each couple with grass rope from the mill, they set out in a long procession. Donald led, on this occasion, and Rob brought up the rear – for he reckoned that it was from there that any trouble might be looked for – with MacAlastair and Mary in the centre. They made an irritatingly deliberate cavalcade, necessarily reduced to the pace of the slowest laden garron.

They headed back by approximately the same route that

they had come – but of course there was no possibility of doing so secretly; sixty-odd horses in a string take a deal of hiding on bare hillsides. Rob imagined that once they were beyond the Pass of Aberfoyle, and so into MacGregor territory, no persons short of the military would dare to interfere with them. But they had five or six exposed miles to cover before that.

They were crossing the long rolling heather flanks of Creag Dubh, the southern buttress of the shapeless Menteith Hills, and still a couple of miles short of Aberfoyle, when MacAlastair, mounting a knoll ahead and looking backwards, gestured urgently, pointing. From the rear of the long column, Rob turned to stare. Following them, and just emerging into sight from out of the birch-clad braes below, was a scattered but extensive concourse of people. Concourse was almost the only name that could be put to it, so far, since it seemed to have no shape nor form nor any coherence; but it was composed of a lot of men, quite clearly, a lot of horses, and the afternoon sun glinted on a notable amount of steel of one sort or another.

Rob hurried forward to the knoll at a canter, where Mary had already joined MacAlastair; Donald was away at the front with the leading pair of garrons.

'Many men,' the gillie greeted him grimly. 'You will not talk *these* round one at a time, I'm thinking!'

'No – more there are than I bargained for!' his master admitted, shading his eyes with his hand. 'There seem to be some good horses in the front – Graham lairdies, no doubt. They must have gathered together more of their folk than I thought possible at short notice.' He frowned, eyes busy. 'There could be a hundred in it – though, och, a lot will be come out to stare rather than to fight, at all.'

'With the half of them starers even, we still have scarcely the advantage!' the other observed dryly. 'Three of us – and all these beasts to be managing...'

'Four!' Rob corrected sharply. 'Do not be forgetting

Mary.' And he glanced sidelong at his wife. 'A quarter of our strength – and her making the better men of us!'

'We fight them then?'

'If we must.'

'What can you do ... against so many?' Mary asked, a little breathlessly. 'Save flee?'

'We cannot flee with all these laden garrons – and I will not flee without them,' Rob declared.

'What, then ... ?'

'See you – they are not just rushing upon their fate, these heroes,' her husband pointed out. 'Circumspect they are, for so many.' That seemed to be true. The concourse, now fully revealed in its ragged and far-flung extent, appeared to be anything but impetuous in its advance, following them with a caution that seemed excessive for so large a company in pursuit of three men and a woman. Rob gestured. 'That could be meaning one of two things, maybe. Either that they do not wish to be fighting us at all, but only to be scaring us away from the garrons and the grain – in which case they do not know Rob Roy at all! Or else they think, maybe, that they know Rob Roy too well, and do not believe that he is ever attended by less than a regiment of the fierce Gregorach! It could be that they think that there must be many more of us – but in hiding.'

MacAlastair nodded thoughtfully.

'If that is so, since we must disappoint them in the first notion, it would be a great pity to do so in the second, would it not?'

Mary shook her head in mystification, but the gillie began to look about him keenly.

Rob did the same, making one of his swift surveys of the lie of the land. He pointed here and there and there again, swinging his arm round. At each gesture MacAlastair nodded briefly.

'You down below, by the burn-channel there. In those hollows,' Rob went on. 'Donald up above – making noise enough for many. Och, it is worth the trying.'

'Aye, then. And the garrons . . . ?'

'I will lead them,' Mary interposed. 'I think that I see what you would be at. I will look after the garrons – keep them moving.'

'Nothing could be more convenient,' Rob agreed, smiling. 'Off you get then, forward – the pair of you. Myself, I will just be taking a bit of a rest, see you!'

*   *   *

For a while it almost looked as though Rob Roy meant what he said about taking a rest. While the other two hurried forward, and Mary relieved Donald at the head of the cavalcade, Rob dawdled on at the rear. In fact, he fell further and further behind. Occasionally he glanced behind him at the pursuit – which, however restrained their ardour for the attack, could not help overtaking this dilatory quarry.

If Rob's outstanding person and identity must by then have been entirely clear to the enemy, the same, to some extent, could be said of the chase. At five hundred yards or so they were still too far away readily to pick out individuals from the mass – though the great fat man on the enormous horse well to the front could be none other than Graham of Rednock, cousin to Gorthie. What was evident was the motley nature of the force, comprising young and old, aged ploughmen and stripling herd-boys, bonnet-lairds and men who might be grooms or house-servants. All were mounted on as extraordinary a selection of horseflesh as ever assembled in one company, and appeared to be equipped with an armoury of which scythes and hayforks were the chief components. The MacGregor snorted strongly at the notion of such a crew daring to sally out against Rob Roy – though he reminded himself that there almost certainly would be many good muskets and pistols, and numerous stout hearts, amongst them quite sufficient to deal effectively with even three MacGregors and a woman.

The sudden yittering call of a curlew, high, clear and prolonged, from well above him on the hillside, answered almost immediately by a similar call from below, produced an extraordinary effect on Rob. His lounging was replaced by action. Raising two fingers to his mouth, he produced a series of shrill and penetrating whistles that shattered the balmy atmosphere of the afternoon. Again and again he whistled, and there was no doubt that all within a good mile's radius must hear him. Then, striking a posture on his garron, he began to point. And to shout.

His shouts were not wild or disconnected. Indeed, they were noticeably clear and were very distinctly amplified by his gestures. Obvious for all to see, he was directing various unseen persons to move from where they were hidden to somewhere else – and, by the sweeping and dramatic motions of his arms, to move fast in large numbers. Jabbing, pointing and signalling, he continued to bellow his commands. Any fool could see, even from a distance, that they meant close in and attack the pursuit from above and below.

Much yelling from hidden points up and down hill thereupon ensued. It seemed quite extraordinary that it could all be made by two men, one of them so preternaturally silent as MacAlastair. Savagely threatening those cries were, with 'Gregalach! Gregalach!' in various keys and intonations prominent amongst them. That terrible war-cry was worth a score of broadswords in itself.

Behind them, on the lower ground, the hunt came to an abrupt and most obvious halt. Despite its lack of form and cohesion, this step at least had every appearance of unanimity. A council-of-war, many councils-of-war, developed spontaneously.

Rob moved up on to an eminence from which he could, as it were, direct the battle. He was growing a little hoarse from all his shouting. His two henchmen must be still more so – and breathless too, for clearly they were darting about, out of sight, seeking to give the impression that their cries came from many men scattered over quite an area of the broken hillside.

A shot rang out. Startled, Rob glanced to his right – for the report had come, not from the ranks of Menteith nor yet from either of his busy lieutenants above or below, but from the westwards, in front of the now distant column of ponies. Anxiety flickered across the man's mind. Could it be an ambush of some sort – with Mary alone up there? Had he sent her into danger . . . ?

Another report echoed over the braes. It sounded like a pistol rather than a musket. Not the volleys of fire that might be expected in an ambush. More like a signal. . . . No cries or shouting sounded from there – if only his two collaborators would cease their wretched braying for a moment, to let him listen properly! It could not be Mary herself? She had no pistol. But she might just have borrowed one from Donald – Donald who was always armed to the teeth like any desperado? If it was herself . . . ?

Whatever it was, the shots had by no means put new heart into the halted and thoughtful pursuit. Increased agitation became plainly discernible. The noise of gunfire always sounds daunting to unprofessional warriors – more so than mere shoutings and slogans. The councils-of-war appeared to be breaking up.

Then a new noise smote Rob's anxious ears – also coming from the west – the drum-beat of hooves, many hooves, that rose swiftly to a rumble, to a thunder. There could be no question as to what that meant. Horses, garrons, in panic flight.

Biting his lip, Rob started forward. He could see, now, the confusion in front. Some part of the long string of ponies was still plodding ahead, but the leading beasts of the cavalcade had turned and were coming plunging back in scrabbling swaying alarm. Their train was no longer a column but a frantic stampede of various pairs and groups linked together and straining this way and that, their burdens jouncing about crazily. And above this tide of frightened horseflesh, like a raft riding a torrent, Mary MacGregor came, her arms waving wildly.

Cursing, Rob urged his mount onwards. And then, something about his wife's seat on her garron's back, the fact that she seemed to be shouting, gave him pause. He realised that she was actually whacking laden ponies on either side of her as she passed them. The man perceived that she was far from flotsam whirled helplessly on the spate of events, but indeed was directing the flood, probably was the creator of it. His held breath escaped from him in an exclamation, part oath, part chuckle, wholly appreciative. That was his Mary, to be sure.

If the effect of the woman's activities on her husband had been dramatic, the effect on the opposition was still more so. Possibly from their distance off they would not perceive that it was a woman, or just one person, at all; probably all that they saw, in the main, was a mass of horseflesh galloping over the hill towards them. Whether any large proportion of them realised that these were the same packhorses that had plodded patiently away from them, was not to be known. What certainly counted with most was that these horses were coming back, towards them – and in a hurry. That, added to the cumulative effect of the shouts and the shots, the gesticulations and the war-cries, completed the weight of evidence necessary to convince the vast majority there that the entire expedition was ill-advised, frought with danger, and likely to be unprofitable. Incoherent and unconcerted to the last, the company began to break up piecemeal, first in ones and twos, then in groups and parties. Soon all were streaming away whence they had come – only a lot faster – save for the little group of lairds at the front, whose dignity at least demanded that they give the others a start. No excessively lengthy start seemed to be called for, however, and with the dreaded slogan of 'Gregalach! Gregalach!' coming down to them with redoubled vigour and clarity, these too turned for home. There are occasions undoubtedly when even the instincts of bumpkins and ploughboys are to be trusted.

As Rob rode forward to halt Mary's headlong career – and that of such of the runaway garrons as he could influence – he was laughing hugely. But Mary did not laugh as she came up. Breathless she was, and flushed, her eyes brighter than the man had seen them for many a day; but she did not laugh back at him. She did not even smile.

'They are gone, I see,' she said. And if she had difficulty in controlling the enunciation of her words, she appeared to have none in keeping their tone cool and impersonal. 'For good?'

'Aye, they are gone, lass – thanks to yourself at the latter end. And I'll wager they won't turn again. *A graidh*, you were magnificent! You sent them running like a flock of sheep. Och, that was the woman I married, whatever!'

'It was not,' she answered, shortly. 'That woman is dead. I did little – only what it was obvious should be done. And what I did, I did that it might hurt the Grahams. That only.'

The man, his laughter gone, shook his red head. 'I don't understand you, Mary,' he said unhappily.

'No – you do not,' she agreed. 'Do you not think that it is time that you went and gathered together these foolish scattered beasts?'

Tugging at his beard Rob went, muttering.

With the help of MacAlastair and Donald they managed to get the dispersed and demoralised ponies back into some sort of order and on their way once more. A little of the grain was spilt, but it was only a small fraction of the whole. Donald was uproariously gleeful, but MacAlastair permitted himself no hint of elation – it was to be doubted indeed whether that man knew what elation was. So that, despite their bloodless victory and the notable haul of excellent cattle-feed acquired, it was a less jubilant party than might have been anticipated that found it's way back, without further interference, into the MacGregor mountains – for Rob had become markedly silent and preoccupied, and Mary had reverted to her former reserve.

In the anonymity of that night, many very willing hands took and distributed the treasured feeding-stuff to secret stores over a wide area, from which conveniently and judiciously it could be crushed and bruised and dolled out to the hungry MacGregor cattle. All acknowledged it as a Godsend. Since it could be anticipated that Montrose, in his wrath, would bring to bear every weapon at his wide disposal against his former partner, including Major Selby's redcoats at Inverarklet, Rob slipped away northwards again at first light next morning, duty done and his given word implemented. The last thing that he wanted was, by lingering in the neighbourhood, to bring down trouble on his clan's people.

On the journey back to Auch, Mary rode her own garron – and tended to ride it as far out of talking distance of her husband as she might. Yesterday's excitements might never have been. Rob did not enjoy defeat on any front, and it is to be feared that on this occasion he did not entirely succeed in hiding the fact.

It was perhaps as well that his political mission in Badenoch and Speyside was still far from completed.

CHAPTER THIRTEEN

ROB ROY put in another couple of months of fruitful activity on behalf of King James, amongst the clans of Badenoch, Inverness and Lochaber, in the doing of which, to some extent, he was able to put his personal problems behind him. Then, one thundery evening in mid-July, Gregor of Glengyle ferreted him out in a glen deep in the Chisholm country of Strathglass; his nephew had been on his trail for days, tracing him across the breadth of Highland Scotland. He came chock-full of news, local and national, that could not but affect his uncle's activities.

First of all, Queen Anne was very ill and sinking fast. A new Government had evolved in London, so-called Tory but in fact neither one thing nor another, a Government of time-servers and fence-sitters, more or less waiting to see which side in the dynastic struggle was likely to be the most advantageous to support. This was less than had been hoped, but at least it meant that no very vigorous anti-Jacobite measures were likely meantime; indeed, that the more public support for King James was evidenced, the more impressed and helpful this apology for a Government was likely to be. Mar, that expert jockey, had managed to change horses skilfully and timeously, and was still Secretary of State for Scotland; Montrose also retained the Privy Seal – but he was less happily placed, his background being too notoriously anti-Jacobite. Moreover, General the Duke of Argyll, Red John of the Battles, had been brought back from Spain and appointed Commander-in-Chief in Scotland – and though he was a firm Whig, he was also a personal enemy of Montrose. The Campbells and the Grahams were ever at loggerheads.

Already this situation, Gregor revealed, had had its repercussions, in Scotland in general, and in the MacGregor country in particular. No longer were the military forces, now under Argyll's command, at the beck and call of the Lord Privy Seal and available to advance his private enterprises. The garrison at Inverarklet, guarding the fort-builders, had been cut down by two-thirds and Major Selby transferred elsewhere. Work on the fort itself still went on, and was indeed nearing completion, but the military escort's attitude towards the MacGregors had changed noticeably. No longer was there oppression or any parade of authority. In consequence, the Gregorach were reverting contentedly to their normal activities, and Rob's orders about not being aggressive or provocative had become out of date and point-less. Again, rumours of an imminent Jacobite rising were filling the country, and since the MacGregors knew that they would be in the thick of anything of the sort, a martial and defiant spirit was becoming predominant. Without hinting that his own chieftainly authority was insufficient to control his people, Gregor indicated that it was perhaps time that Rob Roy came home.

Moreover there was another aspect of the impingement of the murky politics of the day upon the Gregorach. Since Archibald MacGregor of Kilmanan's presumed death in Ireland, in 1708, there had been no High Chief of Clan Alpine, the chiefly line of Glenstrae dying with him. Rob was Captain of the clan, yes – but that was a different thing. Now, this curious Government in London was seeking to buy the allegiance of the Highlands by offering pensions to the clan chiefs, at the rate of over four thousand pounds Scots per annum – £360 sterling. Alastair MacGregor of Balhaldies, who was one of the claimants to be senior cadet of Clan Alpine, thought it a pity that such splendid largesse should pass good men by when it could be had, as it were, for the picking up. Admittedly its acceptance was meant to insure that the recipient did not join in any rising against the Government – but that was not a matter that need weigh heavily with sensible men. Accordingly Balhaldies proposed that he should be elected High Chief of Clan Alpine, in the room or the late Kilmanan, and he in turn would agree to apportion out the pension amongst the other senior cadets who might otherwise be his rivals. For this laudable purpose there must be a council, a meeting of the chief men of the clan – and Rob of course must be there. In fact, it was to be left to Rob to convene and preside at the meeting, as Captain.

Rob smiled grimly at this information – for he did not trust Alastair of Balhaldies much further than he could see him. But it was true that the clan needed its High Chief, for various reasons – more especially with its Captain outlawed. And Balhaldies was a cunning fellow, highly intelligent, educated, and married to an influential wife, a daughter of Lochiel, no less. And her brother, Alan Cameron, was powerful in court circles – which in such times might have its advantages. They might do a lot worse for their figure-head – so long as Rob himself remained Captain and in effective control of the clan. He might come south, as Gregor suggested, and amongst other things convene this meeting.

Rob had every intention of returning south fairly soon anyhow, of course – for the pursuance of his quarter-day vendetta with the Grahams. It would soon be Lammas term, the first day of August, three months on from Whit-sun, and it would be a pity to disappoint anyone. He had naturally been turning over in his mind sundry possibilities in this connection – though undoubtedly Montrose and his minions on this occasion would be taking every precaution. It all seemed to mean that he must travel south just a little earlier than he had intended. . . .

So, since Rob's commitments and negotiations with the

northern chiefs did not permit of any hasty and unceremonious breakings-off, Gregor was dispatched forthwith to the south again, with various instructions, his uncle promising to follow in a few days' time. It occurred to Rob that Mary's peculiar state of mind, which was probably the result of too much solitary meditation, might well benefit from some enforced company of her own kind. He told Gregor, therefore, to summon, not a clan council, but a meeting of the principal MacGregor cadets, chieftains of septs such as Glengyle's own Clan Dougal Ciar, for Auch itself, to consider the matter of Balhaldies. And since the Lammas Quarter-day fell on the first of August, and Rob was liable to be busy about then, let the meeting be called for, say, five days previously; that is, for the twenty-seventh day of July. That would give Gregor twelve days in which to make the arrangements – time enough, surely. As an afterthought, Rob mentioned that he had better warn his aunt in passing, that she would be having visitors.

* * *

Rob Roy as it happened, delayed after a riotous night with young MacIan of Glencoe, was the last of the select band of Gregorach notables to arrive at the little house of Auch under Beinn Dorain's frowning brow – with something of a frowning brow himself, as a consequence of a splitting head; young MacIan, with bloody memories to drown, was a hard man to outdrink.

The company awaiting him was colourful and resounding. It included Gregor MacGregor of Roro – who probably had a better title to the High Chiefship than Balhaldies, but who lacked the necessary ambition – and his son; Duncan of Dunan, and his son; Donald of Coiletter; Malcolm of Marchfield; Gregòr of Bracklie and his sons – another possible contender; Gregor in Ardmacmoine; and of course young Gregor of Glengyle himself. Curiously enough Alastair of Balhaldies was not present – though he sent numerous apologies, assurances and affirmations; Rob Roy was neither astonished nor seriously disappointed at this. Balhaldies was a shrewd man if hot-tempered, and probably reckoned that in that proud and touchy company his case would go better lacking his presence.

Mary seemed to be coping with the invasion with a cool competence that failed nothing in the demands of hospitality, yet conceded nothing in warmth and approval. No man there failed to be aware of the fact. Her long-absent husband she greeted as one more guest to whom, unfortunately, courtesies must be extended. Rob should not have been disappointed in this either, by now – but he was.

He hid it, of course – better perhaps than he managed to hide the effects of MacIan's brand of hospitality. He turned to greet the galaxy of red MacGregor tartans and eagles' feathers, gallantly.

'Gentlemen, you do my heart and spirit a power of good – as Royal's our Race you do!' he cried. 'A nobler array of our Highland spirit and valour never assembled together, I declare. Welcome to this poor hovel – all that his Grace of Montrose has left to a humble but honest cattle-dealer.'

There was considerable outcry at this sally, and the visitors obviously began to feel more at ease. Since the little house patently was quite incapable of accommodating the twelve of them, not to mention their attendants – for each had felt it necessary to support his style and dignity by bringing at least two running gillies – Rob proposed that they hold their deliberations on the greensward outside, the weather being fine. This was another relief, for the somewhat daunting presence of their lovely but difficult hostess was less potent out of doors, undoubtedly. Moreover, Rob had taken the precaution of bringing along with him a pony's load of liquid refreshment, the distilled perfection of various glens on his route – including that of Glen Coe – and this quickly served to thaw out any residual stiffness. Eloquence very soon began to mark the day, and continued to wax and flourish increasingly, like an exotic bloom in the smile of the sun – for the Gregorach were ever as notable in talk as in action. Only Roro, who inclined to the pompous, perhaps failed to measure up to the full flowering of MacGregor oratory. Rob, who himself barely sipped at the regalement, made a point of plying Roro's horn lavishly until such time as pomposity faded into incoherence.

When he judged the atmosphere to be approximately right and suitable, Rob turned to business. 'You all will be aware that Balhaldies has gained the notion that he might adorn the office of High Chief of Clan Alpine,' he mentioned. 'Likewise that the government is after looking for chiefs to give fine pensions to, out of the depths of its wisdom. Now, I am not the man to be saying that I agree entirely with Balhaldies – nor even to be sure in my mind that the pensions will be paid for very long. But it seems to me that, as practical men, we might do well to support Balhaldies in this matter. I do not necessarily believe that he will make any heaven born chief, see you – any more than I recognise his claim as being established. Roro here, or Bracklie, or young Glengyle, all have as good a claim, no doubt, as chieftains of septs as senior as Balhaldies. But . . .'

'My God, yes!'

'Damnation – that is the truth!'

'Yes. But there is more to it than just that, my friends,' Rob went on. 'Such a chief would be of great value to the clan – more than many hundreds of pounds of pensions. A chief who can speak for the clan in high places – as I cannot do, being outlawed, and a humble man moreover. A chief who moves in circles close to Edinburgh and London, who hears of moves and intrigues long before I can do so. How many can do that?'

There was no answer.

'And another way of it. This rising that is projected – if it is a success, that will be fine. Och, just fine. The clan will come well out of it. But it was to be failing, now – and risings *can* be failing, mind you – that would be a pity. The Gregorach would be in trouble, then. It would pay the clan, in such case, to be having a High Chief that the Government could be making an example of . . . if you understand me? Instead of the clan itself. Och, they like a man, those ones, that they can punish, instead of a whole clan. Easier it is. Don't I know it! One man then might save many.'

'*Dia* – you do not mean a, a sort of a *sacrifice*!' his nephew exclaimed, shocked once more. 'Not that, Rob?'

'To be a sacrifice can be no light honour, Greg. Does your Bible not tell you so?' the older man answered.

'But deliberately to use a man so . . . ?'

'Tush, lad – if a man would bear the honour and title of High Chief of Clan Alpine, then surely he must be prepared to give all for the clan. The style has no meaning, otherwise. Just as I, being Captain, must take the forefront of the battle, and risk death first, so much the High Chief, in his sphere, be bearing a similar risk. Glory never lacks its dangers. I but remind all here of the fact.'

Gregor was silent, though others proclaimed hearty agreement.

'The clan is what counts whatever – in this as in all else,' Rob declared vigorously. 'I charge you not to forget it.'

'Rob has the right of it,' Bracklie substantiated loudly. 'It is the clan first, for sure. Up, the Gregorach!'

'Aye.'

'Then, I take it you will not challenge Balhaldies appointment, Bracklie?' Rob asked, mild of a sudden.

'Me? Och, no – not me, Rob.'

'Nor you, Roro?'

Roro was in no position to do more than blink owlishly, but his son shook an urgent head for him.

'And what say you, Dunan?' That was merely a gesture,

though a calculated one, for Dunan was far out of line for the chiefship.

'I say let Balhaldies have it, Rob. So long as you are Captain, it matters not.'

Coiletter and Marchfield, both far-out cousins of Rob's own, and therefore junior to Gregor of Glengyle, looked at their young chieftain – as did his uncle. That man of honour shook his blond head.

'I do not seek the High Chiefship on this occasion,' he said slowly. 'But not because I would see Balhaldies made scapegoat for the clan. If our enterprise for the King should fail – which God forbid – then we all must pay the price equally.'

'Bravo! Spoken like a hero!' Rob declared, but dryly. And swiftly, 'Then we are all agreed. The thing is unanimous. Balhaldies it is. We will draw up a paper to the effect that Alastair of Balhaldies is hereby elected and appointed rightful, lawful and undoubted Head, Chief and Chieftain of our clan of MacGregor, commonly called Clan Alpine, *et hoc genus omne* and we will all sign it, as is proper. Drink up, gentlemen – for this business is thirsty work. I will get me quill and ink. . . .'

In the house as Rob sought the writing materials, Gregor came to him.

'That was ill done, I think,' he said quietly.

'Do you, then? I am sorry for that. And how would you have done it, lad?'

'Honestly, I hope. Without ill-will to the man who will be our chief. Without appeal to, to the baser instincts of these others.'

'So! And you think that by such lofty means you would ever have prevailed upon these prideful men to abate one jot of their own pretensions? Think you that they could ever be got to agree to forgo their own claims and dignity, save by playing upon what you priggishly name their baser instincts? *Dia* – for all I taught you, you know not men yet!'

'I know that men can be easily corrupted, yes. You taught me that, too. But not that *we* should be the corrupters!'

'Save us, boy – enough of this! Mind your tongue. Can you not see it – we play for high stakes, for survival as a clan. A clan that is hated in high places, proscribed, all but landless – doomed unless her leaders are farseeing, cunning, single-minded . . .'

'Single-minded, say you? Or double-tongued?'

'Aye, single-minded. Where the clan is concerned – always.'

'For the clan, then you would forget honour?'

'Honour! Lord – always you prate of honour! What is honour? Answer you me that. No two men will answer that alike. Aye, for the clan, Greg, I will do all things – all things that my conscience permits.'

'Your conscience, now! *You* speak of conscience!'

'Aye, I do so,' his uncle said, sombrely. 'But *my* conscience – not yours, boy! A man's conscience, not a stripling's. Now – leave me to cherish it, if I may, for sweet mercy's sake!'

As he turned his head, in an imperious gesture towards the door, his eyes met those of Mary as she stood there behind them. It was Rob's that fell.

Muttering into his red beard, he stamped outside behind his nephew. He was scarcely at his best or sweetest, that day – MacIan of Glencoe's fault, perhaps.

* * *

His manner changed noticeably, after he had dashed off for signature an affirmation much briefer and less florid than was usually considered suitable. Rob set about collecting from the assembled company the numbers of men whom they might provide for the MacGregor contingent of the Jacobite army. In this case he adopted a technique, Gregor noted, markedly different from that he had used amongst the clan chiefs of the north and west, not merely refraining from using mutual jealousy and pride to work up the numbers promised, but actually damping down undue ardour. Numbers were not everything, he pointed out. A good well-disciplined, well-trained, compact force for special duties, was a much more valuable contribution to King James's cause than any mere swollen rabble. Let them be selective. A total of three hundred would perhaps meet the case – a handy, manageable number.

Keeping the numbers down to three hundred, as it happened proved to be quite a task – for Gregor himself had proposed to bring out fully two hundred. But Rob was adamant – and autocratic – and as Captain of the Clan claimed that decision lay with him. At length he lost patience with the business, declared that he would inform them all, in due course, exactly what numbers he would require of each, and announced that meantime he required to rest himself. He was tired. Food for their journey home his wife would provide. But if any of them would see some sport, he added, as an afterthought – let them meet with him in the Pass of Aberfoyle two days hence at sundown. He thought that on that occasion he could promise them better entertainment than he had done here.

Gregor, for one, wondered. He could not remember his uncle ever complaining of feeling tired before.

*   *   *

Rob Roy usually was as good as his word. Two evenings later, he did not fail such of his fellows as had accepted his invitation to entertainment. Most of them had come, intrigued – all, indeed, except old Roro from Glen Lyon.

The promised sport was not confined to the wooded defile of the Pass of Aberfoyle; it proved to be neither more nor less than the greatest raid that had ever taken place upon the much-harried fair land of Menteith, the ancient

172

Graham earldom that was now Montrose's. Rob had worked hard and fast at the organisation of the affair – reassured by the knowledge that it was changed days for the Lord Privy Seal, and that his own old friend and patron, Argyll the Commander-in-Chief, probably would not for his part frown too heavily on any high-spirited cantrips by the Mac-Gregors, so long as they were merely directed against his personal foe and rival Montrose and were innocently un-seditious in character. From what Rob had learned, his own people of Inversnaid, Craigroyston and Glen Arklet were in need of his firm directing hand, also. This night's enter-tainment, therefore, had a dual objective.

In consequence, for the first time since Rob's outlawry, large numbers of MacGregors were involved – though dis-creetly, of course, and not so that they would be evident or readily identifiable. They were not even evident in the Pass of Aberfoyle for the visitors to see, being scattered by then far and wide, in little groups, over a great area of that green level country that surrounded the vast waterlogged wilder-ness of the Flanders Moss and the Lake of Menteith. Some few men there were in the Pass – no more than a dozen – whose efforts would be engaged near at hand, and who therefore must await the cover of darkness.

Rob entertained his guests first at the little ale-house on the MacGregor side of the Pass, until the shades of night were well advanced. Then, mounted on garrons, he led them quietly – or as quietly as he could enforce – through the shadows, slipping to the south of the Clachan of Aber-foyle and heading eastwards into the low country of Gart-more and Shannochill – Graham territory. But they were not provocative, avoiding all habitations. Presently the ground beneath their garrons' hooves became wetter and wetter, and the great empty flats of Flanders Moss spread dark and mysterious before them. Rob ordered his party to ride exactly in file behind him, treading only where he trod. None were so foolish as to disobey, for the name and nature of this place were only too well known and respected.

Flanders Moss was a land unto itself – a land that consisted largely of water. Covering an area of some fifty square miles, where the stripling Forth, new won out of its confining womb of mountains, poured out extravagantly into a huge level plain so low-lying as to be in places only a foot or two above the level of the distant sea, it became a vast trap for the drainage of hill ranges to north, west and south. A wilderness of endlessly twisting, coiling rivers and streams and burnlets, of lochs and ponds and pools, of meres and bogs and slimy morasses, it remained useless, shunned of men, feared even, empty save for the wildfowl and the flitting roe-deer – unknown and unknowable. Save to Rob Roy MacGregor, that is – and therefore to MacAlastair his shadow, and to a lesser extent to Gregor. Rob all his life had revelled in the place's strange atmosphere and loneliness – and some knowledge of its secrets was part of the learning that, as Tutor of Glengyle, he had imparted to his pupil. For it held secrets worth knowing to bold men. There were routes, tortuous and intricate, through that quaking emerald treachery, islands of firm ground amongst the endless reed-beds, fords in the still network of waterways, even causeways sunken beneath the dark surface – for in times beyond ken it had served as a last place of refuge from the invader. Here even the Roman legions had come to a final halt, baffled at last.

On this occasion, of course, Rob had no intention of penetrating really deep into the benighted fastnesses. He was only concerned meantime with one comparatively small north-western corner of it, known as the Gartrenich Moss. Into this he now led his careful following, twisting this way and that, frequently doubling almost back on his path, pausing every few yards to align his crazy course by unseen landmarks. He did not speak, so keen was his concentration – and none sought to disturb him. Only the squatter and quack of disturbed wildfowl, the creak and whistle of pinnions and the lonely calling of the night birds broke the hush.

After something over a mile of this plowtering, by which time all concerned were wet and mud-spattered to their waists, mounted as they were, Rob called a halt. They found that they were actually based on solid ground, and though in the darkness it was difficult to perceive their position, it became evident that they were on a fairly extensive island in the marshes. Trees of a sort grew here, willow and alder scrub, instead of the man-high sedges and bulrushes.

Refreshments had been brought along, and Rob urged his guests to make themselves comfortable. Meanwhile, he and Gregor, with MacAlastair, had a night's work to do.

That was no exaggeration. The three of them had few idle moments for the rest of that night. Separately they each made their way back through the moss to previously appointed positions, not on the outer edge of it, but, as it were, on an inner secret ring. To these points, north, west and south, presently began to arrive mud-stained weary cattle, in the care of MacGregor gillies, from small parcels of four or half-a-dozen to fair-sized herds – beef-cattle, stirks, breeding-stock and heifers. And as soon as a sufficient number was made up, a gillie was left to meet new arrivals, and the guide, be he Rob, Gregor or MacAlastair, set off with the rest, deeper into the quagmire, to lead the beasts by devious watery routes to the chosen island in the centre – a tiring, trying task that demanded an infinity of patience, though indeed the cattle seemed to have a better instinct than had men for where to tread. At their destination they were turned loose; there was lush pasture in plenty amongst the surrounding water-meadows – and no danger of beasts straying far.

All the night the cattle continued to arrive, so that soon Rob's guests were enrolled to do duty as guides for limited stretches. None complained, for nothing appealed more to

MacGregor fancies, high and low, than the handling of other men's cattle – as Rob well knew.

By the first rosy flush of dawn on the thirtieth day of July, the MacGregors were all slipping away quietly out of the Flanders Moss, through the white early-morning mists, to their several homes, duty done. They left behind them under the supervision of a mere two or three watchful gillies, fully a couple of thousand head of prime cattle, the cream of Menteith's livestock. No tenant of any substance had been spared. It had been done quietly, advisedly, solicitously; no heads had been broken, no roofs lit, no woman harried – and where foolish opposition had unfortunately been offered, the shouting of varied clan slogans other than MacGregor, and yells of Balquhidder! Balquhidder! had served to make rash and sleep-bemused farmers think again, and think moreover along suitably mistaken lines. None would be able to swear that it was Gregorach work, any more than any would be able to assert just whence their beasts had disappeared – even though some might have a shrewd idea; that Moss would hold its secret from more potent folk than these, for an entire army could remain hidden in those endless reed-beds, and if the lowing of a querulous beast or two sounded faintly across the miles of sedge, that provided no uncomfortable proof for peaceful husbandmen who valued their own skins.

So it was that, two days later, on Lammas Term-day, the first of August, the Duke of Montrose's representatives – excluding John Graham of Killearn once more – escorted this time by bands of specially hired bullies in lieu of the military, were met by a solid phalanx of vociferously protesting tenants, none of whom had the wherewithal to pay their rents – all, indeed demanding protection from their landlord whose duty it was to guard and insure them from such disgraceful spoliation and pillage. This was the quarter before the cattle-sales, when rents were necessarily paid in livestock – so that the factors could nowise obtain cash instead of kind, bluster as they would. Sadly frustrated, at each assembly-point they were forced to turn away empty-handed. No MacGregor showed his face in all Menteith.

But Rob was not finished yet. He had no particular quarrel with Montrose's tenantry, as such, and the cattle taken from them far outvalued their quarter's rents. Accordingly on the next two or three nights after term-day, there was considerable if unadvertised movement of livestock northwards by devious ways from the vicinity of Flanders Moss through the mountain passes into Breadalbane. And thereafter, the word spread around Menteith, started who knows how, but sustained and factual, that the missing cattle would all be put up for sale at Killin in a few days time; it might well be seemly and profitable for former owners to be present.

Killin, of course, up at the head of Loch Tay, was well inside the Highland Line, indeed the capital of the Camp-bell kingdom of Breadalbane, under the very walls of the Earl's castle of Finlarig, and so safely out of reach of Mont-rose. And there, a few days later, at a special sale, the dis-puted livestock changed hands once again. It was a very special sale indeed. Rob Roy, though unseen, very much dominated the proceedings. And though large numbers of spectators had turned up, bidding was low, almost non-existent. In fact, it became known at an early stage in the proceedings that any offers for these beasts, from others than their former owners, not only would be frowned upon but simply would not be accepted. In consequence of which the Menteith tenants, or their representatives, were able to buy back their missing stock at mere token figures, with none other than themselves bidding – a quite extraordinary proceeding. Cattle that day made the lowest prices ever recorded in Scots agrarian history, before or since – such token moneys being merely to cover the cost of transportation, as one whisper put it, while other sugges-ted that the small proceeds were to form a contribution to

King James's war-chest. It was a mysterious affair altogether, and many must have wondered at the whys and wherefores of it – as they were meant to do. But the results were plain for all to recognise, and to draw their own conclusions. The Menteith tenants were soon all driving their errant beasts home through the passes of Glen Ogle and Strathyre – with the aid of a quite surprising number of suddenly available Highland volunteer drovers – at a cost to each which worked out at almost exactly the amount of their quarter's rent, a rent which they had nowise been able to pay to their ducal landlord. Nor would Montrose be able to claim any sort of back-payment, for each tenant could justifiably assert that he had had to buy back his own stock, at whatever price he chose fit to state, for no receipts or figures were produced on this occasion. All the land seethed with the story, its refinements and elaborations and mirthful implications. Never had a great landlord and national figure been made to look more foolish, inept, and utterly helpless than his Grace James of Montrose.

Rob would have admitted the affair's over-elaboration; but then it was all planned with the multiple purpose of humiliating Montrose to the utmost degree, rather than merely depriving him of his rents; of involving John Campbell Earl of Breadalbane to some extent, if possible; of making a combined operation for his MacGregors, to demonstrate to them that the Rob Roy hand was once more firmly on the helm, and undisciplined private enterprise no longer to be tolerated; and of offering the Gregorach chieftains not only the promised entertainment but an intimation that though Alastair of Balhaldies might be elected High Chief, Rob Roy MacGregor remained undisputedly the master of the clan.

There is no doubt that little of this ambitious demonstration missed its mark. Certainly it would be talked about and magnified and chuckled over when many others of its perpetrators' more valuable exploits were gone and forgotten. There was only the one man on whom it all fell rather flat – and that was Rob himself. Though he carried on with his scheme, as planned, to the end, his preoccupation was apt to be elsewhere. Partly up at Auchinchisallan, where his manhood suffered continual defeat, but more urgently even further away; for that Lammas Term-day of 1714 was conspicuous for another event altogether. On August the first Queen Anne died in London, and word to that effect from Nathaniel Hooke reached Rob Roy in the midst of his stirring activities.

CHAPTER FOURTEEN

WELL might Rob be preoccupied. So much was to hinge on the Queen's death – poor, weak, unlamented Anne. All the Jacobite plans were geared to this event – the sudden vacancy of the throne. All Rob's missions had been to prepare for action now. This was the moment of fate.

And yet nothing seemed to happen. Everything went on exactly as before. No orders came for Rob from Hooke or anyone else. On his own authority he sent orders round the MacGregor chieftains, requiring them to have given numbers of men armed and ready to join him at a moment's notice. No doubt other chiefs who had given their word to him were doing the same. But as for orders, directions and declarations from the centre, nothing happened.

A peculiar inertia, indeed, seemed to have stricken both sides in the dynastic tug-of-war. Perhaps the heat of high August had something to do with it. The feeble semi-Tory Government in London sat still in office and did nothing, apparently only awaiting a new monarch to appoint a successor to it. Its days were numbered, anyway, for Anne, unpredictable and unreliable to the end, had on her death-bed handed the Treasurer's white staff of office to the Whig Duke of Shrewsbury. Constitutionally, therefore, the Whig and Hanoverian party may have had authority to take over in the interim. But there were doubts and hesitations there also, as well as bitter jealousies. The old Electress Sophia, grand-daughter of James Sixth and First, had died only a few weeks before Anne, and it was said that her son George of Hanover was extremely reluctant to leave his Germanic fleshpots for a disunited country that had a bad habit of dethroning and even executing its kings. He temporised. In the meantime a Regency Council of eighteen noblemen of England, with seven Lord Justices, sat over the affairs of state and twiddled their thumbs likewise. Though they did issue a proclamation ordering the payment of one hundred thousand pounds sterling to anyone who should seize and secure the Pretender should he land in Great Britain or Ireland. This was practically the only official notice taken of James, Prince of Wales, that some called King James the Eighth and Third.

All this was unedifying, but less fraught with consequence than was the inactivity of the Jacobite side – for, after all, these people represented the *status quo*, and as ever possession amounted to the major part of the law. It was up to James's supporters to take advantage of the situation. But this, despite all the plans, no one in authority seemed ready to do. James himself, instead of sailing forthwith, issued an erudite and historically accurate Declaration to the world, setting forth his undoubted right to the three thrones of his fathers, and then went from Lorraine to the French court – but to obtain formal recognition of his new status rather than to raise any French expeditionary force apparently. The Duke of Berwick, an illegitimate half-brother of himself and of Anne, and a professional soldier, whom it was expected would be appointed Jacobite commander-in-chief, was not sent – it was said because the ageing King Louis refused to release him, as a French Marshal and subject. In London, Bolingbroke was still nominally Prime Minister, but he had quarrelled with Oxford and did not seem to be prepared to act on James's behalf alone. No others of that curious administration were of sufficient statue, vigour or Jacobite leanings – save perhaps Mar. And Mar was Mar.

Bobbing John was the biggest question-mark of all. Despite all his intrigues and time-serving, he chose this moment to embrace conjugal bliss for the second time. A few days before the Queen's eventual expiry, he married the Lady Frances Pierrepont, a Whig, and daughter of the powerful Duke of Kingston. Thereafter, though he was still Secretary of State for Scotland, he deserted high politics apparently for choicer delights, and no more was heard of him meantime.

In Scotland, no one was appointed leader. Nathaniel Hooke was an emissary, not a commander, and of the many Jacobite lords and chiefs, none was given any authority over another. King George was proclaimed in Edinburgh by the Lord Advocate.

Restless in their mountains, the MacGregors fretted and fumed, waiting while the ship of state swung this way and that, rudderless. It was all ominously like what had happened in 1707 and 1708.

Rob sent urgent messages to Hooke, in Angus. He went and saw old Sir Hugh Patterson of Bannockburn. He himself proclaimed King James at the Cross of Crieff – and though not all cheered him, none shouted him down.

So passed an unsatisfactory and uneasy August.

Then, in mid-September, word swept the country that George of Hanover at least had made up his mind. He had declared himself to be King, dismissed Bolingbroke as Prime Minister at long range from Germany, and had actually set sail for England. Now there could be no more holding back, surely? The issue must be put to the test before it was too late.

But no. Word came that James had dispatched £4,000 in specie, to aid his brave supporters in Scotland – but nothing more militant transpired. George arrived, unopposed if not riotously welcomed, at Greenwich, with his extraordinary entourage of fat German mistresses, and sat down stodgily on the throne. A man of no enthusiasms himself, he appeared not to notice the lack of the commodity in his reception. The fact that he knew no English, nor had intention of learning any, undoubtedly helped. Gott save the Koenig!

Then occurred an incident that might have changed the course of history – an incident variously interpreted. John, twenty-seventh Earl of Mar, premier earl of Scotland, Hereditary Keeper of Stirling Castle, and his Majesty's Secretary of State for his ancient Kingdom of Scotland, emerged from domestic felicity and presented himself before the occupant of the throne. And Majesty did not see him, would not look upon him, turned its dumpy back upon him – and a day or two later had him relieved of his seals of office. George's manners were bad, admittedly – but this almost seemed to indicate that he had had better information services over in Hanover than had been realised. Mar, seasoned trimmer as he might be, could not smile away such studied and public insult from the source of power and patronage. Within the week word was reaching the north that he was now body and soul for King James and would in due course put himself at the head of his Majesty's loyal subjects in Scotland. The Jacobite cause had at last, it appeared, found its reluctant and belated champion.

Rob Roy, when he heard this intelligence, stormed out and sought solace in the empty hills.

Rob had been living, since Lammas, in a new cave, less remote and more convenient than his old one on Cruach Tuirc – indeed, less than a mile over the hill from his burned-out house of Inversnaid, on the wooded side of Loch Lomond. Here he was entirely free, yet could face a winter with some degree of comfort; he could keep an eye on his own folk, and at the same time on the small and now very unambitious garrison at Inverarklet guarding the fort-builders. The fort itself was practically completed, most of the masons having gone, and only the carpenters remaining on interior work. On this too, needless to say, Rob kept an eye.

Such was the position at the onset of winter of 1714, one eventful year after Rob's outlawry and the shattering of his home.

Donald MacGregor was waiting with the news when Rob returned to his cave after a visit to Glen Gyle, one early evening of November.

'A man has come,' he said excitedly. 'The chief contractor man it is no less, they say. All the way from Edinburgh. For the fort. They do be saying that the fort is finished now. This man – Nasmyth or suchlike the name is – has now to be inspecting it, and to give it to the soldiers, some way.'

'Nasmyth? Yes, that was the contractor's name,' Rob nodded. 'He is here, then? Now? Where? And how did he get here, at all?'

'At the damned fort he is, now. He came with six redcoats. They were after meeting him at Aberfoyle. Some of our people followed them, and brought me word. The soldiers were from Inverarklet, and they went to meet him. They were saying to Callum the Inn, at Aberfoyle – while they were waiting for the man, see you – that they would not be shivering in their tents many nights more, but would be snug in the fort.'

'So-o-o!' Rob tapped his knee, in thought. It had come to a decision for him too, now. He had been wondering about that fort. And hesitating – which was not like Rob Roy. He had been hoping, rather feebly perhaps, that with the coming of hard weather again, the military might return whence they had come, with the workmen, until the winter was over. If he himself did not provoke them. They had been little trouble to each other, that summer. Argyll clearly was for *avoiding* trouble, offering no provocation to his old protégé. But this news changed the situation.

'If Nasmyth has come it can only be to hand over the completed fort to the soldiers,' he agreed, as much to himself at to Donald and MacAlastair. 'It is still the contractor's property – och, he will not be able to get his money for it until he has the local commander's acceptance of it in good order.'

The others nodded.

'If the soldiers are for moving into it, out of their tents, then that means that they are going to garrison it all the time – that they are not going to be leaving us for the winter. And, *Dia* – they will be a nuisance in there, whatever!'

He was not contradicted about that, either. 'I have wondered, my own self, why you have not swept that fort away again before this,' Donald admitted. 'The thing is an insult, just, to our clan.'

'Aye,' Rob said heavily. 'I will tell you why. I like it less than you do – but it has been the lesser of two evils. *Mac Cailean Mhor* – Argyll – has been using me gently, see you. As is only right and just. To strike at Montrose is good and well – that is a *private* matter, and Argyll need not be concerned. But to strike at this fort is different – even though Montrose it was who ordered it to be built. It is for the Government, the fort – for the military. If I should strike at it, Argyll likely cannot be looking the other way, even if he would. We do not want an army of red-coats here at Inversnaid again. Not when we ourselves may be off to the wars any day.'

There was silence in the cave, now.

Rob was tapping at that hairy knee again, a sure sign of deep cogitation. 'And yet, and yet . . .' he said. 'The fort is an ill thing, there – and could be dangerous for the King James's cause, garrisoned against him. I am wondering – wondering whether Argyll would take it less hard, maybe, if the fort was to suffer some damage *before* the military took it over, at all – while it was still by way of being the contractor's property? Och, he might just prefer it that way, see you!'

'But . . . but . . . the man is here,' Donald pointed out. 'It is too late, Rob.'

'Maybe not too late yet. The man Nasmyth will need tomorrow for his inspection. He will not hand over the place until tomorrow, I'm thinking. We have tonight.'

'Tonight!' the younger man cried. 'But can we do it? We cannot get the clan roused, in the time . . .'

'There will be no rousing of the clan,' Rob declared sternly. 'This is against the Government, you will remember not just Montrose. I will not have the clan involved – not until there is a general rising. Myself, I dealt with the fort before – I must needs do so again.'

'But, how? The fort is strong, now. Barred and locked at night. It is not just foundations any more. . . .'

'Wheesht, you! Hush your chatter man, and let me think. That one – the man Nasmyth from Edinburgh – will not have much love for tents of a November night, I'm thinking . . . ?'

*　　*　　*

There were lights shining from the small barred windows of the fort on the top of Tom na Bairlinn that night, a thing that had not been seen before – for the builders throughout had been taken down at nightfall to the safety of the army camp at Inverarklet and the place locked up, with two sentries posted. Those two sentries still patrolled faithfully, patiently, after almost a year's fruitless vigil.

Their fall, that night, was not exactly simultaneous, nor was it entirely soundless – though fortunately it was the second victim who emitted a small squawk and so did not alarm the first. This lack of fullest synchronisation was occasioned wholly by Rob's insistence that on no account must either of the sentries be killed. Half-hearted methods always tended to be the more clumsy.

A little later – but not so late that the lights in the fort were out and all bedded down – two red-coated figures came up to the great iron-studded and barred door, thumping thereon with their musket-butts and calling to be admitted. It was Rob's voice that did the calling, however, in his best Cockney.

The visitors had been prepared for a certain amount of questioning, and Rob was ready with his answers. But such were not required. A lamp was brought to the iron-grating, its light was shone out, less than efficiently, on the two uniformed men. Then, its bearer apparently satisfied, the bolts were drawn and the small wicket door opened.

What followed happened more swiftly than it may be described. The two red-coated figures stepped within, one at either side, and Rob Roy leapt in between them, pistol in one hand and broadsword in the other. The door slammed shut behind him. A musket-butt shattered the lamp upheld by the door-opener – who proved to be the foreman mason – and left only the firelight's flicker to illuminate the scene within.

In the main room of the fort three men stood staring, over by the fire on its wide hearth – and none were in uniform. If there were other men elsewhere in the building, the noise had not brought them out. These three clearly had just jumped up, startled, from a table by the fire, whereon lay papers and tankards.

Rob strode into the room, eyes busy. 'Your pardon, gentlemen, for this intrusion,' he jerked. 'Sometimes I must be more precipitate than I would wish. Do not be alarmed – no hurt is intended towards you. Tell me only – is there anyone else in this building, at all?'

None of the three moved lips to speak, but one managed to shake his head.

Rob came forward, and laid his weapons on the table, as though no longer required. 'My name is MacGregor of Inversnaid,' he mentioned modestly. 'You may not have heard of me – but, och, it is my land on which you stand.' He bowed towards the better dressed of the trio, a heavy red-faced man with spectacles. 'You, sir, I take to be Mr Nasmyth, of Edinburgh?'

The other still did not answer. He was looking now past Rob to the two red-coated imposters, obviously bewildered.

'Ah – I see. These are friends of mine,' the Highlandman explained. 'I am fortunate in my friends. But sit down, gentlemen. It may be sometime yet before I need request you to vacate this building.'

Mr Nasmyth drew a sharp breath at this. 'What . . . what do you mean, sir?' he got out unsteadily.

'Just that it will be necessary for me, unfortunately, to demolish these excellent premises that you have so efficiently erected, sir. You see, contrary to all law and civility, my permission was not sought when it was decided rashly to build this place on my land. As proprietor here, I find it an inconvenience and an obstruction to the view. Therefore I must take steps to clear it away. It grieves me to lay violent hands on such excellent craftsmanship.' Here Rob bowed to the foreman mason, the foreman carpenter and the little clerk of works, who had elected to spend the night with their employer going over the plans and estimates. 'But perhaps you were remiss in not ascertaining that the land had been properly conveyed by me to . . . to your clients. Och, a small thing – but important, whatever!'

'But . . . my God – you cannot do this!' Nasmyth cried. 'You cannot . . .'

'On the contrary, sir, I can – and shall! My only regret is that I have insufficient gunpowder available to do it with fitting thoroughness. But we have enough to serve, see you – and these excellent plans of yours will be helping me to be placing my charges to the best advantage!'

'I protest . . . !'

'Yes, sir – that is to be expected. I suggest that you make your protest – and a strong one, whatever – to his Grace of Montrose. I hear that his Grace is newly appointed Secretary of State for Scotland, in room of my Lord of Mar. Since his Grace it was who made the original mistake here, it is most appropriate that now he should right it. I should demand heavy compensation, Mr Nasmyth – you deserve it. And then I further suggest that you take your workmen and build your fort elsewhere – preferably in his Grace's property of Buchanan! It would look nicely there.' Rob bowed again. 'Now, gentlemen your pardon – but we have labours to perform.' And he took up the plans from the table – also his weapons.

So while the unhappy builders sat there, under the fleering eye and cocked pistol of Donald MacGregor, Rob and MacAlastair went to work. They went outside to the hidden ponies and brought in the kegs that represented the residue of the Gregorach stock of gunpowder. These they disposed in strategic positions, amongst the foundations, under arches and lintels, in corners – the plans proving valuable in showing constructional key-points. Then systematically and with vigour and ruthlessness that must have wrung the hearts of the watching craftsmen, they wrenched off, broke down, shattered and smashed up all the woodwork in the establishment, using tools amply to hand on the premises. It was all pitch-pine, and would blaze like a torch.

Rob had lengths of fuse this time, procured by nimble fingers mainly from the stone-masons' own quarrying equipment. When these were fixed and all was ready, the prisoners were conducted outside into the night.

'Think you that she will go up bravely, or not?' Rob asked of Nasmyth, interestedly. 'We have less powder than I would have liked. You will be knowledgeable about such matters, I have no doubt?'

He obtained no reply from the unfortunate contractor.

Rob lit the various and adequate fuses himself, and on this occasion there was no unseemly scramble for safety necessary. There was time even for the panting Rob to stand back with the others, and watch.

It made a peculiar explosion. There was scarcely any effect of blast or detonation to be observed. A couple of unexceptional flashes, and Tom na Bairlinn seemed to shrug itself beneath the watchers. Then one end of the fort appeared to lift slowly upward, while the opposite end sank and shrank in on itself. But neither of them violently, eruptively. There was a hiccupping sort of rumble, more flashes, and a further heaving and twisting of the building. Finally a sort of sigh on the night air. That was all. Compared with the blowing up of the dam that other time, it was all most undramatic and disappointing.

But, after a due wait – in case of any delayed fuses – close inspection supplied a different impression. The entire building, though superficially it retained its outward shape, leaned and sagged drunkenly. The gables were riven, no wall was sound, cracks and seams forked everywhere, and craters yawned amongst the foundations. What had been left of the woodwork was already blazing furiously. That fort would require to be rebuilt from the bottom up. A year's work had been destroyed in a few seconds.

Rob forebore to look at Nasmyth and his men just then.

They lit the bonfire of the carpenter's handiwork, using the working plans and estimates as tinder, and in a few moments the resinous wood was sending great crimson tongues of flame leaping skywards. There would be no need to stoke that fire.

Rob turned at length to the contractor. 'Mr Nasmyth – you have my sympathies,' he said, courteously. 'But no doubt you will console and recoup yourself with other Government contracts. But I advise that you act smartly about it – as about your claim for compensation. For there may be a new Government very soon, which may not smile kindly on contractors who built forts to harry loyal Highlandmen. A difficult position for men of business? Now – no doubt your companions will conduct you safely down to the tents at Inverarklet for the night? Och, yes. If you will wait for one minute, just, my two friends will restore to a couple of soldiers their borrowed clothing. Och, we would not wish to misuse any Government equipment, see you. Then you can all go down together, and at a good pace – for the soldiers may be cold a little. A good night to you gentlemen.

Oh – there is a small matter that you might be mentioning to the officer down there. It is that this operation was performed by the proprietor of the lands personally, as a private transaction whatever. Not by the Clan of MacGregor – who indeed know nothing of the business. You will not forget. . . . ?'

And so the two little parties went their different ways – and the ruins of the fort on the Hill of Warning stared gauntly across the Snaid Burn at the ruins of Inversnaid House, by the red light of the flaming pile.

CHAPTER FIFTEEN

It took Rob Roy some little time to learn the reaction of Red John of the Battles, Duke of Argyll, to that night's performance – Argyll having much on his mind just then. His was a difficult position, commander-in-chief in a country – and his own country – for an unsteady Government and a new and unpopular monarch, with neither of whom the majority of his countrymen had any sympathy. A Highlander himself, he knew the pull of loyalties and interests only too well – for his own clan was split, the Campbells of Argyll following their chief as good Whigs, and the Campbells of Breadalbane being Jacobites. He was none too sure of the loyalty of his Scottish troops, at a pinch, and had to place his reliance on English soldiers and foreign mercenaries. Moreover, despite his battles and victories, he was a humane and reasonable man, and like most good soldiers, abhorred above all else the idea of civil war. And, of course, Rob was an old friend, and indeed a very faraway relation.

Then there was Montrose to complicate matters, his fellow-duke and traditional enemy, who had once more, on the political see-saw, manoeuvred himself into a strong position with King George, and was now Mar's successor as Secretary of State for Scotland – the man with whom Argyll must deal most closely, in fact. Montrose, enraged by Rob Roy's campaign against him, was demanding the use of troops against the MacGregors – especially with the Martinmas Quarter-day nearly upon them – claiming that the entire Highlands were in danger of blazing up in seditious rebellion, and that a strong hand must be shown. Argyll temporised, claimed that he must concentrate his available forces to hold the strong-points of Edinburgh, Stirling, Dumbarton and the like, in case of a rising, not scatter them over the face of the land. But the pressure was strong, and the effeminate but steely Montrose had all the civil power in his pocket.

The demolition of Inversnaid Fort was a bad blow, that could nowise be overlooked. And then, only a few days later, the countryside rang with the story of a new provocation. Despite the utmost secrecy, intricate last-minute changes of venue, the eventual appointment of remote Chapellaroch as meeting-place, and the darkness of evening as cover, individual tenants being met and escorted by sheriff-officers and hired bravoes – despite all this, Rob Roy was there first, concealed himself in the inn loft above the place of payment, and, towards the end of the business got his minions to set the place afire by the age-old method of firing burning arrows from a distance into the thatch. In the subsequent panic and confusion, he leapt down through the smoke and showering sparks, grabbed up most of the bagged rent-money, and bolted for the nearby Flanders Moss – in the first quagmires of which, presently, he bogged his rash pursuers.

Montrose now was like a man possessed. There was no containing his rage and spleen. But he was shrewd, still. He claimed it all as a Jacobite outrage – robbing law-abiding citizens to fill the Pretender's coffers. He demanded energetic measures by the State – and was in a fair position to insist upon them. Edinburgh rang with alarmist and inflammable speeches.

Argyll had to go some way to meet him. Though he refused to parcel out his all too few reliable troops in small numbers and put them at the disposal of sheriffs and other civil authorities, he did accede to Montrose's demand that loyal and faithful tenants of areas flanking the deplorable

Highland Line – by which he meant Montrose tenants – should be supplied with arms and ammunition to preserve King George's peace and their loyal lives . . . if the military were unable to do it for them. The Commander-in-Chief would have to have been very sure of his position indeed to refuse such request to the Secretary of State.

And so the royal arsenals were thrown open to the Grahams. Into lairds' houses and farms, villages and mills, cottages and change-houses, the stream of weapons flowed.

Meanwhile, on the wider scene, action hung fire. Bolingbroke fled to Lorraine, where James appointed him his Secretary of State. The Duke of Ormonde and other prominent English Jacobites followed him – so that it seemed obvious that there was going to be no uprising in England. Scotland must act first, and probably alone, if the cause was not to go by default.

And in Scotland, though talk there was in plenty, gestures were made, and even some enthusiasts locked up, action did not follow. The winter of course, was no time for any sort of military campaign in the Highlands – and it was to the Highlands that Scotland looked. But the Highlands, as Rob Roy had so often pointed out, though warlike and ready for the fray, were split into numerous mutually antagonistic clans. The men were there, but they would not unite save under someone high above their own prideful jealousies and feuds. None such had been appointed. If James had come over in person, the clans would have flocked to him in their scores of thousands – his half-brother Berwick, likewise. Any royal appointee, provided that he was sufficiently warlike and distinguished for proud chiefs to serve under, would have done. But none emerged. There were some who suggested that Rob Roy himself should take the lead in this impasse, at least for a start – Gregor of Glengyle prominent amongst them. But Rob shook his red head. He was no general, he said; a guerilla commander, yes – but no field officer. Besides, the great chiefs, though they might accept him on occasion as an equal, would never consent to actually serve under such as himself. Moreover, daring and incautious as he could be personally, Rob was not the man to plunge his clan into armed revolt prematurely, where others might not follow; too much was at stake for the MacGregors.

Strangely enough, the only prominent man who seemed to be deeply agitated by the continuing delay was John, Earl of Mar. Whatever else he might be, of course, Mar was a manoeuvrer, with a keen eye for the main chance, a shrewdness for the moment of advantage. He bombarded with urgent letters both James in Lorraine and the Jacobite notables in Scotland, succeeding in offending both by his importunity to action, and the implication that he himself was authoritatively involved. He did not urge his own name as commander in the field – for he was a politician and no soldier – but others with a more military background suspected and resented his eagerness nevertheless.

Thus the months went by, and while some supporters of James grew the more frustratedly impatient, others' ardours cooled noticeably. The Duke of Atholl, who had long flirted with the Jacobites, went south to make his peace with King George. Others did likewise. Breadalbane, claiming to be too old and sick to attend at Court, sent fervent protestations of loyalty – though privately the old scoundrel assured his good cousin Rob Roy that five hundred Campbell broadswords under Glendaruel would be available for King James at three days' notice. In the north and west the clans were deep in winter hibernation and local homicide.

Rob maintained his feud with Montrose, in quarterly instalments – but automatically, now, as a duty, with most of the fire and verve gone out of the business. Killearn might have emigrated to the furthest Indies for all that was heard of him, and stealing rents from this unseen ducal adversary began to pall on Rob. The current disease of inertia and frustration seemed almost as though it might have infected even Rob Roy MacGregor. Curiously enough, it was Mary MacGregor who saved him from that.

Rob still visited Auch at irregular intervals, making duty calls as father rather than husband. During one such visit in the early spring, after snowstorms had kept Rob in the small house amongst her feet for three days on end, Mary abruptly if temporarily abandoned her rigidly maintained attitude of chill aloofness for one of sheer and very human exasperation.

'Mercy upon us!' she cried out. 'Can you be a man, at all, Robert MacGregor – sitting there day after day with nothing in the world to concern you, your hand as idle as it will be in the grave! Is it dead you are, before your time, or what?'

Startled, the man jumped up. 'Lord – what's this?' he said. '*Me* dead! Save us – I think you have it head to tail, woman!'

'Naturally mine is the fault!' she flung back at him. 'Not the great Rob Roy!' The sudden surge of animation did wonders for her, bringing a flush to her almost too perfect features, sparkling her lovely eyes, flaring her chiselled nostrils. The man, despite all, was not unaware of it.

He shook his head. 'Why do you hate me so, Mary?' he asked.

Only for a moment did she hesitate. 'I said naught of hating you,' she answered. 'I cried out upon your idleness.'

'But, what is there to be doing in this snow? The beasts are safe and well. There is wood and peats in plenty, for the fire. What would you . . . ?'

'And is your life, your world, these small four walls? Is not a king in danger of losing his crown, and do not the Grahams ride ever higher – while you sit and watch my peats burn?'

'*Dia* – think you that *I* can win James Stewart his throne for him? I have done my best – I have done more than most. More than he has done himself, whatever! I am ready for his orders. I cannot *make* his orders for him. And have I not done as I said, and made Montrose keep me? Have I not made him a laughing-stock? Snapped my fingers under his woman's nose? Killearn is beyond my reach . . . as yet, God's curse on him! But him I will have too, in time. Till then I make a fool of him also. He is his master's factor, responsible for Montrose's rents. Those rents I take each quarter-day. . . .'

'Rents! Money!' Mary broke in. 'Think you that is all that matters – money, beasts, fodder? Is that all that you would take from the Grahams? Montrose has money in plenty. And cattle. He rules Scotland now. You will never make a pauper of James Graham. Will a few pounds, a few cattle-beasts, redeem your honour – since mine will never be redeemed?'

'But . . . what can I do more? How else can I come at them? You know how I am limited.'

'I know that you have the means of hurting James Graham, and aiding your king, both. If you would.'

'Eh? How could that be? What mean you. . . . ?'

'I have heard that Montrose arms all his tenants with weapons from Argyll. That is true, is it not? Those weapons lie now in each Graham house – for the taking, one by one. They could arm men for King James.'

Rob stared at her, lips moving for a moment wordlessly. 'Merciful Mother of God!' he got out, at length. 'Why thought I not of that? Heaven's angels could not have conceived a choicer design, whatever! Mary,' he declared, looking at her admiringly. 'I think sometimes that you should have been born a man!'

'Would to God I had!' she said, wearily, suddenly deflated again, and turned away.

Rob was now the excited one. 'If this thing, this notable conception, could be done – and I believe that it could – would you aid me in it, lass? Come with me?'

She shook her head.

'But it is your notion, your concern. You would see it successful?'

'I want no part in it – nor any of your man's concerns,' she answered dully.

'Not even against the Grahams?'

'That is *your* duty, not mine.'

'But, woman – you have just said . . . you have told me . . .'

'I have told you your duty. It is for you to do it, not me.'

'But, Mary . . . see you – if I do this thing, if I succeed in this plan of yours – will you then perhaps smile upon me a little more kindly, in return?' That, from Rob Roy Mac-Gregor came as near to complete surrender as was in the man.

She turned to look at him, slowly, deliberately, strangely, her expression at once wondering, scornful, perhaps even a little pitying. 'No,' she said briefly, finally, and left the kitchen.

Rob, of course, was not the man to let personal disappointment interfere with the course of duty – and such pleasant duty. Very shortly thereafter, despite the weather, and the failings and inertia of others, began a prolonged campaign that was to keep himself, MacAlastair and Donald MacGregor fairly fully engaged throughout the spring of 1715 and well into the summer. It was not a concentrated revolution; by its very nature it had to be a sporadic business, comprising innumerable small incidents, wide-scattered and sometimes with quite lengthy intervals between. And other activities, local and national, were not entirely neglected. But it was a recognisable campaign nevertheless, and no one failed so to recognise it – more especially the House of Graham.

All along the borders of the Highland Line no Graham house was safe, no tenant of Montrose, or of any of his cadets, slept at peace in his bed – until relieved of the controversial weapons issued from Government arsenals. Raids were unpredictable, varying in character, and almost impossible to counter. Many were modest in scope and simple to a degree, but others were ambitious and elaborately planned; most were perpetrated in darkness, but others in broad daylight. Physical violence was eschewed wherever possible – but immunity was by no means guaranteed to stubborn men. No hiding-places were inviolable – as ravaged marital beds that had concealed muskets, and the harried crypts of Graham churches, bore witness. Indeed, hiding was worse than useless, for the MacGregors appeared to have veritable noses for powder and shot, and smelt it out no matter how closely hidden, leaving a trail of ruin, burned thatches and the like behind them. Defence against attack proved equally unavailing, even for the larger lairds, for none could afford to maintain an armed guard permanently on duty, day and night, waiting for a blow that might never fall – and where the enemy seemed to have a most excellent intelligence system warning him of the presence of opposition; anyway, the name and fame of Rob Roy paralysed most local resistance at source, most wise men preferring to be rid of arms that they had never particularly wanted rather than clash with the dreaded freebooter – especially as they all duly received a receipt for the weapons, signed by Rob Roy, taking them over in the name of and for the use of King James the Eighth, God save him.

In the circumstances, perhaps, it was not surprising, as time went on, that many of the as yet unraided tenants had second thoughts about the whole business, and ended up by insisting on having the arms returned whence they had come, for safety's sake. News of this move spread, and presently it became something of a race between Rob and the prudent ones as to the ultimate destination of the guns and muskets.

The MacGregor arsenals grew apace. Instead of being a

disarmed clan, as the law described them, they were well on the way to becoming the best armed in all the land.

Rob almost forgot wider disappointments.

CHAPTER SIXTEEN

WHAT drove Mar to take the final drastic step is not to be known. Some said that he feared for his life in the south – though why that should be it might be hard to explain, even admitting that Oxford was impeached on 16th July and committed to the Tower of London; others suggested that the move was to forestall somebody else – who, was not specified. The more probable explanation was that the man just suddenly got sick and tired of waiting. Certainly his letters both to France and Scotland had been growing increasingly urgent and importunate. Whatever the reason, he abruptly changed the entire course of his life. Secretly, on 2nd August, he left London, stealing away on a coal boat of all things, and sailed from the Thames for Fife.

And now there was no more delay. Once in Scotland, Mar announced himself to be King James's Lieutenant in Scotland – omitting to mention that he held no commission to that effect – and summoned all loyal supporters of His Majesty to assemble for a *tinchal*, or hunting-match, on the Braes of Mar – the traditional and accepted step to raising the standard of revolt – in one week's time.

Bobbing John had bobbed up again to some effect.

It is eloquent of the climate of impatience and frustration prevailing in Scotland that so many men of name and fame did flock to Aberdeenshire in answer to that summons – for Mar, despite his anicent lineage and premier earldom, was held in scant esteem throughout the land, and known as a turncoat. Yet they rallied to his hunting-match in their scores and hundreds – eight hundred it was said attended the *tinchal*, of which three hundred ranked as nobility and major gentry – not to mention the still more exclusive company of twenty-six Highland chiefs and captains of clans.

Rob was there, of course, as was Gregor – and Balhaldies, or the Laird of MacGregor as he now preferred to be called also, the first occasion on which both the new High Chief and the Captain of Clan Alpine had appeared together officially. Happily there was no embarrassment or clash of interests; Rob did not even wear the three eagle's feathers to which, in war, his captaincy entitled him, contenting himself with the single plume of a modest cadet; whilst Balhaldies, who was a discreet and diplomatic individual, however ambitious, dressed on this occasion in Lowland garb, deferred to Rob on all matters military, and indeed appeared almost to have more interest in the position of his wife's clan, the Camerons, than the MacGregors; Gregor it was who provided the splendour for the trio, a yellow-maned giant clad in fullest panoply of Highland magnificence, his two feathers the tallest and proudest ever grown by eagle.

As *tinchals* went, the one on the Braes of Mar was a success. The need for action and an end to delay was so evident to all concerned that it was possible to reduce the preliminaries to a minimum. Inevitably there was a certain amount of argument over precedence, but this was on a minor key, and social rather than military. Men held their hands, and to some extent their tongues, meantime.

Hunting was not altogether neglected, and numerous deer died in Glens Cluny and Quoich.

Some of the island chiefs and the Lowland lords from the Borders, with long distances to travel, could not but arrive late. But there was one other who came late who had not that excuse. He was Alexander, Marquis of Huntly, heir to the old Duke of Gordon, celebrated Cock o' the North. Others of the Gordons had been present from the first – the young Earl of Aboyne, General Alexander Gordon, Glenbucket. But Huntly, the acknowledged leader of the great half-Lowland half-Highland house that could put men into the field in their thousands, Huntly came late and came sulking. Probably he did not come purposely to make trouble – but trouble followed nevertheless. He was proud, headstrong, and he despised Mar. He could call out a hundred broadswords for other men's ten. He was heir to a duke – and it was for dukes to lead armies. And he was Cock o' the North. To most people it should have been obvious who should lead the King's forces. He did not actually say this in as many words, of course. But a few misunderstood him, and not a few tended to agree with him. He could not be any less of a soldier than Mar, at any rate.

But Mar was cautious. He did not say that he himself wished to be Commander-in-Chief. He seemed to go on the assumption that James himself, or at least the Duke of Berwick, would be over from France in a week or so to take command, and that his task therefore was merely to organise and set the campaign moving. In fact, a loyal address to his Majesty urging him to do that very thing was one of the first matters attended to. In the circumstances it was difficult to accuse Mar of seeking to impose himself upon them.

Fortunately or otherwise, there were so many practical details to discuss and arrange that the inevitable battle of personalities that bedevils any and every Scottish corporate venture was much restricted. Thanks to Mar's undoubted flair for organisation and his keen eye for priorities, decisions were reached at a remarkable speed, all things considered. It was agreed that the actual standard of revolt should be raised, and by Mar himself, in one week's time, and as nearly simultaneously as possible King James should be proclaimed in as many towns and cities as the Jacobites could control. Sundry small and local expeditions should be made, where victory was assured, for the sake of prestige and to encourage waverers. Meanwhile, the components of the army should be assembling – the main striking force and backbone therefore, naturally, in the clan territories to north and west. The strategic south Highland passes should be closed, and held for King James. It was now the 28th of August. Two weeks should suffice to assemble the clans, or most of them. They should then march south, to place themselves somewhere near the edge of the Highland Line, and in convenient communication with Perth, by the end of September. At Perth, dominated by the staunchly Jacobite house of Drummond, the Lowland forces would assemble. By then, it was hoped, His Majesty would be present to take over the command, and a two-pronged advance on Stirling and Edinburgh would commence.

Rob had considerable part in all these decisions, and it was noticeable that Mar placed much reliance on his views and advice. Rob himself would have liked, of course, to return to the MacGregor country, raise his own clan, and see to the blocking of the passes of Balmaha and Aberfoyle. But Mar, no doubt wisely, had more vital work for him; his assistance in co-ordinating and bringing the main clans to the assembly in the north-west would be invaluable – others could bring out the MacGregors. This latter duty and privilege, therefore, fell to Gregor of Glengyle, for Balhaldies had volunteered to go and use his influence with his brother-in-law Locheil and the Camerons, who were hanging back. Gregor was nothing loth.

The *tinchal* broke up on an unfortunate note. Huntly, disappointed and offended, went off home to Strathbogie before the end, refusing any assurance of active support. Others followed his lead, notably the Lord Erroll, Traquair and Stormont. But that was only to be expected. By and large the meeting had succeeded.

The rising was launched. The majority were committed. Mar remained in effective control.

* * *

The weeks that followed were thrilling or alarming ones for Scotland – and for England too, to a lesser extent – depending upon one's point of view. Inverness fell like a ripe plum to the veteran MacKintosh of Borlum. Aberdeen opted for James, and the King was proclaimed there by the Earl Marischal. In Dundee, Viscount Dundee, though a Graham, performed a like service, and was cheered to the echo. In Dunkeld, Montrose, Brechin, Forfar, indeed all the North-East, it was the same. In Fife the rival factions came to blows, but steadily the Jacobites gained the upper hand. Almost all over the Highlands the clans were mustering, and only the small Government garrison at Fort William remained, practically beleaguered. The Mac-Gregors held the Highland Line – and not passively, either – the best-armed Jacobites of all, thanks to Montrose, and panic spread far further south than Stirling. Argyll, arriving in Edinburgh from the west, complained bitterly that he had a striking force of no more than 1400 men – four regiments of foot and four of cavalry. How was he to defend Scotland with that?

No battles had been fought, but more than half the land was King James's already.

It was in these conditions that, at the end of September, with Mar's headquarters already set up in Perth, Rob Roy led a glittering and colourful array southwards through Lochaber, Glen Coe and Glen Orchy. Perhaps even Rob, hardened campaigner as he was, felt a surge of pride to be marching at its head – for this was the main Highland Division of King James's army, the largest massing of clansman seen for centuries – and largely the fruit of Rob's own work. It might even be suggested that it was the said pride that brought the great company by that route at all – for this was by no means the only road south; but it was the route that passed the little house of Auchinchisallan, under Beinn Dorain.

So Rob rode up to Mary's doorstep in the most resplendent and resounding company that any Highlandman could imagine. Clanranald was there, and Glengarry, and two brothers of Sir Donald of Sleat, with all Clan Donald at their backs. MacDougall of Lorne and the Laird of Mac-Kinnon; Grant of Invermoriston and MacIan of Glencoe; Maclean of Duart and Chisholm of Strathglass; and Mac-kenzie of Applecross, forerunner of Seaforth's great clan, still assembling. And behind them followed the endless serried ranks of their clansmen, in their gallant thousands.

Some might possibly have sensed a degree of pathos in the way that Rob Roy presented this offering before his wife, in the eager, almost anxious fashion in which he watched her reception of it. More perhaps might have found it in their hearts to pity him for the utter blankness of those glorious eyes as they turned away from him and what he brought.

The chiefs rode on, and Rob with them, to camp in Strathfillan – where the Robertsons of Struan, the Stewarts of Appin and the Breadalbane Campbells were to join them. It took their followers two hours to pass the door of Auch, and the flourish of their bagpipes filled the glens. The young MacGregors cheered until their throats would croak no more. Their mother watched expressionless – but her strong slender fingers tore and tore at the edge of her red and black plaid.

Major-General Gordon of Auchintoul was appointed to take field command of the Highland Division, and Rob returned to his MacGregors, who were manning the passes of the Highland Line.

King James did not appear.

CHAPTER SEVENTEEN

JOHN, Earl of Mar, now styled Captain-General of King James's army – some said that his commission to that effect was not only a forgery but was in his own handwriting – faced his officers and commanders with that expression of mild distaste which was habitual with him, even when, as now, he seemed slightly on the defensive, and which did nothing to endear him to his associates.

'I think that we dare wait no longer, my lords and gentlemen,' he said. 'His Majesty undoubtedly is coming – but he is delayed. As you know, King Louis of France has died, and on the representations of Stair, Ambassador from London, Orleans the Regent has refused to allow King James's flotilla to sail. There are twelve good ships lying in Havre de Grace, loaded with 2000 men, 12,000 muskets, 18,000 swords, 4000 barrels of powder, and a dozen brass field pieces. But Orleans has ordered them to be unloaded. I have urged that his Majesty sail without them, secretly if need be – but others advise differently. We cannot be sure that he will leave France within the month.' He did not add that he had in his pocket a letter from the same Majesty declaring that he wished that his supporters in Scotland, however loyal, would not move in advance of his royal authorisation.

There was some muttering amongst his hearers. The less knowledgeable and more ingenuous amongst them had been daily expecting the King's arrival.

Mar went on, a little wearily. 'Argyll, as you are aware, is at Stirling. His skirmishers are as far out as Bridge of

Allan – not much more than a score of miles from this city of Perth. He has no more than two thousand regular troops – but I have reliable tidings that he is daily expecting reinforcements. Six thousand Dutch mercenaries are on the sea, to aid him, and the first have actually landed. Every day that we wait for His Majesty, Argyll grows stronger.'

'We have waited over long already, by the good Lord God!' the fiery Clanranald cried.

'Aye, we have!' Campbell of Glendaruel, Breadalbane's lieutenant, exclaimed bitterly. 'There is scarce a bag of meal, a living cow, a stick of firewood, or an unravished woman left in all Breadalbane – thanks to the MacDonald horde!' And he glared angrily at the tight group of Clan Donald chiefs. 'Let us be on – and see if some can fight as well as they pillage!' The Highland Division of 10,000 clansmen, enforcedly idle, had been a little hard on Breadalbane of the Campbells, admittedly. It had been too good an opportunity to be missed.

Clanranald's hand slapped down resoundingly on the silver basket-hilt of his great broadsword. 'Did a toad croak?' he demanded of the room at large. 'Did a sheep bleat?'

As from a pack of dogs the growls arose.

'Gentlemen! Gentlemen!' Mar cried, his rather thin voice cracking. 'Peace, I beseech you. Let us mind what we are at.' But the altercation, so typical, so normal, had given his nimble mind another aspect of their situation to stress. 'An army inevitably bears hardly on any local population. The burghers of Perth are not backwards in their complaints either, I can assure you! And idleness in irregular troops is helpful to none. Even the bravest.' And he glanced placatingly at the MacDonalds. 'It is time, I think, that we put our case to the test.'

No man could in honesty say differently. It was 9th November, and since 22nd September Mar had lingered at Perth, ostensibly awaiting the King's presence. He had been reinforced by the reluctant Marquis of Huntly with 2500 more Gordons, the Earl of Seaforth with nearly a thousand MacKenzies, the Earl Marischal with 700, the Mackintosh with his clan, and many others, so that Perth groaned under the crushing weight of its deliverers. At the behest of the impatient and to relieve the pressure, as well as to attempt to keep spirited men from each other's throats, Mar had sent off sundry minor expeditions, probing attacks, and feints. Practically all his cavalry, eating its head off on the Inches of Perth, had been dispatched to Fife, under Lord Drummond and the Master of Sinclair, and now that semi-island county was strongly held for King James and threatening the Lothian coast across the Firth of Forth. Brigadier Mackintosh of Borlum, possibly the best soldier in the Jacobite ranks, had crossed from Fife to Leith in a daring seaborne escapade, capturing that seaport and its citadel, and menacing the Capital itself. The pugnacious MacGregors had been detailed to make a comprehensive sweep of Loch Lomond to capture every boat on its lengthy surface – for it was feared that Argyll, denied the use of the Forth estuary, would bring in his Continental mercenary reinforcements at the Clyde, and use the loch and its boats as a means of outflanking the insurgent line to the west. Rob Roy had been recalled personally from this congenial occupation – in which he had been able to deliver a few shrewd blows at the southern Graham lands of Buchanan and Endrick – to take part in still another diversionary expedition, which pleased him less. This was a raid on Inveraray, Argyll's own capital town on Loch Fyne, made in the hope of distracting the Government Commander-in-Chief into making a rescue bid and dispersing his forces, and at the same time giving the restive Highland Division still camped at Strathfillan something to do. It had not been as successful a business as it might have been – for Inveraray was in a strong water-guarded position and did not lack Campbell manpower to defend it – and it may be that Rob Roy was not too unhappy about that, for he had some sympathy and kindly feeling towards the harassed Argyll. It was from this employment that Mar had abruptly recalled the Highland Division leaders, Rob especially named amongst them, for this special council in Perth.

None would deny, then, that the insurgent army had waited long enough for its royal commander, or that it was not time to put the cause to the test. Already Simon Fraser of Lovat had whistled home 300 of his clan, and others from the glens were drifting away from lack of employment.

'You have a plan of action, my lord?' It was Huntly who spoke, stressing the word action, and not troubling to disguise the scorn in his voice. He made no secret of his continuing hostility to Mar and his conviction that he was militarily incompetent.

'I have taken good advice, my lord,' the other answered mildly. 'I believe it to be sound.' And he glanced over towards Major-General Gordon, a veteran of Czar Peter's wars.

Huntly could not publicly question the advice given by so notable a member of his own clan. He shrugged, and with but ill grace held his peace.

'Here is what I – what *we* – propose,' Mar went on. 'Argyll holds Stirling Bridge, and watches it like a hawk. There is no bridge lower across the Forth, nor any higher save up at Aberfoyle, twenty miles away. Only boats – ferries. Argyll knows that we cannot bring an army over those, in his teeth. To our cost it has been a wet autumn, and the rivers are running high. So Argyll concentrates his force at Stirling, watches Aberfoyle – and has us held.'

His hearers knew that, every one, all too well. They waited.

Mar, examining his nails went on. 'Our good friend Mac-Gregor of Inversnaid tells me that there are certain fords across the Forth, known to few. Indeed, I understand, known to practically none save himself and one or two of his people. He has, it seems, sometimes found them useful, in the past.'

There were smiles, there – and it was not often that Bobbing John raised a smile.

'These fords, which I believe are set in the midst of a great bog or moss, will be in no good state after these rains. Indeed, to speak in a general way, they will be impassable. They are always impassable, save under skilled guidance. Ordinary troops could not use them, certainly. But Rob Roy believes that he could get special troops across – lightly armed men, used to fording torrents, linked together, using ropes. He believes, gentlemen, that he could get most of of the Highland Division across, given time.'

There was no doubt that he had the interest of all now. An eager hum of talk broke out. A dozen men turned to question Rob.

Mar made his thin voice heard only after banging on his table. 'Once across these fords, the Highland Division could outflank Argyll's left, move in behind him, and cut his communications with Edinburgh and the south. And with the west likewise, so that his reinforcements from the Clyde could not reach him. He would be in a hose-net, gentlemen, surrounded. Lost.'

'If he did not learn about the crossing of the fords, and strike before the fording was finished,' the Earl Marischal objected.

'Precisely, my lord. I said, you will recollect, that Rob could get the Highland Division across, given *time*. That time, my lord, *we* would have to give him.' Mar paused. 'We should have to move forward from Perth here, directly down as though for an attack on Stirling Bridge itself. Our main horsed army. Openly. Very openly. At the same time, our forces in Fife would also move westwards, towards Stirling. Even the Highland Division would break camp and march eastwards, by Strathyre, Callander and Doune, as though making likewise for Stirling Bridge – and only at the last moment, at night, would turn back to make for these fords. Argyll has all too many spies. He would not fail to hear that we are moving on Stirling and the bridge. There is nowhere else that we could be moving against, there. He lacks men. He would concentrate all to hold the bridge. He could do no other.'

There was silence as men digested this, and many nods of approval and agreement. There were head-shakes too, of course. The plan was far from foolproof.

'The venture seems to me sound,' Panmure declared.

'I do not care for it,' Huntly mentioned, shrugging.

Choosing his time Mar brought Rob Roy into it. 'Rob,' he said, 'have you anything to add?'

'Only that I must have time *first*, to be visiting all the fords. I must see the state that they are in, with all this rain. And send you word, before you move, whatever.'

'That is understood.'

'Why are these fords passable only to Highlanders?' that same Viscount Fentoun who had been so anti-Highland at Kelly Castle two years before, demanded. 'Why the Highland Division? If men can cross, horses can cross. Let the cavalry do it. Once across, we can overrun the land faster and to better purpose, cut off Argyll more swiftly. This is work for horse, not foot.'

There was considerable sympathy with this point of view, the Lowland cavaliers much objecting to having to make in effect a mere feint in order to offer the Highlanders a chance for glory.

Nothing more was needed to swing the clan chiefs solidly in favour of the project. Loudly, hands on their claymores, they swore that they would ford that river or nobody would. Neither flood nor man nor devil would stop them – certainly not any trousered Lowlanders.

Mar, who had been prepared to temporise and compromise, as ever, hurriedly changed his mind. All would have their fill of fighting and glory, he assured – though it is doubtful if many heard him in the uproar – for Argyll was not the man to surrender tamely. And promptly, probably wisely, he closed the council.

Rob Roy was given two days to make his inspection and report on the state of the fords of Forth. Meanwhile the entire army in its three divisions would make ready to move.

CHAPTER EIGHTEEN

WEARY, mud-spattered and soaking wet, Rob, stripped to only his kilt, stood back as two MacGregors with great mallets drove a stake firmly into the sloping river-bank and tied the stout grass-rope securely thereto. But though wet, and the night chill and indeed frosty, Rob was far from cold; all night he had laboured as hard as any of his men, much of the time in the icy waters of the swollen Forth, probing, directing, even swimming. The fords, all four of them in the Frew area, had been marked, tested and roped, and reasonably sound tracks through the quaking moss to each of them surveyed and roughly but clearly signposted. Gregorach guides were placed at every difficult point along the routes that the clans would use, scores of men being required for this task; indeed, the entire MacGregor contingent was engaged on this special duty. The river was running high and the fords were not pleasant to use; but with care, and the use of handropes, bold men should be able to retain their footing, and cross.

This Frew area that Rob had chosen was not in the deepest and most daunting part of the Flanders Moss; even he could never have got an army through that. But it was sufficiently desolate and remote for secrecy, the actual fords lying some three miles out into the wilderness south of the village of Thornhill and half that distance north of Kippen on the enemy side, roughly midway up the winding Forth between Stirling and Aberfoyle. There was a fair track down as far as the Mill of Goodie, a mile north of the fords – the miller of which found his lonely premises requisitioned as the night's headquarters. It was near the mill that Rob stood now – for this Goodie Burn had to be crossed also before the clans could reach the main fords, and though a comparatively small stream, it was running faster than the great river, and required to be roped likewise.

It was nearly four o'clock on the morning of 13th November, and Rob was growing just a little anxious. He had been looking for advance parties of the Highland army for over an hour now. Around midnight a courier had brought him the information that the clan army, after marching east and south all day, according to plan, had duly turned back westwards at Doune, under cover of darkness, heading for here. Doune was a bare seven miles away, and he had expected the vanguard ere this. It would be daylight in three hours, and it was vital that at least the majority of the army should be across the fords and fanning out beyond by that time. It would be a slow process, inevitably.

The drumming hooves of a fast-ridden horse sounded on the frosty night. Rob heard it draw up at the mill, and then hurrying footsteps as a gillie brought the messenger to him. This would be General Gordon's forerunner, announcing that the army was approaching.

But as he loomed out of the dark, Rob perceived that the courier was no Highlander but an officer dressed in Lowland fashion.

'Are you MacGregor? MacGregor of Inversnaid . . . Rob Roy?' he demanded, peering doubtfully at the half-naked and mud-stained apparition.

'None other, sir.'

'I have had the devil's own trouble finding you,' the other complained. 'I have orders for you, from the Captain-General. You are to leave here at once, and proceed with your MacGregor contingent with all speed to Ardoch on the River Allan, there to rejoin the Highland Division.'

Rob Roy stared. 'Good God, man – are you crazy?' he

215

cried. 'Ardoch, you said? Near to Dunblane? Rejoin the
Highland Division . . . ?'

'Yes, As quick as you may. Those are my lord of Mar's
orders.'

'But . . . *diabhol* – the Highland Division is here, whatever! Or nearly. What folly is this?'

'The Highland Division is turned back, sir. Has been
these four hours. Marching for Ardoch. It is joining the
main army there. It should be there before daylight. All
plans are changed.'

'But . . .' Rob swallowed, his great fists clenching. 'Why?'
Why, man – in the name of Heaven?'

'Because Argyll has outwitted us. Stolen his march on us.
He did not wait for us behind Stirling Bridge. Hearing that
we were on the move, damn him, he has moved himself,
north to meet us – it is believed in order to drive a wedge
between our main force and the Highland Division. He lies
on the south slopes of Sheriff Muir now, and we lie on the
north.'

'*Dia* – he does? Red John of the Battles is a man for you!'
Rob exclaimed in involuntary admiration. 'With less than
half our numbers, he does not sit and wait for us. He attacks!
But . . . what is Mar at, man? Why has he changed the
plan?'

'I should have thought that would be obvious, sir. Argyll
seeks to drive up the Allan Water between our divisions,
and so split us. The Captain-General, by quickly altering
his plans will bring in the Highland Division to join him
at Ardoch and so spoil the enemy's manoeuvre. By acting
thus swiftly he will present Argyll with a united army.
There was just time for it to be done . . .'

'By acting thus, Mother of God, he is throwing away his
greatest advantage!' Rob interrupted. 'Can you not see it?
We still have to cross the Forth. The Highland Division
behind Argyll's back, would be worth three times what it is
facing him. Red John's move forwards make our move

twice as good as it was, whatever. Clearly he knows naught of our plan – of this crossing of the fords – or he would never have dared to leave Stirling. It is all the more important that we cross here, as arranged. We can sweep round behind him, take Stirling and its bridge like ripe plums – and he is trapped between the Forth and Mar. Can you not see it, man?'

The officer shrugged. 'Whether I see this or that is no matter, sir. Your orders are to retire to Ardoch forthwith.'

'But this is folly. Your orders are folly. What fool gave Mar such advice?'

'It is the Captain-General's own decision, sir.'

'Then the Captain-General is a fool!' Rob roared. 'Curse him for a fool, as well as a craven and a turncoat! Men's lives hang on this – many lives of better men than Bobbing John. Not to mention a throne, whatever!'

The courier had stepped back a pace or two in the face of Rob's towering wrath – as many another had done before him. But he held his ground in other respects. 'Sir, I think that you forget yourself,' he said, if with little confidence. 'It is not for you, nor myself, to question the orders of the Captain-General. . . .'

'Orders can be changed,' Rob rapped. 'Especially the orders of a fool! They *must* be changed. It may not yet be too late. The Highland Division must be turned again – back to cross these fords. You must turn them. . . .'

'I will do no such thing, 'fore God!' the other declared strongly.

'Then *I* will! I will ride, at once, I will see Gordon. If he will not heed me, then Clanranald will. And Glengarry. And Duart, and the rest. I . . .'

'You are too late, MacGregor. However fast you ride, they will be at Ardoch before you. Hours before. Even now they will be nearing the camp. You are too late. Battle may be joined before you could get there.'

Panting with his anger and frustration, Rob glared at the

man – and knew that what he said was true. It was too late. The die was cast. The sinews of neither man nor beast could bring him to the clan army before it joined Mar. Nor bring him to Ardoch before daylight. Even if foolish men would listen to him when he got there. Something like a groan escaped him.

The courier heard – and wisely reckoned that the time was ripe to take his departure. 'You . . . you will bring your MacGregors as quickly as may be?' he reminded falteringly – and without awaiting any answer, turned and strode back towards the mill and his horse.

For long Rob Roy stared into the empty darkness, biting his lip, tugging his beard, a prey to his most savage emotions. Then, at length, he sighed, and turned to the matter on hand. It would take time, considerable time, to reassemble his men. They were scattered widely, individually and in parties, at strategic points over a large area of the morass and its approaches. And Gregor, with an advance party, was already across the fords of Frew, keeping watch on the enemy side. Wearily, Rob sent for his running gillies.

*　　*　　*

The MacGregors, reinforced by a detachment of Badenoch MacPhersons from Cluny's contingent, sent by General Gordon to aid them at the fords, were delayed in rejoining the main army for a number of reasons. The first was obvious; there were almost a score of rough miles between Frew and Ardoch, and the Gregorach had been arduously employed for thirty-six hours without a break already. Then, about 10 o'clock on a sparkling cold morning, another courier found them, up on the long Braes of Doune, from General Gordon. He informed them that the two armies were already in contact, manoeuvring for position about the long ridge of the Sheriff Muir, and that the MacGregors were now to change direction and make to cross the Allan Water at Kinbuck, and so to connect up with the right wing of the Highland Division, which was of course on the right of Mar's line. Rob Roy accordingly turned his tired company south by east.

Long before they reached the neighbourhood of Kinbuck and its ford, the sound of gunfire was rumbling across the wide strath to them. That could only be Argyll's cannon, for the Jacobite artillery unfortunately was still in France. Everywhere men's lips tightened and weary bodies tensed.

Then, as they hurried down the green haughlands of the Lodge Burn, still a couple of miles from Kinbuck, one of Rob's scouts came back to report that the way ahead was blocked. A party of cavalry was halted in the grassy valley around a bend in front, apparently eating mid-day lunch – and though they were not red-coated dragoons there were red-coats amongst them. Cursing, Rob and Gregor crept forward to investigate.

Sure enough by accident or design, their road was barred. What looked like a full squadron of light horse filled the haughland. By their motley dress they might have been Jacobite insurgents – were it not for the few red-coated regulars vivid amongst them. Almost certainly they were a mounted detachment of the Glasgow Whig Fencibles that Argyll had recruited, stiffened by Light Dragoon officers. Whether they were here as providing defence in depth for the ford at Kinbuck – the first point at which the Allan Water could be crossed above Dunblane – or whether they had merely halted for a meal on their way elsewhere, could not be known. But there they were.

A council of war followed. To attack, or to move back discreetly and cross this Lodge Burn higher up, to seek to come at Kinbuck by another approach? Discussion of the matter was little more than a formality, of course – for these were Gregorach and not noted for discreet withdrawals; moreover, fatigue not withstanding, they were spoiling for a fight, what with one thing and another. And with their 300, against little more than half that number – even of cavalry – self-respect was at stake.

'Three parties of a hundred each,' Rob directed. 'Glengyle on the right, Coiletter on the left. Myself, I am getting old and will take the centre, for peace and quiet! The enemy are all on this side of the burn. Coiletter will make a wide circuit and come up at them from below. Glengyle will cross the burn up here, out of sight, and come down on them openly on the far side. They will have to cross to get at him – and while they are at it and their backs turned, myself I will descend upon them safely! Och, it will be simplicity itself, just.'

The best military manoeuvres are always the simplest. After Coiletter's hundred had been given some fifteen minutes to get into position further down, Gregor and his men, stripped to only their kilts, plunged across the stream. It was running high but came only up to their breasts – nothing to men who had spent the night coping with the swirling Forth. Once across, they proceeded down the far side – and the moment that they came within sight of the enemy, still some three hundred yards off, they fired a random volley of shots, drew their broadswords, and with a wild shouting of 'Gregalach! Gregalach!' charged downstream.

The effect on the Fencibles was remarkable. It was as though an ants' nest had been disturbed. The shouting there was almost as loud as was the MacGregors'. But bellowed commands gradually prevailed, reinforced by blaring bugle calls, and in some fashion the squadron proceeded to mount and raggedly to cross the burn to meet its insolent attackers.

Gregor and his men, in consequence of this delayed reaction, were almost at the waterside to meet them as the first troopers came splashing and clambering out. Broadswords clashed with sabres, pistols banged, men bawled, and horses whinnied and screamed. In effect, Gregor's clansmen were lining the far bank, waiting for the cavalrymen as they came straggling over.

The dragoon officers soon saw the folly of this, and the bugles blew again and again to bring order and cohesion to the excited volunteers. It was then that a wild slogan-shouting from downstream turned all eyes thitherwards. Coiletter's party was coming storming up, on both sides of the burn, distant yet but vociferous. Orders and bugle notes grew the more urgent, if no less confused.

Grimly laughing, Rob waited behind the summit of the steep bank above, holding back his impatient men. One troop of the enemy, seeming to be somewhat better disciplined than the others, was beginning to splash across the stream, half-right, towards a point where they could clamber out unimpeded and so keep the two Gregorach parties from joining up. Gregor, perceiving the danger, promptly detached a proportion of his men to head them off – thereby weakening his retaining force. Orders for a concerted charge towards him were shouted.

Rob glanced over at Coiletter's racing warriors, nodded, and raised his arm, broadswords drawn. With a roar, in which the MacPherson slogan mingled with that of Mac-Gregor and dreaded name of Rob Roy, the third party hurled itself directly down the steep slope.

It was too much for amateur soldiers, however gallant. Not knowing which way to turn, which officer to obey, nor where the next blow might fall, and obviously outnumbered, the Fencibles lost their heads completely. Better trained men than these have done the same at less provocation, frequently – without Rob Roy's terrible name being thrown into the scales.

There was comparatively little blood-letting, in the end, most of the actual killing being done by Gregor's men on first reaching the bank; mounted men at least have this advantage that they can usually extract themselves with greater success from the clutches of the unhorsed. Thus, as with one accord if in varying directions, the Fencibles proceeded to do without further delay. Their regular officers appeared to see no point in lingering far behind. Whooping with triumph, the Highlanders speeded their departure from the scene as best they might, and stared resentfully at those who had insisted on surrendering.

There was more plunder, undoubtedly, than would have been the case with a regular unit. And the midday meal had happily been left almost untouched.

It was some little time before Rob was able to resume his march for Kinbuck. The Artillery fire had died away, he noted.

*   *   *

Climbing out of the valley of the Lodge Burn, in order to cut off a corner, the MacGregors reached the crest of the little ridge that separated it from the wide gently sloping strath of Allan. And there they halted abruptly to stare.

As well they might. A far-flung, complicated and astonishing prospect greeted them. Before them lay the Allan Water running broad and yellow and fast through grassy levels, with the baggage wagons of the Jacobite army drawn up just across from them, and the hamlet of Kinbuck a little way to the left. Beyond, the land lifted and lifted, out of the green of grassland into the dark brown of heather moor, up and up through rolling undulations to a long ridge more than two miles away, that was but the outlying rampart of the Ochil Hills. That ridge and its heather flanks was known as the Sheriff Muir, a lonely place of barren desolation. But today it was not desolate, not in its usual sense – though to many men undoubtedly it represented the ultimate desolation itself. It was in fact a battlefield, spread out before the newcomers like any stage backcloth, the steady lift of the land to the final ridge offering an almost unbroken prospect to the beholders.

But however clear the prospect visually, its interpretation was anything but clear. No battlefield, probably, is ever clear, during the actual fighting, even to the generals who seek to order it. But Sheriff Muir was in a category by itself for confusion. In the early afternoon of that frosty November day it represented chaos, widespread, comprehensive and appalling.

Men were moving everywhere over that extensive panorama. They moved in every direction, too, in large numbers and small – and many, it could be seen, did not move at all. There was nothing resembling a line anywhere to be seen, a front or any recognisable formation of either side. There seemed, at this stage, to be surprisingly little actual fighting going on – though that might be a misconception. Clouds of smoke lay heavily on the still air – but this appeared to emanate mainly from one or two points where the heather had been set on fire, rather than from artillery and gunfire. The sound of scattered and ragged musketry echoed across the strath, punctuating a more continuous sound that rose and fell like the sigh and sob of the tide on a distant sandbar, remote and impersonal – but which represented the voices of men, wailing, shouting, commanding, imploring, screaming and moaning; a peculiarly futile and weary sound, with less reality to it than the yittering of the curlews amongst the hillocks at the MacGregors' backs.

Rob gazed urgently, seeking to probe, distinguish, assess. The vivid scarlet uniforms of Argyll's regular troops at least ought to have been a guide to dispositions – but the scarlet was just as much scattered and dispersed over the scene as were the less outstanding colours of other men. Certainly there seemed to be a fairly large body of red-clad men up on the summit ridge to the right, stationary and seeming partly to block out from view an even larger nondescript mass of men further back and slightly to the north. But that was of little help. Groups of red-coats, mounted and foot, were moving hither and thither elsewhere over the wide vista, some hurrying, some not – but the same applied to other men; who were advancing and who retreating was impossible to tell. All that could be said for certain was that many of both sides lay fallen and unmoving.

Shaking his head in perplexity, Rob transferred his gaze from the wider scene to a vicinity closer at hand, where Gregor was pointing excitedly – to the left foreground, in fact. A continuous stream of men was coming down off the higher ground. Men were plunging into the rushing Allan Water at the Kinbuck ford and struggling across, many to cast themselves down on this side as though exhausted, others to hurry on, through the hamlet and beyond. These were almost all Highlanders, many of them wounded and bloody, others naked or nearly so, some without arms or targes. Not a few stumbled and staggered as they ran. They looked like defeated men.

'Campbells! Stewarts of Appin! Murrays of Atholl!' the keen-eyed Gregor cried. 'Dark tartans.'

'Aye,' his uncle nodded grimly. 'But what of these?' And he pointed, in his turn.

Coming upstream, from the Dunblane direction, were more men, many men, strung out down the valley as far as eye could see. These too were Highlanders, large numbers of them still wearing the Jacobite white cockade. There seemed to be few wounded amongst these, all were well armed, and any staggering and stumbling appeared to be occasioned by the heavy and miscellaneous burdens with which they cheerfully loaded themselves. There was no dejection in this stream, no falling down exhausted. Their fording of the river seemed, compared with the others, more in the nature of a frolic.

'Clan Donald,' Gregor observed, rubbing his chin. 'The Macleans. Glengarry's people. What means this?'

Rob shook his head. 'It behoves us to find out,' he said. 'Myself, I do not like it. Greg – go you down there to the ford, and bring me up two men, one of each sort, of each company. Intelligent men if it may be, who can answer questions.'

Gregor came back presently with three informants – a

young MacDonell who said that he was second son of
Arasdale in Glengarry's country, and much pleased with
himself; a brother of Campbell of Inverlyon, a Breadalbane
man known to the MacGregors; and an unhorsed Lowland
officer called Skene, one of the Earl of Panmure's corps,
with a musket ball through his shoulder. The last two were
less than cheerful.

'All is lost, Rob!' the Campbell declared without pre-
amble, as he came up. 'We are cut to pieces. My brother is
dead. As is Cononish and Ardmoine. Glendaruel himself
is sore wounded. God knows how many others. The Robertsons are broke and Struan a prisoner. The Atholl men are
scattered. The horse it was that failed us, damn them. . . .'

'You lie, fellow!' the Lowlander broke in. 'We failed
nobody. We were transferred to the right. We but obeyed
our orders. . . .'

'Orders to desert us – to abandon us to Argyll's cavalry,
while you rode off after the MacDonalds, you Lowland
scum!'

'Peace, gentlemen!' Rob commanded. 'Quiet you, Ewan –
I want news, not bickering.'

'Och, you will be getting it from neither of these, whatever,' the MacDonell cried. 'They are poor creatures, who
know not one side of a claymore from the other. Heed
them not. *We* won the day for them. Clan Donald ate up
the Sasunnachs like stubble, my God! Before our broadswords they fell like corn, just – like ripe corn, I tell you!
Och, it was magnificent! All the way to Dunblane we
chased them. . . .'

'And the accursed horse followed you, and left us naked!'

'We were *ordered* to the right, I tell you. "Horse to the
right" we were ordered. We could not but follow them.'

'And left us dead men! The Greys rode through us and
through us. . . .'

'We cut them down like thistles, just. We took their

banners. We spoiled them. The sons of Donald drank blood!'

'Strathmore fell. Huntly was dragged off his horse, and is a prisoner. My own beast was shot under me, and I have a ball in my shoulder ...'

'The Mackenzies are slain! I saw Seaforth fall. The Chisholms are no more ...'

'We smote them hip and thigh! We chased them off the field, whatever! They begged for mercy on their trousered knees. . . .'

'As Royal's my Race – *I* beg for mercy!' Rob Roy roared, slashing his hand down in a fierce cutting motion. 'Enough of this babble! Answer only my questions. Speak you only when I bid you. Men are dying while you deafen us. Now – you MacDonell. Tell me ...'

By means of careful questioning and cross-questioning, Rob presently obtained what he hoped might be a reasonably clear picture of what undoubtedly was a highly confused battle. In effect, the right wings of both armies had triumphed. The Jacobite right, after winning the race for the ridge about an hour before noon, under the proud command of the impetuous Clanranald, had flung themselves into the attack first, before their left wing was in position.

Two battalions of his own MacDonalds, two of Glengarry's MacDonells, one of Mull Macleans and one of lesser clans. They had driven irresistibly through the Hanoverian left, smashing four of Argyll's best regular regiments of foot – the Royals, the Devons, The West Yorks and the Worcesters – and not only these but cavalry backing also, the 3rd and 7th Dragoons, chasing them all in headlong rout southwards right to Dunblane town. General Witham who commanded had last been seen spurring hard for Stirling and the south. They had, of course, found plenty of plunder in Dunblane – and that had been the end of the battle for many of the brave sons of Donald. Clanranald's fall at the height of the engagement had not helped in the bringing of his corps back under control. The second line, Mackenzies under Seaforth and Gordons under Glenbucket, had followed on, to turn Argyll's flank.

The left wing, Struan's Robertsons, young Locheil's Camerons and the Breadalbane Campbells, had had further to go to reach the ridge. They were forming up ready to charge in turn, when Argyll acted. Perceiving what was happening to his left, he did not wait for a similar fate to overtake his right. He had held back his infantry and flung in right away his main cavalry support – and the best cavalry in the world, at that, the Royal Scots Greys. Hundreds of them thundered down on the waiting mid-Highland clansmen. The clans stood firm. It had apparently been at this moment that Mar, seeing a situation that no infantry on earth could face successfully, had sent the urgent warning to his own supporting horse, hidden behind a fold of the moor – 'Cavalry on the right!' It had been a warning, yes, and a wise one – but it was not wisely worded. Cavalry on the right, the Angus and Fifeshire cavaliers had heard, and taken it as an order. And off to the right they had trotted forthwith, obediently, to go pounding after Clanranald's victorious warriors: And the left-wing clans were indeed left, abandoned, to face the avalanche of grey horses. They had been cut to pieces where they stood, as to and fro, backwards and forwards the troopers rode them down. No less than six times they turned and faced right-about. And after the Greys, Argyll had thrown in everything that he had left to command. The second line, the Atholl men, the Drummonds and the rest, could not hold them. The entire Jacobite left had collapsed.

After that, evidently, the Sheriff Muir belonged to anybody and nobody. Utter confusion had reigned. But whilst one disordered horde had had Red John of the Battles to command it, one of Marlborough's most experienced generals, the other had only Bobbing John, the agile politician.

That was the situation, so far as Rob Roy could unravel it. It left him in no little quandary and turmoil of mind.

Not so Gregor of Glengyle. He had no doubts. 'Lord!' he cried impatiently, as his uncle turned from his questioning. 'We wait here while others fight – as you said yourself, while good men are dying! Come – let us be doing, for God's sake!'

'Aye, lad,' Rob nodded, set-faced. 'But, where?'

'What do you mean?'

The older man waved his arm. 'There is the battlefield. Miles of it, man. Who do we fight? And where?'

'I care not – so long as fight we do, whatever!'

'Spoken like your own self, Greg! Myself, I prefer a more definite target! Mar had 15,000 men, and more. 10,000 of them must still be over there, somewhere. Our 300 will not ...'.

He paused. A more localised noise had been growing through the general hubbub for some little time. Now it attracted more attention, drawing the eyes to a point a little way upstream where a fold in the land created by a tributary burn opened on to the Allan Water. Out of this fold a trickle of men was issuing, a trickle that grew rapidly into a flood, that surged on down towards the ford also.

These were Highlanders, likewise. Soon they were identifiable as mainly Camerons. There were many wounded amongst them, too. But this contingent was different from either of the other two streams of men already straggling through Kinbuck. It did not straggle, for one thing; there was discipline here, command, control. Presently a banner came into sight torn and tattered but still fluttering proudly above the heads of marching men.

'The Arrows of Locheil!' Rob said. 'One flag that still flies.'

As the mass of the newcomers debouched into the main

228

valley, parties broke off to right and left quickly to take up defensive positions covering the line of retiral. On through these the pacing ranks came, the banner in their midst.

'*Dia* – Locheil is master of Clan Cameron yet!' Gregor exclaimed. 'But . . , think you that they are leaving the field?'

'Aye. It seems so. But, see you what they are at? The enemy must be close behind for them to act so.'

'Yes. Yes – we must go to their aid, then.'

'Wait you,' his uncle said. 'What is the river for?'

The Camerons came on, and presently, after a sizeable gap, another smaller tighter group of them came hurrying out of the side valley, broadswords drawn – the rearguard. They took over the positions of the defensive picket, who then came on.

'We can at least aid them at the ford,' Gregor urged.

'Do that,' Rob nodded. 'Take a score of men.' He himself remained in front of his serried ranks of MacGregors up on their vantage point.

It was there, presently, that John Cameron, Younger of Locheil, came to him wearily, his bannerman at his side. Blood dripped from a graze at his temple.

'Heaven's mercy, Rob,' he greeted. 'This is an ill day – and you with the best of it.'

'Aye, John – I believe you. An ill day. We are new come from the fords at Frew. And you – you have had enough of it?'

'By all the powers, I have!' Locheil's son and heir cried. 'I came to fight not to be made a fool of. This is not a battle – it is a fool's playground! We have not a general – only a posturing ape! I have not received one command, one order, this day!'

'Mar has lost his head?'

'Aye – if he ever had one, God's curse on him! We have suffered four hours of his folly, and I have lost four score of better men than he! I will hazard no more, for naught.'

'Is the King's crown naught?' Gregor demanded, but with less than his usual conviction.

'You were being followed?' Rob put in quickly, and waved his hand towards where the Cameron's rearguard crouched.

'Aye. By a regiment of Fusiliers, and others – a plague on them. We have had them on our heels this hour back. But we have kept them at arms length. They are little trouble – not like the Greys. Those ones are devils incarnate. All day they have haunted us. There is no peace from them. Without them I think Argyll would have achieved little.'

'And these others – the Fusiliers. Are they close?'

'They were. Och, but they have been the less keen as we neared this river. Now I think that they hang back. They may not wish to face the crossing. It may be that their scouts have seen you MacGregors waiting here, fresh.'

'It may be so. Where is General Gordon, John?'

'I know not, and I care not!' the younger man declared.

'And Mar?'

'They say that he is up there on the ridge, biting his nails. Waiting – for what, God above only knows! He has still many men up there, they say – most of the horse, and the Lowlanders and half the Gordons. But what difference does it make? He will not use them aright. . . .'

A new surge of men appearing now from one of the undulations across the river, downstream, drew their attention. It did not demand any very keen perception to see that these were actually fighting their way – indeed more and more of scarlet came into view behind them, until the lower valley on the far side was a mass of red. There was comparatively little musket-fire, though a great deal of other noise; no doubt both sides would be running very low in ammunition by this time. As yet it was not possible to identify the retiring force.

'We can advance to the aid of these, at the least,' the eager Gregor asserted.

'And throw away the strongest position in sight?' his uncle gave gack. 'No, lad – we can do better than that.' He turned to his waiting men, raising his voice, and gave the command for three volleys of musketry, aimed into the air above the approaching combatants, at the same time ordering the MacGregor banner to be raised aloft.

His strategem was highly effective. The three distinct and regular salvoes crashing out, orderly and disciplined and massive – for the MacGregors had had ample practice with their fine Government weapons, thanks to Montrose's lavish provision – gave new life to the retreating men and brought the pursuing red-coats to an abrupt halt. Here, obviously, were Jacobite reinforcements, fresh troops evidently with no shortage of ammunition. Perhaps someone even was able to identify the MacGregor banner. Caution could not have been more clearly indicated.

The newcomers proved to be the Robertsons, a badly decimated version of the fine body of men that Struan had put into the field, but still in good heart. With them were a fair sprinkling of Appin Stewarts – all, like the Camerons, part of the broken Jacobite left wing. Eager hands aided them across the ford.

The red-coats, keeping their distance beyond effective musket range, contented themselves with harrying the broken men who still thronged down all along that valley to reach the comparative safety of the far river bank.

Rob was surprised to see a lean and ascetic-seeming man of middle years limping at the head of the Robertsons. 'Struan!' he cried, 'Here at least is something to offer thanks for. I heard that you were captured.'

'Aye, and so I was, Rob. But they could not hold so aged and wily a campaigner.' Alexander Robertson. 17th of Struan, was a veteran of Dundee's campaigns and had served in exile with the French army. 'But I'll not say that I was not glad to see you here.'

'You were hard pressed?'

231

'Hard enough. I tried to rejoin Mar, but the enemy cavalry is everywhere. Those accursed Greys! And Mar keeps our own horse standing up yonder on the ridge like any royal bodyguard. Perhaps to support the honour of his new dukedom!'

'Dukedom . . . ?'

'Aye – heard you not? Just before the battle was joined, a courier from France arrived. King Jamie did not come himself – but turned Bobbing John into a duke instead! *Dia* – likely that is what has been on his mind this sorry day, instead of soldiering! God save us all, but it is a mad world! Ha – is that young Locheil? I heard that he was down. . . .'

More and more Government troops were converging now on the east bank of the Allan Water, cavalry as well as foot, the Greys' pale horses amongst them.

John Cameron, a fire-eater himself, if somewhat over-shadowed by the reputation of his fierce old father Sir Ewan, was staring back unhappily at the enemy. 'Think you, Rob,' he said, 'with your people and mine, and Struan's, as well as some of these broken men – think you we might not yet fall on the red-coats? If we crossed the river above and below them, we could turn their flank.'

'To what purpose, John?'

'We . . . we might rally this whole wing.'

'Again, to what purpose, at all? So long as Mar sits up there?'

'At the least we could kill some of the creatures!' Gregor broke in.

'Aye – kill and be killed. Without cavalry we cannot effectively fight theirs. We would still be a prey to the Greys.'

'We fought cavalry a while back, and had them running.'

'Only because we surprised them. There can be no surprise here. In morass or on a mountainside, foot may fight cavalry, and win maybe. But never on open ground such as this.'

'Rob is right I dare swear,' Struan Robertson said. 'There is no profit here. Myself I am tired, and my lads are tired. Many are wounded. With you it may be different. I am going back to Ardoch and the camp. Would it was to Struan itself! Shall we march in company, Rob?'

'God forbid . . .!' Gregor began, when Rob cut in swiftly.

'No. We wait. At the least, we can cover your retiral. And that of others.'

'As you will. For myself, I have seen enough madness and to spare for one day. . . .'

In the end, with a fair show of reluctance, young Locheil went with the Robertsons, lurching off on the arm of his brawny bannerman.

In compact martial array the MacGregors stood their ground on their hillock, like a stout rock in a flood of waters.

*   *   *

'I will stand here no longer, and see my honour spat upon by all who pass!' Gregor of Glengyle exclaimed hotly. 'I have borne it as long as I can, God forgive me!'

'Your honour, it is a great trouble to you,' his uncle declared heavily. 'I think that you would be well advised to take it in hand, Greg!'

'The clan's honour, then! Will you scoff at that?'

'The clan may have more to lose than honour on this field, lad. Are you wholly blind?'

'I see all to clearly, more's the pity! I see a battle lost for want of wit and want of courage and want of a man to take a decision. I little thought to see the MacGregors standing by these two hours, watching, their hands empty, their swords unblooded! The Gregorach!'

'You had rather that we had gone hot-foot in, and died uselessly?'

233

'I had rather only that we had acted as men!'

'Men,' Rob repeated. 'What is a man but his life, whatever? Is a corpse a man? How many MacGregors would you have die for a king who twiddles his thumbs in France, and a general who twiddles them up on yonder ridge?'

'But . . . but.' Shocked, the younger man eyed his former tutor and mentor.

'This from you, from Rob Roy MacGregor! This woman's talk!'

'Perhaps I have a thought for the women, this day,' the older man said sombrely. 'They are Clan Alpine also, are they not?'

'Lord – you will not fight for thinking of the women!' Gregor exploded. 'Upon my soul – what has come over you? A while back, at the Lodge Burn, you were not loth to fight. You had no ear for women's wails then. . . .'

'Then it was otherwise, Greg – as you must see. The die was not cast. We were still hastening to this battle – that is no longer a battle. That was but a local skirmish, where I had no fears but that we should triumph, and at little price. Even if we had failed, the price would have been small, in those circumstances. Now . . .' Rob shrugged heavy shoulders. 'We can *only* fail – and at a heavy price, a terrible price. The price of the future existence of our small and harried clan. A price that I am not prepared to pay, whatever. Look at these men at our backs, boy – look at them, I say.' The older man's voice quivered, but powerfully. 'They are all that malice and envy and strife have left of a once-great people. Clan Alpine, the sons of kings – there it is! Save for the boys, the dotards and the women. Would you squander it all on a lost battle, a dilatory king, and a timerous fool of a general? Would you?'

Before the pent-up emotion, almost the ferocity, of that demand, Gregor faltered. But only physically and momentarily. 'If . . . if it was my duty – yes.' he said thickly.

'Duty! Duty to whom, man? To James Stewart in France? To this new Bobbing Grace up on the hill there? Or to your own people whom you were born to serve? I thank God that *you* are not Captain of Clan Alpine this day! But *I* am – and I know *my* duty. It is to the clan first. Here we stand.'

For a full hour since the Robertsons and the Camerons had gone, the MacGregors had stood drawn up on their hillock, in solid silent ranks, plain for all to see, while the aftermath of battle eddied crazily around them. Cries, appeals and taunts had been directed at them, fists shaken. Only one or two of the broken lost rabble that streamed off blood-soaked Sheriff Muir had blessed them for standing there fast and firm in a disintegrating world and holding the ford of the Allan safe for all who could reach it. For their stand had been not altogether negative. The Government forces, wary and suspicious of that strongly placed threatening and uncommitted body of men, had kept their distance, and taken up defensive positions, out of range, to seek to contain them if they moved over. Even a detachment of the Greys had sheered off.

But none of this was enough for Gregor of Glengyle. As his uncle had pointed to the men at their backs, so did he. 'The clan! The clan!' he exclaimed. 'Always you name the clan. But there stands the clan – there! Ask them. The Gregorach are nothing if not fighting men. Think you that these feel as you do? Think you they have no minds of their own? They would fight, to a man!'

'They will do my bidding,' Rob said, without turning his head. 'So long as I am Captain, every man here will do my bidding. *Every* man!'

Gregor scanned all those faces behind him appealingly, hard strong faces. All stared directly ahead of them, grimly, fiercely, or blankly. None met his eye.

Only one man spoke, and he was no MacGregor, but one Alexander Macpherson, a burly drover from Laggan, in charge of the small party of Cluny's men attached to Rob's force.

'I am with Glengyle, Rob,' he declared, and his announcement was almost a shout, to bolster his resolve to oppose Rob Roy. 'I say that we can do no other than fight, whatever!'

'*You* say?' Rob turned now. '*You* say, Sandie?' The scorn was withering.

'Aye, I do.' Not liking the MacGregor's look, the man turned to his own Macphersons. 'Let us endure this no longer!' he cried. 'If he will not lead you, I will!'

There was a tense silence.

Rob broke it, his voice now, strangely, more pleasant. 'Were the question about driving Highland stots or kyloes, Sandie, I would yield to your superior skill.' These two had co-operated on many a cattle drive. 'But as it respects the leading of men, I must be allowed to be the better judge.'

'Did the matter respect driving Glen Angus stots, the question with Rob would not be which was to be last, but which was to be foremost, whatever!'

'Very good,' Rob nodded mildly. 'If you, Sandie – or any other man soever – would be foremost now, let him stand forward.' His hand slid down to the hilt of his broadsword. 'We shall settle the matter promptly, once and for all, I promise you.'

No man moved, no man spoke, almost it seemed that no man so much as breathed.

'Aye, then,' Rob almost sighed, and turned back to face the front, stocky, steady, firm-rooted as any tree.

Gregor all but groaned. 'There goes King Jamie's crown, then!' he said bitterly. 'Yonder sits Mar – and here stands MacGregor! And nothing achieved.'

'If they could not do it without me, they would not do it with me,' Rob Roy answered heavily, levelly, but finally. 'Peace, Greg.'

CHAPTER NINETEEN

ROB topped the long climb from Strathfillan to the pass, wearily, and drew rein at the summit to look down on the small fair oasis of Auchinchisallan, green amongst the sombre brown even in mid-December. And he sighed. He was alone; not even MacAlastair rode at his back. Better that way.

It was four weeks since Sheriff Muir, four sorry weeks for Scotland – and sorrier ones still for Rob Roy. The Jacobite cause was not so much defeated as suffering spontaneous disintegration. Sheriff Muir, despite all follies and failures, had not been a victory for Argyll; indeed, he had withdrawn from the field under cover of night, back beyond Dunblane, to lick his wounds, harder hit than anyone knew, leaving Mar still standing unmoving rather than immovable on the ridge where he had stood so stubbornly and unaccountably all afternoon. But in the morning, stiff and cold after another bitter night, instead of exploiting this residual advantage of being left in possession of the field, Mar had tamely retired back to Ardoch and Perth. And thereafter, since nothing more grievously disaffected Highlanders than retreat and indecision, the clans had begun to trickle off homewards into their mountains. One after another, under this pretext or that, or none at all, they had gone – MacDonalds, MacKenzies, Camerons, Macleans, Robertsons, Gordons, in large numbers and small they slipped away, having lost faith in their leaders and their cause.

A scapegoat inevitably had become necessary, for the cause in general and the army in particular. Mar himself did not suffice – for no one had held him in high opinion anyway, and criticism of Bobbing John was nothing new; moreover he still remained Commander-in-Chief, and so was unsuitable for open raillery. Others' reputations suffered likewise, of course – but then most of these were not sufficiently well known outside their own districts and spheres to fit the part.

But Rob Roy MacGregor was different. He was a hero, a paladin, an idol – now fallen. And there is nothing more satisfactory for angry and humiliated men to kick than a fallen idol. He had failed them, failed the army, failed the King. There were no doubts, no question about it. Everyone knew – whatever they themselves had done – what *he* had done, or not done. He had stood by while others fought and died. He had taken no part in the battle. He had held back his clan when they wished to fight. None, not even his own kith and kin, could deny it. Rob Roy was branded in the eyes of all men as rogue, craven – or worse, traitor.

Many things about Rob had been forgotten, then. But again, others were remembered. For instance, that he was a far-out connection of Argyll's, and that the Duke was said to have been notably gentle with him over his activities when outlawed. Might he not have been bribed to play the part that he did? And was his mother not a Campbell? Again, was he not famed for his fondness for other folks' goods? Had he not held his men back, perhaps, so that they might rob the baggage trains of whichever side lost? Was that not typical of the man? Certainly Mar's baggage down at Kin-buck, had been harried by somebody....

And so Rob, after four grim weeks of it, had resigned his command to Gregor, turned his back on his fellows, and come home, more of an outcast than he had ever been in his outlawry. Why he came to Auch, the home that was no home to him, he might have found it hard to explain – save that it was Christmastide and his sons might possibly be looking for him. The fact was, of course, that he had nowhere else to go; his journey, even through a corner of his own clan country, had quickly demonstrated that.

He came down the hill to the cottage, snug under the remote snow-capped Beinn Dorain, and, though he did not realise it, his wide shoulders were bowed as though under a heavy load and a great tiredness. A few hundred yards from the house, the three boys emerged from the doorway and came running at their varying speeds to meet him – and his heart lifted a little. But their greetings were brief and perfunctory. Where was MacAlastair, they wanted to know? And Donald? And all the fine chiefs that had passed this way before? And how many men had their father killed in the battle? As they turned away disappointed, Rob saw himself as all but a stranger to them.

He walked his garron up to the cottage, bent of head. He perceived that Mary was standing in the doorway. He looked at her, and then looked quickly away. 'Well, Mary,' he said.

'Well, Rob,' she answered quietly, 'You have come, then.'

'Aye, I have come. You do not object to that, I hope?'

'No. No, Rob.'

'I am glad of that. I see you well, I hope?'

'Well enough, yes. And . . . and you?'

'I am tired,' he said.

She led him indoors, to the chair by the fire. She put before him whisky and cold venison and bannocks and honey. She spoke no more than he.

But she watched him, hunched there, staring into the fire, and presently she touched his shoulder lightly. 'Take them,' she urged. 'Eat and drink. It will help.'

He gave a single twitch of the head. 'Let be,' he said. 'I am tired, just.'

'Tired yes – but more than tired.'

Her tone turned him round to look at her. 'What mean you?' he asked.

'I mean that you need not carry your load in this house, Rob. Not here.'

He stared. 'Then . . . you *know*?' he said hoarsely.

'All the world knows,' she answered simply. 'Even I.'

The man swallowed, and his fist clenched. 'Then you know that your husband is a coward, a dastard and a traitor!' he exclaimed. 'In this very chair, one time, you named me no man. It seems that you were right, does it not?'

She shook her dark head wordlessly.

'You will know, since all the world knows, that I have cost King James his crown, lost a battle, sold my honour, failed the clans and tarnished the name of MacGregor for ever! That you know, also?'

'Should I know it, Rob?'

'Why not? No others doubt it.' Something in her voice made him look up, lost as he was in himself. 'But what has come over you, woman? It is nothing to you . . . now.'

She smiled at him, actually smiled, for the first time in what seemed an eternity – and though there was no mirth in that smile, neither was there bitterness. Indeed, there might have been a hint of warmth, of sympathy, of kindness there.

But the man if he saw it with his eyes, did not consciously perceive it with his understanding – though almost certainly it was the sub-conscious effect of that smile that broke down the tottering wall of his pride and self-esteem and hardihood. His red head dropped within his hands, and the pent-up hurt and misery was released on a flood of words.

'Did I do wrong, then? Did I fail?' he cried. 'Should I have sacrificed the clan for nothing, just? For some idea of honour? Was I wrong to be holding men's lives of more worth than that – the men who were mine to lead, whom I had brought out? Those same men, my God, who will not meet my eye now, and who turn away when they see me? Was it not to the clan that I owed first duty – the duty to use my head, my judgment? The battle was lost before ever we reached the field. Nothing that we could have done would have changed the issue, whatever. We could only have gone over and been broken. Died uselessly. Myself I would have gone, yes. But not to throw the clan away. Never! Never that! the clan that I have cherished and schemed and fought for all my days, that I would die a hundred deaths for – the clan that now turns its face from me! Aye, I care not for the rest – let other men point their fingers at me, spit at my back, say what they will. I care not. But my own people, the Gregorach . . . ! Gregor will scarce exchange a word with me, I tell you – Gregor whom I have loved as a son. Coiletter hides lest I see him. And Marchfield. And Bracklie. And young Roro. Donald will have none of me. All keep their distance. In our own country, women turn back in their doorways as I pass – the women whose men I saved! I am like a bearer of the plague, whatever – a leper! No man is my friend any more.'

It was a strange scene indeed, the great Rob Roy MacGregor, master of men, bugbear of authority, scourge of the Grahams, self-sufficient outlaw – brought low, broken, smitten to his knees, his potent armour pierced and penetrated in its one weakness, in his need for the esteem and worship of his own Gregorach. He did nothing by half-measures, did Rob Roy – and in his fall and abasement and hurt, the Celt in him reserved nothing. The woman, biting her lip, made as though to speak, but he went on, clenching and unclenching the fists that held his head.

'If I had not hastened from the fords of Frew, hoping yet that it might not be too late to save the folly and bloodshed of a frontal attack on Argyll, all would have been well . . . for me! Aye, even if I had turned back with Struan and young Locheil, retired with them, there would have been no outcry, I swear. God – if I had sat all day up there on the ridge with Mar, and never raised hand or voice, I would still be a man of honour and fame! But because I held the Allan Water to cover other men's retreat, because I stood my ground on the only spot that was worth the holding, because I did not throw live men after dead – because of this, I am a broken man this day! Because I was not a fool, I am a craven, a knave and a betrayer!' All but breathless, he raised a ravaged face that scarcely was to be recognised as that of the proud MacGregor. 'Was I wrong, Mary? Was I wrong?' he demanded.

And Mary MacGregor, lips parted and trembling, lovely eyes brimming with tears at last, raised open hands in a strange gesture at once surrendering, beckoning, enfolding and running forward flung herself bodily upon the man.

'Rob! Rob!' she cried, chokingly. 'My dear, my own dearest! My poor beloved Rob . . .' And her voice broke and failed her.

* * *

The man shook his head – but not so hard as to disturb the woman's head leaning against his neck and cheek. 'I cannot understand it, at all,' he declared. 'What has changed you, Mary?'

'You have, Rob. What else but yourself?'

'I have? How can that be? I have done you no kindness – been no other than I have always been.'

'You have needed me,' she said simply.

'Eh? Needed you? And have I not always needed you, Lass?'

'No, no, no!' She sat up within the circle of his arms, suddenly vehement, passionate. 'That you have not! Can you not see? For long you have not needed me. You were the great Rob Roy MacGregor – who needed no one but his own self. All men bowed to you. You were sufficient. You had need of none. . . .'

'*Dia*, Mary – what folly is this?' the man complained. 'You I always needed. . . .'

'A woman to keep your house, it may be! But you were

just as happy in a cave! The clan was your true love – not me! The heather was your home – not my fireside. . . .'

'Mercy upon us – what's this?' he gasped. 'You are not after telling me that *this* is what you have held against me all this time, Mary? That for such daftlike notion you have denied me your bed and kindness?'

Eyes blinking, lips tight pressed, she shook her head.

'I thought it was the Grahams,' he went on. 'Killearn – curse him! That you deemed me to have failed you, then. When they burned our house, and I was not there to be saving you. . . .'

Urgently, as with anguish, she turned to him. 'Do not say it, Rob,' she pleaded. 'That is past. I have put it from me, as well as I may. At a price. A nightmare – an evil dream! Leave it, I pray you, to time. And to God's mercy. Maybe that will be sufficient. This is otherwise. Now you have come back to me – to me truly, your wife. Needing me, as you never needed me before. Oh, Rob – *I* needed . . . just this. I am a wicked sinful woman, I think. I needed this – for all men's hands to turn against you. For you to be broken, scorned, lost. This I needed, to find you again. I have been far away, Rob – further than you, by far. Far, far, wandering, lost also. For so long. And cold – oh, so cold.' Her voice broke, but she recovered it. 'But now your need has guided me back to you, my dear . . . and I think that I will not go away again, God aiding me. Not ever. Will . . . will I serve, Rob? Now – in place of all the rest? Of fame and the regard of men? Of power, and a clan's acclaim? Will I serve?'

'As I hope for Heaven, you will!' Rob cried, his voice powerful and vibrant again. 'Lord – already you have made a new man of me, whatever! The clan may think what it will of me, and make do without me. It has Gregor, and Balhaldies – High Chief of Clan Alpine, forsooth! Inversnaid and Craigroyston may go to whomsoever can take them. Myself, I will bide here with you and the boys, Mary *a graidh.* And we will let Scotland and the world go to the devil in their own way. From now till the rim of time! And be sorry for nothing but that I had not the wit to do the same years before!'

The woman shook her head slowly. 'No Rob – that would not serve. Not for you. You are too old to change yourself into a different man – and too young to settle down at any fireside, mine or other. Memories are short, in war, and before long the clan will find that it needs you again. Sooner or later you will go back to them – for you are Rob Roy MacGregor still, and always will be, And James Stewart is still your rightful king, no matter how weak. But it may be that he, and the clan, will take second place from now on . . . ?'

'Aye – by the Holy Powers, they will!' Rob cried. 'Nothing surer. I have learned my lesson, Mary my love. You have raised me up and given me back my manhood. One thing only I ask of you, now – and do not be lying to me. Did I right at Sheriff Muir . . . or wrong?'

'I have never lied to you, Rob – and never shall, I hope. I believe that you did right. Yes, right.'

'Thank you for that word, my heart's love – and thank God! Thank God!'

EPILOGUE

THE night wind blew cold and gusty, with a hint of rain in it – though that was hardly noticeable in the spray that drifted inboard from the dark and angry waters of Loch Katrine. MacAlastair rowed the small boat, and in the stern, huddled in a plaid, sat Mary MacGregor.

'What is behind this folly?' she demanded, not for the first time. She was forced to shout, to counter the noise of the wind and water. 'Surely you must know, MacAlastair?'

The gillie shrugged his straining shoulders. 'Rob ordained it,' he declared briefly. 'He was after telling me nothing more than to bring yourself to Eilean Dhu, two hours after nightfall.'

'But why? Why?'

'I know no more than you, at all. Rob, these days, does not be honouring myself with his confidence!' That, from MacAlastair, was a remarkable statement, and the measure of the taciturn gillie's hurt. But it was not untrue. His master was a different man from former days, undoubtedly.

It was the November term again, Martinmas 1716, one year on from Sheriff Muir, eleven months from the reconciliation in the cottage of Auchinchisallan – the same cottage under Beinn Dorain that now stood a blackened and roofless shell, like the House of Inversnaid, mute witness to the zeal of General Cadogan in the cause of pacification.

Out of the squally dark loomed the blacker mass of the pine-clad islet of Eilean Dhu, in mid-loch. MacAlastair edged the boat into a point where undercut roots provided a landing-place of sorts, and aided his passenger ashore.

It required only a moment or two to establish the fact that, as yet, they had the island to themselves. It was a tiny rocky place, no more than an acre or two in extent, containing only the ruins of some ancient building against which a rude shelter of turf had been erected. Mary preferred even the gusty night to the black depths of this. In the angle between stone and turf walls, out of the wind, the gillie installed her, and lit a tiny fire, screened from all distant view, for what comfort it might offer. Here they waited, wordless.

Mary had been brought thus secretly from the small remote house of Portanellan on the rugged north shore of the loch, for Glengyle House, where she would always have found a welcome, like many another was now a burned-out ruin likewise; shelter for MacGregors had to be remote and well hidden indeed to escape the Teutonic thoroughness of the army of German, Dutch and Swiss mercenaries that King George had brought over and put at General Cadogan's disposal to teach the Highlands their lesson. Argyll was out of favour and superseded, as being too lenient and kindly disposed towards the traitorous clans, and his successor, General Carpenter, held no such views. He gave Cadogan a completely free hand. The latter could not avail much against the far and inner Highland fastnesses – but he could make an example of the fringes along the Highland Line. And with Montrose still Secretary of State and crowing louder than ever in Scotland now, official encouragement was readily forthcoming. The MacGregor country was occupied territory, for the first time in its history.

King James had come – and gone – spending a fantastic month in the North-east, holding reviews, levees and investitures, conferring honours, and then quietly departing for France again, taking Mar with him. The clearing-up process was now in full swing. So much for the cause.

They had fully an hour to wait on that island in the loch, under the sobbing pines, till the creak of oars sounded during a brief lull of the wind, followed by the sound of a powerful voice barking evident and imperative orders. There was no doubting whose voice that was.

Presently two men materialised out of the gloom. Rob Roy's figure was unmistakeable. His companion was smaller, though still a big man and heavily built.

'Ha, my dear,' Rob cried. 'You are here, then. See, my love – I am after bringing you a present.' And with a sudden explosive thrust, he hurled the other man, heavy as he was, headlong, to fall full length almost at the woman's feet.

Mary gasped – and then her exclamation changed into a choking scream as MacAlastair tossed a couple of pine branches on the fire, and it blazed up to reveal the fallen man beside her as John Graham of Killearn.

'Fear nothing, *a graidh* – he will not hurt you now.' Rob called out. 'That one's days for mischief are done. He is empty now – empty as his master's rent-box!' And he tossed down on the other side of the fire a heavy bulging leather bag that chinked musically.

Mary said nothing. Eyes wide, she stared at Killearn as he dragged himself slowly and unsteadily to his knees, panting – stared as though mesmerised in horror, but seeking, as it seemed without success, to draw back, away from him.

'Och, lass – look not so!' her husband cried, 'I thought that you wanted him? *Dia* – I have been at pains to get him for you! I vowed I'd have him, you'll mind – I vowed 'fore God he would die for what he did to you. It has taken time – but we have him now.'

The woman had managed to get to her feet, and had stepped back and back until brought up by the ruined walling. Her breath was coming in great gulps, and it seemed that she sought to hold it down with a hand across her breast, hysteria not far off. Killearn rose and stood swaying, shoulders hunched, wig askew.

Rob looked from one to the other in the flickering firelight, perplexed. 'Are you not well, my heart?' he wondered. 'What ails you? Was it the boat . . . on the loch?'

'That . . . that man!' she got out. 'Why . . . did you . . . bring him here?'

'The best place it was for him, whatever – where we could be sure to be undisturbed. Och, the country is infested, just, with these Germans. None will find him, or us, here on this island.' To give Mary time and opportunity to recover herself, he went on heartily. 'Aye – the bold fellow ventured out of his hole at last! He was after believing the tale that I set afoot that I was fled to Ireland. He conceived that it might be safe, now, with the soldiers thick as maggots, to risk showing his face to his master's tenants this Martinmas term. He chose Chapellaroch again, the man – as nearest to his bolt-hole at Buchanan Castle. But, och – not near enough, by God! Not with Rob Roy still above the sod! His fat Germans are chasing a dozen nimble gillies through the Flanders Moss – and he is here, to face his end! Montrose will be after needing a new factor from this night on, whatever!'

Mary, despite her husband's thought for her, did not seem to be listening. She did not appear to be able to take her eyes off John Graham. That unhappy individual's glance was not similarly drawn to her. He looked indeed everywhere but at the woman.

'MacGregor,' he blurted, 'You canna do this! In sweet Jesu's name o' mercy. . . .'

'Quiet you, cur! Did that name of mercy prevail with you at Inversnaid two years back? Mary – the choice is yours. How shall we reward him?'

'No,' the woman whispered, head shaking. 'No, Rob. . . .'

'Come, lass – this is not like yourself. You are a Mac-Gregor, daughter of kings. . . .'

'I want nothing of this man. Only, never to see him again. Never!'

'That I can promise you, *a graidh*. But the manner of his end is surely of concern to you? Your vengeance. . . .'

248

'I want no vengeance.'

'But, *Dia* – did you not charge me to avenge you? That day at Corrycharmaig. Would that he should die, you said, as *you* had died those nights before!'

'I . . . I was beside myself, just. I spoke wildly, sinfully.'

'You spoke justly. You asked how he should suffer sufficiently. What was just a little pain, before the end, you asked? A little fear? Did I think that would serve, you said? And I swore that I would make it sufficient – I swore it before the throne of God Almighty, that he should pay in full. Now it is time to redeem my vow, Mary.'

'No! No, Rob. I will not have it. I want none of it.'

'But why, in the name of Heaven? Why?'

'Because . . . because I have put it from me. At great cost. I have fought and fought this thing, Rob. I thought . . . I thought that I had won. Now, I cannot be sure, any more. But this I know – that this man's hurt will not help me. Let him go in peace, Rob.'

'No!' It was her husband's turn to cry out. 'That I will not, by the Powers! Your soft heart may melt, your woman's will may flag and fail – but I am made otherwise. This is not a man – it is a murderous animal! While yet he lives, men will suffer. And women and bairns. Such as he are not to be spared.'

'If *I* can forgive him – as I pray God's aid to do – cannot you, Rob?'

'Forgive, is it? Do you forgive a snake that has bitten you? A wolf that has savaged a child? This animal mishandled *our* children, burned our roof over their heads, and cast them out into a winter's night. He even struck yourself, you said, my God! For that, there is no forgiveness in *me*!'

Mary MacGregor and John Graham actually looked at each other then, exchanged glances – an exchange that was as brief, furtive and strange as it was almost guilty. The woman had never told Rob the full enormity of what had been done to her that November night – had told no living

249

soul, indeed. Now, suddenly, it dawned upon Killearn that that must be so – otherwise Rob Roy would scarcely have emphasised this mere striking of his wife as the major injury. The man's abrupt tenseness betokened the first gleam of hope.

Rob, in the uncertain light of the fire, perceived nothing of all this. He went on. 'I will not forgive him – but I will do for him a deal better than he deserves. I will not kill an unarmed man, however evil. He shall even have the choice by which means he shall die – have the means to defend himself, whatever. None shall say that Rob Roy makes war on the helpless. By sword, dirk, pistol, or bare hands, we shall fight, here and now. And the choice shall be Graham's.'

'No, Rob. . . .'

'But, yes. Can I do more than that? When all that he deserves is to be cut down like any dog?'

'Pay heed to her, MacGregor,' Killearn put in, urgently. 'It would be murder, just the same. I am no fighting man. . . .'

'You were fighting man enough that night at Inversnaid, when it was women and bairns to be fought!'

'It was but my duty, man. As Sheriff.' Again that swift glance at Mary. 'In law, your goods and gear were forfeit. As an outlaw avoiding arrest. . . .'

'*Diabhol* – enough!' Rob roared. 'Would you hide behind the law now, you snivelling whelp? Choose you your weapon!'

'No – I tell you, I will not fight. Kill me, defenceless, if you will. But MacGregor – what value is my death to you? Killing me would result only in reprisals against your people. His Grace would avenge me, I assure you. But alive, I could serve you well. I am the Duke's instrument, and I could carry out his orders but gently, interpret his will towards the MacGregors more kindly. I swear that I will do this, if you spare my life. . . .'

'Faugh! Think you that I will bargain with you?' Rob

cried. 'What you have done is no more to be chaffered over than forgiven. Save you your breath, Graham.'

'Rob – heed *me*, at least!' Mary interposed, stepping forward from her wall. 'If you will not think of this man, think of ourselves. If you kill him, his death will be between us all our days. I know it. He will be like a shadow over our lives. Do you wish that? Have we not had sufficient of shadows? Oh Rob – do you not see? If you kill him, his blood is on *my* hands! And that is a thing that I could not live with.'

'Och, lassie – wheesht! Here is nonsense. You are distrait. . . .'

'Distrait, yes – and like to remain so, if you do this thing. I vowed, Rob, that nothing would again come between us. But *this* would – I know it, I swear it! Is that nothing to you? Nothing, whatever?'

'Dear God, Mary – you cannot mean this? It cannot be so.' For the first time uncertainty, indecision, sounded in the man's voice.

Quick to perceive it, Mary slipped to the ground on her knees before him. 'Look, Rob – I kneel to you!' she exclaimed. 'To ask, to beg of you, that you do not do this thing. I have never knelt to you before. . . .'

'Lord! Get up, woman – get up!' he cried hoarsely, striding forward to her. 'Never do that. Never kneel – you must not! And for this worthless cur!'

'It is not for him – it for myself. For us,' she answered, as he lifted her up. 'It is our future, our happiness, that I beg for. Will you not heed me, Rob?'

He stared at her, so close now, this strange new Mary, humble, pleading. He had never known her thus, all their days together. And he shook his head. 'I do not think . . . that I can deny . . . anything that you ask, lass,' he muttered.

'Then – you will spare him?'

'If I must.'

'Oh, Rob – thank you! Thank you! She clung to him

tightly in her relief and emotion. 'You will not regret it, Rob, ever. The other would have been unworthy of you. And it will be for the best, too.' She was whispering now, in his ear, held close. 'For the clan. For all of us,' she went on eagerly. 'Make him swear to treat the Gregorach kindly ever, as he promised – on pain of fullest retribution. Even have him write it down. He will do it – he will do anything for his life. Then let him go. Ourselves we will go, too. Away from here, right away. West into Argyll. To where MacCailean Mhor has offered us refuge, deep in his country. None will dare seek us there. Argyll is still king in the Campbell country. We shall be safe, and live at peace, Rob. There is nothing here for us, any more. Nothing. Let us go there, to Glen Shira, and have done with hatred and fighting. We have had more than enough. Let him, let this man that is no man, go his way, Rob, and us ours.'

He nodded slowly, to her breathless anxious spate of words. 'And my vow?' he asked.

'You swore another vow, once – before an altar. In my presence, Rob. It takes the precedence, I think!'

'Aye, lass, you have the rights of it – as ever.' He turned, one arm still around her, to Killearn. 'You owe your life to this woman whom you have wronged,' he said, flatly, evenly. 'I trust that you will value it accordingly. You will write me a paper, swearing by all that you hold sacred that you will deal kindly at all times with all of the name and race of MacGregor in acknowledgment of this life of yours. Break that bond, and I will seek you out, wheresoever you may be – and no pleading of even this woman shall save you then. Is it understood?'

'Aye. It is understood.'

'Good. And tell you James Graham of Montrose, from me, that our account is not yet closed, whatever. I think that it will not be closed while he and I still live. You will tell him that?'

'Aye.'

'MacAlastair – paper, inkhorn and quill. And more wood for the fire.' He turned to his wife, ruefully. 'As Royal's my Race – I had not thought to end this night with a quill!'

She pressed his arm. 'The night is not ended yet, Rob,' she said gently. 'Indeed, it has hardly begun!'

Gold for Prince Charlie

Book Three

CHAPTER 1

'BLOW, damn you – blow!' Glengyle cried. 'If you call yourselves pipers, pipe now, by God! And no dirge, no lament!
Give us ... give us *The Gregorach's Challenge!* Aye – give
us the *Challenge.* As you've never blown it before. Yonder's
the Prince. Let him hear that MacGregor is with him yet.
That all is not lost. Blow, in the name of God!'

Even Gregor Black Knee MacGregor's great voice was
hoarse and uneven with much shouting and much emotion.
Red Knee indeed would have been an apter description of
him this day, for the famous black mole on his left knee was
completely hidden under the dried and caked blood which
coated the entire leg below a bayonet thrust in the thigh, that
had also torn a ragged rent in his kilt. Limping, he gestured
forward, with the stained broadsword that he had not yet
thought to sheath, towards a cot-house beside a group of wind-
blown stunted trees across the high moor, where a scattering
of horses and men were grouped.

At Glengyle's broad back, his son spoke thickly. 'They
cannot do it. They're done. Done, I say – finished! It is more
than flesh and blood ... '

'As Royal's my Race – they can! And shall!' The big man
turned round fiercely – though he did not leave hold of the
semi-conscious figure that slumped only approximately upright
on the plodding garron at his side – turned, he to whom fierce-
ness of manner had never come naturally despite his style
and reputation. 'Lord – must I play them my own self? 'Fore
God – have we come to that!'

It would be an exaggeration to say that this aroused a smile,
a single smile, in all that weary, tattered and blood-stained
company; but sunken heads were raised momentarily, dulled
and hollowed eyes gleamed here and there. And from somewhere in the stumbling trudging throng, the first uncouth
wails and groans of filling bagpipes sounded. One man handed
over to another the arm of a comrade whom he had been
supporting, and reached across to a baggage pony for his pipes.

Another, who had been staggering along with difficulty on legs lacerated by grape-shot, had himself hoisted on to the broad back of a second garron, already overburdened with two wounded men, and perched ludicrously thereon sought air to fill his instrument. Slowly, unsteadily, amidst outlandish discords and howls, the three pipers strove to respond to the summons of their colonel and chieftain.

Only three sets of pipes, it seemed, had survived the holocaust – or only three pipers.

Gradually the painful caterwauling evened and steadied and merged into something recognisable, though still quite fantastic in the circumstances, into the savagely martial strains of a ranting march, a proud, swaggering, damn-your-eyes flourish that was not so much defiant as purely, scornfully triumphant. Louder and stronger the music swelled as the instrumentalists forgot their pain and hunger and wretchedness in their playing, and all along the shambling ranks teeth gritted, drooping shoulders squared, strides lengthened, and defeated, shocked and betrayed men became fighters again, the warriors that their name and fame demanded.

Up at the front of the straggling column, the young captain immediately behind Glengyle – who was in fact his youngest son Duncan MacGregor, sometimes called Duncan Beg or Little Duncan because he lacked fully three inches of his father's six feet four – Duncan MacGregor was behaving strangely. Stripping off the red-and-green plaid which he had worn folded about his torso and one shoulder, he began to turn around in little circles even as he walked. Men near him looked at him askance, as though the sights that they had so lately left behind had turned his head – as well they might. Then it was seen that he was in fact unwinding something from his body – the colourful silken tree-and-sword banner of Clan Gregor, soiled and rent, which had been wrapped shaftless around his person. He drew his claymore, and thrusting the bloody point through and through like a skewer beside the torn socket for the shaft, he raised sword and standard arm's length above his head.

A ragged snarling sound, part growl, part cheer, issued from hoarse dry throats behind him.

And so, pipes playing and banner flying, after a fashion, the remnant of Glengyle's Regiment of the army of King James

the Eighth and Third, marched, not off the field of Culloden
– for they were already a couple of miles from that shameful
blood-soaked place – but across Drummossie Moor to where
rumour said that the Prince had halted.

Duncan MacGregor kept his arm held high, although presently it demanded his other hand to support it thus.

The thin rain, now and then laced with sleet, blew chill in
their faces off the grey shrouded hills.

Despite the wet, the party for whom they headed were
congregated outside the lonely cot-house, not within it, under
the doubtful shelter of the dark dripping Scots pines. All there
were far past noticing the effects of rain or cold, that late
afternoon of the 16th of April, 1746. In twos and threes and
little groups they stood or sat or lay about, in various attitudes
of exhaustion, anger or despair. Yet however preoccupied they
were, each and all, in their own distresses, it was very noticeable how frequently all eyes turned in the direction of one
man who sat alone, a little way apart, on a fallen tree-trunk.
Head in his hands, he crouched, a picture of utter despondency.

Apparently it took the sound of the pipes some time to
penetrate to this man's inner consciousness, deep sunk as he
was in grief and dejection. When at last, affected more perhaps
by the cries of his companions than by the message of the
music, he looked up, it was to reveal a handsome sensitive face,
too young, at twenty-four, to be so drawn with hurt and care,
large eyes ringed with fatigue, high forehead bruised from a
fall and streaked with dirt below natural fair hair sadly in
need of powder and curling-tongs.

Heavily those tired, rather prominent brown eyes stared,
and lightened a little at what they saw – though only a little.
Charles Edward Stuart rose to his feet, however, a graceful
well-made figure of a man, with a strange distinction of bearing by no means always to be observed in royalty, tall, slender,
bare-headed, dressed in long tartan jacket and tight riding-
trews, with a buff waistcoat, and no single indication of his
rank and position. Shaking his head, he awaited the Gregorach.

By the time that the clansmen came level, two or three
others had joined the Prince – O'Sullivan, the Adjutant-
General and Quartermaster; old Sir Thomas Sheridan,
Charles's second-cousin and former tutor; and Lord Elcho,
commander of cavalry. When Gregor of Glengyle held up his

9

hand to halt his followers and still the pipes, it was indeed O'Sullivan who spoke, frowning, before his Prince.

'Very stirring, i' faith, Glengyle – very dramatic!' he said, in his curious Frenchified Irish, into the hush. 'But have you no thought for His Highness's safety? Do you want to bring Cumberland himself and all his baying pack down upon this wretched spot, with your brayings and squealings? It has been sore enough, by the Blessed Virgin, to bring him so far, undiscovered, without your shouting aloud . . . !'

'My God, sir – is that the way of it now!' Gregor Black Knee burst out, hotly. 'Is our Prince sunk so sudden from Captain-General of his army to a skulking fugitive who hides from his own fighting men . . . ?'

'Gentlemen! Gentlemen!' Charles Edward intervened. 'What talk is this? Be silent, both! Colonel O'Sullivan – you forget yourself, I think.' His attractively musical voice, with its foreign intonation, was unusually strained, with an edge to it. 'I still command here, God pity me!' Then quickly he relented, he whom many blamed for being ever too ready to trust and overlook and forgive. He touched his friend's arm lightly. 'Though well I know, John, that it is but anxiety for my safety that moves you.' Turning back to the huge MacGregor, he mustered a smile – and he had a particularly sweet and disarming smile, however wan and brief it was today.

'Glengyle – I rejoice to see you,' he said. 'If joy is a word that I may ever use again, *mon Dieu!* Your coming thus lifts my heart . . . a little. I had feared that you, too, were, were . . . '

'We are fewer than we were, Highness – but still at your service,' Glengyle told him, simply.

'Aye, *mes braves* – I should have known that if any could cut their way out of that sorry ruin it would be my gallant MacGregors . . . '

'Provided always that they left in good time, of course!' a voice murmured from behind the Prince, where Hay of Restalrig, the Military Secretary, had come up.

There was a choking indrawing of breath from every MacGregor near enough to hear. Hands dropped to broadsword hilts, involuntary paces were stepped forward. There was little love lost between the Highland and the Lowland components of that army – or indeed between many of the units of either persuasion themselves – witnessed to by the sourly laughing

10

voice that spoke as Captain Alexander MacLeod, aide-de-camp, came strolling over even as Charles Edward raised a hand to still them all.

'You have your clans mixed, I think, Colonel Hay! It was the MacDonalds who were, h'm, over dainty on this occasion!'

'Aye – they would not fight! They would not charge, damn them! Because they had not the right of the line, by all the saints!' That was O'Sullivan again. 'And who denied them it? The Lord George. The Lord George again! For his accursed Athollmen...'

'Sawny! John! Peace – I command you!' the Prince cried, and now his voice was vibrant with emotion. The fine eyes flashed, the glazed weariness momentarily gone. 'This is insufferable! Enough of it! Has there not been hurt enough, sorrow enough, for one day...?'

'Aye, sir – and treachery enough, too! The Lord George knew well that the MacDonalds would not fight, denied the right of the line. I heard Keppoch tell him so, with my own ears. Yet he took it for himself...'

'Christ God!' Glengyle roared, that quiet giant who could out-shout them all on occasion. 'Who talks of Clan Donald not fighting, Storekeeper? If they were slow to charge, they were slower still to leave the field! They did not leave the field, I say. They have not left it yet, whatever. Because they are dead, all dead. They died where they stood, I tell you, around Keppoch and Lochgarry and the others, because they would not run Keppoch is dead...'

'Keppoch!' the Prince cried. 'Keppoch, my good friend...!'

'Aye. And most of his own and Clanranald's and Glengarry's officers with him. Those that did not die then are being butchered now, my God! Cumberland's Hessians are butchering the wounded and the prisoners, like dumb animals. Now, at this moment, they are dying like slaughtered cattle.' Glengyle's voice broke. 'I ... I have never seen the like, nor heard it.'

'Yes. Yes we ..., we heard of it.' Charles nodded, biting his lip. 'It is monstrous, beyond all belief. *Ma foi*, they are barbarians, brute beasts! But, you – you escaped?'

'By holding together, just. By holding close, we fought our way out. Some of us.' Gregor Black Knee glanced back at his ragged battle-worn veterans. There were perhaps one hundred

11

and twenty men there, mainly MacGregors, many of them Rob Roy's former freebooters, but with forty or so of the hundred Perthshire Stewarts who had been attached to the regiment. Few there were wholly unscathed. 'These, out. of four hundred! We Gregorach have been cutting our way out of ill places from our mothers' knees. But not as today. Never the like of that!'

'No. No – it is a cataclysm, a disaster! And Locheil? My good brave Locheil? Do not tell me that he has fallen, *mon Dieu?* And the Duke? My lord of Perth? You were brigaded with him, in the centre, were you not? What of the Duke?'

'I think that he escaped, sir. I saw his brother, the Lord John, leading him off the field. They tell me that Locheil fell, both ankles shot with grape. But his Camerons carried him off in time. They were on the right. I did not see . . . '

Captain Duncan MacGregor touched his father's arm, and gestured behind him, wordlessly. Glengyle nodded.

'But, sir – my men are in no state to be standing by, while we talk here. You can see their need. I ask Your Highness's permission that they may stand down. Rest for a little . . . '

'*Certainement*, Colonel. Forgive me . . . '

Both Elcho and O'Sullivan spoke at once. Elcho, son to the Earl of Wemyss, prevailed.

'Your Royal Highness – this is folly!' he exclaimed. 'All these men will but bring down Cumberland upon us. Your immediate safety is all-important, now, if the Cause is to be saved. That is why we brought you here. Already there were over-many of us. My pickets tell me that dragoons are scouring all around for you. Videttes are all over the moor, searching. Already they may have spied us. These MacGregors will bring them down on us like a swarm of locusts! You must order them to leave us, Highness. At once.'

'God in Heaven – is that what you think of the Gregorach, now!' Glengyle cried. 'Is his Highness safer in the midst of a hundred MacGregors, every one of whom would die for him? Or amongst a wheen Sassunach secretaries and storekeepers!' And his hand swept in scornful gesture over the dozen or so of the Prince's company.

'Gentlemen – I pray you! A truce to this talk . . . '

'His lordship is right, Highness,' O'Sullivan insisted. 'In this matter, at least. The fewer men about your person now, the better. What could a hundred of infantry, MacGregors or other, do against a regiment of dragoons? Yourself it is that Cumberland wants – the rest he can hunt down at his leisure. Send them away, sir.'

'Very well, gentlemen. Glengyle – you will take your gallant regiment yonder. Behind these trees there is a hollow where a stream runs. Take your men there, Colonel. Rest them in that hollow. They will be out of sight. Then yourself come back here. For a council.'

'But, sir – here is no time nor place for a council!' Elcho protested. 'You should be gone. Ere this. As far from this fatal place as is possible. Southwards into Badenoch. To join up with Cluny. To Ruthven . . . '

'My lord – your advice will be welcome. At the council. Others give me contrary advice. We must decide what is best. What is wisest. What is possible, *mon Dieu!*' Charles drew a hand over his bruised brow. 'Glengyle – you have your orders.'

'Yes, sir.' The MacGregor hesitated for a moment. 'Highness – might I ask? For my men. Your Quartermaster – has he any food? Any provisions? Anything . . . ?'

'Alas, Glengyle . . . '

'I have nothing, sir. Nothing nearer than Inverness,' O'Sullivan said.

Gregor Black Knee inclined his head. The entire Jacobite army had had one biscuit apiece for sustenance that whole grim day. And not much more the day before – with an all-night march of abortive folly in between. 'Your servant, sir,' he said. 'I shall be back.' And raising his voice. 'Pipes! *Dia* – let us have the pipes!'

' 'Fore God – not again!' Lord Elcho burst out. 'Not again, Glengyle! No more of that damnable noise . . . !'

The rest of his protest was lost in the clansmen's growling wrath and contempt, and in the bubbling ululation of the bagpipes.

In a fold of the high moor, eight hundred feet above the sea, where a burn ran down towards the River Nairn, Glengyle left his men to bathe their wounds and fill their empty bellies with water if with nothing else, and limped back towards the cot-house, taking his son with him. Four miles away to the north, down at sea-level, the towers of Inverness Castle could just be distinguished through the grey curtains of the rain squalls. Beyond, although the massive outline of Ben Wyvis itself could not be seen, the stark white streaks of snow in the mountain's corries stood out strangely.

Under the dripping trees the MacGregors passed Charles Edward's personal bodyguard, dismounted and waiting, sixteen troopers of FitzJames's Horse. Their French officer eyed the two bare-kneed Highlanders with unconcealed scorn, and offered no greeting.

Back at the Prince's party, they found the council already in progress, after a fashion. Another couple of officers had arrived – Major Maxwell of Kirkconnell, of Elcho's Horse, and the Master of Lovat. Tempers were brittle, and words were high.

Young Lovat was speaking, son of the wily Fraser chief.

' . . . nor do I trust Cluny. He has held off all day. He is but six miles off, with five hundred Macphersons. He might have tipped the scales had he thought fit to join us. It would be folly for Your Highness to turn south into his country.'

'How do you know that Cluny is but six miles off?' Lord Elcho demanded. 'The Lord George Murray left him yesterday at Ruthven, fifty miles away . . . '

'This is Fraser country, my lord. I learn quickly all that passes in it.'

'Then perhaps, Master of Lovat, you could tell us where the rest of the great Clan Fraser is hiding? Only two hundred men were here to face Cumberland . . . !'

'Damnation, sir! Do you jest – or must I teach you that in Fraser country no man speaks so to . . . ?'

'My lords! Gentlemen!' the Prince intervened wearily. 'May I remind you that this is a council-of-war – not a tavern brawl? Here is Glengyle. And Captain Duncan. Sit in, Colonel. You are wounded, I see. Your leg . . . ?'

'A scratch, Highness – no more. A bayonet prick.'

'You were at close quarters, then?'

'Oh, aye – we were close enough. Too close for Barrel's fusiliers, I warrant you! But yourself, sir? Your head? Your brow?'

'Nothing, *mon ami*. A bump, a bruise. My horse was shot under me – that is all. No more honourable scar! *Alors* – we have but now heard more of the battle, from the Master of

Lovat here, and Major Maxwell. And ill tidings they bring! The Mackintoshes are cut to ribbons. The Chisholms died where they stood, like the MacDonalds. Dillon's Regiment is no more. The Drummond Horse were decimated by cannon-fire and grape, and my Lord Strathallan is dead. As is Mercer of Aldie. My Lords Kilmarnock and Balmerino are prisoners. All gone. My brave army is no more. There is nothing left — nothing!'

The MacGregor shook his head, fair still, the golden hair only faded a little by silver-grey. 'It is bad, sir — bad. But there is much left, see you. A battle lost, it is — not a campaign. Och, sir, the half of your army were not here, at all. No more than four or five thousand men faced Cumberland this day, and him with twice that number.'

'And there we have it!' Hay of Restalrig interjected. 'Your Royal Highness had twelve thousand at Perth. Many more than that at Edinburgh. Where are the rest?'

'Aye, sir — there's the rub,' O'Sullivan nodded. 'Sure, more than a battle is lost.'

'I fear that you are right, John.'

'But much may yet be saved, Your Highness,' Elcho insisted. 'Go south to Ruthven. That is where Lord George and his Athollmen are making for. And the remnant of Drummond's Horse. With the Duke. Both your Lieutenants-General. It is Cluny's country . . . '

'And claim you that as recommendation!' Young Lovat cried. 'The Lord George Murray and Cluny! My beloved brother-in-law. Better put your life in the hands of honest men . . . '

'Like my Lord of Lovat?' Elcho gave back.

The Prince had to beat on the tree-trunk with his sword-hilt to quell the uproar.

'I will have none of my good friends and faithful officers mis-called!' he exclaimed. 'We have had that, a-plenty! I seek true and wise counsel, not raillery and malice.'

'There is but the one true and wise counsel for Your Highness in this pass,' O'Sullivan declared earnestly. 'Go back to France, sir. King Louis has promised men and arms and money. If we had waited, and brought them with us at the first, this whole endeavour would have turned out differently, I swear. Go back to France and raise them now. Then return with them. Next year, mayhap. There is the only wise and practical course, sir.'

'And what of the men who have come out for your Cause, sir?' Glengyle demanded. 'If you sail away and leave them, for France? What is to become of *them*?'

'They will disperse to their homes. Such as have not already done so!' Hay said. 'I agree with the Adjutant-General. The only sound course is to return to France ...'

'Sound for whom?' the MacGregor cried. 'My God – think you that there is any safety in their homes for the thousands you leave behind? Think you the Government will forgive and forget?'

'And King Louis has been promising men and money for years, Your Royal Highness,' Maxwell of Kirkconnell pointed out. 'You still have an army, if you will but collect it, re-assemble it. Scattered wide it may be, now. But it can come together again. Go to Ruthven in Badenoch. Assemble there.'

'Or in Lochaber. In Cameron's country. Better there, in the West. It is more remote. Bid the clans assemble there,' Young Lovat proposed.

'Safely away from *your* doorstep ... ?' MacLeod the aide suggested softly.

'Damn you, sir ... !'

'There should have been a rendezvous appointed,' Elcho interrupted, looking accusingly from the Prince to O'Sullivan. Of them all, Elcho had ever been most critical of Charles's leadership and his Irish friends. 'That was elementary. Had there been such, we should not be in this pickle, at least. But since neither Captain-General nor Adjutant-General ordered a rendezvous in case of defeat, surely it behoves us that we all seek to join the two Lieutenants-General. Lord George has left word that he is making for Ruthven, with the Duke of Perth. To Ruthven, therefore, all should go. And swiftly, before Cumberland thinks to close the passes of Moy and The Slochd.'

'I agree,' Glengyle said, although he frowned. 'That is what an army should do. Not that I wouldn't sooner see your Highness making for the north-west, for Kintail and Torridon and Gairloch – the wild MacKenzie country where the Redcoats could never come at you. The Earl of Cromartie is north of Inverness, with eight hundred Mackenzies, watching Sutherland. MacDonnell of Barrisdale likewise. I left them there but two days ago. I say, go south now to Ruthven, and join Lord George and the others. Then head you north through the mountains, by the Corryarrack Pass, Fort Augustus, Glen Moriston and over to Kintail, with your men. I will guide you by high ways where no dragoons nor fusiliers may follow. Bring in Cromartie and the others to join you there – and you have an army again. The summer is coming . . . '

'Och, heed them not, me boy,' old Sir Thomas Sheridan, at the Prince's back, said in his thin reedy Irish voice. 'Ye will not turn the clock back, thus. The die is cast. 'Tis France for ye now, lad. The only thing, at all, at all. 'Tis but foolishness to be knocking your dear head against the wall . . . '

'God in Heaven – the *Tutor*-General now!' Elcho snorted.

A new uproar sank and dwindled at the hollow beat of horse's hooves on the heather. A single rider came pounding across the moor from the north-east, from the direction of the battlefield, on a shaggy and sweat-lathered Highland garron. A tall lean handsome figure this, dressed in MacGregor tartans and a major's insignia.

'James Mor!' Glengyle exclaimed. 'So we have not lost him yet!' Gregor Black Knee muttered something else below his breath, and he and his son exchanged glances.

'I sent him back to endeavour to reach Locheil,' the Prince said. 'To bring him here, if he might. Alas, it appears . . . otherwise.'

The newcomer flung himself dramatically off his foundered pony, and came swaggering up to the waiting group. Everything that man did was done with a swagger – whether it was leading a charge, seducing a woman, cutting a throat, or merely undermining confidence in lesser men than himself. His bonnet, with its single eagle's feather, now swept low in an exaggerated yet somehow fleering obeisance to the Prince.

'I thank God for your safe return, Major MacGregor,' Charles said – who, unlike some others, esteemed him highly. 'But . . . you are alone, I see!'

'And, on my soul, devilish lucky to be that itself, Highness!' the horseman replied, grinning. 'But, then – the devil aye looks after his own, does he not? Eh, Gregor?' And he glanced side-long at his cousin. 'You preserved your soul also, I see. And even dear Duncan Beg here, likewise!'

'And Locheil?' the Prince asked urgently. 'We have just

heard, from Glengyle, that he is said to be wounded. But in the hands of his own people . . . '

'That is more or less the way of it, yes,' the new MacGregor agreed, elaborately stifling a yawn. 'Locheil sends suitable greetings, Highness, and suggests that he will see you another day!'

'Another day? You mean . . . ?'

'I mean, sir, that Locheil is off home to Achnacarry on Loch Arkaig-side as fast as some hundreds of running Cameron heels can carry him. And the Camerons were ever good at running!'

'James Mor will have his little jest, sir,' Gregor of Glengyle interpreted quietly. 'If Cameron of Locheil is shot in both ankles with grape, then he is in no state to be sending greetings, nor yet ordering his clansfolk. And Achnacarry is the best place for him, whatever – and the faster there, the better. Ewan Cameron is as true and sure a man as your Highness commands.'

'Yes, indeed, Glengyle. I know it well . . . '

The two MacGregors looked at each other. They were full cousins, although James Mor was considerably the younger – only a little older, indeed, than Gregor's son, the Captain Duncan. He was a dark, sardonically good-looking man, hawk-faced with just a wicked wisp of moustache and beard, almost as tall as Gregor although less broadly built. He was a son of the famous Rob Roy, now dead some eleven years, but a very different man from his father. Nominally second-in-command of Glengyle's Regiment, which he had led with great gallantry and no less than five wounds at Prestonpans, he had latterly spent most of his time in the Prince's personal entourage as a sort of extra aide-de-camp and courier. His cousin made no complaint at this development – nor his second-cousin either.

'Do not tell me that your own self and Duncan are the sole survivors of our graceless band, Gregor?' James Mor asked.

'There are some six score behind the trees younder. We cut our way out. You were . . . otherwise engaged, I take it, James?'

'Exactly.'

'Have you heard aught of Glencarnock? How his regiment fared?'

There were two MacGregor regiments in the Prince's army, for the clan was split. A part of it recognised Balhaldy as chief

18

of the name of MacGregor, long with King James in France, and of these Glengyle was the foremost chieftain; the other part claimed the leadership for Murray MacGregor of Glencarnock, and he had brought his own following to the Jacobite array. It had been brigaded with the Mackintoshes in the centre of the first line.

'They fared but ill, I fear,' James Mor said. 'Unlike the MacDonalds, the Mackintoshes charged too soon. And Glencarnock with them. Ah, well – they paid the price of impetuosity! Glencarnock ever lacked judgement, did he not? Though they say that he is a prisoner, himself . . .'

'Your Highness – may the MacGregors be permitted to discuss their private affairs on some other occasion!' Lord Elcho interrupted. 'At the moment we have more urgent matters to decide. We have lingered here too long already. At any moment the dragoons may be upon us. A decision must be reached, sir.'

'Yes, yes, my lord.' Charles pressed hand to head again. 'Jamie – did you see aught of skirmishers? Videttes? Are Cumberland's dragoons indeed anywhere near?'

'I dodged three or four parties, yes, on my way back,' the Major said. 'I came by Aultlugie and Daviot Castle. A picket was at the castle – I saw their red coats. And I saw a troop cutting down stragglers along the Nairn's banks below. Another troop were shooting what looked like Menzies men – bright red tartans, at any rate – that they had cornered just over yonder ridge . . .'

'Lord – so close!' the Master of Lovat exclaimed. 'Then it is time that we were gone, by the Rood! Sir, to horse, I say!'

'Indeed yes, Your Highness.'

' 'Tis folly to remain here longer.'

'Very well, gentlemen.' The Prince rose to his feet. 'So be it. If the dragoons are already along the Nairn at Daviot, then the route to Ruthven and Badenoch, by Moy and The Slochd, is already closed. To go northwards again, the way we came, to Inverness, would be foolishness. It is what Cumberland will expect, where he will look for me. He will make for Inverness, *certainement*. We part here, therefore, gentlemen – to my sorrow. I go south by west, up Strathnairn, as the Master of Lovat advises, for Fort Augustus, the Cameron country and the sea. Whence I came. God pity me!'

'And at Ruthven . . . ?' Elcho demanded. 'The Lord George and the Duke? Cluny Macpherson and the rest? What of them?'

'You will convey to them my love and devotion and grateful thanks, my lord. And my last orders – that they disperse forthwith to their homes.'

'Then . . . Lord God above! All is over! Done with! The Cause is lost – and Scotland with it!'

'I am sorry, my lord – desolate. But . . . I have no choice.'

'You have choice enough, sir – but you choose ill!'

'Enough, sir! You forget yourself. My father's cause will be saved now in France, not here. Not here.'

'Thank God that your Highness has listened to reason!' O'Sullivan cried. 'To wise and proper counsels.'

'A hundred MacGregors, yonder, would not call them that!' Gregor Black Knee said heavily.

'I grieve that you think not, Glengyle. But I must do what I believe is best,' Charles Edward told him. 'For yourself, you also will do what you deem best. For you and for your regiment. It is now every man for himself, I fear.'

'I have no doubts, sir, as to what is best for me and mine. We march north to Inverness, picking up such other stragglers as will march with proper men. Food there is there, and food my men must have. Inverness is still your town, with a garrison and provisions. Cumberland will not take it tonight, with his own wounds to lick! Then we march ever north, into the Mackenzie country of Cromartie and Seaforth. None shall take us, there. Nor take *you*, if you will but come with us . . . ?'

'No, my friend – that is not how it must be. For me. For yourselves, God be with you. We shall maintain contact, for so long as I am in Scotland – for, who knows, I may need your gallant Gregorach yet. No doubt Major Jamie will be with me, to serve as courier between us, if need be . . . '

'Alas, Highness, I think not!' James Mor intervened lightly, smiling yet. 'As you yourself so aptly put it, now it is every man for himself. Myself, I confess that I'd sooner trust my skin to one hundred MacGregor broadswords, in Cumberland's Scotland, than to, h'm, your royally select band! I pray to be excused the honour!'

The Prince looked at him steadily for a moment, brown eyes into black. 'I see,' he said.

Quietly Duncan MacGregor spoke into the brief silence. 'I will come with you, sir. To serve as link,' he said.

His father opened lips to speak, and then closed them again. 'Valiant cousin!' James Mor murmured.

'Very well, Captain,' Charles said. 'That is all then, gentlemen, I think. This is . . . farewell. God's blessing on you all . . . and the undying gratitude of your Prince. And of your King. I . . . I . . . ' His voice broke, as he held out his hand to Glengyle.

That man stooped low, to kiss it. Others formed up to do likewise – but not all. Elcho bowed stiffly, from a little way off.

Charles Edward Stuart turned quickly away, and went striding through the trees, towards the troopers of FitzJames's Horse, Young Lovat, Sheridan, O'Sullivan, Hay and Captain O'Neil following. Also, at a decent distance, Ned Burke the Prince's valet.

Duncan MacGregor looked at his father, and clasped his hand silently. Then he glanced at James Mor. 'I will take your garron,' he said. That was all.

Vaulting lightly on to its lather-flecked broad back, he rode after the Prince.

CHAPTER 2

DUNCAN MACGREGOR had to drive the stocky short-legged Highland pony hard indeed even to keep in sight of the Prince's fast-riding company, mounted as they were on tall and comparatively fresh horses. Heading almost due south, they skirted a number of small lochans and peat-pools amongst the heather, making for the long southwards slope towards the River Nairn. They thundered past many fleeing Highlanders, singly and in pairs and small parties, not a few of them carrying or supporting wounded comrades, but stopped for none of them. Duncan noted one party of horsemen on the skyline to the east, but whether they were dragoons or some of their own leaderless cavalry he could not tell, with a storm of sleet lowering its grey curtain between them. The troopers of FitzJames's Horse formed a tight cordon about Charles and his group, and drove their mounts unmercifully.

They reached the river in the vicinity of Faillie and galloped along past the ford of the same name, the water running high and yellow with the rains. The floor of the strath, on both sides of the river, was dotted with hurrying fugitives from the battle, of various clans. Of a company of Frasers, in better order than most, his own people who, like himself had arrived too late to take any notable part in the fighting. Young Lovat demanded in the Gaelic whether any of Cumberland's dragoons had been seen thus far up-river – to be told that a troop of light cavalry in blue tunics, Brunswicker hussars by the description, were indeed in front on this side of the Nairn, ignoring the fleeing infantrymen and apparently making each laird's house in the strath their target. Duncan came up on his pony while this information was being translated, and saw the effect of it upon Charles and his companions. It was decided to turn back a little way, and to cross the ford.

By the time that they had splashed across the river, making a difficult task of it in the flood-water in which they could not see the bottom, the Prince had come to the conclusion that he would be safer without his bodyguard, the sixteen troopers being liable only to draw attention to his little party, whilst being insufficient to protect them against any formation of the enemy that they might be expected to encounter. They were instructed to take themselves off, therefore, to head straight into the trackless mountains of the Monadh Liath south by east, to make their way as best they could to Ruthven. Duncan MacGregor at least was sorry for them; mainly Spaniards and Frenchmen, he believed that their chances of reaching Ruthven, fifty terrible miles away, were slender indeed – even if they never saw a Redcoat.

The Master of Lovat now led the Prince's party of eight. They went more discreetly, no longer in headlong gallop, by little-used tracks and by-ways. The main route up Strath Nairn followed the other bank of the river, and this side was more broken, wooded, and with less of habitation – more apt for fugitives altogether, although innumerable burns coming in off the mountains had to be crossed, often in deep and precipitous ravines and with never a bridge to any of them.

Some five miles up the strath they came to the house of

Mackintosh of Tordarroch. The laird himself had last been seen, wounded but still swording, on Culloden Moor. His house, however, provided his Prince with no sustenance that night, for it stood dark and shuttered, with every appearance of having been but recently and hastily abandoned. Whether indeed anyone lurked within, they could not tell; none answered their banging at the locked and barred doors, at any rate, and all cattle, horses and even poultry were gone from the out-buildings.

It was dark, and raining steadily, before their guide brought them to the next hoped-for sanctuary, some eight miles further – the House of Aberarder. They were in Lovat's own clan territory here, but although the Master had sought Aberarder's aid only the day before in enlisting a second battalion for the Fraser Regiment, tonight his house was as black and deserted as that of Tordarroch. Clearly word of the defeat had preceded them, with the uncanny swiftness by which news can travel in the seemingly empty Highlands – with this result. The implications, the acceptance that all was lost and only savage reprisals could now be expected, did nothing to cheer hungry, weary and disheartened travellers.

'By the Cross of Christ – they have not waited long before scuttling into their hills!' O'Sullivan exclaimed, disgustedly.

'Would you – with German Cumberland charged to teach Scotland a lesson?' Sawny MacLeod demanded.

When, at Farraline, another Fraser house a few miles further, and over the watershed into Stratherrick, they discovered the same state of affairs, Young Lovat, crestfallen and angry, came to a decision. They would make for Gortlech House, across at the other side of Loch Farraline, even although it would involve a long and arduous circuit of the loch. They would find that house open and occupied, at any rate – for no less a person than the great MacShimi, his father the Lord Lovat himself, was presently lodging there. That he had not proposed to conduct his Prince to Gortlech and his father – who held a Jacobite lieutenant-general's commission from King James – before this, might have appeared a little strange in the circumstances; but perhaps the Master had his own reasons, and moreover knew the great MacShimi better than most.

Heavily, wordlessly now, the tired and dispirited party splashed and floundered and stumbled its way around the

23

flooded boggy shores of Loch Farraline, the horses now as weary as their riders. Indeed, in the pass, Duncan MacGregor's sturdy garron made the best showing, making up in stamina for what it lacked in pace and style, sure-footed and with an apparent ability to see in the dark. Until near the house itself, on rising ground to the west of the loch, Duncan led the way in fact.

The Master had been right. Lights shone in friendly fashion from the windows of Gortlech House. Nevertheless, the little company's welcome was less than reassuring, warm as it might be. When still approaching uphill through dripping birch trees and shadowy junipers, the horsemen were suddenly and without warning surrounded by a horde of Gaelic-shouting fighting-men who seemed to rise out of the very ground at their horses' hooves, swords and dirks in their hands. They had old Sheridan, O'Sullivan and Ned Burke dragged off their mounts and naked steel at their throats before the Master of Lovat could make his identity recognised. The Prince and O'Neil were hurriedly drawing their own swords and at the same time seeking to control their rearing steeds, when MacLeod and Duncan Mac-Gregor managed to convey to them that these were only MacShimi's guards and loyal Frasers all.

In an atmosphere compounded of relief, resentment and lingering suspicion, all came to Gortlech House.

Fraser of Gortlech himself appeared to be a man torn by conflicting emotions. When the quality of his guests was made known to him, he most evidently did not know whether to express first his sense of honour, his commiserations or his own agitation and alarm. That he also had heard the news of Culloden was apparent – and the fact that he had had a son in the battle, of whose fate the Master could tell him nothing, did not help to soothe him. He and his lady, in fact mislead by a garbled report of the supposed success of the Jacobite army's abortive night venture against Cumberland's birthday celebrations at Nairn, had that day been preparing a great feast to celebrate the Prince's anticipated victory, and his old chief's imminent translation to his coveted dukedom. Now, in incoherent gabbling perturbation, he led Charles and his followers upstairs to the principal room of the house.

There was nothing of incoherence or apparent perturbation about the man who sat at ease, decanter in hand, alone at the head of a long and groaning table therein. Coming in out of the

24

wet and windy night, after that prolonged and perilous flight from horror and disaster, the quiet comfort, plenty and air of assured and established well-being in the lamp-lit and richly provisioned apartment, was sufficiently striking to bring up the dishevelled and travel-stained newcomers with an almost physical start.

As indeed did the appearance of the room's sole occupant. Simon Fraser made an extraordinary figure. Squat and heavy and immensely broad, almost toad-like, he sprawled there, gross, repulsively ugly in form and feature, yet of an undeniable and strange distinction. Sagging-bodied, blotchy of face, physically corrupt, but shrewd-eyed, glittering-eyed indeed, his thick gouty legs stuck out before him like great logs, he was slovenly clad in a mixture of Highland and Lowland dress, the tartans so stained as to be unrecognisable, the disordered lace at throat and wrists torn and discoloured, wig askew, small-clothes undone. An old man, nearing his eightieth year in fact, he sat there dissipated, potent, ageless.

'MacShimi,' his son announced, from the Prince's shoulder. 'His Royal Highness the Prince of Wales, Duke of Rothesay, and Chevalier de Saint George.'

Lovat stared, silent for a moment or two, and then made a mere gesture at rising to his feet – an action of which he was obviously incapable without assistance. 'My esteemed and beloved sir, my precious Prince and true paladin,' he said. 'Scotland's fair hope and future King – behold your most humble, loving and devoted servant!' That was enunciated in courtly French, in a voice singularly and unexpectedly musical, clear and youthful-sounding. 'I rejoice that these old eyes should be thus blest. Your Royal Highness – will you come close that these poor lips may kiss your hand?'

Charles Edward, distrait and weary as he might be, was not a man who could fail to respond to such a greeting. Lack-lustre eyes lighting warmly, he strode forward beside the table to its head, hand outstretched, smiling. 'My lord,' he exclaimed, 'I rejoice that we meet at last! I have heard much of you ...'

'And not all of it to my credit, I swear, lad!' the old man took him up swiftly, kissing the royal fingers. 'Wae's me, there's a-many who would see me low that they might ride higher – many who would make bad blood between MacShimi and your gracious father, to their own advantage.' He continued to hold

25

and plant kisses on the Prince's hand, in embarrassing and almost maudlin fashion – but his shrewd little eyes darted and probed.

'My father, like myself, is assured of your faithful love and devotion, my lord,' Charles declared. 'I would only that I came to assert it on a happier occasion.'

'Aye – so does MacShimi, lad! So does MacShimi! An ill night, this, for true men, by all accounts.' Lovat cast a quick glance at his son. 'There will be a price to pay for the day's work, I warrant. That some of us will pay dearer than others! Who have less to lose! Were you in it, at all, Sim? Were you in it? I'm thinking likely you would not have been in time to be actually drawing a sword, at all?' There was little doubt as to the answer that he hoped for, in that.

'All was lost by the time that I came up,' the Master told him. 'As you know, I had been raising a second battalion. I was only in time to strike a blow or two. And help cover His Highness's retiral . . .'

'Fool!' his father spat out unexpectedly, almost viciously. 'What good in that? To draw sword when a fight is lost is the work of a half-wit! Naught is achieved, save to bring down punishment upon the innocent and the helpless!' He gestured, and most clearly included his own gross helplessness in the sweep of his hand. 'There is a time to strike – and a time to withhold, 'fore God!'

'Your lordship knows well, sure, the difficulty of nicely judging such time,' O'Sullivan mentioned tartly, from down the table – in scarcely veiled allusion to Lovat's own long-delayed and indeed only recent public commitment to the present Jacobite venture.

The great head jerked round with almost reptilian speed. 'To whom have I the honour to listen, Your Highness?' he snapped.

'To Colonel O'Sullivan, my Adjutant-General and Quarter-master,' the Prince informed. And quickly. 'Here also is Sir Thomas Sheridan, Colonel Hay, Military Secretary, Captains O'Neil and MacLeod, aides, and . . .'

'Aye, aye – to be sure. Worthy warriors all, I'll be bound! Welcome to MacShimi's poor table, gentlemen. It was prepared to signal your victory – not your defeat! But draw in, draw in – we must e'en do as we're done by. Your Highness – a glass. Fill up. We shall drink a toast to better days . . .'

'My lord,' Colonel Hay said stiffly. 'The Prince – all of us – have not eaten more than a biscuit all day. Nor much more yesterday, indeed. This food . . . ' He waved at the laden table, all but licking his lips. 'I . . . we . . . '

'Why – set to then, gentlemen. God save us – set to! Victory or defeat – and I'm waiting to hear why it was the latter, mind – victory or defeat, the belly must be served. Highness – sit you here, by me. Gortlech, man – fetch more meats, cates, provision. And the claret's low. Though poor MacShimi may die for it, none shall say that his Prince came to his table and was not filled, sought shelter and was turned away!'

'It is only a bite and a sup that we seek, my lord,' Charles told him. 'We must be far from here before the night is out, I assure you. I must reach the sea, the Western Sea, as soon as may be, to my sorrow.'

'Say ye so?' Lord Lovat considered the younger man thoughtfully.

The others, without ceremony or delay, fell upon the spread food.

The pangs of his hunger appeased for the moment, Duncan MacGregor sat back in the lowest place at that table, and eyed his host and provider with but little of the gratitude that would have been seemly. He did not trust the noble mountain of flesh one inch further than his broadsword tip would reach – being a MacGregor and of an uncomplicated mind. The man had changed sides so often, was so well known to have sold the Stuart cause time and again, that this guest at least wondered indeed how the Prince could have anything to do with him. Presumably it was because he was still one of the greatest chiefs in the Highlands, and could raise a thousand Fraser swords. Could – but would he? Ever? He was clever, too – too clever by half; but had he ever turned either his talents or his power to any purpose other than his own private satisfaction or advancement? The Gregorach would have known how to deal with MacShimi.

But Charles Edward, as ever, was apparently prepared to believe the best of him. As he ate and drank he answered Lovat's probing questions about the battle unreservedly, accepted his belching strictures and improved strategy patiently, and only gently corrected the Fraser when his outspoken denunciation of practically all others exceeded the allowable. Duncan marvelled

27

at his forbearance – and would not believe it weakness.

Suddenly Lovat changed his tune. 'And what's this about making for the sea, young man?' he demanded. 'The sea will be winning you no battles. What is your meaning?'

'My meaning, sir, is to return to France. French ships were to keep patrol along that seaboard, where I landed those months ago. To seek to prevail upon King Louis to honour his pledge and send us the men and arms and money which he promised. That, as I see it, is the most effective way in which I may serve my father, and you all, in this pass. I cannot ... '

'France, eh?' the old chief interrupted. 'You are for France again? On which knave's advice would you be fleeing away to France, man? Will you leave your loyal and faithful Highlands, because of one reverse?'

The Prince frowned. 'You call this day's disaster but a reverse, my lord ... ?'

'A ruffle, sir – a ruffle, no more. There are as many bold lads in the heather within fifty miles of this house as Cumberland can count in all Scotland!'

'But no guns for them, no ammunition, no provisions, no money. And but few trained officers,' Charles shook his fair head, heavily. 'I have discovered, my friend, that more than bold lads are needful to win a throne, and to defeat trained and disciplined soldiers ... '

'They did it at Prestonpans and Clifton, did they not? Even at Falkirk ... '

'At Preston they were fresh, light-hearted, full of confidence, of hope. We all were full of hope. Today, it is ... otherwise. We have retreated six hundred miles, from Derby, six hundred long miles. Have you ever been in a very long retreat, my lord? I think not.' Even Charles could sound bitter, on a rare occasion. 'We have been losing men, whole companies, by desertion, through offence, through petty squabbling, for months. *Mafoi* – today's ruffle, as you name it, was the end, the culmination, of many reverses, not the first.' The Prince's voice wavered, and his head sank forward almost to his arms upon the table.

Lovat's urgent glance considered him, and all of the other heavy-eyed, weary and dishevelled men around his table, probing, calculating – and Duncan MacGregor, of them all, watched him. Then the old man's great swollen hand clapped down on the younger's shoulder,

'Och, och, lad – you are tired, that is all,' he cried. 'Here is no way for Scotland's future King to talk! Damnation – your great ancestor talked not so, sir! King Robert Bruce, who lost eleven battles yet won Scotland by the twelfth! Take heart, man!'

Charles slowly raised his head. 'You think . . . you believe . . . that I can yet rally the cause? At this late hour?' he faltered. 'That there is still support for me in Scotland, to win the day? *You* think that?'

'By the Mass, I do! Would MacShimi, with his own head and fortune and a province to lose, be sitting here persuading you to it, otherwise. Hech, hech, sir – what do you take me for?'

That question more than one man was asking himself, at Gortlech's table, Duncan MacGregor not the least searchingly. He who would die for his Prince, doubted strongly whether the Lord Lovat would do so. Why then was he counselling resistance? Duncan himself, like his father, was for the continuance of the fight, at all costs, and should have welcomed this powerful ally. But why did MacShimi so urge, when clearly the fight would be long and arduous, and success far from assured? He, who knew only too well the difficulties, the weaknesses of the clan system, the fatal jealousies of the chiefs, the unending intrigues – he, indeed, who had instigated so many of the intrigues himself? Lovat had delayed to the very last moment, before reluctantly joining the Prince – and even so, maintaining a loophole of escape by pretending to the Government that it was really his headstrong son's doing against an old man's wishes. Why should he now talk as thought victory could be just behind the next hill?

Charles himself, it seemed, however forgiving, was not wholly blind to this curious contradiction. 'And yet you, my lord, not so long ago, were naming me . . . what was it? A mad and unaccountable gentleman, I think. Yes, such a one, for coming to Scotland at all, without a French army, urging me to return thither, and assuring that all that you could offer me, in these circumstances, were your prayers! Here is a notable change, to be sure?'

For a moment Lovat's extraordinary face was wiped clear of all expression. Then he smiled, almost reproachfully. 'Your Highness will be recognising that circumstances can alter prospects, whatever! You have proved, bonny sir, that you can win battles as you can men's hearts. That the Highlands will rise for you – even if the Lowlands and the Englishry will not. That MacShimi was mistaken yon time. Sink me, lad – now that Cumberland is at our very doors, will not the Highlands rise the more readily? If ten thousand rose to march with you away to yonder London, how many more will rise to defend their own glens, their own rooftrees?'

'I would that I could believe you, my lord . . .'

Duncan thought that he saw it now. The phrase of Lovat's – now that Cumberland is at our very doors! Was that the key to it all? Nearer to Clan Fraser's doors than any other. That could be the reason for MacShimi's fervour. He would have the Rising prolonged, the clans reassembled, the battle renewed – to save his own territory from being over-run, his own rooftrees spared. That made sense out of MacShimi. It was entirely in character for the man to seek to sacrifice a host in his own protection.

Perhaps even MacGregor was not wholly unbiased in this conclusion – and something of Prince Charles's problem in holding together a clan army exemplified.

It was noticeable that the Master of Lovat uttered no words in his puissant father's presence.

'His lordship's faith is touching, sir – but, I fear, too late!' O'Sullivan put in, out of a full mouth. 'A thousand Frasers *yesterday* – and all might have been otherwise!'

'The Irish, I have ever observed, are an unhappy race,' Lovat mentioned conversationally. 'As over-ready with their tongues as they are backward in judgement. And manners, forby . . .'

'Sir!' O'Sullivan's chair scraped back over the floor abruptly. 'I will take such words from no man, by God! Not even you . . .'

'At MacShimi's table, eating MacShimi's victuals, you have scant choice, man! Sit you down and fill your belly, Quartermaster. Belike you'll travel far and fare worse!'

'Your Royal Highness, I protest!' That was Captain O'Neil rising in support of his fellow-countryman.

'Gentlemen, gentlemen!' Almost automatically, and so very wearily, the Prince called his followers to order – as he had been doing for nine months. 'We are beholden to Lord Lovat, and our need is great. His lordship did but jest, I am sure. We have no time to waste on such foolishness. We must be gone forthwith. We cannot linger here.'

Lovat turned back to the speaker swiftly. 'Where?' he demanded. 'Where go you now?'

'Where, but through Locheil's and Glengarry's country, to the sea?'

'Not waiting for the clans to assemble again?'

Charles shrugged his shoulders, helplessly, hopelessly.

'See you,' the old man pressed. 'Send you out orders, from here. Now. My gillies will carry them. Through our own country. Into Lochaber and Locheil and Ardgour. Into Glengarry and Glenmoriston. Into Badenoch and Atholl. To rally to Your Highness. Not here – not just here, mind. This is not a convenient place, at all. At Fort Augustus, maybe. Aye, at Fort Augustus – that would be best . . . '

'I have not the time, my lord. I must be well beyond Fort Augustus by daylight. You do not understand – Cumberland's dragoons are at our heels. They are scouring the country. *Mon Dieu* – some of his light cavalry was actually ahead of us, coming up Strath Nairn!'

'*Dia* – you say that? They were that far?'

'They were. I cannot wait for the clans to reassemble. Long ere they could do so, I would be in Cumberland's bloody hands.'

Lovat's thick fingers beat a tattoo on the table. 'What of Cluny? My good-son. Cluny and his Macphersons cannot be that far away . . . ?'

'No doubt they are now hurrying back into their own mountain fastnesses in Badenoch. They may have joined with the Lord George and the Duke, making for Ruthven.'

There was a sombre pause. Into it, since no one else saw fit to speak, greatly daring, Duncan MacGregor raised his voice.

'Your Highness,' he said. 'MacShimi. There is a middle course. Whereby much may be saved, much gained – and Your Highness's person preserved from capture. Your army, your officers, scattered as they may be, will be looking for orders from their Captain-General – nothing is surer. Send them orders, from here, sir, as MacShimi says, by his gillies. To assemble in two days, three days. Somewhere that is suitable and safe. In the Cameron country – Loch Arkaig. The dragoons will not dare to penetrate yonder for some time, where they could be trapped like rats. And for immediately, tonight, tomorrow – have MacShimi's runners go out to his own people. And to

31

others near at hand, Glengarry's people, Grants of Glenmoriston, and to the Keppoch country. Ordering them to meet with you at Fort Augustus. At dawn, if you wish it. The hour is barely nine. By dawn, in eight hours, many could reach Fort Augustus.' Duncan looked directly at Lovat. 'I have no doubt that the great MacShimi alone could have five hundred Frasers there by then! With these, your Highness could then retire westwards meantime, safe into the Cameron country. Then join the main assembly at Loch Arkaig or elsewhere, later.'

Lovat glowered at the MacGregor heavily. 'Here's a young cockerel crows loud and clear!' he growled. 'Out of a Gregorach roost, by the colours of him! Cattle-thieves, of course, are aye apt for night work and dodging in the heather!'

Duncan's knuckles gleamed white as he clenched his fists on the arms of his chair. But he held his tongue.

'And yet, my lord, Captain MacGregor – who is son to Glengyle – speaks good sense, does he not?' the Prince observed. 'And largely in accord with your own suggestions, it seems?'

The old man pulled at his fleshy chin. Although superficially Duncan's proposals might seem but an extension of Lovat's own, in fact they were quite otherwise. Quite clearly the course that the younger man envisaged would drain Fraser manpower away from Fraser territory, committing Lovat to a major role in any resurrection of the campaign, and at the same time leaving his own lands largely unprotected. It did not demand any great percipience to recognise that this was a very different matter from having the Jacobite army reassembling at Fort Augustus, less than twenty miles away on the verge of Fraser country, where it would serve to keep Cumberland's marauding cavalry at a distance. Minds round that table, of course, were sluggish and fogged with fatigue.

'Ah. H'mmm.' Their host cast darting glances round them all. 'I will do what I can. What I can. Och, yes – MacShimi will do what may be done, whatever. But . . . what sense is there in getting swallowed up away yonder in Locheil's country? Barren empty mountains, just . . .'

'But secure, my lord – secure. Hemmed in and guarded by the same barren mountains. The enemy may only approach yonder by one route, which is easily guarded.'

'Aye. But once in there, the clans themselves will be trapped.

Better assemble in some more central place, Highness. Where all may readily come together. Fort Augustus, I swear, would be the best . . . '

'For Augustus will be warming with Redcoats by noontide tomorrow, sir. No – if assembly there shall be, it had better be in the west. Loch Arkaig is as good as any.' Charles Edward stood up – and perforce all others, save only Lovat himself, must do likewise. 'Let that be the way of it, gentlemen. Though God knows if aught will come of it!'

'How shall all these be fed? In these so notoriously barren mountains, sir?' O'Sullivan demanded.

'They must just fend for themselves. As ourselves must do . . . '

'Let the orders command those coming from their own homes, at least – the Frasers and others – each to bring a pouch of oatmeal enough for a week, sir,' Duncan advised, quickly.

'Orders . . . !' The Prince ran a hand through his hair. '*Ma foi* – never did I feel less like writing orders. Sawny MacLeod – write to Cluny. And to Lord George. To meet at Loch Arkaig in three days. I shall sign it. You yourself will carry the message. See as many chiefs and commanders as you may. You understand?'

'Yes, sir. And what of those to the north? Beyond Inverness? Glengyle's and Barrisdale's Regiments? My Lord Cromartie's force . . . ?'

'I shall go for them,' Duncan said.

'No,' the Prince decided. 'There is no time for them to come. Inverness and all around it will be in Cumberland's hands by morning, by now it may be. To reach these others, and bring them all the way south and west to Loch Arkaig, round through the Mackenzie country, would take many days. Let them remain north of Inverness meantime, as a threat to Cumberland's rear. Sawny – write your orders, and I shall sign them. My lord – you need no written orders from me to your people? To have them at Fort Augustus by the dawn? In eight hours. You will send them your own instructions?'

Lovat toyed with his wine-glass. 'No doubt you are right, Highness,' he said at length. 'Aye – MacShimi will send his own instructions.'

'Very well. Then, as quickly as we may, gentlemen, let us be

33

on our way. With our grateful thanks to my Lord Lovat. And to the Master.'

The old man cackled a laugh.

CHAPTER 3

THE little group of men huddled together behind the broken ramparts of the fort, to gain such shelter as they might from the thin driving rain. None had spoken for the best part of an hour, other than to mutter a curse or two. In the grey light of early morning the scene was as desolate as were their spirits. The shattered walls of Fort Augustus, named after Cumberland himself and strengthened and enlarged by General Wade only six years before, had been stormed and demolished by the Frasers only a month ago – the sign and symbol of Lovat's belated public adherence to the Jacobite cause. Today, however, they spoke nothing of victory, or triumph; only of dripping ruin and owl-haunted desolation. The surrounding hillsides were blotted out under low mists and rain. Some of the men had dozed, as they crouched there, at the first, all but stupefied by lack of sleep; but the chill had soon awakened them again to their miseries.

It was only a small company that waited there. Captain MacLeod had departed southwards, with a Fraser gillie as guide, making for Ruthven by Glen Tarff and the Corryarrack Pass – no easy journey in such conditions. The Master of Lovat had remained behind at Gortlech with his father, meantime. Only the Prince, Hay of Restalrig, and three Irishmen and Ned Burke the servant, apart from Duncan MacGregor, kept their trying vigil by the ruined fort.

That it was a vigil as fruitless as it was trying, had become ever more evident as the comfortless minutes had lengthened into hours. No one had been found there when the royal party had arrived, at around three in the morning; no single man had approached the rendezvous since. The seven fugitive were quite alone in the grey cold world of the mountains.

The Prince had been fretting almost from the start, his reluctant agreement to an attempt to resume the campaign fading like snow in summer. Nor did the three Irishmen, Charles's closest intimates, seek to maintain his resolve – nor yet Colonel Hay, whose views were quite otherwise. Only the young Mac-Gregor sought to counter the tide of reaction and pessimism, and that with the inevitable lack of authority of a very junior regimental officer – although he was in fact a couple of years older than the Prince himself. Even Duncan fell silent as time wore on.

At last Charles would stand it no longer. '*Dieu de Dieu* – this is intolerable!' he cried. 'What profit is there in further waiting? Are we lepers, to lurk and skulk here, shunned of all? None come. None rally to us – not one man! So much for Lovat's bold clansmen! A thousand Frasers within a few miles of me, and not one will rally to my banner! Not one to draw sword for his King!'

'Belike scarce one knows that you are here, sir,' O'Sullivan said. 'My Lord Lovat may have changed his mind, I think! Not for the first time!'

'The old fox has sent out no orders, at all, I swear!' Hay asserted. 'He has held his hand, curse him! I never trusted the man. Though it was but a crazy project from the first . . .'

'Even in his disappointment and despondency, Charles would not hear so ill of the Fraser chief. 'No, no, my friends – Lovat would not act so ill,' he declared. 'He is a strange man – but one of my father's oldest friends and supporters. It will be his people. They will have perhaps fled into the hills. Left their homes. For fear of the dragoons. That will be it. His messengers will still be seeking them . . .'

For once, Duncan MacGregor tended to be in agreement with O'Sullivan and Hay – although he did not say so. 'No doubt Your Highness is right,' he acceded. 'And eight hours is but a short time, at dead of night, to arm and leave all and come here . . .'

'But we dare not wait longer here, Charles.' Old Sir Thomas Sheridan had roused himself and risen, still bent and aching, from the fallen masonry on which he had been sitting. 'You have delayed overlong already,' he said, his teeth chattering. 'Danger there is, all around us, here. The main road, it is, between Inverness and Fort William. Cumberland is bound to effect a junction with his garrison at Fort William, forthwith. Sure, it is madness, lad, to linger here.'

'That is true, sir. Your Highness's safety demands that we go from here. At once . . . '

'Yes, John. Yes. We shall go. Forthwith. To Glengarry's house. It is not any great distance, I believe. Our beasts can do it – and so can we. How far, Duncan my friend?'

'Eight or nine miles, perhaps. No more.'

'Better that we do not halt there, sir – that we go on westwards,' O'Sullivan objected. 'We should still be on this same road from Inverness, at Invergarry. Better to go on through the Cameron country, to the sea. I' faith, the sooner we reach the sea . . . '

'No, John. I told Lovat that I would move on to Glengarry's house from this rendezvous. His people may reach us there.'

'And others, likewise, Christ God!'

'I think not. Not so soon. It lies more secure than this, if I mind aright? How think you, Duncan?'

'I do not think that dragoons will reach Invergarry today, sir. Nor attack the castle if they do. It is in a strong position. And since Your Highness said that you would go there . . . '

'Very well. So be it. Gentlemen – to Invergarry. And, pray God, a bed!'

The rain had stopped and the sun had risen above the mountain ramparts to the east before the fugitives reached the long narrow sheet of Loch Oich, further down the endless gut of the Great Glen. It transformed all the upheaved world of the high places into a wonderland of colour and dazzlement, of light and shade, of the deep sepia of old heather streaked with the emerald of moss and bog and the crimson of raw red earth, of the bottle green of the old Scots pines and the tender verdance of the budding silver birches, the blue of the loch and the white mist-wraiths rising out of the high corries, water glistening and gleaming everywhere and the heady sweet scent of the bog-myrtle ascending like incense to the praise of the new day.

All this brilliance but little lifted the spirits of the travellers, however – more especially when, midway down the west shore, on a jutting green peninsula where the turbulent River Garry joined its peat-brown waters to the loch, they saw the tall reddish-grey walls of Invergarry Castle rising forbiddingly before them, and not a plume of smoke from a chimney, not a flicker of movement from window or doorway, nor any sign of life about the place. In silence they rode up to the obviously empty, barred and deserted stronghold of the Glengarry chief.

It was a doubly bitter moment for Charles Edward Stuart. Here, within these walls only eight months before, he had been welcomed and feted by young Aeneas MacDonnell – who now lay buried at Falkirk. His father, John, twelfth of Glengarry, was a less successful fence-sitter than Lovat, and, unknown to his would-be guests, was even now lodged securely in Edinburgh Castle. His elder son Alastair, Young Glengarry, was still an officer in the French service. But Aeneas, nineteen years old, had brought out six hundred of the clan for the Cause. Here, last August, the Clanranald MacDonalds and the Appin Stewarts had also joined the Prince's standard, amidst high hopes. And now – this.

Sleep they must have, however. Unable to gain entry to the securely locked and barricaded castle, they hid the horses in a deserted stable and bedded down near-by in a loft and sweet-scented bog-hay. Duncan MacGregor volunteered to keep the first hour's watch.

For most of that day they lay at Invergarry. They were neither disturbed nor reinforced. No dragoons came near; no armed parties of clansmen came to join them, Frasers, Mac-Donnells or other; no living soul indeed approached that green peninsula in the blue loch. In the afternoon, Duncan, waking refreshed and hungry, searched the place for possible food – and found nothing. He did, however, notice salmon-nets permanently staked out in the loch across the mouth of the in-coming Garry. Taking a chance, he threw aside the clothes which had not been off his back in ten days and nights, and plunged into the water, gasping at its chill but glad of its cleanly purging. He was fortunate enough to find two salmon caught in the stake-nets, and brought them back to the shore in triumph. Although neither were monsters, they were quite substantial fish. Ned Burke cooked them on a modest fire of twigs and driftwood, roasted on spits. None complained that they were charred on the outside and under-cooked within. They were all the hospitality that Invergarry offered the Prince that day.

There was no argument, this time, as to moving on. That they could not stay here was self-evident. With the sun low over the massed abruptly rising hills to the west, a start was made. They turned south again, down the lochside, heading for Loch Lochy, the next sheet of water, where they could turn away westwards out of this Great Glen which cut Scotland in half, off through the narrow defile of the Dark Mile, into the Cameron country. They planned to ride all night again, towards the Hebridean Sea.

They had gone no more than a mile or so down the shore of the loch when they were abruptly brought to a halt. From the high rocky bank on their right fully a dozen armed men leapt down on to the drove-road at their sides, broadswords and dirks in hand. Ahead, a group of men appeared, kilted and plaided, barring the way.

'Stand, you!' a voice commanded fiercely, in the Gaelic. 'And never a hand on your weapons at all, if you value your lives!'

Twisting round in their saddles, the horsemen perceived three more Highlanders standing where they had just ridden, cocked pistols in hand.

Duncan MacGregor, unlike O'Neil, did not waste time in seeking to draw his sword. In the same motion that he whipped the plaid from around his shoulders, he flung himself bodily off his short-legged garron and on top of the nearest attacker. Two pistol shots cracked out as he plunged down. One ball tore a hole in the flapping corner of the plaid.

The folds of loose tartan cloth enveloped the unfortunate ambusher below, engulfing himself and his upraised broadsword even before Duncan's body knocked him flat on the ground. The MacGregor fell with him, inevitably, and the two men immediately became a struggling, rolling entity of flailing limbs and heaving tartan – into which none of the others might plunge steel for fear of striking the wrong man.

Captain O'Neil was indiscreet enough to unsheath his sword. One of the pistols had been aimed at him. The shot went low, scored a glancing wound along his horse's croup and went on just to sear the skin of O'Neil's thigh. With a whinny of pain the beast reared, throwing its rider sideways out of the saddle, and cannoning heavily into the Prince's mount. Charles, tugging at his own sword, was all but unseated, and found the retaining of his balance as much as he could do before half a dozen fierce hands grasped him and pulled him down to the road.

O'Sullivan, who had been shouting to the Prince to spur and

bolt forward, to ride down the men in front, at sight of his master's downfall, cursed, folded his arms, and so sat. Hay and old Sheridan prudently did nothing.

On the ground near-by the struggling pile had become larger, for Duncan, perceiving a pair of dancing feet near his head and assuming that they represented menace to himself, had thrust out an arm to encircle their owner's ankles, and brought down a second attacker with a crash upon himself – thereby unfortunately partly winding himself.

The MacGregor's object in all this, of drawing the onslaught of as many as possible of their aggressors upon himself, in order to allow the Prince to effect an escape, although it did not gain its ultimate aim, certainly attracted attention. When, in fact, no other fighting was going on, fully half the score or so of assailants were able to concentrate on him. That his somewhat ridiculous situation ended with a crack on the head from a pistol-butt wielded by the leader of the company, rather than many dirks being thrust into his body, was significant for more than Duncan Beg. (However it struck the others, its significance eluded the MacGregor just then.) His twisting thrashing body suddenly went limp, and his consciousness slipped away into welcome darkness.

Turning to the rest of the Prince's party, the spokesman of the enemy considered them all briefly and barked some orders in Gaelic, which evidently had to do with the holding and quietening down of the alarmed horses. Then, in English, he spoke – and it was noticeable that it was to O'Sullivan that he addressed himself.

'You are my prisoners, gentlemen,' he said, and it was apparent that the language did not come easily to him. He was a small wiry man, with a pronounced limp, dressed in a mixture of tartans, keen-eyed, swift of movement, with something of the aspect of a lame terrier dog. 'If you will not be foolish at all, no hurt will be coming to you. Come down from your horses, if you please.'

Those still mounted did as they were ordered.

'Are you Campbells, from Loudon's Regiment at Fort William?' O'Sullivan found his voice to demand.

The small man did not answer. He issued more swift orders to his followers, who proceeded to relieve the prisoners of their weapons and hemmed them in in a tight group. Others picked up the unconscious MacGregor, and threw him unceremoniously, like a sack, across the back of the most convenient horse, which was his own short-legged garron. Some took the other horses in charge, but none mounted. The leader put two fingers to his mouth and blew two ear-piercing whistles. In a few moments two men came running to them from around the twists of the drove-road, one from up-loch and one from down. Obviously they had been pickets set to watch the road for possible interruption. When these had joined them, without any further delay or discussion the small man led the entire company off the road, directly up the rocky bank at the west side and into the birches and alders of the steep wooded hillside above. The Prince and his companions had to use their hands, and sometimes even their knees, to aid them up the abruptly-rising and broken slippery slope, and the led cavalry horses made but a poor task of the ascent unlike the sure-footed pony that carried Duncan MacGregor.

No delay of man nor beast was permitted.

It was quite high above the road in the valley floor before they were granted a respite, very near the tree-line indeed, and the prisoners were panting heavily, Sir Thomas Sheridan especially being in much distress. There was a fairly well-defined track up here, running parallel with the road below but quite hidden from it. Along this, northwards again, the company turned. It was only on protests from the Prince and O'Sullivan that their principal captor agreed to a brief halt.

'Where are you taking us?' Charles Edward asked, of the leader, breathlessly. 'Why are you forcing us to climb this hill? Can you not see that it is too much for this gentleman? He is no longer young . . . '

The Prince was interrupted by Duncan MacGregor, coming to himself draped over the garron's back, and being violently sick. Charles promptly transferred his attention to him, aiding him down off the pony and supporting him as he staggered dizzily.

'My poor Duncan,' he said. '*Mon brave, mon ami* – you will feel very ill. See – take this. It will help.' And he drew a slim silver flask out of the capacious pocket of his long-skirted jacket of Stewart tartan, unscrewed the cap, and set it to the other's lips. 'Drink!'

Duncan sipped the fiery whisky gratefully. There was not a lot left in the flask. As, choking a little, he was handing it back to its owner, the small limping man stepped forward and snatched it from them. Briefly admiring the handsome craftsmanship and the Prince of Wales's feathers engraved thereon, he thrust it inside the folds of his own plaid, and turned away, pointing forward peremptorily.

'You are welcome, of course, friend,' Charles commented, shrugging, with a half-smile. 'So long as you will spare us the contents. Sir Thomas Sheridan, here, could well do with a mouthful, I swear.'

O'Sullivan who, like the other prisoners, had taken the opportunity to sit down amongst the young sprouting bracken, spoke up. 'That is no way to behave towards His Royal Highness, fellow!' he protested.

'Royal Highness . . . ?' the other repeated, looking from the speaker to Charles, and back. 'Are you not then the . . . the *Prionnsa*?'

The man looked along at the tall but slight and graceful figure supporting the unsteady MacGregor. It was perhaps not altogether strange that he had made his mistake. O'Sullivan was considerably older than the Prince, with a haughty and authoritative manner. The way that he had sat his horse, arms folded, after the attack, had been dignified, whatever else it was. Charles had lost his bonnet on Culloden Moor, and wore no distinguishing marks of his rank; and he was the one who appeared to be concerned for the welfare of the rest, rather than the master of them all. Their captor stared at him thoughtfully – and then turning about abruptly, gestured for the march to be resumed, and went striding ahead at a great pace.

Willy-nilly the prisoners followed, the Prince still assisting Duncan – that is until the leader, glancing back, noted it and sent a gillie to take the MacGregor's arm instead. When Charles called out that Sheridan would delay them less if he was mounted on the garron, since they seemed to be in an unconscionable hurry, the small man nodded shortly. Sir Thomas was allowed to ride thereafter.

Thus, with the gloaming all about them, they travelled northwards, dipping down presently through thicker woodland, to cross the rushing Garry by a dangerous-seeming ford perhaps a mile above the loch, the gillies plunging in up to their waists

41

without the least hesitation, although the saddle-horses required a deal of coaxing, with the Prince's party mounted again for the moment. Beyond, they entered the cover of the woods once more.

It was dark by the time that they crossed to the other side of the Great Glen, avoiding the Bridge of Oich and fording that river considerably further up, an unpleasant proceeding in the gloom. Then, despite protests from the tired and stumbling captives, they turned due eastwards up the long slow slope that lifted eventually, beyond the tree-level, to a bare shoulder of heather hill. All made it unmistakably clear that they were in no condition for hill climbing – not that they seemed to make any impression on their captor, who appeared to be tireless despite his limp. He pressed on down into the deeper shadows of a lesser glen beyond.

'This must be Glen Tarff,' Duncan told them. 'General Wade's new road runs up it, on the way to the Corryarrack.'

'What do we here, then?' the Prince demanded. 'Where are we being taken?'

Nobody answered him that.

Sure enough, presently they came down to the long pale scar of the military road, which after reconnaissance by their guards, they crossed and without delay plunged into a country of more woodland, scattered lochans and innumerable hummocks beyond. They had to stumble and flounder through almost a couple of miles of this before the small man acceded to the pleas of his prisoners and made a camp for the night.

They were back into the Fraser country again.

Round a fire of resinous and aromatic pine branches they sat thereafter, fed after a fashion by their escort on tough dried venison and *dramach*, or oatmeal and cold water mixed in an unappetising paste. Some of the gillies were posted as sentries, but most just cast themselves down amongst the blaeberries and slept without ceremony, but close to their captives. These continued to sit around the fire, and discussed their plight, at first in lowered tones. Only a few yards away the small limping man sat and watched them, alert, silent. More than once the Prince sought to question him, to engage him in the conversation, to find out where he was taking them – but without avail. He had a great gift for silence, that man.

'Clearly we are not being taken to Fort William,' Charles

declared, outspoken now. 'Nor yet, it seems, to Inverness. We have been avoiding all roads where we might meet with Cumberland's troops. Or our own. *Ma foi* – it is a mystery, is it not?'

'Perhaps Lord Loudon has moved on up Laggan-side? For Badenoch and Ruthven,' Hay suggested. 'To attack Cluny and any of our people who may have gathered there. It may be that we follow him. By the Corryarrack.'

'Would you not believe that they would lodge us more secure at Fort William, than following a fighting force half across Scotland?'

'Perhaps it is intended that we strike south, beyond the Pass, for Breadalbane. That is Campbell country. These may think that Your Highness would be more secure there. While there are still pockets of our people in Lochaber and Badenoch. It would be a likely course for Campbells to take.'

Duncan spoke. His head was splitting, seeming to open and shut to a curious steady rhythm of its own. 'These are no Campbells, I think. They wear half the tartans of the west – but I have seen none of Campbell amongst them.'

'Then who . . . ?'

'My friend,' the Prince called out, to their watchful warden – though almost certainly he had heard every word that they spoke. 'Tell us – are you of the Clan Campbell? Like my Lord Loudon, Inverawe, and so many others in the Government service?'

The man, although he would answer none of the others, did not wholly ignore the Prince when he spoke to him. 'My name is my own, sir,' he said, tight-voiced.

'Undoubtedly, sir. But, as a gentleman, you will agree that it would be fair that we should know into whose hands we have fallen. As prisoners of war, I presume?'

Beyond the fire the other inclined his head at that, but made no comment.

'You will get nothing out of these barbarians, Highness,' O'Neil declared sourly. His wound, though only superficial, was very painful, and bound up only very roughly. 'They are no doubt some independent brigands, who will sell us to Cumberland for what we may fetch! Savages would be more to my taste . . . '

'You will be well acquaint with savages and barbarians, Captain – in your Irish bogs?' Duncan asked.

43

'Curse you, MacGregor . . . !'

'Felix, *mon cher*,' the Prince said. 'Your leg – does it pain you? You should seek to sleep. Like Sir Thomas. Lie down here . . . '

'I thank Your Highness – I do very well as I am.'

'*Eh bien* – as you will.' Charles Edward reached into a pocket for his snuff-box. Before taking any himself, he offered it to O'Neil and then passed it round the company. Only O'Sullivan and Hay partook. The Prince was about to take a pinch with his own fingers when, recollecting, he rose to his feet and went round the fire to offer the open box to the man who sat alone there. 'Pray, sir – join with me, if you use snuff,' he invited courteously.

The Highlander sat motionless for a moment, before getting up suddenly, without a word, and stalking a little way off, his limp pronounced, there to stand with his back to them. The Prince, sighing, returned to his seat beside the others. Their captor turned to watch them, just outside the circle of the firelight.

For the best part of an hour they sat there, weary dispirited men, hunched around the fire, coughing now and again with its acrid smoke, staring into the flames and seeing therein all the ruin of their hopes, their careers, the possible ending of their lives indeed. All save Charles Stuart, who chose to talk rather than merely to stare. He chatted easily, genially, but at length, recalling other camp-fires that he had sat beside, in this present campaign, at the Siege of Gaeta and in the Italian wars, re-counting anecdotes of his father's impoverished Court at Rome, and of the serio-comic straits to which the royal exiles' household were constantly put to preserve even an illusion of dignity. Frequently he laughed softly. Clearly his theme and object, however lightly implied and hinted at, was the necessity for a philosophic attitude towards human fortunes and misfortunes, and the temporary nature of both trumpets and reverses. Perhaps he was talking as much to himself as to his companions – none of whom joined in on the royal reminiscences. Indeed, it would have been hard to say who were actually listening and who were either deep in their own thoughts or three-parts asleep.

Indeed, the main effect of the Prince's monologue appeared to be upon their dark kidnapper. Coming back to the fire with

44

an armful more fuel, he sat down again, clearly listening intently. In the flickering firelight his black eager eyes seemed to be concentrating on the royal lips. Perhaps it was necessary for him to attend thus if he was going to understand fully the foreign accent of a tongue with which he was not greatly familiar anyway. More than once Charles, smiling slightly, quite evidently addressed his remarks to him.

At last the speaker fell silent. O'Neill, at his side, was lying muttering in his uneasy sleep. The faithful Ned Burke was snoring heavily. Of the others, only Duncan MacGregor looked up, raising an aching head from between his hands.

It was then that their captor rose to his feet, in his abrupt jerky way, and began to limp back and forth at the other side of the fire. He might have been chilled or stiff from long sitting, or merely keeping himself awake – save for some tension, some urgency, in his uneven pacing. For a time he strode thus. Then halting for a moment, he swung round and came over to the Prince, his features working strangely.

'Highness,' he said, 'I cannot do it. No. It is not possible. *Och, ochan! Mise'n diugh.* You understand? *Tha mi'g iarraidh maitheanais.* I ask your pardon.'

Charles looked up, perplexed. 'What is this, friend? What ails you?'

'*Cha'n fhiuling mi sin.* It is not to be borne.' The other struck a clenched fist against his kilted thigh. 'You are free, Highness.'

'*Dieu de Dieu!*' The Prince got to his feet. 'Are you ... are you crazed, man?'

'No. No. It is the truth. *Tha mi cur romham.* '*Sann orm tha naire. No dean tair orm.* You will go. *Na h'uile le gu math duit.*'

'*Ma foi* – what is all this? Duncan – what does he say? What is the man at? Has he taken leave of his wits?'

The MacGregor had risen now. 'It is most strange, sir – extraordinary! He is telling us to go. That he is sorry for what he has done. He says that we are free to go.'

'But ... this is incredible! What is the meaning of it? Tell him ... tell him, Duncan, to speak slowly. To speak plain. Slowly, man. You understand?'

Duncan spoke in Gaelic to their agitated captor, who presently nodded, seeming to take a grip upon himself.

'Highness,' he said, almost bringing out each word separately. 'A great wrong I have done to you. My heart is sore. I did not know you. Did not understand. What I had to do, I cannot do, at all. You shall not suffer by my hand. Go you. Where you will.'

The Prince stared, from the man to MacGregor. 'You mean . . . you mean that you are changing sides? Now? At this late hour? When so much is lost?'

'I have no side. But. . . . I cannot sell my Prince,' the other said simply.

'Sell . . . ? Then O'Neil was right? You intended to sell us? To the Government?'

The man inclined his head, unspeaking.

For a moment or two Charles Edward was silent, also. 'I do not know what has changed you, my friend,' he said at length. 'But I thank God for it.'

'You, it is. *You* have changed me, Highness.'

'I? How can that be?'

'I was not knowing Your Highness. When I came to do this thing. Now I see you. Now I know you. I know you as my Prince. Och, I cannot do it, at all. It is not possible. The money – it would be choking my throat.'

'I rejoice to hear it, *mon ami*. But . . . this money that you speak of? You must have been very sure of money, to do all that you have done . . . ?'

'The man Cumberland, Highness – he will give a great lot of money for you. For your body. *Dia* – much gold. Thirty thousands of pounds, no less. Be Your Highness dead or living.'

'*Mortdieu!* Money? For my person? Dead or alive? *Ciel* – this is beyond all belief!'

'Thirty thousand pounds!' Duncan MacGregor exclaimed. 'Lord preserve us – to seek to buy Your Highness like, like a stirk at a mart! To buy a Prince . . . !'

'At least, it is a princely sum, Captain!' Charles observed grimly.

'It is monstrous! The work of a huckstering German pedler! Does he think that, in Scotland, in the Highlands, your Highness can be, can be . . . ?' MacGregor looking at their captor, faltered and was silent.

'*Exactement*, Duncan!' the Prince murmured. To the small man he said, 'Your masters, sir? When you return to them, without me – how will you do then?'

46

I do not serve any master, Highness. I am a Highland gentleman.'

'Ah, yes. Of course! Forgive me.'

'Go you now, sir, if you would be safe out of this country by daylight. You should not be slow, be lingering.'

'No. That is true.'

'A gillie you shall have. To guide you to the Cameron country.'

'Ah – so you know that is where we go, do you?'

'Yes. And, Highness – do not go to Arkaig by Lochy and the *Mile Dorcha*, the Dark Mile. As you were going, I think. There are Redcoats. The Campbell, Loudon, has there a troop. Go you by Garry.'

'I see. You are very good, sir – very kind. If I might have your name? To thank you.'

'My name, Highness, matters nothing. *Tha mi duilich*. Only that the wrong is . . . only that I make right the wrong that I have done to you.'

'Fear not for that. It would seem that I am *your* debtor. My thanks, friend – your Prince's grateful thanks.'

'You will go, now?'

'But yes. At once. Duncan – rouse the sleepers . . .'

As the somewhat bemused and astonished party was at length marshalled and about to move off into the night, their late captor, whose only wish now appeared to be quickly quit of them, came limping over to the Prince's horse.

'Highness,' he said, eyes lowered, head down – and held out the silver pocket flask.

'Why, sir,' Charles exclaimed. 'On my soul, I had forgotten it, quite. Keep it, friend, I pray you – as a momento of this occasion.'

The other shook his dark head wordlessly, and thrust the thing at the Prince's hand.

'No. I swear, I will not take it. Keep it, sir. I'faith, that is a royal command, do you hear? A souvenir. Instead of thirty thousand pounds, *mon Dieu!*'

The Highlander bent and kissed the outstretched fingers.

CHAPTER 4

BACK through the night they went, across Tarff and Oich and lesser streams, mounted again, with O'Neil riding pillion to O'Sullivan – who, as befitted the Quartermaster-General, had the best horse in the army. Ahead, apparently tireless, trotted the running gillie who was to guide them beyond the Garry.

Picking their way in the dark precluded talk, but did not prevent even sleep-clouded minds from turning over curious circumstances and possibilities.

When the party was safely back across the ford of the Garry, with the wilder roadless country ahead, the Prince called a halt. 'It is time to consider our future progress, gentlemen, I think,' he announced, dismounting. 'It would be wise to weigh well the lessons of this adventure.'

By the splashing headlong river they gathered round.

'We must change our mode of travel, my friends,' Charles went on. 'If I am considered so valuable to the Government that they will spend thirty thousand pounds on my poor person, then most clearly I must deny them the satisfaction of laying hands on me. Equally certain, however, is the fact that with such splendid fortune available for so slight a labour, many will be seeking swift enrichment. Is it not so?'

'Every accursed soldier in Cumberland's army, to be sure, will already be accounting himself rich as Croesus,' O'Sullivan agreed. 'And worse, every peasant and cottager of this be-nighted land, likewise – and that's the devil of it!'

'I think not,' Duncan said shortly.

'They are not all going to change their minds at the last moment, MacGregor!'

'Nine out of ten would not be needing to, Colonel.'

'Either way,' Charles intervened, 'it behoves us to take pre-cautions the more stringent. My father's cause demands it. We may not proceed as now – we are too apparent, too noticeable. We must separate, gentlemen. We must go more discreetly. We must seek other clothing. And for myself, I go afoot from now on. Horses are a luxury I cannot afford, unfortunately.'

'You would skulk, Charles – like any common fugitive?' Sheridan protested, shocked.

48

'I would indeed, Cousin. The commoner the skulker, the more likely he is to reach France alive.'

'I cannot go trudging the heather, Highness,' O'Neil declared. 'My leg . . . '

'Do I not know it, my good Felix. For you rest is necessary. And also a horse. You will return to Invergarry Castle, to wait there for a day. To direct any of our people who may come to the meeting at Loch Arkaig that they avoid this Dark Mile, where Loudon's troop waits. Thereafter you must find your own way to Arkaig.'

O'Neil did not look as though he relished these orders.

'Thomas, you require to ride. Skulking in the heather is not for you. Nor for Colonel Hay, I think.' Something, possibly the curious demonstration of his own influence back there in Glen Tarff, had revived Charles Stuart, given him back his powers of leadership which weariness and dejection had sapped. 'You will go together, mounted, to Arkaig. There to supervise the meeting. Duncan – you best know the country. How shall they ride, to avoid this Dark Mile? There must be a way?'

'There is, yes. Six or seven miles further south, three miles beyond the foot of Loch Lochy, there is another way through. By Glen Loy. Ride to the head of that, and over the little pass into Glen Mallie. That will bring you down to Arkaig beyond Locheil's house of Achnacarry.'

'Good. That is your road then, gentlemen. You hear?'

'Sir,' Duncan interposed. 'Most of those who will answer your message to come to Arkaig will be coming from Ruthven and Badenoch. Down Loch Lagganside and Glen Spean. They will know nothing of this danger at the Dark Mile. If Sir Thomas and Colonel Hay are to be riding in that direction anyway, would they not wait awhile within the mouth of Glen Spean, to warn at least the first comers . . . ?'

'Well thought of, Captain. You understand, Colonel? At the mouth of Glen Spean.'

'But, Highness,' Hay objected. 'It is no more than ten miles yonder, I vow, from Fort William itself! On the very road to the fort. To linger there would be as good as to surrender ourselves. By daylight, every trooper of Loudon's garrison will be scouring the country for this money on your head. It may be that they are doing so now. To say nothing of Cumberland's dragoons following us down.'

'Not so, I think,' Duncan asserted. 'How shall they know that His Highness is in this part of the country, at all? Or even, as yet, of the damnable reward?'

'Eh? This fellow we have just left knew it, did he not? Knew of our route exactly, enough to ambush us yonder . . . '

'Aye – and there's the whole point,' the MacGregor said grimly. 'How did he know so well, so exactly? And so soon?'

'Damme – how can we tell that? But knew he did. And if he knew, others knew. Why not the whole garrison?'

'It depends, does it not, who gave him his information, Colonel?'

'Why – who but General Lord Loudon? Or one of his staff.'

Duncan shook his head again. 'How could he? We rode fast from Culloden. No courier of Cumberland's could have so greatly outdistanced us as to reach Fort William last night. To have received the news of Cumberland's victory, to have discovered that His Highness was in this district, to have planned and despatched that expedition against us, and for it to come north to here – that would all have taken a deal more time than Lord Loudon has yet had.'

'He is right,' the Prince said. 'It could not have been Loudon's doing.'

'Whose, then?'

'Some independent group of clansmen. Campbells probably. They had stumbled on the information . . . '

'Those were no Campbells, Colonel,' Duncan assured. 'Nor was the information such that they could stumble upon. They knew that the Prince was making for Loch Arkaig and the sea. Where would they have learned that?'

'Christ God!' O'Sullivan burst out. 'Lovat! The double-dyed traitor! The old dastard!'

'No! *Mon Dieu* – no!' Charles cried. 'I will not believe that. Lovat would never do that. It is not to be considered.'

'Thirty thousand pounds is a lot of money, Highness. Even to Lord Lovat!'

'It need not have been Lovat himself,' Duncan agreed soberly. 'But only at Gortlech House was it known that Your Highness was in this district, that the decision to make for Arkaig and the sea was made. And at Gortlech House, I mind a small limping man calling off those guards who attacked us when we arrived!'

'Mother o' God!'

'They were Frasers, then . . . ?'

'I do not know that they were. But it seems likely . . .'

'The guide,' O'Sullivan exclaimed. 'Put it to the guide, MacGregor. We shall get it out of him, 'fore God!'

But their silent shadowy guide, when they looked round for him, had gone.

'Frasers were coming back from the battle, to the Gortlech district,' Hay pointed out. 'Some could have arrived, bringing the word of Cumberland's reward. If he had announced it at once. Almost on the field . . .'

'Frasers, or not,' the Prince said strongly, 'they did not betray me. Tempted they may have been, and sorely – but, my friends, in the end they did not betray me, for the gold.'

'That is what I say, Highness,' Duncan declared. 'They did not – whoever sent them. Nor will most in the Highlands, of whatever clan, I think.'

'Of whatever clan! There you have it!' O'Neil put in bitterly. 'Faith, it could have been the Clan MacLeod as easily as the Frasers! Captain Sawny MacLeod also knew all this, did he not? He departed over the Corryarrack, for Ruthven. He could have been captured . . . and talked!'

'Save us all . . . !'

'Damn you, O'Neil . . . !'

'I never trusted the man. He was altogether too smiling. And his chief, the Laird of MacLeod, is a perjured turncoat, as we all know. Like so many another. Trust none of them, I say. As we should not have trusted the MacDonalds, back at Culloden Moor. Traitors all . . .'

'*Diabhol!* I will not hear such talk from any man!' the MacGregor cried. 'If you were not wounded, O'Neil, you should pay for those words in blood! Highness, I . . .'

'Be silent, MacGregor! And you, Felix – for shame! Were you not injured and, as I believe, scarçe in your right mind, I could not forgive your folly. The clans have spilled untold blood for my father's cause and for me – the MacDonalds in especial. Sawny MacLeod is my friend. You shall apologise to Captain MacGregor.'

'I desire no apologies from such as O'Neil . . . !'

'Be quiet, sir! *Mortdieu* – here were we, but two short days ago a band of brothers, comrades in arms, who had fought the

length of Scotland and half of England together. And now –
this! Only suspicion, treachery, the black shadow of treachery
over us! If this is the first fruits of defeat, *Nom de Nom* . . . !
But, enough. This talk profits us nothing. Better that we should
be on our ways. You have your orders, gentlemen. O'Neil, here,
to Invergarry. Sir Thomas and Colonel Hay to Glen Spean,
and thence by Glen Loy and this other glen, to Arkaig, to await
the Lord George, the Duke, and the others. And later bring
their word to me.'

'And yourself, sir?' Hay wondered.

'With John here, I shall make for the sea forthwith. For
Arisaig, where I landed. One of Sir Anthony Walsh's French
privateers was to be ever patrolling there, to slip in to land at
Loch nan Uamh each second night or so. Such was the arrangement.'

'Then you do not come yourself, to the meeting at Arkaig,
sir?'

'No. Better that I should not be there, I think. Better for all.
Safer for all, also. But I shall not be far off. Arisaig is in Clanranald's country, but I shall also be near Locheil and yet suitably far from Fort William – at least for the time being. You
will send and let me know how matters stand, and whether my
friends can undertake to continue the struggle. And, meanwhile, at the least guard some corner of the country to serve
as a base. If they believe that they can do this, then it is best,
I think, that I go myself to France. At once, or as soon as may
be. We have no money, nor arms. Without these it is impossible
to keep together or to subsist. No – I will go myself. I will
then bring succour of money and men. I believe that my
presence will do more to move His Majesty of France than
anybody that I may send.'

A silence fell upon them all, as what this implied sank in.

'I shall take Captain MacGregor with me, meantime, since
we cannot speak the Erse. And Ned Burke, of course. Mac-
Gregor tells me that there is a track, half-way up Loch Garry,
that leads over the hills to Arkaig. It is no road for horses.
That way we shall go. Is all understood, my friends?'

Hay still wondered. 'If Your Highness is to be at Loch
Arkaig, somewhere. If you are to be there anyway, would it
not be best that you should attend this meeting in person?
It will be expected, sir. And you might sway many.'

The Prince shook his fair head sadly. 'Yesterday I would have agreed with you, Colonel. But not now. Not tonight. Now, there is thirty thousand pounds upon my head. A fortune. It behoves me to put temptation in the way of as few as possible. To my sorrow, the fewer who see my face hereafter, the better. Accursed be the mind that conceived this foul thing, and the hurt and dark suspicions that it must breed. How malevolently understanding that mind was, *mon Dieu!* But the deed is done. Even amongst ourselves here the poison has begun its work of base mistrust. You have seen. I shall not add to the trials of my good friends by imposing this new burden of temptation on them and theirs. You understand, gentlemen?'

Wordless now, men eyed the ground. There was nothing to be said, to that.

'So it is *adieu*, my friends. Here we part – let us pray to meet again in happier case. Till then, may a kinder Heaven guide the steps of each of you. Go with God.'

Charles held out his hand to Sheridan, Hay and O'Neil. Sheridan sought to say something, but his tremulous old voice choked on his emotion. The other two kissed the outstretched hand in silence.

Abruptly the Prince turned away, and went to his horse, to remove the tiny bundle of his effects from its saddle. Then, without a backward glance, he set off on foot up the wooded side of the rushing Garry. O'Sullivan and Duncan MacGregor were behind him. Ned Burke, a faithful shadow, brought up the rear.

CHAPTER 5

WITH the early morning sun flooding golden glory at their backs, and setting ablaze all the head of long Loch Arkaig, the four men trudged wearily up the gentle grassy slope towards the pleasant white house that sat so snugly in the mouth of the narrow glen ahead, backed by its ancient trees. That house seemed to have beckoned them for the last hour, as they rounded the marshy meadows at the head of the interminable loch.

When, still a mile away, they had perceived the blue column of peat smoke rising from its chimney, against the dark brown of the heather hill behind, it had been the first lift to their hearts for hours. Someone there was stirring, and the smoored and banked overnight fire had been replenished for the new day. Involuntarily they had lengthened their limping, lagging strides.

For three out of the four were indeed limping. They had covered nearly twenty long and gruelling miles from the Garry in eight hours of benighted walking, the last ten of them along the northern shore of the loch – and only the MacGregor's feet were proof against such treatment. O'Sullivan was in particularly poor way. Time and again his companions had urged the Prince to halt and rest, to seek shelter and food at one or other of the many little townships of scattered cot-houses which they had so cautiously skirted and avoided in the darkness. But always Charles had insisted on pressing on. They would put Loch Arkaig behind them, he declared, with its populous northern braes, before they sought rest. On occasion he could be extraordinarily obstinate.

Now, that resolution had faded somewhat. The long trough of Arkaig between its massed mountains, forked into two narrow side glens at its head, with the great thrusting prow of Monadh Gorm between – Glen Dessary and Glen Pean. It was into the latter that they headed, facing south-westwards towards Morar and the sea. Within the jaws of it, this goodly house was as a magnet to their dragging feet. So normal-seeming, so secure, speaking to them of friendly settled living, of ease – even of a cooked breakfast. Charles had declared that they must avoid all substantial houses, all townships and clachans, lest their passage should be traced, lest the dread contagion of reward-seeking should be spread; they must call only at isolated humble huts and remote sheilings. Yet here they were, passing by the scattering of cabins and blackhouses of this Glen Pean, and making directly for the long low two-storeyed whitewashed house of what must be a laird of some substance.

None had actually voiced the decision that they might halt at it, admittedly.

It was a pair of great grey wolf-hounds that came loping down towards them from the house, baying the heavens, that settled the matter. To turn away now would brand them as furtive fugitives, inevitably. Without debate they pressed on, even though the dogs looked less than welcoming.

Then, above the deep baying another sound reached them – the clear high belling of a woman's voice upraised. At its insistence the hounds fell silent, and halted.

A young woman had appeared at the porch of the house, watching from under a hand that shaded her eyes against the glare of the early level sunlight pouring in from the east behind the newcomers. Under her scrutiny the four travellers approached, unconsciously squaring their sagging shoulders.

'You speak with her, Duncan,' the Prince directed. 'In her own tongue. We are travellers who have lost our way – innocent travellers. Seeking refreshment. For which we will pay . . . '

'You are in Cameron country, sir. None here will think ill of us for being what their own chief, Locheil, is – part of Your Highness's army.'

'Nevertheless, you will do as I say. What the good people do not know, they cannot bear witness to. And, *mon Dieu* – no more of this Highnessing and Sirring! Or we are lost.'

The tall hounds stalking stiff and suspicious behind them, to Ned Burke's distinct alarm, they approached the house. The woman proved to be little more than a girl, and a bonny one – a warm-eyed, well-built creature with a mass of auburn hair which the streaming yellow light turned into a gleaming halo, dressed neatly but serviceably in a gown of bottle-green handspun stuff, shorter skirted than was the southern mode, worn over a white linen bodice, brief sleeved and generously open at the neck, the white spotless enough to emphasise the honey-brown of arms and face and neck, to where it faded into white between her breasts. Her dress was caught round the slender waist with a broad scarlet girdle, and with it she wore a white apron. This also was notably clean, like the bodice – as indeed was everything about her, even to her bare feet. Her glowing cheeks and general air of new-washed freshness, in fact, were almost an offence in the lack-lustre eyes of the jaded, grimy and travel-stained men, unshaven and dishevelled, so early in the morning.

'Good morning,' she called out, in English, before Duncan could address her in the Gaelic. 'You come early to Glen Pean, gentlemen. But you are welcome, if you come in honesty –

even though you are not those for whom I looked.'

Charles Edward, clad now in Ned Burke's plain grey coat, gave her a courtly bow but left Duncan to do the talking.

'We are travellers making for Arisaig and the islands, lady,' he said. 'We fear that we have gone much astray from our road. We have had certain misfortunes, owing to the unsettled state of the country. We seek, of your kindness, only refreshment and direction. You need not be afraid of us, I promise you . . .'

'I am not afraid of you, sir! But one word from me, and my hounds would have their teeth in your throats, faster than you could draw that pistol that I see hiding in your Gregorach plaid!' Those warm eyes could flash as fiery as her hair. Young and fair she might be, but it was apparent that she considered that she was well able to look after herself.

'I beg your pardon,' Duncan said, hurriedly. 'I had forgot, ma'am – "Sons of the hounds, come and eat flesh!" '

She laughed at that, pleasantly, the Clan Cameron's age-old slogan. 'You are not wholly without knowledge of the country you are in, sir, lost or not!' she said. 'But your Lowland friends must not think that we feed our dogs on strangers, as of habit!' Looking at the others, and particularly Charles Stuart, the girl's wide-open hazel-green eyes changed expression – a thing that they could do, apparently, with as great clarity as speed. 'You are tired, gentlemen – weary. You have travelled far and fast, I think?'

'Far, yes,' Duncan admitted cautiously.

'And fast. Those who fall into bogs, as you have done, do so by night. And those who travel by night in this country do so for good reason. Is it not so?'

'Mistress – how we travel, and where, surely is our own concern,' O'Sullivan said tautly. 'If you prefer not to offer us the refreshment we require, then faith we must press on . . .'

'I said before, sir, that you were welcome to Glen Pean – if you came in honesty. I think if you were truly honest with me, you would tell me that you had come hot-foot, and from somewhere nigh to Inverness! And that white cockades were probably in your pockets!'

None of the four answered a word to that.

'I am right, then. Or I hope so – for I am a Cameron, and would not like to think that you were of the other persuasion!'

'You are indeed right, Mademoiselle,' Charles said then,

56

with his engaging smile. 'We should have declared it at the outset. We are of King James's army, and hasten to Arisaig where we have business . . . ah, on his account.'

'Where two French ships have been sighted, off and on, this past week and more, I am told!' the young woman added, significantly.

'You say so? Is it a fact?' The Prince looked at once disconcerted and enheartened. 'It is known that they are there, Mademoiselle?'

'Why yes, sir. Also that three Government warships keep chasing them around the islands and the lochs in a cat-and-mouse game.' She shook her head. 'But, come inside, gentlemen. My father would not have any of the Prince's army kept standing on his doorstep. He . . . he is not here to welcome you in person, I fear, for he is himself with the Prince.'

'Oh!' Charles said. 'I . . . ah . . . am distressed to hear it.'

Quickly she looked at him. 'Distressed? Then . . . then it is true? That there has been a great battle, and that our cause is sore stricken? Only last night we had grave tidings. We heard that Locheil, our chief, was sore wounded. That the Prince's army had been defeated, near Inverness.' Her words tumbled out now in a rush. 'I feared, when I saw you coming. It was my father whom I was looking to see. And my brother. My father is Donald Cameron of Glen Pean, a captain in Locheil's Regiment. And my brother Colin is an ensign. You would not know . . . ? You will not have heard . . . ?'

In silence the men before her shook their heads, or looked down at the grass.

'We did not know whether or no to believe the word of it,' she went on. 'Ill news travels fast, they say. It was but a few words that reached us here. But now, you . . . you make it true by your presence, do you not? That you should have come so fast, so far. And in such state – you who are clearly officers. Was it – was it so great a defeat? A disaster?' That was almost a whisper.

Charles swallowed. 'It was an undoubted set-back,' he admitted.

'The Prince's cause will recover from it, never fear, ma'am,' Duncan assured stoutly.

'Yes. Oh, yes. Pray God it be so. If Locheil was sore wounded, then his regiment must have been . . . have been . . . ?'

'They were hard engaged, yes,' Duncan told her, as gently as he knew how. 'But many escaped. They carried Locheil off the field – both ankles shot. Your father and brother may well have been with them. It is likely . . . '

She bit her red lip, nodding her head a number of times, jerkily, determinedly. 'Yes. Yes indeed. No doubt you are right, sir. But – come inside. I have kept you standing here too long as it is. You will be hungry, and very tired. Only my two young sisters are at home. Lazy they are – not yet out of their beds . . . !'

In the pleasant and comfortable old house, unpretentious but commodious, the newcomers were offered unstinted hospitality by their young hostess. Breakfast had indeed been a-cooking, and more oatmeal was added to the porridge-pot and more eggs and smoked salmon to the frying-pan, which, with milk laced with whisky, bannocks and heather-honey, would keep them in being, as the girl declared, until she could cook them a regular meal. In the interim, they should wash and tidy themselves somewhat, and she would make up beds for them while they did so.

Charles, heavy-eyed as he was, demurred. Her kindness made them eternally her debtors – but they would not sleep under her roof. It must have seemed a curious scruple to Caroline Cameron, as the young woman named herself, that although her visitors would partake heartily of her provender and the other facilities of her house, they insisted on sleeping outside, in any shed or outhouse, apparently solely on account of possible repercussions by the authorities on people who sheltered rebels – a narrow distinction, perhaps, in the house of a militant rebel, to his own daughter. It was the Prince himself who insisted on this – or Monsieur Dumont, a French officer, as Duncan introduced him, along with Mr. Butler from Ireland, a commissary, Ned Burke and himself retaining their own identities. Caroline Cameron eyed them all a little thoughtfully thereafter.

It was after they had fed and washed, their entire bearing and appearance quite transformed and spruced up thereby, that the keen-eyed young woman, whilst Charles and O'Sullivan were inspecting a hay-barn in which it was proposed to bed down, drew Duncan aside.

'Mr. MacGregor – or Captain, should I say? I have no reason to doubt your word, or that *you* are what you say – an officer in Glengyle's Regiment. Or that Mr. Butler is not an Irishman, and may well be a commissary, for all I know of such. But your Monsieur Dumont is a different matter, I swear. He has an extraordinary manner. For a mere French officer, you treat him with notable deference. When he speaks, no other speaks. He must sit first at table – and when he half-rose to collect his eggs from me, tired as you are you were all on your feet in a moment. Is it not so?'

Duncan coughed. 'He is a, h'm, an important French officer,' he said.

'So I must believe! Even so, I would not have thought that a Highland officer, *any* Highland officer, would have been so respectful towards any mere French mercenary! Or has the Prince's army French generals now?'

The MacGregor was silent. His mind was much too heavy with fatigue for this sort of thing.

'Moreover, I would not have you think that I am part-blind, Captain. Do I seem it? When you emerged from washing yourselves, your Monsieur Dumont was a different man! And a *young* man. So young to be so important. Not much older than myself, I vow. Younger than your sober self, I think? And that fair hair, that noble brow, that commanding countenance? Captain MacGregor – if I have the honour to have His Royal Highness in person under the roof of Glenpean House, pray tell me so!'

Duncan all but choked. 'Ma'am ... Miss Cameron ... you go too fast. Altogether too fast. You must not be carried away by, by such imaginings. Monsieur Dumont is ... '

'Is *not* the Prince?' she put to him squarely.

He bit his lip. 'Ma'am, surely it is no part of our travellers' duty to provide you with papers of identity to support our statements ... !'

'Hoity-toity!' Caroline Cameron said. 'But you do not deny it, I see! Here he is. Now we shall see!'

Charles and O'Sullivan came out of the barn. Without a moment's hesitation, the girl ran forward and took his hand.

'Is it permitted that I kiss your fingers, sir?' she asked.

The Prince, startled, stared at her, and then swiftly turned on Duncan. 'Captain MacGregor!' he exclaimed. 'What is the meaning of this? Your instructions were sufficiently clear, I thought ... ?'

'It is no fault of the Captain's, Your Royal Highness,' Miss Cameron intervened sweetly. 'He is painfully concerned that I should believe you to be some junior French mercenary officer. His fault is that he does not credit me with eyes in my head or any modicum of wit. He would have me believe that a prince, Scotland's own Prince, is a prince only in name! That by giving him the name of Dumont he transforms him into merely some ordinary Frenchman. Surely you, Highness, know better than that? Think you that the Highlands would be willing to die for any such changeling?'

Charles shook his head helplessly, wordlessly. Then with a Gallic shrug of the shoulders, he smiled at her ruefully but engagingly. 'I capitulate, Mademoiselle. And apologise. I am Charles Stuart, yes – and yours to command.'

Caroline Cameron dropped in a swift but deep and graceful curtsy, and pressed her lips to those outstretched fingers. When she rose, she looked at none of them. She turned away quickly – but not before Duncan MacGregor at least had seen that her hazel-green eyes were swimming with tears.

She hurried back to the house, and, somewhat sheepishly, the men followed her.

Now that she knew that it was the Prince whom she was entertaining, their young hostess would not hear of him sleeping in any hay-barn. On the other hand, Charles was adamant about not sleeping in the house – explaining the significance of the £30,000 reward and the hue-and-cry which would inevitably take place, and what might be expected in reprisals from a commander-in-chief who could conceive such a thing, and slaughter the defeated wounded and prisoners on a field of battle. Moreover, there was the little township of cabins and cot-houses near by; their dwelling here in the house could not be hid from the clansfolk there, and however loyal and true they might be, their presence represented exactly the situation that the fugitives had made up their minds to avoid. The girl's indignant protests that these were the very families from which her father had taken a score of men to fight for the Prince, could not alter his stubborn although courteously expressed decision.

A compromise was reached – since Charles recognised that not only must they have a period of rest and refreshment forthwith, but that somewhere in this vicinity it was necessary for him to wait awhile for news of what transpired amongst the other leaders of his cause. There was a more secure place, a lonely shieling or summer lodging for the upland pastures, another four or five miles up the glen, near the head of the pass over into Morar. Unoccupied at present, here the travellers could lie up safely – yet near enough to be supplied daily with food from the house. Although O'Sullivan for one groaned aloud at the thought of those additional four or five miles, all agreed that this appeared to be the best solution.

Miss Cameron insisted on escorting them in person to this refuge. Moreover, she provided sturdy garrons for the journey, so that at least they did not have to walk. Declaring that the cottagers below would merely assume that she was hospitably setting the travellers on their way over the long steep pass, she led the way, skirts hitched high on shapely legs straddling the broad-backed pony, the two wolf-hounds bounding joyfully ahead.

O'Sullivan fell asleep twice on his mount's back on that ride up the lovely quickly climbing glen of the River Pean, the second time actually tumbling off into the old bracken, fortunately without hurting himself although a heavily built man of middle age. Even Duncan had much ado to keep his eyes open, Charles, however, riding ahead with the girl, seemed to be able to exchange chatter with her readily enough, to his companions' wonder.

The shieling proved to be admirably suited for their purposes. It was a stone-and-turf cabin of but the one simple room, with a thatch of heather, hump-backed and so much part of all its surroundings as wholly to fade into the hillside, a few hundred yards above the track and a small blue lochan. Behind it rose the two enormous three-thousand-foot peaks of Sgor Thuilm and Sgor nan Coreachan, and, across the glen, the long long ridge that ended in Monadh Gorm, the Blue Mount, above Gleanpean House. From its door indeed they could see all around, both far and near, a whole world of the high places – and notably in both directions from which danger might come, east down to Loch Arkaig and west towards Morar and the sea. The interior, although windowless and dirt-floored, strewn with heather, was clean, there was a central fireplace with a hole in the turf roof above for the smoke to escape, and there were built-up shelves or benches, with deerskins stuffed with heather-tops as mattresses. A sparkling burn splashed past down to the lochan, and there was bog-pine outcropping from all the hill-side around about for fuel.

The visitors scarcely appreciated the full excellence of this sanctuary at first sight, however. Somewhat owlishly they stood, swaying slightly, whilst Caroline Cameron demonstrated its advantages. Once inside, nothing would bring them out into the sunlight again, those built-up mattress benches seeming to have a hypnotic effect upon them all. When at length the young woman turned away back downhill with her horses and hounds, promising to come back again in the evening, her charges collapsed on the bunks like men felled. All except Ned Burke, that is, who knelt first to ease off his royal master's boots. Before he had so much as undone the second spatter-dash, Charles had dropped solidly sideways, asleep.

He was barely the first, at that.

Eight hours later, Duncan MacGregor was swimming in the lochan below the shieling, swimming vigorously for the peat-stained amber water was icy cold, fed from the snows not yet melted high on Sgor Thuilm above. Surface-diving, blowing water like a grampus, turning on his back and kicking up water-spouts with his feet, he was alone, with his companions still asleep in the cabin – or thought that he was. About to clamber out on to a thrusting rock, preparatory to a deep dive, he suddenly was aware of the sound of clapping hands and the tinkle of laughter. And seeing who sat the pony up there, between the two panting hounds, he slid down into the brown water again, hastily.

'Bravo, Captain MacGregor!' she called. 'You swim mightily. Like the monster, the water-horse! Are you trying to catch the trouts – or to frighten them out of the water?'

'I am trying not to freeze to death!' he answered her, pant-ingly. 'If you can do better, come you and join me! Warmer with the two of us!'

'I do very well watching you,' she assured. 'I prefer to do my swimming some months hence, when the water is warm. I shall wait here and guard your clothes for you, sir!'

'No, no. Go away. I want to come out.'

'But I have brought you whisky. And new-baked cakes. Would you not be wise to have one now, Captain? To stop you shivering.'

'No.'

'Or do you not shiver? The Gregorach – perhaps they are too hot-blooded to shiver?'

'Go away.'

'You are most discourteous, sir. When I hold you all in the hollow of my hand!'

'Go and tell that to the Prince. Woman, I warn you – whether you go or stay, I am not remaining in this water another moment!'

Laughing, she turned and rode up the hillside.

Wrapped only in kilt and plaid, he came up with her as she waited outside the cabin.

'They are all still asleep,' she told him. 'You, it seems are the only lively one.'

'They are *Sassunach* – Lowlanders,' he pointed out, explaining all. 'This country is hard on them. And there has been little enough sleep for any of the army these last six days. Let them sleep.'

'Very well. But I brought you news, see you. Good news. At least, for me and mine. For the Camerons. Locheil is back at Achnacarry, and my father with him. But not my brother. He is wounded, poor Colin. But left secure in the house of some Macpherson in Badenoch. He will be safe. It is not good news? I am so very happy. See – have a cake. Take a drink of this. You *are* shivering, I vow.'

'I thought that you sounded in good spirts, Miss Cameron! I am happy about your father . . . '

'Yes. It is wonderful. I have been very anxious. Now I could dance! And sing!' She trilled a laugh, gay, infectious, her eyes flashing and sparkling with joyous relief. When this young woman was happy, it appeared, she was very happy. Indeed, whatever she did she seemed to do with all her heart.

'Have you seen your father? Did you tell him about . . . us?'

'No. He is still with Locheil. Only a gillie brought us the news. He came for clothes and gear and money. This afternoon.'

'And did you hear have any others reached your country?

63

From Badenoch? From Ruthven? The Lord George Murray? the Duke of Perth...?'

'The gillie did not say so. He was concerned only with Locheil and my father.'

'If Locheil, crippled, could be brought thus fast, others surely could have come also. It is important that the Prince should know...'

'What is so important to me, my friends? Miss Cameron – you catch us at a distinct disadvantage, of which I am grievously aware. My humblest apologies.' Charles Edward, crumpled, tousle-headed and flushed with sleep, stooped in the low doorway, smothering a yawn.

Caroline Cameron curtsied. 'Your Highness – I am sorry if I disturbed you. I but brought up some more provisions. I should have been quieter. I brought some Cameron plaids to wrap around you all. And a kilt of my brother's. Which may enable you to attract less notice in this country...'

'You are kind. Thoughtful. But, *mon Dieu* – in this matter of attracting notice, will you not pay heed to your own self, Mademoiselle? For you, like my friends here, these salutations and talk of Highness must cease. My name is Charles. And if Dumont displeases you, then I give you leave to choose me another.'

'But... but, sir...!'

'No "sirs" either. Not said that way, at any rate.'

Duncan intervened. 'Miss Cameron has brought news. Locheil is back, and Glenpean with him. At Achnacarry. Others no doubt. But the messenger did not say.'

'Ah – say you so? My brave, good Locheil! Praise God for that. He will give me good honest advice. Always he has done so...'

'What better advice can Locheil give you, if he be honest, than to reach the Court of France with all possible speed?' O'Sullivan's voice came thickly from behind. 'Locheil, nor any other, can alter the fact that we have lost this throw. Lost totally. And without money and arms, we cannot make another throw – not another that has any hope of success.'

'These French ships in the offing, John, may be bearing arms and men.'

'May be – or may not. That remains to be seen. Even so, the

64

sooner you are aboard one of them, the better for King James's cause, sir.'

'You . . . are not *leaving* us?' the young woman burst out, staring. 'You are not going away again, sir? To France?'

Charles frowned a little, and plucked his unshaven chin. 'I must do what is best for all. Or for most. Take the longer view. Think you I would not rather stay, *ma foi*? Here, with my brave and loyal Highlanders. But . . . '

'Wait a while, at the least, sir,' Duncan urged. 'Until you know the true position clearly. Until . . . '

'Until Cumberland's dragoons, or his filthy money, catch him, you mean, MacGregor? If Locheil can reach Arkaig from Culloden so fast, wounded as he is, how far behind ride Cumberland's cavalry thirsting for a fortune? If the Prince is taken, all is lost – once and for all. No waiting, I say. Let us press on to the sea at Arisaig, and seek these ships with all speed. If they are being harried by Government frigates, they may not tarry much longer. Faith, it may be too late, even now. They may have been caught. Or sailed back to France. I say move on tonight. Now.'

The Prince paced a turn or two outside the cabin, running a hand through his fair curls.

Caroline Cameron looked from one to the other, unhappily now. 'At least eat, gentlemen,' she said. 'While you decide what is best. I have brought your supper . . . '

Over an adequate meal, spread before the shieling in the vivid sunset light that streamed through the pass to them in gold and crimson glory from the Western Sea, they came at length to a compromise. Duncan MacGregor should hurry down Arkaigside through the night, to Achnacarry, to find out what he could of the true position, and consult Locheil in the Prince's name. Charles and O'Sullivan would wait here at the shieling until dawn – for the route over the pass was very rough, and inadvisable in the dark anyway – and then proceed down to the lower ground of Morar, and on as best they could to the sea at Loch nan Uamh, near Arisaig. Here it was that they had landed all those eventful months before. It was Clanranald's country, and Young Clanranald himself might well have reached home, by then, if he had escaped from Culloden. Anyway, MacDonald of Borrodale would shelter them, as he had done when they had arrived. He would know about the French ships, if anybody did. Duncan should rejoin them, as quickly as he might, between here and Borrodale, with his tidings.

None were satisfied with this arrangement. O'Sullivan's age, experience and authority undoubtedly had a greater weight with Charles than could have the representations of the young Mac-Gregor or this mere girl.

And so, in the lovely quiet half-light of the north, aftermath to the blaze of the sunset, Duncan strode down the glen at the side of the young woman's pony, very conscious of her presence above him, of the distracting nearness of a long shapely leg which she made ineffective attempts to cover with a skirt stretched tight by the garron's broad back, of her mood of thoughtful quiet that had succeeded the happy gaiety of her coming – yet himself preoccupied with oppressive thoughts of the sorrowful fruits of failure, the suspicion of motives, and ashamedly, of just the first faintest stirrings of the canker of doubt as to the moral strength and fibre of the so gallant, admirable and gracious prince whom he had so nearly worshipped.

The bitter fruits of failure, indeed.

CHAPTER 6

DUNCAN neither rode nor walked down the rough dozen miles of Loch Arkaig, that night – he rowed. It was Caroline's suggestion that he take one of the Glen Pean boats, and so spare his limbs. She offered the aid of one of her gillies as boatman, to spare his arms also, but this he refused. It was a long long row admittedly, but the simple square sail hoisted, and the prevailing breeze which blew unfailingly down the lengthy funnel of the valley from the south-west, should be a help. For coming back, she advised a garron borrowed from Locheil.

For a MacGregor, used to boat-work amongst the strong currents, great depths and unpredictable winds of Loch Lomond, Arkaig was comparatively uncomplicated. He indeed enjoyed the soothing slap-slap and creak of his progress down the loch, and the feel of oars in his hands again – even although a prolonged neglect of such useful implements, for sword and pistol, produced blisters in due course. It was a fine star-lit night, and the great silent hills crouching black against the deep blue of the sky spoke their age-old peaceable message to him, as did the whispers of the many waterfalls cascading down to the shore on the steep south side, the sigh of wind over endless leagues of heather, and the lowing of cattle from the water-meadows of the northern shores. The loch was nowhere more than a mile wide, and frequently only half that, and no problems of navigation obtruded.

He reached the foot of Arkaig before midnight, in just under three hours – which was a deal less, he reckoned, than he would have taken with a garron over that broken stream-furrowed terrain. Hiding the boat in a clump of water-side alders, he made his way along the river-bank to Achnacarry Castle.

Duncan did not gain Locheil's house without being challenged, but he managed to convince the Cameron guards of his status as a bearer of important tidings for their chief. House servitors declared that Himself and the gentlemen were not yet retired for the night, and the newcomer was led upstairs to the first floor hall of the castle, a modest place enough by southern standards but palatial compared with the Prince's sanctuary, and ushered into the great smoke-filled chamber.

Quite a gathering sat around the long table or about the flaring fire of pine logs. Donald Cameron, nineteenth of Locheil, a fine-looking leonine man of middle years, with the calm reflective eyes of a scholar rather than a warrior, sat on a settle near the fire, his bound-up legs outstretched before him. Although Duncan had seen him often, as a regimental officer he had never had occasion to speak with so great a dignitary; but Locheil welcomed him courteously, even warmly, apologising for being unable to rise to his feet to welcome an honoured guest and a son of Glengyle to his house. He was hospitably offering food and drink, and enquiring after his visitor's journey and comfort; when interrupted by many of those around him, demanding to know the state of Prince Charles, his whereabouts, intentions and plans.

True to traditional Highland civilities, the young man ignored them all until he had assured his host of his well-being, of the honour he felt at coming under so notable a roof, and asked politely for the chief's wounded legs, the safety of his sons, and the general welfare of his people.

Many of the company chafed observably but ineffectually at

this display of Gaelic manners. Donald Cameron might be known as the Gentle Locheil, but he was not a man with whom any would trifle, especially in present circumstances or in the heart of the Cameron country. Despite his preoccupation with his host, Duncan's keen eyes had not failed to note amongst the other guests Sir Thomas Sheridan, Colonel Hay and Captain O'Neil, as well as the impetuous cavalryman Lord Elcho and his friend Major Maxwell of Kirkconnel.

At last, due courtesies over, the MacGregor informed the company of the Prince's situation and proposed programme. His Highness sought Locheil's advice in this pass – but no doubt MacDonuill Duibh would give him that later, and privately, to transmit to the Prince?

This assumption by no means precluded a large part of the assembly giving their own advice vigorously there and then. The sum of it all seemed to be fairly evenly divided, the fighting men, plus Elcho and Maxwell, considering that Charles must stay in the Highlands to rally his scattered forces, and the staff officers counselling an immediate return to France to replenish the sinews of war. It was evident that these two courses had already been the subject of hot debate.

Waiting patiently for the clamour to subside somewhat, Locheil at length intervened. 'I am privileged that His Highness should seek such poor advice as I may be able to offer him, Captain MacGregor,' he said. 'But I could have wished – we all could have wished, I am sure – that he could have come here, under my roof, honoured my house, to receive it. Since he is here in my country.'

Duncan nodded. 'I said the same to His Highness. But he is determined that he will endanger no man's roof by sleeping under it, MacDonuill Duibh. He believes the Government will wreak unmerciful vengeance on any who are thought to have sheltered him. He will not further imperil any, he says.'

'The Government will seek to do so, no doubt – although they do not need the Prince's presence for excuse, 'fore God! They burn and slay and harry already, indiscriminately, without distinction. Young and old, women and children. Even the houses of those who have ignored the Prince's cause are not safe, we hear. Cumberland and his jackals are behaving like madmen.' Locheil paused. 'But surely, if the Prince will but draw his strength to him again, make a stand with such as he can assemble still, he will *save* the houses of his friends, not destroy them?'

Duncan was in no position to controvert that, since it was his own strongly held opinion. 'How many men can I tell His Highness can be assembled to make such a stand, MacDonuill Duibh? At once, I mean?' he asked.

Locheil looked away, across the room at the tight group of his own Cameron lairds who sat around the foot of the long table – not a few of them still bandaged from the battle. The Mac-Gregor noted and recognised amongst them Locheil's sons John and Charles, Major Cameron of Erracht, second in command of the regiment, Cameron of Glenevis, of Torcastle, and others. No doubt Caroline Cameron's father was there too. The chief sighed.

'We have suffered sorely. I have sacrificed so many of my people. God forgive me. Hundreds. Yet . . . ' A low rumbling growl from the foot of the table seemed to hearten him, for he raised his head perceptibly. ' . . . yet we still can fight. I think . . . yes, I think I can promise two hundred men by this time tomorrow.'

'Three hundred, Donald,' Erracht said.

'More, by God!' Torcastle amended.

'That is worth the hearing!' Lord Elcho cried. 'That is how King James will gain his own again – not by talk of defeat and pleas to the King of France.'

'How will three hundred men serve against Cumberland's thousands?' Colonel Hay demanded.

'We have heard the like before,' O'Neil observed. 'My lord of Lovat made some such pronouncement, I recollect! But not one man arrived at the assembly.'

'Sir – have you the effrontery to doubt a Cameron's word!' Erracht cried, half-rising from his chair – and others with him.

'I but speak from recent experience,' the aide said. 'Lovat urged His Highness to fight on. But I do not see a Fraser here! Any more than at Fort Augustus.'

'To what other chiefs can the Prince look for men, in this pass?' old Sir Thomas Sheridan intervened hurriedly, probably seeking to pour oil on troubled waters. 'The MacDonalds? Clanranald and Glengarry and Keppoch?'

There was a moment's pause. Tempers were still somewhat sore over the Clan Donald's role at Culloden; Locheil's Regiment, like others, undoubtedly had lost heavily on account of the MacDonalds' offended failure to charge. Moreover, both Clanranald and Glengarry were rather too close neighbours of the Camerons to be the best of friends.

'How many of the MacDonalds escaped?' Duncan asked. 'They were dying fast, it seemed, as we retired.'

'Many of their officers, of all three regiments, are dead, undoubtedly,' Locheil nodded. 'But some survived. Young Clanranald himself passed here this very afternoon on his way home to Moidart.'

'Young Clanranald? He escaped, then?' the MacGregor exclaimed. 'That is good news. I had feared otherwise. So had the Prince.'

'He could raise another two hundred, at least,' Erracht declared.

'His cousin Kinlochmoidart's company will still be intact,' Locheil pointed out. 'They have been keeping Loudon and his Campbells pinned down at Fort William. There should be a hundred-and-fifty men with Kinlochmoidart, never at Culloden.'

'And would you trust MacDonalds again? After Culloden?' O'Neil demanded. 'And now that treachery is to be rewarded by £30,000!'

There was a sudden and complete silence in that room, so that only the hiss and spurt of the burning logs sounded. Then Erracht's chair toppled backwards with a crash as he leapt to his feet. 'God in Heaven – this is too much!' he cried. 'I am no MacDonald – but my wife was a daughter of Keppoch. Does this . . . this parlour-soldier judge Highland gentlemen by his own Irishry? Does he believe that any would sell the Prince for dirty money . . . ?'

'If they will do it for pride and vanity . . . !'

'Silence, fellow – or a Cameron will teach you manners . . . !'

The sharp crack of his chief's hand smacking down on the settle halted the speaker in mid-phrase. 'Cousin – Captain O'Neil is my guest, I'd remind you,' Locheil said evenly. 'Also he is a wounded man.'

'Then let him not presume upon your hospitality! Or on his scratched leg, by the Powers!'

'My *guest*, I said, Donald! And as such, secure at my table.'

'Then I will no longer sit at your table with such a guest, sir. Goodnight to you, MacDonuill Duibh!' Erracht clapped on his bonnet and stormed out of the hall.

'Goodnight to you, Eoghain 'ic Eoghain,' Locheil returned, but sadly.

Most of the other Camerons rose, saluted their chief, and stamped out after Erracht.

'My apologies, gentlemen,' their host said to his remaining guests, quietly. 'Such displays do credit to none of us.' His level glance rested directly on O'Neil. 'The Prince needs our united strength – not foolish strife and suspicion. But we are all tired, my friends – over-taxed. And the hour is late. I advise that we take to our beds. Who knows whether we may be so fortunate as to have the opportunity again! My gillies tell me that the troop stopping the entrance of this valley, at the Dark Mile, was reinforced at dusk by a full squadron of dragoons under no less a scoundrel than Major Lockhart. Tomorrow, it seems, we probably shall be in the heather!'

'Dare they attack you here, sir?' Duncan wondered.

'I think they may. They know that we are without ammunition – that we have only swords and dirks against their guns. I shall not attempt to defend this house. My grandfather built it for prospects of peace, when our old stronghold was cast down. It is not sited for war. We shall do better in the heather when it comes to fighting.' He gestured towards his bandaged legs. 'Even a cripple!'

'I shall not avail myself of your bed, Locheil,' Lord Elcho announced. 'I have travelled through these last two nights, and shall travel through this. I go on to Kinloch Moidart, where at least I can join a body of armed men – a disciplined unit, Mac-Donalds though they be. I shall endeavour to bring them here to Arkaig, to join you.'

'As you will, my lord . . . '

One by one the others bade their host goodnight, until only Duncan was left. The older man eyed him closely.

'You are not one of the Prince's regular aides, Captain MacGregor,' he said. 'Have you replaced your cousin, James Mor?'

'After a fashion, I have, sir. He has, h'm, rejoined the regiment.'

'I see.' The other sighed. 'So His Highness seeks my advice? Do you believe that he will heed it – with Colonel O'Sullivan at his other ear?'

71

'I do not know, MacDonuill Duibh.'

'Nor do I! O'Sullivan's advice is unlikely to be mine.' Locheil shook his greying head. The Prince's Irish friends, Captain, are loyal. They love His Highness. But they do not love Scotland. And, God save us – they are but doubtful strategists!'

'I know it, sir . . . '

'Aye. What to tell the Prince, then? Tell him that I believe that he can have five hundred fighting men in a week. Two thousand in a month. But, until ammunition comes from France, they can only serve as a threat to Cumberland and a bodyguard to himself. Tell him that, somehow, although we have not a penny-piece left in our sporrans, we will manage to hold the men together until the promised aid arrives. But not if the Prince leaves Scotland. His presence is essential. We shall never hold them, otherwise. Tell him that my country of Arkaig and Locheil will support and hide him meantime, with Clanranald's Moidart and Glengarry's Knoydart – but that he and his gathering forces should move north and still north. Into the Mackenzie country of Ross and Kintail and Torridon. It is remote, easily defended and untouched by war. The Mackenzies of Cromartie and Seaforth can there bring him another thousand men, at least. That is my advice.'

'And what of Lord George Murray? The Duke of Perth? Cluny Macpherson? We had hoped that they would be here by now, from Ruthven. The Prince sent Sawny MacLeod to bid them come here.'

'No doubt they will come.'

'But if you could get here, wounded, by now . . . ?'

Locheil shrugged. 'They hold it against His Highness that he did not appoint a rendezvous in case we lost the battle. That not having done so, he did not come to Ruthven where his two Lieutenants-General went. Give them time, lad . . . '

'Time, sir! Time is what we have not got! If one thing is certain, it is that the Prince will not wait for long. That I prophesy.'

'A week. Ask him for but a week, MacGregor. Aye – and tell him to send O'Sullivan and O'Neil and the rest of them to France, to talk with King Louis! As his ambassadors. Not to go himself. Give that as my advice also, man!'

'As you say, sir . . . '

When Duncan MacGregor left the house to collect the

garron which Locheil was going to lend him for his return journey, he found a man waiting for him at the door. He proved to be Glenpean, a broad stocky man of similar age to Locheil, who had walked out of the hall above with the others, behind Erracht. He spoke to the MacGregor, there in the dark.

'My friend,' he said. 'I believe that you are to be happier than I in that you will be passing my home within a few hours? That you have seen my daughters? Indeed, that the Prince is even now in my shieling of Allt Ruadh? You are carrying a message to His Highness from Locheil – will you carry one to my girls from their father?'

'Assuredly, sir,' Duncan declared. 'I saw your daughter Caroline this very evening. She lent me the boat by which I came here. And the other two I saw early in the morning. All were well and in good spirits. And . . . and very bonny.'

'Aye, bonny. I had hoped to see them – but every Cameron sword is like to be needed here in the morning. A company of foot, we have just heard, is making a night march up Lochy-side. From Fort William. With Lockhart's squadron at the Dark Mile, it can only mean an attack on Arkaig.'

'You think that they know of the Prince's presence here?'

'It is possible. But not necessarily. Enough that they should know that Locheil is home. Loudon has sworn to have Locheil's head.'

The younger man bit his lip. 'I should be staying here with you,' he said. 'One extra sword. It is a bad business when a MacGregor turns his back on a fight . . . '

'Your duty is to the Prince, not to Locheil,' Glenpean said. Duncan could sense the smile that he could not actually see. 'And even a Gregorach sword might not wholly turn the scales! *Dia* – if only we were not devoid of powder and shot, Camerons would be *rejoicing* that the Redcoats should pay a visit to Arkaig-side!' He sighed. 'But, enough of this. Here is my message. It is to Caroline, for the others are too young to understand fully. Tell her that if she hears that the Redcoats are nearer than half-way up the loch, she is not to wait. You understand? Not to wait an hour longer. She is to take to the heather with her sisters. Deep into the hills. The deeper the better. To leave all. And to send all our people away also. She is not to let the soldiers come nearer Glen Pean than half-way. On no account. She is to be ready to leave . . . '

73

'Young girls, sir?' Taking to the hills? In April . . . '

'Yes, by God! There are scores this night, hundreds, who will be wishing that they had done just that, in Badenoch and Strathnairn and Lochaber. Those who are still alive! I have seen . . . Lord forgive these eyes for what they have seen! I was behind Locheil's main body on my journey here, you understand, with just two gillies. We had been settling my wounded son in a safe place – I pray Heaven that it *is* safe – high in the Badenoch hills. So that Cumberland's savages had got before us down Spey. We saw . . . ' The other swallowed audibly. ' . . . we saw bonny young women's bodies lying in the heather, naked as the day they were born, with bayonets between their thighs! We saw women who had been burned alive in their houses. We saw children with their brains dashed against rocks . . . '

'Good Christ!'

'Aye – well may you say it! We saw a minister of the gospel crucified against his own church-door. And everywhere, the dead, the wounded and the survivors, stripped naked of every stitch. Women raped and mutilated, even those big with child. Men shot dead while at work in their fields. And, see you – these were, in the main, Strathspey Grants, who had never come out for the Prince, people of the Laird of Grant who supports the Government, a curse on him!'

'But this is unbelievable! In a Christian country . . . '

'Christian! MacGregor, Cumberland is said to have given orders, not only that there was to be no quarter on the battle-field but that the Highlands are to be made into a desert. He says that the only way to ensure that the country will not rise against the Hanoverian again is that there should be no one left to rise! So . . . so, you will carry my message carefully, will you, Captain? And see that my daughter understands. In case it should so be that I cannot myself come to them in time . . . ' Glenpean's voice quivered, and he gripped the younger man's arm tightly.

Duncan wrung the other's hand wordlessly, and turned away.

'And . . . if you would convey a father's affection, my friend . . . ?'

The young man rode up the dark lochside thereafter, and knew none of the night's peace that had encompassed him on

74

the way down. For too long, it appeared, he had been looking at war like a part-blind man, first from the viewpoint of a fighting soldier and these last days from that of the generals and leaders; now he was seeing it for the first time as the people, his own Highland people, were being brought to see it. And the sight affronted him, sickened him. That men could so act . . . !

The picture of such as Caroline Cameron and her sisters, lying before the smoking ruins of Glenpean House, projected itself unbidden time and again upon the shocked retina of his mind's eye – and he bore the leaden nausea of it in his belly all the way up Arkaig.

Duncan came in person to Glenpean House again in the grey hour before sunrise – and had his weary approach trumpeted by the baying of the hounds. Before he could dismount, the door was opened and the young woman stood waiting for him, rosy with sleep, her hair a tumbled glory, but fully dressed and with a plaid around her shoulders. Obviously she had not undressed all night; by her swift appearance at the door she had probably been sleeping in a chair downstairs.

'You are back. And . . . and alone?' she welcomed him.

'I am sorry,' he said. 'I would have brought your father back with me if I might. But Locheil – he needs all his support . . . '

'I know, I know. It was not to be thought of. But come away in. You will be tired. It is a long weary ride back. I have food for you, ready.'

'Always you are for feeding us, woman!' he smiled. 'I think that the Camerons must be a hungry clan – those hounds ever eating flesh! But I will not come in, no – lest I fall asleep at your kind table. I must get to the Prince. He was going to start for Morar this morning.'

'But that is so foolish,' Caroline exclaimed. 'Where could he be safer than at the Allt Ruadh shieling? Have you not brought word that will keep him? From Locheil?'

'That remains to be seen. I do not know. I hope so, but . . . ' He shrugged. 'Anyway, I must press on.' Duncan hesitated, 'But, before I go, I promised your father that I would deliver you a message, *mo caraidh*. Indeed more than a message – a command. A father's command.'

She laughed at him. 'La, sir – how solemn-sober! That, Captain, for your solemnity!' And she snapped her fingers. 'As for my good father's commands! I was twenty-one nearly a year past – probably he has forgotten! He needs reminding, does he not, that I am not one of his poor gillies?'

The man pulled at his lower lip. 'This is no jest, Miss Cameron,' he assured. 'You will please pay heed to it. The Redcoats – Cumberland's dragoons – are massing at the Dark Mile. Your Camerons, like the rest of us, have nothing but swords and dirks to fight them with. Most had neither powder nor shot even at Culloden Moor. So that there is no certainty that the soldiers will not reach here, even – to Glen Pean.'

She nodded, silent now.

'Your father's commands, in that case, are certain. And very emphatic. You are to take to the hills, with your sisters, before ever they come near. Before they get more than half-way up the loch. You are to wait for nothing. You must arrange for signals to be sent to you from down the loch. You are not to let them nearer than that, before you go. And see that the rest of your folk go likewise. Deep into the hills. Be ready. You understand?'

She searched his tired face in the grey half-light, all the laughter drained from her eyes. 'You mean . . . ?'

'I mean that we are dealing with brute-beasts, not men! No – that is unfair to the beasts, whatever! Even a cat with a mouse, even the ravens with a deer-calf, would not do what Cumberland's pitiless dragoons are doing. By order. In the name of King George! If God Himself can forgive them, I . . . !'

'Hush!' the girl protested. 'Surely, surely you make too much of it! You have been listening to tales. Such rumours grow . . . '

'It is what your father has seen with his own eyes. Do not ask me to tell you of it, girl. I would not have you even begin to imagine it. Just believe that it is so. And promise me that you will do what your father says.'

'Yes,' she whispered. 'Yes. If it is . . . if it is so, of course I promise.'

Almost fiercely the MacGregor glared at her. 'I should not be leaving you. If it was not for the Prince, I . . . I . . . could at least keep watch for you. Provide one sword to guard you. Aid you, if it comes to the heather. But . . . '

'How foolish! Of course your duty is with the Prince. Foolish to fear for me also – for us. I am very well able to take care of

76

myself, on the hill. We have been going to the shielings, at the high pastures, all our lives. In summer time. If ... if we have to go, it will be just a month or two early, that is all. And up there, we do not need wild MacGregors, with swords, to protect us from the deer and the eagles!' She mustered a smile again. 'But – thank you, Gregorach, nevertheless.'

He shook his head, wordless.

Caroline turned away. 'See you – if you will not come inside for a bite, at least you shall take as much of it with you as you can. There is cold meat and bannocks ... '

So, provisioned again, but strangely leaden-hearted, Duncan rode away once more from that hospitable house under Monadh Gorm. He had meant to leave the garron there, but the young woman said to keep it for the extra miles up the glen, and if the Prince should insist on going on over the pass to the sea, to leave the beast tethered at the shieling. She would ride up in the evening, as before, and could bring it back.

He turned and waved, once, some little way from the house, and thereafter did not look round again.

Five miles further, he came to the shieling above the dark lochan by the tumbling Allt Ruadh, just as the lemon-yellow sun was piercing the slate-blue cloud-banks low behind him on the jagged horizon of the Lochaber mountains. No drift of blue smoke yet lifted from the hole in the turf roof. A tired man's momentary resentment at the prolonged sleeping of others changed abruptly as he dismounted and stooped in at the dark doorway.

The cabin was empty. The ashes of the central fire were almost cold. No other trace of his companions remained. They had not waited for sunrise, or even dawn; they had been gone for hours.

Perhaps it was his weariness, but to Duncan MacGregor there seemed to be an ominous significance about that precipitate departure which struck him like a blow.

For a while he stood heavily outside the hut, staring westwards, biting his lip. Then, tethering the garron to a bog-pine root, he removed the folded handkerchief that Caroline Cameron had insisted on him using to cover the sticky patch amongst his hair that a pistol-butt had broken, under his bonnet. Over at the uncaring chuckling burn he washed it clean; he would have liked to have kept it, with its C.C.

77

initials stitched in one corner. Taking off the signet-ring with
the MacGregor crest of a crowned lion, indicative of their
royal descent from Kenneth MacAlpine – a thing that his
father had given him on his reaching man's estate – he threaded
the wet linen through this, and placed it inside the leather
satchel that had contained his breakfast. He hung this from the
cabin doorpost. She would understand.

He turned to look eastwards, down towards Arkaig, sketched
a salute with his hand, and then set off heavy-footed in the
opposite direction up the stony pass that crossed the watershed
between this country and the sea.

CHAPTER 7

IT was almost exactly eight days before Duncan came back to
the head of Glen Pean, although just a little later in the morning. Eight days of fretting inaction, frustration, alarms and
disappointment. Eight days whilst the balance tipped and
swung and wavered, finally to come down to sound the knell
of Jacobite hopes for many a long day to come. Prince Charles
Edward had given Locheil the week that he pleaded for – and
one day more. Now, alone and disillusioned, Duncan Mac-
Gregor came trudging eastwards over the high stony pass
again, and headed down by the side of the bounding stripling
Pean. No sun shone this morning up the long deep trough
of Arkaig.

He was skirting the lochan in the floor of the glen, where he
had swum nine evenings before, and in two minds whether to
press on the five more miles to Glenpean House or to climb up
to the shieling above and rest there, even on an empty stomach
– for he had once again walked all night – when a faint sound
on the still morning air caught his attention. He heard it only
for a moment, so brief was it – but he was fairly sure that it
had been the high baying of a hound, muffled and somehow
swiftly cut off.

That halted him. Stare as he would he could see nothing to
account for it amongst the heather and bracken around him.
The shieling up there was not in sight from the track or the

lochan – one of the distinct advantages of its position. He started to climb the hill.

He reached the cabin, and paused a little way off. Its doorway stood dark, empty. No sign of life showed there, no sound emerged. He noted that the leather satchel was gone from the doorpost. Then, on a sudden impression, the man knelt down – in order the cause the roofline to be outlined against the brown heather rather than the leaden sky. Sure enough, there was just the faintest eddy of bluish smoke lifting above the chimney-hole. His hand on his sword-hilt, Duncan stepped forward softly.

A cry from the heather stopped him. 'Duncan! Captain Duncan! Captain MacGregor!' Out of a fold in the hillside fifty of sixty yards above, Caroline Cameron came running, skirts kilted high, holding the wolf-hound back with one hand and dangling a pistol in the other. Behind her, after a moment or two, appeared her two younger sisters, Anne and Belle.

He started towards the young woman, long-strided – and stopped short. She, who ran as though to hurl herself headlong upon him, stopped short also. So they stood, only a couple of yards apart, the girl's breathing unsteady, her breasts heaving, her eyes filmed – and the hound reached out between them to bridge the gap.

Duncan looked from Caroline to the pistol in her hand, over her shoulder to her sisters, and back to the cabin with its telltale wisp of smoke.

'What does this mean?' he asked, throatily. 'What do you here, all of you?'

'We have been here three days,' she said, panting a little. 'We came ... because it was as – as you said.'

'You mean ... ?'

She nodded. 'They came. The soldiers.'

A sort of groan escaped him. 'You were in time?'

'We were in time. We did not wait.'

'Thank God! And your home? Glenpean House?'

She bit her lip, blinking hard, and then shook her head, wordless.

'My dear,' he said. 'I am sorry. More sorry than I can say, whatever. I did not know. I thought that ... all was well. I saw your father but two days ago, at Borrodale. He said that the Redcoats had not come as far as the head of Arkaig, that they had burned Achnacarry and Muick and Achnasaul – but that he had been home and seen you, and that Glenpean was untouched . . . '

'They came the next day. After he had gone. They were making for Doctor Archie's house in Glen Dessary. They burned it, too. And all the cot-houses – his and ours.'

'I see. And your people? You got them away in time also?'

'Yes. Father had warned them all the day before. They are scattered about the hills, now. There is one family up behind us here, in a sort of cave on Sgor Thuilm. All are safe. Save . . . save old Seana.' The young woman's voice faltered. 'She went back. For something that she had left behind. She . . . she was not very right in the head, you see. And old. They caught her. And they . . . old as she was, they . . . ' Caroline shook her auburn head, glancing back at her sisters, and left the rest unsaid.

But the girls had heard. Belle, the youngest, a plump and vivacious nine-year-old, spoke up in shocked excitement.

'We found her. Old Seana. The next day, when we crept down for some things. When the soldiers were gone. She was bent right over her table. Out on the grass. She was tied that way. With ropes.' The child giggled unevenly. 'And she had no clothes on! Not even a plaid!'

'She was dead,' Anne, the elder by three years, declared reprovingly. 'You should not laugh, Belle.'

'Hush, dear God – both of you!' Caroline said. 'Come you and pay your respects to Captain MacGregor, properly. Aren't you glad to see him? Belle, pull your skirt down. We ran from the cabin in a great rush,' she explained to Duncan. 'Luath must have scented you, and began to bay. I had to quieten him at once – he would have given our presence away. But at least he warned us of someone approaching . . . '

'Cuilean is dead,' the factual Belle informed. 'The soldiers shot him too.'

'We found his body. At the door of the house,' Caroline explained jerkily. 'They had been away somewhere – the two hounds. When the soldiers were signalled. We could not wait for them. Luath came up here to us, later. Alone. Following our scent. But not Cuilean. Poor Cuilean, he was ever the headstrong one . . . '

'Cuilean was brave,' Anne said. 'He could run down any deer. I loved Cuilean very much.'

Duncan stooped to take the pistol from Caroline's fingers, as a diversion. 'And this?' he asked, glancing at it and shaking his head. 'Unloaded? Unprimed?'

'We have no powder and shot either. But it might have kept a soldier away. For a little. So that we could run.'

'We could run faster than any Sassunach soldier in a red coat, I swear!' Anne asserted stoutly.

'And Caroline has a *sgian dubh*, too – a little dirk,' Belle informed, confidentially. 'She keeps it in her . . . '

'Belle! For Heaven's sake!' her elder sister cried. 'Off with you! Into the cabin, and get the fire going again. Quickly, now. The Captain will be wanting his breakfast.' Flushed a little, she turned to Duncan. 'We had just new-made the fire for breakfast. When Luath barked, I covered it over, to hide the smoke, as best I could . . . '

'It was the smoke that warned me that you – or someone other – were here, nevertheless,' he told her. 'It could be a danger. There is a trick that we have in the Gregorach that I will show you.' Deliberately he smacked his lips at them all. 'But I am hungry as any horse. Always I come to you for food. Let us get that porridge boiling.'

It was time that the subject was changed.

The interior of the cabin was transformed from the somewhat stark appearance it had worn when the man had last seen it. The girls had managed to bring up many items salvaged from the wreckage of their home to give the place a domestic and lived-in air, with the indefinable touch of feminine occupancy about it – however dark and constricted it must remain. Plaids hung against the bare stone walls, deer-skins, most of them burnt and charred in places, strewed the earthen floor and that was also now coated with rushes from the lochan. There were wicker baskets of clothes, which presumably had been ready packed for their flight. Even a mirror, broken admittedly, was set to gain the best light opposite the doorway, and a jug of yellow cowslips from the crannies of the hillside lit up a dark corner.

The man was moved. Here was quiet courage, a clear determination not to dwell on sorrows and discomforts. He did not voice his recognition thereof, however.

Bustle and assist as he would at the remaking of the fire and the preparation of breakfast, the inevitable question was not long in coming.

'The Prince?' Caroline asked. 'How is he faring? Where is he now? And how comes it that you are back here alone? Are you carrying messages again?'

'After a fashion, I am,' Duncan admitted heavily. 'The Prince has left me a mission to perform for him. For he no longer needs me . . . where he has gone.'

'Gone? He has gone?'

'Aye. Last evening, with the sunset, he set sail in an eight-oared boat from Loch nan Uamh. For the Outer Isles. For Loch Boisdale. I watched him go.'

'But . . . but this is folly, is it not? Duncan – here is madness, surely? How will he serve his cause yonder? It is here that he is needed, the leader, where his men are to gather. He will gather no army on Lewis.'

'He is not going to gather an army. He has gone seeking the French ships. Word came that they were hiding from the English frigates in Loch Boisdale. Lewis is but the first stage on his journey to France.'

'So-o-o! It is done, then? He has left Scotland.' The young woman gave a long quivering sigh. 'After all. All! So all is over – save paying the price!'

'He will be back.' Strongly, loyally, Duncan declared it, to himself as much as to his hearers. 'He goes only to win the aid that we need. From King Louis. Money to pay his regiments, to buy provisioning. Guns. Ammunition. Powder and shot . . . for such as this pistol.'

'Could someone else not have done that? His own father, even? King James? Is he not the one to have gone to the King of France? The Prince's place is here, with those who have fought for him . . . would fight again . . .'

'Think you that we did not tell him so? Young Clanranald told him, pleaded with him. Locheil sent him that advice, by myself. Elcho arrived two days ago, with Kinlochmoidart, and said the same – although he said it differently, wrongly unforgivably, for he is a passionate, impatient man and he has ever criticised the Prince. He said . . . what he should not have said.' Duncan ran a hand through his hair. 'But others spoke more suitably, reasoned with him. Your Doctor Archie Cameron of

Glendessary – who cannot have known that his house was burned. You father was with him. And others. It was of no use. The Prince – he has a stubbornness, and obstinacy, at times, that there is no moving. And the Irishmen were ever at his private ear.'

'Are they false, then, think you?'

'No, never that. But they see it all differently. It is all just politics to them, a sort of game that they play for high stakes. But it does not mean to them men's lives and homes, the fate of Scotland. Adventurers they are, without a country – more French than Irish, indeed . . . '

'They are with him still? Have gone with him?'

'Yes. O'Neil joined us again at Borrodale. That is where the Prince has been waiting these last days, in a shieling near Mac-Donald of Borrodale's house. Waiting for these ships, waiting for word that the clans were gathering, waiting for Lord George and those who went to Ruthven. Doctor Archie and your father brought O'Neil and Sheridan from Achnacarry. But Sheridan did not sail with them. He was ill again. He is too old for this kind of life. Locheil sent them because he is now taken to the heather himself . . . '

'Yes. Achnacarry Castle is no more. There has been fighting. But Locheil seeks not to come to blows until he has been able to gather the clan again, and equip his men in some fashion, my father told me. He has abandoned all the strath of Arkaig to the dragoons, but they dare not follow into the hills themselves.'

'Where is Locheil hiding, then? I have to find him.'

'Father said just above his own house of Achnacarry. Up the hill, in a cabin like this. He cannot travel easily, injured as he is. But his men are not there. Most of them are in the high valleys between here and Loch Eil itself. A party passed here yesterday, from the north, to join them. Forty men from Glen Kingie. Old men and boys. We were frightened until we knew that they were our own people.' She stirred the phuttering porridge. 'Your mission, then, is to Locheil? Not back to your own Mac-Gregors?'

'It is not to Locheil himself, no. It is a curious matter. While we were waiting in Glen Borrodale, one of Glengarry's people brought the Prince word that a courier, Young Scotus – he will be MacDonnell of Scotus itself now, for his uncle, cousin to Glengarry, fell at Culloden and he is heir – Young Scotus is bringing money to the Prince from his brother the Duke of York. How much money is not known for sure. He came in a small vessel from France, meaning to put in at his own Glengarry country at Loch Nevis. But Government ships chased them and they had to flee far to the north, landing in the end up in the Mackenzie country. This Scotus was making for Inverness, to the Prince, when he learned of the battle. Not knowing then where to find His Highness or to take his money, he made for his own country. Lochgarry, colonel of Glengarry's Regiment, heard of him on his return home from Culloden – I had been told that Lochgarry was dead, but it seems that he was only wounded. He sent one messenger after Scotus, to bring him to the Prince, and the other to tell His Highness himself.' Bitterly Duncan shrugged. 'I do believe that it was the waiting for his money that kept Charles at Borrodale biding as long as he did!'

'But it did not come, the money?'

'No. At length he would wait no longer. That is the mission that the Prince has put upon *me* – to find this Scotus, and get the gold. To keep it safely for him, until he sends me instructions.' The man grimaced. 'It is not an employment that I esteem!'

'It shows that His Highness trusts you. Trusts you more than this MacDonnell of Scotus, it seems. Or many another.'

'That may be. But I am a soldier, not a banker! I would rather that he had chosen someone else. Or left the gold with Scotus – who after all must have been sufficiently trusted by the Duke of York, and has brought it all this way.'

'What do you now, then?'

'First I must see Locheil. Scotus may have come to him, at Achnacarry. He is now the recognised leader of the cause, the most respected man left, whom all trust. Round him all circulate. If he knows nothing of MacDonnell, then I suppose that I must go to Scotus itself, seeking him. It is on the Knoydart coast, opposite to Skye.' Duncan sighed. 'Chasing gold pieces!'

Caroline laughed – the first laugh of the morning. 'Some do nothing else all their lives!' she pointed out. 'But before you do that, or anything else, my good banker, you will eat your breakfast. And then you will sleep. If you have come from Borrodale, then you have covered a score of the roughest miles in all Scotland, and by night. You look as though you have, too. You are not the man you were, even when first I saw you. Rest you need – and this is as good a place for it as any. We shall keep watch for you . . . '

'You are kind,' he said.

Duncan found it a pleasant interlude indeed, up there in the lap of the mountains, and a most welcome change from the atmosphere of manoeuvre, perplexity, anxiety and mistrust in which he had been living these past days and nights. A joy also to relax in easy idleness after all his hurried and furtive travelling – however soon it was to resume.

Not that the girls lived a life of inactivity up at the Allt Ruadh shieling. When the man awoke, in the early afternoon, it was to find Anne Cameron rooting about in the heather near by for bog-pine roots, relics of the noble forests which had once clothed all the Highlands, even up to these altitudes far above the present tree-level. These, when dried in the sun, made excellent fuel, being impregnated with resin, burning with a hot flame and a minimum of smoke. Caroline and Belle apparently had gone for the milk. This involved climbing up the broken hillside above into one of the high hanging corries of the mountain in which some of the Glen Pean cattle had been temporarily penned, well out of the way of marauding Redcoats – with whom it was a major point of policy to round up and drive off all stock, to whomsoever it belonged, as a means of starving the countryside, and at the same time feeding and enriching themselves. It seemed that the Cameron cattle were in fact scattered all over these lofty and inaccessible pastures, in little groups, and the people likewise. It was as well that this enforced dispersal had not been imposed upon them in the autumn or winter, when, apart from the cold and the snows for the refugees, there would have been no herbage for the animals; now, the new growth was already burgeoning, and would provide excellent feeding until September. That indeed was the object of the shieling system – the annual migration of the young people, with the flocks and herds, to make use of the brief rich summer growth of the high places, and thus preserve all that could be grown in the little fields of the lower glens for essential fodder during the long winter months.

Duncan went down to the lochan in the pass to wash and refresh himself with a swim, and then set out over the heather, on Anne's directions, for the corrie about a thousand feet above. Here, in a great cauldron scooped out of the summit massif of Sgor nan Coireachan, ringed with frowning cliffs but floored in bright green grasses and wildflowers, he found not only about forty cattle, cows and calves, but almost a dozen people, living in improvised caves amongst the great rock-falls that choked the mouth of the place – including amongst them a wounded survivor of Culloden.

Caroline, chiding him for not having slept longer while he had opportunity, made him known to her people – who seemed on the whole surprisingly cheerful considering the circumstances and the burnt-out state of their homes down in the glen. Then, shouldering the leathern bottles of milk, and a shoulder of venison from a young stag which one of the men had managed to trap in a pit, they headed downhill again, Belle and Luath the hound running before.

On the way down, the young woman took him to another hidden hollow in the long hillside, not a corrie this time but rather a widening of a deep ravine scoured by a tumbling torrent, where another little party was ensconced. Instead of cattle these had a herd of goats and three or four garrons. It was one of the ponies that Caroline wanted, for Duncan's nocturnal visit to Locheil. That man was relieved to know that the three girls were not quite so isolated and alone as they had seemed.

Later, as Duncan's suggestion that some fish might provide a welcome change to the necessarily somewhat restricted diet that oatmeal, milk, dried beef, fresh venison and honey produced, they all trooped down to the River Plean. Throwing off all but his kilt, the man stepped into the rushing peat-brown waters, encouraged vociferously from the bank, and sought to balance precariously on the slippery river-bed pebbles. In his boyhood he had been an acknowledged expert in the gentle arts of tickling, gudding, or otherwise extracting trout from their element without the aid of lines and hooks. Now, feeling cautiously around boulders with both hands, crouching under the overhang of the banks, testing the eddies, concentrating all his senses in his finger-tips with head on one side as though he listened, eyes half-shut, mouth half-open, he proceeded to demonstrate that he had not entirely lost his cunning – whilst pointing out to his admiring gallery that these Cameron trouties were wee, terrible wee, compared with the giants of his own native Glen Gyle far to the south.

It was not long before he had first Belle and then Anne in the water beside him, modesty cast on the winds, and producing much squealing and splatter if not actual fish – and challenging, daring their elder sister to do better. She came in, too, after a suitable display of reluctance, and with stern warnings to Duncan MacGregor to keep his roving eyes steadily upstream and not down in her direction, under direst penalties – a precaution which she quite omitted to see stringently maintained in the subsequent excitement and thrill of the hunt, even to the extent of summoning the man urgently to her side on one occasion to assist in cornering a monster which, unfortunately, escaped through a certain preoccupation on Duncan's part. All this with her skirts tied approximately round her middle.

Altogether a stirring and enjoyable afternoon, far removed from thoughts of war, suspicion and treachery – and productive of more than brown trout.

It was with much disinclination, then, as the sun sank behind the high pass to the west, that Duncan gave ear to the call of duty, in opposition to the siren-songs of his eloquent hosts and tempters – the two younger of whom punctuated his pleas for delay with giggled wonderings as to the propriety of a man sleeping overnight in the one room with themselves, but deciding magnanimously that, since one room was all that the cabin contained, it was that or poor Captain MacGregor catching his death in the dewy heather outside, to the general hurt of the Stuart cause. Duncan declared that it was clearly high time that Donald Cameron of Glenpean was home to keep his daughters in order – but asserted that he must go, nevertheless.

Caroline, leaving Luath with her sisters, accompanied him down the glen; she wanted to see if her cat, which had been missing since the day the soldiers came, had returned to the vicinity of the house. So they rode down through the gloaming on garrons, now side by side, now one behind the other.

Although they started out smiling and at ease, a silence and a sombreness descended upon them as they neared the foot of the glen and the long trough of Arkaig. The realities of their situations came flooding back upon them both.

Even so, the sight of Glenspean House came as a shock to Duncan MacGregor. He had accepted that it had been burned, devastated, but the sudden recognition that those black-stained, roofless, gaping walls, surrounded by heaped rubble and charred timbers, were all that remained of the fair white house with its garden and trim farmery, brought a lump to his throat and a swift blinding fury to his heart. For a few moments he did not trust himself to speak, nor even to look at his companion.

Caroline Cameron did not speak either.

They scanned the area before them carefully, beyond the house and the scattered ruins of the crofts, to all the open ground about the head of the pewter loch and the wide mouth of Glen Dessary opposite, before emerging from the last trees of their own glen. No sign of life showed therein.

Duncan was still racking his brains for something to say to her, anything, that would not sound either hopelessly shallow or quite unsuitable, as they rode up to the broken premises themselves, still yielding up the evil smell of fire, when the girl herself found words.

'I do not see Min. Mineag, the cat. Do you?' she asked, in a flat factual voice. 'Small. Black-and-white.'

'No. No, I do not.'

'I suppose, if she is here, she will be . . . inside.' Caroline dismounted, and moved towards the gaping doorway, stiffly, unsteadily.

The man came after her.

At the threshold she paused, staring straight ahead of her. For moments she stood so, her back to him, rigid, still. Then, after one or two false starts, she got out a husky uneven call. 'Min! Minnie! Mineag – come, puss . . . ' Her voice broke.

Duncan's hand reached out to take her forearm and grip it.

Twisting round abruptly she buried her auburn head against his chest, and her body shook to great sobs against his own.

Holding her tightly there in the doorway, the man stroked the down-bent head, wordless yet. He saw them both standing in this same doorway last time he had been here, refusing to come inside, saying that it was his duty to hurry on after his Prince. He saw Charles himself standing here, declaring that they must not sleep in this house lest harm come to it and its occupants. And he did not know how hardly he gripped the young woman as he thought of it – so that she stirred and looked up at him, blinking away her tears.

He was not looking down at her – for something else had

caught his blackly frowning glance. He gazed over her head, northwards, towards the mouth of Glen Dessary, out from the dark gut of which a group of mounted figures had just appeared, shadowy in the dusk.

'Men!' he jerked. 'Horsemen. Coming out of the glen.'

She turned, to stare. 'I . . . I cannot see.' She wiped her swimming eyes with the back of her hand.

'There are four or five, I think. It is difficult to tell in this half-light.'

'Are they Redcoats? Dragoons?'

'I think not. I think that I would see scarlet. But all Cumberland's cavalry do not wear red coats.'

'We must not be caught here, Duncan.'

'No. But they may well be going down the north shore of Arkaig. If so they will not come near here. It is the best road, after all. They probably have not seen us, amongst all these broken walls. But if we ride off now, they are bound to see us.'

'What is best, then?'

'Inside. Quickly. The garrons too. They will not see us then. Even if they come this way they will not likely trouble to look inside this burned house. They will have seen many such . . . '

So into the shell of Caroline's home they moved, pulling the reluctant ponies in after them, to stumble over the charred fallen rafters and pathetic rubble within, into a corner that had once been part of the kitchen. There, amongst the debris, they waited, the garrons restless, the girl holding herself tightly under control.

An empty window space allowed them to peer out, northwards. Soon they perceived that the newcomers had not in fact turned eastwards down the north shore of Arkaig, but were coming across the marshy flats at the head of the loch, towards them.

'Surely, if they were Government soldiers, they would have gone by the north shore,' the girl said tensely. 'Where the road runs. It may be that they are our own people?'

'May be. But I think that the man who rides in front is dressed like an English officer, nevertheless.' Duncan was straining his eyes in the gathering gloom. 'Yes, I am sure of it. There are three mounted gillies and two pack-ponies. But the leader is a Southron.'

The horsemen were perhaps a quarter of a mile away. They rode ploddingly as though after a long journey. Soon it was perfectly clear that the foremost was dressed in military clothing with gold facings and a cocked hat. His three followers wore dark tartans and seemed to be armed to the teeth. Equally clear was the fact that not only were they coming in this general direction but that they were actually heading for Glenpean House.

'We . . . we would have been better to have bolted,' the girl faltered. 'While we had opportunity. Better still, perhaps . . . ?'

The man shook his head. 'Their horses are better than ours – long-legged beasts, not garrons. They could ride us down easily. Save on very rough ground.' He looked around him, in that desolate shadowy place, urgently. 'See, Caroline,' he said. 'We cannot get the garrons out of here now, unseen – too late. But *we* can get out. Through those windows at the back. Facing the loch. Once they are a little nearer, so that they cannot see the back part of this house, we will climb out. Then, keeping the bulk of it between us and them, we will hurry down to those alders and bushes by the loch-shore. In the dusk we should get away without being seen. Into the trees and then round to the mouth of your glen again.'

'Yes. Yes. They will find the garrons, but . . . '

'Come, then.'

They scrambled over the debris to a shattered window of the rear wall. Assuring himself that they would be hidden from the approaching riders, Duncan helped his companion to climb through, and then followed her. They crouched down behind the walling, hands blackened with soot. The angle of the building to the nearest cover of bushes was such that they could not risk a dash into the open until the horsemen were very near the front of the house. It was unfortunate, for it meant that if they were spotted they would be the more easily captured.

Fretting, they waited there. By peeping through their window, in alignment with another at the front, they could see some of the space before the house. And here in a few moments, they saw the newcomers pull up and dismount, and gaze towards the burned-out buildings. The leader was a handsome young officer clad in what had been a very fine and elegant uniform, now somewhat travel-worn, the long-skirted coat deep-blue with white-and-gold facings. His supporters might have belonged to any dark-tartaned clan. As the fugitives watched, the officer pointed to the house doorway, and came towards it, followed by two of his men. The other stayed with the horses.

Duncan came to a swift decision. Somehow, he had to aid the girl's escape. 'Quick! Off with you now,' he commanded. 'Run. To those bushes. No – alone. Go, now. I will join you later.' And as she began to question his purpose in a whisper, 'Quickly, *mo caraidh*– or it will be too late.'

Obediently Caroline rose, and bent almost double, an ill posture for any well-made woman, ran for the nearest alders, perhaps a hundred yards away.

Duncan did not wait to watch her progress. Crouching still, he edged to the gable-end nearest to the horses. Peering round, he saw the three men staring in at the door of the house. The garrons inside were restless and uneasy at the smell of fire, and even Duncan could hear them. The fourth man, over at the horses, was watching his companions.

As the group at the door stepped in over the threshold, Duncan darted forward and half-right. The barn, in which the Prince had once thought to sleep, was there. He was behind it, unseen, in a dozen strides. He now had cover. Rounding the corner of the wrecked barn and the byre beyond it, he was behind the cluster of horses. Moreover, the beasts were between him and their guardian.

The man did not hesitate for even a moment. Drawing his dirk, he raced forward lightly.

The stirring of the six horses covered any sound of his approach. He was amongst them in only two or three seconds. Edging between the beasts, he worked his way into position directly behind the unsuspecting guard – who stood holding the reins of the four riding horses in his hand.

Even as something of an outcry from within the roofless walls of the house seemed to indicate that Caroline's flight had been perceived, Duncan leapt. One arm encircled the gillie's neck from the back, and the other hand crashed down the hilt of the dirk on precisely the right spot of the unfortunate man's head, bonnet or none. With an incipient cry that choked off into a long shuddering sigh, the fellow went limp in his assailant's arms, still clutching the reins. For any MacGregor weaned on Rob Roy's tactics, it was child's-play.

Letting his stunned victim fall, Duncan vaulted up on to the back of the nearest horse. Kicking out with his brogans and waving his arms, he sought to stampede the other beasts away

from the scene. He was successful with the more highly strung
saddle horses – but the stolid garrons stayed where they were.
He had no time to waste on them. Digging his heels into his new
mount's flanks, he dragged its head round and sent it plunging
after its fellows.

Cries arose behind him, tenor notably changed from a
moment or two before. It was not these, however, that made
the man look back. It was the hollow pounding of hooves
immediately at his back.

The two pack-ponies were hurtling along at his very heels,
their short legs going furiously, the basket-panniers which were
slung on either side of them joucing about crazily. This
phenomenal display of fire and energy was explained by the two
leading-ropes which stretched forward from the beasts and tied
somewhere to the saddle of his own horse. He had selected the
wrong steed, apparently.

Duncan could not see, at the moment, just where the ropes
were hitched; possibly to the buckles of the stirrup-leathers
under the flaps of the saddle. Nor could he spare time to stop,
investigate, and unhitch them. He must just put up with the
garrons meantime.

This resolution was reinforced a moment or two later by the
sharp crack of powder and shot. That would be only a cavalry
pistol, he imagined, and no great threat at this range; but when,
thereafter, a vicious whistle to his left and a louder report came
practically simultaneously, the man crouched low in the saddle
and pricked at the horse's rump with the tip of his dirk. That
was a musket – a different matter altogether.

Only one more shot came after him, however, and not very
close. Presumably the marksmen were not very swift at reload-
ing. Better that they should be shooting after him than at
Caroline, at any rate. And so long as they were shooting, they
were not catching their errant horses for pursuit.

Presently Duncan decided that he was out of musket-shot.
Glancing over his shoulder, he perceived three men running
hither and thither, not far from the house, undoubtedly seeking
to corner their mounts. Since the beasts could not be seriously
upset, that would not take very long.

Pulling his borrowed horse's head round, he headed his trio
for the mouth of Glen Pean, going as hard as the garrons' drag
on his mount would allow.

It was Duncan's intention to go far enough up the glen to be well out of sight, and then to climb up the hillside to the south, to circle round and back, higher up, to try to pick up Caroline. She would have seen what he was doing, and presumably would be looking out for him.

It was just after he had turned off from the narrow floor of the glen, that it happened. The steep braeside meant that the panniers on the two garrons were unbalanced and askew – and no doubt they were already strained and displaced by the rough treatment they had received on that headlong career. At any rate, as one of the ponies stumbled on a loose stone and saved itself from falling only by a mighty scrabbing, the fastenings of its left pannier snapped with a jerk, and the basket fell to the heather.

The impact burst the wickerwork lid open, and out spewed two or three bags. They all looked identical, not very large, made of some sort of cloth, probably linen. One of them, rolling and bounding downhill, struck a corner of rock, and split open. Out therefrom spilled a stream of coins – that even in the fading light gleamed golden.

Duncan pulled up, staring. Many gold pieces were rolling down.

There is something about gold, about money, that few can resist. The sight of it, in large quantities, will even seem sometimes to alter a man's whole character. If it did not do that to Duncan MacGregor, at least it had him down off the horse and grasping for the errant coins in the instant. He picked up two, three. All were of a sort – *louis-d'or.*

'Lord!' he gasped. 'French! French gold *louis!*'

He hurried to the broken pannier. It was almost full of the little linen bags. He weighed two of them in his hand. They were very heavy, and the coins within chinked metallically. He looked into the other pannier, still attached to the garron. It contained only clothing and personal gear. So did both those on the second pony – the effects of an elegant man who liked his comforts even when travelling. A folded paper lay amongst them. It was written in French script.

Duncan turned back, thoughtfully, to gather up the spilled gold. One pannied filled with coin – reason enough for it to be the one that broke loose, heavy as it was and therefore lacking balance. French gold! Could it be, then, that he had made a mistake? A grave mistake?

He stared away down the glen.

Even as he looked, a mounted figure came into sight round a bend down there, riding hard. The pale breeches at least stood out in the gloom.

'So be it,' Duncan said.

CHAPTER 8

It was less than pleasant just to stand there waiting for the irate rider – but Duncan obscurely felt that he owed it to him, somehow. He had moved down to the track in the floor of the glen once more, with the three animals, and now stood in front of them, arms folded on his chest to proclaim, if possible, his present inoffensiveness. He had taken the precaution of pinning his white cockade, distinguishing emblem of the Jacobites, prominently on his bonnet. He hoped powerfully that the approaching man, even in the dying light, would notice all this and not merely pistol him out of hand.

The officer slowed down from his furious gallop as he approached. Undoubtedly it must have seemed a strange development, and probably he feared a trap or an ambush. One of his kilted supporters, mounted again, had now appeared far in the rear.

Duncan raised his hand and waved it.

About one hundred yards away, the horseman pulled up, and drew his pistol, obviously nonplussed.

Duncan raised his voice as well as hand. 'Sir,' he shouted, 'my apologies to you if you are King James's man. If not – shoot and be damned to you!' He was ready, at the first raising of that pistol, to dodge behind the nearest garron.

The other did not answer. He sat there uncertainly, on restless mount, as well he might.

Duncan tried again. 'Are you French? *Frasçais, Monsieur?*'

'I am not,' came back shortly. 'And who the devil are you, to ask?' That certainly did not sound like a French voice. Nor yet, indeed, despite the language, an English one.

'I am an officer of Prince Charles Edward's army. Sir . . .

could it be . . . is it possible that you are Young Scotus? Mac-
Donnell, younger of Scotus?'

'Aye. I thought that was it, by God!' The question seemed
to further infuriate the newcomer. 'Another rogue in need of
shooting, curse me!'

Duncan hesitated. 'But you *are* Scotus?' he insisted.

'What if I am, damn you! Does that make *you* any less of a
thieving robber?'

'I think so, yes,' Duncan cleared his throat. It was tiresome,
this long-range shouting, and the mounted gillie was coming up
fast. 'My name is MacGregor. Captain MacGregor . . .'

'Well I believe it! Always the MacGregors were thieves and
caterans!'

'Also an extra aide to His Royal Highness. Charged to find
Captain MacDonnell of Scotus.'

'What . . . ?'

'It is the truth, sir.'

'You have an uncommon strange way of carrying out your
charge, then!'

'It was a mistake, Captain. I apologise. I took you for an
English officer. Your clothes. None of His Highness's officers
dress so . . .'

'I am an officer of the Irelanda Regiment of His Catholic
Majesty of Spain.'

'No doubt. But you looked devilish like one of Cumberland's!'

The other turned to glance behind him, saw that his henchman was in close support and evidently decided that he could
risk coming near. He moved forward, pistol notably at the
ready.

Duncan stood still, arms folded again.

The gillie came thundering up just as his master reached the
MacGregor, very fierce with musket in right hand and drawn
broadsword in left. Duncan could see now that the fellow was
wearing the dark Glengarry MacDonnell tartan. No doubt he
thought that his superior had been successful in cornering the
miscreant.

With one looking down at him on either side, neither kindly,
Duncan smiled. 'Your money is all safe, Captain,' he said. 'It
was the gold that opened my eyes. A pannier fell off, and one of
the bags burst open. Only one man is like to be travelling the

Highlands today with all that French gold – MacDonnell of Scotus, the man His Highness set me to find. So it is well met, sir.'

Scotus rubbed a pointed chin with the back of the hand that held the cocked pistol. 'I suppose that I must believe you,' he said.

'Indeed you must! I have a paper signed by the Prince . . . '

'His Highness – is he near, then? Near here? I have had conflicting word – that he is with Locheil in Arkaig and again with Borrodale in Arisaig . . . '

'Unhappily he is neither. By now he should be at Loch Boisdale in South Uist. He sailed for the Outer Isles twenty-four hours ago.'

'Good Lord – what does he do there?'

'He seeks ship to take him back to France.'

'But . . . Saints of Mercy! To France? The Prince? How will that serve him? I have just come from France. His place is here. What a plague means this?'

'Well may you ask. Many sought to dissuade him, I assure you.' Duncan sighed. 'But it is a long story, and better places for telling it than this. Moreover, I have a friend that we must find. I was not alone in yonder burned house of Glenpean's. His daughter was there also – Miss Caroline Cameron. Her home it was. We were looking for something there, when we saw you coming. Taking you for one of Cumberland's officers, we hid – for I have no powder or ball for my pistol. I sought to draw you off – and succeeded. Now we must find her.'

'*Dia* – Glenpean's daughter! And his house destroyed. I knew nothing of it. Who did this thing? Why? I intended to pass the night there. Doctor Archibald Cameron's house of Glendessary is also burned. What is the meaning of it, sir?'

'The meaning is that there is much in this sad realm of Scotland today that you will require to learn, Captain. Much of it that stains the very name of common humanity. But that can wait. Here is your second gillie. I hope that I did not damage your third too sorely? Let us be off down the glen, to find him. And Miss Cameron too. When your man has put his pannier to rights . . . '

They found Caroline readily enough, by means of Duncan hallooing and shouting her name every couple of hundred yards or so down near the mouth of the glen. At his fourth or fifth cry they heard her answering call, and she rose up out of the hillside heather some way above them, eyeing them doubtfully. At Duncan's beckoning and reassuring wave she came down to them.

Whatever doubts MacDonnell himself might have about the MacGregor, he appeared to have none at all regarding the young woman. He was off his horse in a trice, bowing low and kissing her hand, and apologising profusely for having inadvertently frightened her. Flushed, breathless and distinctly dishevelled as she was, he most evidently approved of her – for which Duncan should not have blamed him. He was a very personable, gallant and good-looking young man indeed, though his Frenchified manners Duncan felt to be excessive.

Caroline did not appear to share his insular bias, however, and after only a brief period of introduction and explanation, was quickly on easy terms with him, laughing and bright-eyed. Duncan was vaguely resentful, and felt that it was all slightly unsuitable.

Scotus and his gillies were hospitably invited to the shieling up at Allt Ruadh – an offer accepted with alacrity, and seemingly taken as a personal compliment by the former. There was now no need for Duncan to go seeking Locheil, so, after returning to Glenpean House to pick up the third gillie – now fairly well recovered but eyeing his former assailant without love or understanding – and the two garrons, they all made their way up the dark glen once more.

Luath bayed her warning to the mountains long before the party reached the shieling, and, true to their instructions, Anne and Belle were nowhere to be seen when the newcomers arrived at the cabin. Caroline's call brought them swiftly out of the heather, however, small dark shadows wrapped in plaids, and the nound with them. Astonishingly soon their excited laughter resounded on the night, the fire was blown up and revived, and food produced. The Cameron daughters, it was apparent, seldom actually dwelt on the more sombre aspects of life.

Scotus was a success from the beginning, treating the girls like three princesses – with one of whom at least he might almost have been contemplating seduction.

With the gillies bedded down outside in their plaids, the talk went on in the cabin, by the flickering light of the bog-pine fire, well into the night. Suggestions that the youngsters should go to sleep were treated with the contempt that they deserved, and Scotus's assertion that no beauty sleep was required in this company received with acclaim. Duncan MacGregor became a very secondary figure on the shadowy scene, and John MacDonnell took the stage as to the manner born, ably supported by Caroline.

The newcomer's account of himself was as enthralling as it was well and dramatically told. Without his actually saying so, it was clear that he was cast in a pleasingly heroic mould, suitable to his appearance, and if King James's cause had had more like him for support, matters would have been in a very different state by this time. It seemed that he had been expressly recommended to Henry Duke of York, Charles Edward's brother, by Marshal Saxe himself, and had been seconded for this very important mission by the Spanish king. Prince Henry had collected, with great effort, no less than two thousand *louis d'or*, to assist his brother's campaign, and Scotus selected as the trusted courier . . .

'Two thousand!' Duncan interrupted, a little sourly. 'Two thousand is a vast deal of money, and could have made a great difference to the Prince's army – had it arrived in time. But, Captain – there is not two thousand gold pieces in those bags in your pannier, I swear!'

'There is not, no – because they have been stolen, sir!' the other returned warmly. 'Stolen by our own rascally knavish people. By MacKenzies, of my Lord Cromartie's force. Fight as I would to save them.'

'Stolen . . . ?'

'Aye, by God! My ship, a small French barque, had the devil's own luck, buffeted by gales and harried by the English men-o'-war that blockade this coast. We were weeks at sea. It was intended that I should be landed at my own house of Scotus on the north shore of Loch Nevis, but we could not come near it, and the only place where we might eventually put in was far north at Loch Broom in the MacKenzie country of Dundonnell in Ross. A curse on them! At first they received me fairly enough – but when they found that I was carrying this money to the Prince, damn them if they did not attack me violently, while at table, truss me like a fowl, and steal it all! In the house of Laggie, where I landed. On Loch Broom.

98

And Colin Dearg MacKenzie, who was host to me, leading the assault! Every gold piece – of their own Prince's money! It is scarce to be believed ... !'

'It is, indeed!' Duncan observed grimly, above Caroline's incredulous cries. 'But you still have a few left, friend – a pannierful. Have you forgotten them?'

'I got those back. After much trouble I recovered five hundred *louis*. With the aid of my cousin, Coll MacDonnell of Barrisdale, I ... '

'*Dia* – that ... that ... !' The MacGregor controlled himself. 'Are you cousin to Barrisdale?'

'Our fathers were both brothers to Glengarry,' the other informed haughtily. 'The Prince had attached Barrisdale to Cromartie's force, in some capacity. He came to Loch Broom when he heard of my landing. With his help, as I say, I recovered around five hundred *louis*. That was all. Of the rest – *pouf*! Nothing! All gone into black MacKenzie sporrans. Lost without trace.'

'But this is monstrous!' Caroline exclaimed. 'What sort of scoundrels, dastards, could do such a thing?'

'MacKenzies could, and did! Devil-damned rogues! Officers of Cromartie's, as I said. The whole clan of them as thieves, ruffians, like ... like ... ' He glanced sidelong at the MacGregor.

The man smiled thinly. 'The MacDonnells have never loved the MacKenzies,' he murmured obliquely. Lochbroom and Lochalsh and Dundonnell in Wester Ross had once been MacDonnell country, before the MacKenzies took it from them. The very name Dundonnell told its own story.

'It is beyond all understanding,' the young woman said. 'The money that the Prince needed so desperately! His army unpaid and starving. A gold *louis* is as much as a guinea, is it not? Two thousand guineas ... ! What might it not have done?'

'Even yet, it might have worked wonders. Served to hold the clans together,' Duncan said, frowning. 'Properly used, two thousand guineas at this juncture might keep much of the Prince's army in being until it can be equipped again and ... '

'Might or might not,' Scotus doubted. 'It was never expected to hold together a defeated army. But whether it would

99

or no is of no matter now, since most of it is gone. Five hundred certainly will not . . . '

'Gone? You have not said goodbye to it so soon, so entirely, surely? Fifteen hundred *louis* will not disappear into the ground like a burn in summer! Gold pieces will not be so thick amongst the MacKenzies that such a flood of them will not leave any trace. It should be possible to recover much of the money, I would say.'

'How could that be done, man? Who will take it from them now, in their own country? Think you that I did not try . . . ?'

'My father will be with Cromartie's force by now. Glengyle's Regiment – what is left of it – is up there. He could find most of that gold, I swear.'

'Good God – MacGregors, now!' the other exclaimed. 'You propose that a regiment of MacGregors should go looking for gold pieces amongst the MacKenzies! And expect that any should come out of it, for the Prince? Save us, man – you cannot be serious . . . !'

'Sir!' Rising from a deerskin rug on the floor to one's full height in a single outraged movement is no mean feat, but Duncan achieved it like a spring uncoiling. 'Damn you, Mac-Donnell – watch your words!' he cried, hand on dirk. 'As Royal's my race, I'll listen to that from no man – much less a Frenchified dandy who is cousin to that time-server Coll of Barrisdale . . . !'

'Duncan!' Caroline pleaded. 'Gentlemen! Please – do not speak so. Peace, I pray you . . . !' She started up in turn, and came round the fire to clasp Duncan's arm. 'Here is no way to behave. You are my guests – both of you.'

Wide-eyed, the two younger girls stared from one man to the other.

Duncan swallowed, his glance flickering round them all. 'I . . . I am sorry,' he got out. 'But I will not hear the MacGregor name insulted. By . . . by . . . '

Scotus had risen now, also, without haste and gracefully. He bowed to Caroline, and then to her sisters, smiling. 'My profound apologies, ladies. I am desolated that you should have been alarmed. I was but so taken aback at the notion of MacGregors handing over gold pieces to anyone, that . . . '

'*Dia* – it is a notion that you will have to get used to sir!' Duncan broke in. 'For it is your own position, entirely. You are to hand over the moneys that you have brought, to me. That is why I was seeking you. On His Highness's instructions.'

'To you? Never!' Scotus declared. 'Great God above – do you think that I have brought it all the way from France to hand it over to the first MacGregor I meet?'

'It is the Prince's command,' Duncan said gratingly. 'I have the paper here, signed with his own hand. Read it.'

'No! I tell you, no! I care not what paper you have. I will not do it. His Highness of York gave the gold to me with *his* own hands. I'll not deliver it to any save the Prince of Wales himself.'

'But he has sailed for the Isles, man. On his way to France. I told you. You cannot follow him there, with it.'

'Then I shall keep it until he comes back.'

'That was His Highness's command to me – to hold the moneys safe for him, until he sent me instructions.'

'And think you that you can do that any better than I can, sir?'

'Perhaps – since you already have lost most of it! But that is not the point. It is the Prince's orders. Written here . . . '

'Your orders, perhaps – but not mine. I am an officer of the King of Spain, in the Duke of York's service.'

'But . . . you cannot just carry all that gold around the country with you!'

'And what would *you* do with it?'

'I would hide it somewhere. Safe. Send a courier after the Prince. And await his instructions.'

'I propose to do likewise, sir.'

The two men glared at each other, the tall dark MacGregor and the slender fair MacDonnell.

Caroline stepped between them, biting her red lips. 'See you – this is folly. And worse,' she asserted. 'How shall King James's cause be served thus? The money was sent to aid that cause, was it not? And the cause needs aid, desperately. Even five hundred guineas might do much.'

'I do not dispute it, Miss Caroline,' Scotus acceded. 'But if the Prince is not here to receive it . . . '

'Then give it to someone else to use, in the Prince's interests. Give it to Locheil. All know him to be trustworthy – a good man. The best of the Prince's leaders, it is said. You were going to see Locheil, Duncan. Go, and Captain MacDonnell with you. Together. Give him the gold. He will know best what should be done with it. Surely it is not for either of *you* to decide ... ?'

'The Prince's orders . . .,' the MacGregor began.

'My mission is to the Prince himself,' the MacDonnell declared.

'Oh, do not be so stupid!' the girl burst out. She took hold of Duncan's arm and shook it exasperatedly – though she did not do the same for Scotus. 'What stiff and stubborn infants men can be! Anne and Belle, here, could show more sense, I do declare! I will not listen to more of this. I am going to bed. You will kindly go outside, both of you, while I do so. Do not come in again until I call. And when you do, there is to be no more of this talk. Of any talk! You may bed down over there, at that side. Beside Luath. You understand? Not another word out of either of you. Or I will set Luath on you – and she can be a devil! Out with you, now. Anne! Belle! Into your bed. Quickly. Don't sit there gaping ... '

In that tone of voice Caroline Cameron was not to be argued with. The youngsters scuttled for their bunk, and while their sister smoored and banked up the fire again, with slow-smouldering peats, for the morning, the two men hurried outside into the night. There they paced up and down, wordless, in opposite directions and at different sides of the cabin.

When at length a call from within allowed them to return, they went in discreetly, almost on tiptoe, jostling each other in the dark now that the firelight was quenched, stumbling over impedimenta and even the hound – all with muttered apologies. At one major collapse, which was Scotus falling over the legs of his companion – who, being much less elaborately clad was the quicker outstretched on the deerskins – something that might have been a sniff or even a snigger sounded from the other side of the benighted hut, but was swiftly repressed.

When silence and stillness was at length achieved, after a little a quiet 'Goodnight' came from across the floor. Duncan's brief, and MacDonnell's more comprehensive reply, brought forth no further remark.

Late as it was, Duncan lay long thinking. Perhaps he had got out of the way of night-time sleep, these last weeks. Not so Scotus, evidently, who soon was breathing deeply with the regular rhythm of a seemingly untroubled mind – even though, by earlier sounds, he had taken the precaution of tying the pannier containing the gold in some way to his person.

It was neither the gold nor yet its guardian that preoccupied the other man's wakeful mind, nevertheless. When he listened intently, very intently, he believed that he could distinguish Caroline's soft breathing. He was fairly sure that she lay nearer to the door than her sisters. The latter fell asleep as rapidly as did Scotus, he thought – but not so Caroline.

He listened, and thought and considered – and sought not to sleep, indeed. He was well content just to do that.

It was long after he was assured she slept that he allowed his own eyes to droop.

CHAPTER 9

In a morning of bright sun, shouting larks, and the first cuckoos calling hauntingly from the trees deeper in the glen, the girls were up and about long before the men stirred. Although rumpled and unshaven and feeling by no means at their best, it became – or was made – promptly and abundantly clear to the latter that this was no morning for a resumption of the previous night's disagreements, and tacitly both recognised the desirability of a truce meantime. It was a prickly, brittle armistice, but it served to keep the peace. The understanding was that both men should indeed make their way down Arkaig the next night to see Locheil – although no assurances were exchanged as to final decisions.

Meantime, willy-nilly, they were caught up in the carefree, timeless and idyllic life of the shielings. Always, to the Highlanders, the shielings spoke of an annual release, the end of the harshnesses and confinements of winter, the long halcyon days and short northern nights amongst the high pastures, alpine, arcadian, untrammelled by so much of the restrictions, conventions and routines of ordinary settled life, a young people's elysium. As a brief release from the shadows of defeat, savagery, treachery and suspicion which haunted them, and in the company of such as the Cameron sisters, young men would have been churls indeed had they not responded.

The trouble was, to Duncan's mind, that Scotus seemed to respond too whole-heartedly altogether. Very quickly he was taking the lead in everything, all gaiety and gallantry, as free and easy with the girls as though he had known them all his life, taking liberties with Caroline which Duncan would never have dared – and being put in his place therefor with only mild and token rebukes. His effect on the MacGregor was to make him more than ordinarily abrupt, tongue-tied and reserved – which was not how he wanted it to be, at all.

They all went up to the high corrie for milk and meat, and helped to round up some of the straying cattle, Scotus in his elegant Spanish uniform looking particularly incongruous at the task. They visited two or three other encampments of Camerons, from Glen Pean, Glen Dessary and Glen Camgarry. They joined in an energetic and not very effective attempt to corner deer, by seeking to drive them into one of the many corries that scored the stern flanks of Sgor nan Coireachan, the Peak of Corries – but succeeded only in forcing one young beast over a little cliff, where its broken leg changed the girls' laughter to tears of reproach in truly contrary feminine fashion at the despatch of the poor brute. There was a proposal to go fishing again, down in the River Pean, later in the afternoon – although on this occasion, however much he had relished the business last time, Duncan was strongly against the idea, suggesting on impulse that it might be foolhardy, asking for trouble.

Nobody took this seriously, of course. Indeed, it was difficult up here to feel that anything that went on down in that other world of the valleys and lochsides and plains had any relevance, held any immediate threat.

Nevertheless, back at the cabin by the Allt Ruadh, they found a messenger awaiting them, sent by Locheil to warn his clanspeople that Lord Loudon was going to establish a line of posts based on the head of Arkaig and reaching north-west through Glen Dessary right to salt water at Loch Nevis. A barracks to act as headquarters for this force was to be erected out of the ruins of Doctor Archie Cameron's house of Glendessary. This was to seek to subdue the high Cameron hinterland, and to prevent access to the sea and possible French aid. Probably part of the intention, the messenger said, was to bar the route of the Prince's escape – which would not yet be known by the military. And it seemed likely that having decided to take these steps, the Government would not be long in setting up a similar line through Glen Pean to the sea at Loch nan Uamh.

This news was like a douche of cold water on the party. It brought the Redcoats very near indeed. It meant that Scotus, had he been but one day later, would have been trapped. It darkened the future, here at Allt Ruadh.

Scotus declared that this cabin was no longer sufficiently remote to be secure. The Cameron girls must move up to the high corrie. Caroline demurred. From here, if they were approached, they had all the wide laps of the hills to escape into; up there, there was only the other corries and the narrowing summit. Safer here. Duncan agreed. Above, they could only flee in one direction; down here many ways were open to them. Nevertheless, he did not like the notion of them being left alone. The girls might have to consider moving still deeper into the empty hills to the south . . .

Scotus found in this new situation an excellent excuse for not proceeding that night down Arkaig-side to Locheil's hiding place. Their hostesses' protection had the first priority, he asserted. Duncan found himself obliged to counter this, however reluctantly, and much as he would have preferred to stay where he was. As serving officers their first duty was to the cause; moreover, the girls were in no immediate danger. That gold could not be allowed to remain undelivered. And the sooner that something was done about that stolen by the Mackenzies, the better. It is probable that the MacGregor did not even admit to himself that he had no intention of allowing MacDonnell to stay any longer at the shieling. He insisted – and when Caroline saw that he was determined, and prepared to have another scene about it, she added her support and urged Scotus to go. Though clearly ready and anxious to do battle with Duncan, the other conceded that the young woman's slightest wish was his command, and gracefully yielded.

It was decided not to wait until dark – nor to go down Arkaig-side at all. The safety of the gold was vital, and a much less dangerous though more difficult route to the Achnacarry area could be found through the wild hills to the south, taking longer, but where they need look for no Redcoats. This was Caroline's suggestion – indeed she offered to act as guide

105

to set them on at least the start of their journey. Duncan would not hear of this, of course, declaring that a MacGregor could find his way anywhere in the mountains.

With farewells that were as stilted and cramped on Duncan's part as they were elaborate and eloquent on his companion's, with many instructions to the girls as to what to do in various cases of emergency, the pair, with the three gillies and the two extra pannier-ponies, set out.

Their route lay slantwise, uphill not down, with the sunset at their backs, over the long flanks of Sgor Thuilm, across a thrusting shoulder and so down into a quiet valley beyond, filling with the lilac shadows of the night. This was the first of many such that they crossed, for they were going against the grain of the land. It was slow and tiring travelling for man and beast, for, most of the way, the only tracks that they might follow were deer-paths. But Duncan pressed on determinedly, anxious to get the first and most punishing third of their journey over before the short half-darkness of the May night made the going even more difficult. When they would reach the long trough of thickly wooded Glen Mallie, which ran roughly parallel with Arkaig and eventually joined it, it would be easier.

Their arrival, eventually, in upper Glen Mallie, after negotiating eight grim miles and two high passes, was noteworthy for more than mere easement of travel. They had barely entered the scattered Scots pines, black in the gathering gloom, when a baying of hounds from no great distance ahead brought them up sharp. Duncan, dismounting and listening with ear to the ground, could clearly hear the drumming of hooves, many hooves going fast. Scotus, drawing his pistol, was for hurrying back uphill whence they had come – since hiding amongst the trees would be of no avail against hounds' noses – but Duncan argued that it was almost inconceivable that anyone but Camerons would be riding up Glen Mallie at such an hour; no enemy force would dare risk night travel in such wild and ambush-favourable clan territory.

They sat their mounts, therefore, like graven statues amongst the dark pines, waiting, weapons ready. Duncan tossed the MacDonnell his own plaid to cover up the eye-catching Spanish uniform – which, though it might serve to gain for its wearer correct prisoner-of-war treatment from Government troops, was more likely to draw swift ball or steel from Jacobites mistaking its significance.

Soon three bounding slavering deerhounds were barking around them, and it was not long before horsemen were there too – Highlanders obviously, mounted on shaggy garrons similar to their own, and with broadswords drawn. With nothing to lose now, Duncan hailed them, shouting out the Cameron slogan about hounds eating flesh.

This was answered promptly – and by, of all men, the girls' father, Donald Cameron of Glenpean.

Warmly they greeted each other. Scotus was introduced. Nothing was said of the gold, meantime.

Glenpean and his men, it seemed, were acting as advance-guard for a large party of Camerons coming this way, escorting no less a personage than Locheil himself, borne on a pony-litter.

At Duncan's wondering demands as to the whys and where-fores, he gained the surprising information that the two French warships which had been for so long playing hide-and-seek with the English men-o'-war had at last managed to slip unobserved into Loch nan Uamh, and were waiting there now, loaded with guns and ammunition for the Jacobites.

Duncan groaned aloud. 'Lord – at last! And too late!' he exclaimed. 'Mercy on us – two days! Two days only, and they would have been in time! *Dia* – this is the Devil's own doing!'

'Well may you say it,' Glenpean agreed. 'Two whole ship-loads of what we have been gasping for, praying for. And the Prince gone!'

'With what you have brought, this could have saved the day!' Duncan said, to Scotus.

'The Prince can be brought back, can he not?'

'I do not know. Who can tell where he may be?'

'Locheil has sent a courier after him. Hoping to find boat to take him to the Outer Isles. But . . . ' The older man shrugged eloquently.

'At least the arms will encourage the clans. Hold the army together until the Prince's return,' Duncan said.

'Even that I would not swear to,' Glenpean asserted heavily. 'Locheil is not alone, behind us. And not a few of those who ride with him are giving thanks that those ships will carry them safe back to France rather than for the arms that they bring.'

'To France? You mean that they are going? Giving up? The Irish, you mean? Old Sheridan? O'Hara?'

'Not only these, lad. Many of the Sassunach. Even some of our own people who ought to know better. There is a great cry that all is lost. Captain MacLeod, the Prince's aide, has come back from Ruthven, bringing the Duke of Perth, the Lord Tullibardine and others with him, and saying that the Lord George there, in the Prince's name, ordered all assembled at Ruthven to disperse to their homes. To make what terms they could with the Government – God pity them and Cromartie's force was surprised in Sutherland. Cromartie himself is taken.'

'Sink me – I seem to have come home to a sorry crew!' Scotus cried.

'You have come, Captain, to a broken army at the end of six hundred miles of retreat and defeat,' Glenpean informed levelly. 'But there are true men left yet, never fear.'

'I rejoice to hear it, sir!'

'Unfortunately Murray of Broughton, his Highness's Secretary, has arrived. He was ill at Inverness, but has contrived to escape Cumberland's net, and reached Locheil yesterday. In the absence of the Prince and the Lord George, he conceives himself to be the first authority. But the man is a clerk and no soldier, and I fear that his influence will not be for maintaining the fight.' The Cameron sighed. 'Ah, well – I have work to do. It will not do if Locheil in his litter catches up with his vanguard! If you wait here, you will surely meet him. I will leave a man with you.'

Duncan moistened his lips. 'Glenpean,' he said. 'Your house. Your home . . . ?'

'I know it all, lad,' the other told him. 'It is hard – but not so hard as for many another. Clunes' wife and daughter were caught and ravished. He found them wandering naked, his wife completely demented. Achnasaul's lady was more fortunate – with a pistol ball through her head. Myself, I know that my girls escaped, and are safe up in the shielings . . . '

'We have only just left them, sir – at the Allt Ruadh. They are well, and happy enough. Remarkably so. But this new line of posts that Loudon is to set up in Glen Dessary will make them less secure.'

'Aye. But, God willing, when we have these new guns, when we have ammunition, we may be able to do something about that. Now – I am off. I will see you at Borrodale, at Loch nan Uamh...'

With one of Glenpean's gillies, the two younger men settled down to wait for Locheil, while the advance-party trotted off westwards into the gloom.

The importance of this new development, of the arrival of the two French ships, was amply demonstrated by the fact that not only the wounded Locheil, but practically all the prominent Jacobites who had gravitated to his territories in this present crisis, were travelling that night from their hiding-places around the burnt-out Achnacarry Castle to Loch nan Uamh. The ailing Duke of Perth, formerly one of the two lieutenants-general until he had disagreed with the Lord George Murray, was there; also his brother the Lord John Drummond, colonel of Drummond's Horse. Lord Nairn was there, and Lord Elcho with his friend Maxwell of Kirkconnell, the MacKinnon of MacKinnon, Stewart of Ardshiel, Lockhart of Carnwath and Sir Stewart Thriepland. Also Hay of Restalrig, Sir Thomas Sheridan, Colonel Dillon and others of the Irish faction. It was a strange company to find trotting through wild and night-bound Glen Mallie amongst an escort of fully a hundred Camerons.

When Duncan and Scotus were brought before Locheil, it was to find the chief not really in a litter but sitting in a sort of chair slung between two garrons, a mode of transport that at best could only have been grievously uncomfortable. He greeted the two young men courteously, and on Duncan's claim that they had important information for him, invited them to ride alongside his own two beasts meantime. Unfortunately many of the other leaders were there already, or close at hand, and neither of the newcomers had any intention of broadcasting the news of the gold to all and sundry at this stage. They managed to convey this reluctance to Locheil, who however was too much of a gentleman to offend his illustrious companions by asking them to fall back out of earshot. In consequence the disclosure was postponed, and the rival guardians of the treasure found themselves consigned to a more lowly place down the column, their basket of gold with them, and riding westwards again the opposite direction to their former travelling. Something of mutual frustration perhaps brought the pair of them rather closer to each other as a result.

Distressing to an injured man as this jolting journey over rough country must have been, Locheil did not spare himself or his companions. From Achnacarry to Borrodale's house near the head of the sea loch of nan Uamh, the Loch of the Caves, was well over thirty exacting miles, with a pass between the head of Glen Mallie and that of Glen Finlay to surmount, not very high but grievously boggy and wet. It was down near the foot of the latter glen before a halt was called, at approximately half-roads, where Glenpean had surveyed a camping-place in a wood and had fires burning and hot porridge cooking for all. An hour's break was announced, to rest the garrons rather than their riders.

More than half of this period was gone before, watching their chance, the two young captains approached Locheil where he sat by a fire, for the moment alone. Barely had they begun to speak to him, however, when another man came up, a man not old but of a fleshy paunchy build with, nevertheless, a fine-drawn almost ascetic face, sallow complexioned. He was soberly dressed in Lowland clothes, but wore an air of considerable authority. When Duncan paused in his preliminary remarks, Locheil waved his hand towards this gentleman.

'Captain MacGregor – proceed. If, as I take it, your information concerns His Highness's affairs, then there is no one more fitted to hear it than Mr. Secretary Murray of Broughton. All the Prince's business, other than actual military commands, are in his hands. Speak on.'

They bowed, somewhat stiffly, to the newcomer, who for his part ignored them completely and sat down beside the chief.

Doubtfully Duncan looked at his companion, and then shrugged. 'Captain MacDonnell, younger of Scotus, here, has brought five hundred gold *louis* from the Duke of York, for His Highness,' he said baldly.

'That is so,' the other agreed easily. 'To be delivered to His Highness in person, gentlemen.'

Both older men sat up abruptly, as though electrified.

'*Louis*? From France? Gold . . . ?'

'Five hundred . . . ?'

'Five hundred, yes.'

'But . . . brought, you say? You have it here?' That was Murray. 'In gold? With you?'

'I have indeed.'

'But this is extraordinary! Magnificent!' Locheil exclaimed. 'Five hundred *louis d'or* is a fortune. It will solve many problems...'

'It is a goodly sum, at any rate,' Murray said, more cautiously. 'It will be very useful, undoubtedly.' He paused. 'I would wish to hear details as to how came this notable good fortune, sir?' [1]

His hearers listened to John MacDonnell's account of his stewardship, and the theft at Loch Broom, with varying emotions and sundry interruptions. But at the end of it all, Murray of Broughton was quite decisive and certain – and more authoritative than ever.

'I shall take charge of this money, from now on,' he announced briefly. 'And you, gentlemen, will take the necessary steps to recover such sums as have been, h'm, mislaid, *en route!*'

'No!' Scotus objected vehemently. 'The Duke expressly told me to give it only into the Prince of Wales's own hands...'

'Mine are the Prince's hands, Captain, in this pass.'

'And *I* have the Prince's own orders to take the money and hold it secure until his further instructions,' Duncan declared. 'He knew of this gold. He charged me, before he sailed...'

Murray spoke through him. 'You have heard my instructions, gentlemen.' There was some slight emphasis on the *my*. 'In the Prince's absence, I, as his Secretary, give the orders. I will provide you with a receipt for the money you have brought, Captain MacDonnell. And thereafter, that sum...' He paused significantly. '*That* sum, whatever may be decided about the remainder, is no further responsibility of yours.'

'And if I refuse, sir?' Scotus asked, quietly now.

'Then you will be arrested forthwith, Captain. And, no doubt, in due course tried by court-martial for having mislaid

[1] *The equivalent of 500 golden guineas in 1746 today would be twenty times as much and more. Gold pieces, actual specie, had always been rare in Scotland, especially in the Highlands. At this time One Pound Scots equalled only 1s. 8d. sterling, a chicken might cost 6d. and a cow 10s.*

three-quarters of the total sum entrusted to your charge! Take your choice.'

'Damnation – this is too much!' That was Duncan Mac-Gregor, hotly. 'Locheil – he cannot do this . . . !'

'Locheil, as a senior officer, will you kindly inform these individuals as to their duty?' the Secretary said smoothly, rising to his feet. 'Or must I request the Duke of Perth, as former general, to take the necessary steps militarily?'

The Cameron chief shook his grizzled head unhappily. 'You have the rights of it, no doubt, Mr. Secretary,' he said heavily. 'But you are over-hard on these young men, I think. They deserve a kinder reception than this.'

'They have their duties, sir, as I have mine. Let them abide by theirs, and they need fear no unkindness from me.' Murray bowed stiffly, and was moving off when he half-turned. 'Locheil – perhaps you will instruct some of your Camerons to bring me this money forthwith? Lest there be any further . . . mischance!'

Locheil sighed. 'Very well,' he said.

When the march was resumed a little later, the two junior officers rode very far back down the column indeed, side by side but with little to say to each other or anyone.

CHAPTER 10

THE sun was well up before the weary company arrived at the mouth of Glen Borrodale and gazed out over the blue waters of Loch nan Uamh and all the sparkling vista of the isle-strewn Sea of the Hebrides. Islands, skerries, reefs and rocks, from the mighty jagged mountains of Rhum smoking with captive mists, to the tiniest weed-hung islet ablaze with sea-pinks and girt with golden tangle – all was colour and light and loveliness. Few eyes, however, if any amongst that strung out cavalcade, saw any beauty consciously that morning. All attention was concentrated on the two tall ships that lay directly below them, anchored as close to the rocky shore as they dared, hidden from seawards behind a thrusting headland of the lochside.

Young Clanranald welcomed his guests pleasantly enough to his temporary headquarters at Borrodale House amongst the slanting oakwoods – though clearly he was hardly prepared for so many of them. His father, an elderly man and 16th chief of one of the main branches of the great Clan Donald, preferred in troubled times to live out on his territories in the Outer Isles, so that in effect the son, Ranald, was captain of the clan. Grave and quiet of manner, he was one of the Prince's earliest and most loyal supporters, and his regiment had been, until Culloden, one of the largest and most gallant of all the Jacobite army. So far, the Government troops had not penetrated into this mountain-girt and secluded Clanranald land of Arisaig, Morar and Moidart that thrust like an array of spear-heads into the western sea.

A clan chief's house had always to be ready for vast hospitality at shortest notice, and Clanranald did not fail to produce adequate food and drink for the invasion, even though already his resources had been tapped in providing for the ships' companies after long weeks at sea. One of the ships' masters, Captain Lemaire of the *Bellona*, was with him now. He seemed to be an anxious, not to say impatient man. He was not long in getting into earnest, excited but apparently highly secret converse with Murray, Locheil and the Duke of Perth.

Glenpean was able to give Duncan and Scotus a certain amount of information. It seemed that there were at least three English ships in this area of the Inner Hebrides, and the French captains were not at all certain that their presence in Loch nan Uamh was not suspected. Earlier that same morning a small naval sloop had loitered about at the mouth of the loch for almost an hour, before suddenly departing northwards in a hurry. Telescopes on board might possibly have picked out the Frenchmen's tall topmasts rising behind the trees of the sheltering headland. The captains therefore were anxious to be off at the earliest possible moment.

Proof of this disquiet was forthcoming in a practical fashion only a few minutes later. An order from Secretary Murray was circulated that all fit and able-bodied men, irrespective of rank or age, were to repair at once to the loch-shore, there to assist in the unloading of the two vessels. Clanranald was assembling every small boat in the vicinity to assist in the operation.

When the newcomers arrived down at the beach, it was to find a large accumulation of gear – small cannon, muskets innumerable, bayonets, swords, ball and shot, kegs of powder, blankets, clothing, saddlery, barrels of brandy and wine, and so on – already stacked on the narrow apron of shingle. The shore, however beautiful, was a wickedly rocky and broken one, and only the one little strand offered a landing-place for the small boats. The big ships themselves could not approach nearer than three hundred yards off shore. Most of this cargo had been landed the day before by the ships' own boats; now, with the arrival of more local small craft and a sizeable labour force, the work went apace. There seemed to be a vast deal of shouting wherever the French sailormen were involved.

When Young Clanranald himself, with the MacKinnon chief, threw off plaid and doublet to assist in the actual manhandling of boats and gear, Highland pride and the reluctance of most of the officers to soil hands with any sort of manual labour evaporated, and the work went with a will. Glenpean's own group of Camerons were engaged in transporting the landed cargo, on their garrons, up to well-hidden storage in a couple of the large caves in the hillside, for which the area was famous, perhaps a quarter of a mile inland. To this party Duncan and Scotus and the three MacDonnell gillies attached themselves, glad enough of the work to do, tired though they were.

It was heavy and awkward toil, and the terrain over which the ponies had to be coaxed, steep, slippery, rock-strewn and heavily wooded. Stacks of arms and provisions piled higher and higher on the scrap of beach, having to be moved back as the rising tide threatened to engulf part of the precious freight.

In the midst of all this activity, in mid-forenoon a sudden hullabaloo arose out at the ships. Swiftly the word was shouted back, via the busy ferry-boats, to the shore. Three vessels had appeared in the mouth of the loch, heading in – two sloops and a somewhat larger corvette; naval ships, and as obviously English.

Something near to panic developed amongst the voluble Frenchmen and some of the Jacobites. The shouting and excitement rose to a crescendo. Captain Lemaire, superintending the unloading ashore, went hurrying back to *Bellona*, and behind him, in a few moments, a boatload of Jacobite notables hastily put out. Others stood in apparently violent altercation, and still others ran inland in the direction of Borrodale House.

'There go those ambitious of a passage to France!' Glenpean

observed to Duncan, pausing in his task of tying a couple of powder-kegs on either side of a garron.. '*Dia* – it looks as though some are in a pretty predicament. They have had enough of fighting – so to France they would go. But it seems that these French ships are going to have some fighting of their own! A sorry problem for peaceable warriors!' The Cameron sounded unusually bitter.

'What will they do?' Duncan asked. 'The French ships? Cut and run for it? Fight their way out?'

'They must,' Scotus declared. 'They have no choice.'

'If the English are only small craft – like the sloop this morning,' Glenpean said, 'our French frigates may out-gun them. But still much cargo is to be unloaded. They say not much more than half is ashore . . . '

For a little while there was chaos in the sheltered inlet, with the Frenchmen leaving everything to hurry back to their ships, Jacobite leaders demanding boat-room to get out also – although some seemed to be rowing back again. Many of the working parties ashore were tending to abandon their tasks and hurry to high ground to see what was going on. Then stern orders came from Locheil that the work was to go on with re-doubled vigour. The precious cargo must be cleared and secured.

'Thank God for one man with a soldier's head!' Glenpean cried. 'Donald never loses it.' He pointed 'Though there is another who, I swear, does not lose his head either! But uses it to a different tune, I think!'

In a small boat being rowed out to the ships was the dark and sober figure of John Murray of Broughton.

'Is *he* going? The Secretary? To France?' Duncan demanded.

'I heard that was his intention, yes. Small loss, perhaps.'

'But . . . the gold!' Scotus interrupted. 'What of the gold? If he goes. He said nothing of this last night. God – if he takes it with him . . . !'

'He would never do that.'

Glenpean stared from one to the other. 'Gold?' he repeated. 'What gold, man?'

As the pony-party toiled up the hill towards the caves, the two younger men told the Cameron something of the business, briefly, breathlessly. But their minds were not really on what they were saying, preoccupied with the situation down at the ships and with Murray's probable intentions.

From higher ground, where they could see over the intervening headland, they eagerly turned to stare seawards. It took them a little while, against the dazzle off the water and amongst the great multitude of the skerries and islets, to pick out the English vessels – for they were unthinkingly looking for tall men-o'-war and near at hand. In fact the craft were neither large nor very near – fully two miles away, probably, and beating up and down amongst the islets, as indeed they must in a north-easterly breeze and amidst the intricate shoals and channels of the loch.

'They are not much more than half the size of the Frenchmen,' Glenpean said. 'Their guns will be much less powerful. They will not dare to come too close.'

'Perhaps they will only block the mouth of the loch? Bottle the French,' Scotus suggested. 'Until bigger English ships can come up ...'

'How can they inform other English ships?' Duncan wondered. 'Unless there are some near at hand. The French are not trapped yet.'

'Trapped or no, they do not intend to stay hidden behind that cape,' Glenpean observed. 'Look there ...'

The feverish activity round the two frigates was developing now to some purpose. Anchors were up, and the small boats of each ship, with cables attached to the parent craft, were beginning to row outwards, seawards. Obviously the big ships were to be towed into more open water. One or two small topsails were being unfurled to catch the breeze and provide steerageway.

'Damn them – they're going!' Duncan cried. 'Bolting. They're off!'

'Have they got the gold aboard – that's what I want to know?' Scotus demanded. 'I' faith, if that blackguard Murray sails off with it ... !'

'More important than your gold – those ships are still half-full of guns and ammunition,' Glenpean reminded. 'Enough to equip whole regiments. We need every scrap of it. Curse their shrinking French hides ... !'

They were unfair to the Frenchmen, all of them. The *Bellona* and *Mars* were slowly towed out only a short distance beyond the tip of the headland, where they had an uninterrupted view, and there they hove-to, held in position by boats at bows and sterns. The double-banked gun-ports at their tall sides were opened up, and the fierce snouts of ranked cannon appeared menacingly therein. The lilies of France broke at their mast-heads and fluttered proudly in the forenoon sunlight.

'Ha – we spoke too soon, I think . . . ,' Glenpean began. 'They are preparing to fight – that is clear. But they do not look as though they intend to make a dash for it, to shoot their way out. They are furling those sails again.'

'The short boats are going alongside once more,' Duncan reported. 'It looks – *Dia*, it looks as though they are starting to unload again! Yes – see, there are barrels being lowered once more.'

'Bravo! *Vive la France!*' Scotus acclaimed. 'They have given themselves room to manoeuvre, and to sight their guns. We owe *messieurs* an apology.'

That appeared to be the situation. The unloading proceeded apace, with the two frigates held approximately stationary.

The three smaller vessels continued to beat their way up the loch, tacking one way and another, deliberately or otherwise using the scattered skerries and rocks as a screen.

The pony party had not paused in their own task of coaxing the long string of laden garrons uphill, heartened as they were by what they saw. They were unburdening their beasts in a cave entrance when a single loud cannon shot boomed out, seeming to shake the rock around them and echoing amongst all the enclosing hillsides. At the ominous sound, every man paused.

'That is one of ours. A Frenchman. Too loud, too near at hand for the English,' Scotus announced. 'Sounded like a culverin. A twenty-pounder. Just a warning shot, for the others to keep their distance.' He sounded very knowledgeable – but then he always sounded that.

On their way down to the shore again they saw that the English ships had drawn much closer; were in fact less than a mile away, and keeping as close to the north shore as they dared. Indeed they seemed to be intending to use the other side of the same headland behind which the French had hidden formerly, to protect themselves.

'What range have their guns . . . ?' Duncan was asking when

the shattering crash of a broadside drowned his words. The *Bellona* seemed to leap on the calm face of the loch, one side of her vomiting fire and smoke. A barrier of water-spouts rose in front of the English vessels – but a notable distance in front. That had been a gesture only; clearly the range was still too great.

No reply came from the smaller ships – save to edge still closer in towards the land and to gain the fullest shelter of the headland.

'What next?' Duncan wondered. 'What can the English do? They are held, surely.'

'They could put a landing-party ashore,' Glenpean suggested. 'To attack us from the rear. Halt the unloading, at least.'

Locheil had thought of that. He detached a party of Camerons from the unloading, under Torcastle, and sent them to man the summit of the headland ridge, where they could command the approaches from the west. He also sent word to Captain Lemaire urging him to put ashore two or three of his heavy cannon which, sited on the same ridge, could make the English ships keep their distance.

Glenpean's people worked on, and though the two young officers would have preferred more military employment they were offered none. They were setting off with another pony-train when suddenly Duncan pointed back towards a boat that was being rowed out to the French ships.

'See yonder!' he cried. 'I would know those two a mile off. There is only one man in all the army with so long a back as that. And only one who cocks an eagle's feather that long in his bonnet! Two beauties, I swear! Your cousin and mine, Scotus – God forgive us! Where have they come from? What ill wind brings them here? Those two together . . . ? I do not like it – I do not.'

'Coll!' the MacDonnell exclaimed. 'Coll of Barrisdale.'

'Aye – and James Mor MacGregor. A pair indeed!'

'Both gentlemen with gallant records, lad,' Glenpean put in, mildly reproachful.

'Oh, aye – they are bold enough, I grant you. Both of them. Nobody doubts their courage. But I trust neither. And mislike the more to see them together.'

'Perhaps they are for France? Like Murray and the rest.'

'I could hope so . . .'

'Never. Not Coll. What ails you at Coll? Scotus demanded. 'He is as brave a soldier and seasoned a campaigner as any in the army.'

'I do not deny it. Winning, I might trust him – but losing, no!'

'Stuff, man! Coll is a fighter. And a MacDonnell, whatever! He aided me at Loch Broom, there – amongst the ruffianly MacKenzies. He helped me to recover that five hundred . . . '

'You are sure that none of it stuck to his own fingers? That he did not know more than he admitted?'

'Sir! Watch your words, will you! You will not speak so of any MacDonnell. Of your own James Mor, it may well be true. You know your own clan, presumably! But not . . . '

'Gentlemen!' Glenpean intervened. 'Let it be – och, let it be! What does this serve? All know Barrisdale. And we have work to do . . . '

Colonel Coll MacDonnell, younger of Barrisdale, was indeed known to all. The tallest man in the Prince's army, and one of the most handsome, he had first commanded Glengarry's Regiment for his uncle, and later formed another MacDonnell regiment of his own. Daring, brilliant at guerilla warfare, he had actually been knighted, in King James's name, by Charles Edward, who esteemed him highly. But then, the Prince had also esteemed highly his aide-de-camp Major James Mor Mac-Gregor, whom Duncan for one did not. Indeed the two were much alike in many ways, of a sort that the Highlands have always brought forth in numbers, dare-devil swashbuckling blades, attractive, high-spirited, but perhaps a little mercurial – and only mildly troubled by conscience. Barrisdale and his regiment had not been present at Culloden, having been sent north earlier to reinforce Lord Cromartie's force holding Ross and Sutherland.

Duncan's alarm at seeing him here, without his regiment, and in the company of his own cousin James Mor – who also should have been with Glengyle's Regiment in the north – was instinctive.

A party of Camerons were manhandling two massive eighteen-pounder guns from *Bellona* up to the summit ridge of the headland, as Glenpean's pony-train came down once more from the caves, superintended by three French gunners. Glenevis, their leader, called out.

'Donald – have you heard? Of the gold? On yonder ship. A fortune, just! Gold enough to sink her . . . !'

Glenpean glanced at his companions. 'Och, well,' he answered. 'Not just that, man. Not all that much.'

'It is true, I tell you. All the gold in the world! Casks and barrels of it. In the ship.'

'Here's foolish talk, Glenevis! There is no more than five hundred gold pieces altogether. A deal of money, yes – but . . . '

'Murray *has* taken it out to the ship, then?' Scotus charged.

'Eh . . . ? Murray? No, no. How could he do that? The gold is on the ship, I am telling you. It has come from France. In barrels . . . ' Glenevis and his men were pressing on, laboriously dragging and pushing the heavy cannon up the steep hill and the difficult ground.

'Nonsense, man!' Scotus shouted after them. 'You have it all agley. *I* brought the money from France. But not in that ship. Murray has it. Five hundred *louis d'ors* . . . '

But down at the beach, the same story, or versions thereof, was on everyone's lips. Unlimited gold had arrived from France, and they were all rich beyond the dreams of avarice. The excitement seemed to quiver in the very air. The threat of the English warships so near at hand, even the importance of all the accession of arms and ammunition in the circumstances, seemed to have faded into insignificance. The thought of gold filled man's minds, gold in quantities unheard of, undreamed of, hitherto.

Much perplexed and incensed, the two younger men, with Glenpean, left their ponies and went to speak to Locheil, to get to the bottom of the matter.

'The truth it is,' the chief told them, on the grassy bank amongst the sea-pinks, where he had sat all morning supervising the landward handling of the precious cargo. He sighed. 'I suppose that I should be rejoicing, for the money is needed, without a doubt. But . . . ' He shrugged plaided shoulders. 'It will bring its own problems, I warrant. If it had only come two days ago, two short days, when the Prince was here. I could almost wish . . . ' He left the rest unsaid.

'There is much of it, then?' Scotus asked, almost aggrievedly. 'More than I brought?'

'Much, yes. More than I could have believed. Money that, two months ago, even one month, could have changed all the course of the war. What made King Louis send so much – and delay so long in sending – I do not know. But I am told that there are eight great barrels of *louis d'ors* aboard the *Bellona*. And in each, five thousand gold pieces!'

'God in Heaven!'

'Lord save us all!'

'You say ... five *thousand*?'

'In each? Of eight? That is ... that is forty thousand *louis- d'ors*!'

'That is so, yes, my friends.'

Stricken to silence, they looked at one another, scarcely able to comprehend the full meaning of what they heard. Forty thousand gold pieces was indeed almost beyond comprehension in the Scotland of 1746.[1]

Into their stupefaction Locheil went on heavily. 'What it could have done, all this, is almost beyond imagining. The army has not been paid for months. Payment could have held it together. We could have bought the guns that we needed – the powder and shot. Aye, and the food! Hungry men do not fight their best. Even men we could have bought – those Lowland lairds whose souls are in their pockets. And the frightened English Jacobites who turned their well-clad backs on our ragged Highland rabble! Consider proud Edinburgh, and what money could have done for us there. God – when I think of the Prince, selling even his very rings and drinking cups ... !'

'Aye,' Glenpean nodded. 'It is hard, hard. So much, too late by so little! And yet – better now than never, Donald, is it not?'

'You think so?'

'It could be changing much, even yet.'

'Aye – nothing truer. But change it how? To what end? With the Prince gone?' Locheil grimaced slightly. 'It has changed us our Murray, already – the good Secretary! He has decided not to go to France, after all. He is for taking charge of this great wealth and remaining with it! Others may well think similarly.'

'That I can well believe!' Scotus nodded grimly.

[1] *In present-day figures, 40,000 guineas would add up to almost half a million pounds Scots; but in actual gold coin it represented consider- ably greater value than that. Almost certainly it was the largest single consignment of money ever to enter the Highlands. A million modern banknotes would be less resounding.*

'What is to be done with it all?' Duncan asked.

'Lord knows. Many will be asking that, I think – and offering suggestions!'

'The Prince will have to be informed. Somehow. A courier must be got to him – before he can sail for France. This could yet change all – if the Prince came back.'

'That is, I think, my own view,' Locheil agreed slowly. 'The money must be held intact, for another attempt to bring King James's cause to triumph. For that it was sent. It must be held for the support of armed action against the Elector of Hanover – either this one resumed, or another Rising later. It must not be dispersed, frittered away. It was sent for Prince Charles so to use; it must await his return – or, at least, his directions – surely.'

'Are others saying differently, then?'

'They are indeed. Already. Some are talking about arrears of pay. Of compensation. And subsidies. Inducements. Suchlike phrases – fine words that mean just money. Gold in fists and pouches and sporrans . . . '

The crash of cannon-fire halted Locheil. Up on the ridge above the inlet wisps of smoke rose above the trees. The guns dragged up there had found targets to shoot at, apparently.

Young Clanranald came hurrying up. If the firing meant that a force from the English ships had landed, then a company must be sent to deal with them. He could collect forty or fifty of his own men quickly; could he have Glenpean's score or so to add to them? If it was only at the ships themselves that they had opened up, of course, it would not be necessary . . .

The lesser booming of more distant gunfire punctuated his words. The English were firing back – individual shooting, not broadsides. It might be covering fire for a landing-party or it might not. But it gave added urgency to Clanranald's suggestion.

Locheil agreed. Glenpean hurried back to his men, Duncan and Scotus with him, none of them averse to a little more soldierly activity than pack-horse transport.

Up on the ridge, well supplied now with muskets and powder and ball for their pistols, they were able to see the English ships in a bay of the loch something less than a mile to westwards – though still out of range. Glenevis told them that they had seen small boats heading for the shore, and the French gunners had fired a few shots, not at the vessels themselves but into the intervening woodlands along the shore, to discourage any landing-parties from making their way along. The English guns had retaliated in similar fashion, firing at random into the lochside woods at extreme range. Both sides were well aware of the danger represented by these tree-covered approaches. There the matter stood – but the boats had not put back to the English parent ships.

Having thus briefly sketched in the situation, Glenevis was clearly more interested in discussing the gold than the enemy's possible tactics.

Clanranald decided that they should wait where they were meantime. Knowing every inch of the terrain, he declared that no enemy could approach their present position from the westwards without crossing a certain bare area of ground where a landslide of the steep thrusting hillside had scored a wide open wedge of red earth and rock, sweeping away trees and undergrowth almost down to the water's edge. This, approximately half-way between the two inlets, was in full view from the ridge. Time enough to move down to the attack when they observed the sailors crossing there.

So they waited. No sailors appeared. The subject of the gold absorbed them all.

Duncan fretted, lying there in the sun, idle. Little as he enjoyed the heavy and undignified labour of transport, this prolonged inaction seemed as unsuitable as it was wasteful of manpower. Almost a hundred men lay about the crest of that ridge doing nothing, while the precious freight continued to pile up on the shore behind – and men's thoughts dwelt almost wholly, crazily, on glittering yellow *louis d'ors*, innumerable, uncountable. Clanranald pointed out that their presence here was not in fact wasted; since they could see the English ships plainly enough, it was certain that the officers thereon could equally well see themselves through their telescopes, a large armed body waiting and ready – which was no doubt why the shore party had so far not moved forward.

After almost an hour there was a notable diversion. Without warning, what sounded like a full broadside of French cannon crashed out, shaking the very ground beneath the recumbent warriors, and setting the gulls a-scream amongst all the booming echoes. The fall of shot showed in a great line of spouting water much nearer to the English ships than heretofore.

Soon it was clear that *Mars* had left the bay, and was now in full sail out in the loch, where she was in a position to bear down directly on the enemy. Presumably she had completed her unloading and was now either going to make a dash for it alone or was deliberately challenging the English to a fight. Or perhaps trailing her coat, seeking to decoy the opposition away from their landward shelter.

Whatever *Mars'* purpose, the English lost no time in responding – as indeed they must or be trapped in their inlet. Two ships hoisted sail and put out into wider waters forthwith. The third, a sloop, was left, almost certainly to collect the shore party – and even with the breeze contrary the watchers could plainly hear the bugles aboard urgently blaring their message, presumably of hasty recall.

The situation developed rapidly, rather like moves in a game of chess, the two English ships seeking to divide and confuse the Frenchman's attention, while trying to keep out of his range. *Mars* tacked about in open water. Loch nan Uamh was almost two miles in width and roughly twice that length. She did not seem concerned with immediate escape.

Small boats began to straggle out from the shore to the remaining sloop.

The English corvette, the larger craft, was now firing tentative shots from well across the loch. Two could play the decoy-duck, patently.

Mars was forced to swing round. The English ships were lighter and faster; moreover they could risk shallower water. They would be almost impossible to bring to bay.

It was now practical stalemate. Nevertheless *Mars* was creating a diversion – which was obviously her intention, posing a threat rather than pressing an attack, giving time for her sister-ship to finish unloading and sail out.

Perceiving this, Clanranald decided that the main body of his men should return forthwith to transport duty, but that a small scouting party should proceed cautiously along the coast to find out whether or no any English sailors remained on shore. Duncan offered to lead this, with a local guide – and was surprised when Scotus volunteered to accompany them.

It was almost a couple of hours before this group got back, so thorough was their search. They had found no men – only six empty boats riding at anchor well out amongst the islets of the inlet. This discovery had kept them searching and quartering the woodlands, until satisfied that the boats had only been left thus because one sloop could not take them all aboard.

Although Duncan and Scotus had recognised, from a heavy outbreak of gunfire, that *Bellona* had almost certainly joined her consort, and both French ships were now probably gone for good, taking much of the Jacobite leadership with them back to France, they were quite unprepared for the situation they returned to at the beach below Borrodale House. Agitation prevailed. Not at the loss of leaders – but at the loss of gold. And not, it seemed, just at a gold piece or two a-missing. A vast amount was gone – five thousand *louis d'ors*, no less.

Almost incredible as this information sounded, it appeared to be fact. The gold had been packed in linen bags in eight great barrels – and one of the barrels was gone. Or, rather, the barrels were all ashore, but one of them was filled with stones and shingle.

Suspicion, accusation, resentment quivered in the very air.

'Who brought the money ashore?' Duncan asked the obvious question of Glenpean.

'A number of people did that. There lies the difficulty,' the older man told him. 'The barrels of gold were too heavy to put into small boats as they were. They had to be opened up, and the bags lowered into boats one by one. Then the empty barrels. Senior officers rowed back and forth with each boat – Secretary Murray himself, a Major Kennedy who came with the ship, MacDonald of Borrodale Clanranald's kinsman, Sir Stewart Thriepland, Ardshiel. Others too . . . including your friends Barrisdale and James Mor MacGregor!'

'Ah!'

'The missing money perhaps never left the ship?' Scotus put in.

'That has been suggested. But all saw the barrels opened on board and the bags lowered into the boats. All the barrels and all the bags.'

'How, then . . . ?'

'There was much confusion on shore. Guns were firing, men coming and going. Less care, it seems, was taken when unloading the gold from the boats. Some came in at different points in this bay, where there are few landing places. Other boats were landing the ordinary cargo. Our people, with Clanranald's, were all up yonder on the ridge . . . '

'But, man – five thousand gold pieces cannot just be spirited away!' Duncan cried. 'Think of the weight of them! Even the five hundred that we brought in that pannier was a vast weight. Ten times that . . . !'

'Aye. Clearly a number of men were in league. One boatload, whatever.'

'The carrying of it away would be simple enough,' Scotus pointed out. 'The pack-ponies going up from the beach into the woods with the other gear, all the time. Nothing would be easier than just to join in with the rest.'

'Why are Barrisdale and James Mor here at all?' Duncan demanded of Cameron.

'They came with news of Cromartie's capture. Seeking instructions from the Prince.'

'I see. And no doubt they did not travel alone? They would have some of their gillies with them? Enough for . . . '

'I'll thank you not to couple my cousin's name with yours, MacGregor – as though they were equal rogues!' Scotus said, as in duty bound – but with rather less conviction than heretofore.

'Tut, gentlemen!' Glenpean's head-shaking protest was as automatic, conventional and weary. 'But . . . it is a bad business. A bad, bad business. Och, ashamed it makes a man. Ashamed of his own kind. *Dia* – if only the Prince had been here . . . '

'I think it as well that he is not!' Duncan MacGregor asserted grimly. 'There would seem to be too many men here in love with the chink of gold! You will recollect that Cumberland has put a price of thirty thousand pounds on his person, dead or alive! I think it is as well that His Highness got away when he did. Even though it is unlikely that Cumberland would pay his blood-money in gold!'

'Och, hush you, lad – that is a wicked thing to say!'

'My own remark entirely, but a few days back,' the younger man agreed levelly.

'GENTLEMEN, I vow for the life of me that I cannot see the need for all this damned wearisome discussion. Since His Highness has seen fit to leave us, and even now may be on his way to France – like so many of our friends who have felt similarly impelled today – since that is the position, surely it behoves those of us who remain to deal with this money to the best advantage of King James's cause? The Prince's army – or shall we say, King James's army, since His Royal Highness has found it expedient to leave? – the army must be kept together as far as may be. For the next attempt against the devil-damned Elector. It should not be allowed to disperse, to fritter away – whatever the Lord George may say, God forgive him! To that end the money should be applied. The men must be paid, provisioned, re-armed. Only so can the regiments be held together for another campaign. I speak from experience, my friends. My own regiment is still intact – or as much so as battles have left it. It will not remain so much longer, I can assure you, unless I receive money. Few of us in the Highlands are rich men – not in money, at any rate. Myself, I have spent all my scant fortune. Give the money – or most of it – to the colonels, to keep the army in being, I say.'

The speaker was as manly and soldierly as his words – Colonel Coll MacDonnell, younger of Barrisdale, nephew of old Glengarry. An immense figure of a man, fully six feet eight inches in height and broad in proportion, he was handsome in a dark and smiling sardonic fashion, all vigorously masculine, the Highland gentleman *par excellence*, dressed in fullest gallant style to match. More than a murmur of agreement greeted his soldierly demand.

'Certain regiments and units are already dispersed and broken up,' Colonel Stewart of Ardshiel objected. 'Some, less fortunate than Barrisdale's, did not survive Culloden Moor! Others have been sent to their homes already, by the Duke of Perth and Lord George. Are these, who bore the fiercest burden of the battle, to receive nothing?'

'What of those whose houses have been burned, their glens harried, their women ravished? Are they to be forgotten?'

127

Cameron of Dungallon demanded. His own unhappy case, that was. '*Dia* – there must be compensation!'

'Aye, compensation! Some of us have lost all . . . '

'Peace, gentlemen, I pray you,' Murray of Broughton interjected, in his smooth voice. 'All such will be duly considered, I promise you. I shall make it my business to see that this money is properly used, fairly distributed . . . '

'*Your* business, sir! But is it your business, Mr. Secretary?' That was Barrisdale, smiling still, and genial, but contemptuous too. 'Is not this a military matter? The money was sent, with the arms and the ammunition, for the army. Not for, h'm, secretarial administration!'

A shout of approval rocked that crowded room. Barrisdale had the great majority of the company with him, most clearly.

There might have been more against him the previous night. Most of those like Murray, the Lowlanders, the courtiers, the political theorists, the Jacobite adventurers, had gone. Although the great apartment of Borrodale House was indeed crowded still, that evening there were notable gaps. The Duke of Perth was gone, and his brother the Lord James; Lord Elcho, and his friend Maxwell; Sir Thomas Sheridan, Hay of Restalrig, Colonel Dillon; Lord Nairn and Lockhart of Carnwath and others. The ships had carried them away – and as far as could be ascertained, safely; provided no larger English men-o'-war arrived on the scene, they should all make sunny France in a few days. Everyone in the room knew that Secretary Murray would also have been aboard, but for the gold. In the main, it was only the fighting men, Highlanders almost to a man, who remained.

'I know my duty, sir – and will perform it, with or without your advice!' Murray snapped. 'As His Highness's secretary and immediate representative, the responsibility for distributing this money is wholly mine.'

'No!'

'That's a matter of opinion, sir.'

'Let Locheil distribute the gold.'

'Aye – Locheil knows our Highland position. Better than any Lowland lawyer!'

'I want no hand in it,' Locheil said shortly, from his seat by the fire.

Into the clamour in the great room, Duncan MacGregor raised his voice, greatly daring amongst all his seniors. 'I say that it is not for any to distribute, be he secretary or colonel or other!' he cried. 'The gold was sent to the Prince. He only may say what is to be done with it.'

'What puppy barks there?' Barrisdale enquired.

'Glengyle's son,' Duncan jerked back. 'And a different man from Glengyle's cousin there!'

'Indubitably – thank God!' James Mor MacGregor agreed, smiling.

There was a general laugh at the younger man's expense. Stubbornly he went on, however.

'His Highness ordered me straightly, before he sailed, to take possession of the money that was coming from the Duke of York, and to hold it safe for him until he should come for it or direct me otherwise. That money Mr. Secretary Murray now has taken. The Prince said nothing of giving it to him, or any other. I cannot believe ...'

'Must we look to you, young man, to interpret the Prince's policies and best interests?' Murray interrupted haughtily. 'When your sage counsel is required, no doubt it will be asked for.'

'I hold a paper bearing His Highness's signature, authorising the Duke's money to be delivered to me. The Prince did not know of this other money, but ...'

'And I hold King James's commission as Secretary-General to the Prince of Wales!' the other returned sharply. 'Until his Majesty revokes it, I act in his name. Let none presume otherwise. The gold will be properly and fairly distributed ...'

'But, dear God – it should not be distributed, at all!' Duncan exclaimed. 'That is not what it was sent for. To be handed out to all and sundry. It was sent to fight the Elector of Hanover. It must be kept for that. Forty thousand gold pieces could make the difference between success and failure in a new rising ...'

'Duncan, *a graidh* – is not that what we say?' James Mor put in. 'Give the money to the colonels, to keep the army together, to keep their regiments in being. Use it, do not bury it, or hoard it up.' He could be persuasive when he liked. 'Only by holding the army together can the Elector be fought and beaten. For that we must use the money.'

'Aye – he is right.'

'That is the truth.'

'We did not ask for money from the Prince when we drew the sword! We fought the Elector at Prestonpans and Carlisle and Clifton and Falkirk, without payment. What has come over us now, that all must have gold? Arrears of pay, compensations, reliefs – all that will melt away this money like snow in the sun . . . '

'Nonsense, boy! There is plenty for all.'

'To be sure there is.'

'I agree with Captain MacGregor,' Scotus spoke up. 'I did not bring that money from France to pay compensations and satisfactions!'

'And got rid of most of it on the way!' James Mor mentioned.

'Damn you, sir! That from you! Yourself, you were not so far away when those scoundrelly MacKenzies stole it!'

'You impudent Frenchified jackanapes! Are you suggesting . . . ?'

'Gentlemen! In this house you will kindly remember your manners,' Clanranald intervened sternly. 'I will have no incivilities round this table.'

'You are right,' Locheil commended. 'Let us have no unseemly bickering, my friends. We may all hold our own points of view in honesty and sincerity. For myself, I think that I agree with these young men. The money will be needed for the next campaign, and should not be frittered away. Nevertheless, there is point in what Barrisdale says – and Ardshiel and Dungallon too. If some small proportion of the gold is given to the colonels, to keep their regiments assembled, the great part of it can be held intact for another rising when the Prince returns. There need be no clash.'

'Exactly,' Murray concurred suavely. 'My own view entirely. It is in such fashion that I propose to administer these moneys. None need fear otherwise. And now, gentlemen, if you will give me your attention . . . '

The door opened to admit Glenpean, who was captaining the guard.

'Doctor Archie,' he announced. 'New come from Atholl and the Lord George.'

Archibald Cameron of Glendessary, M.D., youngest brother of Locheil, and known all over the Highlands as Doctor Archie, was a fine looking man of early middle years, prematurely grey and stooping a little, but with a humorous twinkle in his eye.

Dressed now in Lowland clothes, less conspicuous for the enemy-held territory he had just traversed, he looked tired and travel-worn. He greeted the company cheerfully, however, and went over to embrace his brother warmly.

Throughout the room frowns faded and tension relaxed, for the Doctor was one of the most popular and respected figures in the entire army, a soldier as well as a medico, and lieutenant-colonel to Locheil. Where Archie Cameron was present, laughter rather than frowning was the rule. Even the burning of his home had not wholly quenched his spirits.

Nevertheless, his tidings now were not calculated to cheer the assembled officers. The news that he brought from Atholl and the south was that everywhere the rising was considered to be over and defeated, that all the Lowland levies were dispersing to their homes, and their leaders fleeing overseas wherever possible. The Lord George advised the Highlanders to do like-wise, to make whatever terms they might with the Government, and to do nothing to provoke further reprisals. As far as the Lowlands were concerned, all was lost. The Doctor's own arguments and pleas had fallen on deaf ears.

Into the gloom, ire and recriminations engendered by this announcement, the Secretary, who, with Sir Stewart Thriepland, was the only Lowlander present, judiciously informed the newcomer of the heartening arrival of the arms and money from France. The mood of the company lightened at once, so potent was the thought of almost limitless gold. Most of those present forthwith conducted and accompanied the Doctor outside to show him the treasure, if not the guns, stowed temporarily in the forecourt. Duncan, Scotus and one or two Cameron lairds were left with Locheil.

'I do not trust Murray,' Duncan declared to the chief, as soon as they were alone. 'Any more than I trust Barrisdale or my cousin James Mor. It is my belief that they will do anything to get that money into their own hands. How much will Barris-dale's Regiment see of it, I wonder? The gold has gone to their heads . . . '

'And to yours, my boy, I think,' the older man said mildly. 'To all our heads, one way or another. Here we have been arguing and squabbling over it like hounds over a carcase – while we should have been deciding on more urgent matters. Those English ships know that we are here, now. Know that much heavy cargo has been landed to us here. They will be back, bringing others with them. When they cannot catch the Frenchmen, they will come back for us. Nothing surer. We must prepare to move from here – and move the arms and ammunition also. The gold, and what to do with it, can wait.'

Duncan bit his lip, rebuked. 'That is true,' he admitted. 'You are right, sir, of course.'

The gold, however, was not to be so easily dismissed. A mounting noise and clamour outside rose to a crescendo as the door burst open and men surged into the room shouting the news. More of the money was gone. Another barrel was empty. Five thousand more gold pieces had been stolen.

Complete chaos and uproar reigned. Sane and reasonable men were smitten with a sort of madness. The precious hoard that had suddenly become all-important, a recoupment and recompense for all the loss and failure and defeat, they saw evaporating under their very noses. Ten thousand guineas gone in the first few hours! Appalled, crazed, they scoured the neighbourhood in the creeping dusk, all but pulling Borrodale House apart, searching again and again possible hiding-places, accusing each other, coming to blows, every man's hand against his fellow, suspicion rampant, indiscriminate.

It was Duncan MacGregor who discovered the powder. Searching in one of Clanranald's cow-byres, already examined by others, he noticed on the cobbled flooring a thin and intermittent trail of black powder. A mere rub between finger and thumb assured him that it was gunpowder. The rail led him to a great pile of last season's bog-hay in a corner. He himself had thrust a hay-fork into this earlier, as no doubt had others, without jarring the prongs on hidden gold pieces. Now, pulling armfuls of the hay aside, he uncovered heaps of loose gunpowder deep beneath it.

No great discernment was required to realise that the missing gold was now in the kegs from which this powder had been emptied. A feverish opening, and spilling, of powder-kegs followed, but no trace of the missing *louis d'ors* was found. Presumably they had been transported away on garrons, amongst the other stores – this work of clearing away the cargo to hiding-places having gone on continuously, even while the officers were at their evening meal in the house. The business would have been simplicity itself, for a small group of men working with the others; finding the hidden gold, however, would be very much otherwise in a densely wooded steep hillside terrain consisting very largely of great fallen rocks, with bracken-filled hollows everywhere and caves innumerable. Any thorough and intensified search would have to await the morning light.

Glenpean and his Camerons, having been on guard-duty, were the prime targets for accusation. Either they had failed in their vigilance – or they had taken the money themselves. In vain did Glenpean protest that their task had been to guard the approaches to Borrodale House from assault from without, not to watch for perfidy within, and point out that all evening working-parties had been moving to and fro with pony-trains. These assertions did little to clear the Camerons, but they did serve to spread suspicions over Clanranald's own MacDonalds who had necessarily largely manned the working-parties. Talk of the MacDonalds' failure to charge at Culloden rose again on the myrtle-scented evening air, dirks were drawn, and even some blood spilled in a minor way.

Throughout Locheil was pleading for priorities, for a council-of-war to decide matters other than financial. At length, by the device of having Clanranald bring all the six remaining barrelfuls of gold into the great room of the house itself, where it would be safely under the eyes of all, he managed to re-assemble the officers within. Though a man gentle by nature and the reverse of self-assertive, he took forceful lead now, even speaking sharply to Murray of Broughton.

How much attention was concentrated on strategy and matters military, and how much remained preoccupied with *louis d'ors*, was doubtful; but it was decided that Locheil, despite his disability, should be accepted as military commander for the time being, with Clanranald as deputy – these being the two colonels with most men presently at their command – and that a move should be made away from this now dangerous area at first light next morning. A small but trustworthy party could be left to search for the lost gold. Doctor Archie, who had travelled westwards by Loch Eil and Glenfinnan, reported enemy units as near as the latter pass; it was therefore agreed to move north into the empty country around the head of Loch

133

Morar, and to take as much of the arms and stores with them as was possible. And, of course, the gold . . .

Later, in the soft darkness of the May night, the two young men sat in a black pool of shadow under trees that crowned a knoll near Borrodale House. It was a carefully chosen stance. From it not only could all the sleeping house be surveyed but, owing to the configuration of the ground, anyone leaving the house area, save to the eastwards, must pass round the base of the knoll. Duncan proposed to keep watch here all night – and Scotus had somewhat doubtfully agreed to share his vigil.

Encouraged by his finding of the jettisoned gunpowder and his deductions therefrom, Duncan reasoned thus; if all were going to move away in the early morning, it was almost certain that whoever had taken that second barrelful of gold would want to have another look at its hiding-place before they left the district. It would probably have been hidden only very roughly, hurriedly, owing to the need for haste and secrecy. A more thorough hiding and covering-up would likely be called for. Moreover, did not gold always draw its hoarders like a magnet, traditionally? He believed that the thieves would visit their booty sometime that night therefore, while more honest men slept.

When Scotus objected that the guard would spot any such movement, Duncan pointed out that the guard was made up of oddments, Glenpean's group having been relieved, and they would not be apt to know who was who amongst the officers, or just what were their duties. Moreover, all would be very tired, having been hard at work all day after travelling through the previous night. Again, who was to say that the guilty men had not got themselves put on guard duty?

So they waited, keeping their own eyes open only with difficulty – for all that applied to the guard applied equally to themselves. Presently indeed Scotus dropped off, and though he made two heroic attempts to rouse himself, thereafter slept soundly, however uncomfortable his posture, a borrowed plaid around his shoulders. To prevent himself from doing likewise, Duncan rose to his feet, to move like some uneasy shade from tree-trunk to tree-trunk, in geometrical order, rhythmic, deliberate.

For how long the MacGregor kept up this grievous patrol he

did not know; it seemed to pass beyond mere time into eternity He imagined frequently that he saw figures moving in the shadows below; he imagined that he heard noises foreign to the night; he imagined that the darkness was decreasing and that therefore the dawn was near and his vigil in vain. Indeed, in time his imaginings grew so constant and graphic, and his judgement so befogged, in the agonising effort to remain approximately awake, that he was no longer in a state to decide what was real and what false. Some men can make their own hells.

Duncan was in fact fully asleep, leaning against a pine-trunk, when he suddenly jerked upright, thereby scratching his face on a projecting twig. Staring about him hurriedly, dazedly, he managed to focus unsteady eyes on two dark shapes moving below him. This time there was no imagining, he would swear. One figure was taller than the other, but it was the smaller that led the way with a gap between them.

Hastily he shook Scotus, and had the wit to put a hand over the other's mouth to prevent him from exclaiming. Urgently he pointed downwards.

Scotus came awake more completely and swiftly than his companion.

The two young men slipped down the side of their knoll. Their quarry was already out of sight in the gloom, but they had obviously been taking the path that ran up into the woodland behind the house. Along this the pursuers hurried, though cautiously.

They presently heard muffled voices of the men in front, without seeing them; here the darkness was intensified by the thickness of the trees. There was nothing about the voices to recognise, no knowing what was being said – but the murmur acted as a guide.

For some distance they followed the track, broad and churned up by the hooves of garrons. This was the main route from house to the area of the caves. Up over the first ridge they climbed, and down into a little valley beyond. They lost the guiding voices here, drowned in the splash and clamour of a swift-running burn threading the wooded valley-floor. Fording this, they pressed on up the much longer slope beyond, with the track rising towards the broken sandstone escarpment wherein opened the largest of the caves. Frequently they paused briefly, to listen.

135

'They seem to have stopped talking,' Duncan commented, at length. 'I have heard nothing since we crossed the burn.'

'Needing their breath for climbing this damned hill,' Scotus suggested. He sounded similarly affected, himself.

Duncan, leading, increased his pace nevertheless.

At the crest of another and smaller intermediate ridge he halted, all ears – and cursing the thudding of his own heart. No single sound, other than the faint whisper of the night breeze in the trees, disturbed the sleeping hills. Frowning, he whipped off the plaid belted crosswise over one shoulder and handed it to his companion.

'Hold it, so that it will hide a light,' he directed, panting a little. 'We have climbed fast – faster than these others were moving before. We should have come close. We should be able to hear them, at least . . . '

Drawing flint and steel, he struck sparks and blew some tinder into a flame beneath the cover of the plaid. He had chosen a wet patch of the track, of which there were no lack. No recent footprints showed thereon amongst the many broad marks of ponies' hooves.

'I feared as much,' Duncan said, quenching the flame. 'They have turned aside. We have missed them. Damnation!'

They turned back, only too well aware that their quarry could have left the track almost anywhere along nearly a mile of its course. Where their feet slipped on another muddy patch, about half-way down the slope again, they made another inspection by hidden light. Two sets of recent footprints showed here – but they identified them as their own. The men they sought had not come even so far.

'A pest! They could turn off anywhere,' Scotus complained. 'We shall never find them now, man . . . '

'They could, yes,' Duncan agreed. 'But . . . I have been thinking. If they are following the route that garrons took – garrons carrying the stolen gold? The garrons could not turn off anywhere – not without leaving clear traces behind. Except in one place, that is.'

'Eh . . . ? I do not take you.'

'The burn. In the burn itself. Garrons could be led down the bed of the stream, and leave no tracks.'

'*Dia*! That is true, yes.'

'It may not be the burn, of course. But it is worth the trying . . . '

They hastened straight down to the stream now. A light, struck by the little ford, told them what they wanted to know. At the sandy edge new-made footprints turned off the track, down-stream, on the north bank, one set of heeled boots and the other of less clear-cut rawhide brogans.

They would have liked to hurry now, for the others had gained a substantial lead – but they dared not. They had no means of knowing how far along this burn their quarry might have gone. It was notably dark down here, in the gut of the little valley, with the trees growing thickly enough to form what was almost a tunnel. Haste was out of the question.

'This burn will be the one that comes out on to the beach – the one we all drank from today,' Duncan said. They were whispering now. 'It cannot be more than half a mile to the shore. Somewhere between here and there . . . '

'We shall get no warning in this darkness,' Scotus pointed out. He drew his pistol, and began to busy himself with the priming. 'We may find ourselves unpopular, I fear.'

The other shook his dark head. 'We do not want that. Fighting,' he declared. 'We want to win the money back. That comes first. Best that whoever stole it should still believe it undiscovered. To challenge them here will serve nothing. They, or others, will only change the hiding-place. We must see without being seen . . . '

'How in the name of mercy shall we do that, in this darkness?'

It was the same darkness, for all that, which solved their problem for them in the end – and as they were despairing of finding what they sought, fearing that the others must have turned off somewhere out of the burn's channel. They were almost down at the outfall to the beach itself when suddenly they saw a tiny light flare in the gloom ahead, quite close apparently. The air here was filled with the sound of falling water, backed by the deeper and more distant boom of the surf.

'Someone else needs to see what he is doing!' Duncan commented. 'Who would have looked for them right down near the beach? There is a waterfall here . . . '

The light disappeared as he spoke. But it came on again in a

137

few moments, seemingly in the same place. Again it died away and came on, appearing to be very low down, near the bed of the burn – lower than they would have anticipated. It must be below the fall, they decided.

They moved on, climbing some way up the bank in order to get a better prospect, drawing as near as they dared. The light came on and off intermittently – no lamp, but bunches of tinder burning out, undoubtedly. The stream evidently dropped here in a sizeable fall, just before it emerged out into the open sand and shingle of the shore, trees still bordering it closely. They could distinguish nothing of who struck the light, but got the impression of much movement about it.

They waited.

Their patience was not unduly taxed. Fairly soon the light striking came to a stop. The watchers from up on the bank could not see any figures below them, what with the gloom and the intervening foliage – and the noise of the fall drowned lesser sounds. But they both gained a distinct sense of movement away from the pool below the fall, movement which continued back upstream, whence they had come. No single glimpse did they catch of those responsible.

After a brief interval the two young men moved quietly down to the waterside, below the fall. There were only shallows here.

'*Diabhol!* They have it in the water, for a wager! The gold!' Duncan declared. 'In the pool itself. Under the fall. It will take no harm in the water – the gold. It must be that. In the pool.'

'That is it, for sure. Clever they are. Under the fall, where the foam and white water will hide it. Where better?'

'What were they doing, then? Just now? That they needed a light?'

They quickly had an answer. Grasping an alder sapling to pull himself up to the frothing pool, Duncan staggered and all but fell back as the entire young tree came away in his hand, rootless. A second grab had the same result, and ended with the MacGregor knee-deep in the water. Investigation proved that the natural screen of bushes and trees around the pool had been reinforced and thickened by a cunning insertion of boughs and fronds and leafage, some planted in pockets of soil, some just entwined amongst growth already there. The result was a sufficient density of verdure to hide the pool from all but the most determined searchers.

'They are thorough,' Scotus said. 'Who is behind this, think you?'

'My cousin, and yours, are both tall men!' Duncan answered cryptically.

'As are many others. Your own self, for that matter! And those two were with us in the house all evening.'

'Barrisdale's men were not.'

'Nor were my own!'

Within the barrier of foliage, they peered down at the foaming swirling pool. The white froth and scum eddying on the surface they could see, but all else was black as pitch. The pool was large for the size of burn – fully ten feet across, and no doubt deep, scoured by the plunging waters of the fall.

Duncan began to throw off his clothes. 'There is but one way to make sure,' he said.

Gleaming palely in the gloom he lowered himself into the chill water.

His shoulders were just going under when his feet touched the stones and gravel of the bottom. He swam two or three strokes towards the splatter and spray of the fall itself before lowering his feet again. At once his toes came in contact with something other than stone – ridged wood, rounded.

'They are here,' he gasped out. 'I feel one of the kegs. No doubt of it.'

Taking a deep breath he surface-dived and breasted his way downwards. Black as it was, his hands quickly found the kegs. They lay anyhow on the bottom, some of them under the fall itself. It was difficult to count them, difficult to stay down for any time. The pounding, rushing waters of the fall seemed to punch all the breath out of his lungs.

Soon Scotus was in the pool beside him. He was a better swimmer than was the MacGregor, diving like a seal. Between them they found nine kegs, by feel. They may have missed one or two, but not many. They could barely move them. Ropes would be required to hoist them out.

Back on the bank, drying themselves with their plaids, and shivering a little, they agreed that this probably represented only one barrelful of the stolen treasure. The powder-kegs would each hold no more, certainly, than had the pannier containing the five hundred gold pieces that Scotus had brought. Nine or ten of them, therefore, could be expected to account for approximately five thousand *louis d'ors* – but assuredly not ten thousand. This most probably would be the second lot filched, not the first.

'They are clever, whoever they may be,' Scotus said. 'To hide all this so near the beach. None would look for it so close at hand. And to use a waterfall, that must always cover its pool with foam and spume, as hiding-place. And to cover their garrons' tracks by using the burn-channel. These are no fools.'

'A pity that they do not apply their wits to better ends! It will be our task to outwit them.'

'Aye. That is easily said. But how? What do we do now?'

'I do not know, at all. Not yet. We must think of something. Something that will not only get this money away from here, but keep it safely for the Prince, too. I do not trust Murray. Where the gold is concerned, by heavens I do not trust many of them!'

'I am with you there,' the other agreed. 'Locheil, I would trust with it. And his brother, the Doctor. And Glenpean. But who else, I would not be too sure.'

They walked back to Borrodale House the simpler, more direct way, by the beach. Half-way there, Duncan paused.

'We must not tell anyone of this, Scotus,' he said. 'That we have found this gold. If we tell any, even Locheil, all will soon know. These others will be warned. We leave in the early morning for Loch Morar. The men who stole the money will seek to come back for it, later. We must come first. We must make some excuse to leave the rest – before these others do. We must come here again, get the gold up, and take it away. To somewhere where it will be safe. Until the Prince returns.'

'You mean – not give it back to Murray and the rest? Keep it ourselves?'

'Yes. The Prince is going to see but little of that forty thousand *louis*. You heard them all. It will all go, one way or another. By the time that all are satisfied there will be nothing left. I wish that it had never been sent. It will do more harm to our cause, I do believe, than did Culloden! Culloden was defeat, yes – but this gold means demoralisation, unmanning us, turning every man's hand against his fellow's.'

'Ours, also?'

'Perhaps. But at least we can save this five thousand for its true purpose. For Prince Charles. And we both have a responsi-

140

bility in the matter of gold, of money, do we not?'

'That is true. As an officer seconded to the King of France, who sent the money, I may have more responsibility than any. I owe no obedience to any here. Aye – I am with you in this, MacGregor. We shall do as you say. And *I* need ask no man's permission, need make no excuses, to leave them at Morar.'

'That may be so. But we shall have to be careful, see you – or we shall merely bring suspicion upon ourselves as being the thieves. There is a risk in all this, mind you – a big risk. If we were caught with the money, later – this five thousand – few would believe that we had not stolen it for our own purposes. We must go warily . . . '

They were in no two minds about that. Wariness hereafter would have to be their watchword. For a start, wariness about re-entering the purlieus of Borrodale House. To be challenged by the guard would involve explanations as to what they had been doing, and almost inevitable suspicions. Better to wait out here until morning, when in the bustle and preparations for departure it would be an easy matter to mix in again with the others.

The two men sought a dry bed of pine-needles beneath a tall Scots pine, and wrapping themselves in their plaids, slept at last.

CHAPTER 12

THE morning was productive of surprises. Not only Duncan and Scotus, and the men they followed, had been active that night, it seemed. Mr. Secretary Murray came out with a most extraordinary story that had the effect of considerably delaying the company's departure for Loch Morar. It seemed that he had been approached, during the night, by one Harrison, a priest, and chaplain to Dillon's Regiment, who had elected not to sail for France. This priest had informed him that a certain Irishman of the same regiment had admitted to him, in the Confessional, that he and another had stolen the gold. This appeared to be the first theft. They had been working on one of the pony-trains, and had taken the bags of money from one of the barrels and mixed them with bags of musket-balls very similarly packed, and so carried them away with the rest. The gold was still stowed away, it seemed, in one of the caves, amongst the ammunition. Which cave was unspecified. The Irishman, whom the priest refused to name because of the sanctity of the Confessional, had suffered a change of heart apparently occasioned by the subsequent attitude of his companion in sin, a junior officer, ensign of the same unit. He suspected that this officer intended to make away with all the loot. It might seem an inadequate reason for Confession to a priest – but such was Murray's story. They should be able to test the validity of it, at any rate, by searching amongst the caves for the missing money-bags.

In the excitement and indignation, the demand for an immediate court-martial and enquiry was put forward. This sort of thing must be nipped in the bud. Barrisdale was particularly urgent on this score, particularly indignant. Despite Locheil's assertion that their survival, in the face of the possible return of the English warships, was more important than this missing money, immediate steps were taken to find the culprits, while a large party of officers hurried up to the caves to ransack the stored ammunition.

There had been a number of Irishmen left behind – it had been only senior officers who had been able to obtain passage in the French ships. It was fairly quickly ascertained that one of them was missing – a corporal by the name of O'Rourke. Search produced no trace of him. His accomplice, however, was more easily found. The priest had revealed that this man was an Englishman, a Lancashire adherent; and the only English ensign who had been working with the ponies was a man named Daniel.

Ensign Daniel was arrested forthwith.

Barrisdale had his way, and a court-martial cum court-of-enquiry was instituted here and then. Messages from the caves area indicated that no money had yet come to light. Daniel, a hulking man of apparently scant intelligence, declared vehemently that it had all been O'Rourke's idea, and that he himself had thought it best to seem to go along with him, and thus be in a position to know where the stolen gold was hidden so that he could dutifully reveal this to his superiors – a thing which he had been about to do as soon as he had had his breakfast. It was in a separate small and inconspicuous cave a little way apart from the others. He was prepared to show the court just where if they would deal kindly with him in consequence.

Being in something of a hurry, the court ingloriously agreed.

Daniel duly conducted them to a well-camouflaged and isolated small cave, and there, sure enough, amongst the bags of musket-balls were other bags of gold pieces. There were only nine of them, however – although Daniel insisted that there should be ten. And one of them was not much more than half full. It seemed that the missing O'Rourke had not departed entirely empty-handed. The full bags were found to contain approximately five hundred *louis d'ors* each, the part-filled one only three hundred. Presumably seven hundred were missing.

In the circumstances, and largely at Doctor Archie's urging, it was decided to waste no more time in any search for this moiety; what was to be done with Daniel could be decided later. There was no sign of the English ships, but they might appear at any time. Orders were belatedly given to pack up and the garrons were loaded, every beast that Clanranald could produce being pressed into service.

It was then came the morning's second surprise – for Duncan and Scotus, at least. It was decided that *they* should stay behind, with the three MacDonnell gillies, to look for the five thousand gold pieces still missing. They had anticipated that there would be some competition for this duty. There was none. No doubt any volunteering for the task would be looked upon with grave suspicion. It was Locheil who declared that the two young men were the obvious choice, with no other duties to perform. Indubitably it was a sign that the chief trusted them – however much askance they were looked at by many others. There were murmurings and objections – but then, there would have been these for whoever was left behind for the search.

Scotus was elated, seeing this as solving their problem about getting away from the others later and coming back for the sunken money. Now they would have a free hand to get it up and away. Duncan was less pleased, however. This was, in the long run, going to add to their difficulties. It would single them out. When the culprits who had sunk the treasure in the burn came back and found it gone, they would have a very shrewd idea as to who had taken it. They themselves would have to deny, to Locheil and the others, having found it – which was bad. Duncan went to Locheil and asked that they might be relieved of the duty.

The chief would not hear of it. They owed it to the Prince, did they not? Who more fitting than themselves? It was an order. They must search the entire area. The gold could not be very far away. They should look out for garrons' tracks in unexpected places, since it was certain that such an amount could only have been carried away on horseback. And might fortune smile on them.

Feeling guilty as sin itself, Duncan acquiesced.

They watched the entire company move off, about two hundred strong, with its long strings of laden pack-horses – watched with mixed feelings. Borrodale House and its vicinity was left to the care of some old servitors, and themselves. If some of the others would have changed places with them, without a doubt the majority preferred to keep company with the certain thirty-four thousand three hundred guineas rather than go searching for the doubtful five thousand.

A discreet distance behind the main company, Duncan Mac-Gregor climbed alone up Glen Borrodale to a point sufficiently high to be able to watch the long train of men and horses heading away northwards across the tumbled watershed of barren rocky hills. He had to be sure that none, on any pretext, turned back. Satisfied, at length, he returned to the low ground. Three sails, he noted, were showing faintly on the far horizon, near the low Isle of Muck.

Scotus had managed to obtain ropes from a fisherman's cottage. With his three gillies and the seven garrons, they set off into the woodlands, taking the same secret route to the hiding-place as had the original conspirators. Their recovery operation was to be as secret as was the depositing.

At the waterfall they carefully dismantled some of the artificial screen of foliage, for replacement later. Then the two young men threw off their clothing and jumped into the swirling peat-stained water, to commence the quite difficult and exhausting task of diving with ropes down to the floor of the pool, against all the pressures caused by the weight of falling water, looping slip-knot nooses round the kegs, and having

144

them hauled up by the gillies. It made a lengthy proceeding – although in daylight it was possible vaguely to see the kegs under water when close to them. There proved to be ten, after all, representing the entire missing barrelful. They had one keg opened, for a check, and found a sealed bag of five hundred pieces intact therein.

It took them more than an hour to recover the lot. Carefully re-erecting the leafy barrier of boughs and saplings, and loading the kegs on to the garrons, hidden under sacks, plaids and the like, they led the beasts back upstream, splashing along the bed of the burn, they hoped and believed unobserved.

Although Duncan and Scotus found much material for argument and discussion in most things that they did together, in the matter of where they should go now, with their precious freight, there was no question, nor even talk. The shieling of the Allt Ruadh up above the high pass between Arkaig and Morar beckoned them both like a magnet.

Their route was east with a little north to it, keeping to the thickest woodland until they were well away from Borrodale, and avoiding the direct road to Loch Morar at all costs.

'If we *should* meet anyone – any of Locheil's people, for instance – what do we say?' Scotus wondered.

'Nothing,' his companion declared. 'We admit nothing, give no account of what we do.'

'That is not so easy, as I found to my cost. Any man can see that we are laden with more than any personal baggage. If they ask . . . ?'

'Then such ill manners must be discouraged, whatever! Better that we see to it that we meet no one, I agree. We must go by round-about and difficult ways. If one always rides well in front, to scout and give warning . . .'

Thus they did travel all that day, by lonely hill tracks and remote valleys, by Glen Beasdale and little Loch na Creige Dubh, by desolate Loch Beoraid and the narrow gut of Glen Caeol. Here they really started to climb in earnest, and as a windy sunset stained all the westermost faces of the hills, they mounted and mounted to the lofty knife-edge ridge between the giants Sgor nan Coireachan and Sgor Thuilm, and looked down into the fair sanctuary of Glen Pean, now filling with the violet shadows of night. Apart from the peat-smoke of a cot-house or two seen at a distance and avoided, the only signs of life that they had encountered throughout were the deer and the grouse, the ptarmigans and the blue hares, with the circling specks that were a pair of eagles following their slow earth-bound progress on tireless wings for many leagues.

Once beyond the ultimate skyline no travellers could remain unobserved, and it was not long before sundry Camerons had spotted and stalked and recognised them. The fact that they had only that morning left Locheil, Doctor Archie and Glenpean assured them of a welcome, and they gathered quite an escort as they proceeded downhill. Duncan's tentative suggestion that Scotus and his gillies might suitably prefer to remain with the larger group of refugees in the high corrie, on account of the limited accommodation at the Allt Ruadh cabin below, was not even granted the favour of an acknowledgement.

The girls spied their approach from afar and came running – Caroline by no means the hindmost until, almost up with them, she recollected her dignity and smoothing down her skirts sought to look ladylike. Her sisters suffered from no such inhibitions, and hurled themselves bodily upon the newcomers, who had hastily dismounted. Somewhat embarrassed, Duncan gave ground a little before the onslaught. Not so his companion; Scotus swept up Anne in one arm and Belle in the other, returned their kisses with interest, and then advanced upon their sister. Undoubtedly his stature grew in the presence of the other sex proportionately as Duncan's diminished.

Caroline did not seem to object to the MacDonnell's embrace – even if she only offered a firm but rather shy handclasp to the MacGregor.

Flattering as was this welcome, after a mere forty-eight hours absence, just a little of the cream was skimmed off it by Caroline's first words – or at least the first she was permitted to enunciate properly.

'Oh, I am glad that you are safe,' she panted. 'So glad. I . . . we were so worried. And Father? Is he safe too?'

'Of course he is, my dear,' Scotus told her genially. 'Why not?'

'The battle,' she said. 'We heard about the battle. Yesterday. We were so anxious. Almost I decided to try to come myself. To find out . . .'

146

'Battle?' Duncan repeated. 'What battle? You mean the ships? The gunfire . . . ?'

'We heard it. In the distance. Boom, boom, boom!' Belle cried.

'Just the echoes of it . . . '

'Did you win?' Anne demanded. 'You beat them, didn't you? Did you kill lots of Englishmen?'

'Anne! Hush! Think shame!'

'Was it exciting, Duncan?'

'But . . . there was no battle. No fighting. Only a few cannon shots exchanged.'

'Oh, but the man told us there was. A great battle. He had just come from it. With French ships and English ships. And many soldiers.'

'Yes, but it came to nothing.'

'What man was this?'

'A soldier who came through the pass. Earlier today. Going east. He said French ships came into a loch at Clanranald's house – Borrodale on Loch nan Uamh, that would be. And the English ships came in after them. There was much fighting, he said. And we heard the echoes of it, even all this way off.'

'Much gunfire, yes. But most of it out of range. The English ships were smaller than the French. They dared not come too close. No blood was shed. Not on our side, at any rate.'

'None?' Anne demanded. 'All those booms and no one hit, at all?'

'I fear not, my trout!' Scotus laughed. 'All noise and bluster. Are you much disappointed?'

'She is a foolish child. Thank God that it is all right – that you are all safe. You saw Father . . . ?'

'Yes indeed. We worked together all yesterday. Like slaves, like very bondsmen. My back is sore, yet.'

'He is well,' Duncan told her. 'Locheil keeps him busy. He asked us many things about you. About you all.'

'Did you give Locheil the gold?' Anne demanded. 'What did he say? Was he pleased? All that money . . . !'

'H'mmm.' Duncan glanced from the questioner to Scotus and Caroline. 'That is rather a long story, I fear.'

'Tell us,' Belle supported her sister imperiously.

'Well . . . another time, perhaps.'

'You shall hear all our adventures in due course,' Scotus

147

assured. 'Give us but a little time.'

'I do not believe that you gave him the gold, at all!' Anne accused. 'I believe that you just kept it!' She pointed dramatically at the string of ponies behind them. 'What is all that you have got? You have as much tied to those garrons as you took away! More! I believe that you have kept the money! You weren't even at the battle!'

'I think so too,' Belle agreed.

'Anne! Belle! This is insufferable!' their elder sister exclaimed. 'Go back to the cabin, if that is the sort of manners you are going to display.' She turned. 'Forgive them. They are running wild, and it is difficult. But we will all go back. You must be tired. If you have come all the way from Borrodale . . . ?' There was just a hint of a question in that last, nevertheless.

To produce a diversion quickly Duncan changed the subject. 'This man you spoke of – the soldier who told you that there had been a battle? Who was he? How did he come to be here? Was he one of your own people? A Cameron returning home?'

'No, no. He was a stranger. A rough kind of a man. Irish, I would think, by his voice . . . '

'Ha! Irish. And alone? His name would be O'Rourke, for a wager?'

'I do not know. He did not tell it.'

'Had he a garron with him? Was he carrying anything? Anything heavy?' Scotus asked.

'He had two, yes. One laden, very much like your own. The other he rode.'

The two men exchanged glances.

'How long since he left? And which way did he go?' Duncan demanded.

'He was here in the afternoon. We gave him food. I said that he should stay and rest. for he seemed very weary. But he would not wait. He said that he had a very important message to deliver – about this battle. To whom, he did not say. He must press on, he said. He went on down the glen, towards Arkaig. I warned him that the Redcoats were apt to be met along the north side of the loch, where the road is. Some were in Glen Dessary yesterday.'

'Afternoon, you say? Late or early?'

Surprised, the girl looked at Duncan. 'Is it important? It was fairly late, I think.'

'How many hours ago? Three? Four?'

'About that, yes. What is it, Duncan?'

'Just that we must catch that man. He has seven hundred gold pieces with him. Stolen. The Prince's money.'

'Seven hundred! All your gold, and more? Oh, the scoundrel, the blackguard! You are sure? And to think that we gave him food and drink! Helped him on his way! All your precious gold gone . . . '

Duncan cleared his throat. 'Have you fresh garrons for us? These are tired.'

'You mean – to follow this man? Yourselves? Now?'

'Yes. If he has four hours' start, there is no time to be wasted.'

'But . . . surely it can wait awhile? You are tired yourselves – you both look weary. Given rest, you will travel the faster. And the man will have halted for the night by now, will he not?'

'All the more reason to be after him at once. Before the Redcoats get their hands on him – and on the gold.'

Scotus opened his mouth to speak, but closed it again.

'You think that is likely, Duncan?' the girl asked.

'Of course I do. The way that you say he is going, the fool is riding straight into trouble. He is not a Highlandman – he cannot know the country. He will take the south shore of the loch, no doubt, you having warned him. But at the end of it, he will be in territory where Loudon's forces are thickest. He must be stopped before he gets that far.'

She shook her head. 'I have only the one garron, just now. The others are away with a deer-hunting party.'

'One will be enough,' Duncan returned briefly. 'A Mac-Gregor does not require help to deal with one Irish corporal!'

Scotus laughed. 'You are welcome to the task, friend. Myself, I feel that you are perhaps over-zealous in this!'

'I have my reasons,' the other answered. 'If we can lay hands on that seven hundred *louis d'ors*, it could ease our situation greatly . . . in other ways. We could return it to Locheil!'

'Eh? Locheil? Ah . . . mmmm.'

'At least you must eat, Duncan, before you set off,' Caroline insisted.

149

'Always you are thinking of our bellies, woman!' he declared, but not unkindly.

With the two younger girls sent to catch and bring in the fresh garron, and Caroline bustling about the cabin at the preparation of a hurried meal, out of a muttered consultation with Duncan, Scotus spoke up.

'Caroline, my heart,' he said. 'We have something to tell you. Something for your ear alone. We could not speak of it in front of the young ones. But they were right, after a fashion. We have, not five hundred gold *louis* tied to our beasts out there – but five thousand!'

'You have *what*? Mercy to goodness – what are you saying?'

'Plain facts, my dear. We lost our five hundred. To the Secretary Murray. But we have brought back ten times as much!'

She turned from him to stare at Duncan, unbelieving.

'It is the truth, *a graidh*,' that man assured. 'The money – more French gold – is out there. Tied to the garrons in ten gunpowder kegs. Five thousand *louis*.'

'But . . . but . . . !'

They told her the story, as briefly as might be, and their reasons for their actions. Appalled, the young woman listened to the tale of greed and folly and treachery.

'It is . . . it is beyond all belief!' she declared, at length. 'That men who have given their all for their Prince, risked their lives, shed their blood – that such should act so!' She shook her head, helplessly. 'But why – why have you brought it here? It is evil, that gold – evil! Why bring it here?'

'Because you we *can* trust,' Scotus told her. 'Here we can hide it, but keep an eye on it. Where none will look for it.'

'There is nothing evil about the gold itself,' Duncan asserted. 'Only its effect on men. Some men.' He smiled. 'We do not believe that it will have this effect on you, Caroline! If we can keep it safe for the Prince, it will yet do much for His Highness's cause. It is our duty, whatever.'

Doubtfully she looked at them both, her lovely eyes troubled.

'Tonight,' Duncan went on, 'When Anne and Belle are asleep, you two, with the gillies, must hide the gold. As well to learn from those others, and hide it in water. Less difficult and noticeable, it is, than digging holes. Down at the lochan there, would do. There are overhanging trees at one corner – under

150

them and their roots might serve.' He paused. The thought of Scotus and Caroline together on such a secret employment in the dark, gave him no pleasure. But he shrugged away the mind-picture this conjured up. 'The gold will take no harm in the water. So long as it may be recovered again without overmuch difficulty.'

'And you . . . ?' the girl asked. 'With all this money saved? And all that the others have? Must you go hot-foot after this seven hundred?'

'I must indeed. Seven hundred guineas is still a lot of money. But, more important – if I can get it, then we can take it to Locheil. The seven hundred. Somehow we must give an account of ourselves to him. If we take him this, then we shall have justified ourselves in some measure. In accounting for it, we may be spared accounting for the five thousand, meantime . . . '

She stared, as though seeing the man with new eyes.

'Man – you are a true MacGregor, after all!' Scotus declared, slapping his thigh. 'I would never have thought of that.'

'I am not proud of the notion,' the other said shortly.

It was Caroline's turn to change the subject. 'Here is cold venison. And oatcakes and honey. And whisky. I think that I hear the girls coming . . . '

CHAPTER 13

THE man rode alone down the shadowy glen, in no contented frame of mind. How much he would have preferred to remain at the shieling he dared not admit even to himself. He found himself to be almost hating Scotus, dwelling upon his insufferable good looks, his deplorable charm and smug superiority, his dandified Continental manners. Was he not positively betraying Caroline Cameron by leaving her to the mercies of such a one? Why could Scotus not have volunteered for this task? Why had it got to be himself . . . ?

Duncan MacGregor was dog-tired.

At the foot of the glen he made no move to swing out towards the wide levels at the head of the loch, northwards, in the direction of the dimly seen jagged remains of Glenpean House. The Irishman was almost certain to have followed the roadless south shore of Arkaig. The loch now gloomed slate-grey and uninviting before him. Mallard beat up from the shallows at its head on whistling pinions. Due eastwards, along the waterside, Duncan headed his mount, trotting wherever the terrain allowed.

He was in little doubt as to the line on which to look for his quarry. Though there was no road on this side, there were paths, deer and cattle tracks winding hither and thither amongst the rock-strewn and broken wooded hillsides. No man in his sane senses, no stranger to the area in especial, would follow any other save that which, intermittent and sketchy as it frequently was, yet clung fairly faithfully to the loch-shore itself. Along this Duncan pressed, watchful. Here and there, in muddy stretches around the innumerable burns that poured down to the loch, he could distinguish, even in the gloom, the hoofmarks of two garrons, recently made.

He calculated that O'Rourke would not be so vary far ahead, now, in spite of his long start. His beasts were bound to be worn out, especially that carrying the gold. With the fellow no hillman, he himself must be nearing the end of his tether. The wonder was, indeed, that he had got so far. He must have been travelling solidly for almost twenty-four hours, over terrible country. Duncan was prepared to come on him, bedded down in the old bracken, round any bend of the loch-shore. His pistol was primed and ready in his hand, and his broadsword loosened in its scabbard.

Despite all this readiness, the MacGregor was quite unprepared for the fashion of the encounter when it did take place. He was nearly half-way down that interminable loch when, following the narrow path through a very dark stretch beneath trees, his hitherto stolid garron suddenly whinnied in fright, and without other warning reared up on its hind legs, throwing its rider backwards to the ground, before bolting sideways off the path and uphill through the dark pines, as though the Devil himself was at its heels.

Much shaken, and with a jarred shoulder and hip, Duncan staggered to his feet, cursing. He had dropped his pistol. Tugging out his sword, he crouched on guard, peering around him. Warily he backed to a nearby tree-trunk, for possible support and cover.

Nothing moved around him, no sound reached him other than the tinkle of burns, the night breeze in the trees and the lap-lap of wavelets on the loch-shore.

He waited. The other man could move first. He guaranteed that he would hear him the moment that he did so. He was a fool not to have clung to his pistol.

After a while, with the hush continuing, Duncan stooped very slowly, picked up a fallen piece of wood at his feet, and tossed it into the dark of a juniper bush some distance back along the track, where it made a distinct stir.

No reaction being provoked by this, presently he edged forward again to the path. He wanted that pistol. Ready to flatten himself on the ground at the least hint of movement, he scanned the area where he had been thrown.

He saw the body, lying, booted feet to the path, only a darker shade, more substantial, amongst the shadows in the young brackens.

He stared, and his sword-tip sank. It was no Highlander who lay there – and the ragged uniform and broken boots would not belong to any soldier of the Government. Undoubtedly it was the man he sought, the Irishman. And by his every aspect, dead.

Only a moment or two's closer inspection was required to confirm this. O'Rourke, even in the half-light, was not a pretty sight. One half of his face was quite shot away, indeed. But two other bullet wounds showed, one in the back and one just above the left knee, blackening the clothing with blood. No weapons remained about the body, or lay near.

Straightening up, Duncan looked about him thoughtfully. No sign of any garrons. He walked slowly further along the path to where he could hear the nearest burn chuckling its way down to the loch. Where the path crossed this there were tracks in plenty. It did not require any great perception to recognise that these were mainly of shod and narrow hooves, not the broad almost circular unshod marks of Highland garrons.

Duncan did not even have to make a conscious reconstruction of what had taken place, it was all so obvious. O'Rourke had been ambushed, or perhaps had merely blundered wearily into a patrol of the Elector's cavalry. Unhorsed, probably by the shot in the knee, he had sought to bolt one foot into the thickets. He had been shot in the back as he ran. Then, later, he had been shot in the face at closest range by a pistol, no doubt as he lay on the ground, and to save the trouble of caring for a wounded prisoner. His weapons had been taken, but his tattered clothing was not worth removing. Both his garrons, with their burdens, were gone.

With the example of his own beast's abrupt bolting before him, it could not be taken as certain that the Redcoats had the Irishman's garrons, and therefore the gold; but it seemed highly probable.

Duncan went back, and dragged the body the few yards down to the shore, where he heaped loose stones on top of it, in lieu of a dug grave. He repeated the Lord's Prayer over the sad pile. It was the best that he could do. O'Rourke had paid heavily for his cupidity, despite the tentative Confession half-way.

The MacGregor found his pistol, but was less successful in recovering his pony. Although he searched the seamed and wooded hillside for some considerable time, he discovered no trace of the brute; frightened by the smell of blood, it might have run for miles.

Duncan had climbed quite high, to get above the tree level and so to somewhat wider prospects, before he recognised the hopelessness of it all, and turned back. It was then, as he began to head downhill again, that he noticed the red gleam of light, far below him along the loch-shore. A mere pin-point, it was fully a couple of miles off, he reckoned, well to the east of where O'Rourke had met his end. This would be his killers, for sure – bivouacked for the night, with a camp-fire to cheer them. Only Government troops, secure in their domination of a cowed country, would light open fires in such a situation.

Purpose about him again, Duncan MacGregor changed his direction half-right, eastwards, and went downhill long-strided, his weariness forgotten.

That fire must have sunk down considerably from its first viewing by Duncan, for it was no more than a glowing red heap of embers when cautiously, stealthily, the man crept closer and closer to it. The soldiers slept, then, no doubt. But equally without doubt there would be a sentry.

The encampment was in a little open bay of greensward and

154

shingle where one of the myriad burns entered the loch. Apart, some distance fróm the glowing embers, a group of horses stood out, a dark mass in which numbers could not be distinguished – though Duncan believed that there could not be very many. Various black shadows on the ground would be recumbent dragoons. For the moment, at that distance of fully a hundred yards, he could perceive no sentries, no movement.

As he began to work carefully round for a better and closer inspection, a chop-chopping noise to the right, inland, turned his head. A crack of splintering wood followed, confirming Duncan's impression that the first sound had been made by an axe. As far as he could see, the noise disturbed none around the fire.

Then came the sound of something being dragged – the chopped wood. Duncan waited. Presently a dark figure materialised out of the shadows of the surrounding trees to the right, pulling behind him what presumably was a bough. One man only.

Over to the fire this individual drew his wood. There followed the sound of more chopping and the snapping of twigs. Then suddenly the scene was illuminated, as the fire blazed up. The stoker had tossed on to the smouldering ashes what must be the top of a dead pine-branch; only large quantities of resinous needles, dead and dry, could have produced that abrupt flare-up.

All was, for the moment, comparatively clear. There was much vivid red about the scene, the red of the busy soldier's coat, red covering the outstretched sleepers. No other men appeared to be on guard; this was the only sentry, intent on improving a fire that he had allowed to sink. Possibly he had been asleep himself. He carried a musket slung across his back.

Duncan was counting. He counted the horses first – eleven in all, nine long-legged southern cavalry chargers and two Highland garrons. He counted eight men lying around the fire, plus the sentry. A small patrol – no more than a picquet; a junior officer, no doubt, and eight men, on some special duty. But enough to have spelt the end to O'Rourke's dream of opulence.

Those garrons, ten chances to one, were the Irishman's. Duncan's glance, in the flickering firelight, searched their

155

vicinity. There was a certain amount of gear heaped about – stacked muskets, accoutrements, saddlery and provisions. But, yes – he saw them. A little way apart. Four small barrels. Gunpowder kegs.

So O'Rourke also had recognised the value of the kegs as disguise! Duncan had scarcely expected four kegs. Two would have been enough for seven hundred gold pieces, surely? Perhaps it was for easy handling, by one man . . . ?'

The sentry, who presumably felt the cold or perhaps did not like the dark, was heading back whence he had come – no doubt for more fuel. Sure enough, in a few moments there was the sound of more chopping, and presently he emerged once more into the circle of firelight dragging a second branch, ruddy-brown and obviously dead. Duncan noted that he carried no axe this time.

Swiftly the MacGregor's mind worked. The man had left the axe behind. There must be a dead fallen pine there – and he must intend to go back to it for more wood. He was alone on guard – since the number of sleepers and himself coincided with the number of saddle-horses. And his musket was strapped to his back.

Action followed swiftly upon these observations. Moving round as silently as he might from bush to bush and tree to tree – with fortunately the hiss and crackle of the now well-going fire, as well as the splash of the wavelets, to cover sound – Duncan worked his way to the area where the chopping had taken place. He found the source of the fuel without difficulty – a great giant of a Scots pine, uprooted in some early winter's gale. Where the amateur woodman had been hacking away was very evident, even in the dark, and closer inspection revealed a small hatchet there, its blade dug into the red trunk.

Duncan did not hesitate. He withdrew the axe from the wood, but placed it on the ground just underneath. Then clambering over the thick trunk itself, he sank down amongst the prickly brushwood and the shadows immediately beyond. And waited.

For a while he was left wondering whether his reasoning had been correct. The sentry, after breaking up more of the wood already transported, unslung his musket and took a stroll down to the edge of the loch. He remained there, staring out over the dark water, for a while. Then he came back to the sleepers, and commenced to pace up and down slowly. Cramped amongst the brushwood, and frowning now, Duncan was considering whether he ought to try some other plan, when tossing some more wood on the fire, the other evidently decided that the store of fuel was still inadequate. Slinging his musket on his back again, he came stalking over towards the fallen tree. Duncan, tensing, gave thanks for the swift-burning qualities of Scots pine.

Events, after this period of inaction, took place swiftly. The sentry reached the tree, stooped to peer for the axe, perceived that it must have fallen to the ground, and bent right down to feel for it below the trunk. And at the other side thereof, Duncan, holding his breath, rose, and all in the same lithe movement leant over and brought his right hand down hard to the back of the other's head. Clenched in that fist was his dirk – but it was the blunt haft that he smashed down expertly. The felt of the dragoon's cocked hat was scant protection against such a well-placed and calculated blow, and the man folded up with a single grunt, collapsing amongst the tree's debris.

Duncan glanced back to the fire, hurriedly. No one stirred there. He had toyed with the notion of donning the sentry's scarlet coat and black hat, but discarded the idea, deciding that speed was more important. Keeping out of the circle of firelight, he ran round light-footed to where the horses were tethered. First things first, he went to the four kegs. They were linked two and two with a sort of rough rope harness. An eye on the sleepers, he lifted one. It was less heavy than he expected – only half-full apparently. Taking two together, he was able to carry them, by their harness, and stagger over with them to the garrons. It took most of his strength to hoist them up over the back of one of the beasts, one on either side. With his dirk he cut through the rope tethers of both garrons. Then he went back for the remaining two kegs. Throughout, his eyes were never off the huddled sleepers for more than a few seconds at a time. One man kept jerking and stirring alarmingly; perhaps he was only a restless sleeper.

With the second pair of kegs placed on the pony behind the first, he paused, panting. To be off at once, or to cut the tethers of the cavalry horses and seek to scatter them, to delay pursuit? That would take some little time – and he was worried about the stunned sentry regaining consciousness quickly and making an outcry. On the other hand he could not hope to move off the scene with the two garrons without arousing the camp.

The decision was taken for him. Suddenly one of the men, not the restless one, groaned loudly and sat up straight, to stare owlishly around him. Whether what his eyes must see, if dimly, over at the horses, registered immediately on his sleep-dazed mind, Duncan did not wait to discover. Grasping the cut tether of the laden horse, as leading rein, he vaulted on to the back of the other garron, and dragging its head round, kicked the poor tired brute violently into motion. In a hollow pounding of unshod hooves, he headed the two beasts away from the loch and straight up into the hillside woodland.

Behind him a great shouting broke out. It crossed Duncan's mind that this was not unlike his introduction to Scotus, the difference being a mere two hundred *louis*. Under the influence of gold he was becoming as inveterate a horse-thief as any of his MacGregor forebears.

More anxious thoughts than these however quickly filled his mind. With something like consternation he realised that the beast that he was riding was lame. There was no doubt about it; the creature's halting gait, slow pace and extreme reluctance was only too apparent. He would have to abandon it and share the other garron with the gold – no hopeful proceeding with an already tired animal.

Ragged musket-shooting began to follow him – though he was only aware of the noise of the reports. Duncan crouched low on his unhappy mount. Fortunately the trees fairly quickly engulfed him. He wished now that he had had time to loose and scatter those saddle-horses.

On the steep hillside his beast promptly slowed to the merest limping walk. This was quite hopeless. Duncan threw himself off, and clambered on to the back of the other garron, straddling uncomfortably between the two sets of kegs. He abandoned the lame brute.

This animal was clearly almost as unwilling as the other for vigorous motion, especially with the double burden. It took the hill only half-heartedly, despite all its rider's kicks and thumps. Even when he pricked the poor creature's rump with the tip of his dirk, only a very slight access of pace resulted.

Duncan was not long in recognising that this would not do.

Only the probability that these troops would not be bareback riders, and would waste time in saddling up their chargers, was presumably giving him this present breathing-space.

Beyond question, it seemed, this weary animal could not carry both himself and the gold to safety. Almost, he would be better on foot. But he certainly could not carry the money, himself. He had to get rid of the gold, therefore – hide it, where the dragoons would not find it. And quickly. Then look after himself. He had little fear for his chances on the hill at night, with any clutch of Southrons, mounted or otherwise. It was the heavy gold that was the problem.

How and where to hide it, then? Water again? A burn? The hillside was scored with burns. But small ones. Could he find one suitable? In time?

Since pools large enough to hide the kegs were more likely to be come across on the lower levels rather than up on the steep hill, he turned his mount's head half-right, westwards.

The first burn that he crossed was a miserable trickle, useless. He halted the garron for a moment, to listen. Distinctly he could hear crashings and stampings and cries below and behind him. The chase was on. His task was going to demand every second that he was likely to be granted.

The next burn, a few hundred yards westward, was rather better-sized, though still too small. But he had no time to pick and choose. Far from liking the process, he turned downhill alongside it. He felt as though every step was bringing him closer to his pursuers.

Duncan dismounted, to lead the garron, the better to see the stream's potentialities – and also with some idea that he might be able to reduce the noise that he made. There were precious few pools at all on this fast-flowing little watercourse, and such as there were would scarcely hide one keg, much less four. Nothing for it but to go right to the foot again. At least his enemies would not be likely to expect that.

The decision made, he delayed no longer at the upper burnside. He went straight down almost at a run, the pony jouncing and swaying behind with its uncomfortable burden.

From the sounds, it seemed as though the chase was scattered fairly wide. This could be an advantage – and the reverse. Fewer to deal with at once, but more chances of being cornered. Some appeared to be unpleasantly close, too. Let him have but a minute or two at the foot of the hill . . .

But at the foot of the hill this wretched burn formed no pool. It spread itself, yes – but only as a sort of apron of surface water over the greensward. The fugitive cursed his luck.

There was only the loch itself, now. Plenty of water there. Under the bank, somewhere? Had he time? There were alder trees there, flanking the water. Their roots partly undermined. There. Only fifty yards or so . . .

He dragged the garron thitherwards across the grassy level at a trot. He could hear men beating about in the thickets directly above him.

Before ever he reached the water's edge he had the first two kegs dragged off the pony's back. Straight into the shallows he splashed with them, up to his middle, to plunge over and push the things under the projecting alder-roots. Fortunately the water seemed to buoy up the kegs a little, aiding him. Panting, he scrambled out again for the second pair, his wet kilt clinging about his legs.

He practically fell into the loch with his burden this time, strained almost to his physical limits. Somehow he got the awkward and unwieldy objects beneath the roots, the rope getting entangled. He hoped that they were hidden – and would remain hidden in daylight. He dare not delay longer. Sobbing for breath he stood back. One last task. Drawing his dirk, he marked a little cross-shaped score on the bark of the tree.

Staggering up on to the shore again, he slapped the garron on the rump, to drive it away. He would be better without the brute now.

The animal was too tired to move, however. It just stood. Certainly it could not be left there, to draw attention to the hiding-place of the gold.

Grabbing the tether, Duncan began to lead the creature westwards. He was too exhausted himself, for the moment, to run.

He had not gone far when there was a crashing of bushes directly in front of him. One of the horsemen, at least, was down on this path ahead – and close ahead.

There was considerable noise just above him. They seemed to be concentrating. He must have been heard. He dared not try to bolt up there now, as he had intended. Desperately he turned back, eastwards – not the direction he wanted to take.

Leaving the garron he began to run, his wet kilt hampering him at every stride.

A dozen yards he had gone, no more, when a dragoon burst out of the trees above and came hurtling down upon him, his charger's hooves scoring weals through the bracken.

With some notion of swimming for it, Duncan swerved to race in the only direction left to him – towards the loch. Could he reach the water's edge before the trooper with his drawn sabre?

He did – but he did not know it. A few yards from it, troubled by his water-heavy kilt and far from watching his feet, Duncan tripped over a root and sprawling, fell all his length. Part-winded, dizzy, he scrambled up and went staggering on, all too well aware of the drumming of hooves immediately behind. The water only a yard or two off, he glanced round – and saw right above him the terrifying sight of the rearing charger and the down-bent and grinning dragoon, sabre raised for a downward slash. To avoid that fearsome steel he flung his unsteady body sideways – and went directly under the horse's flailing hooves. His whole head seemed to explode in a burst of brilliant lights.

Duncan MacGregor pitched forward, unconscious, his upper half splashing into the shallows of Loch Arkaig.

CHAPTER 14

THOUGH vaguely aware of many strange sensations, much general and unlocated pain and discomfort, and the passage of an infinity of time, it was daylight before Duncan recovered fairly full consciousness and any awareness of his surroundings. He recognised, then, firstly that what seemed to have been obscurely puzzling him for some time by its hazy and hypnotic motion was in fact the gracefully swaying bough of a birch tree with its pale green heart-shaped leaves, nodding in the breeze above him, and intermittently almost hidden behind rolling clouds of blue wood-smoke; secondly, that his head ached and throbbed with an intensity and comprehensiveness that he had never hitherto known or imagined – indeed his whole body seemed to be sore in all its stiff entirety; and thirdly, a little later, that the said stiffness was not wholly muscular, but was partly the result of his wrists and ankles being bound.

That was enough for his notably hazy wits for the moment.

The next assault on his consciousness took the form of a man bending over him and addressing him. There was not so much doubt about his manifestation, for the speaker took the precaution of kicking Duncan in the ribs with the toe of a cavalry boot to emphasise the reality of the situation.

'Well, you,' his visitor observed. 'So you ha' come round at last, eh? And you ha' taken your time, b'God! Now, you better do some talking, see.'

Duncan was prepared to talk. 'God save King James,' he thought would be a suitable remark. But, though his lips found the words, no such pious sentiments emerged.

The boot drove home its clear message to Duncan's already sensitive ribs that this effort was inadequate. 'Talk, I said – you bloody rebel!'

The prisoner moistened his lips, and cleared his throat. 'You ... are ... the ... rebel,' he said, and was pleased to hear the words coming distinctly and with authority. 'King James ... '

He got no further in this brief conversation. A vicious back-handed swipe across the mouth jerked his head back, unbearable pain flooded over him, and he slipped forthwith into the much more friendly embrace of oblivion.

For how long he remained unconscious he had no idea. But when he came round once more, two faces were bending over him, one younger and more intelligent-seeming. Unfortunately the other was still that of the earlier interrogator.

It was the younger man, not much more than a boy indeed, by his looks, who spoke. 'Can you hear what I say?'

'Yes.'

'Good. Answer my questions then. You are one of the Young Pretender's staff?'

Blankly Duncan looked at him. He perceived that the young man was an ensign of dragoons, and the older one a sergeant. Desperately he sought to gather his wits. How had they come to connect him personally with the Prince?

As though to supply the information, the other said: 'Come, sir – silence will do you no service. Nor lies. We know that you are Captain Duncan MacGregor, so-called, of Glengyle's Regiment in the rebel army. You were carrying a letter on your person, signed Charles P. That is the Young Pretender, God curse him, is it not? It was dated but seven days ago. Where is he now?'

So that was it! The Prince's authorisation, ordering him to take over the gold that Scotus had brought. He had carried it in his doublet pocket. Just what had it said? Duncan racked his brains, bemused as they were, to recollect the wording.

His efforts were cut short by a rude shaking from the sergeant. 'Speak, damn you! Don't think that we will let you play dumb.'

'I do not know,' Duncan said.

The sergeant raised a hand to strike, but the young officer stopped him.

'That matter may perhaps wait. There is another, more immediate, of which you cannot disclaim knowledge. What did you do with the gunpowder, sir?'

Duncan stared, and his mind reeled. Gunpowder? Did he mean, where was the ammunition that was landed from the French ships? He shook his head – but swiftly desisted at the pain of it.

'Do not be a fool!' the ensign ordered sharply. 'You took it from here, with two horses. One of the horses we found – but not the gunpowder. Where have you hidden it?'

The truth dawned on the prisoner. They did not know about the gold. They had taken the powder-kegs at their face value. They had not been full, of course – not so very heavy. The coins could not have chinked or rattled. Perhaps even they had been covered over with some of the powder.

'I am waiting,' the officer said ominously.

'I . . . I threw it in the loch,' Duncan told him.

'You did? That is what I thought. Where was your man taking it?'

Duncan's head was in no condition to cope properly with all this, and its implications. They accepted that he had thrown the gunpowder into the loch. They must look on the kegs of powder as important in their own right – to the Jacobites, at any rate. As they would have been, of course, even a week ago. They were concerned about the powder's destination. They assumed that O'Rourke was carrying it for him.

'To ... to my father's regiment. Glengyle's,' he lied. 'He is short of ammunition.'

'I daresay. Where is Glengyle's Regiment now?'

'Far away. North of Inverness.' Cumberland's forces must be well aware of this fact, for they had spies widespread.

'And you were taking the powder there?'

'Yes.'

'Well, no treacherous rebel guns will fire that powder, after it has been in the lake,' the young officer said, with obvious satisfaction. He rose. 'We will move at once. Sergeant. We need not have wasted so long, spent so much time over this matter. It is as I thought. Get this fellow tied behind one of the men. Or better, in front. He may need holding up.'

'Yes, sir.'

Duncan's frail and elusive consciousness did not even survive the rough handling of hoisting him up on to a charger's back before one of the troopers. He swooned right away before ever he reached the saddle.

It was a nightmare journey that followed. How far they went, in what direction they rode, or for how long, Duncan had not the least idea. All that he was aware of was continual awakening to jolting agony, and happily as frequent slipping back into blessed insensibility.

At some stage, a lifetime later, he felt himself to crash down on to something hard, grievously solid – but at least something that did not jolt and jerk. He asked no more of existence, just then – nor knew any more.

'Do not deceive yourself, MacGregor. You will talk, sooner or later. They all talk, eventually. Captain Miller, here, has the art of extracting real eloquence. Unfailingly. I suggest that you spare yourself a demonstration.'

Duncan eyed the speaker as levelly as he might, considering the state of his head. This was no youthful ensign, to be beguiled, but an experienced senior officer, Major Monroe of Culcairn, one of Loudon's staff, the man who had burned Achnacarry Castle and practically every other Cameron house in the area – including no doubt Glenpean House. A spare stern man with a strong Lowland Scots accent, he had a cold and hooded eye.

164

'I cannot tell you what I do not know, Major,' he said, steadily.

'But what you do know, you will tell us. Of that I have no doubt. We shall make it our business to see you do. Eh, Miller?'

The third man in the comfortable sitting-room of Clunes House grinned unpleasantly and flexed the fingers of a great hand in and out, in and out. He did not speak, but his appearance lacked nothing in its own eloquence. A huge man, almost as broad as he was long, with a bull-like head and neck, his muscles seemed to be bursting out of his scarlet coat, his massive shoulders splitting the seams. He had his own fame also, this Captain Miller of Guise's Regiment, a professional prizefighter turned King George's officer. He boasted, amongst other feats, that he had raped eight women in one day's operations in Glen Moriston.

Duncan moistened his lips. 'I would remind you, gentlemen, that I am an officer in the army of His Royal Highness the Prince of Wales. I demand the treatment to which a prisoner-of-war is entitled.'

'Pish, sir! You are a bloody rebel, entitled only to a hanging. Or a musket-ball. Which you will get, I assure you, if you do not talk. And quickly. Where is the man Charles Stuart?'

'I have told you – I do not know.'

Captain Miller strolled forward casually, looked the younger man up and down unhurriedly, grinning, and then, hit him suddenly, viciously, first just under the ribs, and then, as the other doubled up, with a chopping blow at the side of the neck. Duncan sank to the floor, choking.

He was not allowed to lie there. The big man hoisted him up by his torn and stained tartan doublet, and threw him like a sack across the table behind which Major Monroe sat, holding him there lest he slide down again – for the prisoner's own hands were still pinioned at his back.

Monroe spoke on evenly, unmoved, as though nothing had happened. 'You may not know that young man's exact where-abouts, but you will certainly know his approximate location, MacGregor. You were with him only nine days ago. You are attached to his personal staff. From the letter you carried on you, I take it that you are an extra aide-de-camp, or something of the sort. Were it not for that fact, sir, you would have been shot out of hand.'

165

Duncan did not doubt that. Apart from the example of
O'Rourke, in the two days that he had been a prisoner he had
seen evidence in plenty of the Government troops' fondness for
enough to carry in his pocket had preserved his life. So far.
such summary methods of dealing with prisoners. And not only
prisoners; it seemed to be considered suitable treatment for
practically anyone encountered in the Highland area. He had
seen an ordinary small farmer who had brought in an old sword
and a fowlingpiece to deliver up – as according to Cumberland's
proclamation all must do – shot in the back as he left to go
home. He had seen a boy in his early teens cut down with a sabre
because he did not speak English. He had seen an old Cameron
woman, half-blind, shot for not being able to tell where Locheil
was hiding – and raped before she was dead. He did not dis-
believe Major Monroe that the letter that he had been unwise

Gasping for breath, sprawled on the table, he found words.
'If you know . . . that I am . . . one of the Prince's staff officers
. . . how can you deny that I am . . . a prisoner-of-war? Entitled
to protection from hired bullies!'

Captain Miller picked him up, turned him round, drove his
bent knee into Duncan's groin, and flung him back over the
table again, a squirming mass of pain, biting savagely at his lips
to keep himself from yelling out.

Monroe hardly paused, maintaining the same tone of voice,
slightly prim. 'We have three possibilities. One, that Charles
Stuart is still in the Arisaig area. Two, that he is skulking
amongst the islands. And three, that he sailed for France in one
of those ships which brought your gunpowder. I do not think
that he did the last. How do you say, MacGregor?'

Duncan had difficulty in making his lips obey him. His first
words were an unintelligible mumble. 'I . . . I cannot tell you,'
he got out at length, panting. 'I was not present . . . when the
ships sailed.'

Miller reached out his vast paw again, but the Major halted
him.

'A moment, Captain,' he said. 'Perhaps MacGregor does not
know about the Government's great generosity? The Duke of
Cumberland, my friend, is offering a vast fortune, no less than
thirty thousand pounds, for information leading to the apprehension of the Young Pretender. You could do much with such

a sum, I have no doubt, sir? And I have no doubt, also, that a pardon for your past treasons would go with it.'

Duncan found words fast enough now, raising his head from that table. 'I cannot stop you misusing me,' he gulped. 'You keep me bound, so that I cannot defend myself against your baboon here! But, by God – you will not insult me, into the bargain!'

Miller laughed raucously, and began to peel off his tight-fitting gold braided red coat.

'Be gentle with him, Captain . . . about the head,' Monroe mentioned. 'Watkins declared that the least tap about the head, and out he goes! Concussion, or something of the sort, I believe. Unfortunate. It would be a pity if he was to miss any of your educative efforts, would it not?'

Captain Miller made his first spoken contribution. 'Watch me! Just watch me, Major,' he said, in a thick London voice.

He grabbed the prisoner and swung him round. Duncan, bent double and swaying, leaned back against the table-top, holding away. But as the other reached to drag him to him, the bound man, summoning every ounce of his remaining strength, forced himself from the table and hurtled unexpectedly forward. Head still down he butted the big man in the middle with all his force and weight.

Miller, sucking air convulsively, and now doubled up in turn, winded, staggered backwards. He fell over a chair and crashed to the floor.

Duncan fell on top of him, unable to control his rush. But difficult as it was with hands bound behind him, he managed to get to his feet. Those feet were not bound. Raising his right brogan, tottering dizzily, he smashed it down with all the fury and loathing that was in him on to the great fleshy face – once, twice, thrice. He would have continued so to do – but sounds behind him, turned him round. Major Monroe was advancing upon him, arm raised. In his hand was a heavy pistol, grasped by the barrel.

Reeling, everything aswim before his eyes, the younger man lowered head and shoulder in a desperate attempt to repeat his former butting tactics. This time, however, there was no surprise. Monroe, shouting for the guard, saw the rush coming, and brought down the pistol-butt, probably with less nice judgement than he had intended. The blow struck the side of the

167

MacGregor's head, and smashed down on to his shoulder with a sickening crack.

Duncan collapsed on to the floor beside his would-be educator, as unconscious as ever he had been.

He was aware of the groaning for some considerable time before he realised that it was not in fact his own groaning. His body being nothing more than one vast and comprehensive pain, the groans seemed to match it most naturally. It was only when, seeking to raise a hand to his aching groin and finding that he could not do so, he groaned in weak frustration – and doing so, he thereafter perceived some difference in the groans and their quality. Presently, reluctantly, he opened his eyes, and perceived that the major groaning was not his.

He had a companion in the stable of Clunes House – a bundle of blood-stained tartan rags and twitching limbs, that muttered and moaned and cried out. He had been alone before, he thought.

Duncan was not greatly interested in this noisy fellow-sufferer. His own agonies and miseries were much too vivid and pressing for him to have much attention left for others. But the man's reiterated denials and refusals that interspersed his groans, the babbled mixture of no, no, no and curses and pleas, struck an answering chord in the MacGregor, and he roused himself sufficiently to give a little more heed to his companion in misfortune.

It was only then that he perceived that this was, in fact, Cameron of Camusbuie, one of Locheil's captains, an older man for whom he had no great fondness, and whom last he had seen riding off to Loch Morar from Borrodale with the rest. How came he here? And in this state?

Duncan tried to speak – but words came only haltingly to his lips. Anyway Camusbuie did not seem to hear.

Much became apparent without the other's conscious answering, however. The man had obviously been as roughly handled as he had himself – more so, possibly, for his features were almost unrecognisable, so bruised and swollen and cut were they. Such extensive damage could only have been caused by deliberate beatings about the head and face. That he had been put to the question was equally clear – his continual denials and objurgations presumably witnessing to the quality of his answers. But how had he been captured? Did this mean that there had been an action? That Locheil's company had been surprised?

Duncan was still wondering about this, between bouts of much more personal concern and the growing conviction that he had a broken collar-bone, when the stable door was flung open and three soldiers came in half-carrying another tartan-clad victim. He was thrown down on the cobbled floor beside them. As they turned to leave, one of the troopers turned back, and picking up a pail of water from a corner, tossed its contents in a single swing over all three prisoners. He went out, laughing, and the doors were locked and barred again. Whether this was done as something of a kindness, or the reverse, would have been hard to say. Perhaps the latest sufferer had been asking for water.

Duncan recognised the man at once, despite the blood all over his face – and despite the fact that he was sobbing convulsively. It was strange to see so fiery a warrior as Ewan MacDonald of Scirinish sobbing. He did it in a curious fashion also, quite openly, vehemently, angrily. He was one of Clanranald's lairds – the one who had demanded most insistently that the French gold should be shared out amongst those who had fought and suffered for the Prince. Now he lay and beat on the cobblestones with his already broken clenched fists, and such a stream, a flood, of furious and profound profanity issued from his swollen lips, in the Gaelic, in and amongst his savage sobs, as Duncan had never heard in all his days.

When the paroxysm had worn itself out, Duncan spoke. 'What happened, Scirinish? How came you here? You and Camusbuie? Was there fighting? Locheil – is he safe?'

The MacDonald swung on him. 'They are swine, foul and filthy swine!' he cried. 'God burn and blister them! God broil and brand them eternally! May the stink of their roasting choke the very devils in hell!'

'No doubt,' Duncan acceded. 'But yourselves? How came you here?'

The other neither knew to whom he spoke, nor cared. He was in no mood for answering questions, at any rate. 'I told them nothing – nothing! Not even that he had sailed. Nothing, I tell you – save what to do with their accursed money! They thought to buy a MacDonald! Or frighten one!' He was sobbing again. 'By the Holy Ghost, I curse them – living and dying, waking and sleeping, eating and drinking, their sons and their daughters . . . !'

The vehemence of these execrations, or perhaps the splash of the water, seemed to have aroused Camusbuie. He spoke lucidly now, if thickly.

'You did not say that Himself had sailed, Scirinish? In the French ships? You did not tell them that?'

The other went on with his cursing, unheeding.

'*I* did not,' Duncan assured. 'I thought of it, yes – but told them nothing. And you?'

'Nothing,' the Cameron said. 'When I would not tell them if he was still in the country, they wanted to know about the French ships. If I had said that he had gone, they would have spread the word that the Prince had left us. To all. That he had gone away to France. It would have been the end of the Rising, the end of all hope . . .'

'Aye.'

'They tried to make me say it – God, they tried! And the money – that accursed thirty thousand pounds! Did they think . . . ? But, Scirinish? Perhaps he said that Charles went in the ships?'

'He says that he told them nothing. Nothing, at all.'

'Thank God! But they will try again! Heaven have mercy upon us – they will try again!'

Duncan could not deny it. The thought was like lead at his heart. It all but choked the words in his throat. This was just the beginning . . .

Thankful to speak of other things, he told briefly of his own capture, and learned details of the others' misfortunes. There had been no general action. Locheil and the rest, as far as Camusbuie knew, were safe. From Kinlochmorar he and a party of Camerons had been sent out on a patrol, by Locheil. There were rumours that the Lord Lovat was hiding in the vicinity, and they were to find him. Scirinish came with them, as it was Clanranald country. They never found Lovat, but were trapped on an island in the loch where it was said that he might be hiding – the Redcoats must have seen them rowing out to it. That was all that there was to tell. The rest, of the Elector's forces' treatment of its prisoners, was no news to him. No doubt these two had not been shot for the same reason that he himself had been preserved. Only for questioning, for torture. The

Prince's apprehension was all important, it seemed. Otherwise they would be but three corpses, by now.

That night, in between fitful bouts of uneasy sleep, which pain never allowed to be prolonged, Duncan had time and to spare for much thought, much dread, and some wonder. Most of the thought, like the dread, comforted him nothing; but the wonder remained. Wonder chiefly on two scores – that men could so debase themselves, far below the level of the animals, could so debase all mankind, as to treat their fellows in the way that they were being treated here; and at the strange tricks and contrary aspects of character as revealed in these two companions in sorrow. Both had clamoured to get their hands on the treasure landed from the French ships, Camusbuie claiming a home burned and family savaged and scattered, Scirinish wounds in battle and losses amongst his men. The gold, which had been sent for the Prince's use in his efforts to gain his father's crown, they would squabble and fight for without conscience, apparently; but this other treasure, Cumberland's vast thirty thousand pounds, the price for betraying the same Prince, they would shun more fiercely than the plague, they would suffer the extremities of agony and indignity rather than compound with. They were Highland gentlemen, who could never betray for gold. And yet, was not the avidity for this other a betrayal? Would not all the rest think the same way? Barrisdale and James Mor, even?

What did he know of his fellow-men, Duncan asked himself? What did he know of himself, indeed? How much more torture could he stand, before proud will gave in to craven agonised body . . . ?

To the prisoners' surprise, they were left alone all the next day – save for the brief visit of a regimental surgeon, a Welshman, whose duties they took to be inspection as to how much more questioning each could stand rather than healing. He did confirm to Duncan, however, that he had a broken left collar-bone, and went so far as to bind that arm tightly to its owner's side, with a sling to support the forearm – an arrangement which necessitated, at last, the untying of the wrists bound at his back and a retying in front. Otherwise they received no attention, not even food – and though they shouted for water, the pail was not refilled.

171

It was evening before their existence was again acknowledged. Two officers came into the stable, with guards. One was the simian Captain Miller – whose unprepossessing features, Duncan was glad to see, still showed signs of his own yesterday's footwork – but the other was not Major Monroe. He wore the insignia of a lieutenant-colonel and looked an angry man, slight and paunchy.

'Which of these barbarians is the Cameron?' he barked.

With the toe of his boot, and ungently, Miller indicated Camusbuie.

The other stooped down, and slapped the bound Cameron hard across the face. Again and again he did this, until obviously his hand hurt. Then he started to kick instead. He staggered somewhat as he did it, seeming to have but imperfect balance. Undoubtedly he was a little drunk. Panting with the exertions, he gasped out in jerky disjointed phrases,

'Animal! Scum! Vermin! So you would murder one of His Majesty's officers! Cutthroat savages! You shall learn . . . what assassination costs.' In his fury, he had difficulty in enunciating the word assassination, kicking still. 'God help me – I'll teach the whole accursed tribe of you the price of Major Monroe!'

At length, exhausted, the colonel sought to finish his exercise by spitting in the squirming Cameron's face – but, like the rest of this presumably little practised assault, it was not entirely effective and most of what spittle his eloquence had left him went down his own resplendent coat. Miller, who could have done it all so much more efficiently, stood by, almost embarrassed.

'And the other? The aide, MacGregor?'

Eyes narrowing in sheer hate under those low craggy brows, Captain Miller kicked Duncan viciously, a much more telling kick than all the colonel's put together.

'That whelp!' The colonel's lip curled. 'Have him sent under strong escort to Fort William immediately. His lordship wishes to question him in person. As for the other two – take them out and shoot them.'

Miller hesitated. 'Now, sir? Tonight?'

'Good Lord, man – why not? Can your men not aim their pieces unless the sun is shining?'

'I did not mean that, Colonel. I mean sending this man MacGregor to Fort William tonight?'

172

'You heard what I said, didn't you, Captain? Immediately, I said. Those were Lord Loudon's instructions.'

'Yes, sir. Very good, sir.'

As the colonel stamped outside, Miller bellowed orders to the guards. 'Bring these two out. No – not him. These. And be sharp about it.'

'Dear God in Heaven – you cannot do this!' Duncan shouted. 'This . . . this is murder! Colonel – these men have done nothing. They are prisoners-of-war. They have suffered enough already. Colonel – listen to me . . . '

A kick on the jaw did not exactly silence him, but it certainly reduced his shouting to unintelligibility.

The stable door was slammed shut, and he was alone.

It was only a few grim minutes later that a ragged volley crashed out, close at hand. Duncan MacGregor knelt up on the cobblestones and said a trembling, distracted and not very coherent prayer for the departed.

A little later, when he was led stumbling out of that stable by a lieutenant of dragoons, and set up on a cavalry charger, the two bodies still lay where they had fallen against an outhouse wall. Duncan could not even raise a hand in salute, with his wrists tied together. But at least he could turn and look with loathing and contempt at the officer of his escort – since there was no sign of Miller or the colonel. The lieutenant had the grace to flush a little.

So, in the grey evening, Duncan left the House of Clunes, that sat so snugly at the end of the Dark Mile. He rode in the midst of half a troop of dragoons. And though he might bite his lip at every other jolt of the trotting horse, his conscious mind hardly registered a pang of physical pain.

CHAPTER 15

'I AM told, sir, that you have a shoulder broke. It will make painful riding, I do not doubt. If you will give me your parole, let me have your word of honour that you will make no foolish attempt at escape, I think that I may be able to ease your discomfort somewhat.'

The officer spoke stiffly. After half an hour's riding at the head of his column down the wooded shore of Loch Lochy, he had dropped back to Duncan's side. He was a man of approximately the MacGregor's own age, square-built, stocky, very fair-haired. His stiffness seemed to apply to all of him, not just to his present tone of voice. He frowned as he spoke.

'Honour?' Duncan repeated. 'Word of honour? A strange term, I think, on the lips of one of the Elector of Hanover's officers?'

That so stiffened the other that he became quite rigid, a ramrod in his saddle. His lips slashed a straight line across his square features, and clamped that way.

Yet, after perhaps five minutes of silence, the lieutenant spoke again. 'Your parole, sir?' he snapped. But it was a question.

'Is my own, sir. All that is left to me, it seems. I shall keep it.'

Again silence. The officer moved his horse forward a little way from the other.

But presently he was back at Duncan's side once more, his voice stiff as ever, the words seemingly forced out with difficulty from between those tight lips.

'You must not judge all King George's officers by those you have seen here,' he said. 'Here is only the dregs of an army.'

'I do not doubt it, sir. And taking its tone from your German George's brother!'

The other did not answer that. 'The true soldiers are all away fighting the French. In the Low Countries,' he said. 'Would to God I was with them!'

Surprised, Duncan turned to look at him. 'You do not enjoy torturing and shooting prisoners-of-war, and killing defenceless women and children, sir?'

'I do not.'

'How unhappily placed you must be, Lieutenant! How do you manage to pass your time?'

The other snorted. 'You are bitter. I do not wonder at it,' he jerked. 'What was done today was inexcusable. But it was done by a frightened man.'

'Frightened? The ape Miller, frightened whatever?'

'Not Miller so much. Colonel Walton. He it was who gave the orders. He killed because he was afraid. That it would be his turn next. Shot from behind a bush. Any bush. And this country is full of bushes!'

'Why so?'

'Do not say that you have not heard? That no one has told you? Monroe . . . ? Man, Major Monroe was shot this morning. From behind a bush. By the lakeside. By Cameron of Clunes.'

'Dead?'

'Aye. Notably so.'

'*Dia* – so that was it. And Clunes? What happened to him?'

The lieutenant paused. 'I would rather that you did not ask that,' he said, at length.

'I see. Clunes must have felt . . . strongly! Did I not hear something about his wife . . . ?'

'Aye. There is the nub of it! It was Lockhart who did that. Major Lockhart who took over Clunes House and ravished Clunes' wife. Lockhart went to Fort William to see General Loudon two days ago. But he had a white Arab stallion, a handsome beast, which he left behind. Monroe chose to ride it this morning – when he was shot.'

'So-o-o! That was the way of it. Poor Clunes. I never knew him, but he was esteemed a quiet and honest man.'

'You do not say poor Monroe!'

'I do not. Myself, yesterday, if I could have killed Monroe, I would have done it! Any way that I could!'

The silence descended again upon the two men.

It was Duncan who broke it on this occasion, finding that talk, any talk, served to keep his mind off the gnawing, grinding pain of his shoulder, in some measure.

'What makes you, Lieutenant, so different a man from your colleagues?' he asked.

'I am a soldier,' the other answered, stiffly as ever.

'So are these others, are they not? Colonels, majors and captains.'

His companion shook his head. 'I warrant that five years ago not one of them knew one end of a musket from the other! Tavern-captains, chamber-majors and lordlings' fancies – that is the style of them.'

'And you are a trained soldier?'

'Aye. From a boy, almost. I was wounded at Fontenoy, and sent home. When I was fit for duty again, damn them if they

175

did not send me up here, with a troop of replacements scoured from the London sewers! My regiment is still in the Netherlands. Soldiers, not bloodthirsty brigands! I would that I was with them.'

'And I that there were more Englishmen like yourself, Lieutenant.'

'Do not blame the English, Captain,' the other retorted. 'There are villains of all races. But the worst here are your own people. Scots. Monroe was a Scot. So is Lockhart. So is that devil Grant. And the ship's captain Ferguson. Lord Loudon himself is a Campbell, is he not? How they can treat their own folk thus, I cannot tell.'

'Nor I – God forgive them!'

They had left the foot of Loch Lochy and were following the road down the west side of the river, a thin rain falling. The lieutenant, who gave his name as Carter, offered his prisoner a cavalry cloak. Duncan refused it, for any weight bearing on his shoulder was too much. Food and drink the other gave him also, the first that the prisoner had received, actually, for two whole days – and though, because of the constant pain, Duncan had not realised that he was hungry, he ate and drank thankfully. There was nothing to be gained through physical weakness – and much to be lost, perhaps.

The possibility of escape was never far from the captive's mind, however improbable such a thing might appear, one man against thirty. Certain circumstances, however, might just conceivably count in his favour. Because of the rain, it would be a darker night than usual; he knew the terrain fairly well; his injured state might make his guards less wary; and the surgeon's tying up of his wrists had never been renewed and was not very tight, or effective as a shackle, so that he believed that he could free his hands whenever desired. Another quite important consideration, which probably did not occur to his escort, was that when savage questioning and almost certain torture face a man at the end of a journey, he is not likely to be seriously worried about any dangers in an escape attempt.

The journey of twenty difficult miles to Fort William would take practically all night. Around midnight, and approximately half-way, Carter halted his company for a brief spell, after having crossed the ford where the River Loy came out of its glen to join the Lochy. No escape possibility presented itself here.

176

Carter guarded his prisoner well, however, humanely. The professional, he took no chances.

Duncan sought, in his tired and aching head, to visualise every yard of the route ahead. Or not all the route, for in only five miles or so they would issue out into the flat low ground of the Corpach Moss where escape would be out of the question and would remain so practically all the way to the fort. Anything to be attempted must be done in the next few miles. He was restricted to the hill-foots of the Locheil mountains, steeply sloping woodlands cut up by innumerable burns rushing down to the Lochy. The road forded all of these, as he recollected it, save one – where the Laragain came cascading out of its high steep glen in a furious torrent. There, to avoid the deep chasm cut by this river, was a bridge.

Duncan's thoughts concentrated on that bridge. It was high and narrow, a pack-horse bridge, a single arch with a steep hump in the middle of it and a stone parapet.

It might be possible, just possible. And with the last two days' rain . . .

Again Lieutenant Carter rode beside his prisoner – and though Duncan appreciated his strange jerky camaraderie, he could have wished him elsewhere. Also, he recognised that what he was contemplating might seem an ill way of showing that appreciation, for if by any chance he made a successful escape, it must result in serious trouble for this the only enemy officer who had treated him decently. He was unhappy about this – but presumably that was war. This professional soldier would no doubt recognise the fact – and almost certainly would attempt the same in a like situation.

Duncan fretted about his shoulder, also. How much would it hamper him? How much might the pain of it, as well as the lack of the use of his left arm, affect the violent physical efforts that he must attempt?

As the land, and their road, began to slant down into the deeper, wider gap in the long hill rampart which they were following, which was in fact part of the western wall of the Great Glen of Scotland, Duncan was working away with the fingers of his right hand to loosen his wrists. Carter had been silent for a while – for however civil, he clearly was no conversationalist; his charge was concerned that he might notice the manipulations at his wrists, and wished that he had accepted the

177

offer of the cavalry cloak, as cover.

They came to the bridge itself, over the Laragain, sooner than Duncan had anticipated. Suddenly the noise of the rushing river was loud, as they rounded a bend of the road. The jostling and breaking of formation of the ranked dragoons in front, as they first bunched and then strung out in single file to cross the narrow pointed bridge, was all the warning that he received. Although that stringing-out was what he had hoped for, depended upon.

It just would be possible for two horsemen to cross side-by-side, he believed; would Carter stick close to him?

No. At the bridge-end, the lieutenant gestured for nis captive to go first. He would have preferred to be behind – but better this than that they should ride together.

Duncan braced every nerve and sinew as his mount climbed the steep cobbled ascent to the hump of the bridge. He had deliberately allowed the trooper in front to get a good couple of lengths ahead. In the clatter of hooves on stone he could not be sure just how close Carter might be behind – and he dare not look round.

As he topped the hump, he drew a great breath. He had forgotten his collar-bone, his pain and weariness. Every sense was concentrated on immediate action.

The hump passed, he acted at once. He was glad that this was a tall saddle-horse. Keeping his left foot in the stirrup he kicked the right free, and standing up on the left swung his right leg over the saddle. For a brief moment he stood poised there, as he twisted his right hand out of its slackened bonds. Then he leapt – two leaps. The first took him the mere three or four feet on to the top of the parapet, and the second straight downwards as, without pause, he jumped into the void below.

The fall seemed endless to the man. If he had miscalculated, if his memory had played him false, if somehow he had jumped a little way to one side or the other – then he would probably be dead in a matter of seconds. Or almost worse than dead. The gorge was narrow and deep beneath the bridge – possibly seventy or eighty feet. There was a large pool there, in a sort of terrace between a series of rapids and falls. How deep he did not know, though it had looked black when last he saw it. But the entire width of it was probably less than ten yards. He had sought to drop straight downwards, but if his jump had taken him too far to one side . . . ? Or even too far outwards, for the pool would shallow fairly quickly he expected . . . ?

It was extraordinary how much of fear, doubt and agonising conjecture could be crammed into what could only have been a second or two. The rock walls on either side were steep and jagged, with thrusting buttresses. The river should be high after the rain, but . . .

He hit the water with an impact which drove the air out of his lungs. No doubt it savagely wrenched his damaged shoulder, but he felt no pain. He did not feel the cold either, or know any sensation other than the sheer terror of the rocky bottom rising up to smash at his feet and legs.

Then he knew himself to be gasping and fighting for air. He was drawing air into his mouth, but not down into his lungs, which seemed to be closed up, clamped off. It dawned on him, then, that he must have come to the surface again, that he had not been smashed by the rocks, that he was only winded in some measure by hitting the water.

Gulping, choking, Duncan sought to strike out. Having only one arm to swim with, he seemed to go round in circles; or perhaps it was a whirlpool motion in the river. He felt himself being dragged down – his clothing losing its air and becoming waterlogged. It was dark down here in the gut of the chasm, and he could not tell which way to swim. But struggling desperately against the direction that he seemed to be pulled, and gasping for air, he felt a stouning pain in his knee. Another in the other knee told him that he was in shallows. Clawing his way forward with an access of crazy energy, he collapsed, gaping like a stranded fish, on a shelf of rock covered by only a few inches of swirling water, and there lay.

Great as was the temptation to do nothing but seek to regain his breath, to rest his trembling and misused body, the man forced himself to consider, to plan, to establish his position. He seemed to be on the north side of the pool. He thought that dimly he could distinguish the black mass of the bridge away above him. He could hear nothing of what was going on up there because of the noise of falling, rushing water. The walls of the chasm were very steep, near the bridge, and it seemed unlikely that any dragoons would be able to get down to his present position save by going up or down stream some distance, climbing down where it might be less steep, and then working

179

back by the riverside. Certainly none could do this mounted. Probably he had some minutes of grace, therefore.

How to use them?

He must do what they would not expect of him – that was certain. What would they least expect? That he should come back to the bridge and the horses. Could this steep cliff-like bank be climbed? In his present state? Could it be climbed at all?

Duncan MacGregor was an expert rock-climber; no MacGregor boy, brought up on the cliff-girt north-east shores of Loch Lomond was likely to be otherwise. But he had the use of only one hand; and he was dizzy.

He staggered to his feet, and peered upwards. It was impossible to see much of detail in the darkness, but the thought that at least this northern bank was less precipitous than the other. Here, then – or above the bridge? Since he had made his jump at the lower side, the dragoons would be likely to look for him on that side first.

He picked his way upstream therefore, clambering over the rocks, splashing through the shallows.

He did not risk going much beyond the level of the bridge itself, for Carter was no fool and would be sure to send searchers upstream as well as down. Since he could not pick out one place as better than another, by sight, he turned to face the bank almost immediately. At least he could see that a scattering of small trees sprouted from it, which argued crannies, soil, ledges.

The motion of climbing was painful; the injured shoulder was like a leaden weight that had to be hoisted separately and individually at each step. Although the arm was still strapped to his side, it seemed as though it was not part of the rest of him, at all. Each move that he made, each upward lift, each sapling or tussock or outcropping spur of rock that he pulled himself up by, had to be considered in relation to the effect on this grinding shoulder. Sweating, panting, biting back the groans which started to his lips, Duncan fought his private war with that shoulder.

Step by step he fought it and cursed it and beat it.

It was only when, sick and for the moment exhausted, he sank down, leaning against a small but stalwart rowan-tree, he came to realise that he was in fact most of the way up the bank, that the worst of the climb was over. So intent had he been of combating that shoulder that the problem of the actual ascent had more or less taken care of itself. As often was the case, it could not have been so steep as it appeared.

Up here the noise of the river was less loud. He could hear shouting, but it was some distance off, and downstream.

Encouraged, he moved on again, in his dazed, zigzag, crabwise one step-at-a-time climbing. There was more of raw earth than of rock, and although it was slippery with the rain, taken slowly and using every root and tree and handhold, it was possible.

At the top he lay outstretched, gasping, for minutes on end. The road was just in front of him, and the bridge-end dimly visible to his right. Neither men nor horses were to be seen on this side.

Forcing himself up, Duncan made for the bridge itself, seeking to screw every sense to the alert. He reached the stonework. Still no movement, no sign of life around him. Keeping close to the right-hand parapet, he climbed the cobblestones of the steep hump. Just before the crest he crouched down, to peer over. He was only a couple of yards from where he had made his leap.

He could see the dark mass of the horses, waiting beyond the southern end of the bridge. He could not distinguish guards – although there were bound to be such. How many? And where?

Carter would want every man that could be mustered to search for his prisoner, undoubtedly; only the very minimum would be left to watch the horses – not more than three or four out of the thirty, probably.

Still bent almost double, to keep below the level of the parapet, Duncan moved on. Thirty horses can take up a lot of space, and these necessarily overflowed the narrow road on either side. The man reasoned that wherever the guards were, they were unlikely to be up on the rising ground behind the road, where the trees came down. Thither he made his furtive way.

In the event, the entire manoeuvre was ridiculously simple. Duncan saw no sentries from first to last. Slipping from tree to tree, he found himself amongst the outermost of the great concourse of horses. He did not wait to pick and choose. The beasts' reins seemed to be tied together in bunches of four. Taking that group nearest to him, he untied the reins, finding a little difficulty in doing so with one trembling hand. Retaining one set, he managed to haul himself up on to the back of the beast they belonged to. With no more ado, and no more valid selection, he dug in his heels and rode away.

He rode carefully, of course, slowly, so as to make as little noise as possible. Not that he greatly feared in that respect, for the stirrings and hoof-scrapings of thirty horses should mask the sound of his one. He rode uphill since he dared not recross the bridge mounted – but not directly so, slanting over to the left, south-westerly, once again reasoning that this would be the last direction that he might be expected to take.

Up through the trees he went, at a walk, a sense of unreality strong upon him. He had to keep feeling the rippling silky muscles of the beast below him to assure himself that this was not all some sort of hallucination caused by pain and weariness.

Dare he believe that he had won free?

Whether any actual pursuit ever developed, Duncan did not know. No hint of it reached him as he rode up the long side of Meall Banavie.

When the trees began to thin away, on the higher ground, he pulled over to the right again, northwards, to retain their cover for as long as he might, and also to regain his desired direction. He wanted to work back to the trough of Glen Laragain, and to follow it up to its head. That way lay safety, and the empty Cameron territory.

He did not push his mount. The animal was a Lowland cavalry charger and no sure-footed Highland garron. With little instinct or training for the hill, on rough and broken ground it could readily damage a leg.

It was a relief when they reached the upper glen. Duncan risked riding down into it. He was two miles above the bridge here, at least, and he could not anticipate that any searchers would come up this far. There was a track of sorts running up the riverside, and he turned along it. His horse did not require so much attention on this.

Duncan forced his lethargic and reluctant mind to weigh up the situation now. Although all of him cried out for the comparative easement of just riding quietly up a track, he dared not linger in this valley for long. It might be quite some time before Carter gave up the search in the chasm, but once he did, once he reassembled his men, and discovered the loss of one horse, he was almost bound to send at least a small party up here, hot-foot. Anyway, this glen trended away south-westwards towards its head. Somehow he must get over the ridge into Glen Loy, north-westwards. And then, God helping him, over the higher ridge beyond into Glen Mallie. Then still a third ridge lay between him and Arkaigside.

Duncan's whole being protested and rebelled against such a programme, such grievous forcing of himself against the grain of that upheaved land, in his present condition. These ridges were miles wide, up to two thousand feet in height, and awkward, punishing terrain even in daylight. At his most optimistic calculation it would be fifteen savage miles to Loch Arkaig, this way. For consolation, all that he could tell himself was that it had to be done, and that nothing of it was likely to be so desperate and formidable as what he had already accomplished.

Another mile up, therefore, steeling himself, he turned his beast's head off the track at the first sizeable burn coming in from the north, to climb in its company towards the first unseen ridge.

That night's travelling remained ever afterwards little more than an evil dream, a nightmare, vague, undetailed, timeless, in Duncan's mind, without coherence or sequence. He could recollect incidents; his mount stumbling and throwing him off part-way down the heathery side of Glen Loy – for how long he lay thereafter before dragging himself to his feet and on to the brute's back again, he could not tell; the creature getting bogged down in a peat-moss somewhere, and the curses of weak fury and frustration that he had shouted aloud at all Creation as he lurched about, seeking to lead the animal and himself out of it; his getting lost in a vast and benighted wood, he who had prided himself that he could never be lost in all the Highlands, day or night – it must have been the great pine woods of Glen Mallie – and the actual shameful tears that he had wept for himself there, tears for poor damned and lost Duncan MacGregor of Glengyle. These and others of the like stood out; the rest was just pain and endurance and eternity.

Grey dawn found him climbing, so very slowly, the last and lowest of the ridges, still dotted with black pines, between Mallie and Loch Arkaig, leading a jaded, mud-spattered, head-hanging charger. When later, at the summit, he stood swaying and watched the sun rise behind the frowning mountains of

Lochaber, to reflect its first red gleam on the leaden waters of the long loch below, it was to sink down with a groan of thankfulness. Crumpled up as he was, he slept where he sank – and the horse moved no foot as the reins dropped into the heather.

It was mid-afternoon when he wakened, with the sun in his eyes and cramped agony in all his person. Wits sufficient were spared to him to recognise that the open summit of a ridge was not the wisest choice of hiding-place for a fugitive in occupied territory, and he dragged himself and the waiting horse over the crest and down to a nearby thicket. There he sought sleep again, and found it without difficulty.

The shadows of evening were long before he roused himself, and slipped downhill towards the loch. He felt but little rested, he sweated profusely with every exertion – indeed almost certainly he was feverish – and his shoulder was if anything worse. Man and horse drank deep at the first burn that they came to.

Duncan took no great note of where he reached the loch-shore, but he was thankful to mount again and turn westwards along it in the dusk.

It was the blackened remains of a fire on a grassy flat, a large fire, that attracted his wandering and hazy attention presently, and he perceived that he was back at the camping-place where he had first been taken prisoner. And where he had recovered O'Rourke's gold. The gold! He had not so much as thought of it for days. How many days? Three or four? Or more? He could not tell, for the life of him. But the gold . . .

He had no difficulty in locating the spot, at the water's edge, where he had hidden the kegs, the alder-tree with the cross scored on it. Despite the toil and misery of manhandling heavy objects with one arm useless, something compelled him to wade into the water and fight and struggle with those four kegs, dragging them out from under the roots, heaving them on to the bank, and then, worst of all, hoisting them up by pairs on to the horse's back – so high a back. It took him a long time to do it – a man who despised the power of gold over other men.

Hardly able to keep himself upright in the saddle thereafter, he set his mount pacing slowly westwards along the shore track. The beast was left to make its own pace, and largely its own way.

It was late that night when Luath the wolfhound wakened all the mountains to welcome Duncan MacGregor to the dark shieling of the Allt Ruadh. Loud and long she bayed, before she changed her tune to ecstatic yelpings as she leapt and bounded around the foundered horse and the hunched and drooping rider.

Caroline Cameron was first to the cabin's doorway, a plaid wrapped around her, staring out into the gloom at the tall strange horse. Then something revealed to her the identity of the slumped figure thereon.

'Oh, Duncan! Duncan, my dear!' she cried, and came running, arms open, plaid quite forgotten. 'Thank God – oh, thank the good God!'

The newcomer tried to say Amen to that – but was not very sure that he managed it. He was not really very sure of anything, thereafter, save a great chatter of voices, including that of Scotus, strong arms reaching up to enfold him, lift him down, and then a glorious feeling of complete surrender, utter lack of any responsibility for whatever followed. That was bliss, beautitude. In an act of blessed relinquishment that was almost deliberate, he sank away, smiling.

CHAPTER 16

FROM a sort of hell to a very heaven – was ever a man translated so swiftly and completely? Duncan asked himself that question time and again, and always received approximately the same answer. It was pleasurable in itself, however, just to go on asking.

There will be flaws even in the celestial Heaven itself, no doubt – as here. Scotus was overmuch in evidence; Anne and Belle, though excellent children, and kind, were distinctly demanding; and his shoulder ached and ached. These, nevertheless, served only to highlight and emphasise his felicity. To lie on a couch of sweet-smelling heather, in the sun, with no activities, no decisions, required of him, nursed, succoured and

185

cosseted, his every need ministered to by Caroline Cameron, the object of admiration, concern and devotion – what more could man desire? To bask, that was all that he had to do. Duncan bent his whole attention on the business.

No very great concentration and drive was demanded for this – for the man was aware of, indeed cherished, a certain lack of vigour, mental as well as physical. Caroline declared that he had a fever, and perhaps she was right. Certainly the cold-water pads which she kept placing on his brow were very pleasant – even though the tight bandaging and strapping with which she had bound up his shoulder were less so. And her insistence on him lying quite still and in one position was a little trying when his comfort was her avowed objective. But then women, however delightful, were inconsistent ever; was she not asking him questions innumerable, but checking her sisters from doing the same – and indeed telling him to be quiet and not talk when he tried to answer them?

'What harm is there in talking?' he wondered. 'A man cannot be speechless like a dumb animal.'

'You must rest,' she said.

'I am resting, whatever. And the sort of questions that I am asked here are no trouble to answer. Unlike some that I was asked elsewhere.'

'They questioned you? Sorely? They . . . they hurt you, Duncan? In the night, you were moaning and refusing . . . '

'Aye. They did. But not as sorely as they did to others. Camusbuie and Scirinish they killed. But, before they killed, they tortured. Savaged. To have them tell where the Prince might be. To betray him. And they did not speak. The money – they offered them that damnable thirty thousand pounds. Cumberland's reward. They spurned it. These men – I misjudged them.'

'They are dead?'

'Aye. They were men that I thought ill of. Men I believed to be next to traitors, God forgive me. Because of the gold *louis*. They shouted aloud for the French gold – these two amongst others. They would have squandered all the Prince's money. Yet this other money, this reward, they would have none of. They would suffer the pains of hell rather than betray their Prince for gold. Yet the Prince's own gold they coveted. They would have betrayed him in that. Why? Why the difference? How can men act so?'

'I do not know, at all. But do not worry about it.' She laid a hand on his head. 'Do not fret yourself, Duncan. This is what I feared. You should not be talking . . .'

'I have learned that I do not understand men as well as I thought. Men are not always what they seem.'

'That I have learned my own self!' Caroline declared, smiling a little. 'Nor women either.' She bit her lip. 'Oh, Duncan – I . . . we were afraid for you. Terribly afraid. When you did not come back in two days, three days, we feared for your safety. Then your garron came back, on its own. And we feared you . . . dead! I did, at any rate. John had more faith, more confidence. He said that you would came back. He said . . . he said . . . ' Caroline's voice quivered. ' . . . that MacGregors could only be killed by hanging! For cattle-stealing . . . !'

John Scotus was John now! 'He may be right. I seem to have been stealing a deal of horseflesh, of late. But I am sorry that you were anxious for me, *a graidh*.' That was a lie if ever he told one.

'What did you expect?'

He did not answer that. 'Scotus would be a tower of strength to you, I have no doubt!' he said.

'He is very good,' she admitted. 'And cheerful. The girls love him.'

'And you?'

'I like him very well,' she said lightly, and wringing out a fresh cold-water pad, placed it on his brow. 'Now, hush,' she commanded.

Scotus himself, with the younger girls, arrived with the milk from the high corrie. He appeared to Duncan to be growing almost fat, a picture of rude health, well-being and smug self-satisfaction. He had something of the aspect of a family-man, which the other found quite insufferable. Obviously the life of the shieling agreed with him – *this* shieling, at all events.

'Milk for the MacGregor!' he cried. 'Saps for the sufferer! The pity that we have not a tender chicken. But we are going to catch a trout from the burnie for your dinner. Faith, we will make a man of you, yet!'

'Be quiet, John,' he was told. 'Duncan is resting. Put the milk in the cabin, out of the sun.'

'Yes, my dear.'

'John milked the cow today, himself. The black one.' Belle reported giggling. 'He squirted milk all over Anne and me!'

'Then he ought to be ashamed of himself. You all should.'

'Is Duncan better now? Can we ask him questions yet?' Anne demanded.

'I am better,' the invalid told her.

'Ask him how he got the gold from O'Rourke? And what he did with the body!' Scotus suggested.

'I buried it under a pile of stones, at the loch-side,' Duncan said. 'At a bay with a whitened tree-trunk.'

There was a sudden and shocked silence at that flat and factual statement. Even Scotus looked shaken.

'You killed him?' Anne whispered. 'That poor tired Irishman ... ?'

'Anne!' Caroline blazed abruptly. 'Be quiet! Duncan would never do such a thing. How dare you!'

Startled, her sisters turned their stares on her.

'Not I – the Redcoats. A patrol, a picquet, met him, and shot him. I found the body.'

'For the gold?' Scotus exclaimed. 'They got the gold? And yet – you brought it back with you? In those kegs. They are down in the lochan now, with the rest. It *was* gold in them ... ?'

'Gold and gunpowder mixed, I think. O'Rourke was clever – but not clever enough. He fooled the Redcoats – but only after they had killed him!'

'But how ... ?'

Even Caroline forgot to halt the invalid's explanations thereafter – until he himself lay back, silent, tired. Then she was all contrition, miscalling herself, hustling the others away, ordaining absolute quiet, repose.

When, presently, she brought him a horn beaker filled with milk mildly laced with whisky, he did not protest as she raised his head gently and held it to his lips; nor did he spurn the stuff nor gulp it down with any unseemly haste thereafter when he found his head pillowed and supported on a warm, swelling, but firm and distinctly-divided bosom that stirred with a gentle rhythm – even with Scotus grinning at him from the cabin doorway. It was most satisfactory, too, when the MacDonnell and the girls went off down to the burn in the foot of the glen to guddle for trout, and Caroline refused to accompany them;

he found that he had been almost dreading her going. Not only for the lack of her presence; the vision of her long graceful legs splashing in the peat-brown pool, and Scotus watching . . . !'

Men can be bewitched and subverted by more than gold.

It was a pity that he fell asleep in the sun almost immediately thereafter, utterly wasting the occasion – and moreover dreaming of much less pleasant things.

Delectable days of sun and light and good company, of cheer and youthful spirits, of tenderness and regard – and of inner strains and stresses too, of course, of longings and questionings and doubts, of the touch of hands, the flash of an eye, sudden laughter, of the interplay of femininity and masculinity frank or covert. Two young men living close to three of the other sex – and even Belle not so much of a child as to be unaffected by the situation.

Nights too, in the dark windowless cabin, when sleep was by no means the foremost preoccupation in any mind, and an atmosphere almost electric in its tension could be generated without a word spoken, when a faint stir of movement, a deep breath drawn, even, from another unseen couch, could set all therein taut, rigid, waiting, or stirring and sighing in their turn. Secret waves that pulsed and eddied unuttered, yet vehement enough to cause a flush or a bitten lip or a slow quiet secret smile. Awareness, too, all the time, of the watching, brooding mountains all around.

Duncan mended apace, with a sound foundation of basic fitness to aid him. So long as he kept his left shoulder tightly strapped and unmoving, the pain was not too trying. Caroline, however, was urgent that he should be seen somehow by a medico as soon as possible; the collar-bone clearly required to be set properly. And the only medico available to a Jacobite in fifty miles and more undoubtedly was Doctor Archie Cameron.

The last word as to the whereabouts of Locheil's party had been brought by a pair of MacIan's men making south for Ardnamurchan, a day or two before. They declared that they had left the company at Tarbet, between Loch Morar and Loch Nevis, where they had made contact with Lord Lovat who was hiding in the area.

Could Duncan ride as far as Loch Nevis in his present condition? Caroline pronounced most definitely in the negative, whatever anyone else might say and despite her anxiety about the shoulder. But good kind John could go, perhaps, and fetch Doctor Archie here to Allt Ruadh?

Scotus saw difficulties. The Doctor might not be at Tarbet any more. He was a very important man, as well as brother to Locheil, with more to do than come scurrying half-way across the country for a broken bone. And the girls should not be left alone at the shieling with what amounted to a cripple to guard them.

It was Duncan's turn to smile. He pointed out, while remaining entirely uncommitted on the need for the doctor, that Scotus could always leave his bodyguard of three MacDonnell gillies behind him.

Satisfaction was only partial when this thorny problem solved itself by the mountain coming most of the way to Mahomet of its own accord. On the evening in question, and with the matter still undecided, Donald Cameron of Glenpean arrived in person at the shieling. Locheil's whole party was back in the Arkaig area, the Morar district having become too hot to hold them, word of Lovat's persence there seemingly having reached the authorities. The company, and Doctor Archie with it, was encamped for the time being in a small and hidden corrie up on the mountain behind Murlaggan, not ten miles away.

Great was the joy at the Allt Ruadh over Glenpean's arrival – and not only there but all over the uplands where his people were scattered. Quickly the news travelled, and soon clansfolk were coming straggling in. It could only be a brief visit, however. Matters were moving at last, it seemed, and there was the hope of action again. Lovat was bestirring himself. The Frasers could still field a thousand men. There was to be a full-scale council-of-war the next day. Lovat would be there. And Lochgarry. And Keppoch, nephew to the old chief who had died at Culloden. Even the survivors of Cromartie's brigade had been sent for from the northern Mackenzie country; Lovat's lieutenant-general's commission, long a source of heart-burning, could now prove its worth as an authority to issue orders to suchlike brigadiers and colonels. Duncan's own father, Glengyle, had been summoned along with MacLeod of Raasay.

Duncan was glad that he would be seeing his father – but unhappy that Lovat was moving into the centre of the stage. Lovat in any circumstances was a dangerous man, he said – not to be trusted; as leader, general, he could be the ultimate disaster.

The others, who had not met the Fraser chief, were less prejudiced.

Glenpean, sworn to secrecy, was told about the recovered gold – both consignments. He accepted and agreed with the young men's decision not to hand over the large hoard; he urged, indeed, that the same should apply to O'Rourke's lot. It was pointed out that this was only being surrendered in the interests of diverting suspicion.

Glenpean stayed the night at the cabin above the lochan, and next morning at sunrise set off back to Arkaig-side. Duncan and Scotus rode with him – and it required a determined parental veto to prevent Caroline from accompanying them, to watch over the invalid, put his case properly to the doctor, and generally assure herself that mere men did not ruin all her fine nursing. As well as O'Rourke's four kegs, dredged up from the lochan, they took with them garron-loads of smoked sides of venison and beef, sacks of oatmeal and other provisions, for the feeding of Locheil's party was a problem indeed.

Duncan rode, shaky but determined.

CHAPTER 17

ALTHOUGH the corrie on Sgor Murlaggan was less than ten miles away, they went by devious ways to give a wide berth to the new Government post in Glen Dessary, and slowly, for Duncan's sake. It was mid-forenoon before they reached their destination.

The place was well guarded, and they were challenged twice before attaining the corrie. It was an admirably chosen defensive position, as well as being suitably secret, with two emergency exits and plenty of wild country immediately behind it.

If the Allt Ruadh party expected their arrival to create even a mild sensation or stir, they were disappointed. The place was already astir with excitement, it seemed. The newcomers were scarcely noticed. MacShimi himself had but newly arrived, it appeared. Men had attention for none other.

This was scarcely to be wondered at. Lord Lovat was ever conspicuous, spectacular, in all that he did – and Lovat in the heather was something to be marvelled at indeed. He had adopted the fullest fig of chiefly Highland dress for the occasion, his great gross figure positively swathed in tartan, studded with silverware and jewellery, and hung with dirks, *sgian dubh*, pistols. He had come, over twenty miles and more of the roughest terrain, in an extraordinary and enormous litter, not slung between garrons but borne by no fewer than a score of running gillies, a thing shaped like a double-sized sedan-chair, with canopy, cushions, a table, containers for flagons and glasses, and even, as an ultimate refinements, a chamber-pot. MacShimi set a new standard in heather-skulking. He skulked too, with a hundred-man escort.

The Fraser dominated the camp by his very presence, irrespective of his lieutenant-general's commission. Sitting up in his litter like some vast grinning Buddha, gouty thick legs outstretched before him, all men must come to him. Beside his gross bulk, toadlike ugliness, hail-fellow bonhomie and sheer overpowering personality, even the noble Locheil seemed dull and ordinary, the tall swaggering Barrisdale a mere lanky posturer, and Young Clanranald a callow youth. As for Murray of Broughton, he might have been some humble if soured scribe in the great man's employ.

Having failed to see Locheil alone, or indeed away from Lovat's side, Duncan sought his brother, Doctor Archie Cameron, and spent a somewhat painful half-hour with him. After a deal of poking, probing and manipulation, the doctor expressed himself as ever wondering at the healing properties of nature as against the idiocies of men, admiring Caroline's ministrations insofar as they went, but highly critical of Duncan's own share in the business. He should have sent for him, not come riding here. He must keep the shoulder more tightly strapped, and so in position. He must not think that he could play ducks and drakes with a broken collar-bone without being permanently affected. Did he want to be a twisted object of pity with a withered arm for the rest of his days? He must return to Glen Pean forthwith and take care of himself. Move as little as possible for a month and more. Broken bones did not knit together in a few days. Some men were born fools, but others only reached their full folly in maturity. Etcetera.

Duncan MacGregor retired abashed.

The arrival of his father and young MacLeod of Raasay completed the company. They were weary, having travelled almost without stop for two days and nights, from far Kintail. They brought messages of support from the northern leaders – and to Locheil not to Lovat.

Duncan rejoiced to see his father. They were good friends. They had much to say to each other.

It was in the midst of confidences and questionings that the council-of-war was summoned – and it was Lovat who summoned it. Field officers only were to take part – that is, majors and above – and all others must keep their distance. Duncan, therefore, and Glenpean and Scotus and other captains, even Sawny MacLeod the Prince's aide, were excluded, much to their indignation.

The council was held round the Fraser chief's litter, and seemed to consist of a question-and-answer enquiry conducted by Lovat rather than any sort of debate. There were raised voices occasionally, protests, objections, but by and large Mac-Shimi maintained everything comfortably in his own hands. With bewildering changes from sweetest reasonableness and genial goodfellowship to savage irony, devastating wit and roaring intimidation, the aged and belated lieutenant-general who had stayed at home throughout the entire Rising took charge of all. Clearly he had made his decision before ever he had come to the meeting. Colonels of regiments, like Locheil, MacDonnell of Lochgarry, Stewart of Ardshiel, Barrisdale, Clanranald, Keppoch and Glengyle, stood or sat silent for the most part. Yet there were smiles, chuckles, too, and nods of agreement, for Lovat was shrewd and lacking nothing in intelligence. He played on practically every emotion represented before him. Undoubtedly he had studied human nature closely throughout a long and eventful life.

At least it was one of the briefest councils-of-war of the entire campaign – there was that to be said for it.

When it broke up for refreshment, Gregor MacGregor came stamping over to his son. 'As Royal's my Race,' he burst out, 'never have I known the likes of that! The man is beyond all belief – beyond all bearing, too! Does he take us for bairns, sucklings? *Dia* – that I should have ridden a hundred miles for this!'

'From here,' Scotus said, 'he seemed to be giving orders rather than taking counsel?'

'Aye, that was the way of it. MacShimi, the God-sent warrior! The Lord's own anointed!'

'What has been decided?' Glenpean asked. 'I care not who gives the orders so long as we fight, so long as we resume the campaign. Hit back at these women-fighters and house-burners and torturers. Is there action planned, Glengyle – united action, at last?'

'M'mmm. Something of the sort is implied, I think,' the giant MacGregor said grimly. 'If only as excuse for the other.'

'Other? What other do you mean?'

'The money. This gold that has come from France. The sharing out of the gold. That is Lovat's main concern, I think. And not only Lovat's!'

'But . . . '

'I might have known it!' Duncan exclaimed, bitterly 'I might have realised that it was the gold that accounted for Lovat's sudden concern for the Prince's cause! That only money would have brought him to the stage of drawing the sword at this late hour. Aye. How is it to be done? How is the rape to be legalised?'

'Each colonel is to declare how much money he requires to field his regiment's fullest available strength. Some will need more than others, he claims – the large more than the small . . . '

'The numberless Frasers more than any, no doubt!'

'That may well be. First requisitions are to be made up forthwith, and money will be paid out this very afternoon. I told him that my Gregorach did not require gold *louis* before they took the field for their Prince – but he told me not to be a fool, that any soldier is worthy of his hire . . . '

'Hirelings, now, does he make us, 'fore God!'

'What does Murray say to this?' Scotus asked. 'He was for keeping the money in his own hands.'

'He does not like it, that is certain. But he cannot stand up to Lovat. He will balk him if he can, no doubt.'

'But Murray is no more to be trusted with the Prince's

money than is Lovat! He would but have the distribution of it in his own fingers.'

'Is it so . . . ?'

'Enough of the damned money!' Glenpean interrupted. 'Forget it for a moment, if we can! I swear, we are all bewitched by it. What is it all for? This distribution? What are the regiments to be fielded for? What action do we take?'

'The plan is to assemble in Glen Mallie, as many men as can be raised,' Glengyle told him. 'When, was not decided, but as soon as practicable. Locheil's, Lochgarry's, Clanranald's and Barrisdale's Regiments to assemble there. Then to move across Lochy, to join up with Cluny's and Keppoch's, on the Lochaber-Badenoch border. At the same time, Cromartie's Brigade and my own Regiment, with others from the northern clans, to move down through Kintail and Glen Moriston, to link with Lovat's Frasers, then to come up with the others across the Corryarrack. The object is to cut off Inverness and the north-east from Fort William and the south – to cut the Highlands in two.'

'It is ambitious enough, whatever,' Glenpean admitted. 'Was this Lovat's devising?'

'In the main, yes.'

'He would thus have his own territory freed early on!' Scotus pointed out.

'No doubt,' the Cameron acceded. 'But let us not split hairs, so long as we have action at last. Lovat could raise three regiments, at least.'

That seemed to be the mood and reaction of most men in the corrie of Sgor Murlaggan.

The frugal meal over, the business of distributing largesse went forward forthwith. Lovat sat at his table in the litter, with barrels and kegs of gold all around, and Murray of Broughton at his side, pen in hand, paper before him, for all the world like some jovial Samaritan and his disapproving articled clerk. Before this pair chiefs and colonels and great lairds must queue up for their doles, as it were cap-in-hand. Not all relished the procedure, obviously – but to stand out, to refuse altogether to take part, would be a costly gesture indeed when others were obtaining large sums. After all, every commander had been dipping his hand deep into his own pocket for months. This was no more than their due, was it not?

Although the Mackinnon chief was first in the line, by the merest accident, and after much clearing of throat and humming and hawing decided that he needed fifty gold pieces — and was allotted forty — it was Barrisdale who came next and who set the tone and standard of the proceedings by demanding a cool and neat one thousand. Even Lovat looked staggered and at a loss for words at this, and Murray gobbled like a choking turkey. Unabashed the MacDonnell repeated his claim.

'My God!' Murray got out. 'This is fantastic, absurd! You are asking for a fortune, man!'

'I am asking for what is required to put my men once more into the field. Modest enough, in all conscience, I swear.'

'Perhaps the good Barrisdale will let us have details?' Lovat suggested, recovering his breath. 'Some indication as to how he arrives at this sum?'

'Certainly. Two hundred and fifty guineas for immediate payment of the men, re-equipping, horses and provisioning. Fifty to defray debts that the regiment has unavoidably run up in Strathcarron in these last weeks. And seven hundred arrears of pay for four months.'

'Ah! Umm. But I would point out, sir, that arrears of pay are not being dealt with at this time,' Lovat said smoothly. 'Only requisitions absolutely necessary for putting the men into the field. The rest must wait.'

'In the Fiend's name – why? The money is there, enough for all. The arrears paid, the men will but fight the better.'

'That may be so, friend – though do MacDonnells fight but for money? Nevertheless, we have to abide by what the council decided – that this payment is concerned only . . . '

'What *you* decided, Lovat! You, who have no arrears to pay whatever! You who stayed at home . . . '

'Mother of God – d'you speak to MacShimi so!' the Fraser roared, smashing fist on table and setting the stacks of gold coins a dance.

'Aye – and to any who would cheat me of what should be mine!'

'Gentlemen!' Locheil exclaimed. 'This is unworthy . . . '

'And nothing is yours, Barrisdale,' Murray declared, thin-voiced. 'All is His Highness's. To be used to best purpose in his cause . . . '

'And let him remember that himself, the same Murray!' Duncan commented.

'Aye – but there is point in what Barrisdale says,' Scotus, his cousin and fellow-clansman asserted. 'Arrears of pay do not interest Lovat, for obvious reasons. That old fox looks after himself.'

'Of course he does. So do they all, it seems.'

Glengyle cleared his throat. 'In a situation such as this, a man must pay some heed to the requirements of his own men, his regiment,' he said.

Duncan looked at his father sharply. 'Aye,' he said.

Lovat was whispering to Murray. He managed a smile again, as he looked up. 'Barrisdale,' he said, 'I will forget what you said in the heat of the moment. We cannot go beyond the decisions of the council, however. Arrears of pay will have to be dealt with separately. On another occasion. The two hundred and fifty and the fifty guineas we shall accept, meantime. Mr. Secretary will count out three hundred for you.'

Murray scornfully jerked his head at an underling, who could perform such menial tasks, and held out a paper for Barrisdale to sign.

With a flourish, but without change of expression, that man appended his signature. 'You will hear more from me, my friends,' he said, and gestured for one of his people to collect the gold.

'Who is next?' Lovat wondered. 'Ah – Ardshiel.'

The lieutenant-colonel of the Appin Stewart Regiment hesitated. With the example of Barrisdale before him, he might well have been rapidly readjusting his requisition. 'My regiment is not so large as Barrisdale's . . . now!' he said. 'Because we lost a deal more men at Culloden Moor! By that very token, I need more money. More to bring in and equip new men. To arm and victual them . . . '

'No doubt, Ardshiel,' Lovat interrupted. 'I commend your fervour. But that is for later. Just now we are concerned with only an immediate muster. It is the costs of that only that we seek to defray, meantime.'

'Two hundred guineas, then,' the Stewart said abruptly.

'I suggest that you might find one hundred sufficient for the moment, Ardshiel? Indeed, I do. Mr. Secretary – one hundred? Very good. One hundred for the Laird of Ardshiel. Lochgarry – are you next?'

Sitting watching, Duncan MacGregor could not contain himself. 'This is beyond all belief!' he exclaimed. 'Hucksters and pedlars at a fair, I swear, could show more dignity! The best blood of Scotland lining up like beggars before that, that basilisk! Bargaining for as much as they can get of their Prince's money. Bah – it turns my stomach!' He gripped Glengyle's arm. 'You? You are not going to touch any of it?' he demanded.

His father tugged at his still-blond beard. 'Well, now,' he said.

Duncan swallowed. 'You would not consider it? His Highness's money? You?'

'Och now, lad – not so fast.' Gregor MacGregor's frank and open countenance was troubled in most unaccustomed fashion. 'I do not see it quite so. It is not the Prince's private fortune, at all. It was sent, was it not, by the French king, for the furtherance of the true cause . . . '

'But not to go into the sporrans and pouches of the Prince's officers! It was for an army in action.'

'Aye. But to get that army into action again will take money . . . '

'If the gold had not come? If not one penny of it had arrived from France, but just guns and ammunition – would the army not have re-assembled? Given the call. Would any regiment have refused to march? Would the Gregorach? Would a single clansman lay down his sword and say that he would not fight?'

The older man shifted his great frame on the barrelful of gold on which he sat. 'Maybe not, Duncan. But the money *is* here. These others are taking it. If the MacDonnells and the Stewarts and the rest get extra money, extra food, gear – will not our MacGregors desire the same? And rightly. The men have earned it better than some of these . . . '

'The men!' his son said scornfully. 'How much of it all will the men get? How much, think you, of Barrisdale's three hundred *louis d'ors* will his MacDonnells glimpse? Since when have clansmen followed their chiefs for money? *Dia* – most chiefs have never seen fifty gold pieces in all their lives!'

Glengyle shrugged. 'I am not Barrisdale,' he said. 'My

people need clothing, garrons. Most of them are barefoot. Would you have me fail them, in this?'

'Fail *them*? See you.' Duncan leaned forward and dropped his voice a little, subconsciously. 'If you must take the money, give it to me, afterwards. To take away and put with the rest. To keep it safe for the Prince. That little more, at any rate.'

His father looked at him blankly, saying nothing.

Slowly, awkwardly, the younger man got to his feet. His shoulder, after all Doctor Archie's attentions, hurt him damnably. 'Then . . . I am going. I shall not stay to watch you shame your own self and the name of MacGregor!' he said, voice trembling. 'I have seen enough, this day . . . !'

'Son!' Glengyle rose up in his turn. 'Here is no way to speak. You are sick – beside yourself . . . '

'May be. But not because of a broken shoulder! I am going back – back to the shieling. And taking back what I brought.'

It was Scotus's turn to start up. 'You mean . . . ? The money? O'Rourke's gold?'

'Yes. It goes back. They have enough here to squander, in all conscience! Thirty-five thousand gold *louis* should be enough, surely – even for this highly priced company!'

'But . . . Locheil? You were going to give it to Locheil.'

'Only to divert suspicion from the rest. But Locheil has been too much taken up with Lovat even to notice that I am here. None know that we have this gold, none are thinking of it. None know that it is here, save you three.' Duncan looked away towards the distant skyline. 'Unless my father feels so strongly . . . that it should go into the general pool . . . that there may be the more to distribute? And tells Lovat!'

Glengyle drew a sharp breath – and then closed his lips tightly.

Duncan turned his back abruptly. 'Do you come with me, Scotus – or no?' he asked.

'Och, wait you, MacGregor. There is no hurry, man,' the MacDonnell declared. 'Here are friends a-many.. Many to speak with. We have much to learn . . . '

'I have learned enough, I think. You wait. I go.' And without another word to any of them, he stalked stiffly off towards the horses.

Glenpean half-started after him, but Gregor MacGregor held him back. 'Let him be – let the boy be,' he said, deep-voiced. 'I know him. Let him alone. But . . . God go with him . . . and God pity us both!'

It was quite some way on the road back to the Allt Ruadh shieling before Duncan MacGregor gave voice to his own prayer. Suddenly, to the empty heather hillside in front of him he shouted it aloud.

'God's curse on this damnable gold! Curse, curse, curse it!' And he beat his good fist on his knee.

CHAPTER 18

'You were right – right, I tell you. It is evil! Once you said that it was, and I laughed at you. I said that there was nothing wrong with the gold – only the foolishness of men. But you spoke truth. It is evil, devilish! Would to God that it had never come amongst us! It has corrupted us all. All. Aye, myself with the rest. I think gold, dream gold! I said unfor-givable things to my own father . . .'

'Hush you, hush you, Duncan *a graidh*,' Caroline besought him. 'You are ill, in pain – not yourself. Forget it all, just now . . .'

'How can I forget it? It is there – the evil, the folly, the corruption. Can I forget what I said to my father? Or what he did? What they all are doing? Not only adventurers like Bar-risdale and James Mor, but good men. Ardshiel, Mackinnon, Clanranald – even Locheil. These were heroes but a few short weeks ago. Now what are they? Lickpennies! Merchants, trad-ing men for money! Defeat and gold unlimited have been too much for them.'

'It may be so – I do not know.' The young woman shook her head unhappily.

It was very late, fully two hours after midnight. Duncan had arrived back at the shieling alone, in a state of near-collapse. The double journey, in his present state, had been too much for him. Now he lay in a corner of the dark cabin, propped against Caroline's shoulder, while she pressed food and drink on him, and her sisters peered, wide-eyed in the gloom, from their bunks.

'I brought back the money,' he went on. 'O'Rourke's money. I could not give it to Locheil. Just more to be grasped at by the others ...'

'Yes, yes. You know best, Duncan. But eat this, now. All that can wait. It is my fault. I should never have let you go. You were not fit to go ...'

'Scotus stayed. Spanish John – that is what they call him, there – would not come. He said that there was no hurry.'

'Perhaps he was right. Since you had gone, you should not have come away. So soon. It was foolish of you, Duncan. But sip this. It is milk and whisky. It will help you.'

'I had to come. I could not stay there. The place was choking me! All those men ... men I have fought with ... my leaders and comrades ... accusing each other, outdoing each other, hating each other! And myself also. For dirty, filthy money. When I thought of the Prince. And all who had died for him – at Prestonpans and Carlisle and Falkirk and Culloden! Aye, and Camusbuie and Scrinish, there, at Clunes ...'

'Och, Duncan lad – do not distress yourself so.'

'I had to come away, Caroline. To come here. Here is the only place where there is sanity. Here with you. I had to come.'

She made no comment to that.

'You see, don't you? You understand?'

'Och, och – quiet now! Hush, you. There, now. You are feverish again, I do believe. Do not talk, *mo charaid*.' Like a child, the girl gentled him, humoured him. 'Just lie there. Lay your head here, against me. Close your eyes, Duncan. Rest, now.' She began to stroke his hair, lightly, slowly, rhythmically, and presently she was crooning a soft lullaby, without words, without beginning or end, repetitive, calm, inevitable as the tide on a long strand.

Slowly the tension went out of Duncan MacGregor, his breathing deepened, and quite suddenly he slept. Anne and Belle slept too, and Luath the hound, lying across the doorway, chittered and shuddered audibly in her half-sleep, to a night-bird's cry. Caroline's eyes remained open for long.

It was thus that Scotus found them, as the dawn reddened the sky to the east, having ridden, with his gillies, through the night. The young woman wakened swiftly, completely, silently, and raised a finger to her lips before pointing it downwards. She breathed a hush to the low-rumbling dog.

Spanish John, gazing in, grimaced and shook his fair head. 'You never did as much for me, lady,' he complained in a conspiratorial whisper. 'What must *I* do to spend the night on your delectable bosom?'

She smiled at him, and said nothing. But she pointed again, to where the food and drink lay near her.

As the man tip-toed elaborately past, his hand went down to touch her shoulder lightly, to slip up the long column of her neck, behind her ear, and over her hair.

She smiled again, warmly, luminously, but did not otherwise move her lips. Nor her person, cramped as it was.

Scotus went to the heap of skins that constituted his bed near by, and sat, munching bannocks and watching her. Once she turned her head slowly towards him, and their eyes met. The next time that she looked, he too had fallen asleep, head sunk down between his knees.

The girl watched the sunrise, alone.

It was almost mid-forenoon before the little company were up and about that morning – and Duncan, even so, was only out and not about, on Caroline's sternest orders; the fine spell of weather continued, and he was permitted to sit out in the sunshine. Scotus had had a word or two with Doctor Archie, it seemed, and brought back instructions, which, when transmitted to the young woman, made of the MacGregor an invalid indeed, under strictest supervision. Whether Scotus for his own purposes, exaggerated or not, Caroline took doctor's orders entirely seriously.

Scotus brought back with him more tidings than these. There had been a council within a council, it seemed, secretly held the previous afternoon, at Murlaggan. Convened by Murray of Broughton himself, with Lord Lovat not invited. Present had been Locheil, Doctor Archie, Clanranald, Glengyle, Sawny MacLeod, Sir Stewart Thriepland and Major Kennedy. Murray had been highly concerned about the way the money was going. Lovat, undoubtedly, using his lieutenant-generalship, would take complete charge of all the remaining gold – if he was allowed to. Somehow they must prevent that – or they might see none of it again. That had been agreed, and it was decided that a goodly portion of what remained should be securely hidden somewhere that same night. Fully half of it, for preference.

'And what did remain, after yesterday's work?' Duncan demanded from his seat in the heather amongst the urgent bees.

Something over four thousand *louis d'ors* had been disbursed, he was told – which should have left approximately thirty thousand. Anyway, a small group, consisting of Doctor Archie, MacLeod, Thriepland and Kennedy – who was close to Murray – secretly left the camp after dark, with fifteen thousand gold pieces. Scotus grinned.

'I thought that it was perhaps my duty, as well as conveniently on my way back here, to follow them! Not too obviously of course!'

He could not complain of lack of attention on the part of his listeners.

'They rode right round the head of the loch and down the south side. About three miles down, just beyond the mouth of Glen Camgarry. There, almost opposite Callich on the north shore, they left three parcels, each of five thousand gold pieces, one thousand to a bag. One parcel they hid under a rock in the mouth of a burn, and the other two in holes dug in the ground near by. I saw it all. I marked the place well, in my mind.'

Duncan nodded in approval. 'Fifteen thousand. This is better news than I had hoped for. Murray, I swear, will not intend to leave it there for the Prince – even though the others do. Still, it is safe for the moment.'

Scotus grimaced. 'Except that, I am afraid, others beside myself thought of following the four good gentlemen! Twice I glimpsed others dodging and hiding. It is not impossible that others glimpsed me, likewise.'

'*Dia* – that is bad! So others know where this gold is hidden, also?'

'It seems likely.'

'You do not know who they were? These others?'

'No. In the dusk . . . '

'They could have been Lovat's men! Barrisdale's! Anybody . . . '

'They could, yes.'

'What do you intend to do?' Caroline asked. 'What *can* you do?'

'Two things we can do,' Duncan said. 'We can set a watch on the place, day and night. Or we can take it ourselves – dig up the gold and bring it here, to safety. To put it with what we have already.'

Curiously, this second suggestion seemed to shock his hearers, however logical a development it might be of existing policy.

'I' faith man, we can't do that!' Scotus protested. 'There is a limit, whatever. That would make us almost as bad as these others . . . '

'No, no, Duncan – not that!' Caroline cried. 'How can you think of it! It would be shameful!'

'What difference – five thousand or fifteen? What matters it who removes the gold, and to where – so long as we hold it safe for its true owner, the Prince? It is only what we have been doing already, on a larger scale.'

'No – this is different,' Scotus insisted. 'Taking it from Doctor Archie and these others. *They* have not stolen it.'

'Nor do we. But . . . there is this, that if we take it, when the loss is discovered, a great search will be put in hand, a great outcry will arise. And you may have been recognised, Scotus, by those others who followed. That might undo all – bring everyone down on us. No – it had better be the watch, day and night.'

'But . . . how can we do that? Only the two of us?'

'We can do it. With your gillies, and some of the Camerons here. We can do it. We must.'

'It will be a weary, taxing business.'

'No doubt.'

'I will help,' Caroline said.

'And I,' Anne put in – and her sister, of course.

'But for how long, MacGregor? We cannot spend the rest of our days on the shores of Loch Arkaig, watching!'

'Until the Prince comes back – or we receive his instructions. Did you hear any word of him, at Murlaggan?'

'Only that he is being chased all over the Long Island. By sailors from the naval ships. That is why the French frigates would win into Loch Nan Uamh so easily. He would like to make for Skye, it is said.'

'Skye? If that is so, then he is for working back. Back towards the mainland. That he should never have left. We may not have so long to wait.'

'We have no proof of that. It is only hearsay . . . ' Scotus shrugged. 'But, this watch. Allowing that we do set it up – what then? A watch, of one man or two, could not prevent an armed party from making off with the gold.'

'That is why there should be two men, if possible. One to follow the raiders, and one to bring us word.'

'But it is seven or eight miles from here, at least. By the time that word reaches us, where will the raiders be, man?'

'We must do what we can . . . '

'Signals,' Caroline suggested. 'With smoke. Smoke by day and fire by night. We could see that, from here.'

'To be sure. That will help.' Duncan nodded. 'It would save much time. A signal from the top of yonder small hill.' He pointed, screwing up his eyes into the south-easterly sunlight. 'That is at the mouth of Glen Camgarry.'

'Even so – what then?' Scotus went on. 'If we catch the robbers? If it is a large party, we cannot hope to master them.'

'No one intending to steal gold will take a large party to do it,' Duncan asserted. 'Secrecy would be their aim.'

'But equally it must be ours. If we fight them for the money, our own identity will be known. Unless . . . it is intended that we silence them for ever!'

'No! God forbid!' Caroline exclaimed.

Duncan rubbed his chin, at a loss.

'Masks!' Anne cried. 'Masks. Like the outlaws wore, of old! The MacGregors would wear masks, I am sure, when they were being outlaws? I shall make you masks. Then none shall know you!'

'The MacGregors had no need of masks!' Spanish John hooted. 'Their deeds were enough to identify them! But it is a notion, I grant you.'

'Tartans that could not be recognised,' Caroline added. 'Stained in peat-broth.'

'That would serve,' Duncan agreed. 'We can only do what we may . . . '

'And you,' the young woman pointed out determinedly, 'are going to do none of it! Except to give advice, perhaps. For a very long time to come. That I promise you.'

'That remains to be seen,' her patient returned, but with no great sense of conviction.

CHAPTER 19

CAROLINE enlisted eight of her father's people, and with Scotus and his gillies to make up the dozen, the watch was commenced. That she trusted her clansfolk entirely, as Scotus trusted his men, was not extraordinary. It was not from such quarters that the Prince's gold was endangered. To the ordinary Highland folk, the people of the glens, gold was too remote and exotic a commodity to offer any real temptation. None would have known what to do with a single gold piece, much less a barrelful. Coin of any sort they would seldom see. It was their betters whom the gold could corrupt. O'Rourke, an Irish mercenary, had been in quite a different category.

The watch was established, in pairs, in a specially-prepared hide close to where the gold was cached. This was simplified by the terrain, which was very rough and broken, selected for just that reason. A code of signals was arranged, and fires laid.

Their trap made a catch only the second night that it was set. Barely had Scotus arrived back at the shieling after a spell of duty at the lochside, with the darkness, when a pinpoint of red light, gleaming far down the glen, raised the alarm. Cursing, he donned black-stained kilt and plaid again, whilst Caroline put the warning system into operation to assemble the others – Duncan cursing even more vehemently that he was not permitted to ride with the party. In only a short time seven men set out, both looking and feeling highly theatrical in their masks – to the great excitement of Anne and Belle, who equally with Duncan had to be restrained from accompanying them.

It was almost dawn before the group got back, triumphant. Three riders, at nightfall, had raided one of the buried hoards at the loch-shore. When they had moved off, one of the watchers had followed them, and the other, after noting the direction taken, had hurried to climb the little hill and light the beacon. He had been waiting for Scotus's party when it reached the scene.

The raiders had gone south-westwards up Glen Camgarry, and as arranged, the other watcher had left signs behind him as to the route taken – an arrow scored here, a new-broken branch there, three stones to form a tiny cairn elsewhere. Since, all unsuspecting, their quarry had held to the track up the glen of Camgarry, it had all been ridiculously easy. The pursuers had come up with their scout in a couple of hours riding, waiting to tell them that the trio were camped for the night just directly ahead. The rest had been simplicity itself. The nine of them had crept up on the sleeping marauders, who had not even troubled to set a sentry. There had not been so much as a struggle. The culprits had proved to be MacDonald of Suiladale, one of Clanranald's lesser lairds, and two of his gillies. Scotus, seeking to disguise his voice, had berated and upbraided them, in the name of the Prince, Locheil, even Murray. He had confiscated the money – which turned out to be a mere fifty *louis* – and sent the alarmed MacDonald off with the warning that if he ever came back for more, or so much as breathed the whereabouts of the hiding-place to others, his life would be short indeed.

They had been nearer to Glen Pean than Loch Arkaig by this time, so they had come straight back here. They could replace the fifty gold pieces the following day.

Why do any such thing, Duncan demanded? Add it to their own store in the lochan, rather, where it would be safe from such gentry. With the other site known, and being raided, it would be folly, and a waste of time, to replace it.

Five thousand seven hundred and fifty gold *louis*.

The next addition to their accumulation came from an unexpected quarter. Glenpean, with a part of his company, came briefly to the shieling one night, urgently requiring forty of his cattle-beasts, for the use of the regiments presently assembling at Glen Mallie for the projected action. Late as it was, all hands were set to the task of rounding up the animals scattered wide over the high night-bound pastures. It was after her father and the beasts were gone that Caroline Cameron came to Duncan who had been left alone at the cabin, breathless and upset. She all but threw a small leather bag at him.

'There!' she cried. 'Take it! More of your gold – your horrible accursed gold! Take it. Add it to our hoard.'

The now so well-known chink of coins came from the bag, as the man held it in his hand.

'Where did you get this?' he asked, astonished.

'From my father. My own father – Heaven forgive him! Whom I would have sworn would never have touched it!'

'But ... but ... ?'

'He gave it to me, to keep for him. He took it, as payment for the cattle.'

'But that is different, Caroline – that is but honest dealing . . . '

'It is not. Do not you make excuses for him! Before this, he *gave* his beasts. He does not ask money for his men, does he, from the Prince? Must he now have it for his cattle? And even so, a golden guinea for each beast! That is what he has taken. Thirteen pounds Scots each! Oh, it is shameful!'

'M'mmm. I think that you are too hard on your father, *a graidh*. It is a good price, admittedly – but the times are hard . . . '

'Is that any reason for robbing his Prince? The sorrow of it, he says that Doctor Archie has done the same. Sold another forty at the same price. I . . . I told him, the more shame on Locheil's brother, then! I had thought better of them both.'

'Och, but this is not the same at all, lassie. I cannot take this money. To put with the rest. This belongs to your father . . . '

'You will take it! You must. Or don't you ever speak to me again about the Prince's money! It goes with the rest. I told my father so. But . . . do not tell my sisters, Duncan. Please.'

Two days later there was another attempt on the lochside cache. Scotus and a companion had just arrived there, to take over a spell of the tiresome duty, and the pair whom they had relieved were about to depart, when, in the opposite direction they spotted a single man coming up the shore, on foot. That he came furtively, secretly, though in broad daylight, was evident in every line and movement of him – a Highlander with a single feather in his bonnet. He kept to the cover of the trees whenever possible, and every now and again he gazed behind him.

The four watchers waited, slipping on their masks.

At the hiding-place area, the newcomer, whom Scotus recognised at Lieutenant Rory Cameron, brother to Camusbuie who had suffered and died at Clunes, began to line up landmarks and pace out distances, before eventually pinpointing and commencing to uncover the same buried and hidden third of the cache which had already been raided by MacDonald of Suiladale.

Scotus and his men descended upon him then.

The Cameron, startled, had his pistol half-drawn before he perceived that Scotus had his own already levelled at him. Snarling like any cornered wildcat, he crouched at bay.

208

At a loss to know what else to do with him, the MacDonnell treated the man to the same homily and threats that he had given Suiladale. The Cameron protested to highest heaven that he had only been going to take two or three guineas, money that was owing to him for garrons that he had handed over to the regiment. Nothing more. Scotus, treating that with the contempt it deserved, repeated the warning about any second attempt or any revelation of the secret to others – and let him go. What else could he do?

Later, Duncan marvelled that he had seen the same Rory Cameron, on the battlefield of Falkirk, go out alone under fire to carry back on his broad shoulders, three times, badly wounded men.

It was decided, at a conference at the shieling, that short of removing all the gold at the lochside to their own store, as Duncan had first suggested, they should take up the buried parcels – not only the one which had been raided but the other also – and put them beside the third consignment in the stream close by, which did not seem to have been discovered. That this would much bewilder those who had deposited it all, when they came to uplift it, could not be helped.

The following night the transference of the buried gold to the adjoining burn was effected – save for one bag of a thousand *louis* which Scotus, with a certain amount of embarrassment and much explanation, brough back with him to the Allt Ruadh. It all just would not go into the said pool without showing, he reported. They had tried every way. And one bag showing might give away all. Rather than hide it somewhere else near by, where it might eventually be overlooked, he thought it wise to bring it back here to add to their own lot.

Duncan MacGregor smiled to himself.

This distinctly unhealthy preoccupation with the gold was upset in salutory fashion the following evening. One of Clanranald's captains, who had been left for liaison with Locheil, brought them grievous news, at Glenpean's request, as he hastened back to Moidart to warn his chief. The assembly in Glen Mallie was no more, broken up, dispersed and abandoned. They had been betrayed. It could only have been treachery. Of the four regiments to muster there, only about six hundred men had so far arrived, most of them Camerons, naturally – when down upon them descended the Earl of

209

Loudon himself with a large force – three regiments of dragoons, one of hussars and two of his own Campbell militia. He had come directly to Glen Mallie. Locheil had had barely an hour's warning. Disorganised and unready as they were, the Jacobites dared not wait to face a disciplined force four times as large. The order to scatter had been given. Locheil, unfit for fast riding, with Murray and Thriepland, had only escaped by taking a boat across Loch Arkaig. Where they were now, heaven alone knew.

Appalled, the little group at the shieling listened. Here was an end to hopes indeed.

'And . . . our father?' Caroline managed to get out. 'Glenpean? What of him?'

'Most of the Camerons fled southwards. Making for Glenfinnan and the head of Loch Shiel – those who could travel fast. I was sent to warn my chief, Clanranald, who is gathering men in Moidart. I need a fresh horse . . . '

'Yes, yes,' Scotus interrupted. 'But you spoke of betrayal, treachery? Who so base . . . ?'

'Well may you ask! We do not know – we have no proof. But we suspect – aye, indeed we do. Suspect friends of your own, gentlemen!'

'Eh . . . ?'

'What do you mean, man?'

'Barrisdale and James Mor MacGregor left the camp the night before.'

'But this is ridiculous! Barrisdale would not do such a thing.'

'Somebody did. Mallie is a secret and secure glen. And long. Ten miles of it. Thickly wooded. Yet Loudon's brigade came directly for the spot where we were gathered.'

'An enemy scout may have spotted them,' Scotus said. 'Or someone else betrayed them. His own men were there – Barrisdale's Regiment was one of those assembling in Glen Mallie.'

'Aye. One hundred and fifty of them. Even so, he left. And in anger . . . '

'It is nonsense. Ignorant and malicious talk.'

'James Mor is no friend of mine, cousin though he be,' Duncan added. 'But I do not believe that he would be a party to betrayal. Outright treachery. Never that.'

The other shrugged. 'Yet they have been behaving strangely for some time. They were suspicious of all, seeming to bear a grudge against all. Especially against Lovat and Murray. It was the money, I think . . . '

'Aye – the damnable money! Always it is the gold,' Duncan grated.

'And what *about* the gold?' Scotus asked. 'The rest of it. Where is it now? Who has it?'

'Only God knows! Murray took some with him – but fleeing in a small boat, he could not take more than a few bags. Lovat had taken some, of course, when he left for his own country some days before. Not as much as he would have wished, I swear! Barrisdale himself got another two hundred, the day that he left – two days ago. For arrears. He wanted a deal more than that. That was why he left in anger . . . '

'Aye – but the rest? There must still be many thousands . . . ?'

'Doctor Archie and Sawny MacLeod have it hidden at the foot of Arkaig. Somewhere by the loch-shore – just where, none but themselves know. I saw them carrying the bags on their shoulders like gillies. As well that it was the Doctor. None other would have been trusted with it – save Locheil himself.'

Duncan and Scotus exchanged glances.

'How much is hidden there?' the latter enquired.

'I do not know. Ten bags? A dozen? I do not know. I had more to do than count.'

'So-o-o! The good Doctor and Captain MacLeod can lay their hands on the major part of the French money! If I add it aright, nearly thirty thousand . . . '

Frowning, Duncan was hurriedly going to interrupt him when Caroline forestalled him.

'Oh, enough of the wretched money!' she cried. 'Can no one think of anything else? Gold pieces, guineas, *louis d'ors* – that is all that you ever think of! What of the greater things? What of the men? Men's lives? What of the Prince's cause? Is all lost?'

There was a moment or two of silence and discomfort. Then the MacDonald shook his head. 'There was no time to make plans,' he said. 'Locheil said something about trying to win over into the Fraser country, where the northern regiments were to come to join Lovat. Then, again, over to Badenoch, to link up with Cluny and his Macphersons.' He shrugged. 'That is all but hopes. And if Loudon has been told so much, no doubt he will have been told this also.'

None protested that anything of the sort was unthinkable.

The MacDonald, refreshed, exchanged his garron for one of Caroline's, and rode on through the night to warn Clanranald. Going, he left it as his considered opinion that, in view of Lord Loudon's new close proximity, his young hosts would be wise to evacuate the shieling and move elsewhere.

Those he left behind debated that, and the rest that they had been told, far into the night.

Two conclusions they came to, before they slept. One was that they probably were as well where they were as anywhere else that they could go. This high and inaccessible watershed area, on the direct route to nowhere in particular, was never likely to suffer the intensive attentions of conventional troops; it might well be that they would be safer here, less likely to be disturbed, now that the Glen Mallie concentration was dispersed and the pressure relieved in the area. And secondly, that there was nothing that the young men could more usefully do, in the circumstances, than guard and protect the Cameron girls and keep an eye on the two consignments of treasure.

Who would blame them?

CHAPTER 20

So commenced an interlude that seemed almost to belong to another existence altogether, a different life – at least for the two young captains; a period in which time itself seemed to stand still, war and politics and dynastic struggles withdrew to become at first distant, then quite remote, and finally almost unreal, illusory; a period in which even the gold seemed to lose much of its fatal spell over men – viewed from the high watershed above Glen Pean, at any rate. It was a strange and relaxed interlude, with small and personal matters looming so much larger, more important, than matters national. The serene untroubled mountains, omnipresent yet detached as the drifting cloud-shadows that slid lightly, unendingly, across their noble brows, the all-penetrating, all-infusive light of great skies, the long sun-filled days and brief northern nights when darkness barely touched this high world, the scents and sights and sounds of high summer on the very roof of Scotland – all this, given time, could not fail to work its own peaceable balm of spirit and easement of soul, as well as health of body.

Time it was given, as days lengthened into weeks and, imperceptibly, weeks into months. Though time indeed seemed no longer to matter, in a little while, up amongst the shielings. For Duncan MacGregor, at least, almost the only gauge of time was the slow knitting and healing of his broken shoulder. Burgeoning May passed into scented exultant June, and June into maturely smiling July of the bell-heather.

This idyllic existence was no idle one, however, even for the strictly nursed invalid. Although there was little of hurry or urgency about the tasks to be performed, the life held its own rhythmic round of duties. The basic provision of food and drink and fuel was a daily and unending preoccupation. The cattle had to be herded – and none must be allowed to stray over those faces of the hills which might be viewed, even through télescopes, from the low ground of the Arkaig valley and Glen Dessary. Hunting was almost as essential and everyday a proceeding. The digging and dying of bog-pine roots, searching for wild bees' nests for honey, gathering edible fungus, guddling for trout, and seeking for the eggs of plover, curlew and grouse, took up a lot of time, however pleasantly. The curing of hides and the smoking of meat, the fashioning of implements and simple furnishings, were wet weather activities. Secret visits down to ravaged homesteads for items that might be salvaged or adapted, were frequent. Also the watch down at the hidden lochside gold was maintained, although less intensively as time went on and no further raids eventuated – until by mid-July it was only a matter of the gillies taking twenty-four-hour shifts, and one at a time, with Scotus, and presently Duncan also, paying occasional visits.

With the dispersal of the Glen Mallie muster the war meantime seemed very largely to have receded and left this corner of the Highlands. The enemy was not far away; there was the post in Glen Dessary, only six or seven miles off, and another at Callich across Arkaig from where the treasure was hidden. But these were occupied now by garrison-type soldiers, static troops, not first-rank units like dragoons and hussars – infantry indeed, mainly scratch militia levies of older men dredged up for service, the scraplings of King George's barrel, with no enthusiasm for climbing hills, bog-hopping or seeking out nimbler adversaries than themselves in God-forsaken secret places.

Word of the doings of Lord Loudon's more active minions came to the ears of the people of the shielings occasionally – of murder and rapine and arson in Clanranald's Moidart and Arisaig, and Glengarry's Knoydart, to set Scotus fearing for his own home, far out on its Atlantic peninsula as it was. Then, one day in mid-June, the war seemed suddenly to come close again.

They were all working on the new extension to the Allt Ruadh cabin, the two men less than enthusiastically – for this was a separate apartment which Caroline, probably wisely, was insisting upon for the accommodation of her guests and the three MacDonnell gillies, and for which neither Duncan nor Scotus could see the slightest need – when two of the Camerons brought to them an exhausted and frightened fugitive whom they had found hiding in the heather not far away. He had bolted when discovered and had been caught only with difficulty – although he claimed to be a Fraser and a fellow-combatant.

'You are far from Fraser country,' Duncan charged him. 'And your clan has scarcely been eager for combat! Why did you run from these Camerons?'

'I was afraid,' the other, a small foxy, darting-eyed fellow, told them frankly. 'To one man in the heather, all others are enemies, whatever.'

'There speaks an evil conscience, I'll be bound!' Scotus declared. 'As well it might – for I would not trust one of your name, from MacShimi downwards!'

The little man drew himself up with an access of unexpected dignity. 'MacShimi – the great MacShimi,' he said sadly, simply. 'God rest the soul of him.'

They stared at him. 'What do you mean by that?' Duncan demanded.

'He is not . . . not dead?' Spanish John said.

'If he is not, then he is as good as dead,' the Fraser asserted heavily. 'Himself is taken. Captured by the Redcoats. Even now they are carrying him off to London to his death.'

'*Dia!* Lovat . . . Lovat captured!' Duncan looked at the others. He had no love for the gross Fraser chief, but it seemed somehow scarcely conceivable that he could be apprehended like any felon in the midst of his own Highlands, where he had ruled like little less than a king, one of the most notable men and proudest lords in all Scotland. 'You are sure, man? This is not just some rumour ... ?'

'The truth it is whatever. I am one of the gillies who bore his litter. I saw Himself taken. Och, an ill thing it was, an ill thing. They were after catching him in a hollow tree, no less. Where he had hid from them. On the island in the loch – Loch Morar. Damned may it ever be! They came in boats, many boats. Treachery it must have been – God's everlasting curse on the man who betrayed MacShimi!'

'Caught in a hollow tree?' Scotus all but choked. 'Lovat – that great mountain of flesh! Lord ... !'

Caroline spoke, with a swift compassion for the obviously grieving gillie. 'They will not kill him, perhaps. Indeed, I think that they will not,' he said. 'He is a great lord. He did not take any part in the Rising. Do not grieve too sorely ... '

'They will take off his head,' the other announced with sad conviction. 'I heard them telling Himself the same – the Redcoat officers. He goes to London to die. The man Cumberland has sworn it.'

They sought to comfort the man, and presently sent him on his way back to his own country of Stratherrick, but neither of her guests at least believed that Caroline would prove right in this instance and the Fraser wrong. No actual tears were shed for Lovat, up there by the Allt Ruadh – yet a gloom temporarily descended upon them all. MacShimi had the power, always, of dominating any issue with which he was involved – as no doubt he would dominate even that London stage on which his scaffold would be built. That he had managed to keep a clever head upon his broad shoulders through four Risings and eighty as difficult years as the country had ever known, only made this present debacle the more ominous.

Less sure word of others for whom they cared more reached them from time to time, often very indirectly indeed. They heard first that Locheil, with Murray and Thriepland, had reached Glencoe, well south of Fort William. This seemed to indicate that the proposed linking with the northern regiments and the Frasers had been abandoned. Later this was confirmed; the Mackenzies no doubt wisely in the circumstances, had refused to venture out of their northern fastnesses, and Lovat had never so much as attempted to raise his clan. Doctor Archie was said to be still in Lochaber – but the next word as to his brother, Locheil, put him as far south as the MacGregor country of Balquhidder in Perthshire; what he was doing there was not explained. Murray, it seemed, had now left him, heading for his sister's house in Glen Lyon on his way south to Edinburgh in disguise, taking with him, it was said, a vast treasure in gold – although Duncan calculated that in fact it could not be more than about three thousand *louis*. Other chiefs and leaders seemed to have dispersed to the remotest corners of their domains.

These sad tidings had their effect on the young people on the watershed, inevitably – but less grievously so than might have been expected. There was unreality about it all, a lack of personal impact. Almost it was like a story that had been told – and one which required an actual effort of will to relate closely to themselves and their situation.

That was Caroline's fault – if a fault it was. Consciously or otherwise the young woman effected a kind of transfer of allegiance and interest on the part of her two self-appointed protectors, in some degree and at least temporarily, from the shattered Jacobite cause to her own more vital one. Any personable young female, in the circumstances, most likely would have been able to do something of the sort. But Caroline was not just a personable young female. In addition to her notable good looks, she was possessed of a sunny nature most aptly to match the sun-filled summer days. She was indeed a true daughter of the lightsome pastoral life of these high places, a laughing, lively vital presence that was the perfect antidote of the atmosphere of despair, treachery, corruption and folly that King James's cause now seemed to engender. When Caroline was happy, she was very happy indeed – infectiously so; conditions had to be very grievous wholly to quench that happiness. And despite the fact that she and her sisters were homeless refugees in the wilderness, her father was a fugitive somewhere unknown, her brother wounded and far away, and the long-term prospects for them all uncertain to a degree – despite all this, immediate conditions up there on the watershed between Arkaig and Morar that summer of 1746 were far from grievous. Was it her fault that she held both young men ever more securely in her gay and zestful thrall, to the undoubted detriment of their Prince's hold over their hearts and minds?

This supplanting thralldom did not however make the two

216

victims move any closer in brotherly comradeship, as to some extent had that which it superseded. Despite all Caroline's efforts, Duncan and Scotus drew no nearer to love and affection than are any pair of stiff-legged dogs circling the same single and desirable bone. The gold, and the need to co-operate in their private campaign, had indeed brought them together in some measure, with each at least perceiving and acknowledging the other's qualities – or some of them. The halcyon days of that summer did not enhance this appreciation; their mutual delight in the young woman did not cement the bond. They grew but the more critical of each other, in fact, the more suspect of each other's motives. As a sad example, Duncan judged the other's preoccupation with doctor's orders, his insistence that a damaged shoulder should be safeguarded against practically all movement for weeks on end, as no more than a device to keep Caroline's company to himself in most of the many energetic activities of shieling life; whereas Spanish John managed to perceive in Duncan's consequent helplessness only an underhand and unfair appeal to the girl's sympathies and an invitation to intimate ministrations.

Restricted in movement as Duncan was, the same did not apply to Scotus. He did not remain solidly at the shieling as the weeks passed, making occasional and clearly reluctant journeys north into his own country of Knoydart, on family and clan affairs. He did not speak much of these, but it appeared that he had a semi-invalid father alive, as well as a mother and younger brothers and sisters, whose affairs merited certain attentions from himself. Whatever he contrived to do for these relatives, and for the Scotus property generally, he never allowed it to keep him away from Glen Pean for very long. Duncan could have wished him to be more painstaking on his family's behalf. Always during these brief intervals the MacGregor opened up and flourished exceedingly with his eldest hostess – although any progress that he seemed to make in that direction tended with sad regularity to be lost whenever Spanish John returned, and Caroline welcomed him back with quite unnecessary and unsuitable warmth, like some prodigal.

Throughout that summer intelligence of a sort reached them with quite astonishing frequency and detail as to the Prince's wanderings – considering that the authorities were feverishly ransacking the land for him, searching as with a fine tooth comb, shouting aloud their vast reward for information as to his whereabouts. By the end of June they knew that he had managed to cross from the Outer Isles to Skye, and by mid-July that he had in fact come back to the mainland – even to such minutiae as that he had passed three nights at Mallaigbeg in North Morar, not twenty miles away as the crow flies. There had been some discussion then as to whether possibly Scotus should hurry thither – although it would be a long and dangerous journey for any but the said crows – to inform Charles of the gold situation. Whilst still debating this they heard that somehow the Prince had eluded the innumerable Government patrols, and was now down in Moidart. They heard nothing thereafter until, curiously enough, one day towards the end of the month, a Glen Dessary man of Doctor Archie's sent home to collect some cattle for beef, told them that His Highness had been for a week north again in Glen Moriston – surprising news, for that glen was some fifty or sixty miles north of Moidart. What Charles was doing there was not known. But to get there from Loch Shiel in Moidart, where they had last heard of him, he must have passed very close to their own Glen Pean – possibly as near as the head of Arkaig.

His captains did not know whether to be disappointed or relieved.

'What does it mean?' Caroline asked, by the cabin door. 'What is he doing? Why does he rush about the country so? To go down from Mallaig to Moidart, through Morar and Arisaig where the Redcoats are so busy, and then back north again to Moriston? Over so many miles of this hard and dangerous land. Punishing himself . . .'

'It may be just that keep moving he must,' Scotus said. 'That he dares not to stay in any one place or district for more than a day or so, lest the Redcoats catch up with him.'

'Yet it seems that he has been in Glen Moriston for a week. What does he there? Is he raising men? More soldiers?'

'Not in Moriston, no.' Spanish John shook his head. 'I fear not. The Grants there, though on the right side unlike most of their clan, are too few to form even a company. Anyway, the glen has been ravaged, devastated.'

'Nothing that we have heard says that the Prince is seeking to raise men,' Duncan observed sombrely. 'He keeps but two or three close companions, that is all. The Irishmen. Like a

218

hunted stag, he is – and no cornered boar. No further fight he seeks, I fear, but ... '

'And will you blame him for that?' Caroline demanded strongly, the loyal one, now. 'Can you wonder at it?'

'Perhaps, not. But ... he must know now the love that the Highlands bear him. Thousands must have known of his presence, in all these wanderings – yet not one has betrayed that presence for this great reward, it is clear. He must be aware by now of the gold, and of the arms and ammunition landed. Yet it is notable, is it not, that this area which he has come back to, and which he seems to circle around and traverse – it has Loch nan Uamh for its centre! Loch nan Uamh where first he landed, where the gold was brought, where the French ships were ordered to keep calling. Despite the fact that the Government ships are ever watching it closely. I fear ... I fear that, gold or none, guns and powder though we now have, even with the call to muster the regiments gone out anew – even so the Prince has but the one intention; to return to France as soon as ship can take him. To leave all. I had hoped ... ' He left the rest unsaid.

There was silence.

Scotus broke it at length, almost with a sigh. 'France is a fair country,' he said. 'Less harsh than this. Where a man is not always battling. *La belle France* – a fair and generous land.' He turned to look at Caroline. 'You would like it, my dear,' he said. 'You would be happy there – safe.'

The girl said nothing, and the silence returned, Duncan all but scowling.

Presently the young woman rose to her feet, and touched them both lightly. 'France is far away,' she said. 'But so, probably, are those wicked cows of ours! It is time that they were milked. And were we not to get a pannierful of flat stones from the lochan for the new fireplace? And whose turn is it to teach my hoydenish sisters their lessons?'

Thankfully, they returned to the life of the shielings, uncomplicated, essential. The hint, the shadow of change, however, was there for all to perceive.

CHAPTER 21

THE shadow of change at first grew only slowly, like a small cloud on the horizon. It was fully two weeks later before the electrifying rumour came up Arkaig that the Prince was back here again in the Cameron country – close at hand, indeed, near Achnasaul at the foot of the loch. Doctor Archie was there, it was said, with two of Locheil's sons and the Reverend John Cameron, Presbyterian minister of Fort William. Charles Edward had joined them. Duncan and Scotus could delay no longer.

The same night they made the journey down to the foot of the loch. Although still calling for circumspection, the venture was not so hazardous as formerly – otherwise of course neither the Doctor nor the Prince could have dared to linger in the vicinity. The scarlet-hued tide had largely ebbed – for the time being. The Government posts at Glen Dessary, Callich and Clunes House were lightly held and only sporadically aggressive. Nevertheless, the two men went cautiously, keeping to the uninhabited and rough side of the loch as far as the mouth of Glen Mallie, where a boat was hidden, and rowing therein across the dark water to Achnasaul.

It proved a fruitless journey. Charles and Doctor Archie were gone, both. Left the district that very day, they were told, for Cluny Macpherson's country in Badenoch.

Surprised, the young men returned whence they had come. What did this mean? Badenoch was a far cry from Loch nan Uamh. Cluny Macpherson, though his castle was burnt, was still able to maintain some sort of chiefly state in the inaccessible mountains around Ben Alder, his clan preserved from the worst ravages, his regiment more or less intact. Why had the Prince gone to Cluny? Could it be that Doctor Archie was persuading him to a more militant course, after all?

No word percolated through from distant Badenoch to answer such questions.

At the beginning of September, with the heather clothing all the mountains in its richest purple and the bracken of the lower slopes already turning golden, people from the west told them that ships were beginning to haunt the mouth of Loch nan

Uamh once more, having been glimpsed not a few times against the screen of islets that lay off it; whether French or English was not known – but the fact that they clearly took pains to hide themselves was probably significant.

It was a few evenings later, with the nights already commencing to creep in, that for the first time for months a gleam of red light from the east announced that the beacon on the hill by the lochside was lit again. Duncan and Scotus were almost indignant, wondering indeed whether the thing could have been discovered and lit mischievously by somebody or other. The Cameron on duty was not one of the brightest. It was in that frame of mind, and with only the three MacDonnell gillies, that less swiftly than formerly, they trotted off down the glen to investigate. Caroline had to call them back, to give them their masks.

Their watcher on duty met them by the lochside path a few hundred yards west of the hiding-place. It had been no false alarm, he assured them. Just as dusk was falling a fair-sized party of men, Highlanders, had arrived at the site of the hidden gold, and had gone straight to the position of the hoard that had been raided formerly. When, digging, they could find nothing there, they had begun to dig up the entire surrounding area. He had left them at this, and gone to light the beacon. When he had got back, they had been gone. They did not seem to know anything of the treasure in the burn itself; he had checked, on returning, that the gold was still there, undisturbed.

'Who were they?' Scotus demanded. 'Did you recognise any of them?'

The other shook his head. 'No. There was a tall swack fellow that gave the orders and swore with a pretty tongue. But, och, I could not be seeing right. There was ten of them, at least.'

'Ten? If they did not know about the gold in the burn, then they were not sent by Doctor Archie or Murray or MacLeod,' Duncan said. 'It was thievery again. But they have taken their time. Months, it is . . . '

'Perhaps Suiladale told them. Or Rory Cameron,' Scotus suggested. 'But they have gone, it seems. Empty-handed. You will not know which way they went, man?'

'I was up the hill there. Lighting the fire . . . '

'Aye. We should never have reduced it to a one-man watch.'

'So long as they are gone,' Scotus said. 'We have not the strength to deal with ten or more, anyway.'

They rode back to the shieling, since there seemed to be nothing else to do.

Belle Cameron came running to meet them, all but in hysterics, before ever they reached the cabin.

'They have taken them away!' she cried, sobbing brokenly. 'They have taken them — Caroline and Anne!'

'What?'

'Who have taken them? What do you mean, child?'

'The men. Horrible men. They came and took away Caroline. And Anne. They were horrible. Cruel. They hurt my arm . . . '

'*Dia* – you mean the Redcoats?' Scotus actually shook her, in his agitation.

'No, not Redcoats. Just ordinary men.'

'Our own people? Highlanders?'

'Yes.'

'Who were they? Do you know?'

'I do not know. They twisted our arms . . . '

'Belle – it will be all right,' Duncan told her earnestly. 'We will find them for you – get them back. Never fear. Just think. Carefully. When was this?'

'I do not know. A long time. You have been long, long. If you had been here, they would not have done it.'

'Perhaps not. I am sorry, Belle. How many were there?'

'I do not know. Many . . . '

'Ten, perhaps?'

'Yes. At first they were nice. They asked for food. They said could they rest here. We gave them food. They asked where you were . . . '

'They did? Us – by name? They knew about us?'

'Yes. They said they were friends of yours. Then they asked us where the gold was hidden. They said that you had stolen it!'

'Ah! So that is it.'

'When we would not tell them, they got very angry. They said that you were thieves, stealing the Prince's money. And that we were very wicked to be helping you. They said that they would have to take Caroline and Anne away.'

'God's curse on them, the vile hypocrites!' Scotus declared.

'But you escaped?' Duncan put to her. 'Why did they not take you away, too, Belle?'

'I was to wait here and tell you. That is what he said. I was to wait here – not to move. Not to go and tell anyone. Until you came back. Or . . . or he would hurt my sisters. I thought that you were never coming . . . ' She was sobbing again.

'And what were you to say to us? When you saw us?' Duncan asked, putting his arm around her. 'Think now, Belle. Something he would have you tell us, to be sure?'

The girl gulped. 'To go to him at our house – our old house. Alone. He said that you must go alone. And unarmed, he said, too. Or . . . or Caroline . . . '

'Glenpean House? To take them there!' Scotus interjected. 'The dastard!'

'Remember, it is alone that you must go,' the girl insisted, clutching at Duncan's wrist. 'He twisted my arm. So that I would not forget it, he said. He was horrible. In that mask . . . '

'Mask? You mean that this man was wearing a mask? Like ours . . . ?'

'Yes. Like the ones we made. Only the one of them. This tall man.'

'Masks!' Scotus said. 'This links them surely with Suiladale or Cameron. They will have been told of our masks. It could be one of them, again.'

'But someone who knew of us here. At this shieling. That brings it still closer.'

'Aye. But what matters it who it is? They have us, and know it. We can only do as they say. Go down to Glenpean House.'

'You have to go alone,' Belle reiterated urgently.

'Yes, yes – we will go alone.' Duncan frowned. 'The devil chose well. He knows what he is doing. The ruined house, out there in the open at the head of the loch. There is no cover near it, to hide any approach. We cannot trick him there, with more men in hiding. All round is clear, open.'

'We can only go there. Hear what he has to say . . . '

'You know what that will be! There is no doubt what the man will say to us.'

The other nodded unhappily. 'We have no choice,' he said.

They left Belle with the gillies, torn between desire to accompany them and see her sisters, and fear of the threat that

223

had been impressed upon her as to the consequences of the men not being alone. After only a brief debate, they left their arms behind also.

Practically wordless the two men rode together down Glen Pean once more, thinking their own thoughts. Was this to be the end of their vigil, their long struggle on behalf of the Prince? Were they trapped – trapped in their most fatal weakness? Had this devil taken their measure?

Where the mouth of the glen opened to the wide levels at the head of Arkaig, they paused. Dimly they could perceive where the roofless house stood. No light gleamed there – only the faint glimmer of once-white walls.

Grimly, still silent, they went on across the flats.

Presently Scotus spoke, low-voiced. 'There are men creeping along behind us, I think,' he said.

'I know it. Three of them, there are. He takes his precautions, this one.'

'I do not like it.'

'Did you think to like it? We can do nothing but go on.'

As they neared the house, other men materialised on either side of them, silent, menacing.

They were almost at the former front door, now gaping black, when a voice from the shadows on the right, that had been the byre and barn, halted them.

'I am glad that you have come, gentlemen. And so promptly. So, I feel sure, are the ladies. We knew that you would, of course.' Ridiculously affable and normal that voice sounded, in the circumstances. There was something familiar about it, too, undoubtedly – even although its owner might well be seeking to disguise it somewhat.

'Who are you, damn you?' Scotus burst out. 'Who in Heaven's name could behave this way?'

'John!' Caroline's voice rang out, from within the ruined barn.

'We are here, Caroline! We will get you out of this scoundrel's hand, never fear!'

'Excellent sentiments, my friend – save for the epithet. That is quite undeserved, I swear!' The speaker stepped out from the deeper shadows, a tall man, muffled in plaids, but obviously lean and lanky. A mask made only a black smudge of his face.

224

'The epithet is entirely just, James Mor!' Duncan said quietly. 'God forgive Clan Alpine for producing you!'

There was a gasp from Scotus, and silence from the masked man. Caroline's cry rose again, with Anne's joining it.

'Duncan! Duncan!'

'Fear nothing, *mo caraidh*. All will be well. I apologise to you for this man that I must call cousin.'

James Mor was clearly put out. 'You have sharp ears, Cousin – to match your tongue!' he said. 'But you would be well advised, see you, to keep that tongue in check. You and your friends are not in a happy position, I would remind you.'

'In the company of you and your bullies, I agree!'

'Good. Go on agreeing, Cousin, and you will be wise. First of all, you had better dismount.' James Mor snapped a word or two aside, and gillies leapt out to grasp the heads of both garrons. Naked steel gleamed in the gloom.

Since they had by no means come here to bolt, the younger men got down.

'If Miss Cameron and her sister are in any way hurt, Mac-Gregor,' Scotus said through gritted teeth, – 'as God is my witness, you will die for it. I will make it my life and purpose . . . '

'Tush, man – spare us the dramatics! They are not in the least hurt, either of them. We have been having a most interesting conversation. Moreover, it is in your power to see that no hurt nor yet distress comes to them hereafter . . . '

'You to speak of distress – who have dragged them here, of all places, to their ravished home!' Duncan charged him. 'You could have spared them that. Your own home was ravished once, you'll mind.' Thirty-three years before, with James a child, Inversnaid House had been burned over his head, his mother raped while it burned, and his absent father Rob Roy made outlaw. 'Your father would not have done this, James Mor.'

'My father had his own methods,' the other returned briefly. 'In an important matter like this, in the Prince's service, I cannot afford to be over-squeamish, over-delicate.'

'The Prince's service! *You* talk of that?'

'To be sure. What else? I am an aide-de-camp to His Highness. Have you forgotten?'

Duncan swallowed. 'This is . . . this is beyond belief! I

225

would not have thought that you would have as much as dared to mention the Prince's name!'

'Why not? For yourselves, I can understand some such hesitation. But *I* have not stolen the Prince's gold! On the contrary – to recover it is my mission. On His Highness's behalf.'

'*Dia* – what foolishness is this?' Scotus cried. '*We* have not stolen the gold, man . . .'

'My information, sir, is that you have! Excellent and circumstantial information. Only, unfortunately, lacking in details as to where you have deposited the money. Hence these, er, dispositions.'

'But it is not true, MacGregor! You have it all awry. We have been guarding it, nothing more. For the Prince.'

'A likely story! Is it worth while, think you, to insult my intelligence, MacDonnell? Come, my friends – let us be frank. You have taken the money. Many thousands of gold *louis*. Since you still linger on in these parts – in delightful company, I grant you – it seems clear that you have hidden it again somewhere in the area. Where you can keep an eye on it, no doubt? I intend to find out where.'

'You have it all wrong,' Scotus insisted. 'You are mistaken, sir, entirely.'

'I told him that,' Caroline's voice came again, from the barn. 'I told him that you had not stolen it. He will not believe me . . .'

'I do not think that he is mistaken, at all,' Duncan said quietly. 'I believe that James Mor knows the true situation very well! It but suits him to pretend otherwise.'

'The true situation, as you term it, Cousin, unfortunately is all too clear. You cannot deny, I think, if you have any truth in you, that you have removed the gold – for whatever purposes you may see fit to claim. Do you?'

No one answered him.

'Exactly.' James Mor nodded. 'You do not deny it. Now, where have you hid it? For it must be returned to His Highness.'

'That was our intention,' Duncan said shortly.

His cousin smiled. 'Forgive me if I seem to doubt your word, Duncan *a graidh*. But I prefer to do the handing back myself.'

'Liar!'

'Come, now – that is no way to speak. Especially to your

senior officer! You will tell me, in the end. You would not wish to cause the Misses Cameron further . . . inconvenience?'

'So there we have it? Caroline and Anne Cameron, it is, for the gold!'

'I' faith – you are crude, Duncan man! Say that I must use all means that I may, in the Prince's cause. That is, if you refuse to obey the commands of your senior officer! I am, after all, major in the regiment of which you are only captain! And I am speaking in the name of the Captain-General.'

'I doubt it. I do not suppose that you have seen His Highness since you refused to follow him after Culloden.'

'How suspicious and ill-natured you are, Duncan. I spent two days with him, but a week ago, in Cluny's refuge on Ben Alder. When he sent me on this mission. So important to his cause.'

'His cause!' Duncan snorted. 'Your own, do you not mean?'

'My cause and the Prince's are, h'm, inextricably bound up!' the other returned, smiling beneath his mask. 'I trust that you can say the same?'

'Oh, enough of this foolery!'

'Aye – enough, as you say! Foolery is right.' Suddenly James Mor changed his whole attitude. Grimly authoritative, his voice hardened. 'Think you that I brought you here to listen to your childish insults? You, who are thieves, rogues, traitors? I tell you, I should arrest you here and now, and take you before the Prince. He is not so far away. To meet the fate that you richly deserve. Only . . . the money is all important. Charles must have it. At once. And for these girls' sake, who in their foolishness have aided you, I will be merciful. Also, for the good name of our clan. Take me to the place where you have the gold hidden, now – and when it is safely in my hands you, and they, may go free. And I will endeavour to keep your complicity from the Prince's knowledge.'

'Ah! So His Highness does not already know of our wicked theft, after all? He did not send you to us, on this mission of yours?' Duncan said quickly.

'The mission, of course, was in general terms. Do you take me to the gold?'

'If we refuse . . . ?' Scotus began.

'You will not refuse. Not if you value the well-being of these young women!'

227

There was silence then, for moments on end. All recognised that wordy sparring was over.

Into the hush, plain for all to hear, came the hurried thud-thud of running footfalls.

Every head turned, as a gillie came long-strided. Straight up to Major MacGregor he ran.

'Men coming, Seumas Mor,' he gasped out. 'Many men. Mounted.'

'Damnation! So – so you think to cozen me, you young fools! You would play tricks on James Mor MacGregor? I told you – alone! Christ God – it will be the worse for you! For all of you!'

'No – it is not these, I think, Seumas Mor,' the runner panted. 'They come from beyond. From the other side. From up the loch.'

'*Dia* – Redcoats?'

'No, not Redcoats. They ride garrons and wear bonnets.'

'Are they after coming this way?'

'Yes. And not far, they are, at all.'

'Quick, then! Inside, all of you.' A pistol had appeared in James Mor's hand, and with it he gestured at the two younger men. 'In, I say. And not a sound out of you. Or you will make no more!'

A gillie guarding the doorway stood aside to let them be hustled into the barn. Scotus was first inside, and Caroline threw herself into his arms. Anne did as much for Duncan, babbling incoherences.

'Quiet, I tell you!' James Mor snapped. Four or five gillies had followed him into the roofless building. 'Dirks,' he jerked at these. 'Hold them fast. See that they make no sound.' He himself grabbed Caroline, and another gripped her sister.

So they waited, a dirk-point tickling the throats of each of the captains.

If the reported party had come from the north side of the loch, they would be apt to pass fairly close to the burned house – but there was no reason to expect them to actually come and look inside. Burned houses were all too common in the Highlands in 1746.

Presently they could hear the beat of hooves, many hooves. Then the clink of accoutrements, and finally the faint murmur of voices.

In the ruined barn the tension was acute. It was the same barn, some corner of Duncan MacGregor's mind recollected, that Charles Edward had inspected with a view to couching in five months before.

The riders were close. How close? It was hard to judge. Would they come – would they stop at the house?

They did stop. At least, the beat of the hooves stopped. But apparently a little way off, still. The voices continued. They must be looking towards the buildings, probably speaking of them. Then the hoof-beats recommenced. Only moments were required to establish that they receded, that the party was moving away.

Caroline screamed. 'Help!' she yelled abruptly. She managed another 'Help!' before James Mor's hand clamped over her mouth. The others heard the thud of his fist striking her, as he spat out an oath.

Anne cried out, before she choked to a whimpered gasping. Duncan, jerking forward, groaned against the agony of the arm twisted behind his back, and felt sharp steel bite at his throat. Scotus too began to struggle – until he sank part-unconscious from a vicious blow with the haft of a dirk.

Now the voices outside were upraised. Clearly Caroline's cries had been heard. Men were dismounting, questions and warnings being shouted.

James Mor MacGregor accepted the situation forthwith. He barked swift orders to his gillies. Duncan suddenly had a bare knee brought up into the pit of his stomach, and he was thrown down doubled-up, winded, upon a pile of rotting bog-hay. Scotus was already lying on the cobbled floor, moaning faintly. Leaving the girls, their captors hurried out through the doorless gap.

Sobbing, Caroline called and called into the night.

Men appeared, after a little, in the doorway, cautiously peering, pistols and drawn swords in their hands, kilted men. To them the girls gasped and gabbled frantically.

'Save us – if it isn't Caroline! And Anne, too!' a well-remembered voice exclaimed. '*Diabhol* – what do you here, my dears? Though och – maybe I should not be asking that, and it your own house. But . . . see you, it is all right. All right. Fine, now – fine. It is just my own self. Archie. Doctor Archie. Och, quietly, quietly now. What is the matter, at all?'

From his hay Duncan sought and struggled for breath to form words – and could only wheeze foolishly.

Other men crowded at the doorway, questioning. Then all fell silent as another voice spoke, an authoritative though melodiously accented voice even in its present urgency.

'Who have you got there, Doctor? Some men seem to be riding off in a damned hurry. From some bushes, down by the lake. *Mon Dieu* – what sort of *tapage* is this? The women – are they still here, Doctor?'

'Yes. It is Glenpean's daughters, Your Highness,' Doctor Archie Cameron said. 'Two of them. Miss Caroline and Anne. There seems to be someone else here, also. Sir. But it is curst dark . . .'

CHAPTER 22

DUNCAN MACGREGOR, still somewhat bent, and breathing with difficulty, stared round the company. It was dark, admittedly, and he was probably not at his most acute; nevertheless, he ought surely to know his own Prince?

Caroline Cameron seemed to be suffering under a similar handicap. 'You say . . . that His Highness is here, Doctor Archie?' she said unevenly.

'Why yes, Miss Cameron – your devoted servant, as ever. I rejoice that, for once it seems, we are of some little service. It has been my lot this long while to take all and give nothing, I fear.'

One man had stepped out from the group outside the barn – and it was at the words only and certainly not the appearance that Caroline, distrait as she was, sank in an unsteady curtsey. Duncan only stared. Perhaps he was sufficiently bowed already.

Charles Stuart indeed was barely recognisable as the gracefully handsome and so notably princely figure of five months before. Bearded, fair hair shaggy and long, topped by a plain bonnet, muffled in old plaid, legs bare to feet that were shod only in rough rawhide brogans, he seemed less tall, as well as lacking all elegance – probably because he had actually broadened and developed muscle out of the grim life of a hunted cateran. Only the voice was the same – and perhaps the smile, though the night's gloom left that in doubt.

'His Highness always overlooks the fact that he gives us what no other can do – faith and renewed courage,' the Doctor said. 'And humility too – or he ought to – in face of sufferings and indignities borne without complaint.'

The girl was speechless.

Duncan found words. 'Highness,' he croaked. 'It is good to see you. My duty. My homage. And my thanks. You came . . . most aptly!'

'My good Captain! Are you recovered? Better? Your shoulder, was it not? The Doctor tells me that you were evilly treated. Shamefully. On my behalf.'

'That was nothing, sir. A cracked bone, no more. Others gave a deal more than that!'

'It is to your honour to put it so, friend.'

'My honour, sir!' Duncan drew a quivering breath. 'My honour was in grave danger this night, I fear. 'Fore God, it was saved only by a hair's breadth, I think. And by your coming.'

'Aye – what is this, man?' Doctor Archie intervened. 'What was to do here? I have not fathomed it yet. Who rode away, yonder? And why?'

A chorus of supporting questions came from the others there.

'That was James Mor. My cousin. Major MacGregor,' Duncan jerked. His brows came down like a black bar across his features. 'What he was about, I had rather some other told you.'

'James?' the Prince exclaimed. 'James left us only a day or two since. Why should he ride off thus . . . ?'

'I will tell you.' Scotus had appeared drunkenly within the barn doorway, leaning against the burnt doorpost for support, his head held between his hands. 'He ran, curse him, because he is a coward who fights women – as well as a thieving scoundrel and a traitor!'

'*Nom de Dieu* – who is this man, who dares to miscall a friend and officer of mine?' Charles demanded.

'He is John MacDonnell of Scotus, sir. A captain in the Irelanda Regiment of Spain,' Duncan told him.

'My cousin, that I told you of, Highness.' That was Loch-garry, standing beside the Prince. 'Spanish John.'

'Ah. I am sorry.' Charles quickly relented. 'His uncle died gallantly for my cause. Scotus, yes. I have heard of you, sir. But . . . you must not miscall my good friend Major James so.'

'Yet what I said is truth, Highness,' Scotus insisted. 'And he is no true friend of yours, I fear!'

'Allow me to know my own friends, sir! Major MacGregor is on a special mission for myself. He cannot have realised who it was who came, or he would never have gone away thus. It is most unfortunate.'

Duncan bit his lip. 'A special mission, you say, sir? About the money? The gold?'

'It was, yes. Much of it has been stolen, unhappily. James believed that he might be able to recover some of it at least, for me.'

Duncan, looking from Caroline to Scotus, was silent.

'Highness – not all men esteem James Mor quite as highly as you do, I fear,' Doctor Archie put in. 'I have told you. Perhaps we are prejudiced. But . . . the matter need not concern us at the moment, need it? We should move from here. This is not the safest place to linger. We are too near the posts at Callich and in my own glen . . .'

'Very well, Doctor. That is probably wise.' The Prince sighed. 'It is sad to see this hospitable house so. We shall move on. Up to yonder cabin of Miss Cameron's belike. Where we stayed once before. A good secure place . . .'

Duncan almost objected. But what point was there in assert-ing that, since James Mor knew of the Allt Ruadh shieling, it was now unsafe? Clearly the Prince would not accept that as any valid objection. He held his peace.

Their late captors having apparently gone off with their two garrons, Duncan and Scotus, like the two girls, were mounted behind members of the Prince's party – which included, as well as Lochgarry, Colonel John Roy Stewart, Captain O'Neil and one of Locheil's sons. Locheil himself, it seemed, with a number of other Camerons, including the girls' father, was not far away to the south somewhere, travelling independently. Making for Borrodale. There was no sign of O'Sullivan.

In this strange fashion they returned to the Allt Ruadh and the waiting, anxious Belle.

Once again, despite jangled feelings and emotional exhaustion, it fell to Caroline to prepare food and drink for the party, aided at least in theory, by her sisters and Duncan. Scotus, still suffering from the blow he had received, was taking his turn at being nursed.

Duncan had great difficulty in gaining the Prince's private ear. Felix O'Neil in especial never seemed to leave his side. He had indeed become Charles's closest companion, throughout all his wanderings. O'Sullivan, it appeared, had become detached from the Prince by accident just before the latter sailed from the Long Island for Skye, and was now thought to be out of the country. Ned Burke was still in faithful attendance. Duncan had never got on well with O'Neil and could not now believe that he was the best influence to be bearing on Charles – especially where Scottish affairs were concerned.

He did at last gain the Prince's more or less undivided attention – but even so, Doctor Archie was with him. Indeed, it was the Doctor's declaration that he wanted to examine his erstwhile patient's shoulder, and Caroline's seizing of the chance to have Scotus's sore head examined also, that created the opportunity. The five of them, with the two younger girls, had the cabin to themselves for the moment.

Duncan interrupted the Doctor's remarks about his excellent recovery. 'Your Royal Highness,' he said urgently. 'About the gold. It is a bad, a shameful business. But I did what I could. As did Scotus, here. We can now render some account of our stewardship.'

'Ah, yes – the gold. *Dieu de Dieu* – that gold!' Charles was scratching himself in less than royal fashion. 'I must confess, my friends, that I am completely at a loss over all this money. The more I hear of it, the more complicated it becomes! To which gold is it that you refer, Captain? There is so much, so many consignments. The good Doctor has, for instance, two consignments hidden away for me. Large sums. How much in these, Doctor?'

'Twenty-seven thousand *louis d'ors*, sir.'

'Less one thousand and fifty,' Duncan amended.

'Eh? What did you say, MacGregor? *Less* . . . ? What do

you mean, man?' The Doctor looked startled.

'H'mmm. The fact is, Doctor, that one thousand and fifty of the gold pieces that you buried opposite Callich there, are now down in the lochan below us here!'

'My ·God!' The other stared. 'You mean . . . you *took* it? Removed it?'

'Yes. For good reason. The first fifty we retrieved half-way up Glen Mallie – from one of Clanranald's people. The thousand we took later, when we found another raider at your hoard – one of your own Camerons . . . '

'I don't believe it!'

'It is true . . . '

Scotus took up the story. 'We put it all in the burn – the rest of your hoard. From where it had been buried in the ground. All except a one-thousand bag which we could not hide. It would have shown. In the water . . . '

'But sink me – what does it all mean?' the Doctor cried. 'How did you know that the gold was there? Who told you? And these others? It is damnable . . . !'

Scotus eyed his finger-nails. 'I, er, followed you, sir. The night that you hid it all. From Murlaggan. As did others . . . '

'Damn you – you did? Follow us? Spied on us? A pest – you admit it, you scoundrel? Of all the . . . '

'Doctor Archie!' Caroline exclaimed. 'John is not well. His head is hurt. You must not berate him. All he did was for the best. In His Highness's service.'

'My service is indeed more complicated than I knew!' Charles said, cracking a louse between his thumb-nails. 'Proceed, sir – I am fascinated.'

'We had already had experience of what might well happen,' Duncan inserted. 'Scotus only took due precautions . . . '

'Precautions, i' faith! Is that what you call it?'

'It was as I feared, Doctor. Others followed you also. Saw where you buried the gold. I glimpsed them myself. So we set a day-and-night watch on the place. To guard it.' Scotus shrugged. 'Only the second night we made our first catch.'

'I was for digging up all your store, Doctor,' Duncan told him. 'All the fifteen thousand there. To bring it here to our own hoard. For safety. But these others would not have that . . . '

'Your own hoard?' Charles interposed. 'What was that?'

'It was money we had brought from Borrodale, Highness. Five thousand *louis*.'

'*Ma foi!* Five thousand!'

'From Borrodale? *Dia* – then it was you who stole it! At the landing?' Doctor Archie challenged, staring.

'No, no. We recovered it, only.'

'You mean, from the Irishman? O'Rourke, was it?'

'No. That was different. That was only seven hundred. We recovered that also.'

The Prince groaned, and halted in his diligent search for vermin. '*Nom de Nom* – have mercy! I am lost! Confounded quite! Gently, my friends, if you would leave me my poor reason. Fifteen thousand! Five thousand! Seven hundred, was it? Fifty . . . !'

'There is forty also, that my father took for the cattle-beasts,' Caroline put in. 'Do not forget that.'

Charles waved a hand limply. 'Captain,' he said to Duncan. 'If my memory serves me aright, was it not to secure a sum that my brother York sent me that I charged you? Alas, with all your figures and thousands I have now forgot how much it was. All this money which, had it but come a month or two before, could have transformed our cause . . . '

'Aye. That is the sorrow of it. Such *was* the mission you gave me, sir. But that money we have not got, I fear . . . '

'It was five hundred, sir. At least, His Highness of York sent two thousand. But it was stolen from me. At Loch Broom. All of it,' Scotus confessed. 'I regained five hundred only. And that the Secretary Murray took – though we sought to keep it from him.'

'As he did much else,' Doctor Archie agreed. 'He has four thousand away with him now, at least. That is why I put the other twelve thousand in the loch, near Achnacarry . . . '

'A truce! A truce!' Charles insisted. 'This gets worse and worse, I vow! I am dizzy with it all. I have no head for such matters. I was telling James MacGregor that, but two nights ago. He was talking in the same way. You are all as bad as bankers, I swear.'

'What money was it that my cousin was searching for, Highness?' Duncan asked. 'This mission you spoke of?'

'It was . . . *parbleu*, I cannot tell now which of them it was! You have me addled. Doctor – do you recollect?'

'Indeed, yes. It was the original five thousand, amissing at Borrodale. At the landing. He said that he believed that he could find it. Perhaps he knew that you two had it?'

Duncan and Scotus exchanged glances. 'I think, not,' the former said.

'It was *your* hoard, Doctor, that he sought. That he was digging for, when first we came on him,' Scotus informed.

'Mine? By the loch? Damme – is this true? You are sure, man?'

'Aye. He dug up all around the spot. But he got nothing. For he did not know about what was hidden in the burn near by. None of them can have seen that. And *we* had dug up the buried lots and put all with the rest in the burn. Save this one thousand . . . '

'You did that?'

'For safety's sake.'

The Doctor shook his head. 'You think, then, that James Mor meant to steal it? Or some of it?'

'But of course . . . '

'Silence! I will not hear of it!' the Prince cried. 'I told you – I will not hear my friends traduced so. James, no doubt, learned of this, this hoard, hidden by somebody, and sought only to secure it for me. He would not know that it was the Doctor who had put it there. He would think it stolen, like the rest. For the last time, gentlemen, I ask you, I *command* you, to have done with such talk. Such spleen and backbiting amongst my officers and friends is shameful and ill becomes you. There has been overmuch of it, the good God knows.'

There was silence in the cabin for a few moments. Belle had fallen asleep where she crouched.

Charles relented. He always relented where personal matters were concerned, stubborn as he could be otherwise. 'But . . . it seems that you have been very good, true guardians of my interests, *mes braves*. I am confused still, and do not understand how you gained it all. But how much, in all, have you hidden away for me?'

'Six thousand seven hundred and ninety *louis d'ors*, sir,' Duncan told him. 'But one thousand and fifty of it really is part of the Doctor's hoard. We can have it up for you in an hour. Less.'

'Six thousand – here! You have done nobly indeed, my

friends. I am grateful to you. With such a sum, much may be done. And with the Doctor's added . . . How much have you now, all told, Doctor?'

'The Devil knows – or perhaps these young men! For I do not,' the older man said. 'With Sawny MacLeod I hid twenty-seven thousand. But what may be left . . . ?'

'We know nothing of the twelve thousand down near Achnacarry,' Duncan declared. 'But there is still thirteen thousand nine hundred and fifty *louis* down in the burn opposite Callich.'

'So-o-o! Altogether I can put my hands on nearly thirty-three thousand,' the Prince said. 'A goodly sum! A handsome sum!'

'Out of forty-two thousand,' Duncan reminded.

'More,' the Doctor averred. 'For old Sheridan had some other money which was landed on Barra, earlier. A deal of it. Murray took it likewise, I am told.'

'No doubt Murray will return all this to me in due course, in France,' Charles said, and yawned.

Duncan's breath caught in his throat. 'You . . . are going . . . to France, sir?' he got out. 'After all?'

'Why yes, Captain. That is why we are here. We are on our way to Borrodale again. Two French ships are waiting off Loch nan Uamh to take me. At last.'

'But . . . but, Highness – what of the Cause? What of the Rising? If you go . . . ?'

'The Rising, alas, is over. This Rising. The Cause remains – but it must await another day, friend.'

'Another day, yes. But not years, Sir! As it will be if you go away, now. If you return to France. Years!'

'A little time it may take, yes. But I will come back . . . '

'But now is the time, Highness – now!' Duncan was leaning forward urgently. 'With all this money. And the arms and ammunition in the caves at Borrodale. Think what it means – the difference it makes. All the land knows of this treasure, now – knows that you are rich. Use it. Use it as a magnet – not for thieves but for soldiers. Buy what you could not win. The men are still in the glens. The clans are still there. The North is untouched. The people still love you – as witness that none have betrayed you all these months. Raise your standard again. Call on the chiefs once more – and those who will not send men for love of you, will send them for your gold! *Dia* – a guinea a man, and you will have an army greater than anything that Cumberland can field against you! Think of those who have held back. Think of Sleat. Think of the Laird of MacLeod. Offer those two hucksters a thousand guineas for a thousand men, and you will have them in a week!' In his eagerness, Duncan had risen to his feet. 'That is what the gold could do. That is what we have guarded and saved it for – not to pay out in doles and compensations. Or to take back to France!'

The Prince looked up at him sadly, and shook his head. 'It is too late, Duncan – too late,' he said. 'I esteem your devotion, your fervour. But that time is past. The money came too late.'

'Not so, sir. Never say it, with you to lead and hearten us. And already many of Cumberland's best troops have been withdrawn. Sent to the Netherlands. It is the scum that is left. I have it from one of the Elector's own officers . . .'

'Think you that I have not weighed all this? These matters are less simple than you think, Duncan.'

'But . . .'

'Your Royal Highness,' Caroline put in, only superficially hesitant. 'Forgive me for speaking. But . . . if not for the Rising itself, for the fighting – think of the people. All the ordinary folk of the glens. Stay, for their sakes. Our sakes. If you remain, there will still be fight in Scotland, still spirit. The Government will not dare oppress the folk too strongly – not with men and arms and money behind you. But if you go – all is lost. Everyone will know it. And the people will pay. The glens will be worse harried than ever, the savagery unending. With no spark of revolt left, the Redcoats will not be held back . . .'

'You are wrong, wrong!' Charles asserted. '*Au contraire*, when I am gone, and there is peace at last, the Government's ferocities will relax. The fire will be out – they need not beat it so. I am sorry, Miss Cameron – but it is better so. Believe me, I have considered well.'

'The fire will be out! And there you have it!' Duncan declared bitterly. 'The fire is not yet out – not while there are thousands of hands to draw sword for you in the heather! But you will put it out, your own self, if you go . . .'

'Enough, man – enough!' Prince Charles started up. 'You forget yourself! I will not be harassed so, browbeaten! Let me hear no more of it. I am weary of it all. Doctor Cameron was at the same talk, but yesterday. You cannot see beyond these Highland hills; I must take the longer view. Enough, then – my mind is made up. Now – it is time that we were on our way. We have lingered too long already . . . '

'You are not staying, sir? Sleeping here?' Caroline cried.

'No. For many a month now the night has been my time for travelling, the day for sleeping. There is much of this night left to us yet – and we must reach Loch nan Uamh by to-morrow's eve. We press on, Mademoiselle.'

'And the gold, sir? What of the gold?' That was Scotus.

'Ah, yes – the gold. I shall take some of it. Enough for present needs. To see us to France. So that we do not land looking like savages. The French, my friends, would not like that! *Mon Dieu* – how I long for clean linen once more. Respectable clothes. And an end to these devilish lice! Save me – I had not so much as seen a louse before I came to your Highlands! And look at me now – eighty I caught on me but yesterday! Eighty! 'Pon my soul, I am become as good a counter of lice as some of you of gold pieces!' Charles paused. 'Now, how much do I need to take with me?'

None of his hearers sought to make that calculation for him.

Charles seemed to become aware of their quiet, their reserve, for he looked round them all, and smiled, kindly again, no longer haughty. It was to Duncan MacGregor that he spoke.

'I think that two thousand should serve. Or perhaps three – for there will be not a few of us going, and not a groat between us all. It will not do to descend on *la belle France* like whipped curs. That will not help my father's cause. Make it three thousand. But . . . take it from the good Doctor's store, Duncan. Not from yours. *Parbleu* – think you that I cannot see what is in your eyes, man, even in this dark? It was not for such that you fought and guarded it, eh? Not for dressing up a parade of exiles, that you hid and stored and saved the gold! I know it, friend – I know it. So save your own hoard, Duncan, and guard it still. Hold it intact. Safe for me, until I come back. That is my charge for you. Keep it secure, as an earnest of my return. For the purpose for which it was sent, and for which you have guarded it so well – for the winning back of my father's throne. I will come back for it, one day – and expect it at your hand. Six thousand . . . ?'

'. . . seven hundred and ninety *louis d'ors.*' Duncan finished for him.

'*Bon!* As for the rest, guard it also. For the Doctor. He and Cluny Macpherson will use it as they see fit, for the furtherance of my cause meantime, the keeping alight of the flame of resistance, the aiding of those whose need is great and who have lost all for me. You will guard it until such time as they tell you. You understand, Captain? Less the three thousand that I take with me. But not your own store. That you hold direct of me. Till I come for it again. As all here are witnesses.' The Prince held out his hand.

Duncan, blinking, wordless, bent to kiss it, but Charles shook his head.

'Not so,' he said. 'It is a compact, a bargain. To shake *your* hand. The hand of a brave and honest man! It is my privilege, sir. You would not deny me?'

There, in the darkened cabin, they shook hands.

'Now, my friends – we ride. Go you to the Doctor's gold, Duncan, wherever it is, and bring three thousand *louis* after me. For my journey. We have not time to wait. We make for Borrodale, by the most secret way, and will not delay. You will require to ride fast, to catch up with us. You have it?'

'Yes, sir.' Duncan still was not trusting himself with words.

'*Eh bien.* Then, Miss Cameron, it is goodbye. And my deep gratitude for many things. For all that you have suffered, too, and lost, on my behalf . . . '

'Not yet, Highness,' the girl said, stiffly for her, jerkily. 'I also will see you again. At Borrodale.'

'You will? You should save yourself the weary journey, my dear.'

'I will be there,' she said.

'Very well. As you will. Would that I deserved all the devotion of my friends! Come then, Doctor – let us be going. *Allons.*'

'Aye, Highness.'

CHAPTER 23

THE eight garrons were driven nearly to exhaustion before Caroline, keen-eyed however tired, perceived the faint drift of blue woodsmoke rising above the lemon-yellow of a clump of scrub birch ahead, and pointed.

It was mid-afternoon. It had taken the six of them – the girl, Duncan, Scotus and his three MacDonnell gillies, with two led horses – until now to come up with the Prince's party. Charles had wasted no time.

They were down near the head of Glen Beasdale, only a few miles from Borrodale and the sea at Loch nan Uamh. They had thought to have caught up with the others before this.

Without comment, they rode on towards the trees.

At the edge of the birches a hidden Cameron sentry recognised them and let them past. They found the Prince and most of his companions asleep, in a grassy hollow amongst the trees and bracken.

Doctor Archie welcomed them, signing them to be quiet, not to wake the sleepers. They needed and deserved their rest, he said – as no doubt did the newcomers themselves. It was planned to move again, over the last stage of their journey, in a couple of hours or so, in order to arrive at Borrodale as darkness came down. Was all well, he added? The money safe?

'Three thousand on the ponies, there,' Duncan nodded, yawning. 'Ten thousand nine hundred and fifty still in the burn beside Arkaig.'

Scotus said nothing. He had been notably and unusually quiet all that day. As indeed had Caroline. There had been a strange tension about them all.

The Doctor did not require to urge them to sleep; all were nodding almost as soon as they sat down. They had been riding for fifteen hours, with no sleep the night before.

They were not permitted to slumber for long, however. A sudden commotion aroused not only themselves but the entire company. Only one man created it – but his coming was sufficiently emphatic and dramatic to transform the slumbrous scene. It was James Mor MacGregor, alone, on foot, gasping for breath, but vehement.

'Where is His Highness?' he cried out, a sentry still running doubtfully at his back. 'God's death – there is danger! Danger, I tell you! You must get the Prince away. Quickly. Away from here . . .'

All around, men stared at him owlishly.

'Quickly – damn you for fools!' he shouted. 'Would you have him captured? Redcoats are a bare mile away! A squadron of them. And if I could see your smoke, they can!'

The camp came to life like an ant-hill disturbed.

'James!' the Prince exclaimed, jumping up. 'What is this? Where have you come from? Redcoats, you say? Where? What is this?'

'Half a squadron of dragoons, Highness – coming this way. Down the glen, there. Another half-squadron at Borrodale.'

'*Diable!* Dragoons? We dare not encounter dragoons . . .'

'No. You must be off. At once. And unseen. For they are better mounted.'

'This could be trickery, Highness!' Duncan said, level-voiced, forcing himself to the words.

'Curse you, puppy!' James Mor flung at him. 'You were born a fool. Think you that I would . . . ?'

'Do not heed him, James,' the Prince intervened. 'He is not a fool, only distrustful. Care nothing. Here is no time for wrangling. How shall we get away from here, unseen? If they are but a mile off?'

'There is a burn-channel. Just beyond this hollow. I came across it,' James panted. 'Deep enough to hide us. Dismounted. Leading the garrons. We could climb up the bed of it. To higher ground. Where they would not see us. They are down in the floor of the glen. They will not see us, once we are higher, owing to the swell of the hillside.'

Duncan took him up swiftly. 'If they can see the trees, we should be able to see *them*! If they are there!'

'Go you and look, then, Cousin. From up above, there. Look you down the glen.'

Duncan did not even wait for him to finish. He ran up the brackeny side of the hollow, crouching down amongst the tree-trunks as he reached the immediate skyline.

Sure enough, the scarlet coats of many cavalrymen were to be seen plainly enough down there, against the golds and browns of the glen-floor. They seemed to be scattered about, searching over quite a wide area.

Biting his lip, Duncan came down to the others again where all were making ready to move off immediately. He nodded his head. 'They are there, yes,' he jerked. 'Scattered about, as though hunting.'

'My lads seek to make a diversion,' his cousin explained, to the Prince. 'To keep them occupied. While I came on here.'

'Come, then,' Doctor Archie said grimly. 'Down first, and into this watercourse. Then up.'

Caroline, leading her garron, moved off at Duncan's side. 'Are . . . are we wrong about James Mor, Duncan?' she faltered.

'God knows!' he said. 'I do not.'

James Mor avoided any speech with his former captives, and clung to the Prince's side, where Felix O'Neil eyed him without affection.

The formation of the hillside gave them cover once they were over the first small shoulder, as James MacGregor had foretold, and thereafter the curve of the slope kept the valley bottom hidden. They could mount and ride unseen from below.

'You said that there were more dragoons at Borrodale?' the Doctor put to James Mor. 'So we cannot go down there. To the rendezvous? How do you know? Have you been there, your own self?'

'Aye. The French ships are anchored out in the loch. Two of them. The other party – Locheil and Cluny and the rest – had arrived. At the rendezvous. Too many people. The Red-coats were watching the ships. The others were seen . . . '

'They did not catch them?' Doctor Archie interrupted. 'Locheil? He is not taken?'

'My father . . . ?' Caroline gulped.

'No. They scattered, in time. Into the woods. I do not think that they have any of them. Locheil himself had enough men to fight a delaying action. And the woods there are thick. But the Redcoats are alert now. Searching. I knew that His Highness would be coming – guessed that he would come by Glen Beasdale.'

'You came to warn us, James? Risking your own life?'

The tall man grinned wickedly. 'Do not say such a thing, Highness! 'Tis as good as sacrilege! You will mortally affront

243

my cousin Duncan. Probably the Doctor here, too. James Mor could never do anything one half so noble! Say that I happened to be passing – running away from the dragoons. And saw your smoke. I could scarce do less than look in? I left my lads to distract the troopers yonder, and came up here myself on foot. Unseen.'

'Brave!' the Prince exclaimed. 'Gallant! My good James – ever I knew that you were true to me. My grateful thanks, *mon ami.* I shall not forget. But . . . what are we to do? Where are we to go, now, to win to the ships?'

'Locheil was telling the others to make for a new rendezvous. At some hidden place opposite An Garbh Eilean. Where there is an anchorage . . .'

'Doire Fhada,' Glenaladale, one of Clanranald's officers, put in. 'The Long Oak Grove. I know it well. A good secure place, where the ships can come close.'

'That is the name. The Doire Fhada,' James Mor agreed. 'To rendezvous there as darkness comes down.'

'Could you guide us there, Glenaladale?' Doctor Archie asked. 'From here? So that we are not seen . . . '

'To be sure. We must go round the back of this great hill, Sithean Mor. Then cross the headwaters of the Borrodale Burn, and so over into the next valley, of the Brunery Burn. That will bring us down through thick woods to Doire Fhada. But it will take us four hours' riding. Rough trackless going.'

'*Eh bien* – so much the better. It will keep cavalry horses away,' the Prince said. 'Lead on, in that case, Glenaladale.'

'I leave you here, then, Highness,' James Mor announced. 'I must go back to see how my lads fare. Keeping the Redcoats occupied.'

'Must you, James? *Hélas* – of course you must! Tell them of my true gratitude. But . . . will you not change your mind and come to France with me, hereafter?'

The other shook his head. 'I think not, Highness. Not this time. There is work to do in Scotland yet awhile. One day, perhaps, I shall join you in France. But not yet.'

'I am sorry, James. This is goodbye, then, my faithful friend?'

'Call it *au revoir*, as you would say in France, sir.' James actually knelt down in the heather to kiss the Prince's hand –

and even with Charles mounted on his garron, so tall was the MacGregor that he did not require to strain upwards. And somehow, because of a basic element of mockery in the man, even this exaggerated gesture did not appear over-humble or in any way servile. 'God bless Your Highness always, and bring you safe to your father's throne. *Slàn leat, Tearlach!*'

The Prince had difficulty with his words, as he bid his devoted friend farewell.

'A touching scene, 'fore God!' Scotus muttered, to Duncan. 'The man is the world's greatest hypocrite!'

'I can imagine what work keeps him in Scotland, whatever!' Duncan nodded grimly. 'He will find the gold if he can – all of it!'

'And yet,' Caroline demurred. 'He could have earned thirty thousand pounds this afternoon, with all the ease in the world! All that he had to do was to go to the Redcoats instead of endangering himself to come here. Nothing would have been more simple.'

Duncan rubbed his unshaven chin. 'Aye,' he said.

'There are two kinds of gold, it seems,' she went on. 'A man can betray his Prince's trust . . . but not his Prince himself!'

'Glenaladale says that James Mor and Barrisdale betrayed the Glen Mallie assembly to Loudon,' Scotus said. 'Presumably not for nothing!'

' I cannot believe that,' the girl declared.

'I do not know what to believe,' Duncan admitted wearily. 'But there goes a very strange man – that much is certain.'

With a gallant flourish of his bonnet to the Prince, a wave to others, and a mockery of a bow to Doctor Archie – who had never trusted him – and no single glance towards his three former prisoners, Major James Mor MacGregor swaggered off, back again into the burn-channel and downhill, a lone but never lonely figure.

'We shall go by a rather different route, I think, to Doire Fhada – for safety's sake!' Glenaladale said, looking after that retreating paladin. But he said it quietly, so that the Prince should not hear him.

CHAPTER 24

DOWN amongst the dense shadowy woodlands that clothed the northern shores of Loch nan Uamh, with the rocky beach opening before them in the last wan reflections of a watery sunset, figures emerged from behind bushes and trees and boulders, many dark figures, to greet their Prince. Locheil came limping; Clanranald ran to kiss his hand; Cluny Macpherson, stocky, burly, middle-aged, strode out sturdily; Bishop Mac-Donald of Morar raised a hand in blessing.

'Father!' Caroline cried, and jumping down from her garron, ran into Glenpean's arms.

With the Prince's party, there were fully a hundred men assembled there, around the deep secluded inlet of the sea-loch opposite the craggy islet of Garbh Eilean. No one, it was thought, had actually fallen into the clutches of the dragoons. These thick woodlands and broken rocky shores were highly unsuitable for cavalry and apt for fugitives. Nevertheless, there was nothing of elation about that hushed and furtive company. The meaning of their presence there, those who would sail and those who would remain behind, lay upon all their hearts like a leaden weight. This was the end of a chapter, if not of the book itself.

Locheil brought forward a dark-clad man, not in Highland dress. 'This is Captain Dufresne-Marion of the St. Malo privateer *Prince de Conty*, Highness,' he said. 'His ship, with another, the *Heureux*, will move closer in whenever the light goes. Clanranald has a boat out, to guide them here. Then the ships' boats will come for us.'

'Ah, my good Captain – well met! I will confess that I am more than glad to see you! Even if your ship, *Heureux*, is scarcely aptly named for the occasion!' Charles forced a wry smile. 'You must have been very bold, very courageous, putting your neck thus into the very noose, for me. I am only too well aware of the risks that you are taking. I thank you, from the bottom of my heart, sir.'

The Frenchman was peering in the gloom, even as he bowed low, no doubt seeking to reconcile this brawny uncouth figure with the elegant prince whom he had been sent to rescue. 'I but obeyed my orders, Your Royal Highness,' he said. 'But . . . I shall not be sorry to see St. Malo port again, I swear by Mary Mother!'

'I do not doubt it, Captain. Nor you only!'

'How many, sir, sail with you? How many do I carry with you? On the two ships?'

'That I do not know, Monsieur. Locheil? Doctor? Can you tell us? If they would pay heed to me, *mon Capitaine*, all here would come!'

'In my party, I think that thirty will sail, Highness,' Locheil told him. 'Some are still undecided.' He shook his grizzled head. 'Despite your Highness's company, would to God I was not one of them! But . . . I am but a handicap to my friends, here, crippled as I am.'

'You will come back, Donald – never fear,' his brother the Doctor told him. And to the Prince. 'Something over a dozen of our party, sir, intend to sail.'

'Fifty in all, then, Captain . . . '

The other Donald Cameron, Glenpean, had drawn his daughter aside – and the two younger men had followed.

'Lassie,' he said, 'you have come a long way to see a sad spectacle. To see your Prince and your chief leave your country – defeated, hunted men. For Locheil goes too. You should not have come, girl.'

'I had to come,' she said. She paused. 'And you, Father? Do you go to France, likewise? With Locheil?' Her voice quivered.

He shook his head. 'No, lass. Think you that I would? My duty to Locheil and the regiment ends on this shore. I am coming home. Returning to that other duty which, God forgive me, I have sorely neglected these many months – looking after my own daughters, my own people.'

She nodded, unspeaking.

It was Scotus who spoke, abruptly, almost harshly for him. 'None the less, sir, Caroline would be better going to France on the ship,' he said. 'Safer. Not to remain just a hunted fugitive in the heather, any more. She should come to France, to a new life.' It was not really at Glenpean that he looked as he spoke.

They all stared at him.

'Me . . . ? Go to France . . . ?' the girl said.

'Yes. Yes, Caroline. It would be best. You must see it? The winter is coming. The life of the shielings will be very different

247

in winter, in snow-bound hills. No life for you, my dear. And once all resistance is finished, hereafter, the Government will know no mercy. Come to France with me, Caroline.'

'You . . . ? You go?'

'Scotus,' Glenpean intervened, a little unsteadily. 'There is truth in what you say, God knows. But . . . it is not possible. Alone – a young woman? You do not realise what you are asking . . . '

'I realise very well, sir. I am asking that Caroline comes to France with me as my wife. We could be married. Here and now. Bishop MacDonald there would marry us.'

Duncan drew a long breath, but said nothing.

There was silence for moments on end.

At last Caroline spoke. 'You . . . you are kind, John. But . . . '

'I am not kind,' he denied. 'This is not kindness – never think it. You it is that I want. I think that you know it. I have never hidden my feelings for you, my dear. Marry me, Caroline. And come away from this unhappy land.'

Tight-lipped she shook her head.

'If it is your sisters – they could follow us. When we have made a home for them.'

'No, John,' she said. 'I thank you – but no.'

'No . . . ?' The man drew himself up – and suddenly, strangely, he was his normal self again. Gone the jerky hesitancy, the unaccustomed stiffness, almost sternness. He was Scotus once more, Spanish John, easy, assured, debonaire, almost as though a weight had been lifted from his mind. 'Alas, alas – I feared as much!' he said, with a sort of rueful humour. 'Aye – it was too much to hope for. I must continue to travel my road alone, then. Ah, me!'

Glenpean cleared his throat. 'Still you go then, lad? To France? Alone?'

'Why no, sir – not to France. That I would have done only to take Caroline there. To safety. No, I do not go to France – not yet.'

'To Spain, then? Back to your regiment?' That was Duncan.

'Nor to Spain either, my good MacGregor. My lone road is . . . my own. However lonely.'

The girl bit her lip. 'You do not stay with us? To guard the gold? Like Duncan . . . ?'

He shook his head. 'You did not hear the Prince put that

charge on *me*, did you? To guard his treasure. Indeed, I do not think that he esteems me greatly. Perhaps it is that I am less enamoured of his royal self than are some of you! I am not Prince Charles's man, you see – but Prince Henry's. The Duke of York's. It is on *his* service that my road takes me, now.'

'Ah!' Duncan said. 'You go north, then? To . . . Loch Broom?'

'Precisely, my friend. I have a little matter to settle still, with the Clan MacKenzie! A matter of a mere fifteen hundred *louis d'ors*. A humble sum – but some responsibility of mine. To recover . . . for His Highness of York, of course!' A flashing smile went with that.

'M'mmm.'

'Must you go, John?' Caroline said.

'I must, yes. And why not, i' faith? What is there for me here, now? The Gregorach has all in hand here, I think!'

'I am sorry, John.'

'So am I, my heart – so am I. But that alters nothing, does it? Faith, it is a sorry pair we are!'

Duncan seemed as though he was going to speak, but changed his mind.

A soft call from the shore announced that one of the ships was nosing in behind the little island. Immediately there was a concerted move down to the beach. Once the ships' boats came ashore, there would be no time to be lost. Captain Dufresne-Marion made it clear that he did not wish to linger close in to this coast.

The Prince, down at the tide's-edge, raised first a hand and then his voice. 'Gentlemen, friends all!' he called. 'In especial those I leave behind me. How shall I say what is in my heart, *mes camarades*? It has been a long fight, a grievous campaign – and the more bitter in that once it seemed that we should win it. And this is the most bitter day of all, God knows. Yet, if the same God wills, it is not the end, my friends. What so many have fought and died for, what so much loyal blood has been shed for, cannot just fade away as though it had never been. Heaven helping me, I will return. For that day we must gather our strength, cherish our faith, maintain our courage. My father's cause is as true, as just, now as when first we drew sword for it, you and I. It has been repulsed only, not defeated.'

'God save King James!' Clanranald cried, and whipping out

249

his broadsword raised it high. 'King James and the right!'

All around the cry was taken up, amidst the skreik of steel – so that Duncan for one glanced around him apprehensively lest the noise should reveal their whereabouts to prowling searchers.

Charles's voice shook. 'Thank you, *mes braves, mes héros!* I thank you with all my heart. Not only for this pledge, this last assurance of your loyalty and affection, but for all the love and care and selfless devotion that you have shown me – especially in these last months when my very name was a menace to you, my presence a death-warrant. And yet, wherever I went, on whomsoever I threw myself, never was I failed, never once rejected . . . much less betrayed . . . ' He gulped, and faltered. 'I . . . I cannot go on,' he said. *'Pardonnez moi, mes amis . . . '*

Only the draw and sigh of the tide broke the hush. Then a creaking sound, that was too regular and rhythmic for the cries of seabirds, caught all ears – the sweep of oars in rowlocks.

'The boats!' somebody called. 'Here they come . . . '

Farewells were hastily said, brother taking leave of brother, father of son, chief of clansmen. Scotus turned to Duncan, and held out his hand.

'I go now, also – the other way. It is apt. So that I may believe that the fair Caroline sheds one tear for me amidst the flood for Charles Stuart! Think you that she will? Heigh-ho – women are contrary creatures, and never know what is good for them! And you – see that you remember it, MacGregor! It is your good fortune – but ill deserved, I swear! Lord – do not be so solemn, man! If you would but laugh a little, now and then, there might be no holding you! Eh, Caroline?' He shrugged, continental-style. 'Though, sink you – who am I to advise you? Save in this, perhaps – do not wait too long for your Prince to return! That would be foolish, I believe. Especially with six thousand gold pieces comfortably to hand, with no one a better claim to than yourself! In the end a man must look facts in the face.'

Duncan shook his head. 'I shall be waiting still, when the Prince comes,' he said flatly. 'And the gold with me.'

'I' faith, I do believe that you will! And it, too. Poor Caroline!' Scotus turned to the young woman. 'You heard?' he said. 'Be warned, woman. Ah well . . . ' He mustered a smile. 'This is *adieu*, then, my dear.'

Blinking her eyes, suddenly she reached out and gripped his arm. 'Oh, John!' she mumbled.

'Aye, poor John!' He touched her hand lightly. 'Poor Spanish John!'

'You will be back?' she said. 'You also? One day?'

'Oh, to be sure – to be sure, I will be back. In, say, five years! For my second string – for Anne! Ha – Anne will have me! I swear it! And if not Anne, there is always Belle, is there not? Sweet Belle. But a year or two later. What is another year or two? On my soul, I am not done yet! Captain John Mac-Donnell, younger of Scotus, no less! Tell them to wait for me, both of them.' He drew the young woman to him, only for a moment, and held her tightly. Then he pushed her away, and turned.

'Your servant, sir,' he said shortly to Glenpean, and swung about on his heel to go striding off, in the opposite direction to the general drift down to the shingle of the beach, into the shadow of the trees, landwards. Out of the same shadowy trees his three gillies materialised and fell in behind him.

Unmoving, silent, they watched him go – the girl, the young man and Glenpean.

The Prince came up to Caroline, the only woman present – although she could not really see him with her eyes swimming. Instead of offering her his hand, he took hers and raised it to his lips. He did not speak.

Some sort of curtsy she contrived, as silent as he, before he in turn made off, for the boats grounding on the shingle.

Duncan leaned over to take the girl's hand, the same that Charles had kissed. She let him hold it. At her other side, her father tugged at his beard.

'Och, Locheil! Locheil!' he muttered.

A smirr of thin rain blew in their faces, cold and salt from the sea.

'The Elector may now sleep secure for a night,' Duncan said huskily. 'Secure on another's throne.'

'John will ... will not come back either, I think,' Caroline said.

'I wonder that you do not go your own self, Duncan man,' Glenpean declared, almost bitterly. 'There is little to hold a young man here, now.'

'There is much to hold me.'

'The gold,' Caroline said.

'More than the gold.'

'Your father and the Gregorach,' the older man suggested.
'Och, aye.'

'More than these.' Duncan's hand tightened on the girl's. 'I have the same trouble as Scotus. But I have less courage. I cannot just walk away from what I want, what I need. I can but wait. And hope.'

He felt the grip within his own hand tighten in turn, and drew a long quivering breath. Gently he loosened that grip and raised his hand behind her until his arm was around her shoulders. It rested there, strongly, authoritatively, possessively. Words had never been the best of Duncan MacGregor.

'Duncan,' she breathed, the merest whisper. 'Oh, Duncan, my heart!'

One glance they allowed themselves, one long, lingering, shining meeting of eyes that glowed. Then they turned again to watch the shadowy boats and ships and islands merge together into the Hebridean night, and so stood.

Though fifty others stood likewise, staring, they might have been utterly alone. For them the night was no longer dark. It was not the end, after all – only the beginning.

NIGEL TRANTER

THE BRUCE TRILOGY

In 1296 Edward Plantagenet, King of England, was determined to bludgeon the freedom-loving Scots into submission. Despite internal clashes and his fierce love for his antagonist's goddaughter, Robert the Bruce, both Norman lord and Celtic earl, took up the challenge of leading his people against the invaders from the South.

After a desperate struggle, Bruce rose finally to face the English at the memorable battle of Bannockburn. But far from bringing peace, his mighty victory was to herald fourteen years of infighting, savagery, heroism and treachery before the English could be brought to sit at a peace-table and to acknowledge Bruce as a sovereign king.

In this bestselling trilogy, Nigel Tranter charts these turbulent years, revealing the flowering of Bruce's character; how, tutored and encouraged by the heroic William Wallace, he determined to continue the fight for an independent Scotland, sustained by a passionate love for his land and devotion to his people.

'Absorbing . . . a notable achievement'

The Scotsman

HODDER AND STOUGHTON PAPERBACKS

NIGEL TRANTER

THE JAMES V TRILOGY

In 1513 – two hundred years after Robert the Bruce routed the English and restored his nation's pride – King James IV of Scotland lies slaughtered on Flodden's field. With Scotland in a state of turmoil, his seventeen-month-old heir lies at the mercy of ruthless rival factions.

Two men have been entrusted with the new king's welfare: loyal and steadfast David Lindsay and David Beaton. Sons of lowland lairds, they struggle in their role as royal protectors. For there are many who would seek to supplant or control the boy-king James V – his stepfather, the power-hungry Earl of Angus, is one; Henry VIII of England, his greedy eyes never far from the tempting realm of Scotland, is another. Even the boy's mother, Margaret Tudor, plots against her son.

And as he grows up, the young and handsome James V proves to be impetuous, hot-blooded, interested more in wine and women than matters of state. The two Davids have preserved him so far but the threats to James and his country seem to grow by the year . . .

In this fascinating trilogy, Nigel Tranter paints a vivid picture of a turbulent period, an unruly, perplexed and endangered nation, and an attractive but weak-willed king.

'Colourful, fast-moving and well written'
                                The Times Literary Supplement

HODDER AND STOUGHTON PAPERBACKS

NIGEL TRANTER

HIGHNESS IN HIDING

The quashing of the Jacobite Rising of 1745 saw an end to the ambitions of the exiled house of Stuart. But somehow the young pretender, Prince Charles Edward, otherwise known as Bonnie Prince Charlie, managed to avoid arrest.

For six extraordinary months the handsome young prince, often starving, sometimes barefoot and in rags, ranged the Western Highlands and the Outer and Inner Hebrides, hiding, lurking, fleeing.

Despite dire threats of punishment to all who might aid and abet him, the royal fugitive was hidden by brave and trusty supporters, each of whom could have betrayed him for the massive £30,000 reward offered by the English.

This story stands as a tribute to the loyalty and staunch courage of the Highland clansfolk.

HODDER AND STOUGHTON PAPERBACKS